A CARNIVAL FILMS/MASTERPIECE CO-PRODUCTION

DOWNTON ABBEY

THE COMPLETE SCRIPTS

· SEASON THREE ·

JULIAN FELLOWES

WILLIAM MORROW

An Imprint of HarperCollins*Publishers*

To Emma and Peregrine,
my fellow travellers on this extraordinary journey.

Contents

NOTE: Dotted lines alongside the script text indicate sections of text that were cut or partially cut from the original script to make the final edited version.

FOREWORD

At the end of the second series, we left our characters facing the new decade and the new postwar world. Matthew may have (finally) proposed, but little else was settled about the future of the Crawley family. As a matter of fact, I have always been interested in the 1920s, and now we were finally there. It strikes me as a curious, almost nebulous, time, an impression that was strengthened by the accounts of my great-aunts, whom I knew well as a young man and who had vivid memories of the era. My eldest great-aunt, Isie, had been born in 1880 and so this was the decade of her forties. Her husband had died of wounds in the last days of the war and, with an infant son, she had essentially to negotiate those years alone. According to her, at the very beginning nobody was quite sure what had really changed, and what would go back to the way it had been before the war. As time went on, it became increasingly clear that fundamental change had occurred and nothing would ever be the same again, but it took a little while for this to sink in, and it was that very uncertainty that attracted me to the period as a background to a family drama.

There were milestones, markers, along the way. When Lloyd George suddenly ended agricultural relief, without warning, in 1922, he struck a blow against the landowners, many of whom had been in debt since the agricultural depression of the last decades of the nineteenth century, and had taken out loans and mortgages, thinking and hoping, Micawber-like, that something would turn up. But of course for the majority nothing turned up. There was also an anomaly, which I am sure was deliberate, that selling land was still regarded as a capital gain, on which, in those days, there was no tax. So your option was either to lumber on with an erratic farming income, subject to heavy income tax, or to cash in your chips for a tax-free lump sum. Inevitably, and I believe as Lloyd George intended, something like a third of England was sold between the wars.

Counterbalancing that, and creating the baffling illusion of continuity, the new rich – and there were many – continued to spend their fortunes in the old way. I don't mean these were war profiteers in a pejorative sense, but wars do certainly make fortunes and, besides them, there were industrialists and manufacturers and, perhaps most prominently in this company, the powerful newspaper magnates, all of whom aped the Victorian model and purchased great houses and great estates on which to lavish their newly gotten gains. So, there was this slightly bewildering contradiction of old families going under all over the place, but huge palaces, in the ownership of Lord Rothermere or Lord Beaverbrook and their kind, being run with an extravagance scarcely seen since the 1890s.

Being rich in a new way was something being developed by the Americans, and it would not really reach these shores until after the Second World War. The Americans never felt the European imperative to separate themselves from the source of their money, and would cheerfully go into the bank or the office every morning, long after they had taken the reins of New York Society. They had their palaces, too, of course, at Newport or on Long Island, but they felt no need to imitate farmers with profitless estates. Their model is much more recognisable to the present generation when, now, riches are more likely to be devoted to helicopters, Manhattan apartments and houses in the South of France than to the purchase of 20,000 acres of the North Riding. But in the 1920s you had this strange contrast: the new rich creating the illusion that the old way of life would continue, while many of the old rich were chucking in the towel.

Then this was also an era of tremendous social change, not just because of organised labour or women's rights or the rise of the Labour Party, but also because of the cinema and sports cars and aeroplanes and all the other tell-tale signs of the fast-moving twentieth century. My own Great-Uncle Peregrine was a Commodore in the Navy, a man as straight as a ruled line who found himself unable to resist the fascination of flight. By the end of the war he had become a pioneer flyer in the Royal Naval Air Service, and afterwards he became one of the first Air Equerries to King George V. Later, in 1933, he would lead the Houston Everest Flight when they flew over Everest in an effort to win public support for government investment in air power, because Germany was so far ahead in the race – one of the many steps that led to the second war and ultimately to the modern world. His journey, from a country Victorian boyhood to fighting a deadly air battle with the Nazis, gives some impression of the speed of change that generation had to live through.

That was the 1920s, the bridge between the old world and the new, and that is what we explore in this, the third series of *Downton Abbey*.

Julian Fellowes

EPISODE ONE

ACT ONE

1A EXT. CHURCH. DOWNTON VILLAGE. DAY.

Daisy pushes a bicycle towards the church.

1B INT. CHURCH. DOWNTON VILLAGE. DAY.

At first this seems to be a simple wedding, with the young couple in day dress and only a few guests sitting in the front pews. Then the sheet tucked into the bride's belt and the three mothers fussing with the four little bridesmaids and the general murmur all round tell us it is only a rehearsal. An immensely important prelate stands by the altar, while Mr Travis fusses about. Mary turns to the first little girl behind her.

  MARY: Are you going to be as naughty as this on the day?
  BRIDESMAID: I'm going to be a great deal naughtier.*

Mary raises her eyebrows to a hovering mother.

  MOTHER: No, she isn't. Arabella, why do you say such things?

Matthew whispers to Mary.

  MATTHEW: I bet she is.

....

* I felt quite strongly we should start with the wedding – at least with all the drama attendant on a wedding. The previous series had ended on Matthew's proposal being accepted, so the next natural milestone in that story would be the marriage itself, and I didn't see much point in delay. That said, I thought we'd get some mileage out of it. These first two lines, which didn't survive into the edit, were said at Emma's and my wedding, because we had this rather *lively* page called William Portal, who was the son of a lifelong friend of Emma's. My niece was one of the bridesmaids and she said, at the rehearsal in St Margaret's, Westminster, 'Are you going to be as naughty as this on the day?' 'I'm going to be a great deal naughtier,' said William, although I'm happy to relate that his nerve failed him slightly at the sight of a full church, so he wasn't very naughty. But Emma in fact controlled all of the maids and pages by eschewing bouquets and designing a thick, flower-decked rope that they were all more or less fastened to, so they came in as a single body and were dragged up the aisle and then dragged down again.

They laugh.

> MATTHEW (CONT'D): Is there any news of Sybil?
> MARY: She's still not coming. She insists they can't
> afford it.
> MATTHEW: That's Branson talking.*
> ARCHBISHOP OF YORK: Mr Travis? Can we move forward?†

The Reverend Mr Travis is getting increasingly flustered.

> TRAVIS: If I could just ask you to come down the aisle
> again? Can we get the troops organised?

The mothers and children shuffle to the door of the church.
Now we see Robert, Cora and Edith in the front row.

> ROBERT: That means me.
> CORA: It seems rather hard on poor old Travis when he's
> doing all the work but the Archbishop gets the glory.
> We'll have to ask him to dine.

Robert stands to walk with Mary to the starting place. But
the pair of them remain for a moment with the others.

> MARY: Papa was the one who wanted a Prince of the
> Church. I would have settled for Travis.

They move off.

....

* In the interim, Sybil has married Downton's former chauffeur, Tom Branson, and they are living in Dublin. I always feel it's very important that if you make your characters do something big, then for heaven's sake let it be big. It's like when Mary goes to bed with the Turk in the first series; it's fine as long as it's an incredibly big thing that she's done. What you mustn't do is make it a modern and therefore casual thing, because then (a) you take all the juice out of it dramatically, and (b) it becomes unbelievable, because then you think, well, she wouldn't do that. But if it's an enormous thing, and she's aware of it, then you're less confident that she wouldn't do it. So we didn't want to play down Sybil.

† When we actually fixed the dates for when we were going to shoot the wedding, which for a variety of reasons you can't change (we had all the extras, etc.), we discovered that Michael Cochrane, who plays Travis, was, alas, working on the day of the wedding itself. So the whole plot here of Robert insisting on the Archbishop marrying them ('Papa was the one who wanted a Prince of the Church') was concocted in order to explain why the vicar was absent.

MARY (CONT'D): Is there really no way to get Sybil over?
It seems ridiculous.
ROBERT: On the contrary; it's a relief. Branson is
still an object of fascination for the county. We'll ask
him here when we can prepare the servants and manage it
gently.

*Across the aisle, Matthew is with Isobel. They have heard
Robert's speech, but they lower their voices.*

ISOBEL: He's making a problem where none exists. Nobody
could care less if Branson were at the wedding or not.
MATTHEW: You must think country life more exciting than
it is, if you imagine people don't care when an earl's
daughter runs off with a chauffeur.
ISOBEL: Well, the fact remains she *has* run off with a
chauffeur and they have to get used to it.*
MATTHEW: Well, I agree with that.
ARCHBISHOP OF YORK: Mr Travis, are we ready?
TRAVIS: Any moment, your grace. Any moment.

Edith has been left alone with her mother.

EDITH: Branson might be hard to explain to Grandmama
when she gets here.

....

* Sybil's romance is based on an earl's daughter running off with a groom at
this time, the great-aunt of a friend of mine who shall be nameless. In that
family the father set off in pursuit, seized the girl before they made it to
Gretna Green and brought her back protesting. But, of course, these things
did happen, as they have always happened. I don't think the way the Crawleys
deal with it, which is to attempt to normalise it, would be terribly unusual
under the circumstances. In some families the young couple would be shown
the door, but it is a characteristic of the English upper classes not to wish to
provide a story. The younger son of a well-known Scottish earl fell in love
with a club housemaid in the 1890s and, in the end, his parents reluctantly
accepted it on condition they could send the girl to the family of a friend for
two years to learn how to be a lady, so she would not attract attention. Nearer
home, I remember when I was young there was a local chap of our age, whom
my father absolutely detested. He pronounced that the boy was 'not to be
invited to this house unless his absence will cause scandal'. That is the
instinct at work here: the Crawleys, and Robert, are anxious not to be a story.
He likes the fact that the Bransons aren't coming because they can't afford it.
This means he won't have to forbid them, so there's no story.

CORA: My dear mother knows all about him. Remember, Edith, our blood is much less blue than the Crawleys'. Your father may be against Branson coming back to Downton, but I'm *not*.

Mary and Robert are at the end of the aisle.

MARY: So I can't send her the tickets?
ROBERT: No. I have already forbidden your mother from doing just that. The fact is, the cost of the journey has settled the matter comfortably, without any need for a row. Please leave it alone.
TRAVIS: Can we? Please?

Mary takes Robert's arm. Travis nods to the organist who starts to play The Arrival of the Queen of Sheba *by Handel. Robert, Mary and the fractious children come down the aisle, Mary still trailing a sheet from her waist.**
The Archbishop steps forward with aplomb.

1C EXT. DOWNTON. DAY.

Daisy rides a bicycle towards Downton.

2 INT. SERVANTS' HALL. DOWNTON. DAY.

The servants are at luncheon. Carson presides.

O'BRIEN: When will they be back?
CARSON: Before nightfall, I think.
O'BRIEN: I see. And am I supposed to dress every human in the house again?
CARSON: Mrs Hughes is not often away, Miss O'Brien. Nor Anna. It is ungenerous to grudge it when they are.

Mrs Patmore has come in, followed by Daisy.

CARSON (CONT'D): That treacle tart just hit the spot. Thank you, Mrs Patmore.

....

* I'd seen this done at certain rehearsals and I've always thought it rather sensible. There is something almost romantic about a pretend wedding dress. And we have *The Arrival of the Queen of Sheba* because that was what Emma and I chose when she came down the aisle in St Margaret's, Westminster.

MRS PATMORE: So Mrs Hughes and Anna are getting the place ready to let?

CARSON: That is the plan.

THOMAS: I'm surprised Anna held onto that house. I thought they confiscated the profits of murder.

CARSON: Mr Bates had the wisdom to transfer it to her before the trial.

THOMAS: I don't think I'd have allowed it, Mr Carson.

CARSON: Then we must all be grateful you were not the presiding judge.

THOMAS: I still think it's funny. Given that he's a convicted murderer.

CARSON: May I remind you, Mr Barrow, that in this house Mr Bates is a wronged man seeking justice. If you have any problems with that definition, I suggest you eat in the yard.

3   INT. DRAWING ROOM. DOWER HOUSE. DAY.

Violet and Isobel are with Cora.

ISOBEL: I suppose you agree with Robert.

VIOLET: Then not for the first time, you suppose wrongly. The family must never be a topic of conversation.

CORA: I'm afraid Sybil's already made the Crawleys a permanent topic.

VIOLET: All the more reason. If we can show the county he can behave normally, they will soon lose interest in him. And I shall make sure he behaves normally because I shall hold his hand on the radiator until he does.

ISOBEL: Well, I don't know this young man aside from 'Good morning' and 'Goodnight', but he strikes me as a very interesting addition to the family.

VIOLET: Oh, here we go.

ISOBEL: And why should he be 'normal', as you call it? I say he should come here and fight his corner. I like a man with strong beliefs. I think I'll send them the money.

CORA: Please don't. Robert's expressly forbidden it. He'd be furious.

4   EXT.   A DUBLIN MARKET.   DAY.

A trader hands Sybil some change.   She is with Branson.

TRADER: Thank you, Mrs Branson.

She takes the money and a bag.   They turn and walk away.

SYBIL: But why not if we travel cheaply? We'd stay free
when we get there.
BRANSON: It's bad enough that we live on your allowance,
without wasting it on a jaunt.
SYBIL: It's not a jaunt. It's Mary's wedding.
BRANSON: But we're going to have a baby now. And I'm
only earning a pittance…
SYBIL: What you write is important. Whether they pay
you for it is not.
BRANSON: It's important enough to me.

He sighs at his own failure to provide.

BRANSON (CONT'D): Why don't you go alone? We could just
about manage that.
SYBIL: Oh, no. Not without you. When I go back to
Downton, it's as a couple — a happy couple, or not at
all.

5   INT.   HALL.   DOWNTON.   NIGHT.

Robert is on the telephone.

ROBERT: But it can't be as bad… Look, I'll come and see
you… Tomorrow. No, I insist… Right… Goodbye.

He replaces the receiver as Mary comes out of the library.

MARY: Papa? What's the matter?
ROBERT: Nothing's the matter. What should be the
matter?

6   INT.   SERVANTS' HALL.   DOWNTON.   NIGHT.

It is after dinner. Mrs Hughes and Anna have just arrived.

CARSON: How was London?
ANNA: We got it all done, but I couldn't have managed
without my helper.
MRS PATMORE: Have you eaten?
MRS HUGHES: We had a bite on the train.

MRS PATMORE: Well, sit down anyway, and have a cup of tea.

Daisy sighs and leaves with Anna, who is taking off her coat.

MRS HUGHES: I'll start on the final lists for the wedding tomorrow morning.
CARSON: I've got the last of the wine deliveries coming on Tuesday.
MRS HUGHES: How will you manage without a footman?
CARSON: I agree. But I haven't time to find one now.
O'BRIEN: I've had a letter from my sister, asking after a job for her son and —
CARSON: Miss O'Brien, we are about to host a Society wedding. I have no time for training young hobbledehoys.*

The bell rings.

CARSON (CONT'D): Her ladyship's ringing.

O'Brien gets up.

    7   INT. CORA'S BEDROOM. DOWNTON. NIGHT.

O'Brien is plaiting Cora's hair.

CORA: Well, I don't see why not. I'll ask his lordship when —

She is interrupted by Robert opening the door.

CORA (CONT'D): There you are, so I'll ask you now.
ROBERT: Ask me what?
CORA: Carson's in need of a footman and O'Brien has a candidate.
O'BRIEN: Alfred. Alfred Nugent, m'lord. He's a good worker.
CORA: I think it sounds perfect. Robert?

....

* O'Brien, of course, has to manipulate the footman into the house because a simple request has not worked. To be fair to her, she tries to play it straight when she says, 'I've had a letter from my sister asking after a job for her son.' If at that moment Carson had said, 'Well, I'd be glad to give him an interview,' she might have left it at that, but of course when he says, 'I have no time for training young hobbledehoys,' she then has to make use of the back stairs and start plotting.

ROBERT: Whatever you say. My dear, I have to go up to London tomorrow. I'm catching the early train.
CORA: That's very sudden. Do you want them to open the house?
ROBERT: No. I'll come straight back.
CORA: What are you going for?
ROBERT: It's nothing to bother you with.

8 INT. MRS HUGHES'S SITTING ROOM. DOWNTON. DAY.

A shiny vacuum cleaner is taken out of its box.

MRS HUGHES: There. You plug it in and switch it on and it sucks all the dirt out of the carpet and off the floor.
ANNA: I'm not sure I like the sound of it now we've finally got one. Suppose it *sucks* everything else up, too?
MRS HUGHES: All I know is Mrs Gannon, at Easton Grange, says it gets the work done in half the time. Anyway I've paid for it now, so let's give it a try.

*Anna looks at the machine as if it were her enemy.**

MRS HUGHES (CONT'D): What are you going to do with that address book we found?
ANNA: Well, first I'll copy all the entries out for Mr Bates —

They are interrupted by the irate figure of Carson.

CARSON: You'll never guess what Miss O'Brien's done now —
MRS HUGHES: Thank you, Anna.

Anna lifts the vacuum cleaner and leaves. Carson stares.

....

* As Mrs Patmore says later on, 'Much more of this and she'll be able to run a house with one servant living in and a woman from the village.' As we know, in the vast majority of these houses that stayed in private hands this is more or less exactly what happened. I always like to show that things and situations we would find very ordinary were once thought as weird as – well, I was going to say iPads, but I suppose they're quite ordinary now.

I was rather sad we lost the vacuum cleaner plot from this episode, but *Downton* is very tight in its storytelling and this means some moments each week must be sacrificed. It is part of the process.

CARSON: What in God's name was that?

MRS HUGHES: The new vacuum cleaner.

CARSON: It looks like something for unclogging the drains.

MRS HUGHES: I'm sure it has many uses, but I doubt you will be training yourself in any of them.

CARSON: I will not.

MRS HUGHES: Can we return to the matter on hand. What has Miss O'Brien done?

CARSON: She's only persuaded her ladyship to hire her blooming nephew as a footman, and I don't have a word to say about it.

MRS HUGHES: But you have to interview him.

CARSON: O'Brien sent a telegram first thing to tell him he's got the job.

MRS HUGHES: Well, he hasn't.

CARSON: I know, but…

MRS HUGHES: You're too soft, Mr Carson. Insist on your rights. What does his lordship say?

CARSON: He'd left for London before I could speak to him about it.

MRS HUGHES: I'm curious. Why have you taken so long to find a footman?

CARSON: I've seen a few, but these postwar boys just don't have the heart for it. They want jobs that let them take their girls out when they get home at night, and money to spend on them when they do.

MRS HUGHES: And free tickets at the funfair, and a free bus ride home.

CARSON: That's about it.

MRS HUGHES: Well, we've got this boy now, so let's see what you can make of him. And there is one good thing —

Carson looks at her, wondering what's coming.

MRS HUGHES (CONT'D): Whatever he does wrong, we can always blame Miss O'Brien.*

....

* Carson is right to point out that the proper forms have not been observed, and it's true that the collapse of this life was demonstrated by the rules starting to break down. Mrs Hughes, who is much more left-wing than Carson and much less convinced by the old system, still registers that his rights are being eroded, and that Carson has failed to stick up for himself.

9 INT. VISITING CELL. YORK PRISON. DAY.

Visiting Time. Bates holds some papers. Anna is with him.

ANNA: It's all there. Every entry.
BATES: Where did you find the book?

....

Continued from page 10:

For a traditionalist like Carson, it must have been very difficult. 'Why have you taken so long to find a footman?' 'I've seen a few but these postwar boys just don't have the heart for it.' The truth is, a lot of the changes had to do with conditioning, and after the First World War fewer and fewer young people were being conditioned for a life in service.

Of course, sometimes this works in reverse. I go sometimes to a school near us in Dorset, distributing prizes and things, and on one occasion I gave a speech about not erecting a glass wall. If you're looking at the Oscars ceremony, those people's backgrounds are no different to yours, etc. Afterwards I said to the headmaster, 'I hope that was all right.' He replied that although it wasn't terribly realistic to invite them to dream of being film stars, he didn't mind because he wanted them to dream of something. 'My problem is that they're being conditioned to work in Tesco, and I want them to resist it.'

The opposite change happened after 1918. The previous generation had accepted they would be in service – in the case of the girls until marriage; in the case of the men, they would be a domestic servant, or in the stables, or they would work in a shop, or whatever was natural to their own social network – for the rest of their lives. But the children of the 1920s, for the first time, started thinking outside that box. New jobs were appearing and there were more and more things a man – and more particularly, a respectable woman – could do. As Carson says, they wanted jobs with better hours. They wanted to go out at night, they wanted money to spend. It must have been difficult for the older generation, who had worked so hard for so little. Mrs Hughes is given the response of many of her contemporaries. A lot of them just didn't understand why their children were all going to have a much easier time of it.

Conveying all this has been tricky because we wanted in a way to give a sense of the house cutting down, but at the same time we didn't want to diminish the cast too much, or keep losing characters from below stairs but not from above. It's been a bit of a balancing act. In real life, with a family like the Crawleys, they probably would have been down to one footman, two housemaids and no under butler, but there had to be a little bit of 'television margin' here.

ANNA: Behind the bureau. We moved it out to clean and there it was. Vera must have dropped it or something.*

BATES: So, what do you want me to do?

ANNA: Make notes on all the names. Close friend, relation, workmate, tradesman and so on. Then I'll copy those and I'll send them with the book to Mr Murray.

BATES: Haven't you anything better to do?

ANNA: I have not. Because I'd rather work to get you free than dine with the King at Buckingham Palace… So what news have you got?

BATES: What news could I have in here? Oh, I've acquired a new cellmate. To be honest, I'm not sure about him.

He nods at a man a few seats down. The man looks back.

ANNA: Well, just remember what my mother used to say: never make an enemy by accident. Now, do you think you can get the notes done before my next visit?

BATES: I don't see what can come of it.

ANNA: Probably nothing. And my next idea will probably lead to nothing, and the next and the next. But one day, something will occur to us and we'll follow it up, and the case against you will crumble.

BATES: Do you never doubt? For just one minute? I wouldn't blame you.

....

* The prison story was hard for Brendan Coyle (Bates) because it meant he was isolated from most of the cast. We used the exterior of Lincoln Prison, but built the interior set at Ealing Studios. While Brendan was in gaol he would see Joanne Froggatt (his wife, Anna), and in one episode the solicitor, Mr Murray, but no one else from the regular cast. It was different for Jo, because she would see other members of the cast at Highclere and Ealing. I think it was quite testing for him and must have been a relief when his character was set free.

We use the address book to establish Anna's sympathies. The public is entitled to doubt Bates's innocence, and they are given sufficient opportunities to do so, but Anna never does because that would undermine their dramatic narrative. Of course, when you say to an audience that we've found an address book and Anna has copied out the addresses, unless they've been living entirely in the jungle and have only just seen their first television, they know that there will be a name in the address book that will take them further in the story.

ANNA: No. I don't doubt that the sun will rise in the east, either.

10   INT.   SERVANTS' HALL.   DOWNTON.   DAY.

An awkward, tall young man in his early twenties stands at one end of the table.   Carson stands in judgement beside him.

CARSON: You're too tall to be a footman. No footman should be over six foot one.
O'BRIEN: That can't be, can it? Since he's already been taken on.
CARSON: But what have you done?
ALFRED: I was a hotel waiter after I was discharged from the Army, but they've cut back…
O'BRIEN: I think to get a job as a waiter shows real initiative.
MRS HUGHES: I suppose he can speak for himself.
O'BRIEN: Why? Is he on trial? This isn't an interview, is it? Not when he's already got the job.
CARSON: No, it is not an interview, Miss O'Brien, but he is on trial. And if he cannot match our standards he will be found guilty.
ALFRED: I mean to try, Mr Carson.
DAISY: Course you do.
THOMAS: Who asked you?
CARSON: As long as you do. Now go upstairs and get settled in. Your aunt will *hopefully* find you a livery that fits.

He says this deliberately to embarrass them.

11   EXT.   GARDENS.   DOWNTON.   DAY.

Matthew is with Mary.

MARY: Just at the start. So we've a place to sleep after the honeymoon. You can't object to that?*

....

* In the 1970s, we had all those American drama soaps, *Dynasty* and *Dallas* and *The Colbys* and so on, where there was never any explanation of why these apparently very rich families – comprising perhaps four or five married couples – would all live together in one house. In real life, one of the main points of being rich is that you have enough money to buy a house and you

MATTHEW: No, it's nice of them. Though I doubt I'll get used to taking you to bed with your father watching.

MARY: He's so relieved we're getting married, he wouldn't mind if you carried me up naked.

MATTHEW: Careful, I might try it.

MARY: Then, when we're back and settled, we can look at all the options.

MATTHEW: I don't want to move to London or anything. I'm not kicking against the traces…

MARY: Just testing their strength.

MATTHEW: I want us to get to know each other, to learn about who we both are without everybody being there.

MARY: It is quite a big house.

MATTHEW: It's a lovely house. It's your home and I want it to be my home, too. Just not quite yet.

....

Continued from page 13:

are not obliged to live with your parents. But that was the way with these shows, and that was what we found ourselves doing here.

I did at one point toy with the idea of giving Matthew and Mary their own house, but then I just felt we'd get into such a fix with their staff and all the rest of it that we decided against it. It doesn't mean we don't understand why Matthew wants to be master of his own home. He's not hostile to his in-laws, but he would like to be alone with his wife, and, as he says here, 'I want us to get to know each other.'

As always with *Downton*, in these arguments I like to feel that the audience can see both points of view. I don't think Matthew is saying anything silly. He is going to lose, but I don't think his position is in the least untenable. On the other hand, Mary has a sense that now she has married the heir she wants to start being part of the management of the place. She wants to pull her weight. She isn't going to inherit, but that blow has now been softened because her husband will, and so for every reason possible she wants to stay there. Of course, she knows how to manipulate Matthew, and if she said, 'I just want to live here,' then that wouldn't be a good move. But she says she only wants to live at Downton at the start, 'So we've got a place to sleep after the honeymoon.' In short, she is quite deliberately putting him in a position where his refusal starts to look stubborn, as opposed to its being fundamentally reasonable, which it is.

11A EXT. TRAIN STATION. LONDON. DAY.

Robert walks out of the station and approaches a taxi.

ROBERT: Chancery Lane.

DRIVER: Yes, sir.

12 INT. MURRAY'S CHAMBERS. LONDON. DAY.

Robert is with Murray.

MURRAY: I've spoken to Frobisher and Curran, and since I am a trustee, should the estate ever need one, we felt that I ought to be the one to tell you.

ROBERT: You make it sound very serious.

MURRAY: I'm expressing myself badly if you think it is not serious.

His tone effectively quashes Robert's attempt at levity.

ROBERT: Why did we invest so much?

MURRAY: Lord Grantham, it was you who insisted we should. If you remember, we advised against it.

ROBERT: But war would mean a huge expansion of railways everywhere. Every forecast was certain. Rail shares were bound to make a fortune.

MURRAY: Many did, but your principal holding, which was very large indeed, was in the Canadian Grand Trunk line.

ROBERT: It was the main railway in British North America, for God's sake. It wasn't just me. Everyone said we couldn't lose. We knew hard times were coming for estates like Downton, and this investment would make it safe for the rest of time.

MURRAY: Charles Hays was the presiding genius, and since he died the management has not… The fact is, the company is about to be declared bankrupt, and the line will be absorbed into the Canadian National Railway scheme.*

....

* Murray, played by Jonathon Coy, my old pal, hasn't been in *Downton* for a while because we haven't had a legal problem, but I think it's nice when you're in a series and occasionally you have a story, which is what he has here: The Ruin of Robert Grantham. I chose the Canadian Grand Trunk Line because it was, at the time, one of the most surprising failures of that generation. To investors, as the major line in British North America, it was thought bound to succeed because of all the trade that was waiting to use it, and it was situated

```
ROBERT:   Are you really telling me that all the money is
gone?
MURRAY:   I'm afraid so.
ROBERT:   The lion's share of Cora's fortune.
```

Murray is silent. Robert starts to realise this is ruin.

```
ROBERT (CONT'D):  I won't give in, Murray.  I've
sacrificed too much to Downton to give in now.  I refuse
to be the failure, the Earl who dropped the torch and let
the flame go out.
```

....

Continued from page 15:

where you literally couldn't lose. For these reasons, Robert has put all his money into it. But the brilliant man who ran it, Charles Hays, who really was a sort of genius, died tragically on the *Titanic*, and after that the line started to go down until finally, amazingly, at the beginning of the 1920s, it failed. All this is real, as any viewer who wishes to look it up on the internet will discover.

I wanted a reason why Robert would put so much money into one concern, but the fact is, it looked an absolutely copper-bottomed way of doubling or trebling your fortune, which is what Robert needs to save the estate. But doubling or even trebling will only make a difference if you invest an enormous amount, and so unfortunately that's what Robert did. Well, fortunately for us, because then it gives us a whole new plot line for the third series. I feel very sympathetic to Robert here, when he says, 'I won't give in… I refuse to be the failure, the Earl who dropped the torch,' because I know that the hardest thing for that generation – and it goes down to the present day – was to be the one who sells. It's much less hard for their son or grandson, but when you are the one who sold the family house, or demolished it… I had a cousin who pulled down his house and built another, much smaller one. Whenever you went there he would get out his album of pictures of the old house and he'd say, 'This is what the place used to look like.' It was heartbreaking, really. Still, at least they hung on to the estate.

For many families, when their personal economy wasn't working, they should have accepted the fact and done something about it, but they clung on and clung on and clung on because they didn't want to be the one who threw in the towel. They borrowed and borrowed and went further and further off-piste, and by the time they did sell, all the money was consumed by the debt, so the family was essentially returned overnight to a perfectly ordinary middle-class existence. Surely one has to be very hard-hearted not to see that this must have been difficult. You think and hope and pray something will turn up – some uncle in Zanzibar will die and everything will be okay. But for so many, nothing did.

MURRAY: I hate to state the obvious but if there's not enough money to run it, Downton must go. Unless you break it up and sell it off piecemeal.
ROBERT: I couldn't do that. I have a duty beyond saving my own skin. The estate must be a major employer and support the house or there's no point to it. To any of it.

END OF ACT ONE

ACT TWO

13 EXT. DOWNTON VILLAGE. DAY.

Edith's walking along when she hears a voice. Anthony Strallan shouts a greeting from a car. She bends to look in.

EDITH: Hello.
STRALLAN: Hello.
EDITH: What are you doing here?
STRALLAN: Meeting a train. But I'm too early.

She opens the door and climbs in, uninvited.

STRALLAN (CONT'D): I mustn't hold you up.
EDITH: I'm not doing anything. I thought I'd get away from wedding panic.
STRALLAN: Don't you like weddings?
EDITH: Don't be silly. Of course I do. Only I've talked of clothes and flowers and food and guests until I'm blue in the face.
STRALLAN: Weddings can be reminders of one's loneliness, can't they? I'm sorry. I don't know why I said that.

She doesn't mind him saying it one bit.

STRALLAN (CONT'D): So, how's it going? Is the family gathered? Is your grandmother coming over from New York for it?
EDITH: She is.
STRALLAN: And Sybil? Is she here yet?

EDITH: As a matter of fact, she wasn't coming but I think she is now. Mary had a letter this morning. Papa doesn't know yet. He's in London today.
STRALLAN: He will be pleased.
EDITH: I do hope so.*

14   INT.   MATTHEW'S BEDROOM.   CRAWLEY HOUSE. NIGHT.

Matthew is dressing in white tie, helped by Molesley.

MOLESLEY: So you'll live at the big house when you're back from honeymoon.
MATTHEW: Not live. Stay. We'll stay there until we decide where to go. It'll be on the estate, I would think. Or in the village.
MOLESLEY: Not here?
MATTHEW: No, but I shall expect you and Mrs Bird to look after Mrs Crawley.

....

* Now we revive Edith's romance with Strallan. Again, this is all very *Downton*-esque. Strallan is a decent man – his reason for thinking he shouldn't court a woman when he's been wounded in the war and that he's too old anyway is perfectly honourable. But Edith was part of the generation Virginia Nicholson wrote a very good book about, *Singled Out: How Two Million British Women Survived Without Men after the First World War.* There's a picture of one of my great-aunts in it. The officer class had suffered a very high rate of death, particularly in the early years. After 1916 they took them out of officer uniforms because the Germans would pick off the officers first. After that, all the men wore the same. Someone tried to complain about this during our second series, when we showed an officer wearing a private's uniform, but they simply didn't know their facts. Anyway, the point is, it would have been difficult for Edith to find a young man of the right age who came from an appropriate family, who was attractive, who had prospects, and, given the shortage, Strallan isn't that bad an option. So I think they're both being sensible in their different ways.

The wound we chose was the disablement of one arm but not the loss of it, as we didn't want to deal with all the trick photography it would have involved. We did in fact have an explanation of what had happened to him at one stage, but it got cut. I rather regretted this, but it didn't seem to worry anyone.

MOLESLEY: You'll not be taking me with you, sir? Only I thought you'd be needing a proper valet, once you're married.

MATTHEW: But I've always thought of you as more of a butler who helps out as a valet, not the other way round.

MOLESLEY: I'd be happy to be a valet, sir. Especially in the big house.

MATTHEW: But we won't *be* in the big house for long. To be honest, Molesley, I want to live more simply after the wedding. And besides, Mother *absolutely* relies on you.

MOLESLEY: That's very nice to hear, sir. Thank you.*

15 INT. ROBERT'S DRESSING ROOM. DOWNTON. NIGHT.

Robert is being dressed by Thomas.

THOMAS: You must be exhausted, m'lord. You can't have spent more than two hours in London.

ROBERT: It was sufficient.

THOMAS: The new footman arrived while you were gone.

ROBERT : What?

THOMAS: Yes. He got the cable this morning and came straight over. *Very* eager. And very tall.

ROBERT: But when did...? Never mind.†

....

* Molesley is really our downstairs Edith, since the pair of them are permanently at war with what appears to be their destiny. Typically, now that Molesley is Matthew's valet and butler, and now that Matthew is marrying the heiress and is going to live at the main house, Molesley thinks at last he's got a lucky break. But no. Matthew tries to be kind to Molesley, ever since he was reprimanded by Robert for not taking Molesley's ambition seriously – 'You've got to remember this is his job, and you have to respect that,' or whatever he said – but of course Matthew still doesn't really want to be bothered with a valet and he doesn't see why he has to be. Before the war, people like Matthew were obliged to live as everyone of their kind lived. But more and more, after the war, that pressure was gone. And when a woman didn't want the nuisance of employing a lady's maid, and couldn't really afford it, the pressure to keep up appearances was very much less than it had been ten or twenty years before. So that was, like other forces, working against the old system and actually unravelling it.

† Here, Robert is informed that there's a new footman immediately after he's got back, having learnt he's got no money. So he overreacts, which I think is truthful.

16 INT. STAIRCASE AND HALL. DOWNTON. NIGHT.

Robert catches up with Cora on the stairs.

> ROBERT: Did you know about the new footman?
> CORA: Of course. He's already here.
> ROBERT: Why did no one tell me?
> CORA: What do you mean? We talked all about it last night. In my room.
> ROBERT: Well… Nobody else must be taken on. Absolutely no one. Until things are settled.
> CORA: What things?

But he does not choose to answer her.

> ROBERT: How's the wedding going? I suppose it's costing the earth.
> CORA: Mary was never going to marry on the cheap.
> ROBERT: Oh, no. Nothing must be done on the cheap.

With this rather bitter observation, he walks off. *

17 INT. KITCHEN PASSAGE. DOWNTON. NIGHT.

O'Brien is removing fluff from Alfred's shoulder.

> ALFRED: I feel quite nervous.
> O'BRIEN: Don't be. You've got the skill and you've got the willingness.
> THOMAS: But he hasn't got the experience.

He walks past them and into the servants' hall.

....

* People like the Crawleys, or quite a few of them, didn't understand how to live differently. What were they supposed to do? Remember, if Robert sold, it wasn't only his own pride that would suffer; it would be a terrible blow for all the people who lived and worked at Downton, on the estate, in the villages. I remember my father telling me about the reaction of his great-aunt when some sort of employment tax was introduced between the wars, and suddenly the cost of keeping servants shot up. 'Doesn't the Prime Minister realise I have twelve servants indoors whom I have to support?' My father said, 'Yes, Aunt Phyllis, but I think the idea is that you're not supposed to have twelve servants.' Her reply to this was quite hard for him to answer: 'But how will it help anyone for them to lose their jobs?'

ALFRED: He's right.

O'BRIEN: Pay no attention. You've a nice manner,
Alfred. You're not vain like Thomas. They'll like that.

Thomas has heard this. Now he sees Daisy, scowling. *

18   INT. KITCHENS. DOWNTON. NIGHT.

Thomas sees Daisy preparing food, angrily.

THOMAS: What's the matter with you?

....

* I remember the read-through in Ealing Town Hall, and Matt Milne, who
had been cast as Alfred, was sitting down, and I said, 'Oh, hello Matt, we
haven't met, I'm Julian,' and he started to get up and he just seemed to go on
and on and on getting up… It was quite extraordinary. Footmen were paid
by height, not so much in the 1920s when the wheels were coming off, but in
the nineteenth century a footman of six foot would command a higher salary
than a footman of five foot six. This was because, while footmen had jobs to
do, they were essentially status symbols. So you wanted them good-looking
and tall, which was no doubt why so many scandals emerged from the
employing of footmen. They were like gorgeous beach boys lined up in
livery. That said, what you wanted was six foot, not six foot six, or whatever
Matt is, because then they would stand out and dwarf those around them.
Hugh Bonneville, who plays Robert, is extremely tall. He doesn't
photograph as tall, particularly on television, because he's in proportion, but
when you're standing next to him he's actually very tall. So, for him, it didn't
matter that we had a very tall footman, but if I had a footman of six foot six
every time I walked into the dining room I'd feel like a midget.

We make the point of Alfred's height with a shot of Carson looking up at
this immensely tall footman. Carson hasn't chosen Alfred, so he doesn't
really warm to him at first, but then he finds in Alfred an old-fashioned soul
who actually wants to learn how to be a good footman, and eventually how to
be a cook, which is his real interest. He's not casual about his work at all, so
everything Carson had feared from a boy who'd been wished on him doesn't
come to pass.

O'Brien champions Alfred. This is not only because he is her nephew,
but because I always like to give unsympathetic characters something
sympathetic to do every now and then. It means the audience must keep an
open mind about them. Remember how in the second series she supported
the shell-shocked valet? Here, she puffs up Alfred to give him confidence,
particularly as she's now fallen out with her old pal Thomas, which strand we
play through this series.

DAISY: I'm fed up… They promised me promotion. She said they'd get a new kitchen maid and I'd be Mrs Patmore's assistant.

THOMAS: Well, if they really promised, you should withdraw your services.

DAISY: What do you mean? Like go on strike?

THOMAS: But don't say I put you up to it.*

19 INT. DINING ROOM. DOWNTON. NIGHT.

The family is at dinner. Carson is serving Robert. Alfred waits with some potatoes.

VIOLET: But what was in the letter?

MARY: Just that Sybil's coming after all. She says she'll be here on Wednesday in time for dinner.

EDITH: Does she mean dinner on Wednesday or the big dinner on Thursday?

MARY: Obviously she'll be here for both.

ISOBEL: Will she be coming alone?

MATTHEW: Don't make trouble, Mother.†

Alfred is on Violet's left. He demonstrates his hotel silver service technique, scooping up potatoes for her plate.

VIOLET: Ugh… can I do it?

ALFRED: If you wish, m'lady. Of course.

....

* We are starting Daisy's new story here. She's been promoted, except that it wasn't really a promotion because there's no new kitchen maid. When you are promoted your first human instinct is to give orders to the people who are doing the job you used to do, and that has been denied her. Of course, going on strike was dangerous in an unprotected, un-unionised job. There was absolutely nothing to stop your being sacked on the spot. But nevertheless, the withholding of labour had begun to creep in, and by the end of the 1920s it would be a serious part of the landscape – an equivalent of the rioting in the eighteenth century. In those days, the Government may have been aristocratic and entirely untrammelled, but that wasn't the whole story. The un-enfranchised working class used the tool of rioting, and they had to be placated. It's not the same as the ballot box, but rioting is nevertheless an expression of public will that has to be obeyed, or at least dealt with.

† Matthew is always trying to control his mother's propensity for deliberately stirring things up.

He gives her the spoon and fork. But they have spoken softly and Carson only faintly notices that something is going on.

VIOLET: Are you really that tall?

ALFRED: Yes, m'lady.

VIOLET: I thought you might have been walking on stilts.

EDITH: Who's coming to stay?

CORA: Not too many. And only for the night of the wedding. I have been deaf to hints for the night before. And the big dinner is all local.

MARY: When does Grandmama arrive?

CORA: She gets into Liverpool on the fifteenth, so she'll be here the day before the wedding.

VIOLET: I'm so looking forward to seeing your mother again. When I'm with her, I'm reminded of the virtues of the English.

MATTHEW: But isn't she American?

VIOLET: Exactly.

EDITH: What about Aunt Rosamund?

CORA: She's driving straight to the church and her maid will bring her luggage on here.*

During this Alfred tries to put potatoes on Robert's plate.

ROBERT: Can I help myself?

ALFRED: Oh, you want to as well, m'lord?

ROBERT: To be honest, I think you'll find we all want to do it 'as well'.

....

* Nobody comes to stay before the night of the wedding. I did that because I knew we were finishing the episode with the wedding, so we would never have to explain who was staying and who wasn't. Otherwise, we would have found ourselves with a whole other chunk of story.

It was a big thing for us to get Shirley MacLaine as Martha Levinson. A lot of people wanted to come into the series and they made approaches, but we were very clear we wanted someone who was of an equal weight with Maggie, but at the same time her opposite, loving the future, loving change, wishing to move forward. Martha has no nostalgia in her. She wants to climb into fast cars and get moving. And there was something about Shirley's persona that made this believable. She and Maggie are almost exactly the same age, actually, and she's always been marching to the rhythm of her own drum in the public eye. Whether it was China, or the aliens, Shirley's always been on her own track. She seemed to bring that quality to the part in such a good way. Anyway, we asked her to do it and very obligingly she accepted.

This time, Carson has seen everything.

> CARSON: What do you think you're doing? You are not in
> a hotel now.
> ISOBEL: Did you train in a hotel?
> ALFRED: I did, ma'am.
> ISOBEL: That *will* be useful, won't it, Carson?

Carson gives a cold smile.

> ISOBEL (CONT'D): Are you all set for the wedding?
> MARY: Of course he is. Carson's motto is: 'Be
> prepared.'
> VIOLET: I'm afraid Baden-Powell has stolen it.*
> CORA: But you have all the help you need?
> CARSON: Well, I wouldn't fight the idea of a second
> footman, m'lady…
> MATTHEW: I don't know about the rest of you, but I
> sometimes think it's time we lived in a simpler way.†
> ISOBEL: I agree. Much cattle, much care.‡
> ROBERT: Always supposing we have the choice.

....

* My little joke about the Boy Scouts' motto: 'Be prepared.' In fact, his great-granddaughter is a friend of ours, so it was also a fun reference.

† Here, Matthew's desire for a simpler life resurfaces, whereas Violet takes the other moral position: 'An aristocrat with no servants is as much use to the county as a glass hammer.' For her, and women like her, their job was to create employment, to be a social centre, to entertain, and to be the hub of the whole thing. And once they're not prepared to do that, then what's the point of them? Obviously many people now would say there is no point to them, and maybe there isn't, once they're not doing all that stuff. But I think you can understand Violet's argument when they were content to take the weight and be the hub of the county.

‡ One of my mother-in-law's phrases. It's true, the more you own the more you have to worry about. One of my great-aunts, Ierne – a rather odd name (I think it's medieval; we always thought they'd misspelt Irene, but they hadn't) – once said, 'There is a time in life when you wish to acquire and there is a time to give away,' and I think that is fairly true for most people. I remember we went for lunch with her and she gave some things to me, including a portrait of herself as a girl. And I knew she was giving it to me because I would then take it on and the painting would become part of the family stuff, long after her death, and so it proved. We have the picture still. She had ensured its passage. Quite moving, really.

VIOLET: Oh, don't say that. It's our job to provide employment. An aristocrat with no servants is as much use to the county as a glass hammer.

20 INT. SERVANTS' HALL. DOWNTON. NIGHT.

Dinner is laid. Molesley enters after Thomas.

THOMAS: I knew this would happen. Typical.

O'BRIEN: What's typical?

THOMAS: That I'd wind up looking after Mr Matthew. That's all I need.

MOLESLEY: He hasn't thought it through. I'm sorry to say it, but he hasn't.

ANNA: Are you worried for your job, Mr Molesley?

MOLESLEY: Me? Oh, heavens, no. I'm essential to Mrs Crawley. She relies on me. That's what he said. Essential.

O'BRIEN: Oh, yes. We're all essential. Until we get sacked.*

She looks up as Carson and Alfred arrive.

O'BRIEN (CONT'D): How was it?

CARSON: Alfred was confused. He thought he'd been transported to the Hotel Metropole.

Some of them laugh.

ANNA: Cheer up. You'll get the hang of it.

ALFRED: Will I?

Alfred sits as Mrs Hughes comes in.

MRS HUGHES: Oh, you're still here, Mr Molesley?

MOLESLEY: I know. I only walked over for a cup of tea and a chat, and I've outstayed my welcome.

MRS HUGHES: Nonsense. Why not have a bite with us? They won't be leaving for a half hour or more.

....

* I had to watch myself and always say 'sacked' and never 'fired', because these Americanisms creep in on us and you find yourself using them. 'Fired' was never used in this country until thirty years ago, or even less time than that. You never heard it.

MOLESLEY: No. I'd better get back. I wouldn't want them to get home and me not be there to let them in.
O'BRIEN: No, you wouldn't. Not when you're essential.

21 INT. HALL. DOWNTON. NIGHT.

Mary is with Matthew as they cross the hall together. The furniture has been cleared in preparation for the wedding.

MARY: Why's he coming all the way here? Why not say it on the telephone?
MATTHEW: I have no idea.
MARY: If Mr Swire's lawyer wants to see you, and it's urgent, it means he's left you something.*
MATTHEW: I doubt it. I would have heard long before this. Anyway, I hope not.
MARY: Why?
MATTHEW: You know why.

She doesn't answer this. Because she does know why.

ISOBEL: Matthew, do come on. The chauffeur is freezing to death and so am I.

She is waiting by the front door with Robert.

MATTHEW: Talking of chauffeurs, do you think Branson's coming on Wednesday?†
MARY: Papa won't like it much if he does.
MATTHEW: I hope Sybil brings him, whatever your father says. Are you looking forward to the wedding?

....

* Hugo Swire, who's an MP, is a friend of ours and he contributed his name. The big question about this storyline is: why, if Matthew has been left something, has there been such a long time lag? Is it likely? When you are left anything you do hear pretty quickly. But of course all will be explained.

† Matthew is quite snobbish about Branson, even though he'd never admit it. He would say he was the intellectual, sensible one and his wife was brought up in Never Never Land. Even so, Mary, who is more like Violet, is inclined to just get over it now. It's happened. She didn't think it was a good idea – she thought it was mad, in fact – but now it's in the past, and so once he shows up she's quite prepared to be friendly and just get on with it. Whereas you still have Matthew referring to 'the chauffeur'. Of course, they all know there's going to be trouble.

MARY: What do you think?

MATTHEW: I'm looking forward to all sorts of things.*

MARY: Don't make me blush.

MATTHEW: My life's ambition is to make you blush.

ISOBEL: Matthew!

Matthew kisses Mary lightly and joins his mother.

22   INT.   MRS HUGHES'S SITTING ROOM.   NIGHT.

Mrs Hughes looks up as Anna passes outside.

MRS HUGHES: Are you off to bed?

ANNA: I am. Goodnight, Mrs Hughes.

MRS HUGHES: How was the vacuum cleaner?

ANNA: All right. Once you've shown it who's master.

They laugh. But something is troubling Mrs Hughes.

MRS HUGHES: Anna, you do know how very much I pray for Mr Bates's release? Only we've never spoken about the trial.

ANNA: Don't think of that now. Mr Bates knows every word you said was true.

MRS HUGHES: Has he forgiven me?

ANNA: Oh, yes. He forgave you long before I did.

And with that cryptic remark, they part for the night.†

23   EXT.   DOWNTON.   DAY.

A car draws up. The family is waiting. Sybil climbs out. With Branson. Sybil walks over to her father and kisses him.

SYBIL: Dearest Papa, tell me, did you send the money? Please say yes.

ROBERT: What money?

CORA: Hello… Tom. Welcome to Downton.

....

* We have this little, slightly vulgar joke, which is about as vulgar as we get.

† Mrs Hughes was in this difficult position because she was forced to testify against Bates and always felt terrible about it. She didn't lie; she just wished she hadn't had to tell the truth.

BRANSON: I hope I am welcome, your ladyship.*
MARY: Of course. Alfred, would you take the luggage from Mr Branson?
EDITH: There's tea in the library.
BRANSON: Thank you.

Cora is greeting Sybil. Branson walks towards the front door.

BRANSON: Hello, Mr Carson.

Carson bows stiffly at the neck.

24 INT. DRAWING ROOM. CRAWLEY HOUSE. DAY.

Isobel has come in to find an amazed Matthew.

ISOBEL: Was that Mr Charkham I saw leaving?
MATTHEW: Yes. He said to make his apologies. He was late for his train.
ISOBEL: What did he have to say for himself?
MATTHEW: I don't know where to start... Basically, it seems that Reggie Swire did not wish to divide his fortune. So, when Lavinia died, he made a new will with a list of three possible heirs, of which I was the third.

While he talks, she has sat down. This is interesting.

ISOBEL: Why didn't the first name succeed?
MATTHEW: He died before Reggie. In the same epidemic that killed Lavinia.
ISOBEL: But surely if he had children...?

....

* Branson (Allen Leech) is a very useful character to me really from this scene onwards, because for the first time we are allowed to have a working-class character in the family scenes. Until this point, all the working-class characters were in service, but now we've got one simply conversing and having different points of view, with completely logical reasons. And although by this time we knew that Jessica Brown Findlay wanted to leave the series at the end of the third year (which we'll talk about when we get to episode five), from now on I had no desire for Allen to leave because he can always come up with a different argument for all of the various issues. We also have the awkwardness of his being served by the people with whom he was formerly working – a useful awkwardness that we mine in several stories. Naturally, Carson sees him as a traitor to his own kind, and an interloper, and everything bad.

MATTHEW: Reggie didn't make it *per stirpes*. That is, the right to inherit did not descend to any offspring. But at first they thought the second heir, a Mr Clive Pulbrook, would be easy to trace.*

ISOBEL: How much money are we talking about?

MATTHEW: A lot. A huge amount. I had no idea. You could never have told it from Reggie's way of life.

ISOBEL: Lucky Mr Pulbrook.

MATTHEW: Well, this is it. Some time before Reggie's death, Pulbrook travelled to the East, to India. To some tea plantations he owned there.

ISOBEL: And?

MATTHEW: He's never been heard of since. They've made enquiries. They've sent out an agent to visit his property, but there's no sign of him.

ISOBEL: That's why they've decided it's time to let you know the situation.

MATTHEW: In a nutshell. I told Charkham that no one will pray more fervently than I for Mr Pulbrook's welfare.

ISOBEL: That must have restored his faith in human nature.

MATTHEW: Maybe, but if he knew the facts as we do, then his view of human nature would not be reinforced.

Isobel doesn't quite know what to say.†

....

*The name Pulbrook came from the florist Pulbrook and Gould. As I was writing this sentence the doorbell went. I opened it and took delivery of a flower arrangement from Pulbrook and Gould, and so I called him Mr Pulbrook.

† The formula here, where there is a list of sole heirs in order of precedence whose rights will not be transmitted in the event of their own death, was, I think, my invention, but I checked it with a lawyer to see if it would work. I had an inheritance from a female relative once and it was made *per stirpes*. The lawyer explained that this means, 'If you died before she did, your heirs would have got it' – in other words, Emma would have inherited (some furniture). Without this qualification, all the possible heirs in the *Downton* situation would have to be childless, and that didn't seem very believable.

Next, we have the business of its being a huge amount, which we needed for it to be enough to save Downton. But one of the things that I have known – although, funnily enough, much more in America than here – is the phenomenon of people who are far, far richer than you would guess from the

25 INT. SERVANTS' HALL. DOWNTON. DAY.

Thomas is rubbing collars clean. Mrs Hughes and Carson watch.

THOMAS: I'm sorry. I won't, and that's flat.

MRS HUGHES: Then you'll have to do it, Mr Carson.

CARSON: I am not dressing a chauffeur.

MRS HUGHES: He is not a chauffeur now. Anyway, you don't have to dress him. Just see he's got everything he needs.

CARSON: I am not often as one with Mr Barrow. But no.

MRS HUGHES: I'm surprised at you. We're talking about maintaining standards here. To quote you, our opinion of the family's antics is not relevant.

CARSON: I repeat: no.

MRS HUGHES: Then Alfred must do it.

CARSON: Alfred? He wouldn't know what to do beyond collecting dirty shoes outside the door.

MRS HUGHES: Well, he'll have to learn.*

END OF ACT TWO

....

Continued from page 29:

way they live. Most of the English live to the absolute outer limit of their capacity; they live in the nicest house they can possibly afford, they have the nicest holidays they can possibly afford, and the whole thing often goes right to the cliff edge. But the Americans, on the whole, are not like that, just as there are some in England who are different. It's quite normal in Los Angeles for someone to be living in a four-bedroom bungalow on Rexford who is richer than a duke. That's just the way they are. They buy the way of life they want, and once they've got it, the rest of the money can stay in the bank or be invested. And that has been Reggie Swire's way.

Pulbrook has gone to India and vanished because we needed him still to be the probable heir at this stage, so he could not yet be irrevocably dead. We have some dramatic mileage to get out of the situation first.

* The refusal to dress Branson because he's been a chauffeur is based on a true incident of a servant who wouldn't wait at the table on a former servant. I think they made it a buffet or something in the end. However, Mrs Hughes doesn't believe the difference between the classes is part of the Divine Plan. She quite reasonably sees serving anyone the Granthams choose to invite as simply a function of the job.

ACT THREE

26   INT.   DINING ROOM.   DOWNTON.   NIGHT.

The family is there, with Isobel and Matthew, waited on by Carson and Alfred. Branson is in an ordinary suit. The other men are in white tie.

VIOLET: Is it an Irish tradition?

BRANSON: What?

ROBERT: She means not changing.

SYBIL: Of course it isn't, Granny.

VIOLET: It might've been. You don't change on the first night of a voyage.

BRANSON: No, m'lady. I don't own a set of tails. Or a dinner jacket, either. I wouldn't get any use out of them.

ROBERT: Well, I hope you own a morning coat, since you're here for a wedding.

BRANSON: No. I'm afraid I don't.

SYBIL: We live a completely different kind of life, Papa.

ROBERT: Obviously.

During this, with an inner struggle, Carson brings the food to Branson's left. He holds it slightly too high.

BRANSON: Could you lower it a bit, Mr Carson?

Silently, Carson does so. Mary speaks into the void.

MARY: You should buy a Downton wardrobe and leave it here. Then you won't have to pack when you come.

EDITH: What a good idea.

BRANSON: I'm sorry, but I'm afraid I can't turn into somebody else just to please you.

VIOLET: More's the pity.

ISOBEL: Oh, no. Why should you change to please us?*

....

* What Branson wears had to be a very gradual transition. He is a proud man, and we felt that for him immediately to start jumping into black tie, never mind white, would look as though he were imitating something that wasn't organic and true to him, and that he was trying too hard to please the Crawleys. So he starts off refusing to change at all. We then get to a point

She smiles at Violet. Mary catches Matthew's eye.

MATTHEW: What is the general feeling in Ireland, now?

BRANSON: That we're in sight of throwing off the English yoke.

ISOBEL: Do you approve of the new Act?

BRANSON: Would you approve of your country being divided by a foreign power?

ISOBEL: Well, won't it bring home rule for southern Ireland nearer?

BRANSON: Home rule on English terms. Presided over by an English king.

MATTHEW: Is keeping the monarchy a problem?

BRANSON: Would it be a problem for you to be ruled by the German Kaiser?

*At the sideboard, a furious Carson snaps the stem of a glass.**

....

Continued from page 31:

where he begins to wear black tie, even when they're in white tie, and finally, when we get to the house party in series four, he puts on a white tie. But he still feels very bad about it – he feels he's let himself down, which makes him vulnerable, as we shall see.

His clothing is all quite carefully mapped so that he doesn't even wear completely appropriate outside clothes. Branson is clever, so it is impossible for him not to start appreciating certain things, and eventually, of course, he fits in. All of which made him a very useful character for me and full of interesting elements. Violet is not above punishing him for his recalcitrance. Robert is very unflinching. Sybil is much freer in all of this. I remember reading an article once about keeping sherry in the fridge, which was a brief fashion, and someone saying the problem with this is you have to know enough not to keep sherry in the fridge before you can keep sherry in the fridge. And rather similarly, because Sybil is perfectly at ease with people wearing white tie, it means nothing to her when they're not. But Branson is the one who is walking on knives all the way through this series.

Naturally Carson makes everything as difficult as possible for him. But when Mary says, 'You should buy a Downton wardrobe and leave it here,' it's not supposed to be a jibe. She's just making conversation. But obviously Branson is offended by it because he's very prickly. And then Isobel immediately feels the need to make things worse by supporting Branson's position.

* If you look at a newspaper from 1920, it doesn't have the Russian Revolution or anything else, it has Ireland on every front page, partly because many families, certainly including my own, had Anglo-Irish relations, whose houses were being burnt down, or, perhaps, hopefully not being burnt down. It was uppermost in everyone's minds. In December 1921 the treaty that led to the creation of the Irish Free State was signed, but the troubles were by no means over. Should formerly English families continue to own land and be the dominant ruling class? Or should their estates be confiscated?

My own great-grandmother was part of the Ascendancy. Her mother's brother, the first Lord Hemphill, was the Solicitor-General for Ireland, but, oddly, she and her siblings grew up very much pro home rule, and as supporters of Parnell. However, her father's father was strongly opposed to all of this, and so when my great-great-grandparents married he was disinherited. Thus the treatment of Ireland was a very hot topic in our family. Even down to my childhood we were taught to believe in Irish independence as desirable, which, for a family like mine, was quite unusual at that time. For all these reasons, I was keen to discuss it in the show. I give Robert the typical response of his own kind – he is not terribly unreasonable or savage, just fairly classic – but I'm probably most in sympathy with Branson's opinion. So his arguments should be taken as perfectly sincere.

As for the Treaty in real life, de Valera, in my opinion, was not nearly the man that Michael Collins was. De Valera got completely sidetracked by the issue of the Crown. Michael Collins was not a soft man – he'd been a terrorist – but he realised the time had come for talking. And he saw that the most important thing, once they'd got the principle of self-government, was to keep Ireland unified. He argued that if they accepted the Crown and dominion status, like Canada, like Australia, then the world would support them in their struggle to keep Ireland unified. But once they turned against the Crown they would lose the support of America, amongst others, and they would be seen as unreasonable and intransigent. If they took this position then Carson, trying to keep the northern counties attached to England, would be seen as reasonable. Collins's point was that, twenty years down the line, they could have a referendum on Crown and dominion status. But de Valera couldn't see it, and as long as the Crown was part of the conditions he declined to go to London for the discussions. The result was that he lost a lot of support from around the world, and in the end Ireland had to accept division, dominion status and the Crown. And then Michael Collins was assassinated. But even if Collins was right, and it was silly to be sidetracked by the issue, still a lot of them did feel very strongly, which is why Branson says, 'Would it be a problem for you to be ruled by the German Kaiser?' Carson, of course, breaks the glass.

ROBERT: Carson? Are you all right?

CARSON: I have been very clumsy, m'lord. I do apologise.

ROBERT: Please don't. I've every sympathy.

This time Cora tries to rescue matters.

CORA: Is it true the Irish gardens have more variety than ours?

EDITH: Oh, yes. Don't you remember Lady Dufferin's ball at Clandeboye? The gardens there were heavenly.*

27 INT. SERVANTS' HALL. DOWNTON. NIGHT.

The servants are finishing dinner.

ALFRED: I thought them very down on him.

THOMAS: That is because you know nothing.

CARSON: And wasn't he down on *them*? Insulting our country, insulting the King… I thought it was a miracle his lordship held his temper.

MRS HUGHES: But it must be hard, Mr Carson. To sit up there, with people he used to drive around —

She stops. Branson is standing in the doorway.

BRANSON: It is hard, Mrs Hughes.

Carson has stood and so the others have to.

BRANSON: Please, sit down.

CARSON: Is there something we can do, *sir*?

....

* Here, Cora, like all good hostesses, tries to save the day and change the conversation. I used Lady Dufferin and Clandeboye because my Great-Aunt Isie was married to a man whose mother had been a Rowan-Hamilton of Killyleagh Castle, and so his aunt was the Marchioness of Dufferin and lived at Clandeboye. As a result, Isie started her honeymoon there, because for marriages in those days they had a rather nice custom. The bride, in ninety-nine per cent of cases, entered the situation untouched, and so they would go to an English country house, or an Irish one, for a few days while they sort of got used to the idea… After which they would set off on their travels round Europe or wherever.

She was called Isie because her Aunt Eliza was known as Isie for short, and she died of consumption in her twenties. Isie was born soon after that.

BRANSON: I just wanted to come down to say hello. I wouldn't want you to think I'd got too big for my boots.

MRS HUGHES: That's nice.

ANNA: I hope you and Lady Sybil are well.

BRANSON: We are, thank you. And we've been following the story of Mr Bates. Mary keeps us informed… Still, I mustn't interrupt your dinner.

MRS HUGHES: Thank you for coming down.

He nods and goes. They sit.

O'BRIEN: He's settled into his new life.

CARSON: 'Mary keeps us informed.'

MRS HUGHES: Well, he knows her now.

CARSON: What's that got to do with it? His lordship would never call her 'Mary' when talking to me. *Never.* If he wants to play their game he'd better learn their rules.*

28 INT. DRAWING ROOM. DOWNTON. NIGHT.

Violet, Sybil, Cora and Isobel are playing bridge. The others sit about.

VIOLET: Is he coming back?

SYBIL: I don't think so. He's going to bed once he's said his hellos.

VIOLET: Tomorrow, let's ask the servants to come up and dine with us. It'll make things easier.

MARY: You must get him to stop calling Granny 'm'lady'. And Mama.

ISOBEL: We need something that doesn't sound too stiff and grand.

ROBERT: 'Lady Grantham', of course. And he can call me 'Lord Grantham'.

SYBIL: That doesn't sound stiff or grand at all.

Robert glares at her. Mary's passing the table. She whispers.

....

* Carson is absolutely right, Robert would never say 'Mary' to him. Robert is not a snob, actually, but the rules mean that between him and Carson she is referred to as Lady Mary. Branson calls her Mary because he hasn't yet picked up all those customs, for which Carson despises him.

MARY: One step at a time.*

She drifts over to Matthew. They talk intimately.

MARY (CONT'D): So what did the lawyer want? I presume
he turned up.
MATTHEW: He did. And it's rather complicated. But you
were right that it was about Reggie's will.
MARY: So he's left you something.
MATTHEW: Well, no he hasn't. Yet. And he probably
never will.
MARY: But he's dead…?
MATTHEW: Never mind that now. Just sit down and tell me
about the relations who are coming to the wedding. I
want to unscramble them in my head.

29 INT. SYBIL'S BEDROOM. DOWNTON. NIGHT.

There is a knock and a 'come in' and Alfred enters.

ALFRED: Oh. You're in bed, sir.
BRANSON: I am.
ALFRED: I was coming to help you. Have you hung
everything up, sir?
BRANSON: I have. And please don't pretend you don't
know my story.
ALFRED: It doesn't matter to me. I used to work in a
hotel and you didn't get a character reference with every
guest there, I can tell you.

Branson laughs. It is the first time he has done so.

BRANSON: Are you enjoying life at Downton?
ALFRED: I've only just arrived.
BRANSON: It's not a bad place to work. And Lord
Grantham's not a bad man, whatever you feel about the
system. But remember, you weren't born to be a servant.
Nobody is.†

....

* In a sense, Robert is allowing Branson, the chauffeur, to address him in a
way he would not have been allowed to before. In service, Branson would
have called him 'your lordship', so for him to say 'Lord Grantham' is a
halfway step.

30 INT. KITCHENS. DOWNTON. NIGHT.

Daisy is putting the pots away. Mrs Patmore looks in.

MRS PATMORE: Go to bed when you're done.

DAISY: I'll go to bed when I'm ready.

MRS PATMORE: What's happened to you? Have you swapped places with your evil twin?

DAISY: I'd like to know where the new kitchen maid is. That's what you promised. They've got a new footman. Where's the kitchen maid?

MRS PATMORE: I know, and I'm sorry. But I spoke to Mr Carson tonight, and they won't be taking anyone new on.

DAISY: Except a footman.

MRS PATMORE: I don't know how Mr Carson managed it because his lordship's put his foot down. But you're called my assistant now, and you've seven shillings extra every month.

DAISY: You've still kept me here with a dishonest representation.

MRS PATMORE: Oh, dear. Have you swallowed a dictionary?‡

....

† I was sad we lost this scene, because it was about being a servant. Alfred, for the first time, is talking to someone sympathetic to his position as a newcomer, and this sympathy comes from where he least looked for it, from the first man he has to valet. Branson's words convey a message of quintessential Branson-esque thinking: 'It's not a bad place to work. And Lord Grantham's not a bad man. But remember, you weren't born to be a servant. Nobody is.' But once again we had to weigh up what else would have had to go to keep it in. On the whole, I think it was the right call.

‡ Of course, this was a problem across England. Arthur Inch, who was the advisor on *Gosford Park* and later wrote the book *Dinner Is Served: An English Butler's Guide to the Art of the Table*, had been a footman and a butler all his working life. He used to say these years were very difficult, because every so often someone just dropped out of the equation and their job was added to yours. So you found yourself being a butler, the footmen, the hall boys, the valet, the chauffeur – each job previously being a full occupation. To an extent, some of the jobs would get easier, with the invention of new devices and gadgets, but nevertheless, when you were a servant in a house with two servants instead of eight, you were doing a hell of a lot more work. And so my sympathies are rather with Daisy at this point, when her workload doubles and they give her seven shillings more a month.

31 INT. DRAWING ROOM. DOWNTON. NIGHT.

Only Mary, Matthew and Sybil are left. The others have gone.

SYBIL: The money came with a note saying it was for the tickets and it was postmarked Downton. I so hoped it was Papa wanting us here.

MATTHEW: I'm afraid not. But it sounds like the sort of thing Mother would do. The writing wasn't familiar?

SYBIL: No. Tom was furious because he couldn't give it back. It's bad enough for him that we're living off Papa. He won't spend a penny on himself. That's why he doesn't have any clothes.

Matthew has gone to the drinks tray and poured some whisky.

MATTHEW: We've run out of water.

MARY: Ring the bell.

MATTHEW: No, it's late. I'll get it.

He walks out carrying a glass jug, leaving them alone.

SYBIL: Somehow none of it seems to matter when we're in Dublin. Class and all that just fades away. I'm Mrs Branson and we get on with our lives like millions of others. But here he feels so patronised, and he hates it.

MARY: But why are you so broke? He works, doesn't he?

SYBIL: He works like a Trojan, but the rebel newspapers pay nothing and nursing's finished for me until after the baby, so we really do count every penny.

MARY: But you don't regret it?

SYBIL: No. Never. Not at all. He's a wonderful, wonderful man. I just wish you knew him.

She starts to cry and Mary puts her arms round her sister.

MARY: Darling, we will know him. We'll know him and value him, I promise.

SYBIL: He puts a tough face on it and says things that make everyone angry, but he so wants your good opinion. I can't tell you how much.

She wipes her eyes with a half-smile.

SYBIL (CONT'D): Anyway. I'd best go upstairs and make sure he's not too suicidal. Goodnight.

MARY: Oh, by the way, I don't know if Mama's told you, but the whole Grey family's coming tomorrow night.

SYBIL: Including Larry? Crikey.

MARY: You'd better warn Tom… Oh, and Sybil, if I were you, I wouldn't tell Papa about being Mrs Branson.*

32 INT. BEDROOM PASSAGE. DOWNTON. NIGHT.

Sybil walks along to her room as Robert comes out of a door in his dressing gown. She smiles at him.

SYBIL: It's so nice to be home again.

He kisses her as she opens the door.

ROBERT: And it's so nice to see my baby. Goodnight.

BRANSON: Goodnight.

He is standing by the open door, also in his dressing gown. Robert bristles. Sybil sees his pain and strokes his cheek.

SYBIL: Goodnight, darling Papa.

....

* Sybil is now acknowledging that their life is much easier in Dublin because none of these issues are present. I think that it is true that when you make a tremendously uneven marriage – I suspect even today, although nobody would admit it – it is easier if you're just outside everyone's context. If you go and live in California, or you go to Spain, all of those differences and difficulties cease to be. My mother was rather looked down upon by my father's relations, and the happiest time after they were first married, before she'd quite learnt to imitate as she later did, was in Africa, where he was posted. Out there, they were just part of the gang. The fact that she was a very pretty woman, young and good fun, was more important than anything else. And all the stuff that made my great-aunts unpleasant, or certainly very cold, towards her vanished in the heat. The Africa sun burnt it away.

Similarly in Dublin Sybil is just Sybil, married to this nice man. Still, even if things are more complicated at Downton, Mary is speaking truthfully – 'We will know him. We'll know him and value him' – because by now she's made the decision that she wants to get on with him. But inevitably, what's difficult for Branson is that when Sybil is back at home she fits into this way of life because it's what she's always known. And he doesn't. If you said to him, 'Well, what do you want from her? Do you want her not to fit in?' he'd say, 'No, of course not.' But that is what he wants, really. He wants them both not to fit in and to be together in their not fitting in, but this is not realistic. And that's what the scene is about.

33 INT. CORA'S BEDROOM. DOWNTON. NIGHT.

Cora is reading in bed and Robert is in his dressing gown.

CORA: I didn't ask for the marriage either, but it's happened now.

ROBERT: If he had just a scrap of humility —

CORA: What do you want him to do? Genuflect and call you Master?*

ROBERT: I want this wedding to be perfect, that's all. A Downton moment. For us to remember as long as we live.

CORA: It will be. And we'll have Edith's, too, and lots of christenings. So we have plenty of Downton moments to come… What is it?

ROBERT: I wasn't going to tell you. Not until after the wedding…

CORA: You're scaring me.

34 INT. SYBIL'S BEDROOM. DOWNTON. NIGHT.

Sybil is getting into bed with Branson.

BRANSON: But who are the Greys? Why does it matter that they're coming?

SYBIL: The father, Lord Merton, is Mary's godfather, but Larry Grey used to be keen on me. When we were young.

BRANSON: And were you keen on him?

SYBIL: No. I don't think so. I can hardly remember, to be honest.

BRANSON: So what are you saying?

SYBIL: Nothing, particularly… But we could run into Ripon and find some tails. We have the money.

BRANSON: I won't spend more of that money.

SYBIL: All right. But please don't talk about Ireland *all* the time.

....

* My sympathies are with Cora here. In any situation, certainly in families, you can fight things and advise against them until you are blue in the face. But when they happen, then the goalposts have moved and you have to wake up to it. Again, I was sad the scene didn't make the final edit, but you have to ask: is there a detail here that we need to understand what they are feeling? I don't think there is.

He tries to read her. Is she being deliberately opaque?

> SYBIL (CONT'D): I just want to make things easier for
> you.
> BRANSON: For me or for you? Don't disappoint me, Sybil.
> Not now that we're here.*

But she pulls him into her arms and kisses him.

35 INT. DRAWING ROOM. DOWNTON. NIGHT.

Matthew has come back.

> MARY: Shall I order the car?
> MATTHEW: I don't think I can refuse a lift with Mother,
> and then make the poor man go out again. I'll walk.
> MARY: It might rain.
> MATTHEW: Then I'll get wet. Come and kiss me.

He sits, holding out his hand. But Mary has been thinking.

> MARY: So, if they can't find Mr Pillbox, what will you
> do with the money?
> MATTHEW: Pulbrook. And they will find him.†
> MARY: But if they don't?
> MATTHEW: Then I'll decide what to do. Or we will.
> Because I can't keep it.
> MARY: No. Of course not.

36 INT. CORA'S BEDROOM. DOWNTON. NIGHT.

Cora can hardly believe what she has been hearing.

> CORA: Why were you so heavily invested in one
> enterprise? Wasn't it foolish?

....

* We're about to set up the humiliation of Branson. Sybil wants Larry Grey
to see the worthy man whom she's married. She doesn't want Larry to look
down on the former chauffeur. And her instinct is to buy him a set of tails
and make him look like everyone else, so Larry Grey will take him seriously.
But to Branson that means she wants to sell out, to placate the enemy by
draping him in their flag. Again, I hope the audience can see both points of
view. 'I just want to make things easier for you.' Of course I sympathise with
her, but I sympathise with Branson's rage, too.

† I always think it's a sort of casual insult when people can't remember your
name right.

Robert sits and buries his face in his hands for a moment.

> ROBERT: Everyone said there was no risk. *Everyone.*
> That the more money we put in, the more we'd make. They
> said the shares were an absolute bargain, and the war was
> going to bring a massive bonanza.
> CORA: Well, obviously there *was* a risk and they *weren't*
> a bargain... Has some of my fortune been lost?
> ROBERT: Some? All. Or almost all.
> CORA: So it's very bad?

*Robert would speak, but when he tries he starts to cry. Cora
stands and comes over, putting her arms round him.*

> CORA: Oh, my dear. How terrible for you.
> ROBERT: It's not so good for you.
> CORA: Don't worry about me. I'm an American. Have gun,
> will travel.*

He is very moved by this. He takes her hand and kisses it.

> ROBERT: Oh, thank God for you, anyway.
> CORA: And you know what? I'm glad we have a wedding to
> celebrate. Let's make sure it's a great day. If it's to
> be our last, let's make it a wonderful 'last', and enjoy
> our lovely home and the lovely people we've spent our
> life among.

He takes her in his arms.†

....

* This was a phrase used by travelling gunmen in the Middle West, an
advertisement they would put in local papers, and if a sheriff wanted a deputy
or to form a posse, if the town was having trouble with Indian raids and you
wanted some protection, you would answer the ad. According to the
philologist Eric Partridge, this phrase may also be found in *The Times*
personal columns from about 1900.

† The point of this scene, I suppose, is to make it clear that this marriage has
long passed the point where Cora's money is a principal factor. The fact that
they've lost it, which is very sad, is not actually going to alter their
relationship in any way, which I think it was necessary to make clear. She
also has a different perspective. She is not an English landed toff, and the
fact that they're going to sell the house and move to another house is not the
end of the world for her. She's mainly sorry for him.

37 EXT. DOWNTON VILLAGE. DAY.

Branson is walking towards the pub when Matthew hails him.

MATTHEW: Bit early for drowning your sorrows.

BRANSON: I thought it might be better if I moved down to the pub.

MATTHEW: You're not serious.

BRANSON: I can't go through too many more dinners like last night.

MATTHEW: You don't make it easy for them. Do you really think you can recruit Cousin Robert for Sinn Fein?

BRANSON: I don't know what gets into me… I can see them staring, and I know they don't want me here…

MATTHEW: Well, don't include me. Or Mary.

BRANSON: She wasn't too keen on the idea of a chauffeur for a brother-in-law.

MATTHEW: Forget that. She's a pragmatist.

BRANSON: She could be a tough fighter, too.

MATTHEW: Well, let's hope she's not tested. Now forget this and walk back. We're brothers-in-law with high-minded wives. We'd better stick together.

38 INT. VISITING CELL. YORK PRISON. DAY.

Bates is with Anna. He hands her a sheaf of papers.

BATES: It's all there. Friends — though there weren't too many — tradesmen, acquaintances… but I can't see what you'll get out of them.

ANNA: I do not believe when Vera decided to kill herself she never mentioned it to another living soul.

BATES: We know she left no note. I wish to God she had. But why are you sure it was suicide? And not murder?

ANNA: Well, I know you didn't kill her. And what's the alternative? A thief broke in, cooked an arsenic pie and forced her to eat it? It's not a very likely scenario.

BATES: You can see why they convicted me.

ANNA: I'm going to write to everyone in the book in case she said or, please God, *wrote* anything that could suggest a desire to die.

BATES: But how long will that take?

ANNA: Why? Are you going somewhere?

39 INT. CARSON'S PANTRY. DOWNTON. DAY.

Carson looks up and stands. Mary comes in and shuts the door.

MARY: You don't mind my sneaking in here?

CARSON: I'm very flattered, m'lady.

MARY: I need your help with his lordship. I want Anna to be my maid, and for that, we must hire someone to dress Edith and to do the finer cleaning. The junior maids aren't up to it.

CARSON: And I want a second footman. Then Mrs Patmore needs a kitchen maid. It's time to bring Downton back up to scratch. Will Mr Molesley move in after your wedding journey?

MARY: Mr Crawley says not… The truth is, I'm having a bit of trouble persuading him to live at Downton.

CARSON: I'm sorry to hear that.

MARY: I shouldn't have told you, really.

CARSON: I won't give you away, m'lady. Your secrets are always safe with me.

MARY: I love Mr Crawley more than anything. You do know that?

CARSON: Certainly. He's a very lucky man.

MARY: And I don't want to bully him. It's just I *know* he'll be happier here.*

40 INT. SERVANTS' HALL. DOWNTON. DAY.

Tea is nearing the end. O'Brien is with Alfred and Daisy.

ALFRED: I should have gone into cooking. I used to watch them in the kitchens and I could pick it up in a trice.

....

* Here we have the alliance between Mary and Carson operating again. It never occurs to Mary, or at least not yet, that there's going to be any kind of cutting down in the scale of life at Downton, and we can see that this is going to be Robert's big problem, explaining it to her. That must have been particularly hard for those men – and there were still quite a lot of them, not only in my youth, but later – who didn't include their women in the business side of their life at all. My mother had a friend whose husband died and she said to her, 'I've never written a cheque.' It's terrifying, really, to think that was in the 1960s.

DAISY: Why didn't you, then?

O'BRIEN: Oh, it's a hard ladder for a man. For every Escoffier or Monsieur Carême, there's a thousand dogsbodies taking orders from a cross and red-faced old woman.

MRS PATMORE: Who's this you're discussing?

O'BRIEN: Hello, Mrs Patmore. I didn't see you standing there.

MRS PATMORE: Obviously not.

ALFRED: My mum and Aunt Sarah thought I'd be better off as a butler, and so that's what I'm trying for.*

DAISY: I think you're right. I know I'd rather be giving the orders.

MRS PATMORE: To a cross and red-faced old woman. Yes, we know.

41 INT. LIBRARY. DOWNTON. EVE.

Edith is fiddling with a flower arrangement, while Mary watches. Robert works at his desk. The clock chimes.

EDITH: Can I have Anna first? I need her to sew on a button.

MARY: Of course.

Edith goes. But Mary has agreed because she has a plan.

MARY (CONT'D): Papa, can I ask you something? Well, two things, really. Matthew ran into Tom this morning. He wanted to take a room at the pub.

ROBERT: Did Matthew stop him?

MARY: He did. But can you imagine the story that would have gone round the village? Darling, you must be nicer to him. For Sybil's sake.

ROBERT: And will he come down tonight, dressed as a travelling salesman, and insult the King of England?

MARY: Sybil's trying to control him. But do please give her some help.

....

* We have already had this situation with William in the first series. His mother didn't want him to be a groom, but instead chose the ladder for him of footman leading, hopefully, to butler. There was, as we know, a very firm class system below stairs, and naturally mothers were ambitious for their children to be at the top of it.

ROBERT: What's the second request?

MARY: Can I have Anna as my own maid? It means taking on someone new, but we've never replaced Jane.

ROBERT: No. We've never replaced Jane.*

MARY: And if I do persuade Matthew to move in when we're married —

ROBERT: Isn't that settled?

Clearly, he is surprised, but there is the sound of the gong.

MARY: We'll do this later. We can't be late down tonight.

42   INT.   EDITH'S BEDROOM.   DOWNTON.   NIGHT.

Anna has almost finished Edith's hair.

ANNA: There. Is that what you meant?

EDITH: Yes. Perfect. Slightly new, but not too different. We'll see if Sir Anthony notices.

She smiles at Anna through the looking glass.

EDITH (CONT'D): I know they all think he's too old for me, but he's not… Bates is older than you and you're as happy as lovebirds.

ANNA: Well, our situation is hardly ideal, but yes, we're very happy together.

EDITH: Which is all that matters. As I keep telling them.†

43   INT.   BEDROOM PASSAGE.   DOWNTON.   NIGHT.

O'Brien is waiting for Thomas by the dressing-room door.

THOMAS: I've no time to talk.

O'BRIEN: His lordship's not come up yet.

....

* The point of the scene was to explain to the audience how difficult it's going to be for Robert to tell them their way of life is over and that they're going to have to sell up.

† New styles arrived in the 1920s, but gradually. We didn't jump them all into flattening their hair and looking like Clara Bow because that all came in the middle Twenties. So we're creeping in the changes. Edith clings to the fact that Bates is older than Anna and yet they're very happy, which gives her hope that everything can work out with Strallan.

THOMAS: Well? What is it?

O'BRIEN: I was hoping you could help young Alfred to find his way about.

THOMAS: As a footman, you mean?

O'BRIEN: As a valet. He's looking after Mr Branson now. Though I dare say a chauffeur can dress himself. But you can tell him what he needs to know. Give him an advantage.

THOMAS: Why? What's the rush?

O'BRIEN: You've heard Mr Matthew has turned down Mr Molesley?

THOMAS: Blimey. You don't want much, do you? Can you remember what I had to go through to be a valet?

O'BRIEN: Of course. I watched it, didn't I?

THOMAS: But young Alfred is to make the great leap in one bound? Well, I'm sorry, Miss O'Brien, but I'm not convinced… If you'll excuse me.*

END OF ACT THREE

ACT FOUR

44   INT.   DRAWING ROOM.   DOWNTON.   NIGHT.

The party, including all the family, numbers eighteen. Anthony Strallan is among the guests.

MATTHEW: It's infuriating, but there's nothing he can do.

MARY: I don't agree. I think it's feeble. He should *will* himself not to be ill and then collapse the next day. Whom will you ask instead?

MATTHEW: I'm not sure.

....

* O'Brien is asking for Thomas's help to train Alfred so that he'll be able to work his way up the ladder, but, by doing so, she infuriates Thomas even more and deepens their antipathy. I always find in life the more similar people are the more they dislike each other, so that seems quite truthful to me.

Branson, in his suit, is talking to a smart, handsome man.

LARRY GREY: I've known Sybil all my life. So you can
imagine how curious I was when I found out you'd be here
tonight. I never thought we'd meet in person.
BRANSON: As opposed to what? In spirit?
LARRY GREY: Well, you see, to us, in marrying you it
seemed like Sybil had left Downton Abbey for ever. If
you know what I mean.
BRANSON: I know exactly what you mean.*
LARRY GREY: Did they lose your suitcase on the way over?
How maddening for you.
BRANSON: No. My suitcase arrived safely, thank you.
Along with my manners.†

He walks off. Across the room, Violet has arrived.

VIOLET: He's still dressed as the Man from the
Prudential, I see.‡
ISOBEL: Yes. It's nice to have someone from the real
world, isn't it?
ROBERT: Hello, Mama. Can I tempt you to one of these
new cocktails?
VIOLET: I don't think so. They look too exciting for so
early in the evening, don't you think so, Carson?
CARSON: Better avoided, m'lady.§

....

* Larry Grey, Baddie of the Week. Sometimes, because I tend to take an
essentially benevolent view of the landowning classes, it's important to have
someone come along who's a complete bastard, just to remind ourselves, and
the audience, that the opposition to my point of view is not a hundred per
cent incorrect. The trouble with any hereditary system is it does empower
some nasty people. This doesn't mean that everyone who's empowered by the
class system is nasty, but obviously it does happen and, here, Larry is that
person. He's infuriated that he should have been beaten to Sybil by someone
whom he regards as vastly inferior.

† It was important for me that we didn't always see Branson as the
downtrodden person being squashed. He can come back fighting, and it's
necessary to show it.

‡ An advertising jingle from the 1890s that survived. The Man from the
Prudential was still going when I was young. It was a phrase they stuck with
for ages. Of course, these days, no catchphrase lasts longer than about two or
three years.

Isobel is talking to Strallan as Edith approaches.

    ISOBEL: What a pleasure it is to see you out and about,
    Sir Anthony. I want to say, 'Can I be of any help?' but
    you don't seem to need any.
    EDITH: He doesn't need help at all, do you? He won't
    let me do anything.
    STRALLAN: Mustn't be a nuisance, you know.
    ISOBEL: Are you coming to the wedding?
    EDITH: Of course!
    STRALLAN: Well, if you really want me.
    EDITH: I do. I really do.
    STRALLAN: You look very nice. Have you done something
    jolly with your hair?

*He smiles at her affectionately, in spite of his more sensible
self. Just then he is distracted by something.*

    STRALLAN (CONT'D): I say. What the devil?
    EDITH: What is it?
    CARSON: Dinner is served, your ladyship.

The company moves towards the door.

45   INT.   KITCHENS.   DOWNTON.   NIGHT.

*We glimpse a group of visiting chauffeurs drinking tea as
Alfred collects the next course. Daisy is working.*

    DAISY: How's it going?
    ALFRED: Awkward. Mr Branson's well away and Lady Sybil
    doesn't like it much. I don't understand it. He only
    had one cocktail.
    DAISY: Maybe he was drinking before he came down, to
    calm his nerves.

....

§ It was in this era that cocktails began. We don't often serve cocktails at Downton – in fact, I think we only do it about twice – and Carson hates them. One of the things that is almost invariably wrong in period drama is giving people drinks before dinner, which was a completely post-First World War phenomenon. It came to London from America, and spread out across the country, but quite slowly. Even in the 1950s, I had great-aunts who were reluctant to give you anything. Drinking wine during dinner was fine, and afterwards you could be as drunk as a lord, but to drink before was just considered excessive.

46 INT. DINING ROOM. DOWNTON. NIGHT.

As Alfred comes in, Carson meets his gaze. Things are bad.

BRANSON: No! I don't agree! And I don't care who knows
it! Well, the Black and Tans are there to restore order,
are they? Why don't they just murder the entire
population, and then you wouldn't hear a squeak out of
any of them!*

The rest of the company is stilled by this.

VIOLET: Is there any way to shut him up?
ROBERT: If I knew how to control him, he wouldn't be
here in the first place.

Cora turns to the man Branson was attacking.

CORA: Are you interested in Irish politics, Lord Merton?
MERTON: Well, I was only saying that I —
BRANSON: He's interested in Irish *repression*! Like all
of *you*!
MATTHEW: Look, old chap. Of course this stuff matters a
great deal to you —
BRANSON: Yes, it does matter, this *stuff*! It matters a
very great deal!

Across the table, next to Mary, Larry Grey is smirking.

MARY: What's so funny?
LARRY GREY: Nothing. I'm just enjoying this vivid
display of Irish character.
SYBIL: Please, Tom, we don't have to wear everyone out…
BRANSON: Why? What's the matter? Am I not being *polite
enough*?

But they are suddenly interrupted by a shout from Strallan.

....

* The Black and Tans (the nickname came from their uniforms) were a
so-called peacekeeping force put in by the British in the 1920s, who were
oppressive and unpopular, and behaved, generally speaking, very badly. It
was still a term of abuse during my teens when I used to spend my summers
in Ireland. My parents had an island near Kerry, and at that time, if you were
English and before they got used to you, you might walk into a pub and hear
someone muttering 'Black and Tan'.

STRALLAN: Wait a minute! This was down to you, wasn't it?

He addresses Larry with his left hand. The room is silent.

LARRY GREY: I don't know what you mean.
STRALLAN: Yes, you do. I saw you. You put something in his drink, didn't you? Just before we came in.
SYBIL: That's not true, is it? Larry?
EDITH: What a beastly thing to do.
LARRY GREY: Oh, come on, Edith. That's not like you. You could always take a joke.
MARY: The bully's defence. Listen, everyone! Mr Grey has given my brother-in-law something to make him appear drunk.
VIOLET: Could it be… drink?
MARY: No, not drink. Some horrible pill. Sybil, take him upstairs.
ROBERT: *Il ne manque que ça.**

He rolls his eyes at Violet.

CORA: But why would you do that, Mr Grey?
LARRY GREY: Well, I'm sorry, Lady Grantham, but the last time I was here you had a sense of humour.
CORA: Tom has been the victim of a cruel prank, which I know you will all be kind enough to forget.
VIOLET: Forgive, perhaps. Forget, never.
MERTON: Is this true, Larry?
LARRY GREY: I don't know why you're all getting so hot under the collar. He's only a grubby little chauffeur chappie, in case you've forgotten.
MERTON: Be silent this instant, sir! I apologise for my son, Mr Branson. Unreservedly. I only hope you recover before the wedding.†

....

* That's all we need.

† I thought the chap who played Lord Merton, Douglas Reith, gave a marvellous performance. He wrote to us later, asking, 'Would you see Merton coming back?' and I must say there can have been few letters written by a member of Equity that produced such results, because he came back with a whole story of his own. It just shows you, there are no small parts, only small actors. It was a very small part, but he was so good that we just had him straight back.

MATTHEW: I hope so, too. Since I want him to be my best man.

ISOBEL: Bravo! Well said.

But the words have stopped Sybil and Branson in their tracks.

SYBIL: Do you really mean that?

BRANSON: Honestly?

MATTHEW: I've told you before, if we're mad enough to take on the Crawley girls, we have to stick together.

Which earns him a round of applause from Mary.

MARY: Thank you, Matthew. Thank you so much.*

47   EXT.   DOWNTON.   NIGHT.

Cars are driving away. Edith is with Strallan by his vehicle.

EDITH: That was rather marvellous of you. To expose Larry Grey like that. You saved the day, really.

STRALLAN: I wouldn't say that. Matthew saved the day.

EDITH: No. It was you. I do hope we'll be seeing a bit more of you, once the wedding is over.

STRALLAN: Well…

EDITH: Wouldn't you like that?

STRALLAN: I should like that very much. Much more than I probably ought to.

There is a voice from the main doorway.

ROBERT: Edith! Let Sir Anthony go!

Strallan takes this as his cue and starts to climb in, but Edith leans over and gives him a quick kiss. Startled, he almost blushes. Edith steps back and goes inside, passing her father as she does so.

EDITH: Goodnight, Papa.

....

* We have here a situation that we've already set up – that Matthew's best man has ducked out and it allows him to offer the post to Branson. In my head, he does this partly for Mary, as a peacekeeping gesture, but also because he is coming to see that now Tom Branson is in the family they might as well get on with it.

48 INT. LIBRARY. DOWNTON. NIGHT.

Robert comes in. Cora is alone.

ROBERT: Well, that's the last of them. Where are the others?

CORA: They've gone to bed.

ROBERT: So's Edith. And so should we.

He sighs as he pours himself a drink.

ROBERT (CONT'D): Golly. What a night for the county to feed off.

CORA: But it was good of Matthew to show solidarity.

ROBERT: I suppose so. We're going to need all the solidarity we can muster.

CORA: When will you tell the girls?

ROBERT: I think I should tell Mary now.

CORA: Not before the wedding, surely?

ROBERT: I must. They're disagreeing about where they should live, so it'd be wrong for me to keep it from them. Then they can discuss it on the honeymoon and decide more sensibly. Do you think we say something to your mother when she gets here?*

CORA: No. She'd go into State Mourning and cast a pall over the whole proceedings.

ROBERT: Thank God she missed tonight's drama or we'd never hear the end of it.

CORA: Don't worry. She'll bring enough drama of her own.

....

* This next scene is to prepare the way for Mary to be told that they've lost all their money. I was very torn about this, because in a way it seems unfair of Robert to tell her before the wedding, so I gave him the rather elaborate excuse about their needing to discuss where they're going to live. I'm not sure I'm completely convinced by it. In real life I think one would have held it back till they got back from the honeymoon. But one mustn't get too precise about real life when writing for television.

49 INT. BATES'S CELL. YORK PRISON. NIGHT.

Bates is checking Anna's notes. His cellmate, Craig, watches.

    CRAIG: Won't work, you know. And if you don't admit your guilt, they won't let you go when the time comes.
    BATES: How can I admit what isn't true?
    CRAIG: Why do you have to be so pious?

Bates ignores him and continues to write.

    CRAIG (CONT'D): You're a touchy fellow, aren't you?
    BATES: Don't push me, Craig.
    CRAIG: Is that a warning?
    BATES: Yes. Yes it is. It is a warning, Craig. I'm warning you.

He puts down his pen and stands over the other man. And somehow, suddenly, he seems very dangerous indeed.*

50 INT. HALL/DRAWING ROOM. DOWNTON. DAY.

The hall carpet has gone. Men are fixing foliage around the walls. Tables for drinks and a cake are in place. Carson walks through, checking the process. He hears the horrible noise of the vacuum cleaner and looks into the drawing room where Anna is vacuuming. She smiles. He winces.†

51 INT. MRS HUGHES'S SITTING ROOM. DOWNTON.
            DAY.

Mrs Hughes is working when Carson looks in.

....

* This story was, as much as anything, to stop Bates looking like a victim. We needed a narrative action in which he became the positive proactive man, instead of just being the reactive wrongly imprisoned man. That was the point of it.

† It's always rather a big thing when we take up the carpet at Highclere, so we can't do it too often, but for a wedding reception it just wasn't possible to keep it down. And I like it when Carson says, 'Mr Bassett's men are doing the foliage.' Mr Bassett, the gardener, is a sort of Ghost of Christmas Past in this show. We talk about him quite often, but he never appears.

CARSON: The carpet's up in the hall. Mr Bassett's men are doing the foliage now. It's too soon for the flowers but we should check it before Mrs Levinson gets here. Is everything ready for her?

MRS HUGHES: I don't think *everything* is ever ready where she's concerned.

CARSON: Anna was using that infernal machine in the drawing room.

MRS HUGHES: I suppose you're nostalgic for the good old dustpan and brush.

CARSON: I think they had more dignity.

MRS HUGHES: Not if you were the woman on her knees wielding them.

CARSON: What do you make of this business of promoting Branson to best man?

MRS HUGHES: So he's not even '*Mr* Branson' now? You gave him that much when he was a driver.

CARSON: If you'd been in that dining room —

MRS HUGHES: Mr Carson, that wasn't his fault. It was just a nasty trick.

CARSON: If he were a gentleman he'd have left the moment he felt dizzy.

MRS HUGHES: Really? I can think of quite a few 'gentlemen' who didn't.

CARSON: All the same, I know Mr Matthew said it to be kind, but I wish he hadn't.

MRS HUGHES: I don't agree. It's good for him to feel part of it all, if you ask me.

CARSON: I haven't asked you.

52 INT. MARY'S BEDROOM. DOWNTON. DAY.

Mary is admiring herself in a smart day suit. Sybil and Edith are with her. Anna puts the final touches to her handiwork.

EDITH: I'm not sure about the hat. Is it supposed to look crooked?

SYBIL: Don't listen to her! I love it! You're not to change a thing!

MARY: Anna?

ANNA: I think you look lovely, m'lady.

There is a knock and the door starts to open.

SYBIL: Stop! Wait! Who is it?

ROBERT (V.O.): Your long-suffering Papa.

MARY: I suppose he can come in.

Robert opens the door and enters.

ROBERT: What's this for?

MARY: Going away. How does it look?

ROBERT: Expensive.

MARY: Twice the National Debt, I'm afraid, but I know
you don't mind.

Robert looks around at the others.

ROBERT: Can I have one moment alone to give Mary my
blessing?

SYBIL: That's lovely. Shoo, everyone.

MARY: Send our best wishes to Bates.

Anna nods and she and the sisters hurry out.

MARY (CONT'D): She's seeing Bates this afternoon.

ROBERT: She'll miss the Great Arrival.

MARY: Go on. Bless me.

ROBERT: Of course. But there's something I feel I ought
to tell you first. I wanted to wait until you got back,
but I don't believe I can…

MARY: That sounds rather ominous.

ROBERT: Last night you seemed to say that Matthew
doesn't want to live here.

MARY: He wants us to start married life on our own, to
get used to each other, but I'd rather stay at Downton.
Now I don't have to leave until I'm carried out in a box…

His expression makes her tail off.

ROBERT: You see, I've had bad news, and if that's how
Matthew feels, it would not be right to keep it from
you.*

....

* This sounds rather repetitive so perhaps it was right it got cut. It is
important that the audience is absolutely clear about what one character is
telling another, but you do try to avoid repeating it. You structure a scene so
that it finishes just as they're about to get the information you already know,
or you start the scene when they've just got it. Sometimes you can't avoid a
slight repeat, but you do work against it.

53 INT. HALL. CRAWLEY HOUSE. DAY.

Molesley has opened the front door to Branson.

BRANSON: Hello, Mr Molesley. I had a message to call on Mrs Crawley.

MOLESLEY: Very good, sir. If you'd like to give me your hat and coat, sir.

54 INT. DRAWING ROOM. CRAWLEY HOUSE. DAY.

Isobel and Violet are together. The sofa has men's clothes draped over it.

VIOLET: Are you going up to the house to welcome the Queen of Sheba?*

ISOBEL: Oh, I think so. Are you?

VIOLET: No. I'll pay homage at dinner.

ISOBEL: I've always admired the way Mrs Levinson is never overawed by the whole set-up at Downton.

VIOLET: Was Napoleon overawed by the Bourbons?

ISOBEL: No, I mean she must have worried when Cora married into such a traditional family. They might so easily have been prejudiced...

VIOLET: Against what?

She stares at Isobel, who is feeling awkward.

VIOLET (CONT'D): She isn't Jewish, if that's what you're on about.

ISOBEL: But her name? I've always assumed —

VIOLET: Oh, no. Her husband was Jewish but she wasn't, and the children were brought up as Episcopalians.†

....

* It is quite an old-fashioned device, when you start a play with two maids dusting saying, 'Oh, when do you think they'll be here?' 'Goodness knows' and so on, all of which is designed to herald a big event. We are doing much the same thing here. But we knew that the advance publicity of the arrival in the series of Shirley MacLaine was going to be such a big story that the work would have been done for us.

† Violet, of course, is refusing to go up for the arrival because she knows that almost the only person in the larger family group who does not accord her any status is Martha Levinson, so she refuses to give her that pleasure. I wish we hadn't cut these lines about Martha's name. Once the series had started going out in America the whole business of her having a Jewish

55 INT. DRAWING ROOM. CRAWLEY HOUSE. DAY.

Isobel and Violet are continuing their discussion.

ISOBEL: I suspect the late Mr Levinson's allowing his
children to be Protestant is a clue as to the prejudice
he faced on Wall Street.
VIOLET: Probably.
ISOBEL: Well, I'm glad if you raised no objections when
Robert brought Cora to meet you. Bravo.
VIOLET: She was American. That was quite enough to be
going on with.

The door opens and Molesley ushers in Branson.

ISOBEL: Come in, Tom. May I call you Tom?
BRANSON: Of course. Good afternoon, m'lady — that is,
Lady Grantham… I'm glad to find you here because… I
want to apologise for last night.
ISOBEL: Oh, there's no need. We know it was not your
fault.
VIOLET: You weren't the first drunk in that dining room,
I can assure you.
BRANSON: Only the first republican.
VIOLET: Well, you've got me there.

Molesley has slipped in behind Branson.

BRANSON: Why was it you wanted to see me?
ISOBEL: We've asked Molesley to look out Matthew's old
morning coat. He's confident he can make it fit.
BRANSON: That's very kind, ladies. But you see, I don't
really approve of these costumes. I see them as the
uniform of oppression, and I should be uncomfortable
wearing them.

....

Continued from page 57:

name became an enormous factor – people wrote letters, there were questions
in the papers, most of which took me by surprise. I simply thought it was
quite interesting as an element. We do have later stories that touch on the
casual anti-Semitism of the English upper classes at that time, which has
always fascinated me. I have never understood it, what it was based on, why
they went on with it, but even today you can still pick up traces. But Violet is
not anti-Semitic. She just sees everything in terms of the survival of the
Crawley family. As usual.

VIOLET: Are you quite finished?

BRANSON: I have.

VIOLET: Good. Please take off your coat. Molesley, do help him.

MOLESLEY: If you'll just slip it off, sir.

VIOLET: Shouldn't he put on the waistcoat first?

Matthew walks in.

MATTHEW: What's going on?

BRANSON: They're forcing me into a morning coat.

MATTHEW: He has no say in it?

VIOLET: No, he doesn't. And nor do you. Well, what do you think, Molesley?

MOLESLEY: Well, it'll need lifting a little here, m'lady. I'll move the buttons so.

He continues to pin the silent, doll-like Branson.

VIOLET: I think the shoulders look odd.*

56 EXT. DOWNTON. DAY.

A huge, shining, modern automobile is coming down the drive. The servants, minus Anna, are on parade. The family emerges from the front door. The car stops. A flashily uniformed chauffeur holds the door. Mrs Levinson, that is Martha, steps out. She is magnificent.

MARTHA: Come war and peace, Downton still stands and the Crawleys are still in it.

Robert and Cora register this.

MARTHA (CONT'D): Cora…

CORA: Mother. How lovely to see you.

MARTHA: As long as it is. Robert? Aren't you going to kiss me?

ROBERT: With the greatest enthusiasm. Tell me, where does this come from?

....

* Branson must have a proper morning coat if he's going to be best man. Even Isobel would see that, because by having a best man who's not in a proper outfit you're making some sort of eccentric statement, which wouldn't be acceptable. Despite Branson's protests, there is no moment when Violet is prepared to be swayed. Branson is beaten and that's that.

He gestures at the shimmering limousine.

> MARTHA: I hired it in Liverpool. Why?
> ROBERT: I thought it might be a gift from the US
> Government. To help Britain get back on its feet.

This sends a ripple through the servants. Martha turns.

> MARTHA: Carson and Mrs Hughes. The world has moved on
> since we last met.
> CARSON: And we've moved on with it, madam.
> MARTHA: Really? It seems so strange to think of the
> English embracing change… Mrs Hughes, this is my maid,
> Reed.

*Reed is young. As Mrs Hughes takes her in charge, Martha
smiles at her granddaughters.*

> MARTHA (CONT'D): Sybil, tell me all about the
> arrangements for the birth. These things are managed so
> much better in the States. Edith, still no one special?
> Oh well, never mind. You must take a tip from the modern
> American girl. Ah, Mary. Dearest Mary. Now, you tell
> me all your wedding plans and I'll see what I can do to
> improve them.

*Cora and Robert are united as they go in.**

57 INT. SERVANTS' HALL. DOWNTON. DAY.

*Mrs Patmore reads a recipe book as Daisy sits by, doing
nothing. O'Brien, Thomas, Anna and Alfred are there.*

....

* Martha is not a sentimentalist. We make that statement immediately. Her clothes are very up-to-date quite deliberately, whereas Violet's clothes are up-to-date technically, but they always look back to the Edwardian era, and the inspiration for her appearance was always Queen Mary, who managed to die in 1953 but never got much beyond 1910 in terms of style. Martha wants to look and be modern. And she makes a certain amount of fun of them all for trying to resist the future.

There is also an ironic statement in here, when Martha talks about the arrangements for the birth – 'These things are managed so much better in the States' – although actually eclampsia was fatal in the States at this time, too, but even so…

O'BRIEN: Mrs Levinson always hires them young and pays them nothing. Then she gets three years out of them at least, before they realise they're working for slave wages.

REED: Mrs Levinson likes to train her maids herself, and not be stuck with someone else's bad habits.

She is standing in the open doorway, listening to them.

DAISY: Just don't let her take advantage.

O'BRIEN: What's the matter with you?

DAISY: Mrs Patmore knows.

She looks at Thomas, who winks.

REED: Should I tell you Mrs Levinson's requirements during her stay?

DAISY: No. Tell her.

MRS PATMORE: Yes, Miss Reed. How can I help?

REED: Well, to start with, I will need goat's milk in the mornings —

MRS PATMORE: Goat's milk. Fancy that.

REED: She drinks only boiled water —

MRS PATMORE: Really?

REED: In England, that is.*

ANNA: Shouldn't Daisy be doing this?

ALFRED: I ought to take the tea up.

He stands and so does Mrs Patmore.

MRS PATMORE: I'll have it ready in a moment.

ANNA: Daisy? Won't you help Mrs Patmore?

MRS PATMORE: She is helping me, aren't you, Daisy?

As she walks out, Reed follows her. The others are flummoxed.

....

* Reed also belongs essentially to the modern world, which, naturally, makes Mrs Patmore despise her. With her requests for goat's milk, and no fats, no citrus, and all the rest of it… It was an American thing to specify all the things you couldn't eat long before it came here. When I was a child, and later than that, we were expected to eat everything, and if there was something you literally couldn't swallow you pushed it round your plate and hid it under the lettuce, but what you never said was, 'No tomatoes for me.' And anyway, before the war you weren't expected to clear your plate, so it was much less difficult to leave things without people commenting than it is now.

REED: No fats, no citrus, no crab, ever, and nothing
from the marrow family.

Mrs Patmore is dealing with Daisy's strike by ignoring it.

58 INT. LIBRARY. DOWNTON. DAY.

Carson and Alfred are serving the company from a tea table.

MARTHA: Do explain again how exactly you are related to
all of us, Mr Crawley.
MATTHEW: Rather distantly, I'm afraid. My great-great-
grandfather was a younger son of the third Earl.

He knows what's coming, but he tries to be good natured.

MARTHA: My, I'm going to have to write that down so I
can study it.
ROBERT: Look at our page in Burke's. You'll find
Matthew there.*
MARTHA: Good. Because I would so like to understand why
he gets to inherit my late husband's money.

Cora catches Robert's eye, while Matthew struggles on.

MATTHEW: I know. It's funny, isn't it?
MARTHA: Not everyone shares your sense of humour.
ISOBEL: But surely it doesn't matter now they're getting
married.
MARY: In fact, we'd better turn him out or it'll be bad
luck for tomorrow.
CORA: Quite right.
MARTHA: You must be the chauffeur I've heard so much
about.
BRANSON: I am, ma'am.
SYBIL: Tom's a journalist now, Grandmama.
MARTHA: Oh, well, well. I've heard of those journeys on
my side of the water; it's very pleasant to hear of them
happening here.

....

* All Martha understands is that her husband's money is going to this young
man who is no relation to them, which is, understandably, absolutely
infuriating to her. She doesn't have any problem with Branson's marrying
her granddaughter at all, but I suspect her of rubbing this in Robert's face.
I'm not sure how pleased she would have been if Cora had married a
chauffeur. But that is only my secret thought.

Cora, Mary and Matthew have reached the library door.

59   INT.   HALL.   DOWNTON.   DAY.

Mary, Matthew and Cora come into the decorated hall.

MARY: It's all right, Mama. You can leave us
unchaperoned. After tomorrow, all things are permitted.
CORA: Don't embarrass me. 'Bye, Matthew, and get a good
night's sleep.

She goes. They look round the chamber. Mary is pensive.

MARY: How many moments of Crawley history has this room
seen?
MATTHEW: With many more to come.
MARY: I hope so. In fact… what happened in the search
for Mr Pumpkin? Swire's heir? Have you heard anything?
MATTHEW: Yes. Charkham sent a telegram. I've got it
here, actually.

He pulls a telegram out of his pocket and hands it to her.

MARY: 'Convincing proof of Pulbrook's death, stop.
Investigating date.' What does that mean?
MATTHEW: Well, if Pulbrook died after Reggie then his
heirs get money. But if he died first then I do.
MARY: But that's absurd! What right have his heirs to
inherit anything?
MATTHEW: Darling! What right have I? And, frankly, what
difference does it make? I shan't keep it if I get it.
MARY: Well, actually, you will. Because something
rather terrible has happened… You see, apparently Papa
has lost a great deal of money. Enough to ruin him.
Enough for us to lose Downton.
MATTHEW: God, I am sorry. I'm so sorry.
MARY: Yes, but surely, if Mr Prufrock did die before
Swire then we're saved.
MATTHEW: My darling, I don't think you understand.
Reggie Swire will have put me into his will because he
believed I was his daughter's one true love.
MARY: So you were.
MATTHEW: Yes, but I broke Lavinia's heart and she died.
He never knew that. How could I possibly allow myself to
profit from her death? To dine in splendour because I
took away a woman's will to live?

MARY: So you're prepared to destroy us, in payment for your destroying her?

MATTHEW: Darling, please! You know I would do anything for this family!

MARY: Anything except help us! Except save Papa from living out the rest of his days in humiliation and grief! And what about us? What about our children? Oh God, Matthew, how can you be so *disappointing*?

She backs away from him and wards him off with her hand.

MATTHEW: Mary, please —

MARY: No. Don't you see what this means? Don't you see what a difference this makes? It means you're not on our side, Matthew. It means that, deep down, *you're not on our side!*

In tears, she turns and runs upstairs, past a bewildered Edith who looks down at a defeated Matthew. *

END OF ACT FOUR

....

* Here we have Matthew and Mary talking about Pulbrook and this is where we get down to the key plot detail of *'per stirpes'*, which we have talked about already. If it is non *'per stirpes'* then Pulbrook has to die before Reggie for Matthew to be the heir, because if he died after Reggie Swire then his children would already have inherited before they were aware of the inheritance. But there is also the issue of Matthew's decency. He feels he can't keep the money because he believes that he was only included in the will when he was going to marry Swire's daughter, Lavinia. By contrast, Mary is completely pragmatic. To be honest, these points of view represent exactly how my parents would have behaved – and differed. Daddy would have said he couldn't possibly keep it, while Mummy would have thought he was out of his mind. Like these two, he was the idealist, she was the pragmatist. Besides which, to Mary, Matthew's dithering means he isn't a true Crawley, he doesn't believe in the survival of the Crawleys of Downton, which is a horrible awakening moment. Michelle Dockery did it awfully well. They were both marvellous, in fact. But this is an insight into the problems of making a couple happy. You have to find a reason to make them unhappy and full of tension as quickly as you possibly can.

ACT FIVE

60   INT.   VISITING CELL.   YORK PRISON.   DAY.

Anna is with Bates, alongside the other prisoners.

> BATES: I don't envy him. It's a nice gesture from Mr
> Matthew, but it won't make the neighbours kind.
> ANNA: That stuff is so illogical.
> BATES: There is no logic when it comes to class.*

Anna notices Craig looking at them.

> ANNA: How are you getting on with your new companion?
> BATES: I don't like him, but so far I've kept it to
> myself… So, who are the bridesmaids?
> ANNA: You don't care about all that.
> BATES: You're wrong. It's the stuff of my dreams. The
> panic that a dinner won't be ready, or a frock isn't
> ironed or a gun wasn't cleaned. The crises of an
> uneventful life.

She looks at him. She does understand.

....

* Some of this was cut, which I was rather sad about, because Bates's desire for the ordinary reminds me of my own journey back to school at the end of the holidays. We would travel from King's Cross in the afternoon and reach York in the evening, and inevitably it's left me with a lifelong distaste for being on a train in the dark, because it always meant school. But I remember travelling up through the northern towns, past all these back-to-back houses, and I would see the lights on and people sitting in their kitchen having tea, and I remember such envy. I used to think, 'Why can't I be sitting in that kitchen eating that cake?' I've never forgotten it. And I'm sure when you're in prison the things you want to think about are not matters of great import, but the ordinariness of free life: Sunday lunch, watching television… That was the reason for this scene. Bates wants to talk about ordinary things – bridesmaids and such – although he's not in the least a soppy personality. He doesn't want to talk about big issues; he wants to talk about little things. And then we have Anna talking about going to London, but planning to come back so she can go on visiting him, but he insists that she go to France, because she has the responsibility of living life for both of them.

ANNA: The bridesmaids are Miss Drax and Miss Townshend and the Lane-Fox twins.* And her ladyship's mother arrives today from New York.
BATES: She'll keep Mr Carson on his toes… Do you know where you're going for the honeymoon?
ANNA: I want to talk about that. They'll stay in London with Lady Rosamund for a couple of days, just to get used to each other…

She blushes slightly, which makes him smile.

ANNA (CONT'D): And then they go to the South of France. I'll hire a replacement in London and then I'll come home instead. Lady Mary won't mind. I'll pay.
BATES: Why would you do that?
ANNA: Well, to be near you, of course.
BATES: Don't you understand? While I'm in here you have to live my life as well as your own. Go to France, see some sights, get us some memories.
ANNA: But I wouldn't be home for a month.
BATES: And won't we have something to talk about? Go. I insist. For my sake.

61   INT. SERVANTS' HALL. DOWNTON. DAY.

O'Brien and Thomas are both working. Carson looks in.

CARSON: You've found your livery again?
THOMAS: I have.

Reed looks up, enquiringly.

THOMAS (CONT'D): I used to be a footman, so I'm getting back into uniform for the wedding tomorrow.
REED: Mrs Levinson says everything like that is changing over here.
CARSON: Not everything, I hope.†

He goes.

....

* All significant names – the Draxes, the Townshends and the Lane-Foxes are neighbours of ours in Dorset.

† When Reed says everything's changing, we are harping on that sense of disintegration that becomes one of our central themes.

O'BRIEN: Mind you don't push Alfred to the edge of it all. He's First Footman. Let him have his chance to shine.

THOMAS: Alfred, Alfred. I remember when my welfare was all you cared about.

O'BRIEN: But you can look after yourself these days, can't you? And I like to give help where it's needed.

THOMAS: You like to control where you can.

But before she can answer, the dressing gong sounds.

62   INT. HALL. DOWNTON. NIGHT.

Martha is walking downstairs as Violet comes in with Carson.

VIOLET: I was afraid I was going to be late —

Carson slinks away in the background when they start to talk.

MARTHA: Violet. There you are. Oh, dear, I'm afraid the war has made old women of us both.

VIOLET: Oh, I wouldn't say that. But then I always keep out of the sun. How do you find Downton on your return?

MARTHA: Much the same, really. Probably too much the same, but then I don't want to cast a pall over all the happiness.

VIOLET: How could you ever do that?

MARTHA: Tell me, what do you think of young Lochinvar who has so ably carried off our granddaughter and our money? Do you approve of him?

VIOLET: Not as much as you will, when you get to know him.

MARTHA: Has he gone home to change?

VIOLET: Oh, no. We won't see him again tonight. The groom mustn't see the bride the night before the wedding.

MARTHA: Nothing ever alters for you people, does it? Revolutions erupt and monarchies crash to the ground, and the groom still cannot see the bride before the wedding.

VIOLET: You Americans never understand the importance of tradition —

MARTHA: Yes, we do. We just don't give it power over us. History and tradition took Europe into a world war. Maybe you should think about letting go of its hand.

She walks on into the drawing room as Edith comes downstairs.

EDITH: There you are. I see you've said hello to
Grandmama.
VIOLET: She's like a homing pigeon. She finds our
underbelly every time. Dreadful woman...*

63 INT. DINING ROOM. DOWNTON. NIGHT.

Dinner has just started. They are without Matthew or Isobel.

ROBERT: No, it wasn't me.

Robert catches Martha's curious look.

ROBERT (CONT'D): Someone sent Sybil and Tom the price of
the tickets to come over.
SYBIL: What does it matter who it was? It meant we
could be at the wedding. Of course, I wish it had been
you, Papa, but I don't mind. I thank them, whoever they
are.
CORA: Well, I'm very glad you're here, but it wasn't me
either, I'm sad to say.
MARTHA: Well, I love a mystery. Who could it be?
ROBERT: My guess is Cousin Isobel. She always likes to
stick her oar in.
SYBIL: I'm going to ask her.
VIOLET: Oh, for heaven's sake, it was me.†

This surprises everyone, but Branson most of all.

....

* We all felt that we needed a Martha/Violet scene now. And rather than just
drop her into the arrival, we wanted to see the moment when they met, and
for it to be just them. When you watch this scene, they are very evenly
weighted in terms of screen power. You're trying to watch them both, which
is the test of it. In this exchange Martha wins and Violet doesn't pretend
otherwise, which I think is nice. Martha has the ability to face the reality of
the present, which many of the other characters don't, and here we are able to
enjoy their different outlooks.

† The point of this is the shift in Branson's perception of Violet, whom he has
seen, up to this point, as his enemy. I wouldn't say that he now sees her as his
friend exactly, but he has a greater understanding that he has become part of
the overall picture for her. She has accepted the situation, in the sense that
she wants things to be as peaceful as they can be. And, of course, he is quite
moved by it.

SYBIL: You? But it wasn't your writing.

VIOLET: No. Smithers did it. Like all ladies' maids, she lives for intrigue.

BRANSON: You wanted me to come here?

He is genuinely amazed. It is, of course, not the whole truth.

VIOLET: I wanted Sybil and her husband to be here for Mary's wedding, yes.

SYBIL: But why keep that secret?

Violet catches Robert's eye and decides not to expose him.

VIOLET: It was silly, wasn't it?

BRANSON: I'm very touched. I'll admit it.

MARTHA: How democratic. Makes me think maybe I've been mistaken in you.

VIOLET: I am a woman of many parts.

ROBERT: It was very kind. Thank you, Mama.

VIOLET: After all, Branson is a… I mean Tom, you're a member of the family now. You'll find we Crawleys stick together.

MARY: Not always.

Her tone is so harsh that it silences the others.

CORA: Mary, what is it?

MARY: Oh, nothing. It's just…

She can't finish. Pushing away her chair, she stands, tears coursing down her cheeks, and runs out of the stunned room.

VIOLET: Oh, Mary, dear…

64   INT. KITCHENS. DOWNTON. NIGHT.

Mrs Patmore is putting a sauce boat onto Alfred's tray. Daisy still sits, unmoving, on her stool at the far end.

MRS PATMORE: There you are. That's all for this course, don't you think, Daisy?

ALFRED: Is Daisy all right, Mrs Patmore?

MRS PATMORE: Oh, yes. She's being such a big help. Now, I think we should check the pudding, Daisy. Don't you agree?

As she talks, she looks busily into the ovens. Alfred looks across at the increasingly frustrated Daisy. He goes. *

65 INT. DINING ROOM. DOWNTON. NIGHT.

Alfred arrives to follow Carson, who carries a plate of fish.

CORA: It's nerves. Everyone cries at some point before their wedding.†

MARTHA: But what was the quarrel about?

EDITH: I'm not sure. I know she accused him of not being 'on our side'.

VIOLET: Well, I hope she's wrong or that could be rather serious.

ROBERT: Of course he's on our side. It's ridiculous. I'll go and see him.

BRANSON: No. I'll go. I'm his Best Man. I should be the one to go.

ROBERT: What?

BRANSON: I know what it is to marry into this family. I'm not comparing myself to Mr Crawley, but he is another kind of outsider.

ROBERT: Well, I hardly —

MARTHA: Why not? He's the one who'll lose his job if the wedding's cancelled.

66 INT. KITCHENS. DOWNTON. NIGHT.

Mrs Patmore is washing some pots, watched by Daisy.

DAISY: I see what you're doing, you know.

MRS PATMORE: What's that, then?

DAISY: Not responding to my protest.

MRS PATMORE: 'Not responding to my protest.' Very elegant, I must say. Who've you been talking to? Thomas?

DAISY: Well… Oh, just gimme the cloth and I'll dry.

Mrs Patmore has successfully put down this rebellion.

....

* Mrs Patmore deals with Daisy's strike by paying no attention to it and pretending it's not happening, which I always think is quite a good way to manage recalcitrance. It's rather like coping with a naughty child.

† I think it's true that there are lots of brides' tears before weddings.

67 INT. MARY'S BEDROOM. DOWNTON. NIGHT.

Mary is in her nightclothes with Anna brushing her hair.

ANNA: But s'pose he never gets the money?

MARY: It's not about money. It's that he won't save Papa when he could.

ANNA: But he has to be true to himself.

MARY: That's the point. He puts himself above the rest of us, don't you see?

ANNA: What I see is a good man, m'lady. And they're not like buses. There won't be another one along in ten minutes' time.

68 INT. SERVANTS' HALL. DOWNTON. NIGHT.

The table is laid for the servants' dinner. They're gossiping.

MRS HUGHES: Her ladyship is right. It's nerves.

THOMAS: I'm not so sure. They both have very definite opinions.

O'BRIEN: Oh, I see. So now you're going to give advice on marriage, are you?

Carson comes in. Mrs Hughes goes up to him.

MRS HUGHES: Is it true that Mr Branson's gone down to the village?

CARSON: I cannot think of anyone less appropriate, but yes it is.

Anna comes in.

MRS HUGHES: How is Lady Mary?

ANNA: She wants to be left alone for the moment, but I'll go up in a while.

CARSON: It's not her fault if something has gone wrong.

MRS HUGHES: We all know who you think is in the wrong when Lady Mary's involved. *The other person.*

CARSON: Well. As if a husband should have any say in where a couple lives!

69 INT. DRAWING ROOM. CRAWLEY HOUSE. NIGHT.

Matthew and Branson are together.

BRANSON: It seems big, but it's not big.

MATTHEW: And if it happens and I get the money? I can't do what she wants.

BRANSON: It's strange for me to be arguing about inherited money and saving estates when the old me would like to put a bomb under the lot of you.

MATTHEW: But?

BRANSON: But you're meant to be together. I've known that as long as I've been at the house. And at first *this* kept you apart and then *that* kept you apart, but please don't risk it a third time. Because I tell you this: You won't be happy with anyone else while Lady Mary walks the earth.

MATTHEW: Call her Mary, please.

BRANSON: Never mind what I call her. I know what I'll call *you* if you let this chance slip through your fingers.*

70 INT. MARY'S BEDROOM. DOWNTON. NIGHT.

There is a knock on the door. Anna goes to it. Outside, Branson is standing with Matthew.

MATTHEW: I just need a word.

Anna looks round. Mary has risen.

MARY: No. Go away. I'm undressed. You can't come in.

MATTHEW: One word. Come to the door.

BRANSON: Please, just give him this chance.

MATTHEW: I won't look at you.

....

* This, really, is where the friendship is forged that we've already hinted at, and from now on, dramatically, they will be treated in the narrative as friends. Branson is still hovering between his customs as a servant and his customs as a family member, and he goes on batting back and forth. And obviously this is the moment when they have to address Mary's point – it's not about money, it's that Matthew won't save her darling Papa when he could. I agree with her, actually. The issue is not whether Matthew inherits, but that his instinct wasn't immediately to save Robert.

ANNA: It'd be unlucky if you did.

MARY: Only if we were getting married.

MATTHEW: Which we are.

At a nod from Branson, Anna slips out and away. So does he, leaving the lovers on either side of the slightly open door.

MATTHEW (CONT'D): My darling, I refuse to quarrel about something that hasn't happened and probably never will.

MARY: That's what Anna says.

MATTHEW: Then she's right. My darling, I'm sure we will fight about money, and about Downton, and about how to rear our children, and about any number of other things.

MARY: Then shouldn't we accept it? Matthew, I've been thinking, and I'm not angry now, truly I'm not. But if we can disagree over something as fundamental as this, then shouldn't we be brave and back away now?

MATTHEW: No.

MARY: It's not because you're afraid of calling it off? Because I'm not.

MATTHEW: No. It's because of something Tom said. That I would never be happy with anyone else as long as you walked the earth, which is true. And I think you feel the same about me.

MARY: Even if I do, I couldn't bear it if you won't support the family. I have to know we'd pull together.

MATTHEW: I promise I'll do everything in my power to keep this family together as long as it is not against my conscience. My darling, if it comes to it, I'll die for you. Do you really ask more than that?

He is very passionate, and despite herself Mary is persuaded.

MARY: I suppose not.

MATTHEW: Can I kiss you? Because I need to. Very much.

MARY: No. It's bad luck to look at me. That's if we *are* getting married.

MATTHEW: What about if I close my eyes and you do, too?

She hesitates for a moment, but then…

MARY: All right. But you mustn't cheat.

She feels for his face and kisses him, eyes tightly clenched.

MATTHEW: Goodnight.*

END OF ACT FIVE

ACT SIX

71 INT. HALL. DOWNTON. DAY.

Robert is in the hall. Branson comes downstairs.

BRANSON: Right. I'm off to collect Matthew.
ROBERT: You look very smart.
BRANSON: I hope so. Because I'm extremely
uncomfortable.

He smiles as he heads for the door, when…

ROBERT: Branson… that is, Tom, I want to thank you for
what you did last night. I'm grateful. I mean it.
BRANSON: They're both strong characters. I'd say we
have plenty of slamming doors and shouting matches to
come.

Robert flinches slightly, but he recovers.

ROBERT: Forgive me. I was about to be indignant, but of
course you have a perfect right to speak as you do.
BRANSON: I hope you mean that, too.
ROBERT: I do. Now hurry up.

Branson leaves.

* I felt this was a very romantic scene, which we wanted – a romantic lovers'
scene before the wedding. That felt important. I liked the idea of there
being an obstruction, which became his decision to shut his eyes as he
entered the room. And in fact, when they filmed it, using the door as a sort
of Romeo and Juliet barrier, I thought it worked well. But they put in one
detail that I didn't write. Mary opens her eyes and looks at him, and he
doesn't open his. When they did it, it was simply meant as a romantic
gesture, but of course it's bad luck for her to have seen him, and so in
a way it ties into what's going to happen.

72 INT. MARY'S BEDROOM. DOWNTON. DAY.

Mary, in a dressing gown to protect her dress, is at the looking glass as Anna adjusts the family tiara. Cora, Sybil and Edith are with her.*

CORA: You'd ask, wouldn't you? If there was anything you wanted me to tell you. I mean, I'm sure you know —
MARY: More than you did. And relax. There isn't anything I need to hear now.
CORA: Because when two people love each other, you understand, *everything* is the most *terrific* fun.

The sisters laugh indulgently at their mother's innocence.

MARY: Careful, Mama. Or you'll shock Anna.
ANNA: I'm a married woman, now, m'lady.

Which makes them all laugh. Edith stands.

EDITH: I think we should go.
SYBIL: What about Anna? How are you going to get to the church?
ANNA: They're waiting for me in the wagonette. I'll see you there.

Sybil kneels briefly by Mary's chair.

SYBIL: I know mine was a wild, runaway marriage, darling, and yours is the one everyone wanted, but what's so thrilling is that this is every bit as romantic.
MARY: Thank you. For always being so sweet.

....

* I wanted a family state tiara, as a reminder of the responsibilities of Mary's position, and a strong visual statement of aristocratic duty. But in the event they couldn't find a real one they liked, and the false ones didn't look real. The one she wore *was* real, and Michelle Dockery adored it, but it was very 1920s, so in a way we were saying it was a new tiara, bought for the occasion, which wasn't completely right for the narrative. But then, when the show went out, it turned out to have belonged to Princess Maud of Fife, the daughter of the Princess Royal, Duchess of Fife, who married the Earl of Southesk in the 1920s. The tiara had been made for her and subsequently sold by the family, and one of them had recognised it. I found that incredibly interesting, so I then completely forgave the fact that it wasn't the grand family tiara I wanted, and had become a modern one. Really, in terms of logic, if there was no money they could hardly have gone out and ordered a tiara.

EDITH: Love and position, in one handsome package. Who could ask for more?

She and Sybil slip out through the door. Cora stands.

CORA: Never mind Edith. Well. Very, very good luck, my beautiful daughter.

She holds Mary's hands and then she, too, slips away. Anna comes forward and Mary stands to remove the covering gown.

73   EXT. DOWNTON. DAY.

Mrs Hughes and O'Brien usher the bridesmaids into a car. A decorated carriage is waiting.

MRS HUGHES: Now, you've a great big motor car all to yourselves. Just think of that. So we expect you to behave as if you were quite grown up. You can do that, can't you?
O'BRIEN: Have you got everything you need?
BRIDESMAID: Yes.
O'BRIEN: Come on then. Be careful of your dress. Settle down.
ALFRED: Don't do anything I wouldn't do.*

74   INT. KITCHENS. DOWNTON. DAY.

Mrs Patmore is working with Daisy when Mrs Hughes looks in.

MRS HUGHES: Have you got everything you need?
MRS PATMORE: We do. Now, be off with you and enjoy yourself.

The housekeeper leaves. Daisy sighs.

DAISY: I wish we were going.
MRS PATMORE: And who'd get the food ready for when they come back? Still… fetch your coat, and we'll see her off.

....

* Again, details of how this sort of wedding was done, with bridesmaids having their own car and so on. I think people are quite interested in that.

They both hurry out to catch their glimpse. *

75 INT. HALL. DOWNTON. DAY.

Sybil, Edith and Cora, all in hats now, are leaving.

ROBERT: Right. See you in a minute.

They leave. Carson comes in.

CARSON: We're just leaving now, m'lord. As soon as
we've got Anna.

Robert has turned to him, but now they hear:

ANNA: Here comes the bride!

*Anna ducks away as Mary descends the staircase, looking like
a dream. Both Carson's and Robert's eyes shine as the father
takes her arm. She glances at her other father.*

MARY: Will I do, Carson?
CARSON: Very nicely, m'lady.

He hurries away.

ROBERT: Thank heavens you got everything settled. You
had me worried.
MARY: It's not quite settled, I'm afraid. He won't get
off that easily.
ROBERT: But you're happy?
MARY: I am. What about you?
ROBERT: I'm so happy, so very happy, I feel my chest
will explode.†

....

* It was rather sad that Daisy and Mrs Patmore weren't able to go to the
wedding. Some people said, 'Oh, let's have them there anyway,' but I said,
'No, this is a workplace drama. They've got to be where they would be in the
workplace.'

† I loved this shot of Mary descending the staircase, watched by her two
fathers, Robert and Carson, both of them bursting with pride. Charming.

76 INT/EXT. CHURCH. DOWNTON VILLAGE. DAY.*

The Archbishop waits by the altar. The bride's family and friends are on the left, the groom's on the right. Edith sees Strallan enter. She hurries up to him.

EDITH: It's so lovely that you're here. Come behind us.
STRALLAN: But I can't. I'm not family.
EDITH: Well, you almost are.

Matthew is walking in with Branson. They stop.

MATTHEW: Molesley. I'm very grateful to you for keeping Mr Branson up to the mark. We both are, aren't we?
BRANSON: We certainly are.
MOLESLEY: Thank you, sir.

Molesley glows with pride in this public recognition. He catches O'Brien's eye across the aisle and smiles. O'Brien smiles carefully back. Carson is next to Mrs Hughes.

CARSON: This is a proud day, Mrs Hughes.
MRS HUGHES: I don't know if I'm proud, but I'm very glad you're happy, Mr Carson.

Edith has taken her place by Cora, who whispers.

CORA: You're next, darling. You'll see.
EDITH: Will I?

Violet is with Martha on the left side of the aisle.

VIOLET: So encouraging to see the future unfurl.
MARTHA: As long as you remember it will bear no resemblance to the past.†

....

* Actually it was very touching. In Bampton, where we film the village of Downton, the inhabitants were so generous and excited, with the children running round, and the crowd trying to protect us from the paparazzi and the spoilers. We are always very grateful to them for their loyalty and support, which has been unflagging.

† Molesley has earned his spurs by getting Branson into a morning coat, which will pay off for him later. And there's Edith making her move on Strallan, which clearly tells us there is more to come. We have Violet and Martha having a last spar... And at last Mary arrives.

A guest leans in to Isobel.

  GUEST: And the girl is nice?

Isobel thinks. She will not quite concede 'nice' but…

  ISOBEL: I think she's right for Matthew.

Outside, Mary climbs down from the carriage and takes her place by her father. Anna finishes arranging Mary's train and slips in at the back. The organ strikes up and the congregation stands. Mary and Robert start down the aisle. Branson addresses Matthew.

  BRANSON: Good luck.

Matthew watches Mary in wonder, and then steps out to take his place by her side. He whispers to her.

  MATTHEW: You came. To be honest, I wasn't completely sure you would.
  MARY: I'm glad to hear it. I should hate to be predictable.

But the truth is, they are very, very happy.

END OF EPISODE ONE

EPISODE TWO

ACT ONE

1   EXT.   COUNTRY ROAD.   YORKSHIRE.   DAY.

A 1920 roadster races along, with Mary holding onto her hat next to Matthew. Anna is in the dickie seat behind.

MARY: Who will groan first when they see it? Granny or Papa?
MATTHEW: I should think they'll howl at the moon in unison.

The car turns in through the gates of Downton.

2   EXT.   DOWNTON.   DAY.

The car roars down the drive. The family comes running out of the front door. Robert stops in his tracks.

ROBERT: What in God's name is this?

The car skids to a halt. Alfred steps in to open the door.

ROBERT (CONT'D): Well, I never.
CORA: Where did this come from?
MATTHEW: I ordered it on the way through, in London, picked it up on the way back. It's a Humber.*
ROBERT: Well, at least it's English.

Cora is holding Mary's hands.

CORA: Welcome home, my darling.
ROBERT: How was the honeymoon?
MATTHEW: My eyes have been opened.
ROBERT: Don't I know it. Now come on in.†

....

* This car was originally a Humber, a supremely English name and vehicle, and one of the first of my father's cars that I can remember, but in the event we were limited by what we could get hold of, so it became an AC, which was a genuinely lovely car. You will also notice that, in the script, Anna was going to be with them, but in the end, the designer fell in love with a two-seater, so she had to be left behind to deal with the luggage and organise its safe return to Downton. Actually, this is what would have happened in real life, so nothing was lost.

3 INT. MARY'S BEDROOM. DOWNTON. DAY.

Anna is unpacking while Mary helps and Cora and Edith watch.

MARY: What've you been up to while we've been away?
CORA: Mainly just recovering from the wedding... And Mother's still here.‡
MARY: Golly.
ANNA: I think that's everything, m'lady.

Anna takes the suitcase and leaves. Mary looks at Edith.

CORA: Edith, dear. Run down and tell Carson we're ready for tea.
EDITH: You can just say you want to be alone. I won't faint.
MARY: All right. We want to be alone.§

....

† Several people involved in the production were shocked by this, saying that it wasn't very *Downton* to make a vulgar reference. I suppose they thought it smutty or something. But an absolute hallmark of the upper classes is that they don't have any worries about that stuff at all. And so I quite deliberately put in a bit of slightly naughty joshing, because it would be standard. I suppose I was dealing with *bon bourgeois* morality, which was affronted by the exchange, or at least assumed that the Crawleys would be affronted by it. But this is untrue. They have their own rules. Here, the men have separated themselves from the others, because that was always the thing, not to make a *risqué* joke in mixed company. My father once said to me, you can tell an improper joke to a lady, but she must be on her own with you. What you must never do is embarrass a woman by telling a dirty joke in mixed company. If you're alone with her, you can say what you like. That remains right to this day.

‡ Telling the audience that Shirley MacLaine is still in the show.

§ I was sorry this was cut because here we were trying to re-establish the prickly relationship between Edith and Mary. In my experience, siblings have much more difficult relationships in real life than in the movies. You do get families where brothers and sisters are best friends, but they're pretty rare in my book, and usually they tip over into an exclusive closeness that makes it very difficult for the wives and husbands to stay around later. I also thought it would be fun to keep the spikiness going between Mary and Edith; one danger for a writer, when siblings get on too well, is that they start to merge as characters, because they have similar responses. But we have set up Mary and Edith, quite deliberately, as two women who will always have different responses to everything, if only to rub the other's nose in it.

Edith goes.

MARY (CONT'D): Have you told her what may happen?
CORA: About putting Downton up for sale? Yes, your father's told her. And he's told Granny.
MARY: That can't have been easy.
CORA: He felt sick for a week, but he's done it. That's all, though. We haven't told my mother and we haven't told the servants.
MARY: Well, I warn you now. I'm not giving up so easily.
CORA: It's just a house, Mary.
MARY: Not to me, it isn't. Let's go down.*

4 INT. SERVANTS' HALL. DOWNTON. DAY.

Alfred is setting studs into an evening shirt. Thomas is in there, with O'Brien and some of the others.

THOMAS: Who's that for? And why are you doing it down here?
ALFRED: It's for Mr Matthew. It was creased and I brought it down to iron.
THOMAS: You're never looking after him. What about Mr Molesley?
ANNA: He's staying on at Crawley House.
THOMAS: Then why wasn't I asked?
O'BRIEN: Mr Carson thought it best.
THOMAS: Did he, indeed? I wonder how that came about. And if you are learning how to do your job, you should never open a shirt in a room like this where it might be marked, let alone put studs in it. Do that in a dressing room and nowhere else.

....

* We didn't want Downton's future to be panic and terror and sorrow, and so somehow in competition with the excitement of the wedding in the first episode, which justified our keeping the dangers of losing it quiet until the wedding was done. But now we will expand the threat and the drama of their possibly losing their home. All the time in these shows you're trying to put people into trouble or jeopardy. The trouble is, Mary and Matthew are now married. They're well suited, we have no reason to believe they won't be very happy, and it would be an artificial re-casting of their characters suddenly to make them unhappy. Thus we have to make them, and everyone else, unhappy – or at least challenged – for a completely different reason.

ALFRED: Thank you.

O'BRIEN: Yes, thank you, Thomas, for always trying to be so very helpful.*

They hear the sound of the dressing gong.

5 INT. DINING ROOM. DOWNTON. NIGHT.

Dinner is in progress. Carson and Alfred are serving.

MARTHA: So, how did you enjoy the South of France?

MARY: It was lovely, but almost too hot, even now.

MARTHA: I think it's such a shame they close things up during the summer. I love the sun.

VIOLET: So we can see.

MARY: Oh, you couldn't be in Cannes in the summer. No one could bear it.

MARTHA: I could.†

....

* Thomas resents Alfred because he has been wished on the household by O'Brien. Thomas would be perfectly happy to wish a footman onto the household himself. He has completely double standards, and indeed later on brings in a lady's maid for Cora, but he is affronted at the undermining of his power. I do believe in a fully staffed house the gradations of rank were tremendously important, because they were the steps of a career. We make a point always of the different employees defending their positions against all comers, sometimes without hostility and malice, but always with real purpose. Even Mrs Hughes, who is one of the most sympathetic characters in the show, is still quick to jump on it when one of the maids starts behaving out of turn, and Carson is the same. It's not a question of likeability. Service was a real career and so you didn't surrender the progress and the rank you'd achieved.

† The South of France until the Twenties was considered too hot in the summer. The autumn and the spring were the time to go there, when hotels stayed open for people looking for a milder climate. Supposedly it was the Fitzgeralds, Zelda and Scott, who persuaded the owner of their favourite hotel to stay open during July and August, because normally they closed at the end of June. That was the beginning of the South of France summer, the twentieth-century idyll. It was the same with Switzerland. For the Victorians, it was where you went in the summer for the walking and the flowers. Skiing was essentially a peasant way of getting from one place to another. All that would start to change in the Twenties and Thirties.

Violet lowers her voice and leans in to Robert.

> VIOLET: Just how long is she here for?
> ROBERT: Who knows?*
> VIOLET: No guest should be admitted without the date of their departure settled.†
> ROBERT: You won't get any argument from me.

Isobel speaks across the table to Matthew.

> ISOBEL: There's a hideous pile of post, I'm afraid.

....

Continued from page 85:

I like the way things that seem obvious to us are not obvious when you examine them and they have, in living memory, been entirely altered. Part of it must have been the clothes they were required to wear; even the loose and informal versions of them were still inappropriate for a South of France summer, and it wasn't really until the Twenties and the end of the corset that you would get much enjoyment playing in the sun. There's a wonderful letter from Lady Curzon in India describing how her fingers keep slipping when she's trying to do up the buttons of her evening dress because they're so wet with sweat. Look at photographs of the Raj and there are the women in their lacings and triple layers and the men in their uniforms. It must have been boiling. It is difficult to imagine how hot they must have been. But the one thing they did understand was their duty.

* My mother always complained about people who stayed forever and you couldn't get rid of them. In London, after the Second World War, thanks to the bombing, it was very hard to get digs. Some friends of theirs had lost their flat and asked if they could stay while they looked for a new one. 'We'll only be with you for a few days,' they said. 'A week at the most.' Naturally, they were there for months, but everyone managed to keep their temper and finally the guests found what they were looking for and no cross words had been spoken. As they were shown out of our house in Wetherby Place, my parents tore up to the drawing room on the first floor and started to sing and dance. 'They've gone! They've gone!' they shouted, and my mother jumped onto a table and started doing a flamenco dance, while my father stamped around below her clapping his hands in the air. 'They've gone!' Suddenly they stopped. There were their guests standing in the doorway: 'We forgot to give you the keys,' they said. Obviously it was the end of the friendship, which is rather sad.

† My mother was telling this story to an aunt and that was the advice she received in return.

I've put it on the hall table. Don't look at it tonight.
MARY: What have you been up to?
ISOBEL: As a matter of fact, I've found myself a new
occupation. But I'm afraid Cousin Violet doesn't think
it quite appropriate.
VIOLET: Can we talk about it afterwards?
MARTHA: Are there still forbidden subjects? In 1920? I
can't believe this.
VIOLET: I speak of taste, rather than law.
MARTHA: Well, it's not my taste. What about you, Cora?
CORA: I agree with Mama. Some subjects are not suitable
for every ear.

She glances at Alfred, which Martha sees.

MARTHA: Oh. *Pas devant les domestiques*? Come on, my
dear, Carson and Alfred know more about life than we ever
will.*

She laughs gaily. Carson fumes. Robert whispers to Violet.

....

* When my stepmother thought of conversations before the war at dinner
and lunch, she couldn't believe the way they had not been in any sense
restrained by the presence of the footmen or the butler. It was not so much a
question of family secrets, but gossip of a fairly electric kind and certainly
tremendous political arguments, all of which were quite freely indulged in.
Someone hostile to the way of life would interpret this by saying that the
servants were scarcely human to their employers, who paid no attention to
them because they didn't think of them as people. The reverse of this
argument is that, in those days, it didn't occur to them that they might be
betrayed and the idea that their servants would sell some story to the
newspapers, or indeed leak things to an outsider, just didn't seem possible.
And on the whole their trust was merited.

But the phrase '*pas devant les domestiques*' was considered, certainly by my
great-aunts, as very common. By being in French the assumption,
patronisingly, was that the servants would not understand what was being
said, but I think most of them could have worked out that '*pas devant les
domestiques*' was pretty obvious. At any rate, it was a naff phrase, which
Martha is making fun of. In real life, if you felt a conversation was perhaps
inappropriate, you'd simply say, 'We'll talk about this another time.' Besides
which, Martha is deliberately prodding them.

ROBERT: Can't we stop this?

VIOLET: How? She's like a runaway train.

Matthew decides to take charge.

MATTHEW: What have you been doing, Edith?

EDITH: Nothing much. I rather miss the war, really, but of course one mustn't say that.*

CORA: Edith's a treasure. We've a dinner next week and I haven't had to lift a finger. Shall we go through?

MARY: What about poor old Strallan? Have you seen anything of him?

EDITH: I don't know why you call him 'poor' or 'old', when he's neither.

They have all stood. Violet uses the moment to catch Robert.

VIOLET: Isn't it dangerous to let that Strallan nonsense simmer on?

ROBERT: To be fair, I don't think it's coming from him.

VIOLET: Then ask him to end it. It'll be more effective than if we try.

6 INT. KITCHENS/PASSAGE. DOWNTON. NIGHT.

Alfred carries down a tray of used plates.

....

* Edith stands for a lot of those women who took on an activity in the war, having never had much to do before it, and then found it very difficult when the war was over. I had not only a great-aunt but two cousins, all spinsters with boyfriends dead at the front, who ended up breeding dogs – King Charles spaniels – simply to give them something to do. Because, in peacetime, there were so few careers for women like them. For me, there is always a hovering sense of the idleness and boredom of that life, of just paying calls and dining out and dining in, particularly in the country. There's a wonderful house we know in Northern Ireland called Glenarm Castle, where I found a very beautiful, very detailed silhouette, cut out with great skill, and on the back was written that this silhouette was executed by Lady Arabella Someone during 'another long and boring afternoon at Glenarm'. Doesn't that say it all? The war had woken them up to what it felt like to be busy, but the coming of peace meant they were expected to go back to sleep. That is Edith's predicament.

MRS PATMORE: She ate it, then. I'm never sure about Americans and offal.*

ALFRED: I think she'd eat whatever you put in front of her, that one. What a gob. I thought Mr Carson was going to put a bag over her head. Oops.

Reed is listening by the door. Daisy is by the range.

REED: Mrs Levinson knows you make fun of her. But she makes fun of you.

MRS PATMORE: Then we're all square, aren't we?

DAISY: The chimney isn't drawing properly. This oven's not hot enough.

MRS PATMORE: Ooh, a bad workman always blames his tools.

She looks up. Mrs Hughes is in the doorway.

MRS HUGHES: You're busy.

MRS PATMORE: No, I'm not. Well, we're eating in half an hour, but it's all done.

MRS HUGHES: Well, if you could spare a minute.

As they walk out they cross Anna descending the stairs with a mountain of Mary's clothes. Which Daisy sees.

DAISY: Blimey. Is it all for the laundry?

ANNA: Most of it just needs ironing. I'll do it tomorrow.†

....

* I remember thirty or so years ago having some Americans staying with me when I lived in Sussex. I had arranged for them to have lunch at a local house of some historic interest, but they came back clutching their throats. The first course had been a chicken liver pâté and the main course had been kidneys, so it had been a whole feast of offal. For the British like me, this was fine because we eat offal all the time, but for them it was a Poison Banquet. I suppose it's as if one were presented with brains or sweetbread at a lunch party. People eat them, but we would, I think, be wary of serving them up to guests.

† The laundry is the soft underbelly of this show, because the fact is there would have been an operating laundry, and it would have been manned by local women. If it was connected to the house it would be in a remote wing, but more usually the laundry was a separate building, like the stables, and just as the grooms lived above the stables, so the laundry maids were housed in cottages on the estate. They were generally a rougher group – a rowdy and rambunctious class within a class – big and physically tough, because the

Daisy fingers a lace-edged nightgown.

DAISY: Do you ever think of the one that died? Miss Swire. Did you like her?*
ANNA: I hardly knew her, but, yes, I think she was a kind person.
DAISY: I only talked to her once, but I thought she was nice.

7 INT. DINING ROOM. DOWNTON. NIGHT.

Robert and Matthew are alone, with Isis, drinking port and smoking cigars.

MATTHEW: This is very good. I hope you didn't open it for me.
ROBERT: Certainly I did. To welcome you into this house as my son. I can't tell you how glad it makes me.
MATTHEW: Robert, I want us always to feel we can be honest with each other…
ROBERT: Of course.
MATTHEW: Because Mary's told me about your present difficulties.
ROBERT: She was right. Losing Downton will affect you both more than anyone.

....

Continued from page 89:

work was very demanding. The maids were usually discouraged from mixing with the laundry staff, but the fact remains that we ought to have had someone from the laundry staff in the cast. We never have because the amount of servant characters we have in the house fills it up dramatically. In fact, at a house like Downton, even in the Twenties there probably would have been four footmen, and even if they had cut down by the 1920s there would have been six in 1912, when we started. But we just couldn't get the dramatic use out of six footmen. At all events, every now and then I allude to the laundry in a lily-livered way, but we never witness it.

* We needed to mention the dead Lavinia Swire, because her father is going to become a very important absent character.

MATTHEW: I wonder if she's told you about the will of
Lavinia's father… Because if not, I must explain my
decision. You should hear it from me.*

8 INT. DRAWING ROOM. DOWNTON. NIGHT.

*The ladies are being served coffee by Carson and Alfred. Mary
is with Violet, a little away from the rest.*

VIOLET: Your father's told me all about it. But I
cannot understand why so much money was put into one
company.
MARY: I couldn't agree more.
VIOLET: And now we're to be turned out of Downton… Even
Lloyd George can't want *that*.†
MARY: I'm not sure he's a good example.

....

* This is a classic *Downton* situation, in that most of the audience will think,
'Oh, for heaven's sake! If you can save the house and everyone in it, what's
the problem?' But Matthew believes that when Lavinia saw him kiss Mary
she realised he didn't want to marry her, and that this contributed to her
illness and death. Because of this, he feels he cannot, in conscience, benefit
financially from a man who thought Matthew was his daughter's only love,
when he may have been her killer. He betrayed Swire's daughter, and he
cannot take his money for a betrayal. It is an important distinction and I
think Matthew has a point, but of course personally I am nearer Mary: 'It's
happened, so move on.' That would be her viewpoint and it would probably
be mine, but we shouldn't make the mistake of thinking Matthew doesn't
have a leg to stand on, because I think he *does* have a strong and moral leg to
stand on.

† Lloyd George was an avowed enemy of the landed classes. He did not
believe that the rural economy benefited from their large estates. In fact,
history has proved him wrong on that, as many European countries have had
to learn the hard way, and now large estates are the hope of the rural
economy, even when they're owned by corporations or investment trusts. In
his defence, Lloyd George's beliefs – that to destroy the aristocracy was worth
anything, even the destruction of the local economy and the loss of many jobs
– were shared by many people, the Labour politician Manny Shinwell among
them. This seems terrible to me, but then I'm not a socialist. I don't think
the pursuit of a pseudo equality is worth sacrificing people's lives for. But
others do, and quite a lot of them work in my profession.

VIOLET: The point is, have we overlooked something? A source of revenue previously untapped? If only we had some coal, or gravel, or… tin.*
MARY: Well, I can think of someone who's got plenty of tin.†

She looks across the room at Martha. We join her.

MARTHA: So, you help women who have fallen over?
ISOBEL: Not quite.
CORA: Cousin Isobel helps women who have had to degrade themselves to survive. There's a centre in York.‡
MARTHA: Oh, no addresses, please, or Alfred will be making notes.

....

* Women were expected to understand the realities of the situation and also to run an estate if they were required to. It wasn't like being married to a banker. If your husband was the chairman of a bank and he died, nobody rang you up and said, 'Come and take over,' but with an estate, and in the absence of an adult male heir, they expected the surviving women to know how things worked. I think that is, if anything, even truer today, and it was certainly true then. Violet is being no more than typical of her kind, in that she doesn't take out her handkerchief and start sobbing. She immediately tries to think: 'Do we have coal? Might we have gravel?' These women were tough.

† Although the famous Duke of Marlborough is the one who married Consuelo Vanderbilt, it was his father who attempted to save the Churchill fortunes by marrying his own American heiress, a widow called Lillian Hammersley. Her money was less use to the Churchills, because it was only a life interest (when she died it would go back to the Hammersleys), but nevertheless it was a pretty fat income while she lived, and indeed the whole of the long library at Blenheim was put in by Mrs Hammersley, or the Duchess of Marlborough as she became. She also rebuilt the roof, and who knows what besides. At the time, the *New York Times* said the reason for the marriage 'appears to be that the lady has plenty of tin'. I liked the phrase, so that's why I used it here.

‡ By the end of the war a great many women had got themselves into trouble one way or another, either because their husbands had been killed, leaving them with no income, or because they were nursing handsome soldiers and officers who took advantage of the situation. A couple of my great-aunts got involved in helping these women get back on their feet, which is what gave me the idea.

Martha winks at Alfred, who nearly laughs, then he sees Carson's face.

MARTHA (CONT'D): So what do you do for these women?
ISOBEL: Well, first, we like to send them away. To rest.
MARTHA: I should think they need it.
ISOBEL: And then we try to find them alternative employment.
CORA: The war destroyed many households. In thousands of families, the bread-winners are dead.
MARTHA: So, you want me to contribute?
CORA: You don't have to give money after every conversation, Mother.
MARTHA: No? Isn't that what the English expect of rich Americans?

Violet and Mary register this.

9   INT.   DINING ROOM.   DOWNTON.   NIGHT.

Matthew and Robert are still there.   Robert feeds Isis.

ROBERT: But why can't you benefit from the will? You've done nothing wrong.
MATTHEW: When Swire made it he didn't know I'd broken his daughter's heart. It was to reward my fidelity, when in fact I had betrayed her.
ROBERT: So you can never be persuaded?
MATTHEW: If I kept that money, I would be no better than a common criminal.
ROBERT: I see. Well, if that's how you feel then there's no more to be said —

Anna walks into the room from the servery.   She is horrified.

ANNA: I'm ever so sorry, m'lord. I thought you were out of here.
ROBERT: Yes, we should be. Please. We're going now.

10   INT.   MRS HUGHES'S SITTING ROOM.   DOWNTON.
NIGHT.

Mrs Hughes is with Mrs Patmore.   Her shirt is open and she is guiding Mrs Patmore's hand.   It is all intensely awkward.

MRS PATMORE: It's a lump all right. There's no point in dithering about that.

Mrs Hughes nods, and buttons herself up again.

MRS PATMORE (CONT'D): What are you going to do about it?

MRS HUGHES: I don't know.

MRS PATMORE: Well, I do know. Tomorrow, you'll make an appointment with the doctor, and we'll see what he's got to say.

MRS HUGHES: But what if it's…?

MRS PATMORE: If it is, and I'm not saying it is, it's best to know now.

MRS HUGHES: I suppose so.

But she is very frightened and starts to cry.

MRS PATMORE: Now, look. You'll not be alone for a minute if you don't want to be. But we have to get it seen to.

MRS HUGHES: And then there's the expense.

MRS PATMORE: Well, if you must pay money, better to a doctor than an undertaker.

MRS HUGHES: If that's an example of your bedside manner, Mrs Patmore, I think I'd sooner face it alone.*

....

* Cancer is a curious disease, as old as time. This generation seems to be heavily cursed, perhaps because we have far more carcinogenic activities and substances going around, but nevertheless the ancients died of cancer, and whether they called it tumours or malign growths they still knew what it was. For some reason, difficult now to understand, it was a dirty word until the 1960s when, for the first time, you could have cancer without it being seen as shameful. My grandfather died of lung cancer in 1948, and certainly my grandmother was uncomfortable with the term for as long as I knew her. She only died in the 1980s and she couldn't bear the fact that he'd died of cancer, whereas, for the rest of the world, by then it was just a disease that could kill you and had no meaning other than it was very sad. At any rate, this is why, here, Mrs Hughes chooses to say nothing.

This business of not wanting to know always interests me. I don't mean when people fail to have a check-up because everything seems fine. But when they've found a lump and they don't do anything. I always find that very interesting, and it's much commoner than one suspects. I can't imagine not wanting to find out if I discovered a lump.

11 INT. SERVANTS' HALL. DOWNTON. DAY.

The end of breakfast. Carson comes in with some letters, which he distributes. There are about a dozen for Anna.

CARSON: These came while you were away.

She takes them from him and starts to open them.

CARSON (CONT'D): Anna, I'm sorry we can't free you up to be a proper lady's maid, but we're very short-handed. I hope it's not a disappointment.
ANNA: I know you will when you can.*
CARSON: Bad news?
ANNA: Oh, no. I just wrote to some people and two of them have been returned.

She picks up a tea tray and leaves.

12 INT. MARY'S BEDROOM. DOWNTON. DAY.

Anna comes in and puts down the tray on Mary's side, then draws the curtains as Matthew, who is bare-chested, stirs beside his wife.

MATTHEW: It seems rather shocking for Anna to have to see me *en déshabillé*.†
ANNA: I'm made of stout stuff, sir. Don't worry about that.
MARY: Are you seeing Bates today?
ANNA: I am. And I can't wait.
MARY: Give him our best wishes.

....

* Being a housemaid who also did lady's maiding as part of her duties was completely standard, but normally it would be – as it is here at Downton – for the daughters or for a visiting guest. A junior position, in other words.

† This anomaly I always rather like. The ladies' maids, by definition, saw their master in his dressing gown, or even the valets, on rare occasions, might see the mistress in hers. Any lady's maid to a married woman certainly saw her husband in bed when they brought in the tea or her breakfast in the morning, and I always feel, given their quite draconian morality, that it makes for an odd sort of blip. But it was standard, and it was why – as we saw in Season Two – it was the maid who would be sent in if there was a drama and the couple had to be woken up. The first choice was the maid, because she was quite used to it.

Anna smiles and leaves. They are alone.

> MATTHEW: I'm sorry. It still seems odd to be found in
> your bed.
> MARY: But very nice.
> MATTHEW: Oh, as nice as nice can be…

He pulls her into his arms and kisses her.

> MATTHEW (CONT'D): I'm going to see Jarvis today. To
> find out what houses are available.
> MARY: Do you have to? When these are our last days
> here? I thought something might have turned up when we
> were away, but it seems it hasn't.
> MATTHEW: Would you rather wait until we have to go, and
> find a new house then?
> MARY: After all, darling, you're the one who's pushing
> us out.*

But she is just playful enough for it to be a sort-of joke.

END OF ACT ONE

ACT TWO

12A EXT. TOWN STREET. DAY

*Isobel walks down the street and catches a glimpse of Edith,
who runs off before Isobel properly recognises her.*

....

* Mary is going to put up a struggle to stay in the house. Her point being,
reasonably enough, that if the family are going to leave anyway and lose the
house, they might as well live there for the last bit. At least, it would be
reasonable, if that were truly her point of view. But her real plan, concealed
here, is that she doesn't want to move out and, in this, I'm on Matthew's side.
He wants them to have their own place at the beginning, that's all. He
doesn't want anything to be sold or ruined, but he wants to start his marriage
alone with his wife, in their own house, and I believe most of the audience is
on his side rather than hers.

13 INT. LIBRARY. STRALLAN'S HOUSE. DAY.

*Edith is with Anthony Strallan.**

STRALLAN: But Mary's only just got back from honeymoon.
It's a family time.
EDITH: But you are —
STRALLAN: Please stop saying I'm family when I'm not.
I'll be there for the big dinner next week… What is it?
EDITH: I know you don't mean to hurt me —
STRALLAN: Of course I don't. That's the last thing I'd
ever wish to do.
EDITH: Then why do you shove me away?
STRALLAN: I don't want to, not at all, but —
EDITH: If you're going to talk about your wretched arm
again, I won't listen.
STRALLAN: It's not just my arm. I'm too old for you.
You need a young chap, with his life ahead of him —†
EDITH: But *your* life's ahead of you…
STRALLAN: Oh, my dear, if you knew how much I'd like to
believe that.
EDITH: Then it's settled. You're *not* going to push me
away any more, and you *are* coming for dinner tonight.
That's all there is to it.

14 INT. YORK PRISON VISITING CELL. DAY.

Anna is with Bates with all the supervised visitors.

BATES: How'd you get on with Vera's book?
ANNA: I had a few answers waiting for me when I got
back. And two returned 'address unknown'.

....

* Scarlett Strallen gave me the idea for the name, although I have spelled it
differently. She played Mary Poppins on stage in London, and I had written
the 'book' of the show for Sir Cameron Mackintosh. Coincidentally, her
family was known to my mother-in-law, so we'd been involved with the
Vaigncourt-Strallens before this. But the actress daughters dropped the
Vaigncourt, and I suppose one can understand why.

† I feel very sympathetic to Strallan all the way through, because he's trying
to be decent and to behave honourably. He feels he's an old man with an arm
that doesn't work and she's a young girl and she could do much better. But of
course Edith is tougher than that, and if a young and pretty girl is going to
push and push and you're lonely and you're living all alone in your house…

BATES: Who from?

ANNA: Let me see… One was a Mr Harlip, I think. And the other was… Mrs Bartlett, was it?

BATES: Harlip doesn't matter. He was a cousin in the North. She never saw him. But Mrs Bartlett's a shame. She lived round the corner. She was very friendly with Vera.

ANNA: I'll find her. Don't worry.

BATES: Tell me about France. Did you eat frogs' legs and dance the can-can?

She leans across the table, so she can whisper.

ANNA: No… But I bought a garter.

15 INT. CLARKSON'S CONSULTING ROOMS. DOWNTON VILLAGE. DAY.

Mrs Hughes and Mrs Patmore watch Clarkson wash his hands.

CLARKSON: You have no other symptoms?

MRS HUGHES: Not that I'm aware of.

CLARKSON: You're not feeling ill or tired?

MRS HUGHES: I can't swear to not feeling tired, but nothing out of the ordinary.

CLARKSON: Very well. Well, I'm just going to conduct a preliminary investigation.

MRS PATMORE: Do you mind if I stay?

CLARKSON: I should prefer it.*

16 INT. KITCHEN PASSAGE. DOWNTON. DAY.

Alfred, with a tailcoat, runs into Thomas in the passage.

THOMAS: What you got there?

....

* A doctor wouldn't have wanted to be alone with a woman in a room in case later some sort of accusation was made, not that Doctor Clarkson would say that of Mrs Hughes, but I felt it would have been standard practice for him. It strikes me now how sad it is that we've got into this awful fix as a society. I remember being absolutely terrified when I was left in charge of some children of a friend when she had to go and answer the telephone. I just thought, 'Come back, come back, come back.' It was me being hysterical, not the kids, who were fine. I think it is a very unhealthy atmosphere that has been created by the zealots.

ALFRED: Mr Matthew's tailcoat. What do you think that is?

THOMAS: Hard to say.

ALFRED: I've tried it with all the usual things, but I can't shift it.

THOMAS: I'll give you a tip if you like.

ALFRED: Would you, really?

THOMAS: But keep it to yourself. I don't want to give away all my secrets.*

He takes him into one of the side rooms off the passage.

17 INT. DRAWING ROOM. DOWNTON. DAY.

Violet walks in to find Mary reading Vogue.

VIOLET: Oh, there you are, my dear.

MARY: Good morning, Granny.

VIOLET: I've been looking for you. Now, I want to know if we're serious. About getting that wom— about asking your other grandmother to come to our aid.

MARY: She's made of money, and there's only Mama and Uncle Harold to share it when she's gone.

VIOLET: We can't wait that long. She looks as if she'll bury us all. No. We must act now. We must make her feel it is her duty to save Downton.

MARY: But how? What can we do?

VIOLET: Well, get her to sense its value, its vital role in the area. You are her granddaughter; this will be your house if it survives. Surely you can make something of that, if she has a heart at all.

MARY: We'll come for tea this afternoon.

VIOLET: Then we can begin.†

....

* We've lost the whole business of lifting stains now. We went through a brief period of artificial dry cleaning when I was younger, with a substance called Dabitoff, which everyone used, but even that's gone now. We don't try to get any marks out at all. We don't iron out wax or iron out butter or do all of that stuff they used to try. Now you just send it to the cleaners and that's it. It's rather pathetic, isn't it?

† Mary's plotting with Violet to get the money out of Martha seems to me emotionally valid, because the only reason that Violet tolerated Martha in the first place was because of the money that was coming into the family. And

18   INT.   CLARKSON'S CONSULTING ROOMS.   DOWNTON
            VILLAGE.   DAY.

Mrs Hughes is fastening her dress.

CLARKSON: Believe me, there are several stages to go
through before there's any cause for despair.
MRS HUGHES: What stages?
CLARKSON: When you come back in a day or two I will
remove some fluid from the cyst. With any luck, it'll be
clear and that will be that.
MRS PATMORE: How will you do it?
CLARKSON: With a syringe.
MRS PATMORE: Will it hurt?
MRS HUGHES: Since he has to do it whether it hurts or
not, I don't see the point of that question. What I want
to know is, what happens if the fluid is not clear?
CLARKSON: It'll be sent away for analysis.
MRS HUGHES: Because it may be… cancer.
CLARKSON: You're an adult, Mrs Hughes, and I won't
insult you. It may be cancer, but I am fairly certain it
is not.
MRS PATMORE: There you are. It's very, very unlikely.
Isn't it, Doctor?
MRS HUGHES: If the doctor treats me like an adult, Mrs
Patmore, why do you insist on treating me like a child?*

....

Continued from page 99:

now that the money's been lost it is only reasonable to expect her to contribute
some more. I've always made the relationship between Violet and Cora one of
respect rather than adoration. Violet would rather Robert had married the
niece of one of her friends, but she has accepted that the money meant that
the union was important and necessary. But it is still not the way she'd have
liked things, and the fact that her son is happy with Cora doesn't really weigh
as heavily as you would think it might. This is entirely drawn from experience.

* I asked a specialist to tell me what would have happened in the Twenties
and how they analysed whether a lump was cancerous. It would have been
quite a long process, unlike the very quick results we know today. And again
we have the use of the word cancer and Mrs Hughes forcing herself to say the
word, which has been the elephant in the room up to that point. The
business with the injection and the fact that the doctor has to do it whether
or not it hurts comes from my mother. She was with the daughter of a friend

19 INT. KITCHENS. DOWNTON. DAY.

Daisy pokes the coal when Alfred comes in.

DAISY: Does this seem slow to you?

ALFRED: Not really.

He fills a small bowl with water as Reed appears.

REED: Mrs Levinson is going to the Dower House with the others for tea.

Alfred leaves. He smiles at Reed as he goes.

REED (CONT'D): I think he likes me.

DAISY: He's being friendly. That's all.*

20 INT. LIBRARY. DOWNTON. DAY.

Matthew is working, surrounded by letters. Mary comes in.

MARY: Are you all right? You seem to have been slaving away for hours.

MATTHEW: I want to be up-to-date with it all before I go back into the office.

MARY: Anything from Mr Swire's lawyer?

MATTHEW: You can read it if you like.

He hands her a sheet of writing paper. She skims through it.

MARY: So you are definitely Reggie's heir?

MATTHEW: Looks like it. But if they have to get a death certificate out of the Indian authorities, it won't all be settled by Tuesday.

MARY: Good.

MATTHEW: Why is it good?

....

Continued from page 100:

who was having a baby and another woman kept insisting how much it was going to hurt. Finally, Mummy took her aside and said, 'Since she's got to have it, what is the point of going on about how much it hurts?' I thought of that and used it here.

* Just a note to show the freer customs of the Americans, which was why they were enjoyed at every level of society. They had a more relaxed way of behaving. This was not immoral, I hasten to add; just that they were more easy and unconstrained.

MARY: The delay may give you time to change your mind.
MATTHEW: Stop punishing me, Mary. Please. If I accepted the legacy I would be taking money under false pretences. I'd be stealing. Your father understands. Now why can't you?
MARY: I don't think he understands at all. He just doesn't want to beg… Anyway, I'm off to Granny's for tea. I'll see you later.*
MATTHEW: I do love you, so terribly much.
MARY: Yes. I know you do.

21   INT.   DRAWING ROOM.   DOWER HOUSE.   DAY.

Mary, Martha and Cora are having tea with Violet.

CORA: So what's Harold doing now?
MARTHA: His *idée fixe* is yachts. Bigger yachts, faster yachts… something with yachts.†

....

* We had to make the line of inheritance complicated so that we could all enjoy this middle ground when Matthew is, first of all, possibly going to get something, then probably going to get something, but it doesn't become certain until we've had the best part of two episodes. For a start, trying to get a death certificate out of India, how long would that take? Years ago my father asked me to bring the family tree up-to-date at the College of Arms. I thought all you did was photograph a page from *Burke's Landed Gentry* and send it in. Absolutely no chance. They regard this venerable publication as a work of fiction, and everything has to be proved. Everything. Not just birth, marriage and death, but every army rank, every navy rank, every house ownership, every honour, every medal – everything. In the end, it took four years. A lot of the stuff was affected by the history of the time. In the second half of the seventeenth century several of the Felloweses were in Jamaica, and then elsewhere in the West Indies. By the eighteenth century a lot of them were in India and then by the early twentieth they're in Africa. The whole thing took forever, but I'm rather proud of myself. For each generation I proved every sibling, so that any descendants only had to prove themselves up to that sibling.

We've created a real point of difference between Matthew and Mary by this stage, and if I were in her shoes I wouldn't understand it either. I'm very sympathetic to Mary really. Like her, I don't find that his protestations of love ring very loudly.

† We don't meet Harold until the Christmas Special at the end of the fourth year. But I wanted to set him up because I felt, if we ever were to meet, then if no earlier reference had been made to him it wouldn't be very believable.

CORA: Is he happy?

MARTHA: He's much too busy to find out.

VIOLET: It always seems so strange to me that Cora has a brother.

MARTHA: Why?

CORA: You know how things work here, Mother. If there's a boy, the daughters don't get anything.

VIOLET: There is no such thing as an English heiress with a brother. Why do we never see him?

MARTHA: Oh, Harold hates to leave America.

VIOLET: Curious. He hates to leave America; I should hate to go there.

MARY: You don't mean that, Granny. When we're both so drawn to America.

She glares at her grandmother, who remembers their mission.

VIOLET: Indeed, indeed we are. Never more than now. When the bond between the Crawleys and the Levinsons is so strong.

CORA: That's nice, if you mean it, Mama.

VIOLET: I do. It is marvellous the way our families support each other.

MARTHA: You mean you needed the Levinson cash to keep the Crawleys on top.

MARY: I'm not sure we'd put it that way —

VIOLET: I am quite sure we would not.

MARY: But I hope you do feel that Mama's fortune has been well spent in shoring up an ancient family.

MARTHA: Ah, you gotta spend it on something.

Mary catches her other grandmother's eye and gives a nod.

....

Continued from page 102:

One of the problems for me with some of those American soaps was that they were always turning out to have had children they'd never mentioned or had entirely forgotten about, which I didn't find terrifically believable. But I think the fact that Harold hates to leave America got me out of trouble. And now Violet and Cora are both still trying to get Martha's money.

Of course Martha, in a sense, is playing with them here, because she knows perfectly well, as we will discover later, that she only has a life income, but she's allowing them to think she is worth stalking because, I suspect, she enjoys it.

22   INT. MATTHEW'S DRESSING ROOM. DOWNTON. EVE.

Alfred is helping Matthew to change into white tie. Matthew pulls up one tail of his coat. There is a gaping hole in it.

MATTHEW: What happened here?
ALFRED: I… I just…
MATTHEW: You just what?
ALFRED: There was a mark…
MATTHEW: I know there was a mark, but you didn't need to burn it away. What have you done? Well, I'll go down in my dinner jacket. You can send it to my tailor in London in the morning… Come on. Nobody's died. Just find the dinner jacket.*

Alfred looks as if he's going to burst into tears.

23   INT. KITCHEN PASSAGE. DOWNTON. NIGHT.

Mrs Hughes is standing there when Carson appears.

CARSON: Mrs Hughes, there don't seem to be any glasses laid for the pudding wine.
MRS HUGHES: Oh. Are they having one tonight?
CARSON: It's on the menus. I don't write them for my own amusement.
MRS HUGHES: No. I dare say not.
CARSON: Mrs Hughes, I am trying, and so far failing, to persuade his lordship to bring the staff levels back up to snuff. But until he does, it is vital that you pull your weight.†

He is gone before she can defend herself.

24   INT. DINING ROOM. DOWNTON. NIGHT.

Carson and Alfred are serving.

MARTHA: Newport's not a jungle. Not at all. But it is a little less formal.
VIOLET: Well, Matthew obviously wants you to feel at home in his play clothes.

....

* Alfred has been set up, but he does not betray Thomas.

† Carson here is very short with Mrs Hughes. He feels she's not pulling her weight. This is all designed to get the audience's sympathy.

MATTHEW: Don't blame me for this. I'm afraid Alfred and
I had a bit of a disaster earlier.
CORA: Why? What happened?
MATTHEW: Somehow the poor chap managed to burn a hole in
my tails… Don't worry. It can be mended.

During this, Carson pulls a dish away from Robert prematurely.

ROBERT: Careful, Carson. Steady the Buffs.
CARSON: Beg your pardon, m'lord.

But he looks at Alfred as if he would eat him.

STRALLAN: I rather like dinner jackets. And I agree
with you. Sometimes it's nice to be informal.
EDITH: Especially when a couple is alone.*

*She beams into Strallan's eyes, which he responds to.
Silently, Violet indicates the exchange to Robert.*

MARY: But people like us should lead the fight to keep
tradition going.
ISOBEL: If you mean we should never change, I can't
agree to that.
CORA: Nor me. I think accepting change is quite as
important as defending the past.

....

* Violet's resistance to dinner jackets continues for quite a few episodes to come. Inevitably, as the series rolls forward, dinner jackets start to be imposed on her, but at this point a dinner jacket was really quite informal and you would not often wear it. In fact, a dinner jacket would have been the same as a smoking jacket in my youth. When I was young, men like my father would often come home and put on their smoking jacket over their perfectly ordinary trousers, as a way of relaxing in the evening.

Funnily enough, what is happening now to the smoking jacket is what happened to the dinner jacket – it is becoming formal evening wear. In those days, you could wear it in the evening with a black tie, but only in your own house or, a little bit later, if you were staying in that house. But now that's gone and people drive across the county in a smoking jacket. In fact, in Dorset, a smoking jacket with no tie has become an acceptable evening costume, so we are now moving onto the next generation of that. I've been in white tie a few times recently, which is quite unusual and I like the look of it. I think it looks handsome, but you need a valet. It's not a costume to put on with no help, and I think that, as much as anything else, was why it died – putting it on is just a hell of a palaver.

MARY: But the role of houses like Downton is to protect tradition. That's why they're so important to maintain.
VIOLET: Don't you agree, Mrs Levinson? We must do everything in our power to keep houses like Downton going.
MARTHA: Sure. If you think it's worth it. So who's coming to dinner next week?
CORA: Some locals. We thought you'd like to see Downton on parade.

Violet catches Mary's eye.

MARY: That's right, Grandmama. I'm glad we've planned a dinner. We can show you the real point of Downton.

25   INT.   HALL.   DOWNTON.   NIGHT.

Robert, Matthew and Strallan come out of the dining room.

ROBERT: I wonder if I could ask you to come into the library for a moment.

They start towards the library, but Robert turns to Matthew.

ROBERT (CONT'D): Tell Carson and Alfred they can go downstairs. We'll serve ourselves when we get in there.

In other words, Matthew has been ordered to leave them alone.

26   INT.   SERVANTS' HALL.   DOWNTON.   NIGHT.

Reed is reading, while Daisy lays the table. Some of the others are there when Alfred and Carson enter, talking.

ALFRED: I don't know what to say, Mr Carson.
O'BRIEN: What's going on here?
CARSON: Alfred has embarrassed the family. He forced Mr Matthew to appear downstairs improperly dressed.
O'BRIEN: Oh, you make it sound quite exciting.
CARSON: I will not tolerate vulgarity, thank you, Miss O'Brien.
ANNA: I'm sure Alfred didn't mean to, Mr Carson.
ALFRED: I asked Thomas how to get a mark —
THOMAS: Oi, oi. What's this?
ALFRED: The stuff you gave me to clean the tails burned a hole in them.

THOMAS: No such thing. I gave you some soda crystals, that's all. If you used them wrongly, it's not my fault. This is what comes of making him run before he could walk.

This last is directed at a seething O'Brien.

END OF ACT TWO

ACT THREE

27 INT. LIBRARY. DOWNTON. NIGHT.

Strallan is with an awkward Robert.

STRALLAN: If you want me to stay away from her, of course I will.
ROBERT: I know it sounds harsh —
STRALLAN: Please, Robert. I understand completely. Lady Edith is your daughter and you don't want her involved with some cripple who is far too old.
ROBERT: Now you're the one who's harsh.
STRALLAN: The trouble is, she calls round regularly. I can hardly ask for her not to be admitted… I suppose I could write to her. Yes, that's it.
ROBERT: If things were different —
STRALLAN: If I were twenty years younger and had the use of all my limbs?
ROBERT: I hope you won't feel we can't be friends after this.
STRALLAN: But let's leave it for a while. I'll duck out of the dinner next week.
ROBERT: It might be best. Thank you.*

....

* Robert does not want Strallan as a son-in-law, although he's trying to be nice. I don't blame Robert in this, actually. You wouldn't want him for your young daughter, so again it is quite a nice *Downton* situation where essentially you're on both sides. Both men are perfectly pleasant and are only trying to do their best as they see it.

28   INT. HOUSEMAIDS' CLEANING CUPBOARD. DOWNTON.
         NIGHT.

Alfred and O'Brien are staring at the bottle on the shelves.

O'BRIEN: That's the one you should have taken. Soda
crystals.
ALFRED: But he didn't give me that. He pointed to this
one. I promise.
O'BRIEN: You don't have to promise. I believe you.
ALFRED: Why would he do such a thing?
O'BRIEN: I don't know why, but I know he'll be sorry.
That *I* can promise.

O'Brien walks away.

29   INT. ROBERT'S DRESSING ROOM. DOWNTON. NIGHT.

Thomas is helping Robert into his night clothes.

ROBERT: So you think he's not ready?
THOMAS: He's just a lad, m'lord. He can see to the odd
visitor, but permanent valet to Mr Matthew? It's too much.
ROBERT: Actually, I'm pretty sure Mr Crawley would
rather manage on his own.
THOMAS: They wouldn't like that downstairs, m'lord.
ROBERT: I was afraid you'd say that… So what would you
suggest?
THOMAS: Ask Mr Molesley to join us. It'd be kinder to
Alfred in the long run… Kinder than asking more than he
can give.

30   INT. MARY'S BEDROOM. DOWNTON. NIGHT.

Matthew comes in, in a dressing gown. Mary is in bed.

MARY: How is that poor footman? I thought Carson was
going to eat him alive.
MATTHEW: Very glum. To be honest, he has been a clot.
I'll have to send the coat up to London.
MARY: Well, get it done quickly. This dinner has to be
the grandest of the grand.*

....

* The dinner has to be an incredible display of aristocratic seigneurial right so
that Martha is blazed into submission by seeing the majesty of the whole
thing. That's the idea, anyway.

MATTHEW: What do you hope to show her?

MARY: Why Downton matters. Why it mustn't be allowed to fall apart.

MATTHEW: Hasn't Cora had her share of the Levinson gold? I thought what was left was headed for your uncle.

MARY: It's not so laid down in America. He's as rich as Croesus as it is.*

MATTHEW: So you mean to fleece her?

MARY: Since you're the one to get us out of this hole if you wanted to, I won't take any criticism, thank you.

MATTHEW: Will she do it?

MARY: Granny means to make her, or die in the attempt. Now stop talking and kiss me, before I get cross.

Which he does.

31   INT. MRS HUGHES'S SITTING ROOM. DOWNTON. NIGHT.

Mrs Patmore is with Mrs Hughes.

MRS PATMORE: At least it's not long to wait.

MRS HUGHES: Not before I have the test, but how long after that?

MRS PATMORE: Well, you heard him. With any luck, you'll know at once.

....

* One of the reasons why all these American heiresses were so numerous during this period was that a rich man in America would make all his children rich. That was not the case in England, where the eldest son got the lot. The others might be given a nice rectory in Wiltshire, but even that was rare. Consuelo Vanderbilt brought $9 million when she married the Duke of Marlborough, and she had two brothers. That would never have happened in England. An heiress meant literally the sole survivor, the irony being that, inevitably, so many of the English heiresses were bad breeders, because they came from families that had literally died out, whereas in America that wasn't the case at all. An heiress could have plenty of brothers or sisters.

However, this custom (of treating all your children democratically) is one of the reasons why it's very hard for American fortunes to last more than two or three generations, because they keep being subdivided, and one of the ironies now is that this is happening in more and more European families. They don't understand why their importance is fading away, but they will leave a house that has been in the family for 300 years between their children. And the sad fact is, once the ownership is shared, that house will have to be sold.

She breaks off at the sound of Carson's arrival.

CARSON: I wish you could get those maids under control. They've broken one of the serving dishes this time, **and** we've the dinner next week.

MRS HUGHES: We're short of a footman, we're short of a kitchen maid and one house maid at least. That's if **Anna** is to be a *proper* lady's maid, which is what Lady Mary wants.

CARSON: Well, naturally, she likes things done properly —

MRS HUGHES: Oh, for heaven's sake, we can't *do* things properly until either his lordship allows us the staff we need, or until *you* and the *blessed* Lady Mary come down from that cloud and join the human race!*

CARSON: I can only suppose that you are overtired. I bid you goodnight.

MRS PATMORE: You see, she's —

MRS HUGHES: Goodnight, Mr Carson. We will discuss the dinner in the morning.

He nods and goes. Mrs Patmore opens her mouth, but…

MS HUGHES (CONT'D): And no, Mrs Patmore, you may not tell him.

32   INT.   SERVANTS' HALL/PASSAGE.   DOWNTON.   DAY.

O'Brien is in there. Alfred enters. Carson sees him return.

CARSON: Have you finished with Mr Matthew?

....

* Mrs Hughes is not a believer in the aristocratic principle in the same way as Carson. I'm sure that plenty of servants weren't, and she represents them in the series. For them, it was a job. If they had a good employer then that was great, if their employer was less good it was less great, but they didn't have to be paid-up believers, either way. When the end of this way of life comes for Mrs Hughes (and there were many of her kind) and she has to find something else to do, it may be worrying but it won't be a cause for a fit of weeping. She won't regard it as a terrible injustice in the eyes of God that the system has come to an end, and if she can get a job running a small hotel, which she would do well, then that would be absolutely fine. Whereas for Carson the aristocratic principle is woven into his very woof, so we are dealing with sharply contrasting emotions. Here she vents her feelings unusually severely because she's upset. 'I can only suppose that you are overtired,' says Carson.

ALFRED: I have. He's in the dining room.
CARSON: Very good. You won't need to attend to him
again. Mr Molesley will be coming up from the village.
ALFRED: Has Mr Matthew complained?
CARSON: He didn't have to. It's not your fault. We've
hurried you along too fast. You mustn't feel badly.

He walks out of the room. O'Brien whispers to her nephew.

O'BRIEN: This is Thomas's doing… But don't you fret.
I'll make him sorry.

Alfred goes into the passage. He sags back against the wall.

REED: I'm on your side.
ALFRED: I'm glad somebody is.

*Before he knows it, she leans over and kisses him. Then she
hurries away, giggling. This has all been witnessed by Daisy.*

33   INT. DINING ROOM. DOWNTON. DAY.

Matthew is eating breakfast with Edith when Robert comes in.

ROBERT: No Mary?
MATTHEW: She says she's a married woman now, so she can
have breakfast in bed.*

Robert finds the letters, gives one to Edith and serves himself.

ROBERT: I'm sorry about your tails.
MATTHEW: Carson's sending them up on the London train
this morning. They'll have to put a new panel in.
ROBERT: We thought we'd get Molesley to come and look
after you. He knows your ways.
MATTHEW: Well, I'd be perfectly happy —

Carson glances at Robert to stiffen his resolve.

ROBERT: I think it's better if he comes.
CARSON: I do need to talk to you about the other staff
we need, m'lord —

....

* We've always stuck to the distinction of married women having their
breakfast in bed and unmarried women not. Occasionally, which I think is
true to life, if they have an early start or they're catching a train, they'll all
come down and have breakfast in the dining room, but as a rule married
women had it on a tray in their beds in these houses.

ROBERT: Not now, Carson. But you may send for Molesley, if Mrs Crawley has no objection... Edith?
EDITH: Oh, Papa! How could you!

She has burst into tears and now she runs out.

MATTHEW: Golly. Do you know what that was?
ROBERT: I'm afraid I probably do.

34 INT. DRAWING ROOM. DOWNTON. DAY.

Mary is with Cora, who is sewing a tapestry on her knee.

CORA: I'm sorry, but quite enough of my father's money has already been poured into Downton. Why should Harold lose half his inheritance because of our folly?
MARY: So it's all Papa's fault?
CORA: Well, it isn't my mother's and it isn't my brother's, and I don't see why they should pay for it.
MARY: We're still going to ask.
CORA: What are you so afraid of? If we sell, we move to a smaller house and a more modest estate. We don't have to go down the mines.
MARY: You don't understand.
CORA: Mary, this is 1920. The world has changed. A lot of people live in smaller houses than they used to.
MARY: Which only goes to show that you're American and I am English. I shall be Countess of Grantham one day and, in my book, the Countess of Grantham lives at Downton Abbey.
CORA: Your father told me about Matthew's expectations from Mr Swire.
MARY: He refuses to keep any of it. He thinks it would be stealing.
CORA: How frustrating for you, my dear. Two fortunes just out of reach.
MARY: Then I shall have to stretch a little harder, won't I, Mama?*

....

* Cora's very sorry that Downton is probably going to have to go, but she's most sorry for Robert. It is not her own happiness that's tied up in it, whereas her daughter Mary is completely on the other side. Anything must be sacrificed rather than let this terrible disaster happen. So here we separate their positions to make it clear that they have different feelings – another

35 INT. SALVATION ARMY HALL. YORK. DAY.

Isobel's interviewing a woman. The rest sit round the hall.

ISOBEL: What job might you be suited to...? Because we're not simply here to give you food. We need to try to find a place for you in the world.

But she is distracted. A nervous young woman (Ethel Parks) has come into the hall. Isobel stands and walks over to her.

ISOBEL (CONT'D): Do you want to speak to me?
ETHEL: Yes, Mrs Crawley. I do.
ISOBEL: How do you know my name?

But her visitor will not answer that one.

ISOBEL (CONT'D): Have you come for our help? You're very welcome if you have.

But the other woman just shakes her head.

ETHEL: I'm past help, ma'am.
ISOBEL: Nobody is past help. Wait a minute. I know you. You were the maid who brought your child into the dining room at Downton that time.*

....

Continued from page 112:

example of the *Downton* house style that with every issue we have many different points of view being taken by them all. Nor is Cora above poking some fun at Mary.

I'm always interested that Americans as a rule – and this is a generalisation – don't feel obliged to go on with a family house, even when they've got more than enough money to do so. You do get the odd Biltmore or Groton which has gone on down the line of descent but, as a rule, they take the position that this was their grandmother's house in Newport and it's too big for them now. As I say, it isn't much to do with money. They can be rich, with no reason to sell, but they'll sell it anyway. So Mary is trying to evoke in Martha an emotion that the older woman doesn't share. But Mary, of course, is prepared to take her on.

* Rightly or wrongly, I felt we should make this point quickly, even though sharp-eyed viewers will have recognised her and there's no attempt to pretend she isn't Ethel Parks. It is always a challenge in writing this kind of drama that you want the audience to have the information they require in order to follow the story, but you don't want to be too obviously telling them

ETHEL: I'm sorry. This has been a mistake. I thought I was ready to ask you… but I'm not. I'm not ready.

ISOBEL: Wait a minute. Ask me what? Oh, please stay.

But she has frightened Ethel away. She returns to the table.

ISOBEL (CONT'D): Now, where were we? Oh, yes. We have to find something for you to do… I presume you do realise that we can't really recommend returning to your old line of work.

She doesn't seem to be making much of an impression.

36. INT. CLARKSON'S CONSULTING ROOMS. DOWNTON VILLAGE. DAY.

Clarkson enters to find Mrs Hughes and Mrs Patmore.

CLARKSON: I'm sorry to keep you waiting, ladies. The fact is, it's not quite as simple —

MRS PATMORE: Oh, my God.

MRS HUGHES: Mrs Patmore, will you please leave the hysteria to me.

CLARKSON: I'm afraid the test was inconclusive. I had hoped that the fluid from the cyst would be clear, but there are traces of blood in it. Not enough to confirm the presence of cancer, but a little too much to exclude it.

MRS HUGHES: So what happens now?

CLARKSON: I send it away for analysis. And this stage will take some time.

MRS PATMORE: How much time?

CLARKSON: Anything up to two months.

MRS PATMORE: Oh, my —

....

Continued from page 113:

something they already know. We often have arguments with TV executives – though not with my co-producer Gareth Neame, because he feels exactly the same as I do on this topic – who fail to understand why we don't have the scene where she learns that he's dead, or whatever. The answer is because the audience knows it and what they want is the characters' response to that information, not for the same information to be repeated. If you use up a lot of your screen time on exposition of what the audience already knows, then you pay for it in terms of energy and the show runs out of puff.

But Mrs Hughes silences her with a glance. She stands.

CLARKSON: Until then, please try to take it a little more easily. Sit down and put your feet up, if you can.
MRS PATMORE: Chance'd be a fine thing.
CLARKSON: Would you like me to say something to Lady Grantham?
MRS HUGHES: No, thank you, Doctor. I'll speak to her myself, if I need to. Thank you.*

37 EXT. GARDENS. DOWNTON. DAY.

Robert is walking Isis when he hears crying and finds Edith weeping on a bench, in Martha's arms.

ROBERT: My darling girl. What's this?
MARTHA: I think you know what it is, since you asked Sir Anthony to write.

Robert comes and sits next to them.

ROBERT: Edith, you do understand that I only ever want what's best for you?
EDITH: And you're the judge of that.
ROBERT: In this, I think I am.
EDITH: Sybil marries a chauffeur and you welcome him to Downton. But when I'm in love with a gentleman, you cast him into the outer darkness.
MARTHA: She has a point, Robert.
ROBERT: Strallan is certainly a gentleman —
MARTHA: Well, besides which, Edith tells me he has a house, he has money, he has a title — everything that you care about.
ROBERT: You make me sound very shallow.
EDITH: Aren't you? When you make me give him up because he has a bad arm?
ROBERT: Oh, it's not the only reason. He's a quarter of a century too old. Did she tell you *that*?

....

* The test is inconclusive. This is because, throughout my life, I have found that whenever an 'expert' says, 'It should be pretty clear; it'll either be this or it'll be that,' when it comes to it, it never is. Not only in health, but literally in terms of choosing the colours for a room. It's always inconclusive, so here we employ that principle to stretch it out a bit more.

His tone with his mother-in-law is quite harsh.

MARTHA: Your daughter is sad and lonely, Robert. Now, I don't mean to interfere but —
ROBERT: Don't you?
EDITH: If you ban him from Downton, I'll only go to his house. I mean it.
ROBERT: I don't believe he'd see you.
EDITH: Then I'll just wait outside until he does.
MARTHA: I presume you're not anxious for her to catch pneumonia?
ROBERT: Of course not.
EDITH: How can you not like him because of his age? When almost every young man we grew up with is dead! Do you *want* me to spend my life alone?
ROBERT: I didn't say I don't like him. I like him very much.
EDITH: So do I, Papa. Oh, so do I.

Edith gets up and takes her father's hand.

EDITH (CONT'D): Please ask him back. He writes he's not coming to Mama's dinner, but please make him. Please, please, please.
MARTHA: Please?

He looks at them both and gives a weary sigh.

ROBERT: Oh, all right, then.*

....

* Here we have Martha obviously taking the opposite side to Robert when it comes to Strallan. I am on Robert's side, because when Martha says, 'Edith tells me he has a house, he has money, he has a title – everything that you care about,' she is being unfair. Robert has clearly demonstrated that he doesn't only care about these things. He wants his daughter to be happy and he doesn't think a one-armed, middle-aged man who is twenty-five years older is capable of making her happy. So, for me, this is an instance where the audience can get behind Robert. We should not be on Martha's side. Besides which, she's really just making trouble for the fun of it. But Robert will be beaten because, as we all know, when every woman in the house is lined up against you, you don't really have a chance.

38 INT. YORK PRISON VISITING CELL. DAY.

Anna is with Bates.

ANNA: I've found Mrs Bartlett. I wrote back to the
tenant of her old house, explaining, and they've sent me
a forwarding address. I don't know why they didn't
before.

BATES: Just because you know where she is doesn't mean
she'll talk to you.

ANNA: Why not?

BATES: Audrey Bartlett was the nearest thing Vera had to
a friend.*

ANNA: That's why I want to meet her.

BATES: Maybe, but when she looks at you, she won't see
the real Anna Bates.

ANNA: She doesn't have to like me. I need her to be
honest. I'm going to write and ask for a meeting. I can
get to London and back in a day.

BATES: She won't agree.

ANNA: I've the rent from the house so I can make it
worth her while… Why do you think Vera didn't go and see
her instead of sending that letter?

BATES: What do you mean?

ANNA: When Vera was frightened about your visit, she
wrote that letter, saying how scared she was, instead of
walking round to see her friend.

BATES: Maybe she did both… So, what's the news at home?

ANNA: I shouldn't tell you, really. I haven't told any
of the others. It's breaking the code of a lady's maid.†

....

* Bartlett was a surname of my eldest brother's girlfriend in Nigeria where my
father was posted when I was in my early teens. She was called Annabel
Bartlett and my parents adored her, which of course is absolutely fatal
because it means it will never turn out as they would have it. This example
was no exception to that rule.

† One of the most important rules for a maid or a valet was not repeating
what you heard. Inevitably, if you're in a bedroom with a married couple, you
are bound to hear things that are really quite private, and if you gained a
reputation for going straight down to the servants' hall and telling them
everything then it would affect your references and, as a consequence, your
employability. On the whole, nothing was more prized in a valet or lady's
maid than efficiency and discretion. Ironically, this was the reason why the

BATES: Which is what you are now.

ANNA: No, I'm not. Not properly… His lordship's in trouble. It seems they may have to sell.

BATES: What? Sell Downton?

She is silent and simply nods as the news sinks in.

BATES (CONT'D): That makes me sad. I wouldn't have thought there was much that could touch me in here, but that does.

ANNA: Lady Mary thinks her ladyship's mother might save them…

BATES: But you don't agree?

ANNA: The rich don't stay rich by giving away their money, do they?

BATES: They do not.*

39   EXT.   DOWNTON.   EVE.

Molesley is running up the drive.

40   INT.   MATTHEW'S DRESSING ROOM.   DOWNTON.   EVE.

Matthew is putting on a shirt when Molesley knocks and bursts in.

MOLESLEY: It's never come. They promised and promised, and I thought it was sure to be on the seven o'clock. But it's not.

....

Continued from page 117:

foreign governments made such a point of enlisting them as spies, because they would hear things the other servants would not, and if they could get into a senior household as spies they were invaluable. If they were maiding the wife of the Lord Chancellor or valet to the Foreign Secretary then they were hearing things that were worth reporting back to their foreign masters. Here, Anna is aware that she is breaking the code but feels that since this is her husband and Bates is bound by the same code there is no disloyalty.

* I agree with Bates's comments about Mary's chances of getting money out of Martha and, in fact, I am always fascinated by hangers-on of the rich. They cling so fervently but I want to say to them, 'Look, if the food's great and you're just enjoying having a good time, then fine, but please don't think you're going to end this friendship any richer than you were when it started, because it's not going to happen.'

MATTHEW: Well, I'll just have to wear black tie.

MOLESLEY: But Lady Mary, she'll —

MATTHEW: These things don't matter as much as they did. Lady Mary knows that as well as anyone.*

41   INT.   MRS LEVINSON'S BEDROOM.   DOWNTON.   NIGHT.

Martha Levinson is finishing being dressed by Reed.

REED: They think you're going to bail them out.

MARTHA: When are they planning to ask me?

REED: That's what this evening's about. To show you the glorious past that must not die.

MARTHA: But you and I belong to the new world, Reed, and not the old. Where we come from, we look forward.

REED: I thank heaven for it, ma'am.

MARTHA: Now iron that shirt for the morning and bring breakfast at eight on the dot. You were late, today.†

....

* Of course, Mary is not going to understand at all why Matthew is wrongly dressed, but then Matthew doesn't realise that this evening is supposed to be a kind of Hollywood version of an aristocratic dinner.

† I was sad that we lost this scene between Martha Levinson and Reed, because it shows that Martha understands exactly how Mary and Violet are trying to play her. Also, if you have a character who is a body servant to another character, you want to see their working relationship at least once. But anyway, it did go and we are left with Reed coming out of the bedroom and seeing O'Brien.

Also, the irony of the scene, which I like, is that Martha talks about how she and Reed belong to the new world and not the old, whereas in fact the way she treats Reed and issues her with instructions places her quite clearly in the old world. A lot of them, both English and American, thought the new world was going to be a modern version of the old. They didn't understand it was actually going to be a different place, where they boiled their own eggs and ironed their own shirts – although, to be fair, for that generation it didn't usually come to that. They may have had a much-reduced staff, but few of them ended up cooking their own supper. Some of them did, one mustn't forget that, but most limped over the finishing line with their former maid or valet still looking after them. It was their children who had to accept that they were going to live in a completely different way from their parents.

42 INT. BEDROOM PASSAGE. DOWNTON. NIGHT.

As Reed walks down the passage she sees O'Brien ducking out of a door, with something wrapped inside a linen cover…

43 INT. HALL/DINING ROOM. DOWNTON. NIGHT.

Carson has opened the door to Violet.

VIOLET: Thank you. I know I'm early —
MARY: Granny? Come and see what we've done!
VIOLET: Oh, excuse me…

She runs over and pulls her grandmother into the dining room. The table is a mass of silver and flowers.

MARY: What do you think?
VIOLET: Nothing succeeds like excess.*
MARY: When shall we tackle her?
VIOLET: After dinner. We'll get her on her own.
MARY: She won't want to see all this go. Not now she knows it's for her own granddaughter. She won't.
VIOLET: Never mistake a wish for a certainty. Let's *hope* she won't.

....

* A Wilde-ism, so not an original. I have always felt a sort of ownership of Oscar Wilde. His wife, Constance Lloyd, was my grandfather's cousin, not that I knew this early on. From my boyhood, I was told about the governors of Bombay, the rear admirals and the generals in my family tree, but I was never told that Constance was a cousin, and when I was quite grown up, in my thirties, I was having a drink with a relation and looking at his collection of family portraits. One was of a group of children with their mother and when I asked who they were, he said, 'This little girl might interest you. She married Oscar Wilde.' I was absolutely astonished. When I wondered if they had been close, he replied that Constance and my great-grandmother were like sisters. But apparently, once the scandal happened, that was it. Cut off. It gave me such a window on how tough they were. They kept their world going by never bending the rules. There was no such thing as an innocent party when it came to a scandal. After her husband's arrest, Constance began those sad peripatetic journeys drifting around Europe from spa to spa, because nobody would receive her, until she died at thirty-nine.

44 INT. KITCHENS. DOWNTON. NIGHT.

They are working but the atmosphere is slightly smoky.

DAISY: Mrs Patmore —
MRS PATMORE: What is it now?
DAISY: It's smoking. The range.
MRS PATMORE: The wind must be in the wrong direction.
Just rake it through.

There is the sound of running feet. Thomas appears.

THOMAS: Where's Alfred?
MRS PATMORE: Why?
THOMAS: *Where's Alfred!*
DAISY: I think he's in the servants' hall.

Thomas races off. They stare at each other.

45 INT. SERVANTS' HALL. DOWNTON. NIGHT.

Thomas bursts in. Alfred, O'Brien and some others are there.

THOMAS: Where are they?
ANNA: Where are what?
THOMAS: His bloody evening shirts, that's what! Where
have you put them?
ALFRED: I haven't touched his evening shirts. Why would
I?
THOMAS: Have you done this?

He turns a threatening finger towards O'Brien.

O'BRIEN: Thomas, why would I know anything about his
lordship's shirts?
THOMAS: When I find out…
O'BRIEN: Keep your histrionics to yourself and hurry up
about it. Her ladyship's already in the drawing room.
Are you telling me his lordship's not even dressed?

*Thomas gives her and then Alfred a savage look and races off.
Alfred looks at his aunt long and hard, but O'Brien confirms
nothing.*

46 INT. ROBERT'S DRESSING ROOM. DOWNTON. NIGHT.

Robert is in his underwear. He is very angry.

    ROBERT: You can't have lost them all!
    THOMAS: I haven't 'lost' any of them, m'lord. They've
    been taken by someone, stolen, pinched.
    ROBERT: Why would they do that?
    THOMAS: To get at me, m'lord.
    ROBERT: Are you not popular downstairs?

Thomas had allowed himself to lose control. He reins it in.

    THOMAS: Oh, I wouldn't say that, m'lord. But you know
    how people can be. They like a little joke.
    ROBERT: Well, I'm sorry but this is quite unacceptable.
    If you uncover the culprit, refer them to me. But for
    now, what are we going to do?*

47 EXT/INT. DOWNTON. HALL. NIGHT.

*Cars are arriving. Carson is on duty. Glamorous, bejewelled
women are escorted by smart men in tails. Inside, Carson
greets them and the glittering tide moves on towards the
drawing room.*

48 INT. KITCHENS. DOWNTON. NIGHT.

The smoke is getting thick. Panic is setting in.

    MRS PATMORE: It can't be going out!

....

* The one thing people didn't want was a servant that the other servants
detested, because it made for a jangled and unpleasant household. So the
impression you were always expected to give as a servant was that everything
was going swimmingly, rather like an American today. If you ask an
American about their career or their life, everything is always fabulous. They
never say, 'God, I should never have left my last job.' That would weaken
them in their own eyes and therefore (they believe) in yours, and it is, in fact,
a mark of great intimacy and a real compliment from an American when they
tell you their life's going to hell. Thomas immediately has to recover from his
complaint and blame it all on people liking 'a little joke'. This gives
permission to Robert to go on being angry without having to worry that
Thomas is making trouble downstairs.

DAISY: Well, it is. There must be a block in the flue.*
MRS PATMORE: But the dinner's not cooked. We haven't even put in the soufflés.
DAISY: There'll be no soufflés tonight.
MRS PATMORE: And the mutton's still raw.

She stares into the oven. Mrs Hughes coughs in the doorway.

MRS HUGHES: What in heaven's name is going on?
MRS PATMORE: I'll tell you what. We've twenty lords and ladies in the drawing room waiting for dinner, and we've got no dinner to give them.
MRS HUGHES: Oh, my God.

END OF ACT THREE

ACT FOUR

49   INT.   DRAWING ROOM.   DOWNTON.   NIGHT.

The room is filling with a laughing, chattering group. Mary and Violet are by the chimneypiece when Matthew arrives.

MARY: Why are you not in white tie?
MATTHEW: Darling, please forgive me. I'm afraid they never sent my tails back.

Robert arrives in a dinner jacket, soft shirt and a bow tie.

VIOLET: Good God, almighty. You're not in white tie, either? What have you come as?
ROBERT: I am so sorry. Thomas has lost all my dress shirts.

Violet looks across at Edith and Strallan chatting.

....

* I wanted a fire and I just had to accept that I was never going to be able to have a fire in the main part of the house, because the Carnarvons, the real-life owners, would not conceivably tolerate it. So it had to be in an element of the set that was not at Highclere. We could have a fire in the kitchen because it is a standing set at Ealing Studios. Although, actually, this wouldn't be the last fire at Downton.

VIOLET: Why… Why is he still here? I thought you'd given him his marching orders.
ROBERT: I had. But my dear mother-in-law intervened. I've a good mind to tell her —
VIOLET: No, no, no, no. Not tonight. She must have it all her own way tonight, don't you think?

She forces herself to smile as Martha approaches.

MARTHA: Oh, you two are dressed for a barbecue.
ROBERT: I feel like a Chicago bootlegger.*
VIOLET: I don't even know what that means, but it sounds almost as peculiar as you look.

Isobel has arrived, just as Cora approaches her husband.

CORA: Robert, come quickly.
ISOBEL: What is it?
CORA: Apparently the oven's broken down.
ROBERT: It can't have done. What does that mean?
CORA: Well, to cut a long story short, it means we have no food.
MARTHA: Oh… Funny clothes and no food. Should be quite an evening.
CORA: Thank you, Mother.

She leaves. They all go with her into the hall.

50 INT. HALL. DOWNTON. NIGHT.

Mrs Hughes and Carson are standing there.

MRS HUGHES: Nothing's cooked, and nothing's going to be cooked.

....

* Bootlegging had just begun, following on from Prohibition, which became law in the United States in 1920. The English thought Prohibition was mad because it would push the alcohol trade underground, and for Robert to make fun of it would have been completely standard for the period. For us, it was exactly the same as trying to make prostitution illegal, which at certain points in our history has come up. So far, the government of the day has always rejected the measure because a law would push it further underground and encourage the criminal element. But the American Government did not see that, or they persuaded themselves otherwise. In fairness to them, certain states had already outlawed alcoholic drinks and it seemed to work. Kansas had been dry since 1881.

MARY: But surely —

CORA: Shall we just tell them to go home?

MARTHA: Not a bit of it! No, Cora, please, come on. They've come for a party, we're going to give 'em a party!

She smiles at the bewildered group.

MARTHA (CONT'D): Carson, clear the table. You go down to the larders, you bring up bread, fruit, cheese, chicken, ham, whatever's edible. We're going to have an indoor picnic. They're going to eat whatever they want, wherever they want. All over the house.

CARSON: Are you quite sure, madam?

He casts an agonised glance at Robert.

ROBERT: It's not really how we do it —

MARTHA: How you *used* to do it.

ISOBEL: Oh, come on. It might be fun.

CORA: I agree. We'll all pull together and it'll be great fun.

MARTHA: Yes! Now, I know what we need.

She walks back into the drawing room, calling.

MARTHA (CONT'D): Does anyone here play the piano?

Mary is left with her mother and Violet.

MARY: Oh, Mama. This is so exactly *not* what we wanted the evening to be!

CORA: If it's the end of your undignified campaign, I won't be sorry.

She walks away as Mary turns to Violet.

MARY: We can't just give up.

VIOLET: Certainly not. Oh, do you think I might have a drink — Oh, I'm so sorry. I thought you were a waiter.*

She has spoken absent-mindedly to Robert, who stands to one side. He does not reply. He just watches Martha taking over.

....

* My little joke. Because in my head Violet knows, of course, it is Robert.

51 INT. KITCHENS. DOWNTON. NIGHT.

Everyone is helping, Reed included, bringing in food from the various stores. There are hams, ends of joints, salads, cheese. Mrs Patmore and Mrs Hughes are arranging the plates.

MRS PATMORE: Slice that finely, and fetch some parsley. And cut the dry bits off.
ALFRED: You're good to lend a hand.
REED: I don't mind helping. I think it's good to do other things sometimes.
ALFRED: I know you do.

He and Reed smile, all of which Daisy sees.

MOLESLEY: There's not much left of this.
ANNA: Better cut it in squares and put it with the ham. You're very smart in your new valet's outfit.

Molesley blushes with pleasure as Mrs Hughes leans back.

MRS HUGHES: Alfred, go and check the meat larder. Bring anything back you think a human being could swallow.
CARSON: Chop, chop, Mrs Hughes. We can rest later but not yet.
MRS PATMORE: But Mr Carson, would you just —
MRS HUGHES: Mr Carson's quite right. There's not a minute to lose.

52 EXT. KITCHEN COURTYARD. DOWNTON. NIGHT.

At the meat safe, Alfred sniffs a plate and puts it back.

REED (V.O.): Psst. Do you want to know a secret?

She has followed him out. He waits.

REED: Those shirts that Thomas thinks you stole? I saw who took them and I know where they are.
ALFRED: Who did take them?
REED: Never mind that. But I followed. I'll show you if you want.
ALFRED: Why are you being so nice to me?
REED: Because I like you.
ALFRED: And you can say it? Just like that?
REED: I'm an American, Alfred, and this is 1920. Time to live a little.

ALFRED: I thought you were just trying to find something out for Mrs Levinson.
REED: What would she need to find out? When she can read them all like the palm of her hand. She won't help, you know.
ALFRED: Help with what?
REED: Never mind. Just kiss me again.

He does, unaware of Daisy standing in the doorway.

53 INT. DINING ROOM/DRAWING ROOM. DOWNTON. NIGHT.

Martha is in her element, shepherding the guests. The table is covered with food and Carson, Alfred and Anna continue to bring in more. Robert hovers awkwardly.

MARTHA: Now, all of you, find whatever it is you want to eat, and take it wherever you want to sit!
LADY MANVILLE: Anywhere?*
MARTHA: Anywhere. All over the house. If any of you have ever wanted to explore Downton Abbey, this is your chance!

Robert feels as if he's been locked in with a madwoman.

ROBERT: I'm sorry if it's all a bit casual.
LADY MANVILLE: It's exciting, Lord Grantham. I feel like one of those bright young people they write about in the newspapers.†
ROBERT: Thank you, Lady Manville.

She walks off. He sees Carson, who looks like a drowning man.

....

* I'd just been working with Lesley Manville on *Romeo and Juliet*, where she played the Nurse wonderfully, so the name is a tribute to her. We gave the part to Sarah Crowden, daughter of the marvellous Graham Crowden, who is an old friend, and who has raised herself to the honour of Dame Sarah Crowden in our address book.

† The bright young things, the bright young people. In 1920 they had just begun to appear in the news. Their influence would grow and finally 1926 was proclaimed 'The Year of the Charleston', but not before. People tend to think that on 2 January 1920 everyone was doing the Charleston, but of course they weren't. It was a gradual process of loosening up.

ISOBEL: Cheer up. She won't be here forever.

ROBERT: But what damage will be done before she goes?

In the drawing room, a guest plays the piano. Martha is there, singing the verse, until she notices Violet nodding off in a chair. Casually, Martha strolls up to Violet, just in time for the chorus.

MARTHA: 'Let me call you Sweetheart, I'm in love with you.'

Violet does not look anxious to be called 'Sweetheart' as Martha takes her hand and kisses it theatrically.*

54 INT. KITCHENS. DOWNTON. NIGHT.

Mrs Hughes and Mrs Patmore are surveying the detritus.

MRS HUGHES: Is there anything for our supper?

MRS PATMORE: I've hidden a veal and egg pie… Oh, I wish you'd let me talk to Mr Carson.†

MRS HUGHES: I don't want to be a sick woman in his eyes for the next two months. Or a *dying* one, in the months to come after that.

But the strain is too much, and now, at last, she breaks down, sobbing. Mrs Patmore takes Mrs Hughes in her arms.

MRS PATMORE: I know it'll be all right.

MRS HUGHES: No, you don't. But I appreciate the sentiment.

55 INT. DINING ROOM. DOWNTON. NIGHT.

Strallan and Edith are together amid the wreckage.

....

* Music by Leo Friedman, lyrics by Beth Slater Whitsun and first published in 1910. Much recorded down the years by, among others, Bing Crosby, Bette Midler, Stan Laurel and Ethel Merman.

† One of the problems for a cook of a household like this is that you always had to be thinking double – you were catering for upstairs and downstairs all the time. And so we try to make that point every so often.

STRALLAN: Are you absolutely sure you won't wake up in ten years' time and wonder why you're tied to this crippled old codger?

EDITH: Only if you keep talking like that.

STRALLAN: Do you know how much you mean to me? You have given me back my life.

EDITH: That's more like it.

She kisses him gently.

STRALLAN: And you're certain you won't wait?

EDITH: To give you the chance to change your mind? Don't worry. I can get it organised in a month. Shall we tell them tonight?

STRALLAN: No, no. I'll come back in the morning.*

56 INT. SERVANTS' STAIRCASE. DOWNTON. NIGHT.

Alfred carries a bundle and is starting up the stairs…

DAISY: Alfred, can I ask you something? Why do you like that American girl?

ALFRED: Steady! Who says I do?

DAISY: Don't you?

ALFRED: All right. I suppose I do.

DAISY: And it doesn't matter that she's fast? Or that you won't see her again after she's gone home?†

ALFRED: So what? She made me feel good about myself, Daisy. I feel good for the first time since I came here. That's what matters to me.

Carson appears at the top of the staircase.

....

* I don't blame Strallan. He's been more or less forced into this situation by Edith, and suddenly he's got a lovely life coming with this young and adoring wife instead of being alone and sad. He can't be expected to fight beyond a certain point.

† Fast was a Victorian word, normally employed to describe women. It could be used in a variety of ways. You wouldn't call a prostitute fast. It had to be someone who was more or less respectable but pushing the limit. There was a clear distinction between someone who was fast, and someone who was actually *immoral*.

CARSON: Alfred, hurry up. I need you to take round the
claret.
ALFRED: All through the rooms? Won't they spill it on
the floor?
CARSON: If you ask me, we are staring into the chaos of
Gomorrah. But we have to give them more wine and you're
going to help. What's that?
ALFRED: I have to take it upstairs, for his lordship.
CARSON: Then be quick about it.

The men leave. Daisy is thoughtful as she watches them go.

57 INT. DRAWING ROOM. DOWNTON. NIGHT.

*People sit in groups. Young men and women on the floor, piano
music in the background. Mary and Violet are with Martha.*

MARTHA: But of course I'll help you any way I can.
MARY: Thank heaven.
VIOLET: Oh, it seems our family owes Downton's survival
to the Levinsons not once, but twice.
MARTHA: Oh, I'm so sorry, but you've misunderstood me.
No, I cannot rescue Downton. It's a shame if it has to
go, but I can't.
MARY: But… Why not?
MARTHA: Because your grandpa tied the money down. He
felt that the Crawley family had quite enough.
MARY: But you said you'd help us.
MARTHA: I can entertain all of you in Newport and in New
York, and I can add to Cora's dress allowance, but that's
all. My income might be generous, but I cannot touch the
capital. Besides, Mary…

She looks round the room.

MARTHA (CONT'D): The world is changed. These houses
were built for another age. Are you quite sure you want
to continue with the bother of it all?
MARY: Quite sure.
MARTHA: If I were you, and I knew I was going to lose
it, I should look on the sunny side. Both of our
husbands tied the money up tight before they were taken.

She glances at Violet, who is just as angry as Mary.

VIOLET: Lord Grantham wasn't taken. He died.*

57A INT. YORK PRISON. CORRIDOR. NIGHT.

Bates's cell-mate, Craig, receives something in his hand discreetly from a prison guard, which Bates witnesses.

58 INT. SERVANTS' HALL. DOWNTON. NIGHT.

O'Brien and the maids are reading and working.

O'BRIEN: I suppose it's scrap sandwich for the servants tonight.
ANNA: Mrs Patmore's kept something by.

They are interrupted by the arrival of Thomas.

THOMAS: Who put them back?
ANNA: What?
THOMAS: The shirts. Who put them back?
O'BRIEN: Oh? They're back, are they? You mean you overlooked them in the first place.
THOMAS: Don't tell me what I mean, Miss O'Brien. I'm warning you —
O'BRIEN: Listen to yourself. You sound like Tom Mix in a Wild West picture show.* Stop 'warning' me, and go and lay out his lordship's pyjamas.

....

* I like this exchange because I'm always rather amused by these euphemisms, and Americans do go in for their loved ones being 'taken' and people 'passing over' and all of that stuff, but then so do some of the British. The upper classes never employ these phrases. They just say, 'She's dead,' not 'She's left us,' or anything like it. Violet is the one who gets to make the point.

* Tom Mix was a popular star throughout the silent-film era. At this point, I now start using film-star names, because films were becoming more of a standard working-class entertainment, and in the end they would take over from music halls. Although, at this period, in the early 1920s, the music halls were still quite busy, while the cinemas were only just becoming so. The Wild West picture show is very much a period term. We refer to the cinema, but we also have 'kinema' and 'the pictures', but 'the pictures' was — and remained — essentially a working-class term. The word 'movies' hadn't begun at all in England; it was completely American, and that was true until the 1970s. All

The others all laugh and Thomas retreats as Alfred looks in.

ALFRED: What were you laughing at?

O'BRIEN: Seems those missing shirts went for a walk and now they've come home.

ALFRED: Really? Have they?

He gives away no more than she did, but Reed smiles at him.

59 INT. HALL. DOWNTON. NIGHT.

Violet is leaving. A few of the guests are still stretched out here and there. Carson walks about with a claret jug.

ROBERT: Well, Mama. I dare say this has been a novel experience.

VIOLET: It's not the phrase that springs most immediately to mind.

CORA: Mary told me about your conversation with Mother.

ROBERT: What was that?

VIOLET: No matter. I'm sorry Cora was troubled with it.

CORA: But you see, I'm not troubled. By whatever may come.

Violet casts an eye round disdainfully.

VIOLET: What about you, Carson? Have you enjoyed this glimpse of the future? Because it looks to me like a sketch for *The Wreck of the Méduse*.*

....

Continued from page 131:

of this was generational, really, and the cinema crept up on the upper classes slowly.

My parents were mad about films, but what was more unusual was that my grandmother loved films, and so my father went to lots of films when he was a little boy. Naturally, my grandmother's brothers and sisters-in-law thought she was mad. Even in the Thirties (my parents were married in 1935) they took my father's aunt to a film of Fred Astaire and Ginger Rogers and she simply couldn't understand what she was doing there. She said afterwards that she felt as if she had been watching some servants dancing in a Belita competition.

* A famous nineteenth-century shipwreck off Senegal, the subject of a painting by the French artist, Géricault.

CARSON: A good analogy, m'lady. I feel I've been on that storm-tossed raft and only now am I rowing back to shore.
ROBERT: Well, if this is the modern world, I suppose we must get used to it.
VIOLET: Happily, I am past the age when I *have* to get used to anything.*

60   INT. YORK PRISON. BATES'S CELL. NIGHT.

Bates is on his bed. His cell-mate, Craig, is restless.

BATES: What's the matter with you?

There is the sound of a key and the door opens. A warder, Durrant, stands there. He and Craig murmur. Bates looks over.

CRAIG: Keep your eyes to yourself.
BATES: Gladly.

Durrant leaves, locking the door. Craig retreats to his bed.

CRAIG: You didn't see nothing.
BATES: I agree.
CRAIG: 'Cause if you did, I'll cut you.

Bates gets up slowly then, suddenly, like an animal, he seizes Craig and punches him. Hard. Then flings him back against the wall.

BATES: Don't ever threaten me.
CRAIG: I forgot I was sharing a cell with a murderer.
BATES: Don't forget it again.†

....

* When this scene was cut, I must say I was really sad, and so was Gareth Neame. It went for time considerations, like everything else, but it was the only one I really minded about. Carson and Violet are essentially allies. They don't like the passing of the ordered world. Cora has mixed feelings and Robert, although I think he probably would have been happier if things had stayed the same, is going to make a reasonable effort to try and adjust to the new world, but Violet and Carson are really the Colonel's lady and Rosie O'Grady when it comes to this stuff – sisters under the skin.

† We felt at this stage we needed to give Bates a bit more of a prison plot. It wasn't enough for Anna simply to turn up every so often and ask him what he thought of the show so far. We somehow needed more of a dynamic, and so we introduce the villain Craig and various other elements.

61   INT.   MARY'S BEDROOM.   DOWNTON.   NIGHT.

Matthew is in his dressing gown. Anna attends to Mary.

ANNA: Is that all, m'lady?

MARY: Yes, thank you. Goodnight.

MATTHEW: Any news of Bates? Good news, I mean.

ANNA: Not yet, sir. But there will be.

She goes, leaving them alone. Mary sighs.

MARY: It's ridiculous. Uncle Harold gets millions to
waste on girls and boats and we can't save Downton.

MATTHEW: I promise to go into it and see if there's
really no way to keep it.

MARY: We all know there's one way.

MATTHEW: Only if you want me to feel like a thief for
the rest of my life.

MARY: And it's not a price worth paying?

MATTHEW: Not if you love me.

MARY: Of course not. I wasn't serious.

62   INT.   HALL/LIBRARY.   DOWNTON.   NIGHT.

Carson is closing the door. Robert appears.

ROBERT: Don't clear up tonight. Leave it for the
morning.

CARSON: Thank you, m'lord. The maids have already taken
away the food.

ROBERT: I thought Mrs Patmore did wonderfully well under
fire. You all did. Please thank them for me.

He turns away and walks into the library to pour a drink.

MARTHA: This evening has made me homesick for America.
It's time to go.

She is in a deep armchair. Robert does not contradict her.

ROBERT: I don't suppose you want some whisky to take to
bed?

MARTHA: Oh, but I'd love one. No water.

She studies him as he brings it over.

MARTHA (CONT'D): Thank you. I'm sorry I can't help you
keep Downton, Robert.

He looks at her, puzzled.

MARTHA (CONT'D): That's what Mary wanted.

ROBERT: Ah. I thought there was something.

When she speaks again, she is kind, if a little patronising.

MARTHA: You know, the way to deal with the world today is not to ignore it. If you do, you'll just get hurt. Things are changing.

ROBERT: Sometimes I feel like a creature in the wilds, whose natural habitat is gradually being destroyed.

MARTHA: But some animals adapt to new surroundings. Seems a better choice than extinction.

ROBERT: I don't think it is a choice. I think it's what's in you.

MARTHA: Well, let's hope what's in you will carry you through these times to a safer shore.*

63 INT. KITCHEN PASSAGE/MRS HUGHES'S SITTING ROOM. DOWNTON. NIGHT.

Carson is making a last check of the rooms. Mrs Hughes's door is open. He looks in. Mrs Hughes is staring into the fire.

CARSON (V.O.): Is everything all right?

MRS HUGHES: Certainly. Was there something you wanted?

CARSON: The kitchen managed well tonight. In difficult circumstances. His lordship sent his thanks.

MRS HUGHES: Was the evening a success?

CARSON: The odd thing is, I think it was. Though, for me, everyone sprawled on the floor, eating like beaters at a break in the shooting… That's not a party. It's a works outing. Where's the style, Mrs Hughes? Where's the show?

MRS HUGHES: Perhaps people are tired of style and show.

....

* We do actually see Shirley MacLaine again – she comes back for the Christmas Special in the fourth series – but when I wrote this I thought it might be her goodbye, and she played it well. So did Hugh Bonneville as Robert explains that he feels like a creature in the wild whose natural habitat is gradually being destroyed. I believe the audience is sympathetic to him here. In a sense, we say goodbye to them nicely, as Nanny always says.

CARSON: Well, in my opinion, to misquote Doctor Johnson, if you're tired of style, you are tired of life.

This does make her smile a little.

MRS HUGHES: Goodnight, Mr Carson.
CARSON: You'd say if anything was wrong, wouldn't you? I know I've been a bit crabby, but I am on your side.
MRS HUGHES: Thank you for that.

He goes and Mrs Hughes follows shortly after, turning off the light behind her.

64   INT.   KITCHEN PASSAGE.   DOWNTON.   NIGHT.

Mrs Patmore is with Mrs Hughes.

MRS HUGHES: You've just missed an admirer. Mr Carson says you did well tonight.
MRS PATMORE: Did you tell him?
MRS HUGHES: No. And what is there to tell? One day I will die. And so will he, and you, and every one of us under this roof. You must put these things in proportion, Mrs Patmore, and I think I can do that now.*

Mrs Patmore clasps Mrs Hughes's hands and leaves. Mrs Hughes turns off the light and goes out into the passage.

END OF EPISODE TWO

....

* Carson is trying to come to terms with the style of the evening's entertainment as he mourns the changing times, and in an exact parallel, Mrs Hughes is trying to come to terms with the prospect of cancer. In order for there to be an emotional arc that's interesting, she needs to have her own relationship with her illness. We've seen her come through the fear when she can't speak about it, and now she's arrived at a kind of acceptance of her condition, which seemed a good ending for the episode.

EPISODE THREE

ACT ONE

1 INT. GREAT HALL. DOWNTON. DAY.

The carpet is being taken away. Among the servants, Anna is finishing the flowers and tidying up. Edith walks downstairs, revelling in the preparations, as Violet comes in.

VIOLET: Oh, hello Edith, dear.
EDITH: Hello, Granny. Isn't it exciting?
VIOLET: At my age, one must ration one's excitement.

They walk into the drawing room. *

2 INT. DRAWING ROOM. DOWNTON. DAY.

Cora is arranging wedding presents as they enter.

VIOLET: See, I told her everything would come right, but she wouldn't believe me.
EDITH: I still can't. Something happening in this house is actually about me. The dress came this morning.†
VIOLET: I was rather sad you decided against Patou. I would have paid.
CORA: Lucile was safer. We don't want her to look like a chorus girl.‡

....

* We begin as we often begin – with the event that we set up at the end of the previous episode. As the episodes themselves take place over a comparatively short period – sometimes a couple of weeks, sometimes no more than three or four days – we allow ourselves any amount of time between them. The advantage with things like an accepted proposal is that we can just lose the engagement.

† I wrote it, of course, but I am touched when Edith says here, 'Something happening in this house is actually about me.' She is voicing what we all feel. At last, this is her moment. But Violet and Cora are unconvinced by this all the way through, so in a sense they're a step ahead of the game.

‡ Patou was a very, very fashionable designer at that time – not wild, but very much what we would think of as *couture*. In real life, Lucile was Lady Duff Gordon, a *Titanic* survivor, famous really because her husband, Sir Cosmo, was supposed to have paid the sailors in their lifeboat to row away from the ship, although they later defeated this charge in court. The truth may be

```
VIOLET:   How's Anthony?   Excited, I hope.
EDITH:   Desperately.   Just when he thought his life would
never change, he's going right back to the beginning.
VIOLET:   Ah.   What an invigorating prospect.
```

She and Cora exchange a brief glance.

....

Continued from page 140:

complicated, and I'm sure it's very tiresome for the grandchildren every time
it comes up. At any rate, her father was an engineer and she was brought up
first in Canada and later in Jersey. Her sister was Elinor Glyn, the exotic
novelist. After a failed first marriage, she supported herself by dressmaking
until her second husband came along. He was a Scottish landowner and a
thoroughly eligible match, but she was unusual among aristocratic wives in
pursuing her own career after her marriage.

As Maison Lucile, her London business flourished, and later she opened
branches in Paris, New York and Chicago. She also designed for the theatre.
Alfred Worth had been the first designer to use living models to display his
creations, but his models wore protective sheaths to prevent the dresses
actually touching their skin. Lucile had the *mannequins* in her catwalk shows
wearing the clothes as they would be worn by the women who bought them.
She was much admired by the upper middle and upper classes, because her
look was a classy and attractive version of normal, which was what they liked.
But that is to underestimate her contribution to fashion: the looser fitting,
the abandonment of restrictive underwear, all stemmed from her
innovations.

Her *Titanic* experience definitely scarred her. My mother recalled as a
young woman in 1935 going to a cocktail party and, on being introduced to
Lady Duff Gordon, she remarked that the name seemed familiar.
Immediately Lady Duff Gordon burst into a litany of protest: 'We didn't do
it, you know. We didn't do it. We did not pay them to stay away. We offered
them a chance of a reward if we got back, but that's all.' Afterwards, my
mother considered how there was a gap of twenty-three years between the
sinking and the party, and yet it was still so near the surface of the woman's
brain. I'm afraid the rest of her life was obviously blighted by that one
interlude. But one mustn't be too kind. The moment when the ship went
down, she turned to her Italian maid and said, 'Well, Francatelli, there goes
that beautiful nightgown you were so proud of.' I can't believe she was
terribly empathetic to the fate of those still aboard.

3 INT. SERVANTS' HALL. DOWNTON. DAY.

Anna comes in, carrying her coat. Thomas walks down the hall, with O'Brien and Alfred behind.

O'BRIEN: I hope you've got your shirt ready for tonight.
THOMAS: In case you're interested, I've hidden a couple, so I won't be caught out that way again.
O'BRIEN: Why should I be interested?
THOMAS: That goes for you, too.
ALFRED: What have I done?
O'BRIEN: Take no notice.

They pass Anna in the hall.

MRS HUGHES (V.O.): Anna, are the flowers done?
ANNA: Yes. I'll check them on Saturday morning and lose anything that's going over. I've kept back a few in bud.
MRS HUGHES: So, are you away now?
ANNA: I'll be home for the dressing gong.
MRS HUGHES: Oh, we'll manage.

Anna leaves as Mrs Patmore arrives. Mrs Patmore talks in a low voice to Mrs Hughes.

MRS PATMORE: Still no word from the doctor?
MRS HUGHES: I'd have told you if there was.
MRS PATMORE: By heck, they don't mind stringing it out. Shall we go and see him?
MRS HUGHES: Why? I'm sure if he knew anything, he would have said.

Unbeknownst to them, Carson has heard all this.

4 INT. OLD DAY NURSERY. DOWNTON. DAY.

This was a nursery, but it has not been used for years. There is a fireguard and a rocking horse, etc. Mary is with Sybil.

SYBIL: I haven't been in here for years.
MARY: Nor me. But we can talk without being interrupted every two seconds. What did you want to say?
SYBIL: Tom wants the baby to be Catholic.
MARY: Golly. Can we please not tell Papa until after Edith's wedding?

Which makes them both laugh a little.

MARY (CONT'D): Will you mind?

SYBIL: I don't think so. Anyway, I've got worse than that to contend with... Tom's getting deeper and deeper into the resistance to the Treaty.

MARY: But won't it recognise an Irish free state?

SYBIL: Yes. But it divides the country and accepts the Crown —

MARY: Surely it's a start.

SYBIL: I agree, but Tom doesn't.

MARY: Remember what Talleyrand said: *Surtout, pas trop de zèle.*

SYBIL: Don't tell me, tell him.*

5 INT. BEDROOM PASSAGE. DOWNTON. DAY.

Thomas comes out of a door and sees Molesley.

THOMAS: How are you today, Mr Molesley?

Molesley is puzzled by such friendliness and drops a jacket that he was carrying on the floor. Thomas picks it up for him.

MOLESLEY: Er... very well, thank you.

THOMAS: You were talking the other night about your friend's daughter. Is she still looking for a place?

MOLESLEY: She is. You read about the servant shortage in the newspapers, but she can't find a situation for a lady's maid. Not one. She'll end up as a housemaid if she's not careful.

THOMAS: Oh, we can't have that, Mr Molesley. But if I were to tell you something, you must promise not to breathe a word of it downstairs. Miss O'Brien doesn't want it known.

....

* The business of Irish independence, the division of Ireland in 1921, very much concerned Britain at this time and I was keen to reflect that in the show. In the cut material, Mary quotes Talleyrand, because I'm a big admirer of his. I think he is one of the great survivors of history and so I love him, but we're also setting up Branson's Irish story.

6 INT. VISITING ROOM. YORK PRISON. DAY.

Anna is with Bates.

ANNA: I'm going to London tomorrow.

BATES: Wouldn't she have answered your letter if she had anything to say?

ANNA: On the contrary. I think if she had nothing to tell me, she'd have written and said so.

BATES: Maybe. So what else is happening?

ANNA: Lady Edith's wedding, mainly. Lady Sybil's back. And Mr Branson.

BATES: Is it funny having him upstairs?

ANNA: To be honest, I think he finds it more awkward than we do.

BATES: Has Mr Carson relented?

ANNA: I don't think Mr Carson's very big on relenting.

Which makes them both laugh.

7 INT. LIBRARY. DOWNTON. DAY.

Robert is with Cora, Matthew and Branson.

CORA: How will they advertise it?

ROBERT: I don't know exactly. 'Desirable nobleman's mansion with surrounding estate and properties.'

BRANSON: Where will you go?

ROBERT: We have some land further north, at Eryholme on the border with Durham. It came with my great-grandmother. The house is pretty, and we might make something of it. We could always rename it Downton Place.*

....

* The origins here are all in my ancestry. My grandmother was called Wrightson and my great-grandfather, John Wrightson, had a house called Charford Manor in Wiltshire in a village called Downton, where he started something called the Downton Agricultural College. My Fellowes grandfather went there as a student to learn how to manage an estate, fell in love with the daughter of the owner and they married. Those were my grandparents. John's brother, Sir Thomas Wrightson, was a late-Victorian engineer, with an estate called Neasham in North Yorkshire, but they originally came from the bordering estate that's since been incorporated into the whole. It's called Eryholme and for many years it has been the dower house to Neasham Hall. The River Tees goes through their park.

MATTHEW: Who lives there now?

ROBERT: A tenant, but we can come to an arrangement that keeps him happy.

CORA: Let's take a picnic there tomorrow. Take a break from the wedding on Edith's last day of freedom.

The door opens. Mary and Sybil enter.

MARY: Molesley's in the hall. He wonders if he might have a word.

MATTHEW: I'll come through in a minute.

MARY: Not with you, with Mama.

This is mysterious.

MARY: Molesley.

Molesley appears.

MOLESLEY: Your ladyship, may I have a word?

CORA: Of course.

MOLESLEY: M'lady, might I be allowed to put forward a candidate, as Miss O'Brien's replacement?

CORA: What?

MOLESLEY: When the time comes?

ROBERT: Is O'Brien leaving?

MOLESLEY: I hope I've not spoken out of turn. Only I didn't want to let it go and miss the chance. I thought you knew.†

....

Continued from page 144:

Connecting me further to North Yorkshire is obviously my school, Ampleforth. When they said they wanted to set the series in the North, the only part I really knew was the North Riding of Yorkshire, so that's why I had to put Downton near Thirsk and Ripon. At one point we did wonder if we might change houses, and this storyline was going to give us the option, but, in the event, Highclere seemed too central to the whole show to be changed. I had mixed feelings about this decision. The business of having to sell the main house and downsize would have been quite a nice twentieth-century touch.

† Thomas, in trying to get revenge on O'Brien for the shirt plot, has spread the rumour that she is leaving. It's a permanent state of tit for tat, really.

CORA: Of course I know. Thank you, Molesley. I will be happy to listen to recommendations when, as you say, the time comes.
MOLESLEY: Thank you, m'lady.

He goes. They are all rather stunned.

ROBERT: Well, I must confess, I will watch her departure with mixed emotions.
MARY: Mine are fairly unmixed.
SYBIL: Did you have a clue?
CORA: Not a clue. How very disappointing.
ROBERT: But in a way, it raises the big question: when do we tell the staff that the end is nigh?
MARY: It makes it sound so final.
ROBERT: I'm afraid it is final.
MARY: Well, don't spoil Edith's day. Let us get through the wedding first, and then tell them afterwards.

8 EXT. HOSPITAL. DOWNTON VILLAGE. DAY.

Clarkson comes out, carrying his bag. Carson is waiting.

CARSON: Oh, Doctor Clarkson? Do you have a minute?
CLARKSON: Er, one minute, yes. Do you mind if we —?
CARSON: Only, I know Mrs Hughes is suffering from a condition and I wondered if there was anything I can do to help.
CLARKSON: You can help by lessening her duties. That's really all I can say.
CARSON: But you can't tell me how serious it is?
CLARKSON: I'm afraid not. Even if I knew, which I don't… yet. Good day to you, Mr Carson.

This, of course, conveys more information than he wished to.

9 INT. MARY'S BEDROOM. DOWNTON. EVE.

Mary is being dressed by Anna, while Matthew sits on the bed.

MARY: And it can't wait until after the wedding?

Anna says nothing. Mary relents.

MARY (CONT'D): I'm sorry. Of course you must go.
ANNA: Thank you, m'lady… Right. I think that's everything.

As Mary thanks her, Anna picks up some washing, and leaves.

MARY: Shall we go down?

MATTHEW: I had a telephone call from Charkham earlier.

MARY: Charkham?*

MATTHEW: Reggie Swire's lawyer. It seems the death certificate has arrived from India. He wants to bring it here.

MARY: Well, can't he send it?

MATTHEW: He wants to bring it. He was quite definite. I've told him he can come tomorrow. There's nothing going on particularly, is there?

MARY: You know there is. We're taking a picnic to Eryholme to see the house we have to move into. I'm surprised you of all people can forget that.

Matthew sighs but chooses not to rise to the bait.

MATTHEW: Well, he's coming in the morning. I won't put him off.

MARY: So this is the moment when you receive a huge fortune that could save Downton, and you give it away.

MATTHEW: Will you choose where to give it?

MARY: How can I? I'd give it all to Papa.

MATTHEW: My darling, I hope, in some small part of you, you can understand.

MARY: I'm trying. Really, I am. But I can't pretend I'm doing very well.

10   INT. CORA'S BEDROOM. DOWNTON. EVE.

O'Brien finishes sewing on a loose hook. She cuts the thread.

O'BRIEN: Will there be anything more, m'lady?

CORA: No. Unless you have something you want to tell me.

O'BRIEN: What might that be, m'lady?

CORA: I won't prompt you, O'Brien, if you're not ready to say.

Robert enters. O'Brien leaves, completely bewildered.

....

* Charkham is the maiden name of Fiona Shackleton, the famous divorce lawyer. We are very friendly with her and her husband, and in fact we use her name twice. Lady Shackleton (as she is now) is a character in a later series...

ROBERT: Did she tell you why?

CORA: No. Maybe she doesn't want to until she's settled where she's going, but she has let me down.

ROBERT: We should go. Strallan won't be late. He never is, worse luck.

CORA: I know you're not happy, but Edith will be in the same county. Loxley's a nice house, and the estate will give her plenty to do.

ROBERT: She'll be a nurse, Cora. And by the time she's fifty she'll be wheeling round a one-armed old man.

CORA: Edith won't be fifty until 1943. Quite a lot may happen before then.*

11 INT. KITCHENS/PASSAGE. DOWNTON. NIGHT.

Daisy is loading a tray held by Alfred.

DAISY: Alfred, do you ever think about that Miss Reed? What was maid to her ladyship's mother?

ALFRED: I don't know. Maybe. Sometimes.

DAISY: I couldn't get over how outspoken she was. But you liked that, didn't you?

ALFRED: I s'pose I did. It felt… modern. She said what she felt, even though she was a woman. I did like it.

DAISY: Maybe I should be more outspoken and say what I really think —†

....

* I'm sorry this was cut. I am always trying to find opportunities to remind the audience how recent the world of *Downton* was, how someone who was born in 1893 was only fifty in 1943, only sixty in 1953, and would very probably have lived on to the 1960s and 1970s. I had a great-aunt who was born in 1880 and died in 1971. I knew her perfectly well – she died when I was twenty-two – but she was ten years older than Mary Crawley. So this generation really does span the divide between the old world and the new. I'm afraid some of them weren't very happy about it. My grandmother once remarked that she had seen 'too much change', and I think that was the price they paid, but at any rate that is the point of the line.

† Daisy's character is learning to be herself, to have more confidence in who she is and what she wants. And we will continue that journey quite strongly through the fifth series, when she starts to educate herself. I always feel that one of the great advantages of education is the confidence it gives you in your own abilities, and that's why the deconstruction of education has been such a

MRS PATMORE: Er, are you waiting down here 'til they come in search of their pudding?
ALFRED: No, Mrs Patmore.

Alfred leaves. Mrs Patmore turns away, only to find Carson seemingly waiting for her in the passage.

MRS PATMORE: Can I do something for you?
CARSON: Well, I'd better get back upstairs, but while you're here... I saw Doctor Clarkson today.
MRS PATMORE: Oh?
CARSON: I'm worried about Mrs Hughes.
MRS PATMORE: We're all worried, but I don't think he should have told you.
CARSON: He said it would help if we lessened her workload.
MRS PATMORE: I'm sure it would, but she won't be pleased he's been talking about her. Before it's been confirmed.
CARSON: So, it is cancer.
MRS PATMORE: Not until it's confirmed. Don't say anything. She'd hate to think the doctor had told you.

Carson is overcome by conscience.

CARSON: He didn't tell me, Mrs Patmore... You told me.

END OF ACT ONE

....

Continued from page 148:

disaster for so many millions of men and women. As a matter of fact, I find the resistance to the reforms going on at the moment really reprehensible, because we all know – every statistic tells us – that our social mobility has dried up, and the reason for this is because state education has collapsed. Of course, there are many wonderful and hard-working teachers, but the teaching establishment has got lodged in the thinking of the 1970s, and it is hard not to feel that behind the irresponsibility of their fighting change is the realisation of their own failure. It enrages me because it's not their own futures that the Luddites are putting at risk; it's the future of the boys and girls they're supposed to be teaching.

ACT TWO

12 INT. DINING ROOM. DOWNTON. NIGHT.

Robert is with Matthew, Branson and Strallan, all sitting round one end of the table.

> ROBERT: It's a relief to have some men in this family at last.

Strallan eyes Branson slightly nervously.

> STRALLAN: Lady Edith — I mean, *Edith* tells me you're very interested in politics.
> ROBERT: Tom is our tame revolutionary.
> STRALLAN: Every family should have one.
> MATTHEW: As long as you *are* tame…?
> BRANSON: Tame enough for a game of billiards. What about it?
> MATTHEW: Can you tell them where we've gone?*

They leave together. Robert passes the port to Strallan, who pours out a glass for himself, summoning his nerve.

> ROBERT: We're getting used to Tom, and I hope you will, too.
> STRALLAN: We haven't spoken really, since it was all settled… I want you to know that I quite understand why you were against it.
> ROBERT: Yes. Well.
> STRALLAN: I just hope you believe that I mean to do my level best to make her happy.
> ROBERT: I do believe that. It was never at all personal, you know.

....

* This part of the scene was cut in one of the edits, but I argued for it back because I felt we needed to know that the family was genuinely starting to accept Branson, and that Matthew, who is the least set in his ways, certainly of the men, should logically be the first one to befriend him. After all, he got Matthew to the church on time and now, as Robert says here, they're all getting used to Tom, 'and I hope you will, too'. Strallan illustrates what Branson is up against. He is not a bad man, but he is quite awkward with him initially.

STRALLAN: No, of course not. No. It's just… because of all this, and I'm far too old.
ROBERT: Anthony, the thing is done. There is no point in raking it over.
STRALLAN: But are you happy about it?
ROBERT: I'm happy Edith is happy. I'm happy you mean to keep her happy. That is quite enough happiness to be going on with.

13 INT. HALL. DOWNTON. NIGHT.

Robert and Strallan come into the hall and start towards the drawing room. Then Edith appears from the shadows.

EDITH: You will let us have five minutes on our own, Papa. Please.
ROBERT: Very well. But don't tell your grandmother.*

He walks on into the drawing room and they are alone.

EDITH: I couldn't bear it if we spent the whole evening discussing hunting and whether or not the Marlboroughs are finally getting a divorce.†

....

* In the 1920s, they were starting to see the customs of the Victorian age as slightly funny, so things began to be allowed in this generation, like going out for dinner in restaurants, which before the war would have been absolutely verboten. The war had changed that, and by this point there was something humorously naughty about leaving a couple together alone, especially if they were going to marry. In the 1850s it wouldn't have happened and it wouldn't have been seen as humorous. They would probably have been allowed to sit on a sofa and talk, and quite deliberately any others present would sit out of hearing on the other side of the room, but even so, it wasn't exactly wild. There was this rooted idea that to leave a girl alone with a man was to court danger. I said once to my Great-Aunt Isie that it seemed ridiculous to think that if a girl were alone in a room with a man, whom she probably didn't even know, he would immediately say something improper or make some suggestive overture. My aunt nodded and agreed with me that obviously it was absurd, but she added, 'Of course, you were furious if he didn't.'

† The American heiress Consuelo Vanderbilt had married the Duke of Marlborough in 1893. That they were very ill-matched and in fact couldn't stand each other was soon pretty common knowledge. They just about stayed together for a decade, but at some point in about 1904 they separated and her father, Willie K. Vanderbilt, built for her the house that's next door

STRALLAN: The first time I saw the Duchess of
Marlborough was at a ball of Lady Londonderry's. It was
'96, not long after she'd come over from America. She
was the loveliest woman I'd ever set eyes on… Of course,
you weren't even born, my darling.
EDITH: I was. Just not walking very well.*
STRALLAN: And now you're going to wheel me around when I
can't walk any more.
EDITH: Oh, please understand! I don't love you *in spite
of* your needing to be looked after. I love you *because
of it!* I want you to be my life's work.

She takes his arm and squeezes it, but he is silent.

....

Continued from page 151:

to the Curzon cinema in Curzon Street, opposite Crewe House. It was
called Sunderland House when it was first built, because that's one of their
courtesy titles, and originally it had been intended to be the London house of
the Marlborough family. They had built Marlborough House on the Mall
for this purpose, but that had reverted to the Crown in the eighteenth
century, and they were always fairly peripatetic after that.

On their separation, Consuelo lived at Sunderland House and, rather
interestingly, she was allowed to function in Society as a separated woman,
just as after the divorce, which came in 1921, she was also allowed to carry on
in Society. Before then, a divorced woman had a pretty tough time. It can't
have hurt that Consuelo was a multi-millionairess and gave some of the best
parties in London, but it nevertheless meant that the price exacted for
divorce had dropped. Maybe they still couldn't enter the royal enclosure at
Ascot, or present anyone at Court, but they were no longer non-people as
their mothers would have been in such a case. As a matter of fact, if a
divorced woman's daughter was to be presented, someone else had to do it,
and it is true that divorcees were not welcome at King George V's Court.
The rule might sometimes be broken in a private situation, but not publicly.
But the truth remains that, after the First World War, society couples were
no longer prepared to stay together when they were unhappy. In a way, when
the Marlboroughs divorced it was the beginning of a new era. There might
not have been a tidal wave, but there was certainly a bit of a swell of smart
divorces.

* Edith would have been three.

14   INT. PASSAGE. DOWNTON. DAY.

Mrs Hughes is cross-referencing lists as she walks with Carson. There is the sound of the vacuum cleaner. He winces.

CARSON: Have we got to hear that ungodly machine down here?

She chuckles, then indicates her paperwork.

MRS HUGHES: There's been a last-minute change of mind about the wedding menus.
CARSON: Couldn't Mrs Patmore do it?
MRS HUGHES: Mrs Patmore's given me her new order list. She's done her job; it's time for me to do mine.
CARSON: I just don't want you to get tired.
MRS HUGHES: Who have you been speaking to?
CARSON: No one. What do you mean?
MRS HUGHES: Nothing. I don't mean a thing. Now, let me get on.

15   INT. A HALL IN YORK. DAY.

Isobel is organising her fallen women in a sewing class.

ISOBEL: This is a simple stitch, but strong and very useful in a drama.
WOMAN: When do we get summat to eat?
ISOBEL: As I was saying, you should start it about, well, I would say about half an inch away from the centre line —

She looks up as Ethel Parks enters. She goes to her.

ISOBEL (CONT'D): Oh, I'm glad you've come back. I do hope you've come for our help. You'd be so welcome if you have.
ETHEL: You wouldn't say that if you knew what I am, ma'am. I'm past help.
ISOBEL: Nobody's past help. And if you mean by that that you are a prostitute —

She says the word boldly, without apology.

ISOBEL (CONT'D): Well, then you should know that it is true of every woman who has come here to rebuild their lives. And I'm helping them, and I very much hope that I can help you, too.

WOMAN: That's right! Why not come in and help us 'rebuild out lives'?

Several of them start laughing. Isobel's is not an easy task.

ETHEL: That's not why I'm here, Mrs Crawley. That is, I am a… what you've said, but I don't want help. Not for myself, but… The trouble is, every time I make up my mind, I change it.

Which is what has happened now.

ETHEL (CONT'D): I'm sorry. This has been a mistake.
ISOBEL: Oh, please, please, don't go. Not again.

Ethel hurries away as the other women start laughing.

16 INT. SERVANTS' HALL. DOWNTON. DAY.

Some of them are seated. O'Brien is mending as Thomas enters.

THOMAS: Everything all right?
O'BRIEN: Why shouldn't it be?
THOMAS: No reason.

Mrs Patmore is reading Mrs Beeton. She turns to Daisy.

MRS PATMORE: Is Baked Alaska a bit ambitious for the dinner after the reception?*
DAISY: How many will there be?
MRS PATMORE: About forty, I'd say. The rest will have gone home. Now, what is it?
DAISY: Mr Mason's asked me to the farm.

....

* What I wanted to make clear in Mrs Patmore's speech about Baked Alaska and the dinner afterwards is that the modern fashion for having a sit-down feed after a wedding was not an upper-class practice until very recently – some would say after 2000. Before that, upper-class weddings were always stand-up, mill-about affairs. There might have been a lunch beforehand for some of the people who'd comes from miles away, there might even have been a modest dinner for some people who hadn't gone home, but the wedding reception was a walkabout, and that's what we're saying here. I was married in 1990 and the idea of a sit-down dinner was never even mooted. They came in a lot later on.

MRS PATMORE: Say there's a wedding on. You can go when things have settled down. Now, come and sort out this benighted picnic.

She stands, and leads Daisy back to the kitchen.

MOLESLEY: Who's Mr Mason?
O'BRIEN: Her father-in-law.
MOLESLEY: She wasn't married very long.
O'BRIEN: Even so. He's fond of her. She's all he's got left.

Molesley digests this interesting observation.

17 INT. LIBRARY. DOWNTON. DAY.

The lawyer, Mr Charkham, is with Matthew, who holds a letter.

CHARKHAM: It must be strange to receive a letter from a dead man.
MATTHEW: It's very strange.

The door opens and he puts the letter away as Mary comes in.*

MARY: We're leaving. I'm sorry, Mr Charkham, to snatch him away.
CHARKHAM: That's quite all right, Lady Mary. There will be papers to sign.
MATTHEW: Yes. I expect there will.

They shake hands and the lawyer goes. Mary stares at Matthew.

MARY: Papa's asked Anthony to meet us there, so we can all face the future together. He's bringing Isobel and Granny.
MATTHEW: It's hard for your grandmother.
MARY: Matthew, it's torture for all of us. And if I ever look as if I'm finding it easy to lose my home, then I am putting on an act.

....

* This is the all-important letter, which Matthew obviously doesn't want Mary to see, so I'm afraid I fairly shamelessly teased it out.

18 INT. CORA'S BEDROOM. DOWNTON. DAY.

Cora is finalising her tweeds, with the help of O'Brien.

CORA: Are you unhappy here, O'Brien?

O'BRIEN: No, I'm not unhappy, m'lady. Well, no more than anyone else.

CORA: Because, if you are, I wish you'd felt you could have told me.

O'BRIEN: I would tell you. If there was anything you could do to help.

CORA: Or is it just time for a change? Because I understand that. I do.

Robert looks in.

ROBERT: We ought to get going. They're loading the car.

Cora nods and stands, turning to her maid.

CORA: We'll talk of this some more.

19 EXT. DOWNTON. DAY.

Two cars are waiting, and Matthew's sports car. Carson is supervising with Alfred.

CARSON: You're sure you can manage this?

ALFRED: Quite sure, Mr Carson.

CARSON: There's nothing hot. It's not a shooting lunch. Give them some champagne first, and that'll allow you the time to set it out properly.

ALFRED: I'll manage, Mr Carson. What's this place we're visiting?

CARSON: It's one of his lordship's houses, though I'm curious as to why they're going there today. I'd come with you, but I've got the last of the wine for the wedding being delivered this afternoon. I can't not be here for that. Off you go.

ALFRED: Maybe he likes to keep a check on things.

CARSON: Maybe. Off you go.

He has spoken as the family are emerging. His command sends Alfred scurrying to open one car door. The chauffeur opens the other. Carson walks towards the front door.

CARSON (CONT'D): Might I have a word, m'lady?

CORA: Yes, of course. What is it?

CARSON: This is a slightly awkward request, what with
the wedding tomorrow…
CORA: Tell me.
CARSON: Mrs Hughes is very tired. I wonder if it might
be possible for you to divert some of her work my way?
CORA: I don't understand. What do you mean 'tired'?

Carson hesitates.

ROBERT (V.O.): Cora!
CORA: Carson? If you know something, then please tell
me.

Everyone else has climbed into the vehicles.

CORA: Carson?
CARSON: The fact is, Mrs Hughes is ill, m'lady. She may
be *very* ill… I'm extremely sorry to trouble you with
this at such a moment, but I don't want the wedding to
sink her.
CORA: Of course not. But, my heavens, how will we
manage, without O'Brien and now Mrs Hughes…?
CARSON: Miss O'Brien?
CORA: She told Molesley —
ROBERT (V.O.): Cora, please!
CORA: I'm coming!*

And she hurries over to the car, leaving a puzzled butler.

20   EXT.   A STREET IN SOUTH LONDON.   DAY.

*Anna is walking along a dingy street. She stops, checks the
address and knocks on the door. No response. She walks
round to the back of the house, where a narrow alley has
doors in a high wall, corresponding to each house. She turns
down the alley where she sees a hard-faced woman pegging out
clothes. She looks over.*

ANNA: I knocked.
MRS BARTLETT: I heard you.

....

*The point we make here is that it doesn't really occur to Robert that it might
be inconvenient for the people to whom the house has been let that twenty
strangers would turn up and have lunch on the lawn. In those moments, we
do show that, however nice Robert is and however much he's trying to be
modern, there is still an assumption of *droit de seigneur* that goes pretty deep.

ANNA: I've come as I said I would, Mrs Bartlett... I've...
I've brought the money.

She brings an envelope out of her bag. After a moment, the woman walks over and takes it, opening it to check.

MRS BARTLETT: Well, it's your loss, 'cos I've got
nothing to say.
ANNA: All I want to know is if Vera ever —
MRS BARTLETT: Oh? So you were on Christian-name terms,
were you? You do surprise me.
ANNA: If Mrs Bates ever suggested she was depressed or
unhappy —
MRS BARTLETT: Of course she was unhappy. Her husband
had left her and gone off with a trollop.

She stares at Anna, who tries to keep a lid on her feelings.

MRS BARTLETT (CONT'D): He changed, you know. She was
scared of him by the end, and now we know she had good
reason.
ANNA: When did you last see her?
MRS BARTLETT: What's it to you?
ANNA: I just want to find out the truth.
MRS BARTLETT: It won't change anything, you know. You
give me money because you think I can get him off... I
wouldn't if I could, but I can't.
ANNA: Then it won't make any difference if you tell me
the truth.

Mrs Bartlett thinks about this. Then she sighs.

MRS BARTLETT: Well, I don't suppose it matters now. I
saw her the night she died.

Anna is astonished. Mrs Bartlett glances up. Two women are watching them from a neighbouring house.

MRS BARTLETT: You'd better come inside.*

....

* We were very fortunate in the distinguished actress who played Mrs Bartlett – Claire Higgins. I have known her since we were young and in rep. She has since done some extraordinary work and, indeed, I worked with her in a play at the National by Dusty Hughes called *Futurists*, but I hope they will give her her head for this next chunk of her career, as I know she could do some astonishing and definitive things. So it was a real privilege that she

21 EXT. YORK PRISON. EXERCISE YARD. DAY.

The prisoners are walking in a circle. Bates is next to a convict called Dent. They walk under the eyes of the guards.

DENT: Bates. Psst. Watch out.

BATES: What do you mean?

DENT: Search your room. Search your bed. They've set you up somehow. Your cell-mate, Craig, and his mates.

TURNER: Stop talking!

Bates is silent but he looks enquiringly at Dent.

DENT: Just do it.

But when the warder looks round, he is silent, too.*

22 INT. SITTING ROOM. MRS BARTLETT'S HOUSE. LONDON. DAY.

Anna and Mrs Bartlett are talking.

ANNA: Why have you never told anyone?‡

....

Continued from page 158:

wanted to be in *Downton*. Getting that level of actor for these smaller parts layers them so much, and you have a real sense that you're watching one or two scenes out of a much larger performance. She created a character which could have starred in a play called *Mrs Bartlett*, and that's what you want.

Also, to me, it's important that she's on Vera's side. I never like to have a situation where you have an unmitigated black and horrible character, and in this instance Vera Bates had a point. In an earlier series we glimpsed the other side of Bates from his mother, who implied that when Bates used to drink he could become very angry. I don't think he actually beat Vera up, but I am sure he was horrible to her, and now that is what we're hearing from Mrs Bartlett. Vera was clearly pushed to the limit. For a woman to hate a man so much that she wants not only to kill herself but to make sure he's blamed for her death is pretty bad in anyone's book. So Mrs Bartlett is there as Vera's champion.

† This is another opportunity to demonstrate that Bates has not lost his spirit while he's been in prison, that he is still a fighter.

‡ Mrs Bartlett's belief that Bates put the poison in the pie gives a rather Sweeney Todd element to the murder/suicide story. I remember asking myself whether or not the plot wasn't more suited to a melodrama like *Lady*

MRS BARTLETT: Why should I? I've already told you it wouldn't change anything... She was annoyed at first but she calmed down. Their door was open, so I looked in. She was cooking. For him as well, I s'pose. But she had to post a letter, so she walked me down the street. She said Bates was coming back later for his tea. She was terrified.

ANNA: You didn't think to stay with her? To keep her company.

MRS BARTLETT: She wouldn't have it. She was in a strange mood, jumpy and fearful... but determined. I remember she'd made pastry and she was scrubbing it out of her nails, like she didn't care if she took the skin off.

ANNA: So after she posted the letter, she went home on her own?

MRS BARTLETT: She did, poor soul. And I never saw her after. I can remember her now, walking away down the street. It was raining — no, not raining, more like drizzle, and the gaslight seemed to catch in the drops and make a sort of halo round her —

ANNA: A halo? Really?

MRS BARTLETT: You can laugh. But I must have felt uneasy, because I didn't go home. Though I'd no umbrella.

ANNA: Where did you go?

MRS BARTLETT: I just wandered about for a bit. I'd had a suet pudding for my tea, and it was sitting rather heavy. I told myself I was walking to loosen it. But it wasn't that. Not really.

ANNA: When did you hear she was dead?

MRS BARTLETT: Next day. So I knew it was Bates. I nearly told them.

....

Continued from page 159:

Audley's Secret, but I couldn't think of another death that Vera could set up for herself that would look like someone else's fault, other than poisoning herself with something that had been made earlier while Bates was there. If she just took poison it wouldn't be believable that he'd made her take it, and she could hardly strangle herself. It was quite a problem, but anyway we seem to have got away with it.

ANNA: Why didn't you?

MRS BARTLETT: She asked me not to mention how she'd been to anybody. Said she felt cowardly fretting about his visit. That's what came out when the letter was read at the trial. When I heard the verdict I thought he'd swing, and he should have, if the country hadn't gone soft.

There doesn't seem to be anything here to help Bates.

23 INT. STRALLAN'S MOTOR CAR. DAY.

Strallan and Violet are in the back. Isobel is in front, next to the chauffeur.*

VIOLET: This is very good of you.

STRALLAN: Ah, nonsense. You were on the way. I do wish you'd let me sit in the front. I feel most uncomfortable back here.

ISOBEL: No, no, I prefer it. I've ridden in the front seat many times.

....

* Normally, no woman would sit next to a chauffeur, although that was beginning to happen more and more. For her to ride in the front seat meant that someone she knew was driving the car. Sports cars were not built for chauffeurs; they were built for young men to drive. In the days before cars, ordinary gents might have had a trap or a chaise that they could drive themselves around in, but with a coach and horses you didn't get up on the box, as a rule, and drive with the coachman, but driving a car, right from the start, was considered racy and fun. Although a chauffeur was part of a country-house staff for quite a long time, nevertheless it wasn't unusual for a member of the family to drive. Actually, I can never understand how women in particular managed; you can't tell when you look at an old movie and there's Carole Lombard or Marion Davies whizzing along, but without power steering it was incredibly hard to turn the wheel.

What Isobel is really saying in this scene is that she is free. She doesn't need a chauffeur, she doesn't care. She has young friends and she likes to ride in the front. So it is essentially a statement of modernity. Strallan is a man who likes to drive himself, but of course he can't now because it is after the war. In real life probably Strallan would be in the front with the chauffeur and Isobel would be in the back, but it suited us to put her in the front for the dialogue between Strallan and Violet. And so Strallan has to make the point that Isobel has forced him to sit in the back.

VIOLET: Aren't you a wild thing?

STRALLAN: Oh, it's quite safe. There's never been a safer method of travel.

VIOLET: Or a faster one.

STRALLAN: Edith's the speed fiend. She likes to go at a terrific lick.

VIOLET: Do you think you'll be able to keep up with her?

STRALLAN: I'll try.

ISOBEL: What's this place like? Eryholme, is it? Do you know it?

VIOLET: Well, a little. My late husband kept the shooting there, and we'd sometimes have luncheon in the house.

ISOBEL: Is it nice?

VIOLET: Nice enough, as a retreat from the world. I wouldn't have thought it suited to much else.*

STRALLAN: What happened to the shoot?

VIOLET: Robert gave it back to the tenant. He didn't want the expense of it.

STRALLAN: We're all having to rein in.

VIOLET: That's right. We must be practical. It's no good taking something on, however attractive it may seem, if it's not realistic in the long run.

Strallan glances at her, unsettled by her observations.

....

* Here is a memory of another way of life, which came from a conversation I read about somewhere, of the now Dowager Duchess of Devonshire, when she was a young wife, talking to her mother-in-law and discussing all the houses the Devonshires used to have. The older Duchess, Evelyn, was saying that they would always go to Chatsworth for this and that and then they'd go to Devonshire House in London, and then they'd go to Bolton for the shooting and then to Lismore for the sailing, and then came Hardwick… until finally her daughter-in-law said, 'But what about Chiswick?' The old Duchess thought for a moment. 'I think we sometimes went there for breakfast.'

24 EXT. ERYHOLME. DAY.

The picnic has been laid out above the manor house. It is a pretty Elizabethan building, large but nothing like Downton. Folding chairs have been set up around two circular tables and the ten members of the family sit and stroll about, holding drinks. Alfred waits on them.*

SYBIL: Shall we go in after luncheon?

ROBERT: Not today. It seems unfair without giving them warning.

SYBIL: Won't they think it odd, if they look up and see us all here?

ROBERT: I'll drop them a line later.

CORA: Downton Place. How lovely.

MARY: Won't it be a bit cramped?

BRANSON: You do realise that for most people it looks like a fairy palace?

SYBIL: You'll be able to run it with a much smaller staff.

ROBERT: This is it. I doubt we'll need more than eight servants tops. So it'll be very economical. Er…

He makes a slight 'shhh!' gesture as Alfred comes within earshot. He carries something to the table, but then he is gone again.

VIOLET: What about me? Where am I to go?

ROBERT: We still own most of the village.

VIOLET: Oh. Perhaps I could open a shop.

....

* It's always quite nice when we have a day out, although I remember with the picnic we were going through that terrible wet summer and I think we cancelled it five times. If it didn't look marvellous, it wouldn't look truthful, because if Violet woke up expecting to go to a picnic and it was pelting, she just wouldn't come. We found an incredibly pretty house for it, actually. In the script, I made it Elizabethan because the original house at Eryholme was Elizabethan, but in the event it was just a frightfully pretty Georgian house that the location managers found. The scene opened with a very charming wide shot, which I loved. They say they're going to call it Downton Place if they move in, although I'm not sure that they would have, because most people find it rather unlucky to change the names of houses. They might have done, I suppose.

EDITH: Good idea, Granny. What do you think Eryholme needs?
VIOLET: Well, if it's like everywhere else, good manners and some decent conversation.
ISOBEL: Well, there you are, then. You should have a roaring trade in minutes.*

Isobel turns to Edith.

ISOBEL (CONT'D): How's everything going?
EDITH: Very well, I think.
ISOBEL: I think it's rather unfair that Mary should have an Archbishop to marry her, and you've got poor old Mr Travis.
VIOLET: Shall I get you a spoon?
EDITH: No, it's all right. Oh, I don't mind. It was such short notice and he was all booked up, and I prefer it, really. To have the man who christened us.

Mary is with Matthew, a little way away from the rest.

MARY: What had Charkham come for?

Matthew looks at her. He makes the decision to tell.

....

* Violet is teasing them, but her situation was inspired by that of an old acquaintance of mine who rather unfortunately had to sell everything. His mother had been one of my early patronesses and was very, very kind to me, so I was sad that she had actually read in the paper that her own house had been sold, because the whole estate had gone under the hammer and he hadn't told her. We don't accuse Robert of that quite, but I wanted the audience to realise that when an estate goes it affects a lot of people – the whole set-up, in fact, of the neighbourhood.

When Violet refers to Eryholme needing, like anywhere else, good manners and some decent conversation, it is a slight reference to the musical of *Mary Poppins*, for which I wrote the script (more properly called 'The Book' in a musical), where Mrs Corry has the conversation shop. She appeared in the original books, but didn't feature in the film after the opening titles (a slightly odd sequence when you watch it now), but in the musical we worked her in to give an excuse for the famous 'Supercalifragilisticexpialidocious'. In the film, the song comes out of left field really and doesn't have any kind of narrative trigger. We wanted to avoid that, so the shop where you go to buy conversation, which was run by Mrs Corry, made its way into the show. And thence into *Downton*.

MATTHEW: He gave me a letter from Swire. It seems he left one for each of the three potential heirs, when and if they inherited. Mine is the only one to have been delivered.*

MARY: What did it say?

MATTHEW: I haven't opened it. I can't decide whether I will.

MARY: Why wouldn't you?

MATTHEW: Because I know it will be a paean of praise. How Lavinia could not have found a better man, etcetera.

MARY: And you don't want to read that?

MATTHEW: Since she could not have found a worse one, no, I don't. I already feel bad enough, and if I read his words they will stay with me forever.

CORA: It's ready, everyone!

As they start to assemble, she turns to Alfred.

CORA (CONT'D): Alfred, do you know why your aunt is keeping her plans so secret?

ALFRED: What plans, m'lady?

....

* Swire left one letter for each of his heirs. I don't find that unbelievable, nor do I find it hard to understand the reluctance to divide his fortune, because the desire to hold a fortune together was not uncommon. The most extreme case concerned a house, Brodsworth Hall, in Yorkshire where the owner, Peter Thellusson, in 1797, was determined that nothing should split the fortune, which would be allowed to grow for three generations before the heirs could fully own it. He wanted his descendants to be among the richest in the land, and they might have been if his own children hadn't taken the estate to court and ensured that the principal beneficiaries were the lawyers. It was supposed to have been one of the inspirations for Dickens's great Jarndyce v. Jarndyce case in *Bleak House*. It went on and on and on and, of course, consumed practically all the money.

The point was, it has long been recognised that if you can keep a fortune together then the status of your family will rise because there would be a heavyweight player at the head of it, whereas if you divide it with each generation, then within two you've just got people who are quite well off but by no means a force in the land. This is why Swire has chosen to have successive, rather than joint, heirs. Naturally, Matthew doesn't want to read the letter. He doesn't want to read how Lavinia couldn't have found a better man, because he knows he betrayed her. But it is deliberately taunting, and what we are doing is playing with the audience.

They sit down. Robert, Isobel, Edith, Strallan and Violet are together. The remaining five are on the other table.

EDITH: Can I give you some beef?
STRALLAN: Thank you.

Edith serves it and then starts to cut it up for him.

STRALLAN (CONT'D): I'll do it.
EDITH: Don't be silly. How could you?

Violet catches Robert's eye, which Strallan sees.

25   INT. KITCHEN PASSAGE. DAY.

Isobel descends the servants' staircase. She sees Mrs Hughes.

MRS HUGHES: Mrs Crawley?
ISOBEL: We're back from our delicious luncheon, and I was on my way home.

She hesitates. Mrs Hughes waits.

ISOBEL (CONT'D): You had a maid at Downton. Ethel Parks. I was here when she brought her son into the dining room.
MRS HUGHES: Who could forget that?
ISOBEL: Do you have an address for her?
MRS HUGHES: I do. If she's still there.
ISOBEL: You see… You see, I saw her this morning. And I'm afraid she's fallen into a bad way. A very bad way.
MRS HUGHES: Oh, dear. I am sorry to hear that. If you'd like to come with me, I'll fetch it for you.
ISOBEL: Thank you.

They go together. *

....

* In those days, before any adequate poor relief, there weren't many options open to someone like Ethel. Most of the workhouses had closed, which could be seen as an improvement, but what was the alternative? Many women were trained for nothing, and if you had an illegitimate child you either put it out to a baby farm or just survived the best way you could. The baby farms were far from ideal. In Victorian times, there was a real danger that children would be sold for adoption or killed for their clothes, while the 'carer' kept the shilling per week. If they weren't prepared to do that then going on the game was more or less Hobson's Choice. It's a harsh truth that Ethel was not alone.

26   INT.   YORK PRISON.   BATES'S CELL.   DAY.

Craig lies on his bed, while Bates searches his.

26A   INT.   YORK PRISON.   CORRIDOR.   DAY.

Three prison guards are on the march towards Bates's cell.

26B   INT.   YORK PRISON.   BATES'S CELL.   DAY.

*As Bates pulls up the blanket, he spies something pushed into
a crack between the distempered bricks.   It would have been
concealed behind the mattress but he's lifted it.*

26C   INT.   YORK PRISON.   CORRIDOR.   DAY.

The guards are getting closer…

26D   INT.   YORK PRISON.   BATES'S CELL.   DAY.

*Covertly, Bates prises out a substance that has been wrapped
tightly inside a piece of cloth.   Bates sniffs it, without
letting the other man see.*

26E   INT.   YORK PRISON.   CORRIDOR.   DAY.

The guards are here, the keys are jangling…

27   INT.   BATES'S CELL.   YORK PRISON.   DAY.

Bates is reading a letter.   He seems saddened by its content.

  CRAIG: Bad news? I am sorry.
  BATES: Why don't you just —

*The door flies open.   The warder, Durrant, rushes in, followed
by two others, including the warder Turner.*

  DURRANT: Get up, both of you… Against the wall!

They are pushed against the wall.   The others get started.

  DURRANT (CONT'D): Mr Turner, search the bunk, please.

*Turner turns over Bates's mattress and bedclothes, and
conducts a search.   Bates slides the object he has found
towards a gap in the brickwork.*

  TURNER: Nothing here.
  DURRANT: What?

He grabs the mattress to reveal the hole in the wall, but it is empty. He stares at Craig, who's as surprised as he is.

DURRANT (CONT'D): Clear this mess up!

He walks out, followed by the others. The door clangs shut.

CRAIG: Bastards.

Unseen by Craig, tucked into the brickwork, is the tiny package Bates found earlier.*

BATES: There's a lot of bastards in here.

28 INT. SERVANTS' HALL. DOWNTON. DAY.

Servants' tea. Anna is rather silent.

MOLESLEY: I expect you're tired. It's a long day, up to London and back again.
MRS HUGHES: Was it worth the journey?
ANNA: Not really.
CARSON: Miss O'Brien, might I ask what you've confided in Mr Molesley, but have kept from the rest of us?
O'BRIEN: I don't know what you mean.
CARSON: Mr Molesley appears to have given her ladyship the impression that you're planning a change of some sort.
O'BRIEN: What's this?
MOLESLEY: I'm sorry. I thought her ladyship would know.
O'BRIEN: Know what?
MOLESLEY: That you're leaving.
O'BRIEN: *I beg your pardon!* How dare you make such an assumption?

....

* We sometimes forget that the decade of the Twenties was a great drug era, with the so-called dope fiends puffing and snorting away in every night club in London. Most of it was not yet illegal, because the government at that time didn't really make a distinction between drugs and drink (which some would argue now). Although the drug addict was a social type about whom Noël Coward would write in *The Vortex*, and, then as now, drugs were the one thing all parents wanted their children to avoid, nevertheless it was not yet seen as a proper province for the law. The dope fiend more or less died away during the Fifties, not that there were no drugs and not that no one was taking them, but it wasn't on the same industrial scale as it had been. Of course, the Swinging Sixties brought it all roaring back.

THOMAS: Isn't it time for the dressing gong, Mr Carson?

CARSON: Oh. It certainly is. Thank you.

MOLESLEY: But —

Carson has left. Now Thomas stands and heads for the door.

THOMAS: Excuse me, Mr Molesley. I've got work to do, even if you haven't.

O'BRIEN: I'll deal with you later.

She gives Molesley a basilisk stare, then goes, leaving Molesley reeling at his evil luck.

DAISY: You're in the soup. I wouldn't be in her bad books for a gold clock.*

END OF ACT TWO

ACT THREE

29 INT. SYBIL'S BEDROOM. DOWNTON. EVE.

Anna leaves. Sybil is dressed and Branson's in black tie.

BRANSON: Why not just tell her you can dress yourself?

SYBIL: For the same reason that you're wearing a dinner jacket.

BRANSON: I can't have a conversation about my clothes at every meal.

SYBIL: Exactly.

She stands to look at herself.

BRANSON: You know, I think it's a good thing they're leaving Downton.

SYBIL: If you do, keep it to yourself.

....

* I first heard this phrase on *Coronation Street* from Audrey Roberts's husband, Alf. He was building up to his proposal, when she complained that he'd upset her in some way, and he replied, 'Oh, I wouldn't do that. Not for a gold clock.' It's been parked in my brain ever since and I thought it would be nice to give it to Daisy.

BRANSON: Because it's as far away from real life as it's possible to get.*

There is a knock at the door and Alfred appears.

ALFRED: Is there anything I can do for you, sir, before you go down?
BRANSON: I'm perfectly all right, thank you.

Alfred nods and retreats. Branson turns to Sybil.

BRANSON (CONT'D): See what I mean?

30   INT. CORA'S BEDROOM. DOWNTON. EVE.

Cora is with O'Brien.

CORA: You must have said something that Molesley misinterpreted.
O'BRIEN: But I don't say anything to him, m'lady, beyond 'pass the salt', and 'get out of the way'.
CORA: There must have been something. I'm afraid I do feel let down, O'Brien. I really do. And right on top of the wedding…

There is a knock and Mrs Hughes enters.

MRS HUGHES: You sent for me, m'lady?
CORA: Yes. Thank you, O'Brien.

The maid leaves, frustrated by the previous conversation.

CORA (CONT'D): Mrs Hughes, I understand that you're not well —
MRS HUGHES: Whom do you 'understand' that from? Because if the doctor —

....

* Sybil is not a confrontationalist. I am a moderate, in the sense that I admire people like Sybil, who live their own life but don't feel the need to beat everyone over the head with it all the time, as opposed to the type who rants and raves: 'I'm not having this! I can't put up with that!' Tom Branson is torn between these two positions. He arrived in the house much more of a confrontationalist, but he is exhausted with it and has started to come over to the dark side. He will eventually pay the price, which is to feel that his own personality has been eroded and he is living by standards that he doesn't completely endorse. I suppose this is to show that nothing is simple. There is an upside and a downside to most philosophies.

CORA: It wasn't Doctor Clarkson.
MRS HUGHES: It is not confirmed that I am ill, your
ladyship. I've had a test and I'm waiting for the
results. But I am perfectly capable —
CORA: Mrs Hughes, I only want to say one thing. That if
you are ill, you are welcome here for as long as you want
to stay. Lady Sybil will help us to find a suitable
nurse.
MRS HUGHES: I see.
CORA: I don't want you to have any concerns about where
you'll go, or who'll look after you, because the answer
is here, and we will.

Mrs Hughes was not expecting this. Her eyes fill.

MRS HUGHES: I don't know what to say, m'lady.
CORA: There isn't anything more to say until we know
where we stand, one way or the other.
MRS HUGHES: Thank you.*
CORA: Now, what about tomorrow?
MRS HUGHES: I think everything's in hand. The rooms are
ready. And Mrs Patmore's been in a fury all day.
CORA: I can imagine.
MRS HUGHES: I very much doubt you can.

31   INT.   KITCHENS.   DOWNTON.   NIGHT.

Daisy is loading Alfred's tray with a cheese course.

DAISY: If they complain it's dull, tell them it's a
miracle there's cheese at all, the day before a wedding.
ALFRED: I'll send for you and you can tell them. You
said you wanted to be more outspoken.
DAISY: That's not quite what I meant —
MRS PATMORE: Get that cheese up, and if his lordship
asks, tell 'em they must do without a savoury. Her
ladyship'll stick up for you.

Daisy's moment has passed.

....

* Mrs Hughes is slightly wrongfooted by Cora's generosity, because she isn't a
great worshipper of the family. But in life there are moments, in dealing with
the important things like illness or death, which transcend class or political
difference, and this is quite deliberately constructed to be one of them.

32 INT. DRAWING ROOM. DOWNTON. NIGHT.

It is after dinner. They are all there, except for Strallan.

EDITH: He thinks I don't know, but of course I do.
We'll spend two weeks in Rome, then Florence, then
Venice, so I couldn't be happier.
SYBIL: And what about Loxley? Is there masses to be
done?
EDITH: It's not too bad.
MARY: It's not too bad downstairs. The bedrooms are
killers.
ISOBEL: Well, don't do anything too fast. It takes time
to know how a house works.

Edith glows.* Mary is with Matthew, to one side.

MARY: I think you have to read it.
MATTHEW: I don't agree. It's like when someone you love
dies. Don't look at them dead if you don't want that
image in your brain for ever, because it'll never leave
you.†

....

* Edith is the happiest here we have ever seen her, because she thinks her whole life is about to unfold, and also that she can face not just Mary but her contemporaries, having fulfilled her pre-ordained destiny. Very few of us are in control of our own future entirely, we all need a bit of luck, and at last Edith has had a bit of luck. 'It's not too bad downstairs. The bedrooms are killers.' I thought we needed one sharpie from Mary. As for Isobel's advice, this is my own feeling: don't do anything fast, it takes time to know how a house works.

† I was sorry this was cut because it came from quite a vivid moment in my own early years. We were living in Sussex, and my parents' greatest friend there was killed in a car crash. My mother went with the widow to identify the body, as she felt she couldn't let the widow see him first, in case he was too smashed up. They talked about it with the police and Mummy was allowed to go in and identify the body. So she entered the room alone and, as she had feared, the whole of the side of his head was pushed in and horribly damaged. Anyway, it was clearly him so she came out and officially identified him, but she was never able to shake the terrible image from her brain, not for the rest of her life. She didn't regret it – in fact, she was very pleased to have spared the widow from seeing him in that state – but she wished later that they'd taken a professional colleague with them, or a member of staff, to identify him – someone who didn't love him. I've never forgotten that.

MARY: What about if I read it?

But he shakes his head.

MATTHEW: I think I'll burn the damn thing.

Violet is with the girls.

VIOLET: I really think you should go to bed. No bride
wants to look tired at her wedding. It either means
she's anxious or been up to no good.
EDITH: I won't sleep a wink.
SYBIL: Tonight or tomorrow?
VIOLET: Sybil, vulgarity is no substitute for wit.
SYBIL: Well, you started it.

Robert and Cora are with Branson.

ROBERT: Sybil seems to think your politics are
hardening, which worries me.
BRANSON: Really? I wouldn't say I was any more
political. Merely more active.
CORA: Promise you won't be foolish.
BRANSON: First, we'd have to define foolish.

33 INT. KITCHEN PASSAGE/SERVANTS' HALL. DOWNTON. NIGHT.

*The servants are coming in for dinner. Molesley catches
O'Brien as she walks down the passage.*

MOLESLEY: Miss O'Brien. Please, understand that I
didn't mean any harm —
O'BRIEN: Well, why make it up in the first place?
MOLESLEY: I didn't make it up; I was told…
O'BRIEN: Who told you?
MOLESLEY: Well, Mr Barrow mentioned it, but I think it
was an honest mistake…

This has clarified everything for the maid.

O'BRIEN: No, it wasn't honest, and it wasn't a mistake.
But don't worry about it. I can tell it wasn't your
fault, Mr Molesley. So we'll forget about it, shall we?
And when you see Mr Barrow, you can tell him that I may
make some honest mistakes myself in the future.

With this cryptic remark, they walk in and take their places.
Daisy and Mrs Patmore are putting dishes on the table.

ALFRED: Why not sit down and eat with us?

DAISY: Oh, I couldn't do that.

CARSON: Daisy will not sit down because the invitation
is not in your gift, Alfred. She eats with Mrs Patmore.
In the kitchen.*

Even so, Daisy is thrilled. Alfred has another try.

ALFRED: Fancy a game of something later?

MRS PATMORE: Daisy's busy.

ALFRED: Anna?

ANNA: I want to write a letter. Sorry.

MOLESLEY: I'll play.

ALFRED: Let's see how we feel.

34   INT. MARY'S BEDROOM. DOWNTON. NIGHT.

Mary is in bed and Matthew, in his dressing gown, faces her.

MATTHEW: What do you mean you've read it?

MARY: I didn't think it was right to destroy a man's
last words without reading them. I felt it was wrong.

MATTHEW: It wasn't your decision.

MARY: Well, I made it my decision. Do you want to hear
what he says?

MATTHEW: No.

MARY: To start with, Lavinia must have written to him on
her last day, only hours before she died.

MATTHEW: Well, that's nonsense. There was no letter
found in her room.

MARY: Be that as it may, she wrote to him after she
tried to persuade you to call off the wedding and you
wouldn't.

MATTHEW: This is quite impossible.

....

* Carson's fear of the postwar world is that somehow, now that change has
begun to gather momentum, these funny, arbitrary rules that had been
observed for so long, like the kitchen staff eating separately, are all going to
start to fragment, which of course is exactly what happened.

As an answer she takes the letter from beneath her pillow. He does not want to listen, but he no longer tries to stop her.

MARY: 'She loved and admired you for this sacrifice of your own happiness, and she commended you to my care.'
MATTHEW: I can't listen to any more of this.
MARY: You must. 'I have few intimates and so I've decided, in her name, to add you to my list of heirs. I think it unlikely that I'll outlive both the first two, so there is little chance of your reading this letter, but if you do, and if the money has come to you, know it is with my full knowledge of what transpired. Please do not allow any grief, guilt or regret to hold you back in its employment. God bless you, my boy. Reggie.'

They stare at each other.

MATTHEW: Are you sure you didn't write it?
MARY: I assume you know his hand.
MATTHEW: Not well enough to test a forgery.

He has taken off his gown and now he climbs into bed.

MATTHEW (CONT'D): Besides, she couldn't have written to him without our knowing. I'm not accusing you of faking it, but I suspect someone has.
MARY: So it won't change your mind?
MATTHEW: Not yet, it won't.*

35 INT. MRS HUGHES'S SITTING ROOM. DOWNTON. NIGHT.

Carson finds Mrs Hughes working.

CARSON: Time you were in bed. Big day tomorrow.
MRS HUGHES: I'll just finish this.
CARSON: Is it something I could do for you?

....

* We learn later that Swire left Matthew as his heir, even though he knew the engagement was at an end, but we can hardly blame Matthew for not believing it at this stage. That said, Swire didn't have anyone else and Matthew was only the third heir. More to the point, we need a lot of money to save Downton. Which is all there is to it. But obviously Matthew thinks Lavinia couldn't have written a letter while she was ill in bed upstairs without their knowing.

MRS HUGHES: No… Did you say anything about me to her ladyship?
CARSON: I don't know what you mean. Why?
MRS HUGHES: Don't worry. She was very kind, and I was touched. As you know, I don't worship them all like you do —
CARSON: I wouldn't put it like that —
MRS HUGHES: But this time, I freely admit it, I was quite touched.

She goes back to her work and he retreats.

36 INT. SERVANTS' HALL. DOWNTON. DAY.

The servants are at breakfast.

MARY: Am I interrupting?*

Led by Carson, they scramble to their feet.

MARY (CONT'D): No, please. I just want to ask you all something.
ANNA: M'lady, I'm sorry I've not been up.
MARY: Don't worry. I'll change properly after luncheon. But I had to catch you when you were all together.
CARSON: How can we help, m'lady?
MARY: It's a funny thing. Mr Crawley has heard that Miss Swire sent a letter on the day she died. If so, someone must have posted it for her, and we wondered if it were any of you?

Nobody speaks. Carson surveys the table and turns back.

CARSON: I'm afraid not. Given that the poor lady passed away that same day, an incident of this sort would have been reported to me or to Mrs Hughes.
MRS HUGHES: That's right, m'lady.
MARY: I see. Well, thank you very much.

She turns to go as Daisy brings in some toast. She whispers.

DAISY: What were that about?
ANNA: Lady Mary wanted to know if anyone had posted a letter for Miss Swire.

....

* It's always an event when someone from upstairs comes downstairs. We try never to lose that.

DAISY: Oh, I did that.

The words shock the room, including Carson.

CARSON: Daisy? What did you say?

Mary has stopped by the stairs. She comes back in.

DAISY: Poor Miss Swire's letter. She'd written it and she asked me to put it into the box in the hall. Why?
MRS HUGHES: What were you doing in her room?
DAISY: Making up the fire. We started talking and she said she'd written a letter. She was ever so nice. I still get sad when I think about her.*
MRS HUGHES: And it didn't occur to you to tell me?
DAISY: Tell you what?
MARY: Never mind. I am grateful to you, Daisy. You cannot know how much.

37 INT. ROBERT'S DRESSING ROOM. DAY

Robert is with Thomas, who is helping him to dress.

ROBERT: I'll change for the wedding after luncheon.
THOMAS: Very good, m'lord.
ROBERT: Did it surprise you? When you heard O'Brien might be on the move?
THOMAS: Not really, m'lord. She's always been quite a dark horse.

....

* It's completely truthful that Daisy would have gone in to make up the fire in Lavinia's sick room. Normally she would only make up a bedroom fire before the occupant woke up, which was the particular skill of that job, and the maids would do it with very thick gloves so that the fire was burning when they woke up. Then the grate would be emptied and cleaned when they did the room. After that, it would be relit before they changed for dinner and then it would be saved and rebuilt again before they came up for the night. In other words, all the fire duties were done when the family and their guests were either asleep or not in the room, but the exception to the rule was the fire of an invalid. In that case, the person in the bed would be awake and able to watch whoever was making up the fire. I have only ever had the fire lit in my bedroom before I woke up once in my life, at a country house in the North. In fact, I did wake up in time to see the maid finish the job. I think it was the single most luxurious thing I have ever enjoyed.

ROBERT: It seems she's changed her mind, but I dare say we'd recover if she went.

THOMAS: Oh, yes. It'd take more than that to drive us out of Downton.

38   INT.   LIBRARY.   DOWNTON.   DAY.

Robert is with Violet. They are in wedding clothes.

VIOLET: Well, this is the last of them.

ROBERT: I'm glad they've hurried it. So she can be married from Downton.

VIOLET: Are you? I should have thought a little sober reflection would not have gone amiss.

ROBERT: Mama, let's try to be positive. Of all of them, Anthony Strallan is the most traditional choice.

VIOLET: Robert. Edith is beginning her life as an old man's drudge. I should not have thought a large drawing room much compensation.

ROBERT: Why dwell on that now?

VIOLET: Because I want the pleasure of saying I told you so.

39   INT.   MRS HUGHES'S SITTING ROOM.   DOWNTON. DAY.

Mrs Patmore is with Mrs Hughes.

MRS HUGHES: We're not forgetting anything?

MRS PATMORE: I don't think so. One of the maids will supervise the oven and Alfred is staying to manage the wine.

MRS HUGHES: It's a shame they have to miss it.

MRS PATMORE: Not really. They've not been here long enough to know Lady Edith.

Carson looks in.

CARSON: Now, the moment you feel tired, you're to tell me, and I'll take over whatever it is you're doing.

MRS HUGHES: Oh, will you, now?

CARSON: Are you sure you want to come to church? You could stay here and have a lie down.

MRS HUGHES: It would be so nice if people would wait to learn if I really am ill before boxing me up.

CARSON: I don't know what you mean. I don't know anything about any illness.
MRS HUGHES: Don't you? I see.

He goes.

MRS HUGHES (CONT'D): Who told him?
MRS PATMORE: I don't know. Maybe he just picked it up somehow. He's worried about you. He's a good man.
MRS HUGHES: He's a hopeless liar.
MRS PATMORE: But that's quite nice really, isn't it?
MRS HUGHES: I've had a message from the doctor. He'll have the results tomorrow. I'm to call in the afternoon.
MRS PATMORE: Try not to worry.
MRS HUGHES: I'll try, but I won't succeed.

40   INT. MARY'S BEDROOM. DOWNTON. DAY.

Anna is finishing Mary's costume. Matthew is with her.

MARY: That's it. I'll put the hat on later. Go straight to Lady Edith.

Anna hurries out as Mary stands.

MATTHEW: You look marvellous.
MARY: I feel marvellous.
MATTHEW: I'm glad.
MARY: That is, I feel marvellous because we don't have to leave Downton.

He stares at her. What is coming?

MARY (CONT'D): Lavinia *did* write to her father and it was posted from this house. In other words, every word Mr Swire wrote in that letter was true.

Matthew sits down.

MARY (CONT'D): Daisy posted it. The kitchen maid.
MATTHEW: I see.
MARY: Do you, my darling? I hope so. Because if you try to find one more excuse not to accept the money, I'll have to beat you about the head.
MATTHEW: I see. I do have one condition, however.
MARY: Make it a good one.
MATTHEW: Let's not steal Edith's thunder. I'll tell Robert after it's over, and she's left on honeymoon.

MARY: Now that I can live with.

Matthew stands and they kiss.

END OF ACT THREE

ACT FOUR

41 INT. EDITH'S BEDROOM. DOWNTON. DAY.

Edith's in her wedding dress. Anna is finalising a dazzling tiara. Cora, Sybil and Mary are with them.

CORA: The wedding tiara is so much prettier than that fender I have to wear for the opening of Parliament.
EDITH: You should wear this one, then.
CORA: No. Your father wouldn't like it. And I think it's nice that we keep it for all the Crawley brides.
SYBIL: Not for me. I didn't wear it.
MARY: For all the Crawley brides except Sybil.
ANNA: Please say if it's not comfy.*
CORA: You look beautiful.
EDITH: All of us married, all of us happy. And the first baby on the way.

....

*The business of wearing tiaras always interests me because very few modern hairdressers have the skill to put them on. They're always made with a raised gallery with a padded bit at the bottom and straight upright struts supporting the proper jewelled bottom band. The padded bit sat on the brow and the hair was trained through the gallery so that the hair was still raised off the head but the tiara seemed to skim it. There's quite a skill involved, and I notice now at the opening of Parliament, when the peeresses come in wearing their tiaras, very few of them know how to do it properly. Almost all of them are worn, plomp, on top of their hair, as if you're supposed to see the gallery, which of course you're not. The problem is, the wives have to be there so early, by about nine in the morning at the latest, and the thought of shaking your hairdresser awake at dawn to fit a tiara is a bit hard. Of course, when they are put on correctly they look marvellous.

Cora squeezes Sybil's hand. The latter seems nervous.

SYBIL: Mama, will you come over to Dublin when the baby's due?

CORA: Of course, if you want me.

MARY: You ought to have it here.

SYBIL: Tom wants it to be born in Ireland.

MARY: Obviously.

EDITH: Why don't we get the photographer to take a picture of the three of us? When we get to the church.

CORA: What a lovely way to finish our life here. A wedding is a new beginning and that's what we'll have, too, as a family.

MARY: Don't be so defeatist, Mama.

SYBIL: Do you mean we might still pull a rabbit out of the hat? Oh, I do hope so. What do you think, Anna?

ANNA: I think that to take a rabbit out of a hat there must first be a rabbit *in* the hat.

CORA: We should move. The wagonette's waiting for you, Anna.

MARY: Then let us go and marry off… the last of the Crawley sisters.

This makes the three siblings smile as they prepare to leave.

42   INT.   CHURCH.   DOWNTON VILLAGE.   DAY.

The Reverend Mr Travis and Violet are watching Strallan.*

VIOLET: He looks as if he's waiting for a beating from the headmaster.

TRAVIS: Do you think I should reassure him?

VIOLET: How? He's done it before so he must be in possession of all the facts.

TRAVIS: Perhaps the first Lady Strallan was a difficult act to follow.

VIOLET: Or a difficult one to repeat.

....

* We nearly lost this bit – I can't remember why – but it was important for me that we should see that Strallan is beginning to realise he was doing something wrong, because otherwise his dawning awareness would have come too suddenly. I don't remember getting it back being a tough argument, though. I think the consensus was behind it.

43 EXT. CHURCH. DOWNTON VILLAGE. DAY.

Mary, in a ravishing hat, and Sybil, in a modest one, are being photographed with Edith, the bride, while Anna watches. Robert looks at his fob watch.

ROBERT: Well, fashionably late is one thing…
MARY: We're going in. Edith, I know we haven't always got along, and I doubt things change much in the future, but today I wish you all the luck in the world.
EDITH: Thank you.

They kiss and, with Anna, the sisters hurry inside.

44 INT. CHURCH. DOWNTON VILLAGE. DAY.

Mary, Sybil and Anna find their places. The organ strikes up, the congregation stands. Robert and Edith walk down the aisle. The music stops and Travis moves forward. Strallan steps out into the aisle. Edith whispers up at him.

EDITH: Good afternoon.
STRALLAN: Good afternoon, my sweet one.

But as he looks at her, he is aware of a terrible truth.

TRAVIS: Dearly beloved, we are gathered —
STRALLAN: I can't do this.

For a moment, nobody speaks or moves. Then whispers erupt among the guests…

ROBERT: What?
STRALLAN: I can't do it. You know it's wrong. You told me so yourself, several times.
ROBERT: My dear chap —
STRALLAN: No. I should never have let it get this far. I should have stopped it long ago. I tried to stop it.
EDITH: What are you saying? I don't understand what you're saying.
STRALLAN: Edith, Edith… I can't let you throw away your life like this.
EDITH: What do you mean? We're so happy, aren't we? We're going to be so terribly, terribly happy.
STRALLAN: But you are going to be happy. I pray you are. But only if you don't waste yourself on me.
ROBERT: Anthony, it is too late for this —

TRAVIS: Might I suggest we all take a step back —
VIOLET: No. Let him go. Let him go.*

All eyes swivel to her.

VIOLET (CONT'D): You know he's right. Don't stop him
doing the only sensible thing he's come up with in
months.
STRALLAN: Thank you, Lady Grantham.
EDITH: But Granny —
VIOLET: No, no. It's over, my dear. Don't drag it out.
Wish him well and let him go.
EDITH: I can't.
STRALLAN: Goodbye, my dearest darling. And may God
bless you. Always.

*He hurries up the aisle to the amazement of the guests.
Edith looks at her lucky sisters and their husbands. Once
again, the dice have rolled against her.*

45 EXT. CHURCH. DOWNTON VILLAGE. DAY.

*Strallan comes out, wiping away tears. Some chauffeurs
chatting by their cars glance at him. He walks away.*

46 INT. HALL. DOWNTON. DAY.

*The front door flies open and Edith, sobbing, runs to the
staircase, followed by Sybil and Mary. Their husbands linger
below. Robert and Cora join them.*

ROBERT: Should we go up?

....

* Robert Bathurst played all this terribly well, because it was not funny. It
was completely real. In fact, I always admire people who stand their other
halves up at the church or turn the car around on the way. I remember when
Emma came to our wedding, her father was dead and she was given away by
her uncle, Henry Kitchener. He just said to her that everything would be all
right as long as she was sure but she didn't have to go through with it, and my
mother-in-law the night before told her she could still get out of it if she
wanted to. I agree with them. It may sound odd, but I do. I think you
should always give a bride or a groom an out. It's an important duty. I don't
think Robert is right to say that it's too late for Anthony Strallan to cancel
the wedding. I believe one of your jobs as a father of the bride or groom is to
say it doesn't matter what it's all cost.

BRANSON: Leave it to the girls. Let them all cry it out for a bit.
MATTHEW: I think he's right.

46A INT. EDITH'S BEDROOM. DOWNTON. DAY.

Edith pulls off her tiara and cries uncontrollably into her bed.

46B INT. HALL. DOWNTON. DAY.

Robert approaches a gob-smacked Alfred by a glass-laden table.

ROBERT: When everyone gets back, can you clear all this away? I want it gone before Lady Edith comes downstairs. Flowers, glasses, everything. And ask the outside staff to help put back the carpet and the furniture.
ALFRED: Yes, m'lord. But what about…?
MATTHEW: There's been no wedding, and there will be no reception.

47 INT. EDITH'S BEDROOM. DOWNTON. DAY.

Edith's crying on the bed. She has pulled off the tiara and veil, wrecking her hair, but not her dress. Her mother and sisters are with her.

SYBIL: Maybe he'll change his mind.
MARY: Don't say that. He won't change his mind. He won't be back.

Edith weeps some more. The door opens and Cora comes in.

CORA: Is there anything I could say to make it better?
EDITH: No.

She stares at her sisters.

EDITH (CONT'D): Look at them. Both with their husbands, Sybil pregnant, Mary probably pregnant, and what have I got? What has poor, sad, plain little Edith got? Oh, just go. I mean it. Go.
SYBIL: Can't we —?
CORA: Perhaps you should go.

They accept this, and leave. Cora consoles Edith.

EDITH: Oh, Mama.

CORA: You are being tested. And do you know what they say, my darling? Being tested only makes you stronger.

EDITH: I don't think it's working with me.*

48 INT. BEDROOM PASSAGE. DOWNTON. DAY.

Sybil and Mary walk along the passage.

SYBIL: Poor Edith… Are you pregnant?

MARY: When I am, I promise you'll be the first to know. Well, the third.

SYBIL: And you're not stopping it?

MARY: God, no. The sooner we have a baby boy, the sooner we can all relax.

48A INT. HALL. DOWNTON. DAY.

Champagne glasses are cleared, the wedding cake is removed and the carpet is rolled out once again.

49 EXT. DOWNTON. DAY.

Robert is walking when Matthew comes out.

MATTHEW: What should we do now?

ROBERT: There's nothing we can do. Beyond removing all signs of a wedding and holding her hand while she recovers… She will, of course.

Matthew nods.

ROBERT (CONT'D): Meanwhile, it's time to face the business of leaving Downton. Without the wedding to hide behind, there's no reason not to get on with it and astonish the world with the extent of my wretched failure.

He looks about him, at the house and park, with a sigh.

MATTHEW: Actually, Mary and I intended to make an announcement at dinner.

ROBERT: What announcement? What about?

....

* My favourite line in the episode, and one of my favourite lines in the whole show.

MATTHEW: You don't have to leave… I'll explain it later, but I'm going to give you Reggie's money. I'll accept it. And I'll give it to you.

Robert is silent for a second.

ROBERT: Don't be silly. You're not going to give me any money.
MATTHEW: But I am. You don't want to leave, nor does Mary… Nor do any of us, for that matter —
ROBERT: I still won't take your money. What I will allow is for you to invest in the place. If we stay, you'll share the ownership. It'll be your house, your estate, as much as mine. We will be joint Masters.
MATTHEW: But —
ROBERT: And if you don't agree, I will sell and it'll all be your fault.

They shake hands and Robert clasps Matthew's shoulder.*

50 INT. KITCHENS. DOWNTON. NIGHT.

Daisy is working when Anna comes in.

DAISY: What shall we do with the food?
ANNA: I think we should dine very well, in the dining room and down here, and tomorrow we can give the rest to Mr Travis for one of his causes.†
DAISY: I never thought I'd feel sorry for an earl's daughter.
ANNA: All God's creatures have their troubles.
DAISY: Anna —

....

* I believe it is completely believable that Robert would not accept the gift of any money. He is prepared for them to be joint Masters, which, of course, is a hunting image, but it is one that again I think is truthful psychologically.

† We define Mrs Patmore here as a pretty superior cook. In real life they would almost certainly have had a chef and so, despite the fact that Mrs Patmore is a homely body, she must be presented as a very skilled cook or she simply wouldn't have this job. There would probably also have been a *sous chef* and various other members of the kitchen staff – vegetable maid, still-room maid, and so on – or they might have brought in outside help for a wedding, but we never wanted to do that, because if they come in they've got to have a story.

ANNA: Yes?

DAISY: Do you think it's right that women should say what they think? Speak out. About romance and everything?

ANNA: Well, things are changing for us. And the vote won't be long now. So I suppose they must get used to us speaking our minds, but —*

DAISY: But what?

ANNA: With most of the men I've ever met, if you started to court them they'd be so terrified they'd run a mile.

Alfred walks in and Daisy smiles.

51 INT. DINING ROOM. DOWNTON. NIGHT.

The family, without Edith, are at dinner.

ISOBEL: Has she had something to eat?

MARY: Anna took up some sandwiches, but she didn't touch a thing.

ROBERT: This is absolutely delicious.

CORA: That reminds me. Carson, I don't want Lady Edith to see any of the wedding food.

CARSON: Mrs Hughes and Anna are taking what's left down to Mr Travis tomorrow, m'lady. For the poor.

VIOLET: If the poor don't want it, you can bring it over to me.

MATTHEW: How can we help Edith?

ISOBEL: You can help her by finding her something to do.

SYBIL: Then we have the answer. We must find Edith something to do.

....

* Female suffrage came in gradually. First, in 1919, it was only for women who were over thirty, property owners, not domestic servants, and so on. These categories were expanded and loosened during the decade until, by 1930, women were enfranchised by the same rules as men. As with so many other things after 1919, it became increasingly obvious to everyone that full suffrage for women was coming, and why they didn't just get on with it must have been puzzling to some people, but anyway they didn't.

52 INT. SERVANTS' HALL. DOWNTON. NIGHT.

The table is laid with bowls and plates of delicacies.

ALFRED: Is this all we're getting? Just these picketty bits?

THOMAS: Hardly. These are canapés, Alfred. For your first course, some truffled egg on toast, perhaps? Some oysters *à la Russe*?

ALFRED: Then what?

MRS PATMORE: There's lobster rissoles in mousseline sauce or Calvados-glazed duckling, or do you fancy a little asparagus salad with champagne-saffron vinaigrette?

MRS HUGHES: When I think how you've gone to such pains…

MRS PATMORE: Never mind me. What about the pain of that poor girl upstairs?

O'BRIEN: Jilted at the altar. I don't think I could stand the shame.

THOMAS: Then it's lucky no one's ever asked you, isn't it?

ANNA: Poor thing. How will she find the strength to hold up her head?

DAISY: I swear I'd have to run and hide, in a place where no one knew me.

ALFRED: I think she's well out of it.

MOLESLEY: How can you say that?

ALFRED: I mean it. She's young, she's not bad looking. She could do much better than that broken-down old crock.

CARSON: Sir Anthony may have betrayed a daughter of this house, but he still does not deserve to be addressed in that manner by a footman.

MRS HUGHES: Oh, I think he does, Mr Carson. Every bit of that, and worse.

CARSON: Well, maybe just this once.

MRS PATMORE: Right. What's it to be? Lobster, duck or asparagus?

ALFRED: Is there any cheese, Mrs Patmore?

53 EXT. DOWNTON. DAY.

The house seems unaware of the misery within.

54 INT. EDITH'S BEDROOM. DOWNTON. DAY.

Edith lies, staring at the ceiling. Anna comes in.

ANNA: What would you like me to get you?
EDITH: A different life.
ANNA: Let me bring you up some breakfast.
EDITH: No. I am a useful spinster, good at helping out.
That is my role. And spinsters get up for breakfast.

Wearily, she pushes back the bedclothes. *

55 INT. MRS HUGHES'S SITTING ROOM/PASSAGE.
DOWNTON. DAY.

Mrs Hughes is in her hat and coat. Carson looks in.

CARSON: Going out?
MRS HUGHES: Just into the village. I... have to fetch
something.
CARSON: Can I help? I'm going down later.
MRS HUGHES: No, thank you. This is an errand I have to
do for myself.

She is very determined. Mrs Patmore arrives in coat and hat.

MRS PATMORE: Ready?
MRS HUGHES: As ready as I'll ever be.

*Watched by the butler, the two women leave, passing O'Brien
who, in turn, walks past Thomas, carrying some boots.*

56 EXT. HOSPITAL. DOWNTON VILLAGE. DAY.

Mrs Patmore and Mrs Hughes stand outside, biting their lips.

MRS HUGHES: We can be sure of one thing. I won't be
cured by standing here.

Mrs Patmore nods and together they go forward.

....

* One of the greatest tests about being publicly humiliated is being obliged to
deal with it afterwards. The moment of humiliation is bad enough, but it is
facing everyone, when they all know what has happened, that is so hard, and
I admire Edith for not trying to hide. Because you do feel that everyone in
the world is talking about you. Later she will say to Michael Gregson how
nice it is to realise there's someone out there who hasn't heard her story.

56A INT. KITCHENS DOWNTON. DAY.

Carson loads a tray and then checks his fob watch anxiously.

56B INT. WAITING ROOM. HOSPITAL. DAY.

Mrs Hughes and Mrs Patmore wait in silence. A nurse opens the door and Mrs Patmore goes to speak.

   MRS HUGHES: No.

Mrs Hughes walks through the door alone and the nurse closes it behind her.

56C INT. PASSAGE. DOWNTON. DAY.

O'Brien walks down the passage towards Thomas.

   THOMAS: Everything all right, Miss O'Brien?
   O'BRIEN: Oh, yes. Everything's all right with me, but it'll be all wrong with you before too long. Mark my words.
   THOMAS: Oh? And how is that, Miss O'Brien?
   O'BRIEN: I don't know. Not yet. But it will be. You can be sure of it.

57 INT. LANDING/ETHEL'S ROOMS. DAY.

Isobel is climbing a dismal staircase in a slum. At the top she reaches a door and is about to knock when it opens. A man is leaving. He shields his face when he sees Isobel. Ethel is holding the door, in a stained dressing gown. The two women stare at each other.

   ISOBEL: Hello, Ethel.
   ETHEL: How did you find me?
   ISOBEL: I asked Mrs Hughes.

Ethel nods. She looks down at some coins in her hand, and puts them in a box on the table.

   ISOBEL (CONT'D): I would so like to be useful to you. Please. Won't you let me?
   ETHEL: You don't understand, Mrs Crawley. I didn't come looking for help, not for myself. I'm past all that.
   ISOBEL: Then why did you come?

Behind Ethel a child starts to cry. She looks round and back.

ETHEL: I've got to go… Thanks for trying, ma'am. But there's no point. It's all up with me. I'm done.

Almost apologetically, she shuts the door.

58 INT. KITCHENS. DOWNTON. DAY.

Carson approaches Mrs Patmore.

CARSON: Well?

MRS PATMORE: You mean —?

CARSON: Is it? Or isn't it?

MRS PATMORE: It's not cancer, no. It's a benign something-or-other. Nothing more.

CARSON: Don't mention that you've said anything. She doesn't know that I know.

MRS PATMORE: I won't say a word.

He leaves, and she goes into the kitchen taking off her coat. Mrs Hughes comes in.

MRS HUGHES: Did you tell him?

MRS PATMORE: I would prefer to say I've put him out of his misery.

Mrs Hughes chuckles and moves off down the passage. She stops. Someone is singing an old folk song. She moves more slowly and there is Carson, polishing away as he sings.

CARSON: Dashing away with a smoothing iron, Dashing away with a smoothing iron, Dashing away with a smoothing iron, She stole my heart away.

With a smile, Mrs Hughes shakes her head and walks on.*

END OF EPISODE THREE

....

* We all think that Carson is in love with Mrs Hughes, albeit in a very discreet, Carsonesque way, but we also feel it has to be played out. 'Dashing Away with a Smoothing Iron' was a song my maiden aunt, Betty, used to sing to me when I was a little boy. She also used to sing 'Early One Morning'. She is dead now and the songs are forgotten, but I remember both of them well. How strange time is.

EPISODE FOUR

ACT ONE

1 INT. SERVANTS' HALL. DOWNTON. DAY.

Carson is distributing a few letters.

ANNA: Nothing for me, Mr Carson?
CARSON: No, Anna. Once again, I'm afraid there's
nothing for you.

He catches Mrs Hughes's eye. They know this should not be.

1B INT. YORK PRISON. BATES'S CELL. DAY

*Letters are being handed out to the prisoners. There is
nothing for Bates.*

WARDER: Come on.

The warder drags Bates away.

2 INT. SALVATION ARMY HALL. YORK. DAY.

Isobel is with a group of her women. One sits with her.

ISOBEL: Good. You begin on Monday. And you're to come
back and tell us how you're getting on. Promise?
WOMAN: Oh, please promise!

*She shouts this from the side and the others laugh, as the
one with Isobel stands. Ethel comes in. Isobel goes to
her.* *

---

* We decided to bring back Amy Nuttall, who played Ethel in Season Two.
Originally I think I had seen her as simply the girl who was going to be
seduced and then wronged by the handsome officer. But this situation, on
review, seemed to have legs. Because it was very tough for a young woman in
those days, with an illegitimate baby. She was essentially an outcast. How
would she earn her own living? The number of things she could do was
severely limited. Besides which, Amy was very good in the part and nice to
work with, and I think everyone enjoyed having her in the show, so it gave
me the idea of another Isobel story, because we have these different strands
that need to be maintained. We have the main house, the Dower House,
Crawley House and then Doctor Clarkson is a sort of floating piece who goes
between all three according to the demands of the different plots, which I
imagine can be slightly irritating for the actor, David Robb. Obviously in

```
ISOBEL:  Don't run away this time.
ETHEL:  No, I've not come to run away again.
ISOBEL:  Good.  Now once and for all sit down and tell me
what this is about.  I already know you don't want to be
saved, so what do you want?  And why do you keep changing
your mind?
ETHEL:  I won't this time.
```

She takes out a letter.

```
ETHEL (CONT'D):  Can you deliver this to Mrs Hughes?
ISOBEL:  Why not just post it?
ETHEL:  Because I need to be sure she's received it.
Then, if there's no answer, I'll know what it means.
ISOBEL:  That all sounds very mysterious.  Oh, won't you
stay and talk for a moment, now you're here —
```

But Ethel has risen and gone. Isobel stares at the letter.
Then she looks at the others, wearily.

```
ISOBEL (CONT'D):  All right.  Mavis.  You next.*
```

....

Continued from page 194:

Season Two he was never off the screen because it all took place during the war, and he had to deal with the soldiers who came home wounded. He has been less ubiquitous since then, but on the other hand he does still have pretty strong stories, as we shall see in Episode Five, when he has a tremendous one.

* We've established Isobel as a liberal-minded, benevolent intellectual who doesn't look down on the Crawleys, exactly, because she appreciates that they have taken her in, but who does not regard herself as one of them. She sees their philosophies and the world in which they live as essentially limiting. This is a *Downton* situation, as one can see both sides. Anyway, Ethel's plight gave me an opportunity for her to have a consciously liberal story where she would be able to give a fresh chance to this woman who would probably not be touched by a barge pole if Mrs Hughes had anything to say about it. Actually, Mrs Hughes is a kind woman, but, in real life, she would have had to think of the example being set to the other maids. In those days, service was a sort of finishing school where young men and women were trained in various skills, and when the women married and left service, as many of them did, they would take those skills into their married life. For the ones who didn't marry, these skills allowed them, if they were ambitious, to become a lady's maid or a housekeeper and acquire a decent position.

3 INT. DRAWING ROOM. DOWNTON. NIGHT.

Robert has assembled the Crawley clan.

ROBERT: So there we have it. I am delighted to say that our proverbial bacon has been saved by Matthew, and that consequently he is now as much the Master of Downton as I am.
MATTHEW: Which of course is not true —
MARY: It is true, and it's wonderful.
VIOLET: And certainly a very great relief.
ISOBEL: So we are to defy the Age of Change and carry on as before.*

She says it pleasantly enough, but…

VIOLET: I hope you're not too disappointed.
ISOBEL: Not at all. It's an interesting challenge for Matthew. To wrestle Downton into the twentieth century.
CORA: Well, if we are all really sure this is what we want —
MARY: Of course we're sure.
ROBERT: Edith? You're very silent.

....

Continued from page 195:

The housekeeper was in charge of these young women and she was expected by their mothers to be strict. Today, we can still see how things were arranged, with a stout locked door between where the maids slept and where the footmen slept. In some houses the footmen even slept out in the stable yard, while the maids were at the top of the house. There was a strong imperative in all this and if a housekeeper got a local reputation for running a sloppy house where a girl could get into trouble, the girls' mothers would not let their daughters go there to work. As with any system, there were reasons why certain practices became established, and when you think of the age of these girls – many of them started service at fourteen – you don't wonder at the rules being so strict. Rather like the schools of today, where one scandal can set back the work of years.

* An underlying theme of the show is how people deal with change, and whether a particular change is here to stay, or is it a blip and things will go back to normal? So all the characters will be increasingly involved in the changes that are coming. The difference here being that Isobel is thrilled by change and she thinks that if this ghastly, unjust world can be made better then all well and good. The others mainly have mixed feelings.

EDITH: Don't mind me. When you're a maiden aunt it doesn't matter much where you live. You're always in the way.*

4   INT.   CARSON'S PANTRY.   DOWNTON.   NIGHT.

Mrs Hughes is with Carson.

MRS HUGHES: So what's it about?

....

* The world has got better for some people and worse for others. Some aspects of our society work and some don't, but one group for whom it has definitely improved is the single woman, the spinster, particularly the well-born spinster like Edith, because even in my lifetime she really was spare in almost every family. She might be useful. My mother's unmarried sister was charged with the care of their mother who lived to be ninety-nine, but she was essentially under a kind of house arrest, doing community service for the rest of her days. She might be handy for looking after the children or taking them to a museum, but the idea that she had a life that others should respect was simply not there. If such a woman was even upper middle class, never mind posher than that, most careers were closed to her, or at least she closed them to herself. There were women who did do interesting things throughout this period – writers, administrators, some journalists – but I am talking about the majority. They might get a flat in London, but a proper job, a real grown-up career, just wasn't an option for Lady Louise Someone. And so they hovered on the fringes of their family, doing good works, breeding dogs, being helpful, until death claimed them. Even at the end of the 1960s, when I was sampling the delights of debbing, a lot of girls were essentially waiting to marry. They would get jobs but they were 'waiting jobs' – arranging flowers in offices, serving executive lunches, helping at little galleries that belonged to friends of their mothers. Nobody seriously thought they would be doing these things in a few years' time. It was a question of pin money until Mr Right, or preferably Lord Right, came along. In my generation, who are now in their sixties, the women who never did manage to marry are a slightly sad bunch. The daring ones, who trained for medicine or the law or even went on the stage, are fine, married or not, but those who never found an alternative way break one's heart. Whereas the unmarried girls in the next generation, who are now in their forties, seem much less sad – in fact, not sad at all. Edith is someone who is threatened by the spinster fate, which drives her to try new frontiers, to be a writer, to meet new people, and she ends up generating a life. Her future may not be terribly satisfactory in some ways, but still she has a life, which I feel is an improvement on no life.

CARSON: Good news, I think. His lordship seemed very jovial when he asked me to gather them together.
MRS HUGHES: Does it mean the Days of Austerity might be drawing to a close?
CARSON: I don't know for certain, but I am cautiously optimistic.
MRS HUGHES: When were you ever more than that?*

5 INT. MARY'S BEDROOM. DOWNTON. DAY.

Mary is with Anna. Matthew, changed, is sitting on the bed.

MATTHEW: I've got enough on my plate, without going into every detail.
MARY: You're co-owner of this estate. You have to get into the detail.
MATTHEW: Not to challenge Robert, surely?
MARY: You won't have any reason to. But you have to pull your weight. That's all I'm saying.†

....

* Even though it was cut, this is me trying to avoid basing a scene around information the audience knows, but sometimes you have to. When this is the case, you don't dwell on the narrative details that are being given out (which the audience already knows), but on the variety of the characters' responses to it. How is Violet going to take it? Or Isobel? Or Cora?

Cora, in fact, has mixed feelings when she hears that they are going on with this way of life. As an American she's not bound by the past in the way that her husband and daughters are. I am corresponding with an American at the moment: his great-grandparents built a house at Newport; his mother died a couple of years ago; it's been empty since then and they will probably sell it. As it happens, there is no pressing need for anyone to sell anything, but they just don't feel like going on with it. Whereas, were an Englishman to make this decision, he would feel that he was the failure who had dropped the torch. The one member of a gentry or noble family whom everyone feels sorry for is the one who has to make the decision to sell. When you are the great-grandson of the one who sold, the decision no longer bothers anyone. But to be the one to make it, for the English, is a tough one.

† Up to this point, Mary, who is the strongest child, has not had a power base, but that has now changed. Her husband owns half the estate, which means that, in her mind, she herself owns half the estate. She has been the engine of change because she persuaded Matthew to put his money into Downton and, as a consequence, she has also persuaded herself that she is now in a position of authority. Matthew is more diffident. He didn't want

MATTHEW: How is Bates?

ANNA: I've not seen him for a while, sir.

MATTHEW: Oh. Why is that?

ANNA: I'm not quite sure, sir. They've stopped all his
visitors.

MATTHEW: Has he given you a reason?

ANNA: Well, he's not written. In quite some time now.

MATTHEW: And you don't know why?

ANNA: No... But I'm certain I will before too long.

She doesn't sound certain.

6   INT.   MRS HUGHES'S SITTING ROOM.   DOWNTON.
            NIGHT.

*Mrs Hughes is working when she looks up.   Isobel Crawley has
come downstairs.   Mrs Hughes stands.*

MRS HUGHES: Mrs Crawley, how may I help?

ISOBEL: I'm sorry to push in on you again, but I didn't
have time to come down before dinner... and now we're on
our way home...

....

Continued from page 198:

the money in the first place. If the cash has rescued the estate because he
couldn't finally win against Mary's arguments, then fine, but as far as he's
concerned he doesn't really want any further involvement. But as we see
here, Mary isn't going to have any of that, so now we are laying the ground
for the struggle between Mary and Robert.

* I am always quite careful to make the relationship between Isobel and Mrs
Hughes slightly different from Mrs Hughes's relationship with the family.
Isobel does not observe the great social chasm that would be second nature to
people like the Crawleys, however much they like Mrs Hughes, which they
do. You know they would be unlikely to find themselves chatting away in her
sitting room about anything. Whereas that is not quite true for Isobel. And
when Mrs Hughes comes to Crawley House, she talks to Isobel in a friendly
and relaxed way. Then again, she doesn't actually sit down, which is a point
always worth noting, because that was the great marker of social intercourse
between different ranks. As late as the 1980s, if you were talking to your cook
or your cleaner, they did not sit in your presence. That seems to have gone
now, but it's interesting that people carried on with it until so recently. Of
course, real friendships did occur, like that between Carson and Mary, and in
those cases the rules would often be bent or broken, but only in private.

Isobel shuts the door.

ISOBEL (CONT'D): Mrs Hughes, you know I went to see Ethel Parks?

MRS HUGHES: I do, ma'am.

ISOBEL: Well, she wouldn't speak to me then, but she has since sought me out and asked me to deliver this letter into your hands.

She hands over the envelope. Mrs Hughes takes it.

MRS HUGHES: When we last spoke of her, you seemed to think she'd fallen into bad ways...

ISOBEL: I'm afraid that's the case. She has been working as a prostitute.

MRS HUGHES: My, my. That's not a word you hear in this house every day.

ISOBEL: It's not a pretty word, no, but I think it also serves to show the measure of her misery. Ethel has been driven into this, of that I have no doubt. If only she would allow me to help her, but she won't. If this letter can give you any clue as to how I might be helpful, please let me know.

MRS HUGHES: I will, ma'am. Your sentiments do you credit, but I suspect she will be too ashamed to face how far she's fallen.

ISOBEL: Goodnight.

MRS HUGHES: Goodnight, Mrs Crawley.

7   INT. DINING ROOM. DOWNTON. NIGHT.

Carson is with Matthew and Robert, who are in black tie.

CARSON: So, am I to answer to you both?

MATTHEW: Of course not. What Lord Grantham means is that I have made an investment in the estate. That is all. Otherwise nothing has changed.*

....

* Carson is unsettled by the joint ownership because, like a lot of people, he wants a clear chain of command, and it is true that the moment there is any kind of dual monarchy, as we are witnessing today with the Coalition Government, there is constant conjecture. You may remember the American writers' strike a few years ago, when the Writers' Guild were trying to promote certain reforms, most of which I agreed with. But I did not support the demand for writers to have the statutory right to be on the set whenever

CARSON: Very good. And can we bring the staff back up to snuff?
ROBERT: I believe we can.
CARSON: Mrs Hughes is short of a housemaid, Mrs Patmore wants a kitchen maid and I need a new footman.
MATTHEW: Do you, really? I sometimes feel the world is rather different than it was before the war.

....

Continued from page 200:

they wanted during filming. The reason I didn't agree with this is that when a writer goes on a set there is a danger that he or she splits the chain of command and confuses it. An actor playing a scene, if the writer is sitting there, has a tendency to ask what they meant by a line or a stage direction, and naturally you, the writer, can't bear to say: 'Don't ask me, ask the director.' Instead, you babble away about whatever childhood scarring has been the basis of the scene, which may not be what the director wants by then, which is fine. It is legitimate for him to wish for something different. You have only confused things.

Robert Altman wanted me on the set of *Gosford Park* because he was keen to get the details right, and I remember once, we were out at Shepperton studios and Charles Dance asked me a perfectly valid question about his role as Lord Stockbridge. I responded *at length*, and afterwards Bob said to me, 'I can't have that. I can't have them seeing you as the authority on this set instead of me. I don't want to witness that again.' As you can imagine, at the very beginning of what had the potential to be my lucky break, the last thing I wanted was to put the director's nose out, so I took his request seriously. From then on, although I knew several members of the cast and indeed had worked with a few of them as an actor, I always kept myself separate. I used to take a book in so I could hide behind it and I would have lunch with the make-up department or with the grips, rather than sit with the cast and risk upsetting Bob. That is really the emotional area we are mining here. Carson is quite caustic with Matthew. He's sort of forgiven him for stealing Mary's inheritance because he's married Mary to put it right, but he still isn't quite what Carson wants him to be, i.e. Robert Mark II.

We also use this exchange to show that, in real life, a well-established butler enjoyed a liberty of expression, just as ladies' maids did when talking to their mistresses or valets when dressing their employers. Again, there were rules. If a lady's maid ran into her mistress in the body of the house surrounded by the guests in a house party, she wouldn't say anything. Here, because he is alone with Matthew and Robert, Carson can talk back to a certain extent. If there was a dinner going on, he would not.

CARSON: I see. I would like to return to my duties as a butler, sir. But if you prefer that I continue to do the work of a second footman in addition —
ROBERT: Mr Crawley doesn't mean that at all. Do you?
MATTHEW: Certainly not.
CARSON: Well, that is good news.
ROBERT: I suppose it's too late to get into shape before the dinner for the Archbishop of York, but it'll be the last time you have to fudge it.*
CARSON: I will do my best for the Archbishop, with an added spring in my step.

He leaves.

ROBERT: Shall we join the others?
MATTHEW: You don't disagree with me, do you? Oughtn't we to tone things down a bit, eventually?
ROBERT: We're employers, Matthew. Providers of jobs. That is the point of us. For Downton to play its proper role in the area, we must provide jobs.

8 INT. DINING ROOM. DOWNTON. DAY.

Robert, Matthew and Edith are eating breakfast.

MATTHEW: Why don't you have breakfast in bed?
EDITH: Because I'm not married.†

....

* It won't be the last time Carson has to fudge it, because what none of them are really facing is that they are no longer in the pre-war world. It is not a question of just getting back up to scratch, but of whether or not they'll be able to stay at scratch if they do manage to get back up there. The audience thinks, no, they won't. And they're right.

† We've seen before that, at Downton, in a house party all the married women would be given their breakfast upstairs, because it solved a lot of things. For a start, it meant one less outfit, so on a sporting day, if they were going out with the guns, they could change straight into their shooting clothes and skip the frock they would have had to wear for breakfast in the dining room. Over the four days of a shooting party, this would mean four fewer dresses for the maids to plan and supervise, giving everyone more time. The ladies' maids themselves did most of the work of getting the tray ready. The cook or the still-room maid (a character we don't have at Downton) might scramble the eggs, but the tray would be done by a woman's own maid, to just the way she liked it. Again, that lightened the load for everyone else.

MATTHEW: Yes, but now that —

EDITH: Now that both the others are, what difference would it make?

MATTHEW: You know what I mean.

EDITH: I prefer to be up and about.

Robert is reading a newspaper.

ROBERT: Tennessee is going to ratify the nineteenth amendment.

MATTHEW: Meaning?

ROBERT: All American women will have the vote.

EDITH: Which is more than they do here.

ROBERT: Well, they almost do.

EDITH: I don't have the vote. I'm not over thirty and I'm not a householder. It's ridiculous.*

ROBERT: You sound like Sybil.

MATTHEW: I don't think it'll be long now.

EDITH: It's already been much too long.

MATTHEW: You should write to *The Times*.

EDITH: Maybe I will.

ROBERT: Ask your mother if she needs any help with tonight's dinner. Perhaps you could do the *placement*. There's nothing so toffee-nosed as a Prince of the Church, so make sure you put him next to your grandmother. She'll know how to handle him.

She stands and leaves.

....

Continued from page 202:

So far from making work, staying upstairs actually reduced it. But, at this point, Edith is determined to rub everyone's nose in the fact that she's single and jilted.

* Here we have Tennessee about to ratify the nineteenth amendment, giving all women – in that state, at least – the vote. For British women, the right to vote crept in through the Twenties – which we've referred to before – in stages, as the qualifications to make women eligible were broadened. In America it wasn't quite the same. The laws legalising female suffrage were achieved in the different states gradually, but in most states all women were enfranchised completely when they passed the bill. They didn't start with women over thirty, who were property owners, and all the other malarkey the British went in for.

ROBERT (CONT'D): I've been thinking, Matthew. You should look through the books and meet our accountant, all that sort of thing.

MATTHEW: Robert, I know you don't want to feel you have somehow absconded with Swire's money, but this is your house and your estate, and you must run it as you always have.

ROBERT: But I think you ought to be put in the picture. Who knows? You might have some good ideas.

9   INT.   HALL.   DOWNTON.   DAY.

Cora is in the hall as Edith arrives, dressed to go out.

EDITH: I'm going into Ripon. Do you want anything?

CORA: Could you bear to find a present for the Derbys' new baby?*

Mary appears, also in a coat and hat.

CORA (CONT'D): Are you going too?

MARY: No, I'm just off to see Doctor Clarkson. You couldn't give me a lift into the village, could you?

EDITH: Of course.

They go. Cora's curiosity is piqued.

10   INT.   SERVANTS' HALL.   DAY.

The servants are having lunch. A worried-looking Anna waits a moment in the passage before entering.

CARSON: Oh, Anna, you'll be happy to hear that, as soon as we take on a new housemaid, you will be a lady's maid to Lady Mary, at last. I'm not sure about your new name. It might be confusing to call you Bates.

ANNA: Shouldn't we stay with Anna?

CARSON: I disapprove, but you may be right.

ANNA: That's nice, Mr Carson. Thank you.

MRS HUGHES: Thought you'd be more pleased.

....

* I looked them up and in this year the Derbys had just had a child, so that seemed rather fun. Alas, it was cut.

ANNA: No, I am pleased. Really, I'm... I've just got a lot on my mind. Sorry.*

CARSON: I have also advertised for a new footman.

O'BRIEN: He'll be Second Footman, won't he?

CARSON: As to that, I will make no pronouncements at this stage.

THOMAS: Try to find a man with something about him, Mr Carson. I don't like to feel the house isn't being properly represented.

ALFRED: Is that aimed at me?

THOMAS: If the cap fits, wear it.†

....

* I find it useful in this sort of show to keep a sense of ordinary life going. Sometimes with those glamorous shoulder-pad series the conversation is always about the power takeover of the company or the illegitimate child whom someone forgot giving birth to twenty-eight years ago, but nobody ever says, 'What's for lunch?' I feel it is useful to have people complaining that they've run out of stockings, because then the public thinks, I know what that's like. It connects them to the people on the screen.

The question of what Anna is going to be called when she's promoted to lady's maid is something I have exploited before. In *Gosford Park*, Maggie Smith's maid is a young woman to whom she pays a pittance. I didn't want her to be called Harrison or something similar all the way through, because she is really the tour guide for the audience. She is learning about a great house and how a shooting party is managed at the same time as they are. I knew we'd cast the wonderful Kelly McDonald to play the maid, Mary, and it seemed more sensible for her to be Scottish, so I asked a Scottish friend of mine, Mike Emslie, to give me a surname that was really difficult to pronounce, and he came up with Maceachran, which is full of glottal stops. I then had Clive Owen's character asking why Mary is still called Mary and not by her surname, which was the correct form for a lady's maid, and she explains that her employer, Lady Trentham, can't pronounce her surname, and so calls her Mary. 'I don't blame her,' says Clive, which gives us permission to call the character Mary throughout the movie. Here, we didn't want to change Anna's name, because she's fully established as a character, and so we make this special ruling because they can't have Bates and Bates. Obviously, Carson disapproves.

† Will the new recruit be below Alfred or above him? Contrary to O'Brien's argument, the decision would have been perfectly within Carson's remit. It wasn't a question of first come, first served; it was up to the butler to decide who was the more experienced.

Molesley is next to Anna.

> MOLESLEY: What's happening with Mr Bates?
> ANNA: I don't know, exactly. I've not seen him for
> quite a time now.
> MOLESLEY: Still working to get him out?
> ANNA: Don't worry. When he does get out, he won't be
> after your job.

*This last is heard by Thomas. At the other end, Carson turns
to Mrs Hughes, who is silent. He speaks softly.*

> CARSON: You're very quiet.
> MRS HUGHES: You'll never guess what. I've had a letter
> from Ethel. She wants to meet me, but she won't come
> here.
> CARSON: What for? And why not?
> MRS HUGHES: I think she'd be uncomfortable.
> CARSON: Why, particularly?
> MRS HUGHES: Never you mind. I think I'll ask Mrs
> Crawley if we can meet there. Heaven knows what Ethel
> wants of us this time.*

11   INT.   THE OLD DAY NURSERY.   DOWNTON.   DAY.

*Mary is in the room, which has been cleared, and the
remaining articles are under dust sheets. Matthew looks in.*

> MATTHEW: Cora said you were looking for me.
> MARY: Yes. I've stolen the nursery as a sitting room
> for us, and this is the paper… Unless you hate it.
> MATTHEW: Oh. Was that all?
> MARY: Why? What did you think it was?
> MATTHEW: Cora said you'd been to the doctor earlier… I
> wondered why.
> MARY: To get something for my hay fever.

Matthew nods and looks around at the room.

....

* Mrs Hughes is unwilling to give Ethel away. She has an essentially
protective feeling towards her, which obviously we are going to make use of
in the drama. This is reasonable enough, as it was part of the job of the
housekeeper – in this case, Mrs Hughes – to look after the maids in her
charge. And with Ethel, she has failed to do so.

MATTHEW: And what will we use for a day nursery, should
the need arise?
MARY: I think we can worry about that a little further
down the line.*

12 INT. DRAWING ROOM. DOWER HOUSE. DAY.

Violet is with Edith, who has brought her some scent.

VIOLET: Oh. Thank you, my dear. That's very kind. How
much do I owe you?
EDITH: A guinea.
VIOLET: A guinea? For a bottle of scent? Did he have a
mask and a gun? How are you?
EDITH: All right, I suppose.
VIOLET: Yes, I worry about you. That sort of thing is
so horrid.
EDITH: Being jilted at the altar? Yes, it is horrid.
Multiplied by about ten thousand million.
VIOLET: You must keep busy.
EDITH: What with? There's nothing to do at the house,
except when we entertain.
VIOLET: There must be something you can put your mind
to.
EDITH: Like what? Gardening?

....

* At this stage, when I was first writing it, we wanted another sitting room
operating, as I had plans to set up a sort of alternative household within
Downton itself, so that Matthew's and Mary's life together would be lived
more separately from Cora's and Robert's. My idea was, through this series,
to refer to the nursery that's been turned into a sitting room and then to go
on with that separate life in Season Four. However, as things turned out,
Dan Stevens had decided to leave the show, even though he had not yet told
us. We will get to the (perfectly acceptable) reasons for his decision, but the
fact remains we didn't know until we had started to film. And by that time
we had five scripts. It was quite difficult, because I had to decide how to get
rid of him, knowing that the first five episodes – which included one episode
dedicated entirely to Sybil's death – were already fixed, with the cast and the
directors chosen. In the slight hysteria which followed, I must have forgotten
about setting up the nursery/sitting room for the married future that would
never happen. But anyway, at this stage, I thought this room was going to
take a more prominent part than in fact would be the case.

VIOLET: Well, no. You can't be as desperate as that.*
EDITH: Then what?
VIOLET: Edith, dear. You are a woman with a brain and reasonable ability. Stop whining and find something to do.

13 INT. KITCHEN PASSAGE. DOWNTON. DAY.

Mrs Hughes comes out of her room and runs into Anna, who is tearful.

MRS HUGHES: I'm going out, Anna. I've told Mrs Patmore, and I think everything's under control for tonight, but… What's the matter?
ANNA: Nothing. Except… I haven't had a letter from Mr Bates in weeks… I worry… I worry that he's being gallant and trying to set me free… He wants me to make a new life without him.
MRS HUGHES: I doubt it very much.
ANNA: Then why would he be silent like this? And stop me visiting?
MRS HUGHES: Obviously I don't know why, but I do know there'll be a good reason.
ANNA: Do you really think so?
MRS HUGHES: I'd swear to it.

She goes, leaving Anna slightly comforted. As she walks away, she passes Thomas just as Alfred catches up with him.

ALFRED: Thomas, with this new footman coming, I wonder if I could ask —

....

* I have always had rather mixed feelings about gardening. I mean, I do have real gardeners in my life – my grandmother was a real gardener and my mother-in-law is a real gardener – but vague, notional gardening I always find rather irritating. My mother liked to be seen as a gardener but wasn't a gardener at all. She had a sort of trug that was mounted on a stick, like a shepherd's crook, which you could stick into the ground and it stayed upright. You then dead-headed roses and threw them into it. Sometimes, with people coming for lunch, she would go down to the rose garden at the bottom of the lawn, and when they arrived she'd walk up the lawn with her trug of dead-heads playing the role of Judith Bliss. It was all complete nonsense.

        THOMAS: Sorry, Alfred. I've too much on my own plate to
        chew your helping.

He walks on, leaving Alfred, but Carson has been listening.

        CARSON: Don't worry. If you've anything to ask, then
        ask me.
        ALFRED: I will, Mr Carson. Thank you.

END OF ACT ONE

ACT TWO

14   INT.   YORK PRISON.   WORKROOM.   DAY.

*Bates is sewing mail sacks with the others.   Turner oversees
them.   The prisoner, Dent, is nearby.   He whispers.* *

        DENT: They know you tricked them.
        BATES: Who knows what?
        DENT: Mr Durrant's a dealer on the outside.

....

*The whole business of playing ping pong and watching DVDs is a pretty
recent interpretation of prison life and has spawned an interesting debate. To
the liberals, either there shouldn't be any prison at all, or, if there is prison,
then its sole purpose is rehabilitation. For the rest of us, there needs also to
be punishment involved, and society's current suspicions that there is now no
element of it – that on the whole these people are leading the life of Riley – is
deeply disquieting.

Personally, I suspect this is not true and being in prison is considerably
more unpleasant than the *Daily Mail* would lead us to believe. Besides
which, rehabilitation should definitely be part of it. Nevertheless, there is
something about punishment for crime that is natural, and it is disquieting to
me when the liberals refuse to accept human nature. Like leaving children to
teach themselves to read, it is just wishful thinking. If you want a country to
accept the end of the death penalty (which I am sure is right), then people
need to feel confident that a murderer in cold blood is going to have a very
tough time of it. The more who come out after six years and then
immediately murder someone else, the more damage is done. One of the
main arguments against the death penalty used to be that there was a risk of

BATES: What's that to do with me?

DENT: He's working for your cellmate. All I know is that you punched Craig so they set you up, but you hid the stuff they'd planted and turned the tables on them. Now they're angry.

BATES: And what can they do?

DENT: I'll tell you what they can start by doing. Durrant's reported you to the Governor for violence. You're officially a dangerous prisoner.

BATES: The Governor won't fall for that.

DENT: No? So when was the last time your wife came to visit, eh? How many letters have you received lately?

Bates stares at him. To Dent's surprise, he smiles.

BATES: Thank God. What a relief. I thought she'd given up on me.

DENT: Don't thank God until you know what else they've got in store for you.

TURNER: Stop talking!

Bates, full of thought, returns to his sewing.

15 INT. CARSON'S PANTRY. DOWNTON. DAY.

Carson and Alfred stare at six small spoons.

CARSON: Go on, then.

ALFRED: Teaspoon. Egg spoon. Melon spoon. Grapefruit spoon. Jam spoon...

CARSON: Shall I tell you?

ALFRED: All right.

....

Continued from page 209:

wrongful conviction, but the trouble is, far more innocent people have died at the hands of released murderers than were ever hanged wrongly, so it doesn't really hold water. The point being that too many today do not have faith in the legal system.

I remember an argument with a judge who was pleading the horrors of the childhoods that most criminals have endured, but this, to me, was to confuse his role in society. His most important job is to make law-abiding people believe that the legal structure works, not to alienate them. Of course, he was mortally offended, but it does seem to be true, that too many of them have lost touch with their role.

CARSON: A *bouillon* spoon.

ALFRED: But I thought soup spoons were the same as tablespoons.

CARSON: Ah, so they are. But not for *bouillon*, which is drunk from a smaller dish... Off you go, now. I must get on.*

Alfred walks out past Thomas, who's been watching.

THOMAS: You're taking a lot of trouble with young Alfred, Mr Carson. I feel quite jealous.

CARSON: I don't know why. He asked for help. You never did.

16   INT.   DRAWING ROOM.   CRAWLEY HOUSE.   DAY.

Isobel is with Mrs Hughes and Ethel.

ETHEL: It's very hard to begin...

MRS HUGHES: Well, find a way, Ethel. We all have lives to lead.

....

* When I was a child, I remember an all-pervasive sense of a way of life that had only just ended and, in fact, I now know that when I was a little boy it was only just ending. There had been perfectly good butlers in the local manor house until quite a few years after the war (or longer), and one of the signs that they had been in action recently was the array of pieces of equipment that had only recently fallen into disuse. I recall asking my grandmother why all the teaspoons seemed to have different shapes and she replied, 'Because they are not all teaspoons.' Then she started to explain that this one would be used for a melon and that one would be used for a boiled egg, and I saw that the grapefruit spoon was slightly sharper to be able to dig into the fruit, and so on. It was a moment of revelation, that I had arrived just too late to experience a different civilisation from the one I was living in.

For me, this is really the moment when Carson falls for Alfred, because however much he knows the boy was wished on him by O'Brien's plotting, he admires, above all, people who are committed to the work and trying to get it done right. So from this scene on Thomas is going to lose when it comes to Alfred. Carson approves of Alfred, because he is trying to get the details right. 'I thought soup spoons were the same as tablespoons.' This is hardly true now. After the war, manufacturers came up with those little round soup spoons that you find in hotels, and on the whole that's what you are given in a restaurant today. The old giant tablespoons that most people think of as exclusively serving spoons were also once used for soup. And still are, in our house.

ETHEL: Could you write to the Bryants? To say I want them to have Charlie.

MRS HUGHES: We've already been down this path. To no avail.

ETHEL: I know. And I know I said a mother's love was worth more than all they had to give. But I said it for me, not for him.

ISOBEL: My dear, you mustn't do anything until you're absolutely sure.

ETHEL: Mrs Hughes said we all have lives to lead, but that isn't true. I've got no life. I exist, but barely.

ISOBEL: Ethel, we all know the route you've taken —

ETHEL: It's good of you to have me here.

ISOBEL: All I mean is that I work with others like you, to rebuild their lives. Can't we work together to find a way for you to keep your son?

ETHEL: With his grandparents, Charlie can build a life that is whatever he wishes it to be. With all respect, ma'am, you and I working together could never offer him that.

MRS HUGHES: You want me to write to them again.

ISOBEL: But leave it vague. Say that Ethel would like them to keep in contact with their grandson.

ETHEL: I won't change my mind.

MRS HUGHES: Nevertheless, that's what I'll do. Then there'll be no disappointment, whatever comes. Now, if you'll forgive me, we've a big dinner tonight. Good day, ma'am. Ethel.

She has gathered up her things and she leaves. *

....

* We had apparently got to the end of Ethel's story in the previous series when she refused the Bryants' offer and decided to keep the child. And during the gap between series several people were quite vehement, denouncing me for considering this to be a happy ending. 'That wretched child,' they said. 'She's snatched away all its opportunities.' The truth is, we had not yet reached the conclusion. I certainly always intended that Ethel should feel she'd done the wrong thing by trying to keep the child, and we were going to squash it into Season Two, but then the decision came to retain Amy Nuttall, so we didn't have to.

It is true that there was a fashion among social workers in the 1990s for believing that a child must always be left with the mother, however inappropriate, however incapable, which was often almost as bad for the

17 INT. HALL. CRAWLEY HOUSE. DAY.

Mrs Hughes is being seen out by Mrs Bird.

MRS BIRD: She was a housemaid at Downton, before she
went to Mrs Crawley's shelter? You do surprise me.
MRS HUGHES: Ethel has had a very hard time of it since
she left us, Mrs Bird. She's had great difficulty making
ends meet.
MRS BIRD: And we know how she solved that problem.

She is silenced as Isobel and Ethel come into the hall.

MRS BIRD (CONT'D): Give my regards to Mr Molesley.

Mrs Hughes slips away as the others walk towards the door.

ISOBEL: Till we meet again, my dear.
ETHEL: I had a coat.
MRS BIRD: It's there.
ISOBEL: You will help Miss Parks, please, Mrs Bird.

....

Continued from page 212:

wretched young women – who in many cases weren't ready to be a mother –
as it was for the baby. Still, the social workers would deliberately make them
feel terrible about wanting to have their child adopted. Then there was that
weird prejudice against allowing middle-class adoption, which several friends
of ours came up against. One couple – charming, quite well off, living a
comfortable life – wanted to adopt a child, but the social worker told them
their expectations would be too great. They protested that their expectations
would not be any different from those of any parents. Everyone wants the
best for their child, and they don't always get it. That rule applies to any
parent, duke or dustman. But the social worker would not listen, and they
weren't allowed one.

There is now a wind of change in that department and things may be
getting better, but I really felt the madness of those policies. Instead of just
affecting the mad people implementing them, they were affecting the lives of
hundreds of thousands of children, which seemed quite terrible to me.
Anyway, Ethel has come to the same conclusion. Isobel is quite ambivalent
about it, because like all do-gooders she believes in the theory more than the
practice, and in theory the child brought up by its own mother will be happier
than one brought up by horrible Mr Bryant. In practice, as Mrs Hughes is
aware immediately, the child's opportunities will be many as opposed to the
fate beckoning with Ethel, which would have been nil. But Isobel has to take
her time to get there.

Without a word, Mrs Bird ambles over, snatches down the coat and holds it out, like she might catch something from it, for Ethel. Ethel takes it and then nods and slips out.

    ISOBEL (CONT'D): Some manners wouldn't go amiss.
    MRS BIRD: I do not believe it is part of my duties to wait on the likes of her. I'm sorry, but that's what I feel.

*She retreats down to the kitchen.**

    18 INT. DRAWING ROOM. DOWNTON. NIGHT.

There is quite a grand gathering here, the men in white tie, the women in tiaras. Robert is with a prelate in purple.

    ARCHBISHOP OF YORK: I don't want to sound anti-Catholic.
    ROBERT: Why not? I am.
    ARCHBISHOP OF YORK: Not in a real way, I'm sure.
    ROBERT: I don't want thumbscrews or the rack, but there always seems something of Johnnie Foreigner about the Catholics.†

....

* In Mrs Bird's defence, a servant's reputation was their only capital. And when a servant was employed in a house with just one or two servants and no butler to keep them in check then, if anything, their character was even more important. For Isobel to expect Mrs Bird to risk contaminating her reputation by working with an ex-prostitute is not fair. And I very much want the audience to see Mrs Bird's point of view, even if she expresses it in a rather brusque way.

† This is when I start to have my anti-Catholic fun. The anti-Catholicism of the upper classes is something that was still going when I was in my teens and even twenties. By then, they didn't mind you being invited to a daughter's coming-out dance, or staying in the house, or even shooting their pheasants. But they did not want you to marry their child. They didn't want a Catholic in the family and God knows they didn't want Catholic grandchildren. As a result, there was a certain bonding among the Catholics, from the Duke of Norfolk's children down to vaguely toffish families like my own. We were probably all much more intimate than we would have been if we'd been Anglican. A lot of the boys had been to a Catholic school, which is again much less observed now. I went to Ampleforth, but my son went to Winchester, and in fact the present headmaster there is Catholic. I can tell you if someone had asked in 1968 how likely it was that Winchester would have a Catholic headmaster, it would have made fairies seem probable. It was a different world.

19 EXT. DOWNTON VILLAGE. NIGHT.

A village bobby in a cape bicycles past in the rain. A man in hat but no coat emerges from the side of the road and skulks onwards.

20 INT. TELEPHONE BOOTH. IRELAND. NIGHT.

Sybil is speaking urgently into the mouthpiece.

SYBIL: I've no time to talk, but tell them I'm all right. I'm out of the flat. They haven't stopped me —

She breaks off as she sees a man in the street.

20A INT. HALL. DOWNTON. NIGHT

Edith speaks into the receiver.

EDITH: Who hasn't stopped you? Sybil, hello?

21 INT. TELEPHONE BOOTH. IRELAND. NIGHT.

Sybil replaces the receiver and slips out into the night.

22 INT. HALL. DOWNTON. NIGHT.

Edith replaces the receiver.

23 EXT. DOWNTON. NIGHT.

The man we saw earlier is running through the grounds, in the rain.

....

Continued from page 214:

For most of them, it wasn't a question of savage persecution, it was a sort of mistrust. It came from the idea that you were more loyal to a slimy old geezer in Rome than you were to the Queen and your values couldn't be trusted, because you might have a sort of foreign bias. The vague sense of your being a fifth columnist was what put them off. A man like Robert would go six months without giving the Catholics a thought, but when he does he has to reveal his prejudice. 'I don't want thumbscrews or the rack, but there always seems to be a touch of Johnnie Foreigner about the Catholics.' That was completely true of his type.

23A INT. DRAWING ROOM. DOWNTON. NIGHT

Edith comes in, looking flustered. Mary walks over.

MARY: What's the matter?

EDITH: I've just had the most peculiar conversation with Sybil.

Cora has joined them.

CORA: Oh, Lord. Is the baby coming? It's not due for weeks.

EDITH: No, it wasn't like that. She kept on about being 'out of the flat' and nobody had 'stopped her' and — and would we tell someone something.

CORA: What do you mean, 'no one had stopped her'? Stopped her from doing what?

EDITH: That's just it. I don't know. She suddenly put down the telephone.

Carson has entered.

CARSON: Dinner is served, m'lady.

24 INT. KITCHENS. DOWNTON. NIGHT.

Mrs Patmore is working with Daisy on a tray of savouries.

MRS PATMORE: What time are you going Wednesday?

DAISY: I'll get away early, if you can manage.

MRS PATMORE: We'll have to.

DAISY: How is it Mr Carson can have a new footman and Mrs Hughes a new maid, but we can't have a kitchen maid?

MRS PATMORE: Don't worry. I'm working on it. I've put a card up in the shop and asked the schoolmaster.

She bustles away. Alfred is in the doorway.

ALFRED: Glad to see you speak up for your rights.

DAISY: Are you, Alfred? Because, if you are, I'd really like to say —

MRS PATMORE: Alfred, aren't they ever going to get their savoury? Is this some form of rebellion by starvation?*

....

* I never have to invent any reason for a servant character to arrive or leave if Mrs Patmore is in the scene, because she can always send one of the characters upstairs with the food. So she is a built-in dramatic mechanism.

Alfred takes the tray and leaves. Daisy watches him go.

25 INT. DINING ROOM. DOWNTON. NIGHT.

The family and the Archbishop are at dinner. Carson starts to take round the savoury. Alfred follows with the sauce.

> VIOLET: Tell me, Doctor Lang, do you find that the war has driven the people back into the churches or further away than ever?*
>
> ARCHBISHOP OF YORK: Well, as usual, our enemies have been busy. You know there was no truth to the rumour of the chaplains' cowardice?
>
> VIOLET: To the English, all prelates must be concealing their sin.

They are interrupted by a loud banging on the front door. The company chatter subsides. There is more banging.

> ARCHBISHOP OF YORK: Behold, I stand at the door, and knock.

....

* Fifteen years later, Dr Cosmo Lang, by then Archbishop of Canterbury, would make trouble for the Prince of Wales over Mrs Simpson. The son of a Scottish Presbyterian minister, he was made Archbishop of York in 1908 and he would be raised to the See of Canterbury in 1928. Like many of the English, I have rather mixed feelings about the abdication. King George VI was considerably more suited in every way for the role of a constitutional monarch than his older brother. So, like a lot of us, I never know whether to bless or to curse Mrs Simpson. Lang did represent the absolute intolerance that King Edward was up against, and I have a vague sympathy, but I believe privilege must be paid for.

It suits, I would still say, a majority of the British to have a hereditary monarchy, but the other side of it is that we feel we have a right to expect a certain level of personal sacrifice, a degree of unselfishness and concern for the common good, that King George and our present Queen have both consistently displayed, but it is doubtful that King Edward was capable of such things. Obviously, since the dawn of time, some members of the family have cut loose, but happily, at least since Queen Victoria, the monarch has always been able to put the country first. The only one who was going to be the exception to that rule was Edward VIII. So, on the one hand, I see Lang as intolerant, but on the other, I see the new King as personally unsuited to the task. In our present sovereign, we have been given someone who seems to have grasped the true nature of the role from a very early age. Marvellous, really.

MATTHEW: Someone sounds very angry.
CORA: Or very wet.
MARY: Or both.

*Robert looks at Carson, who nods at Alfred.**

26   INT./EXT.   FRONT DOOR.   DOWNTON.   NIGHT.

Alfred opens the door to find Branson standing there, in the rain, dripping. Alfred looks beyond him.

ALFRED: Do you have any luggage, sir?
BRANSON: I barely have the clothes I stand in. Where are they?†

Mary comes into the hall. She is immediately troubled.

ALFRED: They're in the —
MARY: Tom. What's happened? Where's Sybil?
BRANSON: She's fine. I had to get away, and leave her to follow, but I'd made all the arrangements, in case. She'll be on her way by now.
MARY: But why are you here? And why must she follow you alone?
BRANSON: I can explain.
MARY: There's a dinner going on, but I'll go and tell them that you're here.
BRANSON: No, don't. No one must know. I'll tell you it all when they've gone.

Now Matthew has come out of the dining room.

MATTHEW: What's the matter? Tom?
MARY: Go upstairs and find some dry clothes of Matthew's. I'll come for you when the coast is clear.

Branson nods and goes up the stairs. Mary turns to Alfred.

....

* I was a little bit torn here, because when you are in the dining room at Highclere it is pretty difficult to hear what's going on at the front door. There's the whole width of the hall and pretty thick walls. But I felt we would get away with it, because the front door is next to the dining-room windows when you are facing the front of the house.

† In my experience, there is an instinct in some people to normalise a situation, and in others to dramatise. Almost everyone you know falls into one category or the other. I am one of those, like Alfred, who would ask after the luggage.

MARY (CONT'D): Would you please ask Mrs Hughes to sort some food out for him?
ALFRED: Yes, m'lady.

27   INT.   DINING ROOM.   DOWNTON.   NIGHT.

Mary and Matthew come in.   The whole table is looking at them.

MARY: An idiotic man delivering a village pamphlet.   Can you imagine?   In this weather and at this time of night?

She laughs pleasantly and they laugh with her.   She whispers quickly to her father.

MARY (CONT'D): It's Branson.   He wouldn't come in.
ROBERT: Why not?   Is Sybil with him?   What's going on?
MARY: She's not here, but apparently she's coming soon. He'll explain what's happened when our guest has gone.

Violet has overheard.

VIOLET: Something to look forward to.
ROBERT: Other men have normal families, with sons-in-law who farm or preach or serve their country in the Army.
VIOLET: Maybe they do, but no family is ever what it seems from the outside.
ARCHBISHOP OF YORK: And does not every family conspire to conceal its own truths?

He has heard more than they realised.

28   INT.   SERVANTS' HALL.   NIGHT.

Alfred is regaling the others.   Daisy holds a laden tray.

DAISY: Do you think he's on the run from the police?
ANNA: Don't be so daft.
THOMAS: Well, he hadn't got the money for a taxicab from the station.
MRS HUGHES: Maybe he fancied the walk.
O'BRIEN: Yes, that's it.   I should think he loves a night walk in the pouring rain without a coat.
DAISY: What room is he in?

Carson enters, speaking as he does so.

CARSON: I'll take that, thank you, Daisy.

He removes the tray from her and leaves.

    THOMAS: So there'll be no more gossip on that subject tonight.

He picks up a paper. The others return to their activities.

    29 INT. LIBRARY. DOWNTON. NIGHT.

They have all gathered round Branson, who is bathed and wearing some of Matthew's clothes.

    BRANSON: They turned everyone out of the castle, Lord and Lady Drumgoole, their sons and all the servants, and then they set fire to it.*

....

* 'The Troubles' in Ireland were raging by this point, and the burning of the country houses was frequent and ruthless and cruel. I don't believe it was especially bloodthirsty. I cannot say that no one ever lost their life, but the normal practice was to give people ten minutes to get out. That said, it was certainly very hard. There's a story of one man who managed to save a few things – a portrait of his mother, some furniture – and the following day they caught up with him on the road and burned the cart. In those moments the rebels were pitiless. But they were fighting for their very existence. The English establishment had to be made to understand that the days of the Ascendancy were numbered. Although in my opinion the system was due for change by this time, I am not sure that the burnings were necessary, because the political will was no longer there to keep Ireland enchained. But it was a very difficult time there, and it seemed to me we needed one instance where the audience was made aware of what was going on.

Branson's involvement in the riot I have always left slightly nebulous. What I find truthful is that seeing the family watching their home burning affected him much more than he expected. Possibly because he's now a member of such a family, whether he likes it or not. And in this sort of struggle, the one thing you must avoid is letting your enemy become a normal person in your mind, with normal feelings. War propaganda is designed specifically to stop this happening. That was the reason (wasted on some playwrights) why Queen Elizabeth would never meet Mary Queen of Scots, which Mary wanted. Elizabeth knew that the moment she met her first cousin, her nearest surviving relation on her father's side, it would be far harder for her to deal with her as a political pawn in the great game.

This is what has happened to Branson, even if he is only dimly aware of it. The landowning aristocracy have become real people to him, as opposed to heartless tyrants. Later, he starts a romance with a woman who is close to

EDITH: What a tragedy.

VIOLET: Well… Yes and no. That house was hideous. But of course that is no excuse.

ROBERT: No. It is not.

MATTHEW: But what was your involvement?

BRANSON: Who says I was involved?

MARY: Well, you seem to know a lot about it if you weren't.

CORA: And why are you running away? And what was Sybil's part in all this?

BRANSON: She's not involved, not at all, but they think I was part of it. They think I was one of the instigators.

MARY: So the police are looking for you?

BRANSON: That's why I couldn't go home. I knew if they took me I wouldn't get a fair hearing.

CORA: You mean you gave them Sybil while you saved yourself?

BRANSON: I don't think they'll hold her, but if they do, then I'm prepared to go back and face the consequences.

ROBERT: You'd damn well better be!

Cora turns to Robert.

CORA: You must see the Home Secretary.

ROBERT: And tell him what? The police say he was there. He says he wasn't —

BRANSON: I didn't say I wasn't there.

Naturally, this causes something of a sensation.

ROBERT: Why were you? For the fun of seeing private property destroyed?

BRANSON: Those places are different for me. I don't look at them and see charm and gracious living. I see something horrible.

VIOLET: With Drumgoole Castle I rather agree.

ROBERT: Mama, you are not helping.

....

Continued from page 220:

him politically, but she has not made that leap. The upper classes are still generic types to her, machines without feelings, and in the end he breaks up with her because he can't go there. That is what has begun to happen here.

BRANSON: But when I saw them turned out, standing there with their children, all of them in tears watching their home burn… I was sorry. I admit it. I don't want their type to govern Ireland; I want a free state. But I was sorry.

EDITH: Never mind that. What's happened to Sybil?

BRANSON: We agreed that I should leave at once and that she'd close the flat and follow, but I got the last boat so she won't be here before tomorrow.

ROBERT: Good God Almighty! You abandon a pregnant woman, in a land that's not her own! You leave her to shift for herself while you run for it!*

CORA: You have to go to London, Robert. For Sybil's sake if not for his, you have to see Mr Shortt!†

....

* Up to this point, Robert has been trying to get used to the idea that his chauffeur is his son-in-law. He's not keen, which I think is fair enough. I did have some letters from America asking why he would mind, but come on! And he is trying to be just. The problem is when you subconsciously resent someone, and when they then give you a legitimate excuse to resent them they release all your frustrations and irritations. For Branson to abandon his pregnant wife in Dublin while he escapes is, for Robert, to break a basic moral law, which allows him to vent his fury.

Mary's position is different. She thought Sybil was mad to marry the chauffeur, but it's happened, there's no point in going over old ground. Now Branson is her brother-in-law and he's soaking wet, so the first thing to do is to get him into dry clothes and give him some food. She goes in and lies quite easily. As she says in a later episode, 'I don't mind lying.'

I think one of the great reveals of marriage is that until you marry you think you come from one of the most dysfunctional families in the land, but when you marry you see that your wife's family is just as dysfunctional as your own. And as you get older you realise that pretty well all families have dysfunctional elements – grandchildren who have gone off the rails, hippies and drunks and God knows what tucked in the shadows. We've got a sign at home that someone gave us: 'Remember, as far as anyone knows, we are a normal family.'

† Edward Shortt was Home Secretary in Lloyd George's Cabinet. We now get into one of the basic elements of this world, which, in a junior way, I have lived by all my life – string pulling. It started early. My father failed to register my birth when I was born in Cairo and this meant I was an Egyptian national. I was eleven when my father was posted to Nigeria and they tried to get me a British passport so I could join them out there for the school holidays. It was blocked. I remember being with my mother when he

ROBERT: I don't 'have' to do anything!

BRANSON: I never meant —

ROBERT: *Go to bed!* I'll give you my answer in the morning.

29A INT. BRANSON'S BEDROOM. DOWNTON. NIGHT

Branson breaks down in tears as he starts to undress, and he sits on the bed, inconsolable.

30 INT. SERVANTS' HALL/MRS HUGHES'S ROOM. DOWNTON. NIGHT.

There is gossip in the servants' hall.

O'BRIEN: The chauffeur-terrorist. It sounds like an oxymoron.

THOMAS: Sounds like a moron, you mean.

ANNA: I suppose people have to fight for what they believe in.

MOLESLEY: Of course, she married beneath her.

MRS PATMORE: And who are you then, a Hapsburg archduke?

O'BRIEN: You can laugh. What if he has to go to prison? What then?

CARSON: That's quite enough of that, thank you, Miss O'Brien. Bedtime, I think.

He says this as an order, rather than an observation, and walks off down the passage to Mrs Hughes's room.

CARSON (CONT'D): I'm going up.

MRS HUGHES: Goodnight.

CARSON: I'll try to keep them quiet, but, to be honest, I knew it would happen. I knew he would bring shame on

Continued from page 222:

returned. 'Well?' she said. 'I'll tell you what I have done,' he smiled. 'I've bought the boy a fez.' And he took one out from behind his back and put it on his head. I've still got it. Of course, she was furious. In the end they could only solve it by pulling a string; they rang some friend, some cousin, some nephew in the Home Office, and suddenly I had a British passport.

The trouble is that it's easy to lose touch with the frustration of having no strings to pull. Cora knows that when the Home Secretary hears that the Earl of Grantham has asked for an appointment, he will get one. Whether he would now is another thing, but in 1920 he certainly would get one.

this house. It sounds as if he's on the run from the
police and, for all we know, Lady Sybil is languishing in
a dungeon somewhere in Dublin.
MRS HUGHES: I don't think they have dungeons any more,
Mr Carson. Let's wait and see what the morning brings.

She lifts a gleaming machine out of the box. He starts.

CARSON: What in God's name is it?
MRS HUGHES: An electric toaster. I've given it to
myself as a treat. If it's any good, I'm going to
suggest getting one for the upstairs breakfasts.*
CARSON: Is it not enough that we're sheltering a
dangerous revolutionary, Mrs Hughes? Could you not have
spared me *that*?

He gives her a reproachful look and goes.

END OF ACT TWO

ACT THREE

31 INT. SERVANTS' HALL. DOWNTON. DAY.

*We follow a young man down the passage and into the hall
where Daisy and the maids are clearing breakfast away. When
he walks in, they turn to find themselves looking at the most
gorgeous young man any of them have ever seen. They just
stare.*

JIMMY: Hello?

....

* The toaster was to remind people that the Departure of the Servant was
paralleled inevitably and logically with the Arrival of the Gadget. The more
there weren't other people to undertake these tasks, the more electrical irons
and Hoovers and toasters and the like took over. Sometimes it went too far.
There was a great attempt in the 1960s to have drip-dry shirts that did not
need ironing, but they were frightful, which the manufacturers soon realised.
'The shirt you don't iron' had to be abandoned and we returned to labour-
intensive cotton, because they could not get a drip-dry shirt to feel anything
but horrible.

They continue to stare, until...

    ANNA: Can we help you?
    JIMMY: I'm here to see Mr Carson?
    ANNA: What's your name?

Before he can answer, Thomas comes in.

    THOMAS: Who's this?
    JIMMY: Jimmy Kent, at your service.
    THOMAS: I'm Mr Barrow. His lordship's valet.
    JIMMY: And I'm hoping to be his lordship's footman.
    Which is why I'm looking for Mr Carson.
    MRS HUGHES: What's the matter? Have you all been turned
    into pillars of salt?

She has spoken as she approached. Now she sees the newcomer.

    MRS HUGHES (CONT'D): May I help?
    JIMMY: I've come for the interview.
    MRS HUGHES: I see. Well, if you'll wait there.

She can't help giving a look to the staring girls.*

....

* And now we have the very handsome Jimmy, played by Ed Speleers. When I was acting I played a part in a television series about two sisters. One had nothing unusual about her, and the other was a raving beauty. Essentially the story was about how the raving beauty was destroyed by her looks because she was taken by them into all sorts of areas and relationships that didn't work for her, whereas the dull one didn't have a fabulous life, but she had a perfectly livable, satisfactory one. When we got to the read-through, the raving beauty turned out to be played by a completely ordinary-looking woman – quite a good actress, but ordinary. I said to the director that I didn't understand his choice. 'Isn't she meant to be a raving beauty?' He said, 'Oh, I see. You mean we should have gone for outer beauty?' To which I replied that this was the whole point of the story – the destructiveness of outer beauty. But he couldn't see it, so of course it didn't work.

There was a real prejudice then against good-looking actors – not in America, but in England. Even in this case, with Jimmy, I remember some slight resistance when I said that his being good-looking was key. But I thought, no, the whole point of this character is that he is really handsome, and that is what is going to make the trouble with Thomas. Eventually, Jill Trevellick, our wonderful casting director, came up with Ed Speleers, who was clearly gorgeous and exactly what I was hoping for. And he was very good. Anyway, he's here as a heartbreaker.

32 INT. MARY'S BEDROOM. DOWNTON. DAY.

Mary and Matthew are in bed together.

MATTHEW: What will your father do?

MARY: He'll shout a lot, and then he'll do his best to save Tom.

MATTHEW: Even though he doesn't agree with anything Tom says?

MARY: Tom's family.

MATTHEW: You know Robert wants to introduce me to all the secrets of Downton?

MARY: Yes.

MATTHEW: What if I find things *I* don't agree with?

MARY: You won't. You know Papa. He's as straight as ruled line.*

33 INT. LIBRARY. DOWNTON. DAY.

The family watches as Robert blazes away at Branson.

ROBERT: I want to make it quite clear that whatever I do, I am doing it for Sybil, and not for you! I find your actions despicable, whatever your beliefs. You speak of Ireland's suffering and I do not contradict you. But Ireland cannot prosper until this savagery is put away.

....

Continued from page 225:

I think we sometimes forget that, these days, the camera constantly exposes the national audience to immensely good-looking people. Before television and films, you didn't see raving beauties very often, and when you did it was incredible. You have stories of people standing on chairs to watch people like the Countess of Dudley or Lillie Langtry, who had acquired their fame through their beauty, which to us seems strange, but when you remember this was the world before the silver screen it becomes more understandable.

* Mary understands her father and here we go on with the business of Matthew's investigating Downton's management. You keep these story lines alive with the odd reference all the way through, because really what you are saying to the public is: I am not dealing with this storyline here, you will get it shortly, but I am just reminding you about it so that when you do get a scene that takes the narrative further you haven't forgotten what's going on.

MARY: That's all very well, Papa, but you must keep Tom out of prison!

ROBERT: I'll go to London today. I'll telephone Murray and ask him to arrange an interview. I won't come home until I've seen Shortt.

CORA: Thank you. I know it's right.

ROBERT: It's right for him.

He nods dismissively at Branson.

CORA: And for Sybil, and for this family.

ROBERT: I suppose so... By the way, Matthew, I've had the books brought in for you to see. You can look at them while I'm gone.

MATTHEW: I've said before: I really don't —

ROBERT: No, you should, you should... Let me know if Sybil gets in touch.

BRANSON: She won't. She won't want to give them anything to trace her by.

ROBERT: What a harsh world you live in.

BRANSON: We all live in a harsh world. But at least I know I do.*

....

* When Branson says, 'We all live in a harsh world, but at least I know I do,' it seems to me a truthful observation. I am reminded of a story told to me by a friend, an actress, very glamorous, and also very rich because her father was very rich. She was driving home around Trafalgar Square after a show and went through a red light. The police stopped her and pulled her over, and they were perfectly justified, but because she hadn't taken off her stage make-up, and was driving a white Lamborghini, and because she was young and blonde, they decided she was a tart. And she said she suddenly saw the treatment you get when the police think you're nothing. She had always been treated as the daughter of a multi-millionaire and everyone was always very charming. But on this particular evening they emptied her handbag onto the road – just tipped it out onto the tarmac – and pushed her back against the vehicle. She said how, in those moments, you suddenly realise we are all living on a sort of pie crust, and underneath it is volcanic lava. I have never forgotten the image, and how every now and then you glimpse what life could be like if you weren't permanently wrapped in cotton wool. I hope never to lose that awareness, but never to lose the cotton-wool wrapping either, if possible.

34   INT.   CARSON'S PANTRY.   DOWNTON.   DAY.

A young man is just leaving as Mrs Hughes enters.

MRS HUGHES: Any good?

CARSON: Not a lot of fire in his belly.

MRS HUGHES: The next one may start a good too many fires
in everyone else's belly.

She goes into the corridor.

MRS HUGHES (CONT'D): Would you like to come this way?

Jimmy enters. Mrs Hughes goes. Carson nods him to a seat.

CARSON: Now, Mr…

JIMMY: Kent.

CARSON: Kent. Exactly. I have your letter here. I see
you've been working for the Dowager Lady Anstruther…?

JIMMY: Yes. But she's closed up the house and gone to
live in France. She begged me to go with her, but I
didn't fancy it. I didn't think I'd like the food.

CARSON: I see. She 'begged' you, did she?

JIMMY: You know what women can be like.

CARSON: Not, I suspect, as well as you do.*

34A   EXT.   CRAWLEY HOUSE.   DAY

Ethel approaches the house with her son.

ETHEL: Come here, Charlie. Let's put your hat on. Make
you look nice and smart. Be a good boy for Mummy, yeah?

*She licks her finger and wipes his face with it, and then
gives him a kiss.*

ETHEL (CONT'D): Come on.

....

* When Jimmy tells how Lady Anstruther begged him to go with her to
France, we now lay a plot that we don't reap until the fifth series. Carson is
interested. 'She "begged" you, did she?' Even he, loyal as he is to the upper
echelons, picks up the hint of an inappropriate interest in Jimmy by Lady
Anstruther, which we don't develop here, but we do eventually.

35 INT. HALL. CRAWLEY HOUSE. DAY.

Ethel walks in with Charlie. Mrs Bird has opened the door.

ISOBEL: There you are, my dear. Come into the drawing room. Mrs Hughes is already here.

Ethel takes the child past her and into the room.

ISOBEL (CONT'D): When Mr and Mrs Bryant arrive, please show them straight in.

MRS BIRD: Very good, ma'am.

ISOBEL: Mrs Bird?

MRS BIRD: How often is she going to be here?

She speaks softly, nodding towards the drawing room.

ISOBEL: Where is your charity, Mrs Bird? Remember, we must hate the sin but love the sinner.

MRS BIRD: I can forgive sinners, Mrs Crawley, but I don't see why we have to have 'em in the drawing room.

36 EXT. MASON'S FARM. DAY.

Mason and Daisy are in the farmyard. He is feeding the pigs.

MASON: People say they'll eat anything, but it's not true. You must be careful what you give 'em if you want good bacon.

Daisy winces slightly.

MASON (CONT'D): Nay, don't shy away, Daisy. We raise our animals to eat, or for their milk or for their leather.

DAISY: I could never be a farmer.

MASON: Don't say that. I'd like to think you value what I do.

DAISY: So I do. I value and admire it…

MASON: Well, then. That's all I ask.

DAISY: Can I ask you something?

MASON: Of course you can.

DAISY: This will be hard for you, but what would you say if I'd met a man I liked? Because the last thing I'd ever do would be to hurt you.

MASON: What? Did you think I'd want you to be left alone your whole life long?

DAISY: No, but…

MASON: William wouldn't want it, neither. So, tell me. Has he spoken up?

DAISY: Not exactly, but he's very nice. Would it be wrong, d'you think, if I were to show I'd like it if he did?

MASON: This is too modern for me, Daisy. I'd only say this: you have a pure heart, and if he's a proper man, he'll know that. But take your time, prepare what you'll say, make sure your words cannot be misconstrued.*

37 INT. DRAWING ROOM. CRAWLEY HOUSE. DAY.

The Bryants are there, and Mrs Hughes, Isobel and Ethel.

MRS BRYANT: Thank you for letting us come.

BRYANT: And why have we come? To hear more guff about a mother's love?

ISOBEL: Mr Bryant, that's not fair!

BRYANT: Isn't it? We know what you are now, Ethel. We know how far you've fallen. I didn't want to let Mrs Bryant in the same room as you, but she insisted.

MRS BRYANT: What Mr Bryant means is —

ETHEL: How could you know about me?

BRYANT: Do you think it's so difficult to find out about a woman like you? Hah. I could give you a list of your clients.

ETHEL: You mean you've had me followed?

BRYANT: What? Didn't you think we'd keep a check on our grandson?

MRS BRYANT: We're not judging you —

BRYANT: I'm judging her! I judge her and I find her wanting!

....

* I was sorry to lose this. Mason is used as Daisy's *deus ex machina* while we wait for her to turn into the kind of person who can benefit from what Mason intends to give her. That is her character arc. This theme is taken up very strongly in Season Five, where she starts to educate herself. It is also useful for her to have someone else she can be honest with, so she isn't only confiding in Mrs Patmore. Here, Mason gives her permission to have a life beyond William, which, in real life, is always an important development when you are friendly with your in-laws and your spouse is dead.

MRS BRYANT: Ethel, we've decided to offer you some money. To make things easier, so that you won't have to…
BRYANT: Unless you don't want to give it up!

Isobel decides to ignore this last sally.

ISOBEL: Well. That is very generous, isn't it, Ethel? It throws a different light on things.

There is a noise in the hall. Isobel looks at Ethel.

ISOBEL (CONT'D): Oh, there's Mrs Bird with the tea. Would you like to help me, Ethel?

She opens the door and, after a second, Ethel follows. Mr Bryant has brought a teddy bear out of his coat.

BRYANT: Here, Charlie, look what I've got for you.
CHARLIE: A teddy.

He offers it to Charlie, who takes it eagerly.

BRYANT: That's right.

Bryant hugs the boy.

38 INT. HALL. CRAWLEY HOUSE. DAY.

Isobel shuts the door. Mrs Bird is there with a full tray.

MRS BIRD: Should I not take it in then?
ETHEL: I can do that.
MRS BIRD: I'm sure I don't need your help.
ISOBEL: Thank you, Mrs Bird.

The disgruntled woman puts down the tray and goes back to the kitchen.

ISOBEL (CONT'D): Ethel, you don't have to do this. You have a choice.
ETHEL: You mean I should take money from that man? It won't be much. Enough to keep us from starving, but not much more.
ISOBEL: But even if Charlie doesn't go to a famous school or university, what does it matter, if you're there to give him love?
ETHEL: Yet I suppose Mr Crawley went to a famous school and university?

ISOBEL: But Matthew was destined for a different kind of life. He needed a different training, don't you see?*
ETHEL: I see. Thank you, Mrs Crawley.

39 INT. YORK PRISON. CANTEEN. DAY.

The prisoners are eating. Bates whispers to Dent. Then…

DENT: When do you want it to happen?
BATES: Tomorrow night.
DENT: But not Mr Durrant?

He glances at the corrupt officer supervising them.

BATES: No. Any other warder but him. Tell Turner about it. He's straight. But don't tell him till the afternoon.

He hesitates.

BATES (CONT'D): Why are you doing this? Why are you helping me?
DENT: I can't stand Craig.

40 INT. DRAWING ROOM. CRAWLEY HOUSE. DAY.

Ethel comes in, carrying the tray. She puts it down. As Isobel follows, Ethel starts to pour tea into the cups.

MRS BRYANT: You do that very neatly, my dear.
ETHEL: I was trained by Mrs Hughes.
MRS HUGHES: She was a good worker. Even though things haven't gone so well lately.

....

* I was rather sad here, because Penelope Wilton objected to this dialogue and didn't quite say it as it's written. Isobel was supposed to remark that Matthew was destined for a different kind of life, by which I wanted to make it clear that even liberal, forgiving, understanding people can at times accept the status quo unconsciously, in a way that is not cruel exactly but unthinking. Ethel wants to say that if she gives Charlie to the Bryants then he'll be destined for a different kind of life as well. We ended up with a slightly sentimental version of the moment, because we don't challenge the fact that even Isobel assumes that Matthew will have a better life than Charlie, because that's what is ordained. It is the moment when Ethel finally makes up her mind that this time she is going to go through with it, and it sort of works but, for me, not quite as well as it could have.

MRS BRYANT: I hope that you can accept our offer, Ethel, and that we can be friends. Because we both wish you well, don't we, dear? We wish Ethel well.

BRYANT: I don't wish you ill. I'll say that.*

Ethel has been handing round the cups…

ETHEL: I can't accept your offer. And we won't be friends.

MRS BRYANT: What? Not even for Charlie's sake?

Ethel watches Charlie, happy on the lap of Mr Bryant.

ETHEL: I think you love my son, Mr Bryant. I don't think you're a nice man, or a kind one, but I believe you love my boy… So you'll be pleased by what I've come here to say.†

Isobel is anguished, but Mrs Hughes thinks Ethel is right.

41 INT. LIBRARY. DOWNTON. DAY.

Matthew is at the desk. Near him a table is stacked with ledgers of various sizes. Mary comes in.

MARY: Any news while I was out?

MATTHEW: No. Perhaps the Home Secretary won't see him.

She goes to the fire and rings the bell.

MARY: Papa'll pull some strings until he does.

Mary glances at the vast ledgers open on the table.

....

* Kevin R. McNally, who plays Mr Bryant, is married to Phyllis Logan, who plays Mrs Hughes, so there was a certain hilarity off camera when we were filming these scenes. It was fun for them to be back together. He's in all the *Pirates of the Caribbean* films, so they have had to put up with long stretches when he has to go off and do them.

† This is a typical *Downton* moment, in that I don't go on with the scene to the point where Ethel tells them she is going to give them the child, because the audience already knows what she intends. We can imagine the dialogue – 'Oh, are you sure? Oh, that's wonderful' – which, for me, risks a kind of inertia, however emotional a scene may be. If you can't think of a way to repeat the information in an unexpected way, then on the whole it's better not to repeat it at all. That's my philosophy.

MARY (CONT'D): Ah ha. You've started on the Augean task. How are you getting on?

MATTHEW: Not badly. I'm beginning to get a sense of how it all works.

MARY: In a way, it's probably best you tackle it by yourself.

Carson comes in.

MARY (CONT'D): Ah, Carson. May we please have some tea?

CARSON: Of course, m'lady.

MARY: Anna said you were interviewing footmen today.

CARSON: That is correct.

MARY: Have you chosen the lucky winner?

CARSON: Not yet. There were two candidates when it came down to it. One was steady, but not much else, but the ladies downstairs want the other one.

MATTHEW: Why is that?

CARSON: I don't know precisely. Unless it's because he's more handsome.

MARY: Of course it's because he's more handsome. Oh, do pick him, Carson, and cheer us all up a bit. Alfred's nice, but he does look like a puppy who's been rescued from a puddle.

CARSON: Well, this new one seems very sure of himself.

MATTHEW: You can manage that, can't you?

CARSON: I suppose I could, sir.

MARY: Well, it's settled then. Tell the maids they can buy their Valentines.

CARSON: So be it, m'lady. But Alfred is very good, you know. He's very willing. Even if he is Miss O'Brien's nephew.

He goes out and the other two burst out laughing.

MATTHEW: Clearly nothing worse could be said of any man.*

....

* Footmen were status symbols, as we've said before, and in the nineteenth century were paid according to their height. Handsome could also command a pretty good salary, but, as characters in a household, they were fraught with dangers. In the royal family of Mecklenburg-Schwerin in Germany, there was a custom that all the princesses were lit to their bedrooms individually by footmen. Quite inevitably, Princes Marie had to announce that she was

42 EXT. CRAWLEY HOUSE. DAY.

Mr and Mrs Bryant, Charlie, Ethel, Mrs Hughes and Isobel come out, the Bryants, Mrs Hughes and Ethel in their overcoats. *

MRS BRYANT: You'll want to say goodbye.

Ethel kneels and kisses her son for the last time.

ETHEL: I give you my blessings for your whole life long, my darling boy.
CHARLIE: Yes.
ETHEL: You won't remember that or me, but they'll stay with you all the same.
BRYANT: Let's not make a meal of it.
MRS BRYANT: You go on, dear, and settle him in.

Ethel stands and moves back. Bryant takes the boy and goes down to where the car waits. Mrs Bryant turns to Ethel.

MRS BRYANT: I'll write to you. Make sure Mrs Hughes always has your address.
ETHEL: But won't he —?

....

Continued from page 234:

pregnant by said footman and the only person who took pity on her was Queen Victoria. The Queen denounced the custom as absurd. What did they think was going to happen? And in fact, she arranged a marriage for the girl – not a royal marriage, but a respectable one – so Princess Marie did actually have a perfectly acceptable life. Victoria even invited her to stay at Osborne, so she 'lent her face', as they would have said then. I find this an interesting slant on Victoria, who was realistic enough to see it wasn't only the girl's fault.

* We had actually shot an earlier version of this scene in the Christmas Special at the end of Season Two, but we could not do anything with the child, who was having a horrible time, as he made quite clear. This kind of thing is always depressing for actors when they prepare their arc and perform it, only to be rung up by the director who says, 'I'm afraid we've cut the battle. We'll remount it if we can.' Inevitably you don't believe it, but in this instance we did remount it, and Jill Trevellick found a wonderful little boy who was a natural actor, which most children are not. So we were rewarded for giving it a second chance. For Amy Nuttall, Phyllis Logan and Penelope Wilton, it was a really moving moment. And for me.

MRS BRYANT: A little judicious disobedience is a key part of marriage, as I hope you find out, my dear.
ETHEL: He won't let me see him, though, will he? I'll never see my son again.
MRS BRYANT: Never is a long time, Ethel. But you were right. He does love Charlie. And not just for his father's sake. He will do his best for him. His very best. Now I must be going. I'll say goodbye.

She goes, leaving the three women. Ethel is distraught as the car drives away.

MRS HUGHES: You've done a hard thing today, Ethel. The hardest thing of all.

Ethel looks across at Isobel.

ETHEL: You don't agree, do you?
ISOBEL: I don't want to make you doubt now that it's happened.
MRS HUGHES: You've done the right thing for the boy, Ethel. Whatever Mrs Crawley may say. Begging your pardon, ma'am.
ISOBEL: Perhaps you're right.
MRS HUGHES: I am. Until we live in a very different world from this one.
ETHEL: Well, then. I should be away.

She walks off, sadly, to the road, watched by the others.

MRS HUGHES: Let's pray she makes a new life for herself that's worth having.
ISOBEL: You don't sound very optimistic.
MRS HUGHES: What chance is there for a woman like her? She's taken the road to ruin. There's no way back.

She, too, walks away, leaving Isobel thinking.

43 INT. YORK PRISON. BATES'S CELL. NIGHT.

The door is thrown open and the usual posse barges in, led this time by Turner.

BATES: What's this about?
TURNER: Silence. Stand up. Against the wall, the pair of you.

Bates does as he is told, and both he and Craig are
manhandled against the wall.

 CRAIG: What you looking for?
 TURNER: Just keep quiet.

Craig catches the eye of his own warder, Durrant, who has
arrived last and is not in charge of the raid. He is out of
his depth.
 They have stripped Craig's mattress and found a slit in
the material. A further search reveals a package.

 SECOND WARDER: Mr Turner, come over here.
 TURNER: Well, well. A very mysterious package, I don't
 think.

He looks at Craig.

 TURNER: Craig, what do you call this?
 CRAIG: I don't know. I've done nothing.
 TURNER: You'd better come with us, Craig.

Craig looks at Durrant, who almost shrugs, then at Bates.

 CRAIG: You'll be sorry.
 BATES: Why? What have I done?

But Bates smiles as his fellow prisoner is led out.*

44 EXT. DOWNTON. DAY.

A car approaches Downton.

44A INT. HALL. DOWNTON. DAY.

Sybil walks through the hall. Branson, who has run down the
stairs, appears.

 BRANSON: Oh, thank God.

They walk towards each other and embrace passionately.
Branson, by now, is in tears.

 BRANSON: I'm so sorry.
 SYBIL: It's all right...

....

* It was important for the character of Bates not for him simply to be a
bruiser, but to have some lateral thinking in order for him to retain the sense
that he's tough but he's also clever.

45 INT. SYBIL'S BEDROOM. DOWNTON. DAY.

Sybil, who is visibly pregnant, sits with Branson. Mary, Cora and Edith are clearly relieved. Anna is unpacking.

SYBIL: They didn't try to stop me. But it doesn't mean they won't come after us. Unless Papa can persuade them otherwise.

CORA: Tom, how could you have left her all alone, to fend for herself?

SYBIL: It wasn't like that. We thought this might happen and we'd decided what to do. The question is, what now?

MARY: I've telephoned Papa's club and left a message that you're here.

CORA: I'm sure we'll hear from him soon.

SYBIL: Because we can't go home without some guarantee of Tom's safety.

CORA: You mustn't travel any more. Not yet. Not before the baby's born.

SYBIL: But Tom wants it born in Dublin.

MARY: He won't hold you to that now.

She glances firmly at Branson.

BRANSON: Well, won't this be the first place that they look?

MARY: How could you be part of it? The Drumgooles are like us. She came out with me. She was Laura Dunsany then. How could you dance round her burning house, Tom? It's horrible.

SYBIL: He didn't dance. And he isn't dancing now.

There is a knock and Sybil answers.

SYBIL: Come in.

Carson comes in with a telegram on a salver.

CARSON: A telegram for you, m'lady.

Cora takes it and opens it.

CORA: Your father's coming home. He's seen Mr Shortt.
SYBIL: And what happened?
CORA: He doesn't say. Only that neither of you is to leave Downton.*

46 INT. THE OLD DAY NURSERY. DOWNTON. NIGHT.

Mary is there, at her desk, when Matthew looks in.

MATTHEW: Where's Robert?
MARY: He went straight to his room as soon as he got back. He wants us all in the library at eight.
MATTHEW: Did he look cheerful?
MARY: I didn't see him. Why?
MATTHEW: I don't quite know how to put it.
MARY: Try.
MATTHEW: Looking through the books… there seems to be a great deal of waste.
MARY: What do you mean?
MATTHEW: Well, as far as I can tell, there's been no proper management for years. Rents are unpaid, or far too low. There's no real maintenance scheme. And half the assets are underused or else ignored entirely.
MARY: You're not saying Papa is guilty of anything?
MATTHEW: Not in that way, no. Of course not.
MARY: I don't want to pull rank, Matthew, but a country estate is not a city business. There are people, many people, we have to look after —
MATTHEW: But nobody benefits when the thing is badly run.

....

* Dunsany is a name from my own youth – a very old friend was the daughter of Lord Dunsany but she had a different surname, so I use the title as a name, without giving the surname away. Incidentally, Sybil may completely believe Tom's version of events here, but I am not sure I do. I think he did get into it, and went very, very deep in the planning. His regrets did not surface until the event. I am sure there are many burglars who plan to burgle and when they've actually broken into someone's house wonder what the hell they're doing there. That is what Branson has gone through. Initially, he was a convinced rebel; his change of heart has come out of the horror of witnessing the burning.

Mary is by now quite indignant. She stands.

MARY: Obviously, if that's your impression you must talk it through with Papa.*

END OF ACT THREE

ACT FOUR

47 INT. KITCHEN PASSAGE. DOWNTON. NIGHT.

Thomas has come in with two heavy suitcases and a hat box.

MOLESLEY: You're back.

THOMAS: I am. Anything happened here?

MOLESLEY: There's a new footman. Came today. How was London?

THOMAS: Quite fun, as a matter of fact.

MOLESLEY: Has the firebrand been saved?

THOMAS: That's not for me to say, is it, Mr Molesley. Now, I'd better take these upstairs.

He walks away past the footmen's cupboard where the new footman, Jimmy Kent, is trying on livery.

THOMAS (CONT'D): You got the job, then?

....

* 'Nobody benefits when the thing is badly run.' For me, this is the Socialist/Conservative conflict. The Socialists pride themselves on a greater consideration for human need, but the Conservative argument is that nobody benefits if the economy is not working. Here, Mary's position is essentially a Socialist one, where she thinks the people's good must be put ahead of any considerations of efficiency, while Matthew is the Tory, insisting on decent standards. I can see both sides. It is ultimately a fantasy to think that you can do good in a country if you can't run the economy. But on the other hand, there are certainly many measures the Labour party wants to bring in that I agree with. But in the end, I suppose I find that when a Labour government again and again and again leaves office with the economy in a mess, it becomes harder and harder to understand how people will continue to empower them.

Jimmy gives him a ravishing smile.

> JIMMY: I'm on my way, Mr Barrow. They say you were a footman once.
> THOMAS: That's right.
> JIMMY: So can I come to you if there's anything I need to know?
> THOMAS: Certainly. Why not?

He moves on. O'Brien has been watching this exchange.*

48 INT. LIBRARY. DOWNTON. NIGHT.

The family is assembled. Violet is with them.

> BRANSON: *I can never go back to Ireland?* That's impossible.
> ROBERT: If you do, you'll be put in prison. It was the best I could manage.
> CORA: Surely they need proof, to ban a man from his own country?
> ROBERT: They have more proof than Tom will concede.
> SYBIL: Is that fair? He's admitted to being there. He's told you so himself —
> ROBERT: But he did not tell me that he attended Dublin meetings where the attacks on the Anglo-Irish were planned.
> SYBIL: That's not true...

All eyes are on Branson. Sybil takes her hand away from him. At first he says nothing. Then...

> BRANSON: I was always against any personal violence. I swear it.
> VIOLET: Oh, so at least we can sleep in our beds.
> ROBERT: Maybe. But you were not against the violent destruction of property.

....

* We did an unusually audience-directing shot where Thomas walks past just as Jimmy is putting on his shirt. In this way, we have made Jimmy a love object for Thomas from square one, even if he himself is innocent of it. O'Brien is still festering with her desire for revenge on Thomas, and she is a good plotter because, like all good plotters, she has a lot of patience. She now starts to lay a plot that will burn through the rest of the series.

BRANSON: I've told you. The sight of it was worse than
I expected.
MATTHEW: So what was the deal you managed to extract
from the Home Secretary?
ROBERT: They don't want to make a martyr of him. And
with Sybil, they think they could have another Maud Gonne
on their hands, or Lady Gregory, or worse, if they're not
careful.
VIOLET: Lady Gregory, Countess Markievicz — why are the
Irish rebels so well born?
ROBERT: Whatever the reason, I don't want Lady Sybil
Branson to join their ranks. Mercifully, nor do the
Irish authorities. If Tom can stay away, they'll leave
him alone.
CORA: Isn't anyone going to thank your father?
BRANSON: I can't be kept away from Ireland.
ROBERT: You'll be arrested the moment you touch dry
land.
SYBIL: Thank you, Papa. Of course we're very grateful,
aren't we?*

Before Branson can answer, Carson comes in.

CARSON: Dinner is served, m'lady.

....

* For me, it is the romanticising of revolution that is so dangerous. People
like Isabella Gregory and Connie Markievicz did not help, because what they
did was drape a gauze of romanticism over the whole thing, as opposed to
showing houses in flames and young men getting shot and dying fifty years
before their time. This was all the worse because there was a real chance of
achieving everything that was achieved without any of it. But I am against
upper-class rebels, anyway. They always cause more trouble than any
working-class fighter. Better to face the street hero than the Duke of
Orleans any day of the week. Here, Robert naturally wants to keep Sybil out
of it because she would be a story. Sybil thanks him for it, but whether
Branson is grateful is another matter. What I think is difficult for Branson
from now on is that he owes his survival and freedom to the power of a
system that he disapproves of. And it is only because Robert is a product of
that system that he has the power to save Branson. Inevitably, this
compromises the very nature of his freedom.

49 INT. KITCHENS. DOWNTON. NIGHT.

Mrs Patmore and Daisy load the trays for Alfred and Jimmy.

MRS PATMORE: Now then. Do what Mr Carson tells you.

JIMMY: I know what I'm about.

DAISY: Are you all right, Alfred?

ALFRED: Yes, but shouldn't I be carrying the pork and Jimmy the veg? I am first footman.

MRS PATMORE: Never mind that. Up you go.

DAISY: I think Alfred's right. Isn't he first footman, like he says?

MRS PATMORE: That's for Mr Carson to decide.

Which pleases Jimmy. The two young men leave.

DAISY: I like Alfred, though.

MRS PATMORE: And so do I, but look at them. Which looks like a first footman to you? By heck, it's nice to think we're running at full strength again.

DAISY: Really? I'm running at full strength and always have been with no one to help me, neither.

MRS PATMORE: All in good time, Daisy. All in good time.

50 INT. DINING ROOM. DOWNTON. NIGHT.

They are at dinner, being served by Alfred and Jimmy.

VIOLET: What do you mean you wrote to a newspaper? No lady writes to a newspaper.

EDITH: What about Lady Sarah Wilson? She's the daughter of a duke, and she worked as a war journalist.

VIOLET: Well, she's a Churchill. The Churchills are different.*

....

* Lady Sarah Wilson was born a Spencer-Churchill, the youngest of the 7th Duke of Marlborough's eleven children. Her husband was in the Army and was killed at the very start of the war in 1914. Before this, he had fought in the Boer War, where she accompanied him. This was not too unusual. I had an aunt whose sister-in-law, Mrs Duberly, went with her husband to the Crimea and had an affair with Lord Cardigan (Jill Bennett played her memorably in Tony Richardson's film *Charge of the Light Brigade*). What *was* unusual was that, in South Africa, when one of its correspondents was arrested by the Boers, Lady Sarah was recruited by the *Daily Mail* and her dispatches during the Siege of Mafeking made her reputation.

MARY: Have we no Churchill blood?

CORA: I think Granny's right.

VIOLET: Can somebody write that down?*

CORA: It's good to have strong views. But notoriety is never helpful.

EDITH: Well, I've sent it now.

ROBERT: It won't be published.

EDITH: Thank you for that vote of confidence, Papa.

Jimmy is serving Mary.

CORA: This is our new footman, Mama. What should we call you?

JIMMY: Jimmy —

CARSON: James, your ladyship. This is James.

ROBERT: Welcome to Downton, James.

JIMMY: Thank you, m'lord.

He retreats, at Carson's suggestion.

....

Continued from page 243:

When her nephew, the eighth Duke, married Consuelo Vanderbilt and restored the family's fortunes, she was impossible to the new bride. She had been *de facto* mistress at Blenheim and there was a famous moment when she tried to lead the ladies out of the dining room. At the prompting of a friend, Consuelo intercepted her at the door. 'Are you ill?' she said. Lady Sarah said no, why should she be? And Consuelo replied that she thought Sarah must be ill because she was leaving early. At that moment Sarah Wilson's hold on Blenheim was broken.

But she was a brave woman, however difficult she may have been. In 1914 she set up a hospital in France within earshot of the guns at the front and was dealing with really terrible cases when they were brought straight from the trenches. After her husband's death, she went home for his funeral and returned two weeks later. Anyway, I make Edith refer to her because she is a classic case of how the role of women, even upper-class women, was changing.

* It's not that Violet and Cora don't get on, but they are not mad about each other. That seems to me quite true to life. They have an arrangement, but neither is the first person the other would choose for lunch on a birthday.

MARY: Well done, Carson. That must have cheered up the maids.*
VIOLET: He looks like a footman in a musical review.
EDITH: Poor Alfred. We mustn't allow him to be completely overshadowed.
CARSON: Quite right, m'lady. Hard work and diligence weigh more than beauty in the real world.

He goes out into the pantry.

VIOLET: If only that were true.†

51 INT. KITCHEN STAIRS. DOWNTON. NIGHT.

The two young men are coming down.

JIMMY: I've never been 'James' in my life. I was 'Jimmy' to Lady Anstruther —
CARSON: I don't care if you were Father Christmas to Lady Anstruther. You are 'James' now, and you will stay 'James' while you are at Downton.

He has been walking behind them. Now he goes on ahead.

....

* The twentieth century didn't invent scandal and, as I have said, footmen certainly figured in plenty of them. Famously, one was employed by the Comte de Castellane, who was married to a daughter of the Duchesse de Dino and (probably) Talleyrand. She was called Pauline. The Duchess came to stay with her daughter and found herself dining with a man who on her last visit had been waiting on her at table, although in this instance he was having an affair with the master of the house, not the mistress. The Duchess rose, saying that in future she would take her meals in her room. We have already hinted that Lady Anstruther reached a level of intimacy with Jimmy the footman that was not quite right, when he was working for her before he came to Downton.

† I thought the actors playing the two footmen were well contrasted, thanks to Jill Trevellick again. I remember Robert Altman, who directed *Gosford Park*, once telling me why he always tried to get famous people to play quite small parts in his films. It was because when they were famous the audience could tell the difference between the characters and they never muddled them up. The danger of casting unknowns is that the audience may be confused. We can't get stars to play every part in *Downton*, but that's where Jill's skill is shown. She finds actors of the right calibre and age, but so different you are not going to muddle them.

JIMMY: He thinks he's the Big Cheese and no mistake.
ALFRED: That's 'cos he *is* the Big Cheese.

Thomas and O'Brien are standing further back.

O'BRIEN: He's nice, that new bloke, isn't he?
I think he likes you.
THOMAS: Why do you say that?

Thomas looks at her, trying to fathom her purposes.

O'BRIEN: Oh, only an impression, that's all.

O'Brien walks away and, in spite of himself, Thomas is
pleased by this. He smiles and walks away, leaving O'Brien
to her own nefarious devices.

52 INT. DINING ROOM. DOWNTON. NIGHT.

The three men are left alone with the port. Branson stands.

BRANSON: If you'll excuse me, I'm going to bed. Can you
tell the others?
ROBERT: Tomorrow, we'll make some plans.
BRANSON: I don't know how.

He walks to the door, then he stops.

MATTHEW: You've lived out of Ireland before. Surely you
can again.
BRANSON: But Ireland is coming of age now and I need to
be part of that. But I know what you've done for me. I
know you've kept me free. And I am grateful. Truly.

He nods stiffly at Robert and goes, leaving them alone.

MATTHEW: Poor chap. I'm sure he is grateful.
ROBERT: No, he's not. He says it to keep the peace with
Sybil. But then I only rescued him for Sybil's sake, so
I suppose we're even.

He takes a drink.

ROBERT (CONT'D): Did you get a chance to look through
the books they brought in?
MATTHEW: As a matter of fact, I did.
ROBERT: Could you make head or tail of them?
MATTHEW: I think so. Yes. I was waiting for a good
moment to discuss them.

MATTHEW: You came. To be honest, I wasn't completely sure you would.

MARY: I'm glad to hear it. I should hate to be predictable.

BATES: What news could I have in here?

MARTHA: Come war and peace, Downton still stands and the Crawleys are still in it.

MRS PATMORE: She ate it, then. I'm never sure about Americans and offal.

ALFRED: I think she'd eat whatever you put in front of her, that one. What a gob. I thought Mr Carson was going to put a bag over her head.

ANNA: I just want to find out the truth.

MRS BARTLETT: It won't change anything, you know. You give me money, because you think I can get him off... I wouldn't if I could, but I can't.

STRALLAN: I can't do it... I should never have let it get this far. I should have stopped it long ago...

EDITH: What do you mean? We're so happy, aren't we? We're going to be so terribly, terribly happy.

VIOLET: So encouraging to see the future unfurl.

MARTHA: As long as you remember it will bear no resemblance to the past.

MRS PATMORE: Slice that finely, and fetch some parsley. And cut the dry bits off.

THOMAS: Alfred, Alfred.
I remember when my welfare
was all you cared about.

O'BRIEN: But you can look after
yourself these days, can't you? And
I like to give help where it's needed.

THOMAS: You like to control
where you can.

SYBIL: Have you seen her?

BRANSON: She's so beautiful.
Oh, my darling. I do love you
so much.

PHOTOGRAPHER: If you could all form a group around the father.

CARSON: This is a proud day, Mrs Hughes.

MRS HUGHES: I don't know if I'm proud, but I'm very glad you're happy, Mr Carson.

ISOBEL: Ethel? What's the matter?

ETHEL: I had rather a nasty encounter in the village, that's all... Mrs Bakewell refused to serve me. In the end her husband did, but it wasn't very nice.

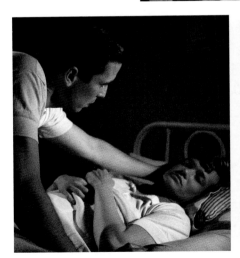

THOMAS: I'm here now.

GREGSON: Well, I hope this means you're persuadable, Lady Edith.

EDITH: I'll think about it, I promise. I just felt I had to meet you and see what it would be like.

ALFRED: But shouldn't I be carrying the pork and
Jimmy the veg? I am first footman.
MRS PATMORE: Never mind that. Up you go.

ROSAMUND: I did think we'd have dinner together.
And then we can have a proper catch-up.
MATTHEW: If that's what you'd like, but please don't let me be a nuisance.
ROSAMUND: I insist. A good family gossip will be my payment in kind.

BRANSON: If I were to say I'd live with you while Sybbie's little, and that we wouldn't move out until she's older, would you mind?

ROBERT: Right, gentlemen. Time's up to resume play.

MATTHEW: I didn't know it was possible to love as much as I love you.

JUDGE: I declare the Downton team the winner!

SUSAN: Would you speak well of me to Rose? Not every day, but sometimes?

CORA: Of course I will. I promise.

SHRIMPIE: What are we going to do about Rose?

ROBERT: Oh?

MATTHEW: Yes. There were some aspects of the way things have been done that I wasn't… quite sure about…

ROBERT: You sound like Murray.

MATTHEW: Do I?

ROBERT: He's always banging on about how we should overhaul this or overhaul that. Nothing's ever right for him.

MATTHEW: Well, I hesitate to say it…

ROBERT: Come on. We should let them get in here. We can talk about it another time if you really want to.

Robert stands. Matthew is able to recognise a brush-off.

53   INT. YORK PRISON. BATES'S CELL. NIGHT.

Bates reads a book when the door opens and Turner the warder looks in and throws a packet of letters onto the bed.

TURNER: These came for you, Bates.

BATES: When? When did they come?

TURNER: They came when you were out of favour. Now you're in favour again.

BATES: Why? What have I done?

TURNER: Just watch out for Mr Durrant. You're not a favourite with him.

He goes, as Bates starts to untie the bundle of letters.

54   INT.   KITCHEN PASSAGE/MRS HUGHES'S SITTING ROOM.   DOWNTON.   NIGHT.

Carson is going through some papers when he stops, and starts sniffing. Smoke is coming from Mrs Hughes's door.

CARSON: Oh, my —

He snatches up a fire bucket from the floor and runs towards Mrs Hughes's door. He bursts in, ready to throw the sand.

MRS HUGHES: Oh! Are you going to tip that over me?

He stops, bucket in mid air. The room is rather smoky.

MRS HUGHES (CONT'D): I was just making myself some toast. You have to set the number on the dial and I had it up too high, but I've got the hang of it now. Would you like a piece?

CARSON: I was worried that Mr Branson might take it into his head to burn the house down. But I didn't think that you would.

MRS HUGHES: No? You should never take anything for granted, Mr Carson.

A young man runs into the room with a fire bucket too.

CARSON: No, no, no — not now.

With a snort, Carson retreats, but Mrs Hughes just chuckles.

55 INT. SYBIL'S BEDROOM. DOWNTON. NIGHT.

Sybil is in bed. Branson undresses.

SYBIL: You never told me you went to those meetings.

BRANSON: I never told you I didn't.

SYBIL: And what else haven't you told me?

BRANSON: All I know is I can't stay here. Not for long.

SYBIL: You must. And so must I. And you must let the baby be born here.

BRANSON: You're very free with your *musts*.

SYBIL: But I will *not* be free with our child's chances! We need peace and safety. Downton can offer us both.

Her tone makes him look at her. She is quite determined.

56 INT. DINING ROOM. DOWNTON. DAY.

Robert, Matthew, Branson and Edith are at breakfast.

ROBERT: God in Heaven… 'Earl's daughter speaks out for women's rights.'

EDITH: What?

ROBERT: 'In a letter to this newspaper today, Lady Edith Crawley, daughter of the Earl of Grantham, condemns the limitations of the women's suffrage bill and denounces the Government's aims to return women to their pre-war existence.'

He lowers his paper in amazement.

EDITH: You said they wouldn't print it.

MATTHEW: Well done. That's most impressive.

ROBERT: Don't say you support her.

MATTHEW: Of course I support her, and so do you, really. When you've had a chance to think about it.

BRANSON: So I should hope, anyway.

This earns him a 'harrumph!' from Carson.

ROBERT: What do you think, Carson?
CARSON: I would rather not say, m'lord.

Which does succeed in amusing all the rest of them.

57 INT. PASSAGE/KITCHENS. DOWNTON. DAY.

Anna is on her way upstairs when Mrs Hughes hails her.

MRS HUGHES: Anna?
ANNA: Yes?
MRS HUGHES: There's quite a packet of letters arrived for you earlier.

She holds out a real bundle. Anna takes them.

MRS HUGHES (CONT'D): Are they all from Mr Bates?
ANNA: Looks like it.
MRS HUGHES: Why so many at once?
ANNA: Oh, I neither know nor care, just so long as I've got them.

Smiling, she runs upstairs.

57A INT. KITCHENS. DOWNTON. DAY.

Daisy is at work when Alfred comes into the kitchen.

ALFRED: Thanks for sticking up for me last night.
DAISY: It won't make any difference.
ALFRED: Oh, no. But it's good to know you're on my side.
DAISY: I am on your side, Alfred. In fact, there's something I've been wanting to say, but I don't want you to take it in the wrong way…
ALFRED: You've got my attention.
DAISY: Well —
MRS PATMORE: Ah. Here we are, Daisy! I'd like to introduce Miss Ivy Stuart, the new kitchen maid. And this is Daisy, *my assistant cook.*

She says it with a flourish, expecting Daisy to grin, and it should have been a great moment for her, but she sees Alfred look at the newcomer with undisguised admiration.

ALFRED: My, but aren't you a sight for sore eyes, Miss Stuart?
MRS PATMORE: That's enough of that. Alfred's a footman, so you'll know enough not to listen to a word he says. Shoo.
ALFRED: Tell me if you need any help.

But before he goes, he remembers…

ALFRED (CONT'D): Sorry, Daisy. What were you saying?
DAISY: Nothing. Doesn't matter now.

Alfred nods and goes. Ivy looks at Daisy.

IVY: I hope we're going to get on.
DAISY: We don't have to get on. We have to work together.

Even Mrs Patmore notices Daisy's voice is very severe. *

58   INT. MARY'S BEDROOM. DOWNTON. DAY.

Anna is dressing Mary.

MARY: And does he explain why the letters were withheld?
ANNA: Not really. In the latest one he says there's been a spot of bother but he's sorted it out. I suppose the reason's tucked inside that.
MARY: You're finishing your husband's 'spot of bother'. I suspect I may just be beginning mine.
ANNA: Why? I thought everything was settled now, and back to normal.
MARY: But Mr Crawley's idea of normal may not be the same as his lordship's.
ANNA: But they won't fall out, surely?
MARY: I don't know. I don't think so. It rather depends on Mr Crawley.

Her tone is not reassuring.

....

* I felt it was useful to have a situation where Daisy is not very nice. She is so warm and sympathetic as a character, there's always a danger she'll become a bit saccharine, but here she's not very pleasant to this girl who hasn't done anything wrong. All she's done, in fact, is to be very pretty and be attractive to Alfred.

59 INT. DRAWING ROOM. DOWER HOUSE. DAY.

Violet is writing letters when the butler announces Matthew.

> MATTHEW: Good morning, Cousin Violet. I'm sorry to barge in on you like this.
> VIOLET: Then sit down and tell me why you have.

Matthew chooses a chair. He is getting his nerve up.

> MATTHEW: A situation has arisen, and I'm not quite sure which way to turn.
> VIOLET: Well, obviously. If you've turned to me.
> MATTHEW: Robert won't discuss the matter, and Mary is affronted by the very mention of it... But, given that I've sunk my own fortune, alongside everyone else's, into —
> VIOLET: Into Downton.
> MATTHEW: I feel a duty, apart from anything else, to do what I can.
> VIOLET: About?
> MATTHEW: Downton is being mismanaged, Cousin Violet, and something must be done. The thing is, how do I do it without putting people's noses out of joint?
> VIOLET: Oh, my dear. Oh, I doubt there is a way to achieve that. I mean, you must do what needs to be done, of course. But I think I can safely say a great many noses will be out of joint.

This is not what Matthew wanted to hear.*

60 INT. BATES'S CELL IN YORK PRISON. NIGHT.

Bates sits on his bed, reading his pile of letters.

61 INT. ANNA'S BEDROOM. DOWNTON. NIGHT.

In exact parallel, Anna lies on her bed, reading her pile of letters, too.

END OF EPISODE FOUR

....

* Matthew's ambition is to make changes without putting any noses out of joint, even though this is unrealistic, which I think is reasonably true to life. And by doing that we have set up a storyline that we will turn through a few episodes.

EPISODE FIVE

ACT ONE

1 EXT. DOWNTON. NIGHT.

A car drives away, its lights illuminating the façade. The door slams, a man hurries inside, carrying a bag.

1A INT. HALL AND STAIRCASE. DOWNTON. NIGHT

We see that the man is Doctor Clarkson, who hurries through the house and up the stairs, his medical bag in hand.

2 INT. SYBIL'S BEDROOM. DOWNTON. NIGHT.

Cora is in there, with Mary and Edith, all in dressing gowns, while Doctor Clarkson examines Sybil. He seems confident.

CLARKSON: The pains have stopped. Nothing will happen yet.

They all smile.*

....

* Jessica Brown Findlay (who plays Sybil) had announced from very early on that she would do the third season but no more. What many in the audience did not grasp, least of all in America, is that no English agent will allow a client to sign for more than three years of anything. In America the actors are generally required to commit for far longer, but we don't do that. And there is no question but that it is harder to lose a character when they are a member of the Crawley family. When a servant wants to leave – and Siobhan Finneran (O'Brien) also decided to leave at the end of the third season, much to my sorrow – that is easy. They get another job. But a member of the family can't just vanish, and if they're not prepared to come back at all, ever, then they must die, because it's not believable that you literally never see them again.

If Jessica had been happy to do one or two more episodes in the next series, then we would have kept her alive and made her live in Dublin, occasionally coming over for visits. But she wanted a clean break. Of course, in a way, for Allen Leech (Branson) it was rather good that she didn't want to come back at all, because he then could stay on as a widower at the heart of the series. The real problem for us arose when Dan Stevens, who played Matthew Crawley, decided he also wanted to leave, but we didn't learn this until the first five episodes had been written and cast. If I had known, I might have killed Sybil in Episode Two and then Matthew could have had an

3 INT. BEDROOM PASSAGE. DOWNTON. NIGHT.

Robert, Matthew and Branson are waiting, also in dressing gowns, as the doctor and Cora emerge.

CLARKSON: Everything is fine.

ROBERT: You mean it was a false alarm.

CLARKSON: Not exactly. These early labour pains show that the womb is preparing itself for birth.

Robert looks rather stunned.

CORA: Doctor Clarkson, I'm afraid Lord Grantham doesn't enjoy medical detail. The point is, can we all go back to bed?

CLARKSON: You can. And so can I.

MARY: I'll see you out.

ROBERT: Sir Philip Tapsell will be here tomorrow.

CLARKSON: Of course. If you think it advisable.

Clearly, this is a slightly touchy subject. He starts for the stairs with Mary. Branson comes after him.

....

Continued from page 254:

accident in Seven, but once we were going to film Five, then we couldn't have another episode all about death. It had to be slam bam. Dead.

Anyway, Jessica wanted to have a new adventure. I thought it might be a useful thing to kill her in childbirth, as a reminder that women still died in childbirth in the 1920s (and can die now). People imagine that had all finished some time around the year 1857, but it absolutely did not. This decision also gave us an opportunity to look at the kind of condition that would kill you. What interested me, having talked it through with an obstetrician, was the commonly held notion that eclampsia and pre-eclampsia have gone away, when it is still a very, very serious condition. The difference being that, in the 1920s, once the fits had started you had no chance. The only tiny possibility of surviving was to deliver the child as quickly as possible by caesarean and hope that the fits would never come. This was no guarantee, but sometimes it did work.

Interestingly, both Napoleon I and Napoleon III were faced with doctors saying, 'I can save either the mother or the child,' and in fact, rather admirably given the dynastic situation, they both chose the mother and, in both instances, the doctor got the child through as well. But they did not require caesareans and these were very risky until the 1880s, at the earliest. Nevertheless, in this instance, it was the only option.

BRANSON: There really is nothing wrong?
CLARKSON: Nothing at all.   She's a healthy young woman
going through a very normal and natural process.
BRANSON: Thank you, Doctor.*

4   INT.   SERVANTS' HALL.   DOWNTON.   DAY.

The servants are having breakfast, waited on by Ivy.

IVY: I think I'd rather be in a city if I were having a
baby.   Where they've got all the modern inventions.
ANNA: Far away from everyone you know and trust?   I
don't think I would.
MRS PATMORE: What are you talking about having babies
for, Ivy?   I think we can leave that for a little further
down the menu, thank you.†

....

* David Robb (Doctor Clarkson) said to me, 'So many stories seem to hinge
on my getting the diagnosis wrong. Can I just have one story where I get it
right?' So that gave me the idea of Robert, who is not at fault – that would be
unfair – holding the belief that he must get in an expert. This allowed me to
tackle the damage that has been wrought by so-called experts in every field,
who of course turn out in so many instances not to be experts at all, but
merely to hold the current fashionable prejudice about whatever it is. Robert
falls for that. He thinks because he is an important man and his daughter is
who she is, he must have a London expert who knows everything and is
fashionable. We start with Clarkson, who thinks everything is going well.
'The womb is preparing itself for birth.' I quite like this line of Cora's in
reply: 'Doctor Clarkson, I'm afraid Lord Grantham doesn't enjoy medical
detail.' That's me.

† Ivy's consciousness about being more likely to come across new medical
developments in the city but not outside it is truthful. People certainly
thought like that. My stepmother's mother was American and she was
expected to have her baby in the family house in Rutland, but when it came
to it, in 1917, she chose to go to London, for exactly this reason. On arriving,
she discovered to her dismay that none of the hospitals would admit her,
because they were all full of wounded soldiers. 'But you're not ill,' they said.
'You're just having a baby.' In the end, she checked into the Hyde Park Hotel
where my stepmother was born. So Maureen was a child of the Hyde Park
Hotel. Rather nicely, years later in 1982 when she married my father, they
were staying their first night at the Hyde Park Hotel before going to Ireland,
and someone (not me) tipped off the hotel that Maureen had been born
there. They were given a wonderful bridal suite and all that sort of generous

She has arrived in the doorway.

JIMMY: It's always an idea to be prepared.

THOMAS: I expect you're always prepared.

JIMMY: I try to be, Mr Barrow.

CARSON: I don't like the direction this conversation is taking. Could we all begin the day's tasks, please? And remember, Lady Sybil is in a delicate condition, so no noise on the gallery.*

IVY: It's exciting, though, isn't it? To have a baby in the house.

DAISY: It won't make much difference to you. Now, get back in the kitchen and do as you're told.

Her tone is harsh. Ivy leaves. She hands Cora's tray to O'Brien.

O'BRIEN: Well, I think that message got through.

5 INT. CORA'S BEDROOM. DOWNTON. DAY.

Robert, dressed, is talking to Cora, who's in bed. The door opens and O'Brien appears with the breakfast tray.

ROBERT: We can't risk her welfare to soothe Clarkson's feelings.

CORA: I know.

ROBERT: I like the old boy. But he did misdiagnose Matthew, and he did miss the warning signs with Lavinia.

CORA: Thank you, O'Brien.

O'Brien puts her tray on her lap.

CORA (CONT'D): Is that fair? He didn't want to get Matthew's hopes up when it wouldn't make any difference, and with Lavinia, the disease could move like lightning.

....

Continued from page 256:

stuff, and a friend afterwards said to the manager, 'That was very, very kind of you to do that, to make such a fuss of them.' 'Yes,' he answered, 'but it wasn't a dangerous precedent.'

* One of Carson's permanent battles is to keep things clean and to stop young men being young men: 'I don't like the direction this conversation is taking.' We see that through all the series, and Mrs Hughes endorses it, because of her responsibility for the maids.

ROBERT: I know, I know. But even so.
CORA: And he's treated Sybil since she was a girl. Sir Philip Tapsell may have delivered many lords and royal highnesses, but he doesn't know us.
ROBERT: I'll ask him to include Clarkson in his deliberations. Will that satisfy you?
CORA: I suppose so. Thank you, O'Brien.

We leave the bedroom with the maid. *

6 INT. KITCHEN STAIRS AND PASSAGE. DOWNTON. DAY.

O'Brien is coming downstairs when she sees Jimmy.

O'BRIEN: You look a bit puzzled.
JIMMY: I am. Mr Carson's asked me to wind the clocks.
O'BRIEN: You must be doing well. In this house that marks you out as First Footman more than anything could.
JIMMY: That's just it. I said 'thank you' and 'right away', but I know nothing about clocks. Lady Anstruther's maid always wound them.
O'BRIEN: You'd better ask Mr Barrow.
JIMMY: Do I have to?
O'BRIEN: He's the clock expert. He used to wind them, but of course it's quite wrong for a valet to do it. Or a maid. And Mr Carson's trying to get back to normal.†
JIMMY: Mr Barrow won't mind?
O'BRIEN: Oh, no. I can see he likes you and that's good. Since he's got the ear of his lordship.
JIMMY: Yes. I suppose he would have.
O'BRIEN: I'd keep in with him if I were you. Let him think you like him back. He could be a big help.
JIMMY: I will. Thank you.
O'BRIEN: Think nothing of it.

....

* Robert is defending his position, which consists of getting what he believes to be the best man for the job, but Cora's view, which might have saved Sybil's life (except that Jessica Brown Findlay was leaving the series), is that we know Tapsell has delivered lots of lords and royal highnesses, but he doesn't know Sybil. He doesn't know the family. So they come to this compromise of including Clarkson, which is, in a way, a recipe for trouble.

† I like to remind the audience of these endless rules of the game.

7 INT. MARY'S BEDROOM. DOWNTON. DAY.

Anna has brought a breakfast tray for Mary. Matthew is there.

MATTHEW: Of course I'm not going to bother him until after the baby's born.

MARY: But you are determined to shake things up.

MATTHEW: My darling, you want to stay here until you die, and for our children to live here after us. For that to have a chance of happening, I can't let the whole thing disintegrate.*

Mary thinks about this. Then she turns to Anna.

MARY: When are you seeing Bates?

ANNA: Three o'clock, m'lady. I'll be back before you want to change.

MARY: Will you ask why they stopped your visits?

ANNA: I'll ask Mr Bates. I don't want to get up the nose of the authorities.†

She smiles and leaves the room. Matthew nods.

MATTHEW: I'm going downstairs. And I swear not to start on Robert.

MARY: Poor Papa. He's in such a state about Sybil. All fathers hate to think of any man touching their beloved daughters, and when they have a baby it's a terrible proof that they have been touched.

MATTHEW: A terrible and a wonderful proof.

For a moment, it seems that Matthew is going to speak again.

MARY: What?

MATTHEW: Nothing.‡

....

* We lost this section, but I was trying to show how Mary sees, in the end, that it is not in anyone's interest for the estate to be badly run. That said, she has to take a little time to get there.

† This scene went, but its motivation did not. We decided we should have an episode without an Anna/Bates scene in prison on opposite sides of a table, because by then we had played that formula so much.

‡ This is a theme of the series. Matthew is not exactly impatient for Mary to get pregnant, but is certainly looking forward to it, an inference which she quite deliberately does not wish to pick up.

8   INT. SYBIL'S BEDROOM. DOWNTON. DAY.

Sybil is in bed. Mary is with her. A nurse fusses around.

SYBIL: I'm the size of a house, my back hurts, my ankles
are swelling and my head aches. Honestly, I cannot
recommend this to anyone.
MARY: I am listening, but of course I'm dying to start
one of my own.
SYBIL: So you're not waiting?
MARY: Waiting for what?
SYBIL: I don't know. But I did wonder.

The nurse has gone and they are alone.

SYBIL (CONT'D): Mary, you know what I said about the
baby being Catholic? I've just realised that the
christening will have to be here, at Downton.
MARY: Blimey.
SYBIL: I wanted the whole thing done in Dublin, out of
sight, out of mind. But we can't wait for ever, and we
can't *not* christen it, poor thing.
MARY: You don't have to do this. It's your baby, too.
SYBIL: I don't mind. I mean, I do believe in God, but
all the rest of it — vicars, feast days and deadly sins —
I don't care about all that. I don't know if a vicar
knows any more about God than I do. And I love Tom, so
very, very much.

The nurse comes back in with a look at Mary.

MARY: I'll let you rest.

Mary stands.

MARY (CONT'D): And don't worry. I'll fight your corner
with Travis if it comes to it.

9   INT. LIBRARY. DOWNTON. EVE.

Thomas has his hand on Jimmy's, as they wind the clock.

THOMAS: There. You feel a slight increase in the
resistance?
JIMMY: I think so.
THOMAS: That's what you're watching for. Never go past
the point where the clock is comfortable.
JIMMY: You make it sound like a living thing.

THOMAS: Clocks are living things. My dad was a clock-maker. I grew up with clocks. I understand them… Never wind them in the early morning before a room has warmed up, nor too late, when the night air cools them down. Find a time when the family is out of the room.

Throughout this, he lets his hand rest on Jimmy's shoulder, until Jimmy is uncomfortable, but someone walks into the room and he removes it. The gong sounds.

THOMAS (CONT'D): There we go. Duty calls.*

10 INT. YORK PRISON. VISITING CELL. DAY.

Bates and Anna are with other prisoners and their wives. Officer Durrant is supervising. He watches them.

ANNA: You should have sent a message.

BATES: But I didn't know. I've only just been given all your letters.

ANNA: But I don't understand. Why was I kept away from you until now?

BATES: It doesn't matter. Whatever the reason, it's over. The point is, someone has to question Mrs Bartlett.

ANNA: I still don't understand.

BATES: You wrote and said she saw Vera on the evening of the day of her death.

ANNA: That's right. She'd eaten a pudding. She went for a walk. The door was open and she went in.

BATES: And she saw Vera scrubbing pastry from under her nails.

ANNA: I wrote because it was such a strange detail for her to remember.

BATES: What was she making with pastry?

Anna is bewildered.

....

*Thomas is behind Jimmy, guiding his hands over the hands of the clock, so we get the message. There's something about the detail of clocks that I find very interesting. I originally made Michael Gambon's character in *Gosford Park* a clock expert, but Michael's speciality is guns and he said, 'Could I possibly change it from clocks to guns, because if I'm dismantling and tending guns, then I know what I'm doing.' This seemed to me a sensible and logical comment and so I did it.

BATES (CONT'D): A pie. She was making the pie that she ate that night, when I was on the train back to Downton.

Anna gasps. They stare at each other as the penny drops.

ANNA: So Vera planned this. She meant for you to be imprisoned. She meant you to be hanged. For her suicide. It was her revenge.
BATES: And what a revenge. For both of us.

Anna has a horrible thought.

ANNA: They'll say you poisoned the milk or the flour or something. To catch her after you'd gone.
BATES: They tested everything in the kitchen. They said it was in the pastry, where I couldn't have put it.
ANNA: Oh, I hope she's burning in hell —
BATES: Don't go down that road. Once you do, there's no way off it.*

11 INT. HALL. CRAWLEY HOUSE. DAY.

Mrs Bird opens the door to Ethel.

MRS BIRD: You, again.
ETHEL: That's right, Mrs Bird. I've been asked to call on Mrs Crawley.

Mrs Bird nods brusquely towards the drawing room door.

MRS BIRD: She's in there.

12 INT. DRAWING ROOM. CRAWLEY HOUSE. DAY.

Isobel Crawley is with Ethel.

ETHEL: Oh, I thought there might be news of Charlie…
But that's not why you asked me to come?

....

* Vera's manner of committing suicide is very malicious. Her poisoning had to be by a prepared substance, as opposed to something natural, because if she just took poison then it would seem like suicide. She had to take poison in a way that would make it seem most unlikely that she would do it to herself. Therefore, to poison a cake or a pie was an obvious solution, because nobody would think that would be the way to finish yourself off.

ISOBEL: No… I've been thinking about you since we last met, and wanted to know how you were living…

ETHEL: I've not gone back to… doing what I was doing, if that's worrying you. I've no Charlie to feed, so now if I starve, I starve alone. And I'd rather starve than do that.

ISOBEL: But I know how hard it will be for you to find employment.

ETHEL: They want nothing to do with me. Not when they hear what I am. What I was… And I won't lie.

ISOBEL: You see, I thought you might work here for a while. Helping Mrs Bird. It would mean that when you moved on you will have had a respectable job, with a respectable reference.

ETHEL: Here?

ISOBEL: Poor Mrs Bird is having to manage everything with one kitchen maid, now Molesley's gone, and I think she finds it very hard.

ETHEL: Hard or not, she won't want me.

ISOBEL: Oh, I think she will. When I've spoken to her.

ETHEL: Are you sure you've thought about this, ma'am? What will Mrs Hughes's reaction be, or Lady Grantham's? And *old* Lady Grantham? Can't wait to hear what she has to say about it.*

ISOBEL: Don't you want to come?

ETHEL: It's not that, ma'am. You're offering a return to a wholesome world, and I am very, very grateful.

ISOBEL: Well, then.

ETHEL: But I think it's going to be a lot more complicated than you allow.

ISOBEL: Then we shall have to face those complications together, shan't we?

....

* Isobel hasn't faced the disturbance that she will bring to her own household, because she doesn't like to think that anyone disagrees with her – anyone who's decent, that is. She pretends she needs another kitchen maid, which of course she doesn't really, and in all of this Ethel is much more realistic. She's grateful, but she understands the complications inherent in this much more clearly than Isobel does, so really we're on her side.

13 INT. YORK PRISON. NIGHT.

It is lock-up. The prisoners are going back to their cells.

DURRANT: You look chirpy, Bates. There's quite a spring
in your step.
BATES: Thank you, Mr Durrant.

*He enters his cell, together with a new prisoner. It is
locked. Durrant sees Craig, who is being shepherded by
another warder, and goes to him.*

DURRANT: I'll take it from here.
WARDER: Sir.
DURRANT: Bates seems very cheerful.
CRAIG: Is he? He had a visit from his wife earlier.
She must have brought him some good news.
DURRANT: Hardly seems fair, does it? You've got an
extra year on your sentence, I've got a formal reprimand,
and Mr Bates, who's done it all, who's made all the
trouble for us, gets good news. What do you think it is?
CRAIG: Well, she can't be pregnant. He was arrested a
year ago.
DURRANT: Well, she might be. But he wouldn't be very
happy about it.
CRAIG: So what do you want to do?
DURRANT: Ooh, that'll need some thought. But first,
what does this good news consist of? When you shared
with him, where did he keep his letters?

14 EXT. FARMYARD. DOWNTON ESTATE. DAY.

*This is a ruinous place. The sheds are open to the elements,
the machinery weed-clogged and rusting. Matthew is with
Mary.*

MATTHEW: Quite a few of the cottages have been renovated —
MARY: Thanks to you.
MATTHEW: Maybe a little thanks to me, but many of the
farms have been left entirely to their own devices.

He looks around him.

MATTHEW (CONT'D): Coulter hasn't farmed this properly
for twenty years. He struggles to pay the rent, which is
too low, anyway. There's been no investment.

MARY: Papa would say you can't abandon people just because they grow old.
MATTHEW: I agree. But it would be cheaper to give him a free cottage and work this land as it should be worked.
MARY: I see. And you don't think Papa understands that?
MATTHEW: Maybe he harks back to a time when money was abundant and there wasn't much need to keep on top of it. I think he equates being business-like with being mean or, worse, middle class… Like me.

He smiles to show he is not hurt, just frustrated.

MATTHEW (CONT'D): But the middle classes have their virtues, and husbandry is one.*
MARY: We ought to get back. Sir Philip Thingy's due on the seven o'clock train, and you ought to be there to hold Tom's hand.
MATTHEW: Poor fellow. He's so terrified but so thrilled at the same time. As I would be… As I will be.

He gives Mary a slightly nervous smile, and they walk away.

END OF ACT ONE

ACT TWO

15 INT. DINING ROOM. DOWNTON. NIGHT.

The family and Violet are with Sir Philip Tapsell, a very grand specialist from London.

VIOLET: The dear Duchess of Truro is full of your praises, Sir Philip, but then of course you know that.

....

* Mary is coming to see that Matthew is not advocating heartlessness. He thinks caring is compatible with efficiency, but he does not believe that anyone benefits from a failing estate. He feels they should have realistic rents and generally exist in the modern world. Whereas Robert would still take the sentimental view that they can't turn out a bad tenant, no matter what they've done. Then again, that is why we like him.

SIR PHILIP TAPSELL: She had quite a time when she was
first married. But I said to her, never fear, Duchess,
I'll get a baby out of you one way or another.

*Robert does the nose trick while Carson closes his eyes in
disgust.*

VIOLET: And so you did.
SIR PHILIP TAPSELL: Three boys and, as a result, a
secure dynasty, I am glad to say.
ROBERT: But you see no complications here?
SIR PHILIP TAPSELL: None at all. Lady Sybil is a
perfect model of health and beauty.
CORA: We told our local doctor we'd send a message to
him when it looks as if the baby's coming.
MARY: Doctor Clarkson has known us all since we were
girls.
SIR PHILIP TAPSELL: Yes. What's needed here, Lady Mary,
is a knowledge of childbirth, nothing more, but if it
soothes you, then of course he is most welcome.*

16 INT. KITCHEN STAIRS AND PASSAGE. DOWNTON.
        NIGHT.

*Mrs Hughes approaches the stairs, where Thomas talks to
Jimmy. The latter is holding a tray of coffee things.*

JIMMY: How d'you keep your shoes so clean? Is there a
trick to it?
THOMAS: I thought you were going to ask how I keep my
nose clean. 'Cos I can show you that an' all.

He laughs as she draws alongside. Jimmy seems awkward.

MRS HUGHES: Mr Barrow, I hope you're not keeping James
from his duties.
THOMAS: Course not.

He walks away into the servants' hall. Mrs Hughes hesitates.

* Sir Philip Tapsell, played very well by Tim Pigott-Smith, is a snob doctor, a
type that we've all come across. His manner is emollient. He's puffing them
all up and of course he doesn't want the local doctor pushing in. This is
because (a) he'll just complicate things, and (b) if it all goes well he has to
share the glory and what's the point? How can this ridiculous local sawbones
know anything that he, the great Sir Philip Tapsell, doesn't know?

MRS HUGHES: You mustn't let Mr Barrow take up too much of your time, James… Now, get that tray up to Mr Carson.

17 INT. HALL. DOWNTON. NIGHT.

The men come out of the dining room. Anna is lurking in the shadows as Branson starts upstairs.

BRANSON: I'm going to check on Sybil.

ROBERT: Anna?

ANNA: I'm sorry to trouble you, m'lord, but I wondered if I might have a word.

ROBERT: Come into the library. Matthew, will you take Sir Philip to the drawing room.

He walks away with the maid, leaving the other two alone. Sir Philip waits but Matthew does not move.

SIR PHILIP TAPSELL: Shall we go in?

MATTHEW: As a matter of fact, Sir Philip, I was rather hoping to have you to myself for a moment… Do you know that I was injured during the war?

SIR PHILIP TAPSELL: I think I did hear something about it from Lady Grantham.

MATTHEW: My spine was very severely bruised, and for a time it seemed I had lost the use of my legs and… everything else.*

SIR PHILIP TAPSELL: But the bruising reduced and you recovered? Yes, I have heard of this. Well… How relieved you must have been.

MATTHEW: Yes. But I wonder now whether the injury might have affected my… I suppose I mean my 'fertility'. If it might have limited my chances of fathering a child.

SIR PHILIP TAPSELL: Is everything working as it should?

MATTHEW: Oh, yes.

SIR PHILIP TAPSELL: Then why do you think there may be a problem?

MATTHEW: We are anxious to start a family. But we've been married for a few months without any… results.

....

* 'Very severely bruised' was a truthful saying at the time and there were cases of some bruising being misdiagnosed as a full spinal break. The *Daily Mail* decided to invent the story that Matthew's spine had been broken and then miraculously came together. This, of course, is not what we said or did.

SIR PHILIP TAPSELL: My dear Mr Crawley, may I point out the word that gives you away? 'Anxious.' Anxiety is an enemy to pregnancy. Don't, whatever you do, feel anxious. Six months is nothing. I know all men spend their youth terrified of making a girl pregnant if they so much as look at her, but I assure you the process is often slow. I can run a test if you wish, but I would urge you not to bother for some time yet.

But this doesn't quite answer the question for Matthew.

CORA: There you are. We were wondering what had happened to you.

She is standing in the doorway. They go to join her.

18   INT.   LIBRARY.   DOWNTON.   NIGHT.

Robert is with Anna. He is amazed.

ROBERT: This is extraordinary. Why did the police miss it so completely?
ANNA: Mrs Bartlett never spoke to them. She never spoke to anyone.
ROBERT: Except to you.
ANNA: She didn't think the truth would make any difference now. She thought it was only further proof of his guilt.
ROBERT: The difficulty is she may not want to accept Bates's innocence.
ANNA: Doesn't she have to?
ROBERT: Not necessarily. She may think he drove his wife to suicide and deserves to rot in prison. In short, she may not wish to tell the truth to set him free.

They stare at each other. It makes a kind of horrible sense.

ANNA: Then we need to get a statement from her before she finds out it could overturn the case.
ROBERT: I'll telephone Murray tonight. He can come up here, and talk to you and see Bates. It might mean using one of your visiting times.
ANNA: Whatever we must do.
ROBERT: You were right, though. The proof was out there and you've found it.

That settled, Robert allows himself a small smile.

19 INT. KITCHENS. DOWNTON. NIGHT.

Ivy is scrubbing the central table. Alfred arrives.

ALFRED: Why aren't you in bed?

IVY: I've still got this to do, and I'm not tired.

ALFRED: You'll be tired enough in the morning. That I can promise. Where were you before you came here?

IVY: I was a maid of all work for a shop-keeper's wife in Malton, but my mum wanted me to better misself, so she put me up for the job here.

ALFRED: And is it better?

IVY: Not as you'd notice. Mrs Mawle was quite nice. But here I'm bossed by Mrs Patmore and bullied by Daisy, and everyone seems to mistake me for a rag to wipe their shoes. What about you?

ALFRED: Hotel trade. But it's harder than service and the pay's no better.

MRS PATMORE: What are you doing down here, chatting? You should be in bed.

She is in the doorway, watching. Alfred nods and goes.

MRS PATMORE (CONT'D): He's a nice boy. Alfred.

IVY: Is he? Yes, I s'pose he is.

Which interests Mrs Patmore.

20 INT. DINING ROOM. DOWNTON. DAY.

Robert, Edith and Matthew are at breakfast. Edith is reading a letter. She gasps and the others look up.

EDITH: The editor of *The Sketch* wants me to write for him. He saw my letter to *The Times* and he wants to give me a regular column.

MATTHEW: How regular? And what about?

EDITH: Once a week. And I can write about whatever I like. It would be the problems faced by a modern woman, rather than the fall of the Ottoman Empire. But even so.

MATTHEW: Will you write under your own name?

EDITH: I hadn't thought.

ROBERT: You won't have an option. That's what he's buying, that's what he wants: your name and your title.

This has put a dampener on the moment.

MATTHEW: Oh, I don't know. I thought Edith's letter to *The Times* was very interesting —
EDITH: Don't bother, Matthew. I'm always a failure in this family.

She stands and leaves. Matthew glances at Robert.

ROBERT: What?
MATTHEW: Lots of people write for the papers and magazines now. The sons and even daughters of people you know.
ROBERT: Mostly drug fiends and sewers.*
MATTHEW: Edith must do something, Robert.
ROBERT: They want to make a fool of her. I can't allow that. When you're a father, you'll understand.

21 INT. DRAWING ROOM. CRAWLEY HOUSE. DAY.

Isobel is with Mrs Bird.

ISOBEL: I'm sad to hear this, Mrs Bird.
MRS BIRD: And I'm sad to say it, madam. But it's kept me awake all night, and I know I cannot work alongside a woman of the — a woman who has chosen… that way of life.
ISOBEL: But Miss Parks has changed —
MRS BIRD: Maybe she has and maybe she hasn't, but if I tolerate her, I will be tarnished by her. Suppose people come to think that I'd followed the same profession as what she has?
ISOBEL: Nobody could look at you and think that, Mrs Bird.
MRS BIRD: Well, I hope not. Because I'm a respectable woman. I may not have much but I have my good name, and I must protect it.
ISOBEL: You shall have a month's wages in lieu of notice. Where will you go?
MRS BIRD: Back to Manchester and stay with my sister. She says there's plenty of work for a plain cook these days.
ISOBEL: And they will find one in you. Goodbye Mrs Bird, and good luck.

....

* From Nancy Mitford's Uncle Matthew in *The Pursuit of Love*.

22 INT. KITCHENS. DOWNTON. DAY.

Ivy is cleaning a saucepan. Jimmy and Alfred are with her.

JIMMY: Is there anything else you need to know about
having babies, Ivy?
IVY: Honestly, if I told Mrs Patmore the things you two
say to me, you'd be up before Mr Carson.
ALFRED: So, what are you doing with your afternoon off?
IVY: None of your business.
ALFRED: I'd like to make it my business.

As Jimmy laughs, we see Daisy watching her and the two men.

DAISY: Have you greased the cake tins?
IVY: Yes.
DAISY: What about the pastry?
IVY: It's in the larder.
DAISY: Then get started on the vegetables for tonight.

She stalks out. Jimmy whistles. *

JIMMY: She doesn't want much, does she?
IVY: She doesn't like me.
JIMMY: Why not?
IVY: I don't know. She just doesn't.
ALFRED: Well, anyone who doesn't like you needs their
head examining.
IVY: I hope you agree with him, Jimmy.
JIMMY: That'd be telling.

With a laugh he goes. Mrs Patmore listens in the doorway.

23 INT. KITCHEN. CRAWLEY HOUSE. DAY.

Isobel is with Ethel.

ISOBEL: I'll put an advertisement in the local paper —
ETHEL: No, ma'am. Don't advertise for a cook to come
and work with me. Because they won't stay. Not when
they find out.
ISOBEL: They aren't all like Mrs Bird.

....

* When Daisy comes in as the spoilsport we immediately see that she has
miscalculated, because by making a 'them and us' situation, with Jimmy and
Alfred both on Ivy's side, Daisy is immediately wrong-footed. She should
never have let that happen.

ETHEL: Don't be angry with her. She had to look after her good name.
ISOBEL: But it's so small-minded —
ETHEL: Beg your pardon, ma'am, but we're not like you. If Mrs Bird lost her reputation, she'd have nothing to bargain with. She did what she had to do. Good luck to her.
ISOBEL: Well, what do you suggest?
ETHEL: That I become your cook-housekeeper, ma'am. You say there's a girl from the village?
ISOBEL: Yes. Meg. She's rather dozy and she hasn't been with us long, but I don't think she'll cause trouble. She's here for the morning and then she comes back later to help with dinner and to turn down my bed.
ETHEL: Well, I should say we're in good shape and all Sir Garnet.*
ISOBEL: But can you cook, Ethel?
ETHEL: I've been in kitchens all my life.†

24 INT. HALL. DOWNTON. EVE.

Mary comes in with Edith, both changed, to find Branson alone.

MARY: Are we first down? How is Sybil?
BRANSON: Sleeping, thank God. She's been restless all afternoon. I don't think it'll be long now.
MARY: I'm sorry it couldn't have been in Dublin.
EDITH: We know how much it meant.
BRANSON: Nothing means more than she does.‡

....

* The phrase 'all Sir Garnet', meaning 'all is in order', came from the super-efficient Sir Garnet Wolseley, who served in the British Army across the globe, becoming commander-in-chief at the end of the nineteenth century.

† I was rather sad at the cuts here, because I felt Ethel's defence of Mrs Bird was quite important for the understanding of the whole business of reputation: 'She did what she had to do. Good luck to her.' So the only realistic thing, if Ethel wants to keep her job, is to be a cook-housekeeper and, of course, she can't cook, but she thinks she can fake it.

‡ The beginning of the alliance between Mary and Branson.

24A INT. DRAWING ROOM. DOWNTON. NIGHT.

The door opens. Matthew walks in. He goes over to Mary, as Cora and Robert arrive with Edith.

MARY: I've hardly seen you all day.

MATTHEW: I've had another session with the books. It gets worse every time.

MARY: Well, for God's sake don't say anything now.

Sir Philip and Violet arrive.

ROBERT: And you're sure you have everything you need?

SIR PHILIP TAPSELL: Quite sure.

EDITH: Hello, Granny. Are you here? How nice.

CORA: Your grandmother will be with us every night until the baby's born.

VIOLET: I hate to get news second-hand.

SIR PHILIP TAPSELL: Well, you won't have long to wait.

CORA: I thought I'd ring up Doctor Clarkson after we've eaten.

SIR PHILIP TAPSELL: Yes, I've been talking to Lord Grantham about the good doctor.

ROBERT: Sir Philip feels the room would be too crowded, what with the midwife and the nurses… It might be better to leave old Clarkson out of it, for the time being.

CORA: But I said I'd telephone.

SIR PHILIP TAPSELL: Well, it really isn't necessary.

CORA: I've given him my word.

Her tone silences the company. Edith takes charge.

EDITH: Why don't I run down in the car after dinner and fetch him?

The matter is settled as Carson comes in.

25 INT. KITCHENS. DOWNTON. NIGHT.

Ivy is slaving away, when Daisy pulls a saucepan off the stove and dumps it on the table. Alfred is waiting.

DAISY: The hollandaise for the fish. Put it in the sauce boats for Alfred. I'm doing the soufflés.

IVY: As soon as I —

DAISY: Will you just do it!

She hurries away. Alfred steps in and takes up the pot.

ALFRED: Out of my way. Quick!

IVY: What you doing?

He puts the sauce on the stove, waits for a while, then takes it off and puts it back on the table. Daisy comes back in.

DAISY: Haven't you done it? Oh, my God!

ALFRED: What's happened?

DAISY: It's curdled, and it's got to go up in a minute! Oh, my Lord!

ALFRED: Ivy can manage it. Don't worry. Go on with what you're doing.

DAISY: Can you really?

Behind her head, Alfred nods.

IVY: I can.

Daisy hurries out. Ivy turns, terrified, to Alfred.

IVY (CONT'D): Now what?

ALFRED: Give me an egg. Quickly.

He takes it and breaks the yolk into a saucepan. Only now do we see Mrs Patmore watching this scene from the shadows.

ALFRED (CONT'D): Dribble it in.

IVY: But it's ruined.

ALFRED: Do what I say.

She does, amazed by what is happening.

IVY: How does that work? It's magic.

ALFRED: One of the tricks of the trade.

Ivy puts the sauce into the sauce boats as Daisy comes back.

DAISY: How've you done that?

IVY: Just… one of the tricks of the trade.

DAISY: Well, go on. Take it up.

Alfred winks at Ivy and goes. Mrs Patmore steps out.

MRS PATMORE: Well done, Ivy. You played a good one, there. Thank her, Daisy.

DAISY: Yes. Thank you.*

....

* Saving a curdled hollandaise came to me from Mrs Field, who used to work for a great friend of mine, and she taught me two things: one was how to

Ivy nods and carries some dirty pots away to the scullery.

MRS PATMORE: That didn't hurt at all, did it? I'll tell you what, Daisy. Alfred won't like you any better for being rough on her.

She goes before Daisy can reply.

26 INT. DINING ROOM. DOWNTON. NIGHT.

Jimmy carries in a plate of fish. Alfred has the sauce.

ALFRED: I should have the fish.
JIMMY: I'll do it.
ROBERT: By the way, Murray will be here in the morning. There's been a development in Bates's case.
MARY: A good development?
ROBERT: I think so. But that's all I want to say at this stage.

Conversation is obviously limping at the table. Cora speaks for them all.

CORA: There's nothing more tiring than waiting for something to happen.*

....

Continued from page 274:

make those very light biscuits – almost wafers – you have with ice cream, and the other was how to save curdled hollandaise, which was to trickle in a yolk, and it does work actually, or it should. This scene tells us various things: 1) Ivy's going to be very grateful to Alfred and he will mistake that for something more; 2) Daisy has played it wrongly and has forced them into each other's arms; 3) Alfred's real interest is food. All three of those storylines are pushed forward here and now Jimmy and Alfred are fighting out the position.

* This is a phrase of my mother-in-law's. It's rather like that moment when you're waiting for people to come for dinner and there's a sort of dead moment when nobody's arrived. In our family it was particularly sharp because my mother, during the Second World War, had been in South America with my eldest brother, who was little (four or thereabouts), and my father was somewhere at the front. She was staying with her sister in Argentina and an English ship had come into harbour. They knew a couple of the officers on board and they'd gone down and invited all the officers to come for supper. Unbeknownst to them, after they left, an Admiral had

MATTHEW: Edith, have you written back to your editor,
yet?
VIOLET: What's this?
MATTHEW: Edith has had an invitation to write a
newspaper column.
VIOLET: And when may she expect an offer to appear on
the London stage?
EDITH: See?

*She shrugs at Matthew as the door opens and a nurse comes in.
Branson jumps up.*

BRANSON: Oh, God. Is it beginning?

27 INT. KITCHENS AND PASSAGE. DOWNTON. NIGHT.

*Jimmy walks in while Mrs Patmore and the rest of the kitchen
staff are hard at work.*

JIMMY: Dinner's suspended, so to speak.
MRS PATMORE: Yes, but suspended, cancelled, or
suspended, keeping it hot? And what should I do about
dinner down here?*
JIMMY: I couldn't tell you.

He walks away towards the servants' hall when Thomas appears.

JIMMY (CONT'D): Looks as if the baby's coming. So I
suppose it's all hands to the pump.
THOMAS: An unfortunate choice of phrase.

*He laughs and rests his hand on Jimmy's shoulder, lightly
stroking his cheek. Mrs Hughes comes round the corner.
Thomas withdraws his hand and goes. Jimmy speaks nervously.*

JIMMY: Mrs Hughes…

....

Continued from page 275:

come on board and they'd all been put on duty and couldn't get a message off
the ship. So my mother and her sister and her sister's husband just sat there
for the whole evening with this dinner for 20, and so, for the rest of her life,
she always had this slight thing, 'Suppose nobody comes.' But anyway, that
was what reminded me.

* A reminder that the cook of a great household had to be something of a
campaign manager as well.

MRS HUGHES: What is it? Because I'm very busy.
JIMMY: It can wait.*

He moves off and Mrs Hughes continues to the kitchen.

28 INT. LIBRARY. DOWNTON. NIGHT.

Clarkson is with Violet, Robert, Cora, Sir Philip, Matthew and Mary.

ROBERT: What do you mean, 'concerned'?
CLARKSON: Lady Sybil's ankles are swollen and she seems… muddled.
CORA: What sort of muddled?
CLARKSON: Not quite there. Not quite in the present moment.
MARY: And what do you think it means?
SIR PHILIP TAPSELL: It means she's having a baby…

Robert lets out a wry laugh.

SIR PHILIP TAPSELL: A word, Doctor Clarkson?
CLARKSON: Excuse me.

The two men leave the room. The others look at each other.

CORA: Sir Philip mustn't bully him into silence.
ROBERT: My dear, this is just Clarkson's professional pride. Like barbers asking, 'Who last cut your hair?' They always want to be better than any other practitioner.
MATTHEW: But we must listen to what he has to say.
VIOLET: I quite agree.
ROBERT: I don't want to hurt Sir Philip's feelings.
VIOLET: If there's one thing that I am quite indifferent to, it's Sir Philip Tapsell's feelings.†

....

* This is the first time Jimmy starts to suspect that Thomas's interest in him is not quite pukka. Up till then they've just been joshing along and, suddenly, a man is stroking his cheek. We're about to begin that story.

† Just my inbuilt resistance to experts. I can't bear them because they never are experts.

29 INT. HALL. DOWNTON. NIGHT.

The two doctors are hissing at each other.

SIR PHILIP TAPSELL: You are upsetting these people for
no reason at all —
CLARKSON: I am not. I think she may be toxaemic, with a
danger of eclampsia, in which case we must act fast.
SIR PHILIP TAPSELL: There is no danger, whatsoever.
Judging by my experience, Lady Sybil is behaving
perfectly normally.
CLARKSON: Do you not find the baby small?
SIR PHILIP TAPSELL: Not unusually so.
CLARKSON: And the ankles?
SIR PHILIP TAPSELL: Maybe she has thick ankles. Lots of
women do.
CLARKSON: But she does not.
SIR PHILIP TAPSELL: I warn you, Doctor. If you wish to
remain, you must be silent. I cannot allow you to
interfere.

END OF ACT TWO

ACT THREE

30 INT. KITCHEN. CRAWLEY HOUSE. NIGHT.

Ethel stirs a mixture in a bowl, when she has a thought…

ETHEL: Oh, Christmas!

She runs to the oven, opens it and takes out a smoking dish.

ETHEL (CONT'D): Oh, don't be burned! Don't be burned!

*But the cloth is too thin and with a scream she drops it.
She runs to find an implement and with the cloth scrapes the
mixture of burned offerings off the floor back into the dish.
She mixes the dirty bits into the bowl when the door opens.*

ISOBEL: Are you all right, Ethel? Only I heard a
shout —?
ETHEL: Fine, ma'am. Everything's fine.

Isobel looks into the mixing bowl. She looks at Ethel.

ETHEL (CONT'D): It's a kidney soufflé, ma'am.

ISOBEL: A kidney soufflé? Isn't that a bit adventurous?

ETHEL: I've seen Mrs Patmore do it a hundred times.

ISOBEL: Yes, but she can't have *begun* her career as a cook by making a… kidney soufflé.

ETHEL: Shall I try something else, ma'am?

ISOBEL: No. If we're to avoid a midnight feast, it's too late to turn back.

She starts for the door.

ETHEL: Is there any news from the house?

ISOBEL: Not yet. But it can't be long now.

She leaves. Ethel sniffs the mixture. It clearly does not smell as she had expected.*

31 INT. DINING ROOM. CRAWLEY HOUSE. NIGHT.

Isobel, with a book propped open, looks at the food Ethel has just put down in front of her.

ETHEL: I'm sorry it's a bit late. I've not quite got used to that stove yet.

ISOBEL: No.

ETHEL: It will get better. If I could have a bit of time before you entertain.

ISOBEL: Yes.

ETHEL: Now, I've had a go at an apple pie for afters…

ISOBEL: Let's keep it simple, Ethel. I'd be quite happy with some cheese.

....

* Now we have Ethel's first failure. I wanted something quite difficult and I felt a kidney soufflé was sufficiently arcane to be a challenge, but my feeling was, with a cook, a real cook like Mrs Patmore, they have certain things they can do very, very easily – they're just part of their repertoire – and other things that they have to concentrate on. A kidney soufflé would be the sort of thing that a cook would perfect so that it would always seem exotic and interesting, no doubt with an anchovy sauce or something, and obviously Ethel's seen it made hundreds of times and has not in any way understood how difficult it is. Isobel is beginning to understand that she's employed a cook who can't cook, but she's determined to make her point.

ETHEL: Very good, ma'am. I take it Mr Matthew hasn't telephoned?
ISOBEL: No. And I worry. But I'm sure there's nothing to worry about.

She goes, leaving Isobel poking at the thing on her plate.

32 INT. PASSAGE/SERVANTS' HALL. DOWNTON. NIGHT.

Anna has just come downstairs, to find Carson.

CARSON: Is everything all right?
ANNA: I'm not sure. I think so. I've just come to fetch some warm milk in case she fancies it.

She walks off, passing Molesley, who carries a letter.

MOLESLEY: Mr Carson. I'm glad I've caught you. I've had a letter from Mrs Bird, who used to work for Mrs Crawley.
CARSON: I didn't know she'd gone.
MOLESLEY: Well, that's the point.

33 INT. HALL. DOWNTON. NIGHT.

Cora comes out of the library to find Clarkson in a chair.

CORA: You don't have to wait out here.
CLARKSON: I'm trying to find the nerve to go upstairs. Sir Philip is quite a formidable opponent.
CORA: If there is something you want to say, then please say it.
CLARKSON: I will, because we must act quickly. But I have no wish to alarm you.
CORA: You have failed in that, as I am already alarmed, so tell me.

34 INT. SYBIL'S BEDROOM. DOWNTON. NIGHT.

Branson sits by the bed, holding his wife's hand.

BRANSON: I've been thinking about what we should do. You know I've a brother in Liverpool and there might be an opening there. It'd mean working with cars again —

SYBIL: No. We're not going backwards. You must promise me that.*

Before he can, she has another contraction.

BRANSON: God. I wish there was something I could do.
SYBIL: Just be here. You don't have to talk, you know… We can just lie back and look at the stars.

This is an odd thing to say. Branson looks around.

BRANSON: Is she…?
SIR PHILIP TAPSELL: It's all just as it should be.

The door opens and Anna comes in with the milk, followed by Cora and Clarkson. Sir Philip rolls his eyes.

SIR PHILIP TAPSELL (CONT'D): Now what?
CLARKSON: I want to test the latest sample of her urine.
SIR PHILIP TAPSELL: Oh, for heaven's sake —
CORA: Just give the order to the nurse, please, Sir Philip.

Clarkson walks over to the bed.

CLARKSON: How's the young mother doing?
SYBIL: Am I on duty, Doctor Clarkson?
CLARKSON: What?
SYBIL: Only, I swear I'm not on duty, otherwise I wouldn't be lying here.
CLARKSON: No. No, you're not on duty.

35 INT. CARSON'S PANTRY. NIGHT.

Molesley, Mrs Hughes and Carson are together.

CARSON: Mrs Crawley has hired a *prostitute* to manage her house?
MOLESLEY: And that's why Mrs Bird felt she had no choice but to hand in her notice.
CARSON: Nor did she, poor woman.

....

* I think Sybil's ambition for Branson is right. One of the things she feels is that they couldn't see who he really was because he was a chauffeur, and she doesn't want him to go on being a chauffeur. It's nothing to do with snobbery. It's to do with his potential.

MRS HUGHES: But Mr Carson, this is Ethel we're talking about. Our Ethel. And Mrs Crawley was just trying to give her a helping hand. Is that so wrong?

CARSON: I do not criticise her for her charity, but she hasn't considered her actions. No respectable person, certainly no respectable *woman*, can now be seen entering her house.

MRS HUGHES: But Ethel's given all that up —

CARSON: I didn't think she was running a brothel in Mrs Crawley's kitchen!

MRS HUGHES: Doesn't it make a difference?

CARSON: Before you accuse me of hypocrisy and cant, I ask you this: would you invite an ex-prostitute to come here? To live and work alongside the other maids?

Mrs Hughes is unable to say that she would.

CARSON (CONT'D): Right. Thank you. So, the question is, what should we do about it?

MRS HUGHES: Can't we say nothing for now? Mrs Bird's gone and I doubt Mrs Crawley can find someone to replace her —

CARSON: I should hope not.

MRS HUGHES: I don't remember Ethel as any great cook, so it may sort itself out.

CARSON: Very well. We shall keep silent for the moment. But I don't want the maids going into that house on any pretext whatsoever. Is that clear?

MOLESLEY: Quite clear, Mr Carson.

A horrible thought strikes Carson.

CARSON: Or the footmen.*

....

*The modern philosophy is that we can leave our past behind us. Victorians believed that we carried our past with us and we were never essentially free of whatever we had done. I think that the extreme of both is unrealistic. Our belief today that some public figure can expect high respect, say, four years after being involved in some sordid scandal, is nonsense. And we see people living this nonsense. So my own feeling is probably not as the Victorians felt – that we have to be blamed for our sins all our life – nor the idea that we are washed entirely clean. We are all the product of our choices and that's what, in a way, Isobel is working against – although we like her for it.

36 INT. LIBRARY. DOWNTON. NIGHT.

There is a row in progress here, too. Branson is not present.

SIR PHILIP TAPSELL: I'm sorry, but I find this interference unprofessional and verging on insolent —

CLARKSON: Insolent! May I remind you I have known this young woman since she learned to walk, while you first met her… what? A month ago? Two?

ROBERT: Gentlemen, please! Must we fall out?

CLARKSON: It's my belief that Lady Sybil is at risk of eclampsia —*

ROBERT: What is that?

SIR PHILIP TAPSELL: A rare condition from which she is *not* suffering!

CORA: Tell him why you think she may be.

CLARKSON: Her baby is small, her ankles are swollen, she's confused and there is far too much albumin, that is protein, in her urine —

ROBERT: Doctor Clarkson, please! Have you forgotten my mother is present?

VIOLET: Peace. A woman of my age can face reality far better than most men.

CLARKSON: Look, the fact remains, if I am right, we must act at once!

MARY: And do what?

CLARKSON: Get her down to the hospital and deliver the child by caesarean section.

MATTHEW: But is that safe?

SIR PHILIP TAPSELL: It is the opposite of safe! It would expose mother and child to untold dangers! She could pick up any kind of infection in a *public hospital!*

CLARKSON: An immediate delivery is the only chance of avoiding the fits that are brought on by the trauma of natural birth. It may not work, but —

....

* I had a lot of responses from people involved in the care and study of eclampsia. They were glad that the condition was being brought back into the public consciousness, because it does need more money for research. It's the usual thing: the creaking gate gets the oil in medicine as much as in anything else. It's the same with the unfashionable cancers. Pancreatic cancer gets almost nothing.

SIR PHILIP TAPSELL: Honesty at last! Even if she were at risk from eclampsia, which she is *not*, a caesarean is a gamble, which might kill either or both of them!

Robert is in agony. At last he looks at his wife.

ROBERT: I think we must support Sir Philip in this.
MARY: But it's not our decision! What does Tom say?
ROBERT: Tom has not hired Sir Philip. He is not master here, and I will not put Sybil at risk on a whim. If you are sure, Sir Philip?
SIR PHILIP TAPSELL: I am quite, quite certain.
CORA: You're being ridiculous. Obviously, we have to talk to Tom.

Robert is shocked. He looks at his mother for support.

VIOLET: Don't look at me. Cora is right. The decision lies with the chauffeur.

37 INT. KITCHEN PASSAGE. DOWNTON. NIGHT.

Anna is on her way downstairs. Mrs Hughes sees her.

MRS HUGHES: How are things going?
ANNA: I'm not sure. The doctors are arguing, and that's never a good sign.

Carson has heard Anna's voice and now he appears.

CARSON: Is everything all right?
MRS HUGHES: Unfortunately, it seems it is not.

38 INT. BEDROOM PASSAGE. DOWNTON. NIGHT.

Branson is with the doctors, Robert and everyone else.

BRANSON: Could we get her to the hospital?
SIR PHILIP TAPSELL: To move her now would be tantamount to murder.
CLARKSON: Sir Philip, admit it. You are beginning to detect the symptoms yourself. You can see her distress.
CORA: Can you?
SIR PHILIP TAPSELL: Yes, Lady Sybil is in distress. She's about to give birth.
CLARKSON: Lord Grantham, Mr Branson, time is running out. We should be at the hospital by now. If we'd acted at once, the baby would be born.

BRANSON: But if she has the operation now, do you swear you can save her?

CLARKSON: I cannot swear it, no. But if we do not operate and if I am right about her condition, then she will die.

SIR PHILIP TAPSELL: If, if, if, *if!* Lord Grantham, can you please take command?

ROBERT: Tom, Doctor Clarkson is not sure he can save her. Sir Philip is certain he can bring her through it with a living child. Isn't a certainty stronger than a doubt?

CORA: Robert, I don't mean to insult Sir Philip, but Doctor Clarkson knows Sybil. He's known her all her life!

BRANSON: So you'd take her to the hospital?

CORA: I would have taken her an hour ago!

We hear Sybil's screams.

BRANSON: God help us.

A nurse opens the door. Branson runs into the room and the others follow, while a worried Robert and Matthew remain. Clarkson looks at the others.

CLARKSON: I'm afraid we've left it too long.

39 INT. DRAWING ROOM. CRAWLEY HOUSE. NIGHT.

Isobel is writing as Ethel brings in a hot drink on a tray.

ETHEL: Any news from the house, ma'am?

ISOBEL: Not yet. Matthew said he would try and telephone if it's not too late.

ETHEL: Lady Sybil was always kind to me.

ISOBEL: Yes, she's a very dear girl.

She takes a sip of the drink and recoils slightly.

ISOBEL (CONT'D): What… What's in this?

ETHEL: Some honey. Was that not right?

ISOBEL: It's perfectly fine for now, Ethel. But perhaps not another time.

She returns to her work. Ethel sighs and goes out. *

   40 INT. KITCHENS/PASSAGE. DOWNTON. NIGHT.

Ivy is finishing up. The two footmen are there.

ALFRED: But if you want to be a cook, does that mean you'll never marry?
IVY: Why should it?
JIMMY: None of the cooks in the important houses are married.
IVY: Then why are they all called 'Mrs'?
JIMMY: It's the title for the job.
IVY: I like the sound of that.
DAISY: Don't you two ever get bored with clogging up the kitchen?

She is standing in the doorway.

IVY: I've finished now, honest.
DAISY: Then go to bed.
MRS PATMORE: No. Run along to the servants' hall. I'll make some cocoa.

The three young ones do as they are told. Mrs Patmore talks as she gets out the milk and puts it on to heat.

MRS PATMORE (CONT'D): There's quite a few will stay up till we know the baby's safe.
DAISY: I s'pose.
MRS PATMORE: Daisy, there's nothing wrong with one-sided loving. You should know that if anyone does… It's not Alfred's fault. It's not your fault. It's not Ivy's fault.
DAISY: But the way she flirts —
MRS PATMORE: She's young and she's away from home. Anyway, I don't believe she's any more successful than you are.
DAISY: No? When Alfred follows her round with a face like a Bassett hound?

....

* Ethel can't even make a hot drink that Isobel likes. I hate honey. I've hated honey all my life and it's always the sort of ultimate health thing that you stir honey into this, that and the other. I can't stand it. I don't know why, but it's just a taste I can't bear. So I've given Isobel the same resistance.

MRS PATMORE: Who says she cares about Alfred?*

41 INT. LIBRARY. DOWNTON. NIGHT.

Violet, Branson, Robert and Matthew are together.

ROBERT: Would you like anything, Mama?
VIOLET: Oh, no. Just good news of the baby and a car to take me home. I don't suppose I shall get either before long.
ROBERT: What about you, Tom?
BRANSON: I just feel so helpless.
MATTHEW: We men are always helpless when a baby's in the picture.†

Mary opens the door, smiling. They jump to their feet.

MARY: You can come up. It's a girl.
BRANSON: And they're both...?
MARY: They're fine.
VIOLET: Oh, thank God and hallelujah.

Branson pushes past her and runs to the stairs.

42 INT. SYBIL'S BEDROOM. DOWNTON. NIGHT.

Sybil, tired, has been tidied up. She holds the baby. Cora is in there with Edith, Mary and Sir Philip. Branson clasps her hand.

SYBIL: Have you seen her?

....

* Mrs Patmore has understood that Ivy's interested in Jimmy, not Alfred. So they're all in love with the wrong person, really. It's a little play out of *A Midsummer Night's Dream* in the kitchen.

† I think it's always good to make these points for the younger generation – they assume that the place for a husband is sitting by the bed, holding his wife's hand, and they don't realise that for several hundred years he was nowhere near. Certainly, for my own father, whose children were born from the late Thirties through the Forties, to have been present would've been an abomination. My mother always said, 'You don't want anyone in the room you know socially when you're having a baby.' She was one of those who then made sure she was made up and had her hair done, with a nice little bed-jacket and some gladioli, and then he was allowed in. There was no coming in until she'd been put back into shape.

BRANSON: She's so beautiful. Oh, my darling. I do love you so much.

SYBIL: I just want to sleep, really.

CORA: Of course you do. You've earned it. She's a wonderful baby. Well done.

SIR PHILIP TAPSELL: I think we should let her sleep.

A nurse steps forward to take the child as Branson goes, shaking Sir Philip's hand on the way.

SIR PHILP TAPSELL: Well done.

BRANSON: Thank you.

SYBIL: Mama.

CORA: Yes, my darling?

Cora returns to her chair by the bed. Sybil lowers her voice.

SYBIL: Tom is thinking of getting a job in Liverpool, going back to being a mechanic. But it wouldn't be right for him. He needs to move forward.

CORA: We'll talk about it tomorrow. We don't need to worry about it now.

SYBIL: I think Papa may see it as some kind of answer. And if he —

CORA: Your father loves you very much.

SYBIL: I know. I know. And I love him terribly, but will you help me do battle for Tom and the baby if the time comes?

CORA: Of course.

SIR PHILIP TAPSELL: Lady Grantham?

CORA: Now sleep, darling.

Cora kisses her finger, lays it on Sybil's lips and stands.

43   INT. BEDROOM PASSAGE. DOWNTON. NIGHT.

Clarkson is outside with Branson, Robert and Matthew when Cora comes out with Sir Philip. Robert smiles at his wife and they kiss.

ROBERT: All's well that ends well.

CORA: I'm sorry we doubted.

SIR PHILIP TAPSELL: As to that, Lady Grantham, it's always a good idea to forget most of what was said during the waiting time, and simply enjoy the result.

MARY: Is there anything more to be done?
SIR PHILIP TAPSELL: Not really. The nurse will stay
with her, and so I suggest we all get some sleep and meet
again, refreshed, in the morning.
ROBERT: What about you, Doctor Clarkson?
EDITH: Shall I run you home? I don't mind.
CLARKSON: No. If it's all right, I'd like to stay up for
a while longer. Just to make sure everything is well.

Sir Philip rolls his eyes at Robert.

SIR PHILIP TAPSELL: There's no reason to.
CLARKSON: I'd like it.
CORA: Then I shall ask them to make you comfortable.

Which settles the matter.*

44 INT. SERVANTS' HALL. DOWNTON. NIGHT.

*Most of them are still up, drinking cocoa. O'Brien watches
Thomas with Jimmy.*

THOMAS: Show us a card trick, Jimmy.

Carson arrives.

CARSON: That's it. The baby is born. It's a girl. Now
you can all go to bed.

Thomas and Jimmy stand.

THOMAS: Good news.
JIMMY: Do you like Lady Sybil?
THOMAS: I do. We worked together in the hospital during
the war, so I know her better than all of them, really.
She's a lovely person. Like you.

*He drops his voice and takes Jimmy's shoulder, sliding his
hand down the younger man's arm. He breaks away and walks
off. Jimmy is disturbed. O'Brien is watching him.†*

....

* A picture was released of Sybil and Branson together. All the papers took it
up and they made a false newspaper, showing the happy couple, which was
handed out. They didn't realise what lay in the last few pages.

† Thomas, who is not usually generous, is generous about Sybil, because they
had that time in the hospital working alongside each other. I think that's
reasonably truthful, because those situations stay with you.

O'BRIEN: Anything the matter?

JIMMY: No… No… But Mr Barrow's so… familiar all the time, isn't he?

O'BRIEN: I'm glad to hear it. That's a very good sign. If he's taken to you, he'll definitely put in a good word with his lordship.

JIMMY: 'Cos I'd like to tell him to keep his distance.

O'BRIEN: Do you want to get your marching orders, then? Why? What are you implying? Nothing unseemly, I hope.

JIMMY: No. No. Nothing like that. G'night.

O'Brien watches the troubled young man walk away. And smiles.*

END OF ACT THREE

ACT FOUR

45 INT. CORA'S BEDROOM. DOWNTON. NIGHT.

Mary runs into the room. She shakes her sleeping mother.

MARY: Mama, Mama! Wake up and come quickly! It's Sybil!

Now Robert is awake. He and Cora share a terrified glance.†

....

* O'Brien hasn't quite brought the situation to the boil yet, so she doesn't want Jimmy saying lay off. She wants nothing said until it gets out of hand.

† We have this very atmospheric moment – there had been an advertisement break here – of looking up through the hall in the dark with one light and Mary's shadow running as the first harbinger of doom as she races in to her parents' room to wake them.

46 INT. SYBIL'S BEDROOM. DOWNTON. NIGHT.

When Mary hurries in, Sybil is pouring with sweat and tossing about. Branson, in pyjamas, is trying to calm her. Matthew is silent, standing with Edith. Clarkson is still dressed and Sir Philip is in a dressing gown, his hand over his mouth, as the nurses also look on.

> SYBIL: I should be — I should be getting up!
> I should be up!
> BRANSON: Darling? Can you hear me, darling? It's Tom!
> SYBIL: I'm needed on the wards! I'm a nurse! I should
> be — help — busy! Help! I have to get back to the
> wards!
> BRANSON: No, darling. All you need to do is rest.
> MARY: Sybil…
> SYBIL: My head… My head… hurts so! It's splitting!
> MARY: Sybil… Let me bathe your forehead.
> SYBIL: It hurts so! It hurts so!

Mary kneels but Sybil won't lie still. She's going into a fit.

> BRANSON: Oh God, oh God. God, God — no! No!*

Now Cora comes running in, followed by Robert.

> ROBERT: What's happening? What the hell is happening?
> Sir Philip?
> MARY: Sybil? She can't hear me. Sybil? Sybil? It's
> Mary. Can you hear me?

Tapsell is in hell. He stumbles forward.

> SIR PHILIP TAPSELL: It looks as if… I'm afraid it very
> much looks as if…
> CORA: It looks as if *what!*
> CLARKSON: This is eclampsia.

Sybil is threshing around wildly while Branson and Mary try to calm her. She's choking now, as she flings out her arms, spilling flowers, water jugs and everything else. As the doctors and Robert talk, we hear the others in the

....

* There was sometimes an interval before the fitting that killed the mother. So you had this awful kind of false dawn of thinking you're through it and then we have this scene.

*background, Branson, Mary, Matthew, Edith desperately trying
to help. 'Shall I fetch some water?' 'Open the window!'
'Darling, please! Wake up! It's me! It's me!' 'Listen to
me, my darling! Just breathe! That's all. Breathe!' And
so on...*

ROBERT: But it cannot be? Sir Philip? You were so
sure.
MATTHEW: *Somebody do something!*
SIR PHILIP TAPSELL: Human life is unpredictable.
ROBERT: *But you were so sure!*
CORA: What can we do?
BRANSON: Help her! Help her! Please... Oh God, no.
EDITH: Dr Clarkson, should we take her to the hospital?
Shall I get the car?

*She has broken away from the others, desperate to help. But
the doctors both know what will happen next.*

CLARKSON: There is nothing that can be done.
MATTHEW: That's not possible! Not now, not these days!
CLARKSON: Once the seizures have started, there's
nothing to be done.
ROBERT: But you don't agree with him, do you, Sir
Philip? Of course there's something!

Even for him, the time has come to stop lying.

SIR PHILIP TAPSELL: I'm very sorry.
BRANSON: Please don't leave me. Help her! Help her,
please! What's happening?
MARY: She can't breathe.
BRANSON: Please, please. Just breathe. Oh, God. Oh,
no. Wake up, my darling! Wake up! *I beg you to wake up!*
ROBERT: There *has* to be something worth trying at least!
BRANSON: Come on, come on, breathe, love. Listen, it's
me, my darling. All you have to do is breathe, right now.
SIR PHILIP TAPSELL: We've given her morphine, and
atropine...

*Cora and Branson are by Sybil now, both of them frantic,
shaking Sybil and imploring her to wake up.*

BRANSON: Please breathe, love.
CORA: Oh, please...
MARY: She can't breathe.

BRANSON: Please, love. Please wake up. Please don't leave me. Don't leave me. Please wake up, love. Please don't leave me. Please, love.*

But Sybil does not wake up. The fight and the struggle is over and she is at peace. Clarkson checks for her pulse. Robert is in a complete daze.

ROBERT: But this can't be. She's twenty-four years old. This cannot be.

Cora holds her daughter, tears pouring down her cheeks. Matthew, Mary and Edith stand, struck dumb. A nurse opens the door and the room is filled with the sound of a baby crying. Branson covers his face with Sybil's hand and continues to cry.†

47 INT. SERVANTS' HALL/KITCHEN PASSAGE. DOWNTON. NIGHT.

A group of stunned faces, all the servants in dressing gowns, old and young, stare at Carson, who has finished speaking.

DAISY: Is there anything we should do, Mr Carson?
CARSON: Carry on, Daisy. As we all must.

He walks out, leaving them to their thoughts. Daisy walks towards Mrs Hughes and breaks down in her arms. Anna notices Thomas slip out into the passage. Silently, she rises and follows. She finds him in tears.

ANNA: Thomas?
THOMAS: I don't know why I'm crying, really. She wouldn't have noticed if I'd died.
ANNA: You don't mean that.
THOMAS: No. No, I don't. In my life, I can tell you, not many have been kind to me. She was one of the few.

....

*Talking to Allen Leech afterwards about when he says, 'Please wake up, love,' I asked, 'Where did that come from?' It was, he recalled, some deathbed he was at and he sort of reverted… I suddenly had an image of this little Dublin boy, in the grip of helpless grief, and that was all him. Not me. Which I thought was really very, very good.

† In fact, they all played this scene terribly well. I think it is one of our best episodes ever.

She hugs him. Mrs Hughes walks by and they straighten up. *

MRS HUGHES: Oh. Don't mind me. The sweetest spirit under this roof is gone, and I'm weeping myself.

She walks on, past Carson's room. He stands there.

MRS HUGHES (CONT'D): Are you all right, Mr Carson?

He looks up and there are tears in his eyes, too.

CARSON: I knew her all her life, you see. I've known her since she was born.

48 INT. SYBIL'S BEDROOM. DOWNTON. NIGHT.

Cora is alone by the bed. Everything is tidy and neat, and a candle burns on the table. She strokes Sybil's hand.

CORA: We'll look after them. We'll look after them both. Don't you worry about that.

The door opens and Mary appears.

MARY: It's time to go to bed, Mama. You'll need some rest to face tomorrow.
CORA: Not just yet. This is my chance to say goodbye to my baby. You go. I'll be all right. I promise.
MARY: I could stay… Or would you prefer to be alone?
CORA: Alone, I think. But thank you.

Mary retreats to the door.

CORA (CONT'D): And Mary, could you ask your father to sleep in the dressing room tonight?

Mary hesitates, then she nods and goes out, closing the door.

CORA (CONT'D): Because you *are* my baby, you know. And you always will be. Always. My beauty and my baby.

And she kisses the dead hand that she holds.

....

* This moment between Thomas and Anna – it's always important to find these different conjunctions of different characters, and a moment like that gives you the opportunity to bring together people who are not necessarily linked in the scenes.

49 INT. DRAWING ROOM. CRAWLEY HOUSE. DAY.

It is morning. Isobel is with Ethel.

ISOBEL: No. I can't believe it, either. But I'm afraid we must… I'll go up there later and see if there's something I can do.
ETHEL: But what can anyone do?
ISOBEL: We can pray, I suppose. But that's about all. We just have to pray.

50 EXT. DOWNTON. DAY.

A taxi arrives at the house and Murray gets out.

51 INT. LIBRARY. DOWNTON. DAY.

Matthew is with Murray.

MATTHEW: I've asked Carson to bring Anna here, Mr Murray, but I don't think it'll be possible for you to see Lord Grantham. Not today. I'm sure you understand.
MURRAY: Of course. I should have guessed there was something wrong when there was no car at the station. What a dreadful, dreadful thing.
MATTHEW: It seems unbelievable in this day and age. Quite unbelievable.

The door opens and Carson ushers in Anna. Matthew stands.

MATTHEW: I'll leave you to it… Mr Murray, I wonder if I might have a word with you before you go. It's not the best day for it, but there's no knowing when you might be up here again.
MURRAY: Of course, Mr Crawley.

Matthew leaves with Carson. Murray nods to Anna.

MURRAY (CONT'D): I am very sorry to trouble you on a day like this, Mrs Bates.
ANNA: You weren't to know. None of us could have known.
MURRAY: Please, sit down, and tell me what it is you think you've discovered.
ANNA: It doesn't seem right. Not today.
MURRAY: Please try.

Slightly hesitantly, Anna does sit down.

    ANNA: I'm not quite sure where to start.

      52   INT. SYBIL'S BEDROOM. DOWNTON. DAY.

Branson is sitting by the bed. He holds Sybil's hand.
Across the room, Mary also sits, keeping vigil. Edith
comes in.

    EDITH: The men from Grassby's have arrived.
    BRANSON: To take her away.
    MARY: Yes. And we must let them.

Mary comes to the bed and kisses Sybil's still face.

    MARY (CONT'D): Goodbye, my darling.

Edith kisses Sybil on the forehead, too.

    MARY (CONT'D): She was the only person living who always
    thought you and I were such nice people.
    EDITH: Oh, Mary. Do you think we might get along a
    little better in the future?
    MARY: I doubt it, but since this is the last time we
    three will all be together in this life, let's love each
    other now, as sisters should.

She hugs Edith and takes a deep breath. The sisters turn to
Branson, who gazes out the window.

    MARY (CONT'D): Can I tell them to come up?

Branson nods but does not move as the sisters leave
*together.**

      52A INT. LIBRARY. DOWNTON. DAY.

Anna is with Murray.

    ANNA: You see, what I have discovered is quite simple,
    Mr Murray. It's proof of my husband's innocence.
    MURRAY: That seems a good place to start.

....

* I think it's truthful that Mary doesn't believe they will remain reconciled,
but they will just be reconciled for this moment.

ANNA: Yes. But the key to his innocence depends on the word of a woman who hates him, and may want him to stay in prison, whatever the truth.
MURRAY: Why not tell me everything you know?*

52B INT. SYBIL'S BEDROOM. DOWNTON. DAY.

Branson walks from the window to the bed and sits on it, taking Sybil's hand as the tears come once again.

53 INT. LIBRARY. DOWNTON. DAY.

Matthew is with Murray.

MATTHEW: Of course, this isn't the right time, but you're here, and it's not a subject for the telephone.
MURRAY: No. But I must confess to you, Mr Crawley, that even at this sad hour your words are music to my ears. Testing times are coming for these estates. Indeed, they've already arrived, and many great families will go to the wall over the next few years. It's never been more vitally important to maximise the assets of a place like this, and run it with a solid business head.
MARY: What are you talking about?

She has comes in without their noticing. Matthew is silent.

MURRAY: Mr Crawley and I were discussing the management of the estate. He was outlining some interesting plans for the future.
MARY: And do you intend to involve my father in these fascinating plans?
MURRAY: Of course.
MARY: Then I cannot think this a very appropriate moment to be deciding the destiny of Downton, Mr Murray, when my sister's body has just been removed from the house and my father is quite unable to see or speak to anyone.

The two men understand that she is extremely indignant.

....

* Again, we try not to tell the audience what they know. What we tell them here is that there's no reason why Mrs Bartlett should tell the truth, which may not have occurred to the audience. We don't tell them the facts again, because they've had those, so we tell them the only element of it they may not have thought of.

MURRAY: I'm really only here to talk to **Mrs Bates** about her new evidence. Naturally, if I'd known —
MARY: No, no. That's quite different. None of us would wish to keep Bates in prison for an hour longer than necessary. Shall I fetch her?
MURRAY: I've already seen her. Now I'm on my way to York. To visit Bates and learn what he has to say about it.
MARY: Then thank you so much for coming all this way.

Mary goes to the bell pull.

MURRAY: Lady Mary, please tell your parents how very sorry I am.
MARY: Of course.

The door opens and Alfred stands there.

MARY (CONT'D): Mr Murray is just leaving.

Murray accepts this, takes up his briefcase and goes.

MATTHEW: I'm sorry, darling. Forgive me. I wasn't thinking. It's just… Murray was in the house —
MARY: Papa has lost his youngest daughter. I think that's enough. Or does he have to lose control of his estate on the same day?*

54   INT. MRS HUGHES'S SITTING ROOM. DOWNTON. DAY.

Mrs Hughes is with Carson and Mrs Patmore.

MRS HUGHES: Mrs Rose, in the village, has just had a baby and she's volunteered to nurse the child.
CARSON: Good. I suppose she'll stay here?
MRS HUGHES: Not for long. The Doctor's sent up a pamphlet on feeding babies with something called the 'percentage method'. Boiled milk, water, honey, orange juice… That kind of thing.

....

* It's a lapse of taste for Matthew and Murray at this moment to be discussing the estate, which Matthew at once sees. It's really not right. They shouldn't have brought it up at that point. I'm on Mary's side there. Matthew wasn't thinking. It was just that Murray was in the house.

MRS PATMORE: I'll take care of it.

CARSON: We don't want to add to your work.

MRS PATMORE: I don't mind. I'm glad to do it.

She dabs her eyes.

MRS PATMORE (CONT'D): She wasn't much more than a baby, herself, poor love. When I think how I taught her to cook. She couldn't boil an egg when she came downstairs, but yet she was so eager…

He sighs.

MRS HUGHES: I'm sure she was very grateful.

CARSON: I'll go up and tell them the child will be taken care of. I wonder how her ladyship's coping. And of course there's Branson. What will we do about him now?

MRS HUGHES: We will show him that we are kind people, Mr Carson. That's what.*

55 INT. VISITING CELL. YORK PRISON. DAY.

Murray is opposite Bates.

MURRAY: I agree the challenge is to get a statement from Mrs Bartlett before she realises its significance.

BATES: That's it…

He stops for a moment and sighs.

BATES (CONT'D): I can't stop thinking about Lady Sybil. A lovely young woman, at the height of her happiness. If I had any beliefs, that would shake them.

A bell rings. The prison warder, Durrant, calls out.

DURRANT: Make your way out now!

MURRAY: I'll keep you informed, Mr Bates. I'll do my very best for you.

BATES: Thank you, Mr Murray.

The visitors stand and start to leave. Craig watches Murray and Bates with Durrant.

....

* I felt we needed to indicate how they were going to manage with the baby, because otherwise it leaves too many unanswered questions. Although this scene didn't stay in, we made it fairly clear later, I think.

DURRANT: I s'pose that's his lawyer.

CRAIG: Lord Grantham's lawyer, more like.

DURRANT: I don't care if he's lawyer to the Prince of Wales. He'll get a shock when he contacts Mrs Audrey Bartlett.

Which is obviously very amusing to them both.

56 EXT. FRONT DOOR. DOWNTON. DAY.

Alfred walks forward and opens the door to Violet, in black.

56A INT. FRONT DOOR. DOWNTON. DAY

Alfred closes the door behind Violet, who approaches Carson.

VIOLET: Oh, Carson.

CARSON: Good afternoon, m'lady.

VIOLET: We've seen some troubles, you and I. Nothing worse than this.

CARSON: Nothing could be worse than this, m'lady.

She nods and, uncharacteristically, pats his arm. Crossing the hall, she stops and almost sags, her shoulders shaking, and she holds onto the wall for support. She takes out a handkerchief and dabs her eyes. But then, as Carson watches, she lifts her veil and straightens up again, as stiff as a ramrod, and walks on into the drawing room.*

....

* It is a marvellous moment when Violet pats Carson's arm. Previously, in the three years of the series, we've never seen any physical contact between Violet and Carson. They're perfectly friendly and they've backed each other up on various things, but they'd never touched each other and, in a sense, her patting him is a kind of equalising gesture – that in the face of grief these social distinctions don't matter. Maggie Smith did this very, very well. She stops and sighs and her whole shoulder shakes, then she straightens up and goes in because, for someone like her, she would think it the height of ill-breeding to make things worse by visiting her grief on them.

One of the things that always irritates me – you know they say of people, 'He was the bride at every wedding and the corpse at every funeral' – is the way, particularly nowadays, that we're all much more sobby than we used to be. People sort of arrogate the grief to themselves as if they're the one really suffering. Sometimes you have to say, 'Look, this isn't about you,' as they're

57 INT. DRAWING ROOM. DOWNTON. DAY.

Cora is staring into the fire as Violet comes in. Robert, Mary, Matthew, Isobel and Edith are with her. They are all in mourning. Robert stands.

ROBERT: Ah, Mama.

VIOLET: Oh, my dears.

ROBERT: You'll be glad to know they've found a nurse for the baby. She is already here.

VIOLET: Good. Good. Where — Where's Tom?

EDITH: He's upstairs. I've asked if he wants anything. He says no.

CORA: He wants his wife back. But that's what he can't have.

She stands.

CORA (CONT'D): I must write to Doctor Clarkson and have it sent down before dinner.

ROBERT: Darling, there's no need for that.

CORA: I should. I want to. I have to apologise for our behaviour.

MARY: What? Why?

CORA: Because if we'd listened to him Sybil might still be alive. But Sir Philip and your father knew better, and now she's dead.

She leaves, closing the door behind her.

VIOLET: Why… Why did she say that?

ROBERT: Because there is some truth in it.

VIOLET: My dear, when tragedies strike we try to find someone to blame, and in the absence of a suitable candidate we usually blame ourselves. You are not to blame. No one is to blame. Our darling Sybil has died during childbirth, like too many women before her. And all we can do now is cherish her memory and her child.

....

Continued from page 300:

sobbing and sobbing away. There's that wonderful moment at the funeral of the Duke of Kent, who had been killed in an air crash in the Second World War, when the impresario Binkie Beaumont said to Noël Coward, who was showering tears, 'Cheer up, Noël, you're not the widow.'

But Robert only stares out of the window, in silence for a moment, before he speaks.

    ROBERT: Nevertheless, there is truth in it.*

58 EXT. DOWNTON. DAY.

From a window on the first floor, Branson looks down. In his arms he holds his newborn, motherless child.†

END OF EPISODE FIVE

....

* The difficulty here is that Cora realises, if they had done what Doctor Clarkson suggested right at the beginning, not that Sybil *would* have lived but that she *might* have lived, and that's just a fact, and Violet is trying to give some comfort. She doesn't usually talk about feelings, so I always think it's quite effective when she does.

† The shot of Branson and the child was filmed in what's called the Portico Bedroom behind the portico, like a sort of fortress that he's locked into, this alien boy with his tiny child.

EPISODE SIX

ACT ONE*

1 EXT. DOWNTON. DAY.

Mourners are leaving, some in chauffeured cars, some workers and villagers on foot, farmers in horse-drawn traps. The male gentry are in black morning coats and top hats, but some of the others wear suits with black arm bands. Robert is there, thanking the guests.†

....

* When Dan Stevens (Matthew) announced his departure, I had already written Episode Five, in which Sybil was going to die. It had already been cast and set up, and now I suddenly learned that by the end of the series another principal player had to go, too. Well, two actually, as Siobhan Finneran (O'Brien) also decided to leave around this time, but O'Brien's departure, as a servant moving on to another job, would not be a problem. The point was, I didn't want to do a second whole episode about someone dying. We'd originally planned to kill Sybil in Five, so we had three episodes for the audience to get over it, but now, suddenly, we had to kill someone else.

I went to Dan and asked if he might be prepared to finish this series and allow us to kill him in the first episode of the following year. That way, we would finish the Special with the baby in the crib and everyone happy. But he couldn't do that as he'd been offered some films and a play on Broadway, and he didn't want to cramp his next chapter, which I don't criticise him for in the least. It was perfectly understandable.

In fact, in the end, his refusal helped me, because if I'd killed him in the first episode of the following season I would have been stuck with funerals and mourning for half the series. But by killing him at the very end of Season Three it allowed me to have a six-month time jump, which we would never do between episodes but we could do between series, and that meant Matthew's death was in the past and it was time to move on. It gave us the opportunity for the series to be about Mary waking up, as opposed to just being in the pit of despair. But it was a bit of a nightmare, because here we were, mining Sybil's traumatic death – the first death at Downton – all the time knowing we had to have a second one before the end.

† I wanted to mix horse-drawn and motor vehicles, because that was a clear sign of transition. It was good visually, to say that at this time a lot of the farmers wouldn't have had a car, and they would use a trap as they always had. I had a great-aunt who ran a great open-fronted Daimler, with the chauffeur sitting in the rain, but she didn't take it out for an ordinary errand,

2 INT. DRAWING ROOM. DOWNTON. DAY.

Matthew is with Branson.

MATTHEW: I know we all sound like parrots, Tom, but I really would like to help if I can. So would Mary.

BRANSON: I've a baby I can't look after, no job, no money. I'm exiled from my country, and my wife is dead. I'm past help, but thank you.

The rest of the family are assembled. Robert enters.

ROBERT: The Southesks looked for you to say goodbye...*

CORA: I was here.

But her voice is heavy with sorrow. Isobel stands.

ISOBEL: I hope you'll tell me if there's anything I can do. Anything at all.

MARY: Thank you.

VIOLET: I'll come with you. Save him getting the car out twice.

ROBERT: You're both very welcome to stay for some dinner.

....

Continued from page 306:

which would still be done in a pony and trap until her death in the early 1950s.

We always think of a car as easy and a trap more difficult because of the harnessing and getting the horse and everything else, but they thought differently. I remember I didn't quite agree with Robert's waistcoat in this scene, which had a sort of blue trim on the black. I didn't feel he would wear anything so frivolous at his own daughter's funeral, but no doubt someone will write in and say that this was absolutely standard mourning stuff.

The black armbands survived into my own time. My brothers and I wore them for my mother for about a month, but not for my father. She died in 1980, he died twenty years later, and by then armbands had gone. It's always quite interesting to see a practice die in your own time. But it's sad in a way – to me, at least.

* We had just been staying with the Southesks in Scotland when I was writing this. We didn't tell them, so when they were watching it they both jumped out of their skin.

VIOLET: I don't think so. Grief makes one so terribly tired.*

She squeezes Robert's hand and pats Cora's shoulder.

VIOLET (CONT'D): Goodbye, my dear. Now that it's over, try to get some rest.

Violet kisses Mary and Edith, and then she and Isobel leave. Cora looks up.

CORA: Is it over? When one loses a child, is it ever really over?†

3 INT. SERVANTS' HALL/PASSAGE. DOWNTON. DAY.

The servants are having tea. Carson looks in.

CARSON: Is the dining room clear?
ALFRED: It is, Mr Carson. I must say, the funeral gave them a good appetite.

Two of the maids giggle.

CARSON: And what, may I ask, is so funny?
ANNA: It's all right, Mr Carson. They didn't mean any harm.

She turns to the young newcomers.

ANNA (CONT'D): We were all very fond of Lady Sybil, you see. We got to know her so much better during the war, and now we're very sad at the loss.
CARSON: If you want to do well at Downton, you should know these things without being told.

....

* An observation of my own. One of the elements of grief that I think people overlook is that sorrow is fantastically tiring. You get to the end of each day, when you're in the grip of a really deep grief, absolutely whacked. Maybe it's the churning around of your system, but anyway, I gave it to Violet to say because it's true.

† Not an original thought from me, but I believe losing a child at any age is the worst thing that can happen. We must all feel that, or almost all. My mother died in her sixties and my grandmother at the time was ninety-seven, but it still practically killed her. Well, it did kill her, really. She went straight downhill and died a couple of years later. You'd think there was a point when a parent was past that, but apparently not.

He turns away. Mrs Hughes is in the passage. He goes to her.

> CARSON (CONT'D): I ask you. In the old days, their mothers used to train them, at least in the basics. Now they arrive knowing nothing.
> MRS HUGHES: Perhaps their mothers don't want them in service any more.
> CARSON: And what are they supposed to do? Become bankers and lawyers?
> MRS HUGHES: And why not, Mr Carson? Why not?*

Back in the Servants' Hall, Jimmy is sitting by Thomas.

> ALFRED: Cheer up, Mr Barrow. A long face won't solve anything.
> ANNA: Leave him alone. He knew Lady Sybil better than any of us.
> THOMAS: Except you. We were the two who really knew her.
> JIMMY: I'd say your grief speaks well for her.
> THOMAS: Thank you for that.

He puts his hand over Jimmy's and squeezes it.

> THOMAS (CONT'D): Thank you for saying that.

Jimmy allows himself a slight grimace to Anna.†

....

* A cut for time… Carson forgets that the young maids would hardly have known Sybil, and he is not prepared for the casualness of twentieth- and twenty-first-century labour. People don't feel now that they have plighted their troth with the company that employs them. It's interesting how Americans seem to feel that loss more than we do. Over there, lots of companies have drives and they all go away for a camping weekend together to try and engender that kind of company spirit that used to be quite common, but I'm afraid that if you live in an era where you have to engender it artificially, it means it's not going to work, whatever you do. Now, even when they're happy and working hard, people are aware that in twenty years' time they'll probably be doing something else. As for Carson's comments on the likelihood of women entering the professions, he is only revealing his own limitations.

† Thomas's feelings for Jimmy are now beginning to get out of control. The difference between someone being sympathetic towards you and fancying you is something that's tripped almost all of us up at some point or another, whichever side we stand.

4   INT. DRAWING ROOM. CRAWLEY HOUSE. NIGHT.

Isobel has removed her hat but has not changed. The door opens and Ethel comes in with a tray.

ETHEL: Are you sure you wouldn't like this laid in the dining room, ma'am?
ISOBEL: No, thank you. I'd like to eat quickly and have an early night.
ETHEL: How was the service?
ISOBEL: Oh, quite nicely done. But you know how it is when you bury someone young. It's hard to find any cause for celebration.
ETHEL: I feel for her ladyship. When you lose your child… There's nothing worse under the sun.
ISOBEL: No. There's nothing worse.

Isobel thinks for a moment.

ISOBEL (CONT'D): I was wondering if I might try to take her out of herself. Perhaps give a little lunch party. Nothing formal. Just Lady Grantham and the girls…
ETHEL: And I could cook something special.

This reminds Isobel of the problem. She sips the soup on the tray. It is disgusting. She recoils slightly from the spoon.

ISOBEL: Well, we don't have to decide that now.*

5   INT. MARY'S BEDROOM. DOWNTON. NIGHT.

Anna is getting Mary ready for bed.

MARY: But I don't understand why they haven't let him out.
ANNA: Mr Murray hasn't been to see Mrs Bartlett yet, and when he does, she may not want to repeat the things she said to me.
MARY: Well, she must be made to repeat them.

....

* Here we have an irony because I know Isobel's son is going to die before her. All of us involved are thinking about that; what we're going to do with her character, how we're going to develop Isobel beyond Matthew's death, because we certainly wanted to keep Penelope Wilton. There was never any question we weren't going to ask her to stay. So we would have to develop her in a slightly different way, and her principal relationship eventually will be with Violet, to replace her relationship with Matthew.

ANNA: Even then, would we have enough to overturn the verdict? How can we prove she was cooking that pie and not something else?
MARY: Because something else would have been found. It had to be the pie.

She smiles at Anna's anguished face.

MARY (CONT'D): Look, I'm not saying it'll all be done by Tuesday. But this is the moment we've been waiting for. What's the matter?

Anna is crying, but she shakes her head.

ANNA: It's so nice of you to say 'we'.
MARY: I mean it. We need some good news in this house, Anna, and this is it. This must be it.*

And the two of them give each other a hug.

6 INT. CORA'S BEDROOM/PASSAGE. DOWNTON. NIGHT.

Cora lies on her pillows. She holds a book, but she does not read. The door opens and Robert enters. He hesitates.

ROBERT: I thought I might move back in here tonight. If you'll have me.
CORA: Not yet. I think I'd rather sleep alone for a while yet.
ROBERT: Well, if you're sure…
CORA: I'm sure.†

....

* We enjoy our moments of bonding: Carson and Robert, Carson and Mary, Mary and Anna, and so on. They're quite consciously displayed as couples, viewing problems sympathetically but from the slightly different perspectives of their contrasted positions, all of which underpins my own philosophy of 'There but for fortune,' which is key to the show. It is the chance of birth that has made Anna work for Mary and not the other way round, and these scenes underline that.

† In these houses, the bedroom where the lady of the house sleeps is her room. Even if she is one half of a couple, it would be called her ladyship's bedroom. If he chose to sleep in it that was his business, but he would have another bedroom. Here we cheat slightly, because we have him sleep in the dressing room every now and then, when, in real life, he would have had another bedroom to himself and either used it or, in many cases, not.

He starts to leave, but then he stops.

ROBERT: Cora —

CORA: Let's not go through it all again.

ROBERT: But I'm not arguing. You listened to Clarkson, and so should I have done. But Tapsell has a reputation as an expert —

CORA: And you believed him. When Doctor Clarkson knew Sybil's history and he did not. You believed Tapsell because he's knighted and fashionable and has a practice in Harley Street… You let all that nonsense weigh against saving our daughter's life. Which is what I find so very hard to forgive.

ROBERT: Do you think I miss her any less than you?

CORA: I should think you miss her more, since you blocked the last chance we had to prevent her death.

This is very hard, but she just looks at him. He nods.

ROBERT: I'll say goodnight, then.

CORA: Goodnight.

He goes and she is left alone. Outside in the passage, Robert closes the door, wipes his eyes quickly and walks away. *

7 INT. DINING ROOM. DOWNTON. DAY.

Robert, Matthew and Edith are having breakfast.

EDITH: How is Mama?

Robert looks at her.

EDITH (CONT'D): I'll go up after breakfast.

Branson comes in. There is a silence until Edith speaks.

EDITH (CONT'D): I hope you got some sleep.

BRANSON: Some. Thank you.

....

* Cora now exposes Robert's weakness here, in that he can't let himself break free of the old ways and the old traditions. She's right, really, and unfortunately she can't resist rubbing it in. I don't think she could be much more severe than she is here. I suspect I'm slightly on Robert's side, because Sybil's gone now and this behaviour won't bring her back.

MATTHEW: How is the baby doing?*
BRANSON: I envy her. She doesn't know a thing about it.
EDITH: We ought to think about getting a nurse. Mrs
Rose will leave once the baby's weaned. Perhaps a local
girl —
BRANSON: But I'm not staying. Or at least, just until I
find a job.

This is clearly something they hadn't thought about.

EDITH: Well, there's no rush.
MATTHEW: God, no.
ROBERT: Tom's right. He has to start to make a life for
himself some time.
EDITH: Some time, yes. But not right away. And anyway,
now that the funeral's over, we ought to think about the
Christening. Do you know what you'd like her to be
called?
BRANSON: I'd like to call her Sybil.
MATTHEW: Of course.
ROBERT: You don't think it might be a little painful?
BRANSON: Very painful, at first. But I think it's
right. I want to remember her mother whenever I look at
her.
EDITH: Of course you do. And she would want to be
remembered. I'll go and see Mr Travis this afternoon.
BRANSON: Why Mr Travis?
EDITH: To fix the date.
BRANSON: But Sybil will be Catholic.
ROBERT: What?
BRANSON: My daughter is Irish and she'll be Catholic.
Like her father.

....

* It's tough to have children in a series like this, because the ageing is so
difficult. You can take an actor through ten years and you don't really have to
age them much beyond greying up their temples a bit. But the changes in a
year of a child's life, from six months to eighteen months, say, mean that
every time you see them you need a different kid. For each episode, you need
to find a child that's right for that moment, and maybe for two or three
episodes more, then it's on to another one. Branson's announcement here
that he is planning to leave is the first strand of a major theme through this
series and the two that follow. So far, Robert doesn't mind if Branson goes,
but the child will complicate everything.

Robert is about to explode but he catches Edith's eye. She shakes her head. He stands abruptly.

ROBERT: It's time I started my morning.*

He walks out, leaving the others slightly stunned.

8 EXT. DOWNTON VILLAGE. DAY.

Mrs Patmore is strolling through the village with a basket.

ETHEL: Mrs Patmore!

The cook stops and looks about. There is Ethel, standing with her own basket. Mrs Patmore doesn't quite know what to do.

MRS PATMORE: Oh… Ethel.
ETHEL: Mrs Patmore, I wonder if I could ask for your advice.
MRS PATMORE: Well, I…
ETHEL: I suppose you know I'm working for Mrs Crawley now? At Crawley House?
MRS PATMORE: I had heard.
ETHEL: She's been ever so kind to me, and I'd hate her to suffer for it.

Mrs Patmore doesn't know where this is going.

ETHEL (CONT'D): You see, she's hired me as cook-housekeeper, but, to be honest, my cooking's a little rusty.
MRS PATMORE: Oh, yes?
ETHEL: She's giving a lunch party, to help her ladyship in her sorrow. I know she'll tell me to keep it simple, but I'd like to surprise her with something really nice.
MRS PATMORE: Our ladyship?
ETHEL: Mrs Crawley wants to show sympathy. I know you don't want to stop her.
MRS PATMORE: Of course not.
ETHEL: So might you help me prepare a few dishes? You just tell me how to make them. I'll do the work. Please.

....

* When Branson announces the Catholicism of his daughter, Robert just about holds it in, but clearly that's going to be a big issue, as it would be for these people, for many years after this.

MRS PATMORE: Look. I don't mean to be rude or personal, Ethel, but Mr Carson has made it very clear —
ETHEL: That no one from the house is to have any dealings with me?

Mrs Patmore confirms this with her silence.

ETHEL (CONT'D): But surely you're not afraid I'll corrupt *you*, are you?
MRS PATMORE: I am not.
ETHEL: Then why should Mrs Crawley be punished for showing me kindness?

9   EXT.   EXERCISE YARD.   YORK PRISON.   DAY.

Bates is walking around with other prisoners.   He passes Officer Durrant.

DURRANT: You don't look as optimistic as you did, Bates. Something wrong?
BATES: Not that I'm aware of, Mr Durrant.
DURRANT: Really? You seem downcast.

The prisoner Craig has seen this exchange and comes over.

DURRANT (CONT'D): I wondered if some scheme to improve your lot had gone awry.
BATES: If you know of something that might suggest my fortunes have taken a turn for the worse, Officer, perhaps you'd be kind enough to share it with me.
DURRANT: Am I kind enough to share it with him, Craig? No. I don't think I am.*

They laugh, as Bates continues walking.

* With these plots you have to decide how much you keep reminding the audience of the information. My ruling is, if the information doesn't really matter then I don't remind them of it. Here, what they need to know is that Craig wants to damage Bates, but the details can become monotonous if they're repeated too often. There are people who disagree with me over this, and they will repeat the minutiae of a plot three or four times so that the audience is solidly in possession of all the facts. Happily, the producers of *Downton*, Liz Trubridge, Gareth Neame and I, all agree on the *Downton* casual release of information without explanation. We do this with contemporary incidents as well as storylines. If the audience wants to follow them up and go on the internet, fine, but if they don't, that's fine too.

10 EXT. DOWNTON. DAY.

Mary is reading when Robert approaches.

ROBERT: Did you hear about Branson's announcement at
breakfast?
MARY: I wish you'd call him Tom.
ROBERT: He wants the child to be a left-footer.*
MARY: Papa, I know it's hard for you —
ROBERT: There hasn't been a Catholic Crawley since the
Reformation.
MARY: She isn't a Crawley; she's a Branson.
ROBERT: The only chance that child will have of
achieving anything in life is because of the blood of her
mother.
MARY: Well, I don't agree. And besides, Sybil —
ROBERT: That's another thing. I think it's ghoulish to
call her after Sybil.
MARY: Well, I don't.
ROBERT: I'm going to see Travis. Get him to come and
talk to… Tom. Try and make him see sense.†

11 INT. SERVANTS' HALL. DOWNTON. DAY.

Daisy folds away a letter and smiles.

ANNA: Good news?
DAISY: Mr Mason wants me to go and see him. On my
afternoon off.
JIMMY: Who's Mr Mason?
ANNA: Daisy's father-in-law.
JIMMY: What does he do? This Mr Mason?
DAISY: He's a farmer.

....

* I have always been puzzled by how this term started, but apparently,
according to the internet, it all goes back to the spade. The incoming
Protestants brought spades with footrests on both sides of the shaft, whereas
the native Irish, who were generally Catholics, had spades with one footrest
that was cut out of the shaft. So, if they dug with their left foot they were
consequently left-footers. This seems a bit neat to me, but perhaps it's true.

† Robert assumes that the child's chances are based on being Sybil's daughter.
It doesn't yet occur to him that Branson could have anything of value to offer.
That is the journey of discovery that he hasn't begun to make yet. Mary
disagrees with him on all counts here.

ALFRED: That's a grand life.

JIMMY: Do you think so? Too much getting up early for me. I'm a town man.

IVY: 'As I stroll down Pic-Piccadilly in the bright morning air?'

JIMMY: That's me.

She has been flirting with him, which he doesn't mind. Mrs Patmore has observed it all from the door.

MRS PATMORE: Ivy? Are you feeling all right?

IVY: Yes. Why?

MRS PATMORE: You look a bit flushed.

DAISY: You don't mind if I visit Mr Mason tomorrow, do you?

MRS PATMORE: Not if you finish your work today.

Ivy is still flirting with Jimmy.

IVY: I'd love to go to London one day.

JIMMY: Then you'll have to save up for a ticket, won't you?*

This makes Thomas laugh. He stares at Ivy, disdainfully.

THOMAS: You have a lot of time off.

MRS PATMORE: Not as much as she thinks. Come on, Ivy. Chop chop.

Jimmy looks up and Thomas winks at him.

12   INT.   DRAWING ROOM.   CRAWLEY HOUSE.   DAY.

Isobel is with Ethel.

ISOBEL: No, there's no need to cook. Just fetch some ham from Mr Bakewell, and make a light salad. You can't go wrong with that, and Lady Grantham won't want more.

ETHEL: I'd like to make a bit of an effort. To show our sympathies.

....

* I don't think there's any question that Ivy is obviously much better suited to Jimmy than she is to Alfred. It's only much later that she starts to realise what she's lost. She sees then that Alfred may not be strolling down Pic-Piccadilly but he's nevertheless more likely to own a house there, because he's actually working at something with prospects. But she doesn't see it here.

ISOBEL: It's a nice idea, Ethel. But I'd like to keep it safe. I'll walk up to the house later.

13 INT. DRAWING ROOM. DOWER HOUSE. DAY.

Violet, in black, is having tea with Robert.

VIOLET: What is your plan for the child?

ROBERT: What do you mean?

VIOLET: Well, if Branson takes her away to live with him in Liverpool, or wherever he comes to rest, then presumably it will be his influence that governs her upbringing.

ROBERT: I hadn't thought about that.

VIOLET: Then I suggest you do, and soon. What does Cora say?

ROBERT: Not much… Not much to me, anyway.

VIOLET: She still holds you responsible?

ROBERT: She's wretchedly unhappy, if that's what you mean.

VIOLET: I will not criticise a mother who grieves for her daughter.

ROBERT: I think she's grieving for her marriage, as well as for Sybil.

VIOLET: Robert, people like us are *never* unhappily married.

ROBERT: What do we do if we are?

VIOLET: Well, in those moments, a couple is 'unable to see as much of each other as they would like'.*

ROBERT: You think I should go away?

VIOLET: Or Cora could go to New York to see that woman. It can help to gain a little distance.

ROBERT: I can't seem to think straight. About any of it.

VIOLET: My dearest boy, there is no test on earth greater than the one you have been put to. I do not

....

* I love this line of Violet's, which is a quote from an aunt, but actually Violet is trying to be helpful. She defends Cora for grieving, but she tries to remind Robert that they must observe the disciplines of their way of life. One of the strengths of the show is that we make it very clear that they are all living under constraints – the family quite as much as their employees – and these constraints are at times very difficult. But that's part of the game they're all playing, and these are the rules they're playing by.

speak much of the heart, since it's seldom helpful to do
so, but I know well enough the pain when it is broken.
ROBERT: Thank you, Mama.
VIOLET: Which won't answer what we are to do about the
child.
ROBERT: I've asked Travis to dinner. I thought he could
talk to Branson.
VIOLET: We shall see. I cannot say I have much faith in
Mr Travis's powers of persuasion.

END OF ACT ONE

ACT TWO

14 INT. KITCHENS. DOWNTON. DAY.

Daisy and Ivy are working. The footmen are lounging about.

DAISY: Don't you two have any work to do?
JIMMY: We're cleaning silver later, but Mr Carson told
us to wait for him.
IVY: I wouldn't mind your hours... What's the matter?*
ALFRED: You look very —
IVY: Very what?
ALFRED: I don't know exactly.
DAISY: Stop gabbing, Ivy, and remember you've my work to
do tomorrow as well as your own.
JIMMY: Are you off to see the rich farmer?
DAISY: Whatever he makes, he earns it.

....

* It is true that footmen had a far easier time of it, and the more footmen
there were, the lighter the load. As living status symbols, they may have had
duties, waiting at table, winding clocks, but a kitchen maid worked from the
crack of dawn until she turned in, with very few breaks. It wasn't a dead end,
because the kitchen maid was on a ladder, first to be still-room maid and then
undercook and eventually cook – that's if she didn't leave in her twenties and
marry, like a lot of them did – but nevertheless, it was very tough. The
footmen were the idle rich among the servants, and spent much of their time
just sitting about.

ALFRED: Oh, it'd be nice to be your own boss.
DAISY: No farmer's his own boss. He takes his orders
from the sun and the snow and the wind and the rain.

Mrs Patmore comes in. She is dressed to go out.

MRS PATMORE: Oh, I see. Is this the new servants' hall?
What have they done with the old one, I wonder?

*The others accept their dismissal and go. Mrs Patmore is
checking a book against some sheets of paper. Ivy watches.*

MRS PATMORE (CONT'D): What are you staring at?
IVY: A cat can look at a king.
MRS PATMORE: But not at a cook. Now get on with
whatever it is you're doing. I'll be back before the
gong.

15 INT. SERVANTS' HALL. DOWNTON. DAY.

*The footmen come in to find O'Brien sorting buttons. Thomas
is in there, gluing a leather sole.*

O'BRIEN: What are you doing?
THOMAS: Sticking it together. It's coming away but
there's no wear in it.
O'BRIEN: I think Mr Dobson's gone off. We should find a
new cobbler. What are you two up to?
ALFRED: We're waiting for Mr Carson.
O'BRIEN: You've been bothering young Ivy. Or she's been
bothering you.
JIMMY: That's more like it.
ALFRED: Speak for yourself.
O'BRIEN: Don't you like Ivy?
JIMMY: Oh, I don't mind her, but she's not my type.

O'Brien sees Thomas listening. She smiles, encouragingly.

THOMAS: What type's that, then?

Jimmy laughs, just as Carson looks in.

CARSON: Why are you here, and why isn't the pantry table
set out for cleaning?

16 INT. KITCHEN. CRAWLEY HOUSE. DAY.

Mrs Patmore walks in and takes out the sheets of paper. Ethel is with her.

MRS PATMORE: I don't know what I'm doing here.

ETHEL: You're here because you're kind.

MRS PATMORE: Am I? Right. I've written down some receipts. They're not complicated but I want you to study them. This is a list of what you'll need. I'll come in on Thursday morning and see how you're getting on.*

ETHEL: Can I really do it? Salmon mousse?

MRS PATMORE: Anyone who has use of their limbs can make a salmon mousse.†

ETHEL: Lamb Chops Portmanteau'd? I don't know…

....

* I'm sad this was cut because 'receipt' is not used much in this sense now, but then it was the standard word for recipe. In fact, recipe was considered common. I would say that the transition was in the Fifties. My mother went on saying receipt through the Sixties and Seventies, but by then it had become rather an affectation. I'm always interested by the evolution of words. 'Receipt' was doomed because it became so ordinary in its other meaning: 'Would you like a receipt?' A meaning that is more used now than ever. Throughout history, when a word has two meanings, one will eventually dominate the other, until either the meaning will be adjusted or a new word will appear. 'Recipe', really, is a corruption of 'receipt', isn't it? The final 't' has been replaced by an 'e'.

† Salmon mousse always makes me laugh, because there was a time in the early Seventies when you seemed to get salmon mousse as a first course in more or less every house you went to, because that generation of women were still learning to be their own cooks. The pre-war cooks had finally tailed away in the Sixties, but today's mass of private caterers hadn't really begun. You quite often hired someone to come in from the village to serve or wash up, but you normally cooked yourself, and yet many of these women had grown up never having cooked anything. The bonus of salmon mousse was that it's absolutely foolproof, and in fact it was one of the very first things I cooked. As time passed, I varied it to tuna mousse, but that didn't make an enormous difference. It was the first course, I should think, at more or less every dinner I gave between the ages of about twenty and thirty. Unlike me, Mrs Patmore has the pride of a real cook.

MRS PATMORE: Surely you can cut up a bit of chicken liver and some parsley?*

Ethel looks at her.

MRS PATMORE (CONT'D): Oh, why not just serve 'em bread and cheese then, and have done with it?
ETHEL: You're right. I'll give it a go.

17   INT. HALL/LIBRARY. DOWNTON. EVE.

Isobel has just arrived.

ISOBEL: Please tell Lady Grantham I'm here.
CARSON: She's in the library, ma'am.
ISOBEL: How is she? How is everyone?
CARSON: This is a house of mourning, Mrs Crawley. It will be for some time.

18   INT. LIBRARY. DOWNTON. EVE.

Cora, in a black evening dress, looks up as Isobel enters.

ISOBEL: Forgive me for barging in, but I have a little plan… Oh, goodness. You've changed. It's much later than I realised.†

....

* Lamb Chops Portmanteau is a genuine recipe from that period. Food was rather fussy then, as it was right up to the era of Fanny Craddock in the 1950s and 1960s. Dishes were trimmed with green mayonnaise rosettes and all that sort of stuff. It took years for the rather cleaner cooking of the USA and the continent to dispose of those frills on lamb chops and all that niminy-piminy presentation. I used to be amused when I was young by the mutual disparagement by Americans and the English of each other's cuisine. Americans would always tell you how terrible English food was, and we would always say how terrible American food was. In fact, on the whole, the Americans were right and we were wrong. Our food after the war was not good. I suspect it was partly because of the departure of the cooks. A woman who was expected to do all the jobs formerly undertaken by nannies and cooks and housekeepers and cleaners can hardly be blamed for not excelling at any of the tasks. At any rate, for whatever reason, this was an uncomfortable period for English food, which started going downhill in the 1920s and probably reached its nadir in the 1950s, before our national menu began to rebuild itself.

† Isobel is quite deliberately the first of the family group who begins to abandon the Edwardian customs. She starts having her supper on a tray in

ISOBEL: Well, I was wondering if you and the girls might
come to me for luncheon on Thursday.
VIOLET: Do I count as one of the girls?

Isobel had not seen her, half hidden by a wing chair.

ISOBEL: Of course.
CORA: You're very kind, but I'm not really going out at
the moment.
ISOBEL: There'll be no one else there, only me. And a
walk to the village might blow some cobwebs away.
CORA: I'm afraid I would only bring my troubles with
me.*

....

Continued from page 322:

the drawing room, she stops changing for dinner, and so on. Violet, by
contrast, continues to dress when she is alone and is served alone in the
dining room by her butler. Both types existed and you find a version of both
types now; those who embrace informality and change and those who do not.
Today there is an obsession with comfort, the logical extension of which is
that we should all be wearing trainer pants with elasticated waists, because
there comes a moment when the discomfort, even of a tie, is almost
impossible to endure. You see it in America with their dressing-down
Fridays, and on the West Coast the universal preference is for jeans and a
T-shirt. I take a dinner jacket to Los Angeles for red carpet evenings but
other than these, it's very rare that you will put it on. Again, the idea is that
you must always be comfortable.

My argument with it is that it is the death of the Event, because it is
impossible to make an evening into an event if everyone is sitting there in a
T-shirt and jeans. So, as in almost everything in life, what you may gain on
the roundabouts you certainly lose on the swings. A particularly strange
anomaly, which you see on the West Coast, is where the women will dress up
terrifically, to the nines, but the men don't match them. The men are in
leather jackets and jeans, and the women look as if they're going to a ball at
the Hofburg.

* I always think people can be curiously obtuse about how to deal with those
in the throes of a death. I remember once, when my mother had died after a
long illness, we were all in the country. We'd had the funeral and we were in
that numb state that follows, when a great friend of mine, who was staying
nearby with her in-laws, rang to see if there was anything she could do to
help. 'Can you ask us for a drink or something?' I said. 'Just to get my father
out of the house. We won't stay long, but he really needs to break it up a bit.'

The door opens and Mary and Matthew come in.

MATTHEW: Hello, Mother. What brings you here?
VIOLET: She's just invited Cora and Edith and Mary to
come to luncheon on Thursday.
MARY: Oh, how kind. Thank you.
VIOLET: That settles it.*

Robert arrives with Edith.

ROBERT: Isobel? Have you come for dinner?
ISOBEL: Oh, no. I'm dressed quite wrongly, and I know
you have a guest.
VIOLET: I doubt Mr Travis has much of an eye for fashion.
MARY: Oh, do stay. We need cheering up.
CARSON: The Reverend Mr Travis.

He is at the door. Travis walks in. He goes first to Cora.

TRAVIS: Lady Grantham, let me first say that I continue
to bear the deepest condolences for your great sorrow.

Cora starts to cry and Violet rolls her eyes.

19   INT.   KITCHENS.   DOWNTON.   NIGHT.

The footmen collect the pudding. Jimmy lifts the tray.

IVY: Can you manage?
JIMMY: Course I can.
IVY: Sorry. I didn't mean to insult your manhood.

....

Continued from page 323:

I later learned that her father-in-law could not understand the point of this.
Why would a man want to go out when his wife has just died? It is in those
moments that you realise the absolute lack of empathy or understanding with
which the English can be cursed. I find Americans are a more empathetic
race. Most Americans I know would not need to have it explained why Pa
wanted to go out. They would see that all he wanted was a rest from being
bereaved in a house of mourning. From that incident came the Isobel story
of asking them out for lunch.

* Here, Violet is once again a pragmatic and positive force. I fairly
unashamedly make Violet a guide to right thinking, most of the time.
Underneath her snobbery and self-importance, she has a fairly stout
grasp of the realities of life.

The two young men look at each other and laugh.

> MRS PATMORE: She didn't mean that, either. Now get on.
> ALFRED: Are you looking forward to your outing with Mr Mason?
> DAISY: I am. It's a lovely place.
> IVY: You should go with her.
> ALFRED: Or I could come out with you.
> MRS PATMORE: You know the trouble with you lot? You're all in love with the wrong people. Now take those upstairs.

As Jimmy walks past Thomas…

> THOMAS: Are you in love with the wrong person?
> MRS PATMORE: That's for him to know and you to find out.

Jimmy has walked off down the passage. Thomas murmurs.

> THOMAS: I will find out.*

20   INT.   DINING ROOM.   DOWNTON.   NIGHT.

The atmosphere is awkward.

> TRAVIS: But isn't there something rather un-English about the Roman Church?†
> BRANSON: Since I am an Irishman, that's not likely to bother me.

....

* I was rather sorry this went. Thomas is trapped in that moment when you think you're making your interest in someone clear, but they don't get it. Which we've all done. You think you're flirting, but if you ask them later why they led you on, they look at you completely blankly, because they don't know what you're talking about. This is where Thomas and Jimmy are. It is so outside Jimmy's consciousness that he should be courted by another man, and an older man at that, that it just doesn't occur to him. Which is a protection of sorts. It all rolls along without his knowing.

† Anglicans always say Roman Catholic, but Catholics only say Catholic. And when a Catholic character in a film says, 'I'm a Roman Catholic,' you know it's been written by an Anglican. This stuff intrigues me. Someone asked if I wasn't rather anti-Catholic in *Downton*. But they can't have been watching very attentively. I have quite a lot of fun with the anti-Catholicism, which I remember from my own youth.

TRAVIS: I cannot feel bells and incense and all the rest of that pagan folderol is pleasing to God.

BRANSON: I see. So is He not pleased by the population of France? Or Italy?

TRAVIS: Not as pleased as He is by the worship of the Anglicans, no.

EDITH: South America? Portugal? Have they missed the mark, too?

TRAVIS: I do not mean to sound harsh. I'm sure there are many individuals from those lands who please Him.

MARY: And the Russians? And the Spanish?

TRAVIS: There must be many good Spaniards.

MATTHEW: And we haven't even started on the non-Christians. There's the whole Indian sub-continent to begin with.

ISOBEL: And the British Empire. Does He approve of that?

TRAVIS: If you mean does He approve of the expansion of the Christian message, then yes, I think He does.

ROBERT: And so do I. Poor Mr Travis. You're all ganging up on him.

MARY: Well, you and Granny are ganging up against Tom.

VIOLET: Not me. The Dowager Duchess of Norfolk is a dear friend, and she's more Catholic than the Pope.*

ROBERT: I simply do not think that it would help the baby to be baptised into a different tribe from this one.

BRANSON: She will be baptised into my tribe.

ROBERT: Am I the only one to stand up for Sybil? What about her wishes?

MARY: Sybil would be happy for the child to be a Catholic.

....

* The Dowager Duchess of Norfolk is a dear friend of Violet, more Catholic than the Pope and perfectly real. The Duke's first wife was childless, and obviously for the premier Catholic of England there was no question of divorce. There was not then, and is not now, any shortage of Howards, but nevertheless, when she died he felt he should marry again and have another shot at it, as direct succession is always seen as preferable. His second and much younger wife had a son, Bernard, and two daughters, Rachel and Winifred, and then he died. So she was quite a young widow, and she had to fly the flag for the Norfolks until her son achieved his majority. I admire that, so I've put her in as a friend of Violet's.

ROBERT: How do you make that out?

MARY: Because she said so. To me. On the day she died.

BRANSON: Did she? Oh, God, did she, really?

ROBERT: I'm flabbergasted.

CORA: You're always flabbergasted by the unconventional.

ROBERT: But in a family like this one —

CORA: Not everyone chooses their religion to satisfy Debrett's.

Naturally, this silences the table. Violet glances at Robert. *

21 INT. SERVANTS' HALL. DOWNTON. NIGHT.

The servants are eating dinner.

CARSON: I've no great wish to persecute Catholics, but I find it hard to believe they're loyal to the Crown.

MRS HUGHES: Well, it'll be a relief for them to know you no longer want them burned at the stake.

JIMMY: I don't believe in orthodoxy.

....

* This is all really a reference to my own growing-up years, because I was a cradle Catholic. My family was not always Catholic, actually, but my grandfather died in the Great War at the age of twenty-nine, and my grandmother married again some years later when my father was eleven. Her second husband was a man called Arthur Byrne, whose family was very Catholic, and whose brother, Herbert Byrne, would end up as Abbot of Ampleforth. My father was summarily converted, much to the horror of his aunts and uncle, but then they didn't like their sister-in-law much anyway. They carried on as if he'd been sold into the white slave trade. As it turned out, my father enjoyed his Catholicism, and even quite enjoyed being part of a persecuted minority, as he then was. I don't mean we were spat at in the street, but among the upper middle and upper classes it was uncomfortable that one was Catholic. My wife's grandmother wouldn't have Catholics in the house, but that was quite rare by then. It was more a sense of our not being properly English, as Travis says here. In fact, his arguments would have been standard for an Anglican vicar of that time, or indeed later. But the family is more reasonable, with the slight exception of Robert, and they won't condemn the world's largest, most numerous Christian religion in this way. Besides which, it is fun to trap Travis. Still, it would have been a big thing for Robert to accept that his grandchild will be Catholic. Even in 1991 it was a big thing for my mother-in-law, so I'm the more appreciative that she has gone along with it so gracefully.

O'BRIEN: That's a long word.

JIMMY: A man can choose to be different without it making him a traitor.

THOMAS: I agree.

He finds Jimmy's observation encouraging.

ANNA: I don't like discussing religion. We'll only fall out, and surely it's our private business.

MRS HUGHES: Amen.

ALFRED: It's funny though, isn't it? All that Latin and smelly smoke and men in black dresses. I'm glad I'm Church of England, me.

THOMAS: Really. And what do you feel about transubstantiation?

ALFRED: You what?

CARSON: Never mind, Alfred. Your heart's in the right place, and I can't say that for everyone under this roof.*

....

*This is a *Downton* moment, because we always like to see a replica of the upstairs arguments going on among the servants. Alfred is anti instinctively, but the majority, on the whole, are tolerant, and I would say that was a fairly accurate replication of middle- and working-class society. Carson, of course, reflects Robert's resistance to Catholics. His remark about it being hard to believe they're loyal to the Crown was the great complaint, that their loyalty to the Pope made them not quite safe. This argument was credible enough in the wars of the sixteenth and seventeenth centuries, when there was a danger that Catholics were fifth columnists, loyal to the King of Spain, who wanted to make England a Catholic country. At least, that was the fear.

In fact, I believe most English Catholics just wanted to be left alone to get on with it, and sadly there is evidence that Queen Elizabeth I would have agreed with them. She did not stoke up the persecution of the Catholics until the Pope issued an encyclical saying that it was not a crime to assassinate her and that all good Catholics in England should rise up against their Queen. With this supremely unhelpful gesture, he turned every English Catholic into a potential traitor, which placed them in an impossible position. Again, the Queen may well have appreciated the spot they were in, but it meant the priests who were being smuggled in were enemy agents.

She also had to deal with the intriguing, in both senses, Mary Queen of Scots. When I was young I had a romantic vision of Mary Stuart, and in fact it was a poster of her kneeling at the block that first really interested me in history. Alas, now I believe she was not innocent of the death of her

22 INT. MARY'S BEDROOM. DOWNTON. NIGHT.

Mary and Matthew are in bed together, lit by the moon.

MATTHEW: When Sybil was talking about the baby being a
Catholic, did you get the sense that she knew?

MARY: I'm not sure. Not at the time, but of course I've
asked myself since.

MATTHEW: You'd think we'd be used to young death, after
four years of war.

MARY: That's why we must never take anything for granted.*

MATTHEW: Which is what I'm trying to get Robert to see.
He wasn't given Downton by God's decree. We have to work
if we want to keep it.

MARY: But not only Downton. Us. We must never take *us*
for granted. Who knows what's coming?

MATTHEW: Well, I have to take one thing for granted,
that I will love you until the last breath leaves my
body.

MARY: Oh, my darling. Me, too. Me, too.

And she pulls him into an embrace.

22A EXT. MRS BARTLETT'S HOUSE. LONDON. DAY.

Murray walks along the street and knocks on the door.

....

Continued from page 328:

husband, nor of several plots against Elizabeth. It is a very complicated issue
as to whether Elizabeth, by executing Mary Stuart, started a train of events
that led to both the execution of Charles I and subsequently Louis XVI.
Certainly that was the Queen's fear, that she had damaged the status of the
anointed sovereign. Anyway, all this is why anti-Catholicism did have
historically justifiable roots, and I'm a Catholic so I can say it.

* Here is a clear example of how, by this point, I was writing towards
Matthew's death, because by now I knew it was coming. I'd had all the
conversations with Dan Stevens, because we certainly didn't want to lose him
at all. But he'd made the decision. From then on he was very cooperative,
but we knew it was happening and so we had to get some emotional mileage
out of it, which is what we're doing here.

23 INT. MRS BARTLETT'S HOUSE. LONDON. DAY.

Murray is with Mrs Bartlett.

MURRAY: But this is quite different from the story you told before.

MRS BARTLETT: I don't think it is.

MURRAY: I'm afraid so. You said you went to Mrs Bates's house after you'd eaten your evening meal, whatever you choose to call it, and that she was in the process of cooking hers —

MRS BARTLETT: Well, I had just eaten when I saw her, that's true, but it was dinner at midday. Mr Bates was going to call on her that afternoon.*

MURRAY: But you described how the light from the gas lamps caught the rain, and made a kind of halo round her.

MRS BARTLETT: That sounds rather fanciful for me.

MURRAY: So you do not remember saying it?

MRS BARTLETT: I don't remember, because I never said it.

MURRAY: I see… As a matter of interest, why did you let me come here today, if nothing you could say would alter the verdict?

MRS BARTLETT: I thought it was time you saw how real people live.†

....

* I'm interested by this. When I was a child we had a cockney char, as they were known then, called Margaret Perrin. She came in every day of the week and worked for my mother, and she would always refer to the midday feed as dinner, and the evening feed as tea, which was, in fact, eaten earlier than our dinner. Then they would have some sandwiches before they went to bed. Interestingly, this is an eighteenth-century structure. They had breakfast very late to our way of thinking, at about eleven or twelve. They would then have dinner, the main feed of the day, at five, and it would go on until about eight. It was quite a palaver, and then they would go to the play or the opera and from there onto gaming and supper houses, and at the end of the evening, after the play, they would have oysters somewhere or they would go to the end of someone's soirée and eat something. So it made a different pattern of feeding, which survived in the working class but not in the upper class. I find that sort of thing fascinating.

† Mrs Bartlett is a match for Murray. I think it must have been very hard for people in this very stratified society, who had been told from birth they did not occupy a very high position, to stand against officialdom, and one of the great changes in my life – which I heartily approve of – is the refusal of the

24 INT. KITCHENS. DOWNTON. DAY.

Ivy is humming as she works, doing the odd dance step.
Jimmy's eating an apple. Alfred watches from the door.

ALFRED: Where's Daisy?

IVY: Gone off to play the milkmaid.

ALFRED: Do you like dancing?

JIMMY: 'Course she likes dancing. Everyone likes
dancing.

IVY: I love the foxtrot, don't you?

JIMMY: It's all right.

IVY: What about you, Alfred?

JIMMY: Alfred wouldn't do the foxtrot, would you,
Alfred? He takes himself too seriously for that.

IVY: Well, I love it. I think it makes you glad to be
young.

*Alfred cannot answer before Mrs Patmore returns.**

....

Continued from page 330:

majority of the population to be bullied by officialdom any more. But such a stand in the 1920s would have been rare and difficult. So, to me, Mrs Bartlett is an admirable figure. She doesn't accept that, just because she is low in the pecking order, she doesn't have the right to kick back. By the same token, I think Murray feels disempowered by people who challenge his authority, as, in my personal experience, civil servants and people are always disempowered, and usually rather fretful and indignant, when their automatic power is challenged.

* I had a bit of an issue over this scene with Ivy and the foxtrot, because the dance teacher, with the best intentions, had altered it to a Charleston, thinking that seemed more fun. People feel that the moment flat chests and hair bobbing came in the Charleston whizzed up on the next lift, but in fact it was some years before that happened. We are in 1922, but the Charleston didn't really arrive until 1925, and The Year of the Charleston, so called when it was all the rage, was 1926, so we had to revert to my original idea. The foxtrot of the Twenties was a wild dance, the precursor of the Charleston, whereas in my parents' day, in the Forties, it was more sedate and you sort of walked it. My plan had been to have the wild 1920s foxtrot, but in the event it was fairly demure, more like the later version.

25 EXT. MASON'S FARM. DAY.

Daisy walks through the busy farmyard towards the house.

26 INT. MASON'S FARM. DAY.

Mason is serving Daisy with another lavish tea. But she can't eat because of what she has just heard.

DAISY: Me? Run this farm? Are you serious?

MASON: Not right away, but eventually.

DAISY: But… I'm a cook.

MASON: And you think there's no cooking on a farm? You could do a cracking trade. With jams and jellies and cake and all sorts. You could sell them at the fairs.

DAISY: But I'm a woman.

MASON: Are you? Well, I never knew *that!*

He laughs. This is definitely his plan.

MASON (CONT'D): There are widows who take on a tenancy and you're liked in the big house. They'll not refuse you. I own the equipment, all the stock and I've quite a bit put by. It's hard work, but you're used to that.

DAISY: I can't answer now.

MASON: No, of course not! But think on it. And think on this an' all. My dream would be if you were to come here and live with me. So I could teach you.

DAISY: But I always thought I'd spend my life in service.

MASON: You have forty years of working ahead of you. Do you think these great houses like Downton Abbey are going to go on, just as they are, for another forty years? Because I don't.

All these notions are difficult for her to take in.

MASON (CONT'D): How's that young man you were talking about? Did you ever tell him how you feel?

DAISY: No… I thought he might like me, but I were wrong. He's keener on someone else.

MASON: Then he's a fool and not worth bothering with. He's seen a diamond and he's chosen glass.*

....

* Mr Mason is one of the moral instructors in our show, and he is also, to some extent, a *deus ex machina* in Daisy's story, offering her a future beyond

Clarkson enters.

CLARKSON: You wanted to speak to me, Lady Grantham.*

....

Continued from page 332:

Downton. We never really worry about Daisy because we know she has the protection of Mr Mason, but she is not yet ready to abandon the old way of life, which is symbolic of the way that generation looked both ways. They clung to the past while planning for the future. They are starting to make feelers and we have different stories of Mrs Patmore buying a house in the fifth series, and of Carson buying another, which is my way of marking the coming of change.

As for widows taking on a farming tenancy after the war, this wasn't unusual if the husband had been killed and the son was not interested or not old enough to take it on. She would know the way the estate worked, and wouldn't have to be taught the ropes. You'd think that society would be prejudiced against the concept of a woman farmer, but actually they weren't particularly. It's one of our misapprehensions. And if you look at a picture of a farmers' market where they were hiring for reaping or lambing, the women farmers are walking around as well as the men. One only has to think of Bathsheba Everdene in *Far from the Madding Crowd.* I'm sure there was a certain paternalistic attitude to women on their own, but they weren't that unusual, which is interesting to me. Here, again, Mason is sounding the trumpet for the end of the way of life they're all committed to, which you will hear more and more as the show goes on.

* With Clarkson and Lady Grantham or Clarkson and Isobel, I try to show the gradations of that provincial, almost Chekhovian society. The doctor, the school teacher, certainly the vicar, were in a superior position to a tradesman or a farmer, but below 'The Family' in the big house. In fact, the vicar would often be the younger son of a landed family, so his case was different, but with the others there was always a slight inequality, indicating that there would be social interaction, but you were not a great friend. So, for example, when the Dowager, Lady Grantham, gives a luncheon or dinner party, the doctor would not expect to be invited (and Clarkson feels honoured when he is invited in the fifth series), but he might be asked to tea, when he'd gossip about the village.

I always feel sorry for people in that society who were neither fish, flesh, foul nor good red herring, and sorriest of all for the governesses and tutors. Tutors less, because being a tutor could be seen as the beginning of a career in the civil service or something – a recommendation from, say, Lord Minto

VIOLET: Yes. On a melancholy matter, I'm afraid.
Please.

Violet beckons for Clarkson to sit, and he does.

CLARKSON: How can I help?
VIOLET: I want to talk a little more about the death of
my granddaughter.
CLARKSON: A terrible, terrible tragedy.
VIOLET: But now I am concerned beyond that.
CLARKSON: Oh. Are you worried for the child?
VIOLET: No, not especially. No. She seems quite a
tough little thing.
CLARKSON: Are you fond of babies?
VIOLET: Of course.
CLARKSON: What's your favourite age?
VIOLET: About sixteen.
CLARKSON: So, how can I help?
VIOLET: Doctor Clarkson, my daughter-in-law is quite
convinced you could have saved Sybil had you been allowed
to.
CLARKSON: Well… One can never speak of these things
with any certainty.
VIOLET: Well, this is the point. What was the
likelihood of Sybil's survival?
CLARKSON: Had we operated? She might have lived. There
are cases where an early caesarean saved the mother after
pre-eclampsia.
VIOLET: How many cases?

....

Continued from page 333:

of his son's tutor would take you to a secretaryship or the start of a political
life. But for governesses it was a dead end, unless she could find a man who
would marry her without a loss of caste. Jane Eyre is an obvious example of
this in literature, superior socially to kindly Mrs Fairfax but not seen as good
enough for the company of Mr Rochester. And in Jane Austen's *Emma*, the
whole business of Emma's governess, Miss Taylor, marrying Mr Weston
disturbs the peace of the household until it is established that Mr Weston is a
gentleman, and so the former Miss Taylor may continue as an intimate of
Miss Wodehouse. I think in the country people do still have acquaintances
in the village that they're friendly with but they wouldn't ask them to a
top-level entertainment. It strikes me as absurd, but it still goes on.

CLARKSON: Not many, I admit. I'd need to do some
research.
VIOLET: Then can you do it?
CLARKSON: It was the way Sir Philip set his face against
any —
VIOLET: Sir Philip Tapsell is a vain and tiresome man.
We won't quarrel over him.
CLARKSON: So why will we quarrel?
VIOLET: Possibly because I want you to tell Lord and
Lady Grantham what you have almost admitted to me.
CLARKSON: But there was a chance…
VIOLET: Doctor Clarkson. You have created a division
between my son and his wife, when the only way they can
conceivably bear their grief is if they face it together.
CLARKSON: So you want me to lie to them and say there
was no chance at all?
VIOLET: 'Lie' is so unmusical a word. I want you to
review the evidence, honestly and without bias.
CLARKSON: Even to ease suffering, I could never justify
telling an outright lie.

Violet looks at him coldly.

VIOLET: Have we nothing in common?*

END OF ACT TWO

....

* I'm always interested by the whole business of the benign lie – what used
to be called a white lie – where you tell a lie and on the whole matters are
improved and people's feelings are spared. But is it right to conceal the
uncomfortable truth? This, for me, is the issue, because Clarkson is really
letting Robert off the moral hook that he ought to have faced, that he was
wrong to trust the London expert, rather than the man who knew Sybil from
childhood. And I think Violet's motives in seeking the Doctor's support are
defensible but flawed. She sees her son and daughter-in-law putting their
marriage at risk because of this difference, and she sees her own moral and
familial imperative as trying to get them back together. I don't criticise her
for that, but it doesn't mean I think she's necessarily in the right in making
Clarkson falsify the truth.

ACT THREE

28 EXT. FARMLAND. DOWNTON. DAY.

Matthew is walking with Branson. He points as he speaks.

MATTHEW: This is the farm I'd like to take back in hand.
It's badly run, and it makes no sense to manage it
separately.

BRANSON: What about the tenant?

MATTHEW: We'd look after him.

BRANSON: He's growing barley and wheat; I'd say he'd do
better with sheep.

MATTHEW: Exactly. We'd merge the grazing — How do you
know that?

BRANSON: How do you? After spending all your growing
years in Manchester.

MATTHEW: I've been on a steep learning curve since
arriving at Downton.

BRANSON: My grandfather was a tenant farmer in Galway,
with black-faced sheep.

MATTHEW: So there's a country boy inside the
revolutionary.

BRANSON: Not much of one.

MATTHEW: You must hate it here.

BRANSON: No, I don't hate it. But I don't belong here,
either. Lord Grantham tries to put up with me, but now
Sybil's gone he cannot understand why there's a chauffeur
at his table.

MATTHEW: What will you do?

BRANSON: I've thought of Liverpool. There may be
something for me there.

MATTHEW: And the baby?

Branson sighs.

BRANSON: I'll hire a woman or get a cousin over to take
care of her. I don't know. But what else can I do?

MATTHEW: You could leave her here.

BRANSON: No. I'll not be separated from her. She's all
I have left of her mother.*

29 INT. KITCHEN. CRAWLEY HOUSE. DAY.

Mrs Patmore is putting on her coat. Ethel is with her.

MRS PATMORE: Right. You know what you're doing?
ETHEL: I think so. Yes.
MRS PATMORE: Use an alarm clock to remind you when to
put things in the oven and when to take them out.
ETHEL: I will.
MRS PATMORE: You've done well, Ethel. Maybe you've also
done yourself a favour.
ETHEL: I'm very grateful.

....

* Having made the decision that Sybil would die, because Jessica Brown
Findlay wanted to leave the show, we then had to decide what to do with
Branson. One option was to send him back to Ireland, maybe leaving the
baby, and occasionally he could return as a guest star. But we all felt Allen
Leech was a great asset to the show. He is also an attractive man, and
knowing we were about to lose one attractive young man, we didn't really
want to lose two. More than this, his character is a bridge between the
people below stairs and the people above. He has been at different points in
the drama on equal terms with both groups, making him unique in the house.
Having brought that about believably (I hope), it felt foolish to throw it away.

So, having decided to keep him, the next question is, what is he going to
do? Someone suggested he open a garage in the village, but that would have
been too self-consciously difficult where Robert was concerned, a son-in-law
running a garage where the locals get their wheels changed is something that
he would not find easy to live with, and it would have been false dramatically
to make him find it easy to accept. But the job of agent, which was frequently
given to cousins or connections of the family, seemed to me believable. My
mother's grandfather was agent to Lord Ormathwaite in Shropshire, and
lived the life of a minor gentleman running that estate, so it seemed quite
possible that a man like Branson would be given the job. In this way, Robert
could absorb Branson into his family group, but in an acceptable and truthful
way. The only problem was, we'd never shown him doing anything but lying
underneath a car with an oil can, so from this point on we start planting the
idea that he has a rural background and some knowledge of the country.

30 EXT. CRAWLEY HOUSE. DAY.

Mrs Patmore walks through the gate and away, just as Carson comes out of the Post Office. He is shocked by what he sees.

31 INT. YORK PRISON. VISITING ROOM. DAY.

Murray is with Bates and Anna.

BATES: I expected her to deny everything. The moment she realised her testimony would release me.

ANNA: You know she did say every word of it?

MURRAY: Of course. But I'm afraid someone tipped her off before I went to see her.

BATES: I think I know who.

Bates looks up at Officer Durrant, who stands nearby.

MURRAY: The question remains as to what we do next. I wonder what Mrs Bartlett is thinking at this moment.

ANNA: That she's glad Mr Bates is still in prison.

MURRAY: I'm not sure. It's a big thing for a woman like that to lie to a lawyer. To flout the law.

BATES: They would have bribed her to do it. Or frightened her.

MURRAY: Well, we cannot offer a bribe. But perhaps we can try to persuade her. Into returning to the path of truth.

BATES: Let me see what I can do.

ANNA: Nothing foolish. You mustn't do anything stupid. Promise me.

BATES: Leave it with me, Mr Murray.*

....

* I like Murray's being practical. In my experience, lawyers are a ruthless bunch, and once they're on one side they stick to it. The question the public always asks them is how they can defend a man when they know he's guilty. They always get round this by saying, 'If he hasn't told me he's guilty, how do I know he is guilty?' Which of course is a straight piece of Houdini. The truth is, they have an amoral streak that allows them to absent themselves from the notion of whether their client is guilty or not. I don't exactly criticise this, because the legal system would not work if every criminal had to be defended by people who believed in their innocence or prosecuted by people who believed in their guilt. So I do understand the system, but for me it has a dark side, and that's what we refer to here.

32 INT. KITCHEN. CRAWLEY HOUSE. DAY.

Isobel comes in to where Ethel is working.

ISOBEL: I don't understand. I can smell cooking.
ETHEL: It's quite simple, ma'am. You'll be pleased, I promise. I've had help.
ISOBEL: And I suppose there's no ham and there's no salad?

Ethel's silence confirms this. The front doorbell rings.

ISOBEL (CONT'D): If this luncheon is a failure, Ethel, I shall hold you responsible.*

33 INT. MRS HUGHES'S SITTING ROOM. DOWNTON. DAY.

Carson and Mrs Hughes wait for Mrs Patmore, who comes in.

MRS PATMORE: Oh, I'm sorry if I've kept you waiting, but I had to send up the luncheon.
MRS HUGHES: It's good of you to spare the time.
MRS PATMORE: It's all right. I've only the men to cook for today and they're easy.
CARSON: What were you doing at Crawley House this morning?
MRS PATMORE: Who says I was at Crawley House?
CARSON: I saw you coming out.
MRS PATMORE: Oh, I see. Well, Mrs Crawley was giving a luncheon party and I...
CARSON: And you were helping Ethel.
MRS PATMORE: I suppose I was.
CARSON: Against my strict instructions to give the place a wide berth.

....

* We always try to make the moments in the day reasonably parallel when we go between the different groups. We may jump so that the next thing they're doing is changing for dinner or having tea, but we try to have one or two scenes between the servants or with the family, or maybe go to Violet, because that's the third camp, to show that they're *all* having tea, or they're *all* having breakfast, or they're *all* in the middle of the morning, just to endorse the time sequence.

MRS HUGHES: Now, Mr Carson, no one disputes your position as head of this household, but I'm not sure that you're entitled to dress down Mrs Patmore in this way —
CARSON: Of course, if Mrs Patmore wants to spend her time frolicking with prostitutes —
MRS PATMORE: Do I look like a frolicker?
CARSON: May I ask who was expected at this precious luncheon?
MRS PATMORE: Her ladyship, the young ladies and the Dowager.

This is much, much worse than Carson had thought.

CARSON: You have allowed a woman of the streets to wait at table on members of our family?
MRS HUGHES: They may be your family, Mr Carson. They're not mine.
CARSON: Oh… I am speechless.

He stalks out of the room.

MRS HUGHES: I would guess he won't stay speechless for long.*

34   INT. DINING ROOM. DOWNTON. DAY.

Robert, Matthew and Branson are having lunch. They're alone.

MATTHEW: I really need to spend a day with the agent. To talk it through.

....

* I would be sorry if the audience saw Carson's position as outrageously intolerant. I think, at that time, for someone to allow a reformed prostitute into their house would have been an enormous thing, and for her to wait at table on the Countess of Grantham and her daughters would have put the family's reputation at risk. So I don't think his position is unreasonable, even if it is very unmodern. We, on the whole, tend to sympathise with Isobel's more advanced views, but if people read into this that I think Carson is completely wrong-headed then they would be mistaken. As for Mrs Hughes, she always has an ambivalent attitude to this sort of thing. She doesn't dislike Ethel. She rather admires her for rebuilding her life. At the same time, she thinks it only works with Mrs Crawley because Ethel is the sole servant employed there. Finally, she believes Ethel will never have a real chance until she moves away from the area where her past is known. So her position is not entirely modern, either.

ROBERT: Jarvis has a lot on his plate.

MATTHEW: Yes, of course, but I want to —

ROBERT: Must we discuss this now? It's very boring for Tom.

BRANSON: I don't —

MATTHEW: Tom is your son-in-law, and his daughter is your only grandchild.

ROBERT: None of which gives him a word in the running of this place. Or would you like to involve Carson? Or the maids? Or people in the village?

BRANSON: Look, I really —

Robert is angry but so is Matthew.

MATTHEW: Robert, we must act if we are to avoid another crisis. At the moment the capital is leaking into the cracks caused by bad management.

ROBERT: Bad manage—?

Alfred and Jimmy arrive with the pudding.

ROBERT (CONT'D): We'll discuss it later.*

But it means he is already furious when Carson arrives.

CARSON: M'lord, I wonder if I could have a word.

ROBERT: Can't it wait?

CARSON: No, m'lord. It can't.

Robert gets up and leaves, throwing his napkin on his chair in anger. The two young men catch each other's eye.

35 INT. KITCHENS/PASSAGE. DOWNTON. DAY.

Alfred and Jimmy carry in full trays of plates.

JIMMY: Mr Carson's got a real bee in his bonnet. What's that about?

....

* Robert's resentment over Matthew involving Branson in running the estate is going to be a story that runs over the next series, but we start to ratchet up the tension from here. Robert has reluctantly accepted that he must share power with Matthew, but he wants nothing to change. In some way he expects everything to stay the same, even though Matthew is now a co-owner. In a sense, Matthew's cash allows him to think that, but Matthew knows that if things don't change, his cash will run out, just as Cora's cash ran out. Ideally, you should see all their points of view.

MRS PATMORE: Never you mind. Ivy? Have you been running?

IVY: No. Why?

MRS PATMORE: Well, your colour's up. I hope you're not coming down with something.*

ALFRED: How was your day off, Daisy?

DAISY: Lovely, thank you.

IVY: What are you doing? With your day off?

JIMMY: What I usually do. I'm going somewhere on me own.

He walks off, passing Thomas who lingers at the kitchen door.

MRS PATMORE: You never give up, do you? He's not interested.

IVY: Well, he must be interested in someone. He's young, isn't he?

THOMAS: But that 'someone' is not you.

He moves on and Ivy takes some plates into the scullery. Left alone, Mrs Patmore talks to Daisy in a gentler voice.

MRS PATMORE: How was Mr Mason?

DAISY: Very well. As nice as usual…

MRS PATMORE: What is it?

DAISY: He made me an offer. He wants me to go and live at the farm, because he wants to leave me the tenancy and all his stock and all his tools and all his money and everything.

MRS PATMORE: My lord. You're a proper heiress.

....

* Make-up became a sort of young rebellion at this time. For years the official position had been that any use of make-up was only suited for loose women – not quite prostitutes necessarily, but loose and fast women – when secretly many respectable women wore make-up and had done for years. There was, in fact, a big market in what we would now call nude make-up, which is make-up that doesn't quite show but just improves you. That was essentially a mid- to late-Victorian concept, of slightly tinted balms and powders that would make an 'un-made-up' woman look prettier. Now visible make-up was on the way in and young girls like Ivy would see photographs in magazines, not only of actresses but of countesses and politicians' wives, all in visible make-up, and want to try it. Mrs Patmore is firmly on one side of this divide. Ivy, as a young woman in the early Twenties, quite understandably is on the other.

DAISY: I haven't said yes, yet.

MRS PATMORE: But he's made the offer. And a very generous one it is, too.

DAISY: He's ever so generous. And so kind.*

36 INT. DINING ROOM. CRAWLEY HOUSE. DAY.

The five women are eating together.

CORA: This was very good.

ISOBEL: It was. It really was.

VIOLET: Don't sound so surprised.

ISOBEL: I am surprised. I owe Ethel an apology. I've underestimated her.

EDITH: I sometimes wonder if I should learn to cook.

MARY: Why?

EDITH: You never know. It might come in handy one day. And I've got to do something.†

ISOBEL: What did you say to that editor who wanted you to write for him?

EDITH: I haven't said anything, yet. It's probably too late now, anyway.

ISOBEL: Matthew tells me Robert was against it.

CORA: What difference does that make?

VIOLET: Oh, really, my dear, shhh —

CORA: We're all family. I'm not letting the side down. I'm just saying that Robert frequently makes decisions based on values that have no relevance any more.

....

* I've made it quite clear that there are strings, namely that Mason sees her as taking over the farm. If she wants a different future, then in a way she is morally bound to tell him, so that he has the option of not making her his heir. That will be a spike that she is on, but much later.

† This was inspired by my grandmother. She was not a very progressive, nor indeed particularly intelligent, woman, but she decided her daughters should learn how to cook. They had a cook then called Carrie and she agreed to give cooking lessons to the three girls. So they all trooped down to the kitchen and solemnly learned how to make pastry or whatever. My grandmother's friends found out about it and thought it was a ridiculous idea. They argued that it made extra work for Carrie and, if it caught on, it would threaten people who needed the work. Obviously, as things turned out, the fact that they had learned how to cook – although not, in my mother's case, particularly well – would be a saving grace after the war.

EDITH: Do you think I should do it?
ISOBEL: I wouldn't countermand your father.
VIOLET: Then why bring it up?
MARY: Well, I do. And so does Matthew.

The door opens. It is Robert.

ROBERT: And so does Matthew what? What else has Matthew
decided for my family?

Isobel stands.

ISOBEL: Robert —
ROBERT: Don't worry. I don't need to be fed. We're
going. All of you. Now. This is completely
astonishing.
CORA: What are you talking about?
ROBERT: Do you know who has prepared this luncheon for
you?
CORA: Yes. Ethel. Our former housemaid.
ROBERT: Who bore a bastard child.
VIOLET: What?
CORA: Robert, Ethel has rebuilt her life —
ROBERT: Has she? Do you know what she has built it
into?
MARY: What do you mean?
ISOBEL: I think Cousin Robert is referring to Ethel's
work as a prostitute.

This is news. Violet recovers first.

VIOLET: Well, of course, these days servants are very
hard to find.
ISOBEL: I don't think you understand the difficulties
she's had to face —
ROBERT: I couldn't care less how she earns her living!
Good luck to her! What I care about is that you have
exposed my family to scandal!
ISOBEL: But who would know?
ROBERT: I can't tell you how people find out these
things, but they do. Your gardener, your kitchen maid,
your…

*The door opens and Ethel enters with a tray of the pudding.
She is neatly dressed in black with a white apron. Violet
whispers to Mary.*

VIOLET: It seems hard to believe, but then I suppose she has an appropriate costume for every activity.
ROBERT: We're leaving.
ETHEL: Is this because of me, m'lord?
CORA: No. It's because of his lordship. And we're not leaving. Is that a *Charlotte Russe*? How delicious.
ETHEL: I hope it's tasty, m'lady. Mrs Patmore gave me some help…
CORA: I'm glad to know that Mrs Patmore has a good heart, and does not judge.

She says this looking directly at Robert.

ROBERT: Is anyone coming?
VIOLET: It seems a pity to miss such a good pudding.

Robert slams out of the room.

37 EXT. EXERCISE YARD. YORK PRISON. DAY.

The prisoners are exercising. Bates has his eyes on Craig further down the line. Gradually he moves up. Some of the others notice, but they do not give him away. As they pass a small recess, Bates acts fast, pulling Craig out of the line.

CRAIG: They'll get you for this.
BATES: Maybe. But not before I get you.
CRAIG: I don't know what you want.
BATES: Who went to see Mrs Bartlett? Who got her to change her evidence?
CRAIG: Who's Mrs Bartlett?

Quick as a flash, Bates pulls a thin stiletto knife out of his pocket and presses it into Craig's neck.

CRAIG (CONT'D): You're out of your bleedin' mind.
BATES: Yes. I am out of my mind and, lest we forget, I am an assassin. Now tell me, who went to see her?
CRAIG: Durrant.
BATES: How did you know about her evidence?
CRAIG: I seen where you hide your letters. When we shared a cell.
BATES: I see. Well, now Durrant is going to tell her the police are on to her, and she's gonna wind up inside if she doesn't change her story.
CRAIG: Change it to what?

BATES: To the truth.

CRAIG: Or else what?

BATES: Or else I go to the Governor. I tell him how you and Durrant are bringing in drugs and trying to get me to sell them for you.

CRAIG: That's a lie.

BATES: My goodness, so it is. But I think he'll believe it, don't you? When you've already had a warning? And Durrant'll lose his job, and you will stay here five years longer.

CRAIG: Or we could always kill you.

BATES: Yes, but you're not a killer, Craig. Not like me. You rob and steal and break into helpless old women's houses. But you're not a killer. It's not in you. I am. It is in me.

He releases his grip on Craig's throat and steps back.

CRAIG: It was only a joke.

BATES: Well, it was a bad joke and now it's over.

CRAIG: He won't like it.

He nods towards Durrant as they come back out into the light.

BATES: He'll like it better than early retirement.

He smiles at a curious Durrant and moves off. *

38 INT. MRS HUGHES'S SITTING ROOM. DOWNTON. NIGHT.

Carson is still horrified.

CARSON: No. He went down there and told them. And none of them came away.

MRS HUGHES: Not even the Dowager? My, my. Perhaps the world is becoming a kinder place.

....

* I was sorry we lost the line about Bates having a killer's instinct, as I always like to keep a slight question mark hovering in the air above Bates's head. Bates is not above using his aura that he's capable of anything. I don't think it's a statement of truth when he says that he is a killer, but even I am not sure, and I wrote it. I suspect he was a ruthless killer in the Boer War, for instance.

CARSON: You say 'kinder'. I say weaker and less disciplined.*

MRS HUGHES: Well, if her ladyship is prepared to visit Crawley House, I dare say you won't object when I do.

CARSON: I won't forbid it, because I have no right to do so, but I *do* object. With every fibre of my being.

MRS HUGHES: Then we must agree to differ.

Mrs Hughes walks away but stops when Carson continues.

CARSON: If we must, we must, but you disappoint me. I never thought of you as a woman with no standards.

Mrs Hughes shoots him a look as she closes the door behind her.†

39 INT. LIBRARY. DOWNTON. NIGHT.

Robert is on his own when Mary comes in.

MARY: I wish you'd come back to the drawing room.

ROBERT: I'd only set your mother's teeth on edge.

MARY: She'll come through it. She will. Which brings me to your performance today. How did that help?

ROBERT: I was angry with Isobel. For exposing you all to gossip.

MARY: You were angry, all right. But not with Isobel or Ethel. I think it's because the world isn't going your way. Not any more.

He pours himself another drink.

ROBERT: Has Matthew told you about his latest plans for Downton?

MARY: I know he wants to change things.

....

* Mrs Hughes says kinder, Carson says weaker and less disciplined. Again, that's a *Downton* moment, because we agree with both of them.

† We often have these moments where Carson and Mrs Hughes recognise each other's rights in the pecking order. Mrs Hughes may be trendier and more informal, but she knows how the system works, and she's certainly prepared to tell Carson. She tells him off earlier for dressing down Mrs Patmore. And here Carson knows he cannot forbid her to go to the house. She is not under his authority in that sense. But, of course, he doesn't mind showing his displeasure.

ROBERT: Oh, doesn't he just. Now he intends to lecture poor old Jarvis on how to do his job, when Jarvis has lived in the area since he was a boy.

MARY: You mustn't let him upset you.

ROBERT: He's more or less told me I've let the estate fall to pieces.

MARY: I'm sure he didn't mean that.

ROBERT: Didn't he? 'A fool and his money are soon parted.' And I have been parted from my money, so I suppose I am a fool.

MARY: You won't win over the Christening.

ROBERT: Not if you're against me.

MARY: I'm never against you. But you've lost on this one.

ROBERT: Did Sybil truly not mind?

MARY: She wanted Tom to be happy. She loved him very much, you know. We all need to remember that.

ROBERT: I keep forgetting she's gone. I see things in the paper that would make her laugh, I come inside to tell her that her favourite rose is in bloom, and then, suddenly…

He closes his eyes in grief.

MARY: Say that to Mama. Please.

ROBERT: She doesn't want to hear it from me.*

END OF ACT THREE

....

* I think it is important in a family drama to contrive moments where only two members of the family are present, because once you have more than two of them there, the quality of intimacy changes; most people don't, on the whole, confide in a group. But also Mary is, in a sense, Robert's eldest son. He has invested her with that. And he doesn't mind revealing himself to her as having been disappointed in his own behavior, which he probably wouldn't say to Edith. We also have a little remembrance of Sybil. It always annoys me in a drama when characters leave and nobody ever talks about them again. It's as if the earth has swallowed them. I always make a point of their referring to Sybil every so often, or later to Matthew, just to make sure that we can't be accused of that.

ACT FOUR

40   INT.   NURSERY.   DOWNTON.   NIGHT.

The room is in shadow save for a night light burning.
Branson looks down into the crib, as Mary and Matthew come in.

MATTHEW: How is she doing?

BRANSON: She's as healthy and blooming as any motherless child could be.

MARY: She's a motherless child and I'm a childless mother. You'd think we could sort something out.

She laughs gently, as if this were a joke.

BRANSON: But she'll always be motherless. There's the difference.

This is kind of him, which Matthew appreciates.

MATTHEW: Thank you.

Mary takes the child from Branson and holds her, while Matthew strokes the baby's head. Matthew and Mary look at one another. *

41   INT.   SERVANTS' HALL.   DOWNTON.   NIGHT.

Dinner's over and they sit around.

MOLESLEY: You mean they stayed in that house? Even after they knew?

MRS HUGHES: I expect they didn't want to insult Mrs Crawley.

MOLESLEY: I couldn't have swallowed another bite. Not once I knew.

MRS HUGHES: Jesus managed to eat with Mary Magdalene.

MOLESLEY: Now, we can't be sure that he ate with her. He did allow her to wash his feet.

MRS HUGHES: I see. Well, I'll tell Ethel she has a treat in store.

....

* The bonding of the young ones becomes one of the themes in the following series. I was sorry this went.

Further down the table Ivy is distracted by Alfred's staring.

IVY: What's the matter with you?
ALFRED: I'm sorry, but… I don't know… You seem even prettier somehow.
MRS PATMORE: Ivy? We haven't finished yet.
IVY: We've never finished.

But as she walks past the cook, Mrs Patmore stops her.

MRS PATMORE: What's this?

She reaches up with her apron and wipes Ivy's cheek.

MRS PATMORE (CONT'D): Rouge? Have you been painting your face?
IVY: It's not like the old days, Mrs Patmore. All the girls do it now.
MRS PATMORE: Not in this house, Miss Hussy! Go and wash! We'll see no more of it!*

Jimmy has been playing the piano all this time. Thomas stands by the piano, watching him.

ANNA: It's nice to know we've another piano player in the house. Unless you think it's too soon?
MRS HUGHES: Oh, no. Lady Sybil was a bright young thing. She'd be glad of some music. You play well, James.
THOMAS: There's no end to Jimmy's talents, is there?

He rests his hand on Jimmy's shoulder. O'Brien has come in.

O'BRIEN: His lordship wants you.

....

* Mrs Patmore's demand that Ivy washes off the rouge is unfair, because by the early 1920s, as I have said, great ladies were beginning to wear lipstick that was quite clearly lipstick, and not a slightly pink balm, but this moment was inspired by an incident in *The Edwardians*, by Vita Sackville-West, when they look out at the servants walking to church across the park, and one of the maids is wearing a flower in her hat. She will be dismissed for this piece of frivolousness, when the hostess and her friend, Lady Roehampton, are both sleeping with their lovers under the same roof and the bedrooms have been arranged to make this easy. Vita Sackville-West is commenting on the disparity between the morals expected of the working class and the morals lived by the upper class. Here, this exchange can be seen as a similar case.

Thomas strokes Jimmy's neck and ear and walks off.

JIMMY: I wish he wouldn't do that.

O'BRIEN: What?

JIMMY: He's always touching me. I'm going to tell Mr
Carson.

O'BRIEN: You'd never.

JIMMY: I'd tell the flippin' police if it'd make him
stop.*

O'BRIEN: I must go. I need to fetch some linen and her
ladyship won't be long now.

She leaves the room as Jimmy plays on. Daisy comes up.

DAISY: I like to hear you play, but it makes me sad,
too.

JIMMY: Why's that?

DAISY: There was a footman here once, William; he used
to play.

JIMMY: But why does that make you sad?

DAISY: Because he died. In the war. He was… he was my
husband.

JIMMY: I see.

With a half-smile, Daisy moves off.

....

* All of us, or all of us when young, have found this situation difficult at some point. You hesitate to object because you're not quite sure that they are making a pass, yet it feels inappropriate and so you're stuck. When you're older, you just chuck their hand off your knee, but when you're young and people are standing slightly too close, it is very uncomfortable. We hear so much about inappropriate behaviour in the office now, but in my youth it was very difficult for a young woman to object to a man leaning over her when she was copying or pressing into her in a queue, because then he'd say, 'Ooh, pardon me for living,' and the woman would be made to feel a fool. For me, a straight pass – 'Would you like to come out for dinner and sleep with me?' – is infinitely preferable to a hand slithering down the side of your leg. But Jimmy is on to him by now. O'Brien, of course, is trying to encourage Thomas to cross the line, which she will use.

42 INT. PASSAGE/SERVANTS' HALL. DOWNTON. DAY.

Daisy carries a tray down the passage and into the servants'
hall. She stops dead. Facing away from her is Alfred,
alone, singing under his breath and trying to dance the
foxtrot.

  DAISY: What are you doing?

He jumps round as if he'd been shot.

  ALFRED: Nothing.
  DAISY: It didn't look like nothing.
  ALFRED: Can you dance the foxtrot?
  DAISY: I think so. Yeah. I can.
  ALFRED: Would you teach me?
  DAISY: Well, I'm s'posed to lay the tea…
  ALFRED: And here's me thinking you'd like to dance with
  me.
  DAISY: Go on, then.*

She puts down the tray and joins him.

  ALFRED: How do you put that hand —?
  DAISY: Like this.

They take up a dancing position.

  DAISY (CONT'D): You do… that foot goes back first.
  ALFRED: Right.
  DAISY: Yeah, it goes: slow, slow, quick, quick, slow,
  slow, quick, quick, slow, slow, quick, quick.

The pair dance clumsily under Daisy's tutelage, though she's
clearly relishing every moment of it.

  ALFRED: What is it?
  DAISY: Nothing. It just reminded me of when Thomas
  tried to teach me the grizzly bear…
  ALFRED: I've never heard of that one.

....

* Alfred's desire to get Daisy to teach him the foxtrot is rather shameful. We
should feel that he is wrong in the way he is using her affection for him. And
it reminds us of the last time Daisy was dancing with a man she was in love
with who wasn't in love with her, when she did the grizzly bear with Thomas
in Season One. So she has a hard time of it.

DAISY: Well, it was a long time ago, and a lot's happened since. Now, come on.

She starts to sing softly, as she dances.

43 INT. BEDROOM PASSAGE. DOWNTON. NIGHT.

O'Brien is carrying some shirts. She passes the dressing room door as Thomas comes out. They talk in hushed tones.

O'BRIEN: Everything all right?

THOMAS: So so. I don't think he's very happy but it's none of my business.

O'BRIEN: Not like your little footman friend.

THOMAS: Why do you say that?

O'BRIEN: I think he's got a crush on you. He was purring when you were with him at the piano. I saw.

THOMAS: Well, he's a nice lad. And he's obviously got good taste.

*O'Brien laughs and walks on.**

44 EXT. DOWNTON. DAY.

Mary and Edith are walking up the drive when Anna comes running towards them, waving a telegram.

ANNA: M'lady! It's arrived! It's here! I wanted you to be the first to know!

MARY: Know what? What's arrived?

ANNA: He's done it! Mr Murray's done it! He's got her to make a statement! Witnessed and everything!†

EDITH: Does he say why Mrs Bartlett changed her mind and told the truth in the end?

ANNA: I don't care why she did it! She's done it! That's what matters!

....

* I was sad we lost this, but the plot seems to have survived its excision. O'Brien is going in for the kill here by talking of Jimmy's crush on Thomas. She knows exactly what she's doing.

† We know how Murray has got the statement and it wasn't very pretty. I like those moments in a narrative drama where the audience knows something that the characters don't. Mrs Bartlett has been frightened to death by Craig and others from the prison, but Anna, Mary, Matthew and Robert just think it's Murray's being cleverly persuasive.

EDITH: So when will Bates be set free?
ANNA: It'll take a few weeks. For the formalities. But he'll be released. Mr Murray's quite clear about that. So Mr Bates is coming home.
MARY: Oh, I am so, so happy for you.
ANNA: I know you are.
EDITH: Have you told Papa?
ANNA: Not yet, m'lady.
MARY: Oh, do. Please do. He's very low just now. And it will be wonderful for him to hear something good.

They all run towards the house.

45 INT. SERVANTS' HALL. DOWNTON. DAY.

Daisy and Alfred are practising the foxtrot.

DAISY: I've got to go. I must get started on the luncheon.
ALFRED: Do you think I'm getting better?

Daisy hesitates. There isn't much sign of it.

DAISY: Why does it matter if you're enjoying yourself?
ALFRED: Because I've got to get the hang of it. I've just got to, that's all.

46 INT. LIBRARY. DOWNTON. DAY.

Robert is working when Cora comes in, with a sheet of paper.

CORA: Have you seen this note from Mama?
ROBERT: I have. I wonder what she wants.
CORA: I can stand anything but a lecture on marital harmony.

He laughs as if she were joking. But she does not laugh.

CORA (CONT'D): Do we have to go?
ROBERT: I think so. And we needn't stay long.
CORA: Good.
ROBERT: You look very nice this morning.
CORA: Don't flirt with me, Robert. Not now.
In case you've forgotten, our daughter is dead.

Cora walks out, closing the door behind her.

47 INT. LIBRARY. DOWNTON. DAY.

Robert is alone now, and sad, when the door bursts open and Anna is standing there, flushed. Behind her are Mary and Edith, still in their coats. Robert gets to his feet.

ANNA: I'm ever so sorry to interrupt, m'lord, but Mrs Bartlett has given a statement that'll clear him. At least, Mr Murray says 'it will make the verdict unsafe'. So Mr Bates is coming back to Downton.

MARY: Isn't it marvellous?

ROBERT: Yes. That is *absolutely* marvellous. Do you want to telephone Murray? If you do, tell Carson. He'll manage it for you.

EDITH: Why? Are you going out?

ROBERT: Your grandmother has asked us to call. But I'll hear what he says later. I really am so very glad.

48 INT. CARSON'S PANTRY. DOWNTON. DAY.

Carson is working on the wine books. He sees Ethel passing.

CARSON: Excuse me. What are you doing here?

ETHEL: I'm sorry, Mr Carson, but I wanted to thank Mrs Patmore, and I've brought these flowers.

CARSON: When we want flowers, there are plenty in the gardens here.

Mrs Hughes has arrived to hear this last remark.

MRS HUGHES: How nice of you, Ethel. Mrs Patmore's in the kitchen.

Ethel moves off as Mrs Hughes gives Carson a severe look.

MRS HUGHES (CONT'D): I hope you never need a favour from your fellow man.

CARSON: You can talk as tough as you like. I know *you* won't abandon me.

MRS HUGHES: Well then, why doesn't that thought make you kinder?

CARSON: Because I am who I am, Mrs Hughes.*

....

* Ethel is taking the bull by the horns. By coming to the house with flowers, she is fighting back from the humiliation that Robert has put her through. I don't think we should see her as an innocent victim of Carson's bullying,

49 INT. SERVANTS' HALL. DOWNTON. DAY.

Daisy and Alfred are dancing.

DAISY: Slow, slow, quickly go back, slow —
JIMMY (V.O.): Oh…

He has come in and he stands there looking at them.

JIMMY: Look at the pair of you.
DAISY: Alfred's learning the foxtrot.
JIMMY: I bet he is, but he's gonna have to do better than that.
DAISY: What do you mean? Why?
JIMMY: Well, he's only learning it to please our Ivy. Aren't you, m'laddo?
DAISY: Is that true?
ALFRED: Well…
JIMMY: Of course it is, you runner bean. Now step aside, and let me show you how it's done.

Without waiting for a response, he seizes Daisy's hand and starts to dance a smooth, accomplished foxtrot, singing to accompany himself as he does so.

CARSON: What is going on here? At a time like this, of sober dignity!

They freeze. Carson is standing in the doorway.

CARSON (CONT'D): Have you lost all sense of shame and propriety, sir? What makes you think you're the stuff of a first footman? It's Alfred who looks like a first footman to me. Take a leaf from his book and learn to conduct yourself with discretion!
JIMMY: But, Mr Carson, he was the one —
CARSON: Silence! You're a disgrace to your livery! And as for you, Daisy, have your years here taught you nothing?

He turns on his heel and goes. Jimmy looks at Alfred.

JIMMY: Thanks for speaking up.

....

Continued from page 355:

though. She is strong in her way and she has decided to take him on. In fact, Carson is the one who loses.

He goes, leaving the others alone.

ALFRED: I don't suppose you want to practise —
DAISY: I'm very busy. Why don't you ask Ivy if she's got any spare time?*

50 INT. DRAWING ROOM. DOWER HOUSE. DAY.

Robert and Cora have come in to find Violet and Clarkson, which is a surprise. Cora is the first to gather her wits.

CORA: Doctor Clarkson.
CLARKSON: Lady Grantham. How are you?
CORA: Much as you'd expect me to be.
VIOLET: Doctor Clarkson has something to tell you, which may alter your view on things a little.
CORA: I don't mean to be discourteous, but I doubt it.
ROBERT: Since you're here, I have a few words of my own to say. I feel I owe you an apology —

But Clarkson holds up a hand to cut him off.

CLARKSON: Please, Lord Grantham, if you'll just allow me...

He hesitates, but he knows he has to say it.

CLARKSON (CONT'D): On that awful night, I'm afraid I may have given you the impression that my recommended course of treatment offered a real chance for Lady Sybil's survival.

They are all silenced by this.

CLARKSON (CONT'D): The truth, and I've done a great deal of research since, as you can imagine, is that the chance was a small one. A tiny one, really. I'd read that early delivery was the only way to avoid the trauma, and it is.
CORA: As you tried so hard to tell us.

....

* Alfred behaves badly in that he doesn't say, 'It was me, I was dancing with her, and he was just trying to show us a step.' I quite like, every now and then, to make an essentially ungenerous or unpleasant character, like Thomas or O'Brien, do someone a good turn. Similarly I think it's good to have a sympathetic character do something wrong, like here, where Alfred is nervous of Carson and doesn't want to forfeit his good opinion. That's life.

CLARKSON: But what I did not quite realise was that eclampsia is almost invariably fatal, with or without a caesarean. Had you agreed, we would have subjected Lady Sybil to the fear and pain of a hurried operation, when in all likelihood she would have died anyway.

CORA: But there was a chance —

Clarkson looks at Violet, nods and then answers.

CLARKSON: An infinitesimal one. The discomfort and the terror would have been all too certain.

ROBERT: So you think Tapsell was right?

CLARKSON: Oh, I cannot go that far. Sir Philip Tapsell ignored all the evidence in a most unhelpful and — I may say — arrogant manner.

ROBERT: But Sybil was going to die.

CLARKSON: When everything is weighed in the balance, I believe that Lady Sybil was going to die.

They are silent as this sinks in.

CLARKSON (CONT'D): And now I'll take my leave.

He walks out and closes the door. Cora starts to weep and stands there, shaking. Then Robert puts his arms around her and they are motionless, crying together.

*Violet has done her work.**

END OF EPISODE SIX

....

* I thought they all played this scene fantastically well, and, for me, it is one of the best in the whole show. Clarkson has been induced by Violet to say that his suggested treatment would have made no difference. At least, he can't quite say it, because he can't bring himself to, but he reduces the chance to an infinitesimal one, in accordance with Violet's instruction, thereby allowing Cora and Robert to be reunited. So Violet has her way. Of course, what Violet really wanted Clarkson to say is that he was completely wrong, that he read the wrong book, that Sybil didn't have a chance and Tapsell was correct. But the Doctor is not prepared to do that, even for her. He wraps it up in as much lace and tinfoil as he can, but he's not quite prepared to say he was wrong. Which is the truth. It wasn't a big chance, it was a small chance, but it was a chance, whereas Tapsell's refusal to accept the symptoms meant there was no chance at all.

EPISODE SEVEN

ACT ONE

1 INT. YORK PRISON. DAWN.

A warder opens a locked door and Bates, in hat and coat, walks through.

1A EXT. YORK PRISON. DAWN.

A car pulls up. Anna is sitting in the back.

1B EXT. MAIN GATE. YORK PRISON. DAWN.

Bates walks towards the main gate, which is opened for him.

1C EXT. YORK PRISON. DAWN.

Anna sits in the car with a chauffeur waiting in the cold, early light. At last a small door, set into the great wooden gate, opens and Bates emerges. Anna hurries out of the car. For a moment they stare at each other, and then Anna runs forward and they embrace.*

ANNA: Thank God.
BATES: Yes. Thank God. And you.

They kiss.

1D EXT. DOWNTON. DAY.

Bates and Anna are in the car, approaching Downton.

2 INT. SERVANTS' HALL/PASSAGE. DOWNTON. DAY.

The servants are all having breakfast.

ALFRED: How do we speak to him?

....

* I was rather fascinated by the technicalities of shooting this scene, because when they did the reverse shot back towards Anna and the car there were dustbins, posters, modern signs, everything. In the old days you would have to get everyone's permission to remove them, shoot the scene and then put it all back. Now none of that is necessary; they just take them out on the computer.

MRS HUGHES: Normally. How do you think you speak to him?

JIMMY: But what about prison, or do we pretend it's never happened?

BATES: I don't think that'll be necessary.

He is standing there with Anna. Everyone crowds round.

CARSON: Welcome back, Mr Bates. I have waited a long time to say that.

BATES: Thank you, Mr Carson.

MRS HUGHES: Too long. Now come and sit down.

MOLESLEY: Give us yer coat.

MRS HUGHES: Mrs Patmore, can you find something for Mr Bates to eat?

MRS PATMORE: I certainly can. Daisy! Ivy! Stir your stumps and get some breakfast for our returning hero!

ANNA: Can't I have some?

BATES: Who's Ivy?

ANNA: The new kitchen maid.

Bates sees Thomas standing there.

BATES: Thomas. Still here, I see.*

THOMAS: Mr Barrow, now, Mr Bates. And yes, I'm still here. And busy as a bee.

CARSON: There have been some changes since… since you've been away. You will have heard about Lady Sybil.

BATES: Yes, I've heard. Anna took a letter from me to her ladyship.

MRS PATMORE: There we are.

She puts some food before Bates.

BATES: Thank you, Mrs Patmore.

MOLESLEY: Can we all have one of those?

They all laugh.

....

* That moment when Bates first sees Downton was, I thought, rather a good one. In fact, bringing Bates back in gave us quite a useful dramatic dynamic. In a sense you reinvent him, because he's been out of the group for so long, so you can have all the collisions with Thomas and everyone else all over again, and when he asks who Ivy is we are reminded how long he's been away.

DAISY: Welcome back, Mr Bates.

BATES: Thank you, Daisy.

We hear Carson introduce the new faces as Anna walks into the passage and removes her coat to hang it. Mrs Hughes follows.

MRS HUGHES: Anna, we've always skirted round the subject, but I hope Mr Bates knows how very sorry I was. To be used in that way at the trial.

ANNA: To be quite honest, Mrs Hughes, he forgave you long before I did. He knew you only said what was true.

MRS HUGHES: Even so, to see justice done at last takes a weight from my mind.

3 INT. DINING ROOM. DOWNTON. DAY.

Robert, Matthew, Branson and Edith are having breakfast. Robert feeds Isis while Edith is reading a letter.

MATTHEW: Something nice?

EDITH: The editor's written back, repeating his offer.

ROBERT: He knows he's on to a good thing.

EDITH: He wants to meet me. He asks if I'm ever in London.

MATTHEW: Why not? You could see Rosamund and buy some new clothes.

ROBERT: He only wants to persuade you to write for his horrible paper.

EDITH: Still, I think I will go. It seems rude not to, in a way, and I haven't been to London for ages. Excuse me.

She stands and leaves. Robert looks at Matthew.

ROBERT: Please don't encourage her.

MATTHEW: But I think it's a good idea.

Robert clearly does not agree. He also stands.

ROBERT: I gather you've trapped poor old Jarvis into a meeting.

MATTHEW: It won't take long. But he *is* the agent and there are things we must get started on, if you agree.

ROBERT: Oh, I'm glad you still think my agreement has a part to play.

He leaves. Branson looks at Matthew.

BRANSON: Are you sure you wouldn't rather just cut and run, like me?

4 INT. HALL. DOWNTON. DAY.

Followed by Isis, Robert is walking away from the dining room when he sees Bates waiting by the staircase.

ROBERT: Bates! My dear fellow! I didn't know you were here already!

BATES: They let you out at dawn. Thank you for sending Anna in the car.

ROBERT: Nonsense. Where have they put you?

BATES: In my old room, m'lord.

ROBERT: Well, that won't do. I'll ask Jarvis how far they've got with finding a cottage.*

BATES: Thank you... About Thomas —

ROBERT: He's called Barrow, these days.

BATES: Yes. He would be.

ROBERT: I'll sort it out, Bates. I promise. But in the meantime, you just rest. Stay in bed, read books.

BATES: If you're to pay me a wage, I have to make myself useful.

....

* As Bates is now a married man, he and Anna need a cottage, because at the moment he's living in the male quarters and she is in the female. On their marriage they had asked for a cottage, but Bates was arrested almost immediately and so the idea has been allowed to go to sleep.

Marriage among servants was a tricky business. The only servant who was always expected to be married was the coachman (and subsequently the chauffeur). He would normally not live in the house, but in a cottage as part of the stable yard. He had to be near the horses and then later the cars, but other servants who were married – and that in itself was uncommon – would not be expected to live in single quarters. One can't ever talk as if there were hard and fast rules, but it was more unusual for a married couple to live in the house. We would think little flats might be arranged on the top floor, but there weren't really married quarters within the houses; rather they would be in another part of the stable yard or a cottage on the estate. Houses differed: Blenheim has a lot of separate quarters where people could live and still be close to the house in order to work there, but it wasn't usual. And Anna's situation, being a married lady's maid, was rare.

ROBERT: For now, just enjoy being free. Heaven knows you deserve it.

Robert leaves, with Isis in tow.

4A EXT. CRAWLEY HOUSE. DAY.

A car pulls up, and Ethel, who is picking herbs from the garden, runs inside.

5 INT. DRAWING ROOM. CRAWLEY HOUSE. DAY.

Isobel is with Violet.

ISOBEL: But you didn't walk out of my luncheon when Robert asked you to.
VIOLET: Well, that luncheon was to support Cora in her grief. It did not seem appropriate to let the whole thing end in chaos and a quarrel.
ISOBEL: So you don't think I should have given Ethel a second chance?
VIOLET: I do not criticise your motives, but did you really consider? Ethel is notorious in the village.
ISOBEL: I don't think so.
VIOLET: I know so. You have surrounded this house with a miasma of scandal, and touched all of us by association.
ISOBEL: I think one must fight for one's beliefs.
VIOLET: And is poor Ethel to be the cudgel by which you fight your foes?

The door opens. Ethel appears with a tray of coffee things.

ISOBEL: Ah, Ethel.

Isobel gets up to close the door behind Ethel.

ISOBEL (CONT'D): I was telling Lady Grantham how your cooking has come on.
ETHEL: I'm studying, m'lady. These days, a working woman must have a skill.
VIOLET: But you seem to have so many.*

....

* Violet thinks Isobel isn't really helping Ethel by keeping her in a place where her past is known. But Isobel feels that, until Ethel has done a job and got good references, she's not going to make the transition to a new life. And, of course, she is also proving her liberal point.

6 EXT. GARDENS. DOWNTON. DAY.

Robert is walking with Cora.

CORA: I don't see how you can just sack him. He's done nothing wrong.
ROBERT: He can't have expected to stay my valet once Bates was released.
CORA: Ask Carson. He'll have some ideas.

In the distance a nurse is wheeling a perambulator.

CORA: Poor little girl.
ROBERT: Has Branson said anything more about moving out?
CORA: How can he move out before he's found a job? How can you want him to? He's our responsibility now, Robert, he and the baby. We owe that to Sybil.

But he does not answer and instead looks away.

ROBERT: I must get on. I've got this meeting with Jarvis and Matthew.

7 INT. SERVANTS' HALL. DOWNTON. DAY.

Bates and Anna are there, along with Thomas and some of the others. Anna cleans a gold fringe, while Ivy lays the table.

ANNA: Stop fidgeting.
BATES: Give me that cloth.

She does. He starts to help sponging and shining the fringe.

THOMAS: You got any plans, Mr Bates?
BATES: It's rather early to say. His lordship suggested I have a rest.
MOLESLEY: I expect you'll be looking for something to do, Mr Barrow. Now that Mr Bates is back.

He has only voiced the thoughts of everyone in the room.

THOMAS: I wouldn't be too sure about that.
ALFRED: They're showing a film tonight in the village hall. *Way Down East*. It's about a wronged woman who survives in the wilderness, through her own wits and courage.
O'BRIEN: Blimey. They've stolen my story.
ALFRED: Lillian Gish is in it.
IVY: I like her.

ALFRED: There's a late showing tonight, half past ten, for local servants. What about it?

Ivy is quite interested, in spite of herself.

IVY: Will you come with us?
JIMMY: I haven't got a ticket.
IVY: You could get one.
JIMMY: Sounds a bit soppy, to be honest.
IVY: Well, I'm not going with Alfred on my own. My mum wouldn't like it.
MRS HUGHES: She would not, and nor would I. You may go if Madge or Alice go with you. But not otherwise.

Alfred looks over to the maids. Two of them smile and nod.

IVY: All right. If Mrs Patmore agrees. Straight there and back, mind.

Alfred is thrilled, Jimmy snorts with derision.*

8   INT. LIBRARY. DOWNTON. DAY.

Robert, Matthew and an elderly man, Jarvis, are standing over some plans on the table.

JARVIS: This means the overhaul of every part of the estate we hold in hand, and some large new parcels in addition. All in an instant.
MATTHEW: But don't you see? If we invest in new machinery, new methods and new techniques, the whole estate must benefit by it. And as for taking new lands in hand, we won't be running it as separate farms. We'll find another use for some of the farmhouses —

....

* I think this is our first real film moment. The movies had been going from about 1905, and were seen as a working-class entertainment. They were not yet taken seriously, but the 1920s would change that, with D. W. Griffith and others raising the status of film-making. But at this point they were considered fairly lowly, to be shown in village halls because there weren't built cinemas outside the major towns. This is a real film, *Way Down East*, directed by D. W. Griffith, and they did have showings for servants. None of this is out of the ordinary. I think it's also quite right that Mrs Hughes would not let Ivy go unaccompanied. Maybe later in the 1920s, when things were beginning to loosen up, but not yet.

ROBERT: This is ridiculous! Downton has existed for
hundreds of years in perfect harmony. We have worked
with the farmers as partners. Now you want to blow it
all to smithereens —
MATTHEW: Of course I don't, but —
JARVIS: If I may, my lord. Mr Crawley, you are very new
to our way of life here —
MATTHEW: I *beg* your pardon!
ROBERT: There's no point biting Jarvis's head off, you
are new to it.
MATTHEW: Must I remind you of the state the place was in
a few months ago?
ROBERT: That was nothing to do with the way we run it!
The money was lost in a bad investment.
MATTHEW: Yes. And you've been bailing the place out with
Cora's fortune. You have been for years. Downton must be
self-supporting if it's to have a chance of survival!

*His voice has been raised and, as he stops, they all three
realise this and become embarrassed.*

ROBERT: Well. You've given us plenty to think about.
Hasn't he, Mr Jarvis?
JARVIS: He has indeed, Lord Grantham.*

END OF ACT ONE

....

* Jarvis's problem, really, is that he can't see the future – which of us can? –
but then again, Matthew's plans for the estate are pretty modern and there
were plenty of estates that wouldn't get to these ideas until after the Second
World War. Most surviving estates would eventually take more and more
land in hand so they could farm in larger economic units, but it left empty
farmyards and they had to be used for something else, which in many cases
was not properly addressed until the 1970s and 1980s. There was the odd
case of forward thinking, and we're saying that Downton was one of them,
but we must be careful. The development of farmyards into cottage
industries and farm shops was still far away, so we can't do much of that, but
what did happen was letting farmhouses as they became empty. That was
quite standard. Robert's difficulty is that he can't see what was wrong with
the way things have been done until now. Matthew points out, quite
truthfully, that he was just bailing out the estate with Cora's money and that
couldn't go on forever, but Robert will not face the truth: that you can't run a
business by bailing it out. In short, they are all cross.

ACT TWO

9 EXT. DOWNTON VILLAGE. DAY.

Ethel comes out of the shop. She is crying and she stops to wipe her eyes. Violet has seen this as she is driven past in her car.

10 INT. HALL. DOWNTON. DAY.

Cora, Robert, Branson and Edith emerge from the dining room. Matthew and Mary are behind them. Matthew talks softly.

MATTHEW: I'm afraid I must involve Murray.

MARY: But Papa employs Mr Murray.

MATTHEW: The *estate* employs Murray, and the estate needs his help.

Edith leads the way with Branson, Robert and Cora.

EDITH: I'll be back on Tuesday.

CORA: Are you going to take the job?

EDITH: I haven't decided.

ROBERT: Don't be ridiculous.

He walks into the drawing room. The others follow.

11 INT. DRAWING ROOM. DOWER HOUSE. DAY.

Violet is with Edith, having tea.

VIOLET: Why would I persuade your father otherwise, when I agree with him?

EDITH: How can you say that, when you keep telling me to find something to do?

VIOLET: I meant run a local charity, or paint watercolours or something.

EDITH: Well, I'm going to London to see the editor tomorrow, and if I like him then I'm going to say yes. I don't want to fall out with Papa —

VIOLET: But you do want to be notorious.

EDITH: No, I don't. Not at all. But I don't want to be invisible, either. I've had enough of it.

Violet considers this for a moment.

VIOLET: Very well. I'm coming up tonight. I'll see what I can do. But I want a favour in return.*

12   INT.   DRAWING ROOM.   CRAWLEY HOUSE.   DAY.

Ethel, looking bleak, has brought in tea for Isobel.

ISOBEL: Ethel? What's the matter?
ETHEL: I had rather a nasty encounter in the village, that's all.
ISOBEL: What sort of encounter?
ETHEL: Mrs Bakewell refused to serve me. In the end her husband did, but it wasn't very nice.
ISOBEL: We shall take our business elsewhere.
ETHEL: There's no need for that, ma'am. I'm used to it.
ISOBEL: You shouldn't have to be.

13   INT.   KITCHENS.   DOWNTON.   DAY.

Alfred and Jimmy saunter in to find Ivy working.

ALFRED: Are you all set for this evening?
MRS PATMORE: If you mean have I allowed Ivy to go out when it's not her half day, I have, but *why*, I could not tell you. Bring them all home safe.
ALFRED: If that's Béchamel, why don't you use parsley or mace?†
MRS PATMORE: I do. But I boil it in the milk beforehand. I made it last night.
JIMMY: Oh, leave her alone, you big ninnie.
MRS PATMORE: There's nothing wrong with a man who can cook. Some say the best cooks in the world are men.

....

* For Edith, this is part of the change in consciousness of women after the war. That's what we're using it for, but we also use it to demonstrate the dynamic of the family. Violet wants a favour in return for supporting Edith. I think we know Violet well enough to accept that if she really disapproved she wouldn't support her at any cost, so she must be open to argument.

† Alfred's interest in cooking will become a major storyline. I used Béchamel here because it is a comparatively simple sauce, but it illustrates how even the plainest things can be cooked well or badly, and Alfred, like a true enthusiast, is fascinated by the minutiae. Naturally, Jimmy despises all this girly nonsense, but Carson approves of Alfred – even if cooking is outside his proper job description – because of his enthusiasm and hard work. He doesn't really like Jimmy, who he thinks too clever for his own good.

JIMMY: And do we think this sad beanpole will be the best cook in the world?
CARSON: Why do you always feel the need to be so unpleasant, James? What's Alfred ever done to you?

He is standing in the doorway. He delivers his next speech towards Alfred as he turns and goes.

CARSON (CONT'D): You can take in the fish and meat tonight. James can follow with the sauce.
JIMMY: But I should be the first footman.
IVY: Course you should.

Hearing this, a furious Daisy appeals to Alfred.

DAISY: Listen to her! You're taller than him! You've been here longer than him! Why are you taking her to the pictures, when she talks like that?
ALFRED: Well, I've got the tickets now. So…

14   INT.   NIGHT NURSERY.   DOWNTON.   DAY.

Mary looks in, to find Branson holding the baby on his lap.

MARY: Don't get up.

She sits down next to him, playing with the baby's feet.

MARY (CONT'D): How's the christening going?
BRANSON: It's all arranged with the Catholic church in Ripon.
MARY: Weren't you going to tell us?
BRANSON: You and Matthew. I didn't think the others would want to know.
MARY: Please give them a chance to behave properly.
BRANSON: I wondered if you'd be a godmother?
MARY: Am I allowed to be?
BRANSON: As long as at least one of them is Catholic, and my brother's coming over. He'll stay in the village.
MARY: No, he won't. He'll stay here.
BRANSON: He's a bit of a rough diamond.
MARY: I'm very fond of diamonds.*

....

* It is true that you can have Anglican Godparents for a Catholic child as long as one Godparent is a Catholic. Our son Peregrine had six Godparents, and only one was Catholic, but one you must have.

15 EXT. DOWNTON GROUNDS/COTTAGE. DOWNTON. DAY.

Anna and Bates are together, looking around.

> BATES: I still can't believe I'm here. I keep pinching myself.
>
> ANNA: Believe.
>
> BATES: Which one would be ours?
>
> ANNA: Well, they won't move Mr Chirk or the Tripps, but Mrs Bow wants to live in the village, so we might get hers.*
>
> BATES: None of which solves the problem of what I'm going to do.
>
> ANNA: Your job, of course. They'll have to give Thomas his notice.
>
> BATES: Mr Barrow.
>
> ANNA: Mr Stick-It-Up-Your-Jumper. He'll have to go.

He looks at her, and smiles.

> BATES: Revenge is sweet.

16 INT. NIGHT NURSERY. DOWNTON. EVE.

This is a converted spare room with a changing table. A nurse tidies up while Branson watches Cora play with the baby.

> CORA: Sybbie, precious? I think she's starting to recognise her name.
>
> BRANSON: Sybbie? Not Sybil?
>
> CORA: The same but different... Mary tells me the christening is all arranged. May we come?
>
> BRANSON: If you want. I didn't think Lord Grantham would feel comfortable.

....

* It was not unusual for a cottage to be allotted in this way. As Robert owned the village it would just mean they were waiting for one to come up. To a certain extent these were dead men's shoes. One of the extraordinary things in the 1950s and 1960s was the number of people who demolished many of their cottages because they couldn't see any other use for them. Once they didn't have the farm workers, the nannies and footmen that were expected to retire into them, they knocked them down rather than pay rates, and in the process succeeded in vastly devaluing their estates.

CORA: Nurse? It's time for our bath.*

The nurse moves forward, takes the baby and goes out.

CORA (CONT'D): We mustn't give them *too* much to talk
about downstairs… So have you made any more plans?
BRANSON: My brother is coming over for the christening.
He's written that he's moving to Liverpool and he'd like
me to go into business with him.
CORA: When does he arrive?
BRANSON: The night before the service. Mary wants him
to stay here, but I'm not sure it's a good idea.
CORA: She didn't say anything to me.
BRANSON: Perhaps it's to be a surprise.

17 INT. KITCHENS/PASSAGE. DOWNTON. EVE.

*Alfred is taking the plate of fish. He walks out first. Jimmy
has the sauce.*

JIMMY: Look at him. He can't balance it.
MRS PATMORE: Leave him alone. Up you go.

Jimmy passes Thomas.

JIMMY: It's a flippin' insult. Just 'cos he's ten foot
tall.
THOMAS: You're right.
JIMMY: I've got a good mind to —
THOMAS: Ah, ah. Don't do anything you'll regret. These
things can be managed, but not by losing your temper.

Jimmy walks on. O'Brien is watching.

....

* Normally we don't let nannies speak, because we haven't really got room to
service them with narrative. And they were a separate group, as a rule. They
didn't eat with the other servants or sit with them much, because they were
always in the nursery. It was one of those slightly uncomfortable, halfway
jobs. She wasn't quite a governess, who would probably be a lady, a curate's
daughter or something, when a nanny would not, but it was similar. She
wasn't just a servant, because she spent a lot of time with the family and she
was also allowed to give the servants orders, which otherwise only the
governess or the tutor could do. Actually, by the 1920s tutors had pretty well
gone. The boys went off to boarding school early on. Only the girls stayed to
be educated at home.

O'BRIEN: You make a cosy couple, I must say.

THOMAS: I don't think so.

O'BRIEN: That's not what I've heard. Alfred says he's
always going on about you. Silly, sloppy stuff.
Alfred's sick and tired of it, and no wonder.

THOMAS: He's making it up.

O'BRIEN: Have it your own way.

Thomas walks on, with a lot to consider.

18   INT.   SERVERY/DINING ROOM.   DOWNTON.   EVE.

Alfred is preparing, nervously. Jimmy comes in.

ALFRED: Right…

JIMMY: Don't put them like that.

He rearranges the spoon and fork at the edge of the dish.

JIMMY (CONT'D): They've got to be able to get hold of
them.

Carson appears at the doorway. He nods.

CARSON: Come along.

19   INT.   DINING ROOM.   DOWNTON.   NIGHT.

Violet, Isobel and the family are all present.

MATTHEW (V.O.): I've asked Mr Murray to come up. So we
can talk it through together.

ROBERT: You've asked Murray? To come here? Without
consulting me?

MATTHEW: I felt I wasn't explaining things well, and I
know he can.*

Alfred has reached Violet on Robert's right.

....

* Matthew wants to involve Murray because he knows Murray agrees with
him, so he's trying to strengthen his own team. He didn't consult Robert in
advance because he didn't want the order to be countermanded.
Nevertheless, Robert thinks it's an incredible liberty to ask the family lawyer
to come up without telling him. We agree with Robert, but on the other
hand we also know that the estate needs Matthew to get his way, so we
should, in good *Downton* fashion, be completely torn between the two of
them.

VIOLET: Oh, lovely. What a treat.

Alfred leans in. The spoons fall into Violet's lap. He makes a grab for them and deposits some fish there as well.

VIOLET: Oh!
CARSON: Oh, my, your ladyship!
VIOLET: No fuss, no fuss. Just scrape me down and get me a spare napkin.
JIMMY: I'll take that.

He removes the dish from a defeated Alfred and hands him the sauce. He moves on to Robert, who helps himself. Violet talks on as Carson is putting her to rights.

VIOLET: I saw your cook in the village today, Isobel. She seemed upset.
ISOBEL: Yes. Mrs Bakewell was rather unkind.
MARY: Mrs Bakewell? In the shop? How odd. Why?

She then remembers whom they are talking about.

MARY (CONT'D): Oh. I suppose we know why.
ISOBEL: It seems a pity that, even in this pretty little village, people can be so unforgiving.†
ROBERT: Some people are unforgiving; others are insensitive.
CORA: What time do you leave in the morning?
EDITH: I thought I'd get the ten o'clock. I'm meeting him for tea.
CORA: And you're sure Aunt Rosamund doesn't mind giving you a bed?
EDITH: She didn't seem to.
ROBERT: You're not encouraging this?
CORA: She hasn't agreed to anything yet.

....

* To carry the main dish was the first footman's job, who at this moment is Alfred, but Thomas and Daisy support Jimmy, who feels he has a right to the position. Here, Jimmy shows that his soul is not entirely spotless in that he's prepared to set Alfred up, which he does by misarranging the cutlery.

† Living in a village is essentially living in a political minefield, and I like to remind people that, far from being a straightforward rural paradise, it is actually much harder to stay out of trouble in a village than it is in a London street. Someone like Ethel, with a known past, in those days (or perhaps in these) would just not be allowed to forget.

MATTHEW: Well, I hope she does agree. I think she'll
get a lot out of it.
ROBERT: Mama, talk to her. Talk to all of them. Say
something sensible.
ISOBEL: Yes. Let's hear how a woman's place is in the
home.
VIOLET: I do think a woman's place is *eventually* in the
home, but I see no harm in her having some fun before she
gets there.
EDITH: Oh, Granny! Thank you!
ISOBEL: Have you changed your pills?
VIOLET: And another thing. Edith isn't getting any
younger. Perhaps she isn't cut out for domestic life.

This casts something of a pall over the proceedings.

MATTHEW: How are your plans proceeding, Tom?
BRANSON: I was telling Lady Grantham. My brother has a
garage in Liverpool. He's asked me to go in with him.
MARY: The brother who's coming to stay?
BRANSON: Yes. Kieran.
ROBERT: Why is he coming here?
MARY: For the christening.

For Robert, this is the tin lid. Silence falls. *

20 INT. SERVANTS' HALL. DOWNTON. NIGHT.

They are finishing dinner. Alfred is in a state.

O'BRIEN: How did he rearrange the spoons?
ALFRED: He put them right on the edge of my plate, but
I'm not saying it was deliberate.
JIMMY: I hope you're not, 'cos I was trying to help.
CARSON: Well, I think Alfred can manage without your
help in future, James. And next time, will you wait to
be asked before you take charge?
MRS PATMORE: Are you still here?

....

* I think we've set up Edith's tea with her editor sufficiently for the public to
be aware that a major character is coming in. Isobel's assumption that Violet
will support Robert and try to deter Edith is the customary assumption of
the dedicated liberal that everyone else is illiberal. In this case she would
normally have been proved right but, contrarily, Violet decides to support
Edith.

She has just come in. Daisy and Ivy are clearing.

CARSON: Perhaps Alfred no longer wants to go to the
pictures. He may want to ponder his mistakes instead.
MRS HUGHES: Of course they're going.
IVY: Are we?
CARSON: Yes. You can go. I will not withdraw my
permission. But as you walk, you might contemplate what
it is to waste a chance when it is given. I believed in
you, Alfred, and you have disappointed me.
IVY: I'll get my coat.*

The young couple leave. Mrs Hughes looks at Carson.

MRS HUGHES: I s'pose you never wasted a chance.
CARSON: Well, if I did, I learned from it, and that's
all I'm asking from him.
MRS HUGHES: That and some ritual humiliation.

Further down the table, O'Brien nods at the defeated Jimmy.

O'BRIEN: Silly duffer. I expect he's waiting for you to
console him, Mr Barrow.

21 INT. MARY'S BEDROOM. DOWNTON. NIGHT.

Matthew is in bed. Mary gets in beside him.

MARY: You shouldn't have rung Murray without telling
Papa.
MATTHEW: You berate me for not wanting to take
responsibility, and now you tell me off for doing just
that. You can't have it both ways.

....

* What one must remember about the life of a servant in those days is that
even if you were working in a nice house for nice people and the whole thing
wasn't bad at all, you still lived your life by permission. Arthur Inch, who was
the butler advising me on *Gosford Park* – a lovely man – couldn't believe it
when he was first in the Army, training to go to war. They'd get to five in the
afternoon and then they'd be told: 'Right. That's it. Tomorrow we'll study
such and such.' Eventually, he realised it was up to him to arrange his own
evening. If some of them were going to the pub or whatever, he'd join them,
but he told me that for the first few weeks it felt wild, because he'd been living
by permission since he was fourteen. He went back into service after the war,
but he said there were a lot of people who just couldn't go back. They'd got
used to deciding how they were going to spend their own time.

MARY: I can if I want to.

She leans in and kisses him.

MARY (CONT'D): What's the matter?
MATTHEW: Do you think I should see someone?
MARY: What?
MATTHEW: If there's anything wrong then it's obviously
my fault. You know what they told us when I was wounded.
MARY: But they were wrong. They said so.
MATTHEW: I wonder. All doctors pretend to know more
than they do.
MARY: Darling, please don't worry. I'm sure there's
nothing wrong.
MATTHEW: That's the point. We're not sure.*

22 EXT. THE DRIVE. DOWNTON. NIGHT.

*Alfred and Ivy walk along. The other two maids loiter
behind.*

ALFRED: It was okay, but I prefer English films with
English stars. They seem more real somehow.
IVY: I like the American actors. They've got more
you-know-what.
ALFRED: And how about Ivy Close in *The Worldlings*? She
makes Lillian Gish look like a village school ma'am.
IVY: Ivy Close. It's funny to think of a film star
having your own name.
ALFRED: There aren't any with my name.

....

* Now Matthew raises again the possibility that there's something wrong. I
have always been interested in how when you're young you are terrified of
anyone getting pregnant and then, for many people (although not for me,
actually – Peregrine was born nine months and two minutes after we left the
church – but for many friends), it is two or three or even four years before it
happens. It can take much longer than you think.

I was sorry they cut 'All doctors pretend to know more than they do', as
that is my voice. Nothing irritates me more than doctors talking as if they
know everything and you know nothing, particularly when you're dealing
with a disease like cancer, when nobody knows anything. And how they hate
to be questioned. They'll do anything to avoid being questioned, because
they just want you to say, 'Yes, Gov,' and go home. Like school teachers who
want to give you a hundred lines if you don't do what they say.

IVY: No… but there's a *king*. The one who burned the cakes.
ALFRED: Well, I hope I won't be burning any of my cakes in future.

*They both laugh. They do seem well suited.**

23 INT. SERVANTS' HALL. DOWNTON. NIGHT.

Thomas is reading a paper when Jimmy comes in.

JIMMY: Where is everyone?
THOMAS: They've gone to bed. Except for the picture-goers. They're not back.
JIMMY: If I'd thrown a bucket of slop in the old lady's lap, I wouldn't be allowed to go to the flicks.
THOMAS: What are you saying?
JIMMY: Mr Carson doesn't like me. No matter what Alfred does, he still prefers him. It's not bloody fair.
THOMAS: Well, I love you.

He says it lightly. Jimmy takes it as a joke.

JIMMY: If you do, you're on your own.
THOMAS: I'm sure I'm not. What about your family? Where you from?

....

* There were lots of popular English films at this time, and although the names of the actors – people like John Stuart and Chili Bouchier – have rather been forgotten, they were big stars then. There was no language barrier, obviously, and in fact one of the big changes when sound came at the end of the 1920s was that suddenly everyone was up a tree. Not just actors with foreign accents, like Vilma Banky, but also producers and distributors. Before then you could take a German film, write some different subtitles and release it in the normal way of things, and so there was a real international feel to the film industry that sound would destroy. Anyway, there were English films and English silent stars, and one of them, Ivy Close, whom Alfred admires in *The Worldlings*, was the great-grandmother of Gareth Neame, our producer.

I think with Ivy's lack of interest in Alfred I'm probably making a melancholy point for all people who were plain when young. Like me. If only she'd seen his potential she would have been glad to get off with him, and I suppose, subconsciously, I was trying to be revenged on all those pretty girls who didn't want to dance with me at the end of the 1960s.

JIMMY: I don't have any family, not really. Cousins.
You know. No one else.
THOMAS: And your mum and dad?
JIMMY: Dead. My dad was killed in the war and my mother
died of the 'flu. I haven't any brothers and sisters, so
there we are. All on me ownsome.
THOMAS: You must get lonely.
JIMMY: Meaning?
THOMAS: I know what it's like, that's all. Funny.
We're quite a pair.

Jimmy doesn't know how to respond, but Thomas's tone is kind.

THOMAS (CONT'D): We both like to look very sure of
ourselves but we're not so sure underneath, are we?
Still, you've no need to worry. Mr Carson may prefer
Alfred, but nobody else does.
JIMMY: Don't they? I wonder. Sometimes I think it's
just Jimmy *contra mundi.*

O'Brien arrives. She finds a book she left on the table.

O'BRIEN: Was that Latin? I should try it on Mr Carson.
Make up some points.
JIMMY: Never mind Latin, I need a magic spell.
O'BRIEN: G'night.

He goes out. O'Brien shakes her head.

O'BRIEN (CONT'D): He's a funny one, isn't he?
All bluster and shine on the surface, but something else
behind the eyes.

Thomas is silent.

O'BRIEN (CONT'D): What? Am I not supposed to comment on
him because you've formed a mutual admiration society?
THOMAS: Whatever it is, it's not mutual.
O'BRIEN: You can't pull the wool over my eyes. I know
what's going on.
THOMAS: You're quite wrong, Miss O'Brien. He's a proper
little ladies' man.

O'Brien gives a snort of laughter. He looks at her.

O'BRIEN: If that's how you want to play it.
THOMAS: What are you going on about?

O'BRIEN: There's no need to bark. I only know what Alfred tells me.

THOMAS: Well, if he says Jimmy's interested in me, he's lying.

O'BRIEN: Oh, dear. Was it supposed to be a secret?

She gathers up her things and leaves.

23A INT. JIMMY'S BEDROOM. DOWNTON. NIGHT.

Jimmy is getting washed and undressed for bed.

23B INT. SERVANTS' HALL. DOWNTON. NIGHT.

Thomas sits alone reading the paper, then puts it down.

23C INT. THOMAS'S BEDROOM. DOWNTON. NIGHT.

A vexed and tormented-looking Thomas starts to undress, then sits down, torn by thought.

24 EXT. THE DRIVE. DOWNTON. NIGHT.

Alfred and a giggling Ivy come up the drive.

IVY: You are daft.

ALFRED: Oh, Ivy. I love to be out with you like this. I wish we could make it a regular thing.

IVY: I can't. I wouldn't want you to get the wrong idea.

ALFRED: Look, I'm sorry, but Jimmy's just not interested. I hate to hurt your feelings like that, but he's not.

IVY: You don't know that. He flirts with me. He does.

ALFRED: If you knew he wasn't interested, would that make a difference?

IVY: I'd have to hear it from his lips.

24A INT. THOMAS'S BEDROOM. DOWNTON. NIGHT.

Thomas continues to brood on his bed.

24B INT. SERVANTS' PASSAGE/STAIRS. DOWNTON. NIGHT

Alfred forlornly watches Ivy, and then he goes up the stairs.

25 INT. MENSERVANTS' PASSAGE. DOWNTON. NIGHT.

Thomas comes out of his room in his trousers and vest. He walks down the hall to another door. There is no sound. He opens it and goes inside.

26 INT. JIMMY'S ROOM. DOWNTON. NIGHT.

Thomas comes in. Jimmy is asleep. Thomas closes the door behind him.

26A INT. STAIRS. DOWNTON. NIGHT.

Alfred makes his way up the stairs.

27 INT. JIMMY'S BEDROOM. DOWNTON. NIGHT.

Thomas kneels down by the sleeping face. He strokes the young man's cheek.

THOMAS: I'm here now.

Thomas sits on Jimmy's bed. He leans over and kisses his mouth. The sleeping Jimmy almost responds, then he springs awake, just as Alfred walks in and turns on the light.

ALFRED: I'm sorry to wake you, Jimmy, but I've got to ask —

He stops dead. In his eyes, Jimmy is kissing Thomas.

ALFRED (CONT'D): Oh, my —
JIMMY: Get off! Get the bloody hell off me! Will you bloody get off! Alfred, it's not what you think!
THOMAS: Don't do that. Please. Alfred doesn't matter. No one'll believe a word he says. He's nothing.
JIMMY: What are you doing? Why are you in here?
THOMAS: Because of what you said. Because of all there is between us.
JIMMY: There's nothing between us! Except my fist if you don't get out! And if you tell any —

But when he looks round, Alfred has gone. Jimmy is standing now, and threatening. Thomas backs away.

THOMAS: But what about… the things you said —
JIMMY: I said nothing except get out! Go on, get out,
Thomas!*

28 INT. MENSERVANTS' PASSAGE. DOWNTON. NIGHT.

Thomas is in the passage when Carson opens his door.

CARSON: *What* is going on?
THOMAS: Nothing, Mr Carson. Jimmy, er, James, had a
nightmare. He's fine, now.
CARSON: Well, go to bed.

Carson storms off to bed, slamming his door behind him.
When Thomas turns round, he sees Alfred looking at him.

END OF ACT TWO

ACT THREE

29 INT. SERVANTS' HALL. DOWNTON. DAY.

This is breakfast, but there is an atmosphere you could cut
with a knife. Jimmy stares straight ahead. Alfred is
nervous. Thomas offers them toast, and they both glare at
him.

....

* If Jimmy had just woken up to find Thomas kissing him and kicked him off
the bed, then for him to take it any further would seem to me unbelievable.
The last thing he'd want would be to introduce the subject as a topic for the
others. He would have told Thomas, 'If you mention this to another living
person you're a dead man,' and that would have been the end of it. But by
making Alfred a witness we force Jimmy into a public response, which can
only be the most hostile one imaginable. Once Alfred has seen, then Jimmy
has no choice. From then on, he must behave as if this is the most horrible
thing that has ever happened in the history of the world. So I have to set up
the question Alfred needs to ask about Ivy in order to bring him into the
bedroom when he gets back from the cinema. In Jimmy's head, once Alfred
has seen him and Thomas apparently kissing, he knows he will go downstairs
the following morning and tell everyone. So Jimmy must act first.

ANNA: What is it? What's going on?
MRS HUGHES: James? What's the matter with you?
JIMMY: Nothing.
MRS HUGHES: Alfred?
ALFRED: Ask Mr Barrow.

But Thomas speaks before she can. He shakes his head.

THOMAS: It's nothing. Really.
MOLESLEY: It doesn't seem like nothing.

*He gives a little laugh and looks round, but nobody joins in.
Ivy enters with some more toast. Jimmy looks up.*

JIMMY: Ivy? Never mind the toast, you look very tasty
yourself, this morning.
CARSON: *What* did you say?
JIMMY: Well, can't a red-blooded man compliment a pretty
girl?
CARSON: Not at breakfast, for heaven's sake!
O'BRIEN: Alfred? What's happened?

She has whispered, and he whispers back.

ALFRED: Not now.
CARSON: Well, if there is anything I ought to know, I
hope I hear about it before the end of the day.

Alfred looks at Thomas, but Thomas just looks away.*

30 EXT. A STREET IN LONDON. DAY.

*Edith pulls up in a car, gets out and walks across the
street. She is dressed in a smart suit. She finds the
entrance she is looking for and goes inside.*

....

* Jimmy now makes the pathetic but entirely predictable gesture of becoming
aggressively heterosexual in order to make his statement, and so he starts
flirting with Ivy. To Carson, this is hideous to see, but that is a young man's
awkwardness. He has to prove his own 'normal' sexuality in order to kick
Thomas even further into touch.

31 INT. GREGSON'S OFFICE. LONDON. DAY.

*Michael Gregson, forty, is a handsome fellow in a solid sort of way. Edith is with him, holding a cup of tea.**

EDITH: This really has been so interesting.
GREGSON: Well, I hope this means that you're persuadable, Lady Edith.
EDITH: I'll think about it, I promise. I just felt I had to meet you and see what it would be like.
GREGSON: I assume your father disapproves.
EDITH: Well, it's the business of parents to worry, isn't it?
GREGSON: Oh, no. All sorts of toffs are writing for magazines nowadays. Some of them even advertise face creams and cigarettes and the rest of it.
EDITH: I'm afraid Papa would not find that reassuring.

Which makes him laugh.

EDITH (CONT'D): In fact, if he were here he'd probably just shout 'Run!'
GREGSON: Will you please make up your own mind, without his advice?
EDITH: I'll have to think about that, too.
GREGSON: Are you going back to Yorkshire tonight?
EDITH: No. I'm staying with my aunt. I've got to look in to the offices of *The Lady* while I'm here.
GREGSON: Not to write for them, I trust?
EDITH: Oh, no. It's just something I promised to do for my grandmother.
GREGSON: *The Lady*? That's, er, Covent Garden. Here's an idea. Let's… Let's have lunch tomorrow at Rules. If you accept the job we'll celebrate; if it's a no, I'll drown my sorrows. How's that?

*Edith laughs and they shake hands.**

....

* Gregson is played by Charles Edwards, a very good actor and for me a real leading man. He's got that gentlemanly decency that used to be the stock in trade of Jack Hawkins, Kenneth More and countless others, but there aren't many of them now.

* It is important in this story that Gregson genuinely likes Edith; there's no side to it. He's not a social climber at all. He comes from an educated,

32   INT. ROBERT'S DRESSING ROOM. DOWNTON. EVE.

Thomas is dressing Robert for dinner. He drops his brush.

ROBERT: You seem nervous today, Barrow. Is something troubling you?

THOMAS: No, m'lord.

ROBERT: We will get things sorted out. We won't leave you in the lurch.

THOMAS: I'd be grateful if you could let me know when you've made a decision.

ROBERT: I'll talk things through with Carson, and we'll see what we can come up with.

33   INT. DRAWING ROOM. DOWNTON. NIGHT.

It is after dinner, and they are all in there.

Across the room, Mary, Matthew and Branson have spread a map of the estate out on the piano.

MATTHEW: It makes no sense to retain this bit as a separate section. No sense at all. But of course Jarvis won't see that because he hates change.

MARY: Just try to carry Papa with you. That's all I ask.

MATTHEW: He'll be with me in the end because this is the only way forward, and at some point he's going to see that.

MARY: Some point in the near future, I hope.

Carson, Jimmy and Alfred are serving. The young men seem distracted.

CARSON: What's the matter with you both? You were in a dream all through dinner.

JIMMY: Nothing's the matter.

....

Continued from page 386:

upper-middle-class background, much the same as Isobel Crawley and Matthew, really. He's not more interested in Edith because she's an earl's daughter, and I think it is one of the first times that she has been in a relationship where that side of it has no significance at all.

I mention *The Lady* several times. It was already the principal publication for domestic service recruiting and had been for some time, so I thought it more fun to use a real magazine. And Rules, also real and an old favourite of mine from my youth, is just around the corner from the magazine's offices.

Cora is talking to Robert.

CORA: Does Mr Murray want luncheon tomorrow?
ROBERT: No. He's in York all morning. He'll come up
here afterwards.
CORA: Followed by Tom's brother for dinner. So it
promises to be a day of contrasts.
ROBERT: God in heaven.

He scratches Isis's ear.

MARY: What do you think, Tom?
BRANSON: I agree with Matthew. The estate can offer
proper compensation to the tenants now, while the money's
there, but if we miss this chance it may not come again.
ROBERT: So says the Marxist.

He has walked over to listen. Violet has heard this, too.

BRANSON: If you don't mind my saying so, you've a narrow
view of socialism.
ROBERT: You seem to have a very broad interpretation of
it.
VIOLET: Now, now, children. If Branson is watering down
his revolutionary fervour, let us give thanks.
MARY: Tom.
VIOLET: Do you know anything about farming, Tom?
BRANSON: A little. My grandfather was a sheep farmer in
Ireland.*
CORA: Oh, Mama. Edith telephoned. She's running your
errand in the morning. She'll catch a train after lunch.

....

* For Matthew, the difficulty is to find a way forward that will carry all the
people who need to be carried. Sometimes in a business you can't persuade
them and you may have to get rid of some employees and replace them. But
with these estates, the people you had to carry with you were the members of
the family, and they weren't replaceable. A lot of houses went down because
the key people couldn't change. Often the agent, the lawyers, sometimes
even the wives and children knew that things would have to be different, but
the owner just couldn't get it, which is what Matthew is afraid of when it
comes to Robert. Here we also have the plan of buying out tenants, which I
use to define Branson as someone other than just a troublemaker who's run
off with a daughter of the house. We need to believe he is intelligent and
capable of addressing problems. As a simple Irish rebel there wasn't enough
scope for him, dramatically.

MARY: What errand is that?

VIOLET: She's just looking for something you can only get in London.

MARY: That doesn't narrow the field. Did she say if she'd taken the job?

CORA: I don't think she's decided.

ROBERT: So there's still hope, then?

By the table, Jimmy whispers to Alfred.

JIMMY: Why do you keep giving me funny looks?

ALFRED: I'm not.

Carson speaks softly.

CARSON: What's going on? Have you both been up to something I don't know about?

ALFRED: Not both of us.

34 INT. CORA'S BEDROOM. DOWNTON. NIGHT.

Robert and Cora are in bed.

CORA: Are you awake?

ROBERT: I can't seem to get to sleep. I don't know why.

He reaches out and turns on the lamp.

ROBERT (CONT'D): Could you credit Matthew summoning Murray without my permission?

CORA: You keep telling everyone Downton's a dual monarchy now. I never realised you didn't mean it.

ROBERT: So, you're against me over Matthew, the christening and Edith.

CORA: Robert, even your mother spoke up for Edith. Think of that.

ROBERT: A facer, I admit. She'll have had some reason of her own, of course.

CORA: Is she really so Machiavellian?

ROBERT: Yes.

With a sigh, he switches out the light again.*

....

* Because of the constant soap opera of any family, there are always new incidents coming up and in my experience you can never quite tell how the family alliances will play out. Every member is capable of changing sides.

35 INT. RULES RESTAURANT. LONDON. DAY.

Edith weaves between the tables, pulling off her gloves.
Gregson stands as she approaches the table.

GREGSON: I was afraid you'd stood me up.

EDITH: I'm so sorry. It took much longer than I thought.

GREGSON: What was it about?

EDITH: Oh, just family stuff. An errand for my grandmother.

GREGSON: Are you very family minded?

EDITH: Well, you know. When you live at home with your parents, you're still in the middle of all of it.

GREGSON: Yes, I saw a picture in the paper of your elder sister's wedding. She looked very glamorous.

EDITH: People say so.

GREGSON: Am *I* allowed to say I'm rather pleased you're *not* married?

EDITH: I'm a little less pleased.

GREGSON: Oh, dear. That sounds like you're hiding a romantic secret.

He is being playful and flirting. Her tone is more acerbic.

EDITH: Not too romantic. A little while ago I was jilted at the altar. Which wasn't much fun.

Gregson looks shocked.

GREGSON: Oh dear. I am sorry.

EDITH: Oh, please don't be. It's a relief to be reminded I'm not an object of pity to the entire world.

He reaches out and takes her hand.

GREGSON: I've clearly put my foot in it, and now you'll turn the job down… Please don't.

But Edith has recovered. She looks into his worried face.

EDITH: I won't. Not if you don't want me to.*

....

* Edith's hideous awareness of her own humiliation is common to us all at a certain stage of our lives. Rather like when you break your leg, you can't understand how everyone else is moving around so easily. In youth, you always think everyone's talking about you, and in middle age you don't care what they're saying; it's only when you're old that you realise they're not talking or thinking about you at all.

36 INT. LIBRARY. DOWNTON. DAY.

Robert and Matthew are with Jarvis and Murray.

MURRAY: Surely, Lord Grantham, you don't question Mr Crawley's goal of making the estate self-sufficient?

ROBERT: No. But I question his plans for the employees and tenants in order to achieve it. Can't we allow things to evolve more gently? As we did in the past.

MURRAY: The past is not much of a model. The third Earl nearly went bankrupt, the fourth only saved the estate by dying, and what would you all have done in the Nineties without Lady Grantham's money?

ROBERT: I say, Murray. When I asked you to say what you think, I didn't mean to be taken literally.

JARVIS: Must we talk in this way?

MATTHEW: Yes. I'm afraid so. Thanks to Mr Swire we have another chance, but we have to change our ways. All I'm talking about is investment, increasing productivity and reducing waste —

JARVIS: Waste!

MATTHEW: Yes. The estate has been run very wastefully for many years —

JARVIS: I won't listen to this!

ROBERT: Now, come on, Jarvis. If I can listen to it, so can you.

JARVIS: No, Lord Grantham, I can't! Am I to stand here, after forty years of loyal service, to be accused of malfeasance and corruption!

MATTHEW: Nothing of the sort!

MURRAY: Mr Jarvis, I don't think that was anyone's intention —

JARVIS: No? That's what it sounded like to me! Can I rely on you to give a fair account of my career here?

ROBERT: My dear chap, think for a moment. We must both see things have to move forward. My goal is to find the way of least disruption. Won't you stay and help me with that?

JARVIS: My lord. Will you give me a good reference?

ROBERT: Yes, of course I will.

MATTHEW: Mr Jarvis, if I have offended you, then I offer my sincerest apologies.

JARVIS: Thank you. But I can see that my time here is done. I'm the old broom, Mr Crawley. You are the new. I wish you luck with your sweeping. My lord.

With that, he goes. The others stare at each other. *

37 INT. CARSON'S PANTRY/SERVANTS' HALL. DOWNTON. DAY.

Mrs Hughes looks in as Carson is comparing a couple of bottles of wine.

MRS HUGHES: Mr Carson. You'd better come.

He stands and together they make their way to the servants' hall, where they are all having their tea. A large Irishman in a tweed coat is holding court.

KIERAN BRANSON: We always said he'd make something of himself, and so he has.
CARSON: May I help you?
ANNA: This is Mr Branson's brother.
CARSON: Then what's he doing down here?
BATES: He won't go up.
MOLESLEY: He says he'd rather stop with us.
CARSON: Can we fetch Mr Branson, sir?
MRS HUGHES: I've already sent Alfred. Here they are now.

Branson, Alfred and Mary are walking down the passage.

BRANSON: Kieran? What are you doing down here? Come upstairs.

....

* Sometimes in life you diddle around a subject for a long time and then you suddenly think, I've got to have this terrible conversation and only when I've had it will we all be able to move on to the next square, and that is what I feel Matthew is doing here. He hoped Jarvis would go along with everything without being punched, but it hasn't happened, so it's time to act. I also feel, as a matter of fact, that neither Murray nor Matthew thinks Jarvis is the man to lead the reforms. He's just not capable of it and that's what they've come to. I don't believe Matthew for a moment thinks Jarvis has been dishonest or corrupt, he's just inefficient – and worse than inefficient, he belongs to an earlier time. Even Robert has calmed down and now sees that things have to move forward.

KIERAN BRANSON: I don't fancy it. Can I not stay put?
Have my dinner down here?
MARY: But we're all so looking forward to meeting you,
Mr Branson. If you come with us, you can see your room
and get changed... If you want to.
KIERAN BRANSON: And what would I change into? A
pumpkin?

*All the servants laugh, but compose themselves at a glance
from Mary.*

KIERAN BRANSON (CONT'D): Come on, Tommy. Can we not eat
down here? They seem a nice lot. What's the matter?
You too grand for them, now?
BRANSON: They know I'm not, but my mother-in-law has
been kind enough to invite you to stay and dine. And
I'll not let you snub her. Now, get a move on.

*Kieran stands, pats Molesley on the back, and they go. Mrs
Hughes looks at the butler.*

MRS HUGHES: I know. You always said he would bring
shame on this house.
CARSON: No, Mrs Hughes. For once, I will hold my
tongue. I thought Mr Branson's respect for her
ladyship's invitation exemplary. And now it's time for
the gong.

He leaves and Mrs Hughes finds herself facing Anna and Bates.

MRS HUGHES: Well. 'Mr' Branson's done something *right*,
for a change.
ANNA: Miracles can happen.*

....

* We found this very good actor, Ruairi Conaghan, who looks like a plumper
version of Allen Leech. His role was to represent what Branson had come
from, so that the audience would be quite clear about the journey he has
made. The death of Sybil means that the negotiation of that journey has
become more difficult, because she was the bridge between the two worlds
and she's now been removed from the equation. Mary is behaving correctly
and comes downstairs to extend her invitation, but she isn't really a match for
Kieran Branson, because once people don't play the game according to the
rules she finds it very difficult to deal with them.

I had a girlfriend once whose uncle was charming but very, very vague,
and one day he arrived at a shooting party dressed in fairly old tweeds. He

38 INT. MARY'S BEDROOM. DOWNTON. EVE.

Mary's hair is being finished by Anna. Matthew sprawls on the bed. He is not yet changed.

MARY: Have they decided which cottage you're to have?

ANNA: Not yet. But I wish we could settle Mr Bates's job, first.

MARY: He's Papa's valet, surely?

ANNA: He will be. But no one seems to know what to do with Mr Barrow.

MARY: He'll have to go.

ANNA: Then I wish we could get on with it. There. That's you done, m'lady.

She picks up some things and leaves.

MARY: Hadn't you better get changed?

She adjusts a necklace in front of the mirror.

MARY (CONT'D): How was it?

Matthew sinks back on to the bed in faux exhaustion.

MATTHEW: Pretty bad. Jarvis has resigned.

MARY: What?

MATTHEW: He's gone, and I'm going to have to make it all work or I've had it.

MARY: But you're certain this is right?

MATTHEW: Come here.

He holds out his hand. She walks over and he pulls her down onto the bed, holding her in his arms.

....

Continued from page 393:

looked pretty rough carrying his gun, and he didn't have anyone with him, so the butler assumed he was a valet-loader and pointed the way downstairs. Off he went to the servants' quarters where they asked if he wanted some tea. Somehow they, too, got the impression that he was his own valet and they showed him a picture of his wife in a magazine and asked if it was a good likeness. He replied that she was prettier in real life, and this went on for quite a long time until someone looked in from the family and told him to come upstairs. The sad result was that the servants wouldn't serve him for the rest of the party, because they thought he'd done it as a joke, which he absolutely hadn't. Anyway, that was what gave me the idea for Kieran's arrival.

MARY: You'll make me untidy.

MATTHEW: Good.

Now he takes her face in his hands. His voice is passionate.

MATTHEW (CONT'D): You see, I know it's right, Mary. I believe I can make Downton safe for our children, if we ever have any. But I can only do it if you're with me. I need to know that you and I are one. In this, as in everything.

MARY: But what about Papa? I do love him.

MATTHEW: Love him by all means, but believe in me. Believe in what I'm doing, in what *we're* doing, or I don't think I can go on.

She stares at him and then kisses him.

MARY: There. Will that convince you?

MATTHEW: Convince me again.

She does.

MARY: And don't say 'if we ever have any'. Because we will.

MATTHEW: I'll believe you, if you believe in me.*

END OF ACT THREE

....

* By introducing change you become responsible for its resulting in improvement, which is why many people shrink away from it, but this is going to be Branson's opportunity. Again, this whole set-up was written in the sure and certain knowledge that Matthew was about to quit the scene, so we needed Branson to step up to the mark, so to speak. For the same reason, we make Matthew and Mary tremendously together and happy now, having had a certain amount of dissension in the first five episodes, written before I knew he was going. After Episode Five we realised they were not going to be together for very much longer, so we could afford a period of perfect unity. If Dan Stevens had not left the series then we would have had to find other ways to make them unhappy.

ACT FOUR

39   INT.   SERVANTS' HALL.   DOWNTON.   EVE.

O'Brien is alone with Alfred.

O'BRIEN: But it's been a while now. What if Mr Carson
finds out you knew all along and you never told him, how
will that look?
ALFRED: Surely it's for Jimmy to tell?
O'BRIEN: Supposing he's in on it?
ALFRED: No. He started yelling at Thomas as soon as I
walked in.
O'BRIEN: Yes, I'm sure he did. As soon as you walked
in. What if you hadn't walked in? I'm sorry, Alfred, Mr
Carson won't tolerate these sorts of shenanigans, and
he'll be furious if he finds out you knew and you said
nothing. You need to speak up. For your own good.

*Daisy and Ivy come in to lay the table for the servants'
dinner, which brings the conversation to an end.*

39A   INT.   HALL/EDITH'S BEDROOM.   DOWNTON.   NIGHT

*Edith comes rushing through the hall in her coat and hat, and
quickly gets ready for dinner in her room.*

40   INT.   DINING ROOM.   DOWNTON.   NIGHT.

*All the family, including Isobel and Violet, are there.
Kieran, still in his tweed coat, seems slightly subdued.*

ROBERT: And what exactly does this business consist of?
KIERAN BRANSON: Automobile refurbishment.
BRANSON: He means car repairs.
ROBERT: I see. And you would live nearby?
KIERAN BRANSON: We've rooms over the garage and we can
get one of the cousins over, to help with little Sybbie.
There's a bit of a park not too far away.
MARY: Well, that's something.*

....

* Automobile refurbishment. I don't blame Kieran for wanting to raise his
own status. Why shouldn't he? Obviously the picture he is painting for a
Crawley grandchild is terrible for Robert, but one of the great phenomena of

How ghastly it sounds. There is a leaden pause.

> VIOLET: I remember an evening rather like this. We were travelling back from Scotland to London when the train was suddenly engulfed by a blizzard, and we spent the night in a tradesmen's hotel in Middlesbrough.

That doesn't seem to get the ball rolling, either.

> EDITH: Granny, I've done what you asked.
> ISOBEL: What was that?
> VIOLET: I'll tell you about it, later.
> MARY: So, who's coming to the christening?
> CORA: All of us, I expect.
> MARY: Granny?
> VIOLET: Well, yes, If Brans— Tom wants me to.
> BRANSON: I would be honoured.
> MATTHEW: Robert, are you coming?
> ROBERT: Tom doesn't want me there, and I wouldn't know what to do. All that crossing and bobbing up and down. I went to a Mass once in Rome and it was more like a gymnastic display.

He laughs, but the others don't really — except for Kieran Branson.

> BRANSON: I would like you to be there very much.
> ROBERT: Why? What difference would it make?
> BRANSON: All I know is Sybil would want you there. She loved you with all her heart and she would want you there.
> CORA: Will you argue with that?
> ROBERT: Not if you think it's so important.

....

Continued from page 396:

the twentieth century has been social mobility – alas, rather frozen now. Of course, people always think social mobility means moving up, and it is good for people to maximise their own potential and achieve what they can achieve, but that said there is also the counter-pull of *down*, and when there isn't an enormous amount of inherited money – true in many middle- and upper-class families – and if there is no great ambition, there is nothing to hold you up in a much more changeable society. These days, you can easily have a situation where someone can be Lord Tiddlypush while his second cousin is working in a garage.

MATTHEW: How did you get on in London?

EDITH: Well, as a matter of fact, I've got an announcement to make and now's as good a time as any. Listen, everyone. You have a journalist in the family.

VIOLET: Since we have a country solicitor and a car mechanic, it was only a matter of time.

MARY: How *was* the editor in the end?

EDITH: Oh, nice. Very nice.

Which makes Mary look at her again.

41   INT.   KITCHEN PASSAGE/SERVANTS' HALL.   DOWNTON.   NIGHT.

O'Brien is with Alfred.

O'BRIEN: So you're ready to speak out?

ALFRED: I think you're right, and I must.

O'BRIEN: Good. He has broken all the fundamental laws of God and man. Report him, as you should, and then stand back and enjoy his fall.

BATES: Enjoy whose fall?

He is standing near them. They did not see him arrive.

O'BRIEN: What?

BATES: You said: 'Stand back and enjoy his fall.' Whose fall?

O'BRIEN: I don't know. I can't remember.

Bates nods and moves on to the servants' hall, where he finds Anna, among the others, reading. He speaks softly.

BATES: Miss O'Brien's up to something.

ANNA: You do surprise me.

BATES: She's plotting misery. I suppose Thomas will be in on it.

ANNA: I doubt it.

BATES: Why not? Don't they hunt in a pack?

ANNA: Not these days. Things've changed.

Which gives Bates something to think about.

42   INT.   DRAWING ROOM.   DOWNTON.   NIGHT.

The company is all in there. Isobel is with Edith and Violet.

ISOBEL: I don't understand. You've placed an advertisement in a magazine to find a job for my housekeeper?

VIOLET: I knew you'd be against it.

ISOBEL: Well, how would you feel if I found other work for your cook or butler?

EDITH: Granny feels that for Ethel's sake she should move elsewhere —

ISOBEL: Oh, nonsense. She couldn't give tuppence about Ethel or anyone like her!

VIOLET: You've been reading those communist newspapers again.*

Kieran is with Branson, Matthew and Mary.

KIERAN BRANSON: I don't suppose there's any beer?

BRANSON: Haven't you had enough?

MARY: Of course we have beer. We must have some somewhere. Carson?

CARSON: I believe so, m'lady. I'll fetch it.

Robert is stroking Isis. He murmurs to Cora.

ROBERT: What's the betting we'll have a chorus of 'Molly Malone' before we finish?

CORA: You're the one pushing Tom into his brother's arms. This is not what Sybil wanted for him. She told me.

On his way to the door, Carson passes Violet.

VIOLET: Ah, Carson. Would you ask Mrs Hughes to meet me in the hall, please?

CARSON: Very good, m'lady. I will bring the beer in a moment, sir.

KIERAN BRANSON: It isn't so bad here, after all.

....

* Here we have Isobel about to be told that Violet is advertising to replace Isobel's cook, which is rather extraordinary. But I don't blame Violet. Her main motive may be to rid the village and the family of a potential scandal, but she genuinely does not believe Ethel will have a new life until she gets away from the scene of her downfall. Her position therefore is, I think, perfectly defensible.

43 INT. MRS HUGHES'S SITTING ROOM/PASSAGE.
DOWNTON. NIGHT.

Carson holds a tankard on a tray. He's with Mrs Hughes.

CARSON: I don't know. She just asked if you could go
up.
MRS HUGHES: I suppose I'll have to.

In the passage, Alfred and Jimmy are coming downstairs.

CARSON: What's this?
JIMMY: They said we could go. They'll ring when they
need the car.

He walks into the servants' hall. Alfred lingers.

ALFRED: Mr Carson, might I have a word?
CARSON: Well, I have to take this up.

But Alfred just looks. After a moment, Carson nods.

CARSON (CONT'D): Oh, very well. Come with me.

As they go, Molesley turns to the others.

MOLESLEY: Well, this is a house of mystery and no
mistake.

But, as usual, no one wants to share his joke.

44 INT. HALL. DOWNTON. NIGHT.

Violet, Edith and Isobel are with Mrs Hughes.

VIOLET: Mrs Hughes, you've always taken an interest in
Ethel. Do you think I'm wrong?
MRS HUGHES: No. While Ethel is in this village she is
doomed to be lonely. But if, as her ladyship suggests,
she could get a job far away from here —
EDITH: She's not a bad cook now, and with a respectable
reference, which of course you can give her…
MRS HUGHES: And I can write another.
ISOBEL: I can't get over how you've planned all this
without a word to me.
VIOLET: Well, I knew you wouldn't agree. I know how you
hate facing facts.
ISOBEL: I resent that. I'm sorry but I do.

VIOLET: Nevertheless. Ethel is unhappy, as you must know. Besides which, her presence in the village —
ISOBEL: Ah. Now we're getting to it. Robert disapproves and Carson disapproves and everyone disapproves except me.
MRS HUGHES: Mrs Crawley, I hope you don't see me as an intolerant person.
ISOBEL: No.
MRS HUGHES: Because I agree with her ladyship. In a new place, where she can start again, Ethel has far more chance of happiness than in re-enacting her own version of *The Scarlet Letter* in Downton.
VIOLET: What is *The Scarlet Letter*?
EDITH: A novel. By Nathaniel Hawthorne.
VIOLET: It sounds most unsuitable.
ISOBEL: I'll talk to Ethel.
EDITH: The advertisement in *The Lady* will appear next month, so there's plenty of time to consider it properly.*

45 INT. CARSON'S PANTRY. DOWNTON. NIGHT.

Carson stands aghast, facing Alfred. They are both in shock.

CARSON: I don't understand what you're saying. Thomas was doing what?
ALFRED: I've just told you. When I came in, it looked as if… No. He *was*… He was kissing Jimmy on the mouth.
CARSON: *Kissing?*
ALFRED: That's what I saw, Mr Carson.
CARSON: And what was James doing?
ALFRED: I think he was asleep, 'cos he just woke and he got very angry.

....

* This is an important scene between Violet, Edith, Isobel and Mrs Hughes. When you want to have a cross-class scene like this, where they are all essentially equal contributors, you don't really want to put it into a sitting room, because then either Mrs Hughes is sitting, which would be unbelievable, or she is standing and they are sitting, which would be awkward. Nor would we believe Violet in the kitchen, but by putting it into the hall, they're all standing without surrendering any status. Mrs Hughes and Violet are simply two women talking to each other. I love the fact that Mrs Hughes has heard of *The Scarlet Letter*, but Violet hasn't.

CARSON: As he should have been, by God.
ALFRED: My auntie says he might have been faking his
anger because I walked in, but it didn't look fake to me.
CARSON: Well, we can always rely on your aunt to take
the ungenerous view.

He thinks for a moment.

CARSON (CONT'D): You will not speak of this to anyone.
Is that clear? I'll decide how to proceed, if necessary
with the advice of his lordship, but I don't want to hear
the subject even mentioned in the servants' hall.
ALFRED: Very good, Mr Carson.
CARSON: The world can be a shocking place, Alfred, but
you are a man now, and you must learn to take it on the
chin.*

46 INT. KITCHEN. CRAWLEY HOUSE. NIGHT.

*Isobel comes in. Ethel sits alone in a chair. A lamp sheds
a feeble light but she does not read. She just sits and
stares. Isobel watches her for a moment. Then Ethel turns
and stands.*

ETHEL: Beg pardon, ma'am. I was miles away.
ISOBEL: That's all right. I just wanted to let you know
I was back.
ETHEL: Would you like some tea?
ISOBEL: No, thank you. I'm going straight to bed…
Ethel, are you happy?
ETHEL: Well, I… suppose I'm happy compared to what I was
before.
ISOBEL: You see, I… Never mind. Goodnight.

47 INT. DRAWING ROOM. DOWNTON. NIGHT.

Robert, Cora and Violet are alone.

VIOLET: How can I still be here when all the young have
gone to bed?

....

* Carson's initial instinct, which I think is truthful, is to try always to contain
potential damage. That is in his blood and his first instruction would
therefore be to tell no one, but despite his resolve he will soon have to admit
the situation is hopeless, because once O'Brien knows anything, then it's out.

ROBERT: The motor's ready when you are.

VIOLET: When is Jarvis leaving?

ROBERT: I'm not sure… It seems a poor return for forty years of service.

VIOLET: Maybe. But he was your father's man. To him, you were always the young master, never the chief.

ROBERT: Which does not alter the fact that now we must find someone else.

VIOLET: But you've already found him.

ROBERT: What do you mean?

VIOLET: Well, obviously the answer to a thousand different questions is to give the position to Branson.

CORA: Tom.

VIOLET: Well, if he's the agent, we can call him Branson again, thank heaven.

ROBERT: That's a mad plan.

CORA: It's not. Tom and Matthew can work on the new ideas together. They're the same age. Well done, Mama.

ROBERT: But what does he know of farming?

VIOLET: His grandfather was a farmer.

ROBERT: In a small way.

VIOLET: Which means he has more practical experience than Jarvis ever had. Think of the child. You cannot want your only granddaughter to grow up in a garage with that drunken gorilla?

CORA: Don't we owe this to Sybil? She asked me not to let Tom slide backwards. And I promised.

ROBERT: I'll do it on one condition. No, two. First, Matthew must agree.

CORA: He will.

ROBERT: Second, you will both admit it when you realise you were wrong.

VIOLET: Oh, well. That is an easy caveat to accept. Because I'm never wrong.*

....

* When Violet says that Jarvis was Robert's father's man – 'To him, you were always the young master, never the chief' – she is speaking the truth. I've seen that in several houses of this type. Until they get their own people into all the key positions the next generation is not really in charge, and the first ten or fifteen years can often be a probationary period before they're actually running things. So that is drawn from life. Violet obviously thinks of Branson for the job because, if he takes it, then they've solved Sybbie's future,

48 INT. CARSON'S PANTRY. DOWNTON. NIGHT.

Thomas stands before Carson's desk.

CARSON: I don't need to tell you that this is a criminal offence.

THOMAS: We hadn't done nothing.

CARSON: But you were hoping to do something if Alfred hadn't come in.

THOMAS: It's not against the law to hope, is it?

CARSON: Don't get clever with me. When you should be *horsewhipped!*

But pronouncing the words has released some of the tension.

CARSON (CONT'D): Do you have a defence? Am I mistaken in any part of this?

THOMAS: Not really, Mr Carson. As for a defence, what can I say? I was… very drawn to him, and I'd got the impression that he felt the same way. I was wrong.

CARSON: It seems an odd mistake to make.

THOMAS: When you're like me, Mr Carson, you have to read the signs as best you can, because no one dares speak out.

CARSON: I do not wish to take a tour of your revolting world.

THOMAS: No.

CARSON: So, are you saying that James is the innocent party in all this?

THOMAS: Yes, Mr Carson, he is. Now, when would you like my resignation?

CARSON: I will take time to consider. And we must first find out what James intends to do. He'd be within his rights to report you to the police.

THOMAS: Oh, my God.

CARSON: Although I'm quite sure it won't come to that.

THOMAS: Are you going to tell his lordship?

CARSON: I haven't decided. Will you give me your word that nothing had happened?

....

Continued from page 403:

but I hope we made it believable by this stage that it's a job he could do. Certainly it is true that Branson's experience of farming would have been much more practical than Jarvis's.

THOMAS: I will, yes.
CARSON: Right. Goodnight.*

Thomas nods and heads for the door. Mrs Hughes comes in.

MRS HUGHES: Mr Barrow looks very grim-faced.
CARSON: Never mind him... Human nature's a funny business, isn't it?
MRS HUGHES: Now, why didn't the poets come to you, Mr Carson? They'd have saved themselves a lot of time and trouble.

49 INT. MENSERVANTS' PASSAGE. DOWNTON. NIGHT.

Alfred is with Jimmy.

ALFRED: I wasn't supposed to mention it to anyone, but I'm not comfortable keeping you in the dark.
JIMMY: No... So what did old Carson say?
ALFRED: Not much. I told him you were as shocked as I was... What are you thinking?
JIMMY: Only that if I can manage this sensibly, I think you can kiss goodbye to being first footman.

With that enigmatic observation, he goes into his room.

....

* This scene is very key to me, because the subtext of Thomas's homosexual story is that it was very difficult to be gay in the 1920s. You took your life in your hands all the time, but what is also true, which I think modern sentimentality sometimes refuses to admit, is that normal, decent, nice people would often take a position on it that would seem to us hostile and unjust. Carson's prejudice would not have been in the least unusual. Obviously there were people who weren't prejudiced, but there were plenty who were, and Carson's revulsion, when we know he is a decent, upright man trying to do his best, would be typical of what the Thomases of this world would have had to put up with. I felt it was useful to have a naked expression of the loathing that they had to live among. Carson later shows some sympathy for Thomas, because I think what happens to Carson during this story is that something he has hated generically has taken a human face, which is always the best argument against extremism. This is why the one thing I'm always against is judging anyone according to a type. It doesn't even matter if it is something positive. All type judgements are worthless, because they generalise the individual. Here, what happens to Carson is that eventually, although he doesn't approve, he comes to see that it is not Thomas's fault.

50 EXT. CATHOLIC CHURCH. RIPON. DAY.

The bells are pealing as the party emerges from the church.
A photographer is waiting.

BRANSON: What's this?

EDITH: I hope you don't mind. After all, we had to have
a record.

PHOTOGRAPHER: If you could all form a group around the
father.

They do. Cora is with Mary and Edith.

EDITH: It seems so strange without Sybil here.

CORA: She's watching. I know.

MARY: I envy you. I wish I did.

PHOTOGRAPHER: Ever so slightly. Thank you very much.

Robert finds himself next to Branson. Matthew is there.

BRANSON: You really mean it? You want me to take on the
running of the whole estate? It's a big job.

ROBERT: Think of it as a christening present from Sybil.

BRANSON: But if you're only doing it because of her, if
you're not sure…

ROBERT: I'm sure we should give it a go. If it doesn't
work out or you get bored, then we can think again.

MATTHEW: It's a wonderful idea, Tom, and I'm ashamed it
wasn't mine.

The camera goes off.

PHOTOGRAPHER: Perhaps one with the grandfather holding
the baby? And maybe the great-grandmother with him?

Robert takes the child nervously. Violet joins him.

PHOTOGRAPHER (CONT'D): And what about Father Dominic,
who christened her?

A Benedictine priest in a long, black cassock steps forward
and makes a third adult in the group. Robert and Violet both
*look as if they are trapped in a cage with a crocodile.**

....

* Father Dominic was based on Father Dominic Milroy, the priest at
Ampleforth who suggested I might become an actor. A rather adventurous
piece of advice in 1965, I may say, when it was like suggesting someone
become a professional gambler or an astronaut. I'd done a couple of plays

CORA: What's the matter, Robert? Are you afraid you'll
be converted while you're not looking?

*The others laugh as the shutter clicks, capturing Robert's
startled face.*

END OF EPISODE SEVEN

....

Continued from page 406:

and he suggested I consider the theatre as a career. Of course, if my father
had known I was being given this advice he would have absolutely hit the
roof, but I had enough sense not to tell him. Years later, when they put me
on *This Is Your Life*, Emma got Father Dominic down from Yorkshire to
come on the show. He is a marvellous fellow.

EPISODE EIGHT

ACT ONE*

1 EXT. DOWNTON VILLAGE CRICKET PITCH. DAY.

Molesley is with his father, old Bill Molesley, inspecting the cricket pitch, which is being rolled.†

BILL MOLESLEY: I think it's held up well, all things considered.
MOLESLEY: Especially after all that rain.
BILL MOLESLEY: How's the house team coming on? Because we're taking this very seriously in the village.
MOLESLEY: Nobody takes it more seriously than his lordship, Dad. Whatever he likes to pretend.

2 INT. CARSON'S PANTRY. DOWNTON. EVE.

Thomas is with Carson.

CARSON: Mr Bates has had his rest now, and wants to get back to work. Mr Barrow, isn't it better to take your punishment and move on?
THOMAS: You mean because…

....

* In the structure of *Downton*, unusually really, the first episode and the last episode of the series are an hour and a half; all the others are one hour, except for the Special, which is two hours. And because the Special is shown in Britain a little while after the end of the series, on Christmas Day, we have to have two endings. We need the end of the series to be essentially a resolution that is satisfactory, but then the Special must be like a movie, carrying its own dynamic and resolved within itself. After that we have a long gap, to recover.

† Bill Molesley (played very well by Bernard Gallagher) comes in every now and then, usually to give Molesley some back story, and here we involve him in this year's climax, the cricket match. We like to have a big event like cricket or a fête or a wedding so that we can legitimately involve the servants, the family and everyone else in our little world. When it came to country house cricket, you often had the house playing the village. Occasionally you could have the servants versus the family, but to have a house team that was a mixture of family and servants was quite usual, as they had it in L. P. Hartley's *The Go-Between*.

CARSON: Let's not go through it all again. I have left things unresolved for too long. It's time to draw a line under this whole unfortunate episode.

THOMAS: So I go out the window.

CARSON: I cannot hide that I find your situation revolting but, whether or not you believe me, I am not entirely unsympathetic. You have been twisted by nature into something foul, and even I can see that you did not ask for it.

Thomas accepts this without comment.

CARSON (CONT'D): I think it better that you resign quietly, citing the excuse that Mr Bates has returned. I will write a perfectly acceptable reference and you'll find that there's nothing about it that's hard to explain.

THOMAS: I see. What about tonight?

CARSON: Well, it's nearly time to change, so you should dress him tonight and let Mr Bates take over tomorrow.

Thomas nods and walks to the door. Then he turns.

THOMAS: I am not foul, Mr Carson. I am not the same as you, but I am not foul.

CARSON: Yes, well. We've spoken enough on this subject. Now, if you will excuse me, I'll ring the gong.*

He walks out, past Miss O'Brien who may have been listening.

CARSON (CONT'D): Come along, Miss O'Brien. Time to stop eavesdropping and do some work.

O'BRIEN: I don't know what you —

But Carson has gone about his business.

3   INT.   LIBRARY.   DOWNTON.   EVE.

Robert, Cora, Mary and Edith sit around. Edith is reading some pieces of paper covered in writing.

CORA: How are you getting on with the cricket team?

ROBERT: We should be all right. We've still got Thomas, thank God.

....

* Thomas is allowed a moment of nobility, just to vary things, and for me, he is noble here. We probably don't dislike him any the less, but we do see what he's up against.

EDITH: Won't he be leaving soon?

ROBERT: Not before the match if I've got anything to do with it. And we've two footmen again and two sons-in-law, so with Carson, the valets and the hall boys, we're almost there.

EDITH: One of the gardeners told Anna their team is in terrific shape.

ROBERT: It's so unfair that the outside staff play for the village.

EDITH: Why don't you support the house and the village? You own both.

ROBERT: But I'm captain of the house team.

CORA: If I were you, I'd be captain of the village. They always win.

ROBERT: Not always. Usually, but not always… Mary? You look as if you're in a trance. What were you doing in London? It's worn you out.

MARY: Maybe. I'll try and rest tomorrow.

She glances at her mother. The gong sounds in the house.

4   INT. SERVANTS' HALL. DOWNTON. EVE.

O'Brien is with Jimmy, who glances at the clock.

JIMMY: Crikey. I'd better go.

O'BRIEN: Before you do, a little bird tells me Mr Carson has made up his mind to deal with Thomas after all.

JIMMY: Well, it's about time.

O'BRIEN: I only meant, if you want to register your anger at how Thomas treated you, now is the hour.

JIMMY: I'm not sure. I'm still disgusted by the whole thing, obviously —

O'BRIEN: Obviously. But if you don't speak out, people might think you weren't disgusted at all… Now, you must excuse me. I ought to be upstairs.

She hurries off, leaving Jimmy to think it over.

5   INT. BEDROOM PASSAGE. DOWNTON. EVE.

Matthew, in black tie, finds Anna waiting outside a door.

MATTHEW: Anna? What are you doing out here?

ANNA: Her ladyship's with Lady Mary, sir. I'm afraid she's going to be late.

MATTHEW: Let me see what's happening.

He opens the door and goes in.

6   INT. MARY'S BEDROOM. DOWNTON. EVE.

Cora is seated by the dressing table, holding Mary's hand.

CORA: You couldn't be in better hands than Doctor Ryder's. Truly.

MARY: I hope to God you're right.

MATTHEW: Anna's worried you're getting late.

They hadn't seen him and they look round.

MARY: Heavens, you made me jump.

CORA: I must go. O'Brien will scold me.

She stands and leaves, letting Anna come in.

MATTHEW: What were you talking about?

MARY: Nothing… Women's stuff. Your ears must have been burning earlier. Papa was discussing the cricket match.

MATTHEW: The village thrashed us last year. I suppose I'll have to play?

MARY: You suppose right. It's because of last year he's absolutely desperate to win this time.

MATTHEW: Bates must count himself lucky to be out of it.

ANNA: I think he'd like to walk normally, sir, even if playing cricket was the price he had to pay.

MATTHEW: Of course he would. I'm so sorry. How stupid of me.

But Anna is laughing. She has caught him out.

ANNA: That's quite all right, sir. I was only joking.

7   INT. KITCHENS/PASSAGE. DOWNTON. EVE.

Molesley, carrying some shirts, is chatting while he follows Mrs Patmore, who gets to the kitchen and joins Daisy and Ivy in their work.

MOLESLEY: Oh, there's absolutely no question that some people have a feel for it. I think cricket's like anything else. When you learn it as a child, there's an

understanding that is hard to come by later. And with a
father like mine, I was brought up with cricket in my
blood.*

MRS PATMORE: I see. And why did you never think of
playing for the county?

MOLESLEY: I don't seek public recognition, Mrs Patmore.
I'm not one of those who likes to trumpet his glory
abroad.

MRS PATMORE: No. Of course not.

DAISY: Why have you never played in the match before?

MOLESLEY: How could I? I didn't work at the house until
this year, and I could hardly play on the village team.

MRS PATMORE: Oh. Hardly.

IVY: We'll have to start a fan club, won't we?

MOLESLEY: That's kind, Ivy, but I just want to do my
best for the house. That's all the reward I seek.

MRS PATMORE: Oh, your modesty is an example to us all,
Mr Molesley.

He leaves, and they all laugh.

8   INT.   DRAWING ROOM.   DOWNTON.   EVE.

Edith is still reading her papers as the others drift in.

MARY: What is that you're so glued to?

EDITH: This week's column. I've got to send it off
tomorrow.

MATTHEW: What's it about?

....

* I am always rather touched by people who talk endlessly and
enthusiastically about things they are not actually any good at. They want to
be good and one of the toughest lessons in life is to realise that because you
want to be good at something doesn't mean that you are good at it. In fact, if
life guides you towards a different door you must go through it. I speak from
experience, because I wanted to be a famous actor, but in the end, although I
had a perfectly respectable acting career, I did not have that something extra
that I seem to have in writing. Now whether that was just luck or not doesn't
make any difference. That was the direction I had to go in. I've seen people
refuse what they regard as the wrong lucky break, but you mustn't refuse the
wrong lucky break because all lucky breaks are lucky breaks. Here, Molesley
believes that because he loves cricket he can force himself to be good at it.
But life isn't like that.

EDITH: The poor soldiers. How many are reduced to begging on the streets. And some officers are working as dance partners in nightclubs.
MATTHEW: After the trenches even the Embassy Club must seem an improvement.
EDITH: You shouldn't make fun of them.
MARY: She's forgetting that you were in the trenches and she wasn't.*

Violet is with Isobel and Cora.

VIOLET: She must be eighteen by now.
CORA: Little Rose, eighteen. How scary.
ISOBEL: It's quite a responsibility.
VIOLET: Well, I couldn't say no. Her mother is my niece and my godchild, and she asked it as a special favour. Apparently, she hates London and they can't get to Scotland until July — poor Shrimpie, his work keeps him nailed to his desk.
ISOBEL: She hates London, so she's coming to a great-aunt in Yorkshire to have a good time. How original.†

Across the room, Robert is talking to Branson.

....

* Edith's column about her soldiers is a truthful reflection of the period. In the early 1920s there were a lot of ex-soldiers knocking around. One of the problems was that the officer class had been heavily decimated early on in the war and by 1916 they were promoting from the ranks far more. These men were called temporary officers, but this was soon corrupted into 'temporary gentlemen'. After the end of the war a lot of them became slightly sad figures, dressed in their blazers, running the golf club. There simply weren't enough job opportunities for men who wanted to sustain the social rank that being promoted to officers had given them. Working as dancing partners in nightclubs was quite common.

† Rose MacClare is going to be Sybil's replacement as a young girl in the series. Sybil was a rebel, but she wasn't a flapper. Rose is. By being ten years younger than Mary, she is a product of the postwar age – she was fourteen when the war finished. And now she is eighteen. And so she is going into the Twenties as a young woman who is not referring back to the way things used to be. She looks forward to the way things are now. She is Violet's great-niece; her mother is Violet's niece, but she drops the 'great', which was quite normal. My great-aunts were all called Aunt – Aunt Isie, Aunt Lorna – they weren't called Great-Aunt Isie. You just dropped a generation.

ROBERT: Well, don't be silly. Of course you will.

BRANSON: No, I won't. I'd like to help, but I've never played a game of cricket in my life. Oddly, the game was never part of my childhood.

ROBERT: Didn't you play last year?

BRANSON: No. Nor the year before that. The fact is, I've never played cricket.

ROBERT: But couldn't you try?

CORA: Robert. Stop being such a bully. Let's just have a nice dinner.*

9 INT. KITCHEN PASSAGE. DOWNTON. NIGHT.

Jimmy is loading his tray. He walks out past O'Brien.

O'BRIEN: I'm afraid I've heard Mr Carson's going to let him off.

JIMMY: What can I do about it?

O'BRIEN: Say you won't tolerate it. That unless he gives him a bad reference you're going to tell the police.†

JIMMY: I couldn't do that... Could I?

O'BRIEN: Why not? And won't you have to? If you don't want folk to think there's something funny about you.

MRS PATMORE: It's a good job that's supposed to be eaten cold.

She is standing behind them. Jimmy runs off. Mrs Patmore turns to find Bates watching. She shakes her head.

10 INT. HALL. DOWNTON. NIGHT.

Violet and Isobel are leaving. Robert and Cora are seeing them out.

ROBERT: Are you sure about Rose? Wouldn't it be better if she stayed here?

....

* Branson's struggle through the rest of this series and into Seasons Four and Five is his fear of being turned into a Crawley and being made to subscribe to their ways of dressing and their opinions and to activities that are not natural to him. But in another way he isn't really acknowledging how he is changing as a person. He sees them differently in some ways, which he doesn't yet want to admit. That struggle will dominate his story from now on.

† O'Brien shows that malice knows no bounds.

VIOLET: Oh, no. I'm quite looking forward to it.

ISOBEL: I couldn't manage an eighteen-year-old. Not these days. I wouldn't know what she was talking about.

VIOLET: My husband was a great traveller, so I have spent many happy evenings without understanding a word.

CORA: I dare say there's a trick to it.

VIOLET: The thing is to keep smiling, and never look as if you disapprove.*

11 INT. ROBERT'S DRESSING ROOM. DOWNTON. NIGHT.

Robert is in his gown, while Thomas clears some clothes away and Bates stands there.

ROBERT: So, Bates, I'll see you on duty tomorrow. Goodnight, Barrow. You do know I wish you every good fortune?

....

* 'Keep smiling, and never look as if you disapprove.' That is from my mother, because she always hated the fact she couldn't really speak any language other than English, and with my father as a diplomat, particularly early on in the marriage, she had constantly been in situations where everyone was talking French and all she could do was smile and nod and hope that it made sense. For this reason, we were all sent away at thirteen or fourteen to learn French. She would even find houses where English was not spoken. She didn't mind so much if the father spoke English, but she hated it when the mother did, feeling that she would just use us to practise on.

I was sent off to the Dordogne, to a very nice family living in a beautiful little château with a Roman tower. My bedroom was at the top of it, and all the doors and windows were curved, the windows being made of ancient concave glass. The main section of the circle was the bedroom and the last segment was the bathroom. I had only just arrived when I went into the bathroom, opened the window and it slipped from my hand and shot back against the wall and broke, falling four floors into the stable yard. Crash! Crash! Bang! Crash! I remember just wanting to be dead. I didn't know these people, I'd come straight upstairs, I hadn't spoken to any of them and I'd broken this clearly incredibly precious, specially moulded glass window, which was presumably the original from the eighteenth century. I just sat down under the window in the corner against the floor, closed my eyes and tried to make it go away. Funnily enough, they must have been kind to me because I have no memory of what happened after. I stayed there for two or three weeks, came back sort of speaking French, then I went again later and we always stayed on friendly terms. Life.

THOMAS: I believe so. Thank you, m'lord.

Robert goes, leaving the others alone.

THOMAS (CONT'D): To the victor the spoils.
BATES: What will you do?
THOMAS: Oh, what's it to you?
BATES: You're right. It's nothing to me.*

12 INT. MARY'S BEDROOM. DOWNTON. NIGHT.

Mary is in bed. Matthew paces the room, in his gown.

MATTHEW: If we can buy out Simpson and Tucker, quite a chunk of the estate will be back in hand. We'll be operating a real business. That's why I think the cricket may have come at rather a good time.
MARY: Why? Because you think if you get a few runs and catch someone out, Papa will accept all this gladly?
MATTHEW: I think the cricket match will show him it doesn't mean we can't keep up the old traditions as well.
MARY: And am I to help persuade him?
MATTHEW: Of course. You're on *my* team now.†

He gets on the bed and leans in to kiss her.

MARY: You can kiss me, but that's it.
MATTHEW: Why? Haven't you missed me?
MARY: Desperately. But London seems to have tired me out.‡

....

* I don't like to make it too sentimental.

† Now we are talking proper management and involving Mary. That will be quite an important part of what leads on from the death of Matthew, so we must build Mary's interest in running the estate from this point on. And now that the Matthew/Mary team is not going to be at loggerheads with Robert, it's going to be Mary herself who is at loggerheads with her father. We start to play that here.

‡ Mary has been to London, but we don't quite know why – nudge, nudge, wink, wink.

13 INT. CARSON'S PANTRY. DOWNTON. NIGHT.

Jimmy knocks at the door. Carson looks up enquiringly.

CARSON: Come.

JIMMY: Mr Carson, is it true Mr Barrow's leaving?

CARSON: Yes, and for what it's worth, I think he was genuinely mistaken over the... incident and he's sorry now. Which, of course, is no excuse.

JIMMY: I want to be sure you'll give him a bad reference.*

If the curtains had spoken this couldn't be much odder.

CARSON: I'm sorry?

JIMMY: I can't let a man like that go to work in innocent people's houses.

CARSON: I will write the character I think he deserves.

JIMMY: Can I read it?

CARSON: Certainly not.

JIMMY: Because I've been thinking, I ought to report him to the police.

CARSON: What?

JIMMY: It's my duty. I know today thinking is much more liberal but —

CARSON: Now, just a minute. I've never been called a liberal in my life and I don't intend to start now! But I do not believe in scandal. Mr Barrow will go, and when he does I would like him to go quietly. For the sake of the house, the family and, for that matter, you.

JIMMY: I'm sorry, Mr Carson, but I can't stay quiet if my conscience prompts me differently. I won't turn a blind eye to sin.

He walks out, leaving a troubled Carson.

END OF ACT ONE

....

* For a senior servant not to have a reference from their most recent job was employment death. I am not saying he couldn't pick up a job as a waiter or something, but as far as his career trajectory is concerned, as a proper servant he would be absolutely finished.

ACT TWO

14 EXT. DOWNTON VILLAGE/CRAWLEY HOUSE. DAY.

A car drives up to Crawley House. Violet gets out with a glamorous-looking young woman.

15 INT. DRAWING ROOM. CRAWLEY HOUSE. DAY.

Isobel is with Violet and her companion, Rose MacClare.*

> ISOBEL: Well, this is nice. I've asked Ethel to bring us some coffee.
> ROSE: Oh, I'm not supposed to drink coffee. My mother doesn't approve.
> ISOBEL: Would you like something else?
> ROSE: Absolutely not. After all, she won't find out unless you tell her.

They smile, but Violet is not entirely at ease with this.

> ISOBEL: How is Lady Flintshire?
> ROSE: Incredibly busy. Daddy works harder than a slave, and so she has to manage everything else by herself.
> ISOBEL: I doubt he works harder than a slave.
> VIOLET: Cousin Isobel is very literal. Now, I have something for you —

She breaks off as the door opens and Ethel carries in a tray.

> ETHEL: Shall I pour, ma'am?
> ISOBEL: No, thank you. I'll do it.

The maid nods and leaves. When the door closes, Violet takes some letters from her bag.

....

* Alastair Bruce, our historical advisor, and I discussed fictional but reasonably noble-sounding names. As Rose was going to be the daughter of a peer, we thought it was probably better that there was no confusion with real Scottish people with those tribal names; the McDonalds and the like. In the end, we thought MacClare was quite convincing. There is no such name as MacClare. Having said that, someone will write in saying my name is John MacClare.

VIOLET: These are the first answers to the advertisement.
ISOBEL: Cousin Violet is trying to find a new job for my cook.
ROSE: That sounds rather inconvenient.
ISOBEL: Cousin Violet has never let a matter of convenience stand in the way of a principle.
VIOLET: As the kettle said to the pot.

16 INT. CARSON'S PANTRY. DOWNTON. DAY.

Carson is once again with Thomas.

THOMAS: I'm to leave with no reference, after working here for ten years?
CARSON: I'm afraid my hands are tied.
THOMAS: I'll never get another job now, Mr Carson... Does his lordship know about this?
CARSON: No.
THOMAS: Then I'm going to tell him.
CARSON: And how would you do that, without telling him the rest of it?
THOMAS: This wasn't Jimmy's idea. Somebody's put him up to it. He wouldn't be so unkind, not left to himself.
CARSON: I'm almost touched that you will defend him under such circumstances. But, there it is.
THOMAS: Well, can I stay here for a day or two? While I come up with some sort of plan?
CARSON: Yes. I think I can allow that. But that's the best I can do.
THOMAS: Thank you, Mr Carson.*

17 INT. THE BATESES' COTTAGE. DOWNTON. EVE.

This is a shabby and cramped living room. Bates and Anna stand alone in it, looking round.

BATES: At least it doesn't smell damp.

....

* Carson is being forced to do something he believes to be unfair and unjust, which we should be absolutely clear about. For me, there is a poignancy in Thomas's refusal to see Jimmy as the bad guy. He's not the main bad guy, but he's bad enough in my book.

ANNA: I think it's nice. Or it will be. When it's got a lick of paint.

BATES: I can do that. I can.

ANNA: You're not climbing any ladders. But, yes, together we can make it really comfy.

BATES: What do they call extreme optimism?

ANNA: They call it 'making the best of things', and that is what we'll do.

BATES: You being in this room is enough to make it nice. Come here.

He takes her in his arms to kiss her. She responds and they fall back onto the ancient sofa, which collapses under their weight in a cloud of dust. They lie there, laughing.*

18 INT. DINING ROOM. DOWNTON. NIGHT.

The family, including Rose, are all present. Carson, Jimmy and Alfred are waiting at table.

MARY: We should think of some things to do while you're here.

ROBERT: Edith, you should take Rose over to Whitby on Wednesday. When they have their market. She'd enjoy that.

EDITH: I can't. I'm going to London on Wednesday.

ROSE: Oh. Well, could I come?

VIOLET: Ooh. But you've only just got here. I thought you hated London.

ROSE: Who told you that?

VIOLET: Susan.

ROSE: Oh. Darling Mummy.

VIOLET: Should I correct her?

ROSE: Oh, no. She's right, really. But I'm planning a surprise for her, and I need to go to London to arrange it. You won't give me away, will you?

....

* I felt it would be quite wrong to show Mr and Mrs Bates going into some kind of *Ideal Home* cottage. Estate cottages were pretty primitive much further into the century, and indeed on one estate where we stay in the West Country, something like eighty cottages had to be given bathrooms and plumbing and electricity during the 1970s. But while the cottage is basic, for Anna, they are on their own. They've got their own house. That is what matters.

ROBERT: Won't you stay with your parents?

ROSE: Well, I can't. That would spoil everything.*

EDITH: You can stay with me. Aunt Rosamund won't mind. And there's plenty of room.

CORA: I don't even know why you're going.

EDITH: To see my editor. To discuss my article.

ROBERT: Someone should invent a new kind of telegram, so you could send a whole document at once. Just like that.

ISOBEL: And if a document, why not a person? Like H. G. Wells's Time Machine. You'd just get in, press the button, and step out in Deauville.

VIOLET: Would we be allowed to take a maid?

19   INT.   DRAWING ROOM.   DOWNTON.   NIGHT.

They are all in there.   Matthew walks over to Edith.

MATTHEW: I think I might come up with you to London. I'll ring the office in the morning. I can stay at my club.

EDITH: Don't do that. Aunt Rosamund would love to have you. And I suspect I'll need help controlling Rose.

MATTHEW: Why do you say that? She seems rather demure to me.

EDITH: I'm not sure. Instinct.

Violet is with Rose and Isobel.

VIOLET: But when your mother finds out will she mind?

ROSE: No. She'll be delighted and so grateful to all of you for helping with my secret. Besides, with Edith as my chaperone, what harm can I come to?

Violet is frustrated by this, which Isobel sees.

ISOBEL: Don't say I didn't warn you.

VIOLET: I wouldn't dare.

Cora is with Branson.

CORA: But how can I help?

BRANSON: If our plan works, we'll be farming a third of the estate directly.

....

* Rose is quite manipulative at this stage. She just wants to get to London without her parents' knowing.

CORA: And you can manage that?

BRANSON: We think so, but we need you to think so too, because Lord Grantham definitely won't.

MARY: Are you drawing up the battle lines?

She has just arrived to join them.

CORA: Poor Robert. The postwar world is not being kind to him.

MARY: How are you getting on with the agent's house? I hope Jarvis didn't leave it a wreck.

BRANSON: No. Not at all. But the furniture was his, so I'll have to begin in a state of Trappist simplicity.

MARY: I'm sure there's some stuff in the attics here. We'll have a look.

CORA: What about Sybbie? Won't it be lonely for her? With just you and Nanny and nobody else for company?

BRANSON: I think it's right for both of us.

20 EXT. KITCHEN COURTYARD. DOWNTON. NIGHT.

Mrs Hughes comes out with a scuttle and walks towards a door when she sees a figure half hidden in shadow.

MRS HUGHES: Good God. Who's there?

The figure moves. It is Thomas, sitting on the wet ground. He has been crying.

MRS HUGHES (CONT'D): Mr Barrow? What in heaven's name are you doing out here?

THOMAS: Have you come for some coal?

MRS HUGHES: I've run out and everyone's busy.

THOMAS: Give it here.

He pushes open the door and starts to shovel in the coal.

MRS HUGHES: I know you're leaving, but things can't be as black as all that. You're trained now. You can apply for a position as a butler.

THOMAS: You don't know everything, then.

MRS HUGHES: Don't I?

THOMAS: Not if you think I've got a future.

MRS HUGHES: Then will you tell me everything?

THOMAS: Look, I'm afraid if I do, Mrs Hughes, that… it will shock and disgust you.

MRS HUGHES: 'Shock and disgust'?   My, my.   I think I
have to hear it now.   Come on.*

21   INT.   HALL.   CRAWLEY HOUSE.   DAY.

Isobel is with Ethel, who has a sheet of paper.

ETHEL: I'm just going out to the shops, ma'am, if you'd
like to see the menus for today and tomorrow.
ISOBEL: This all looks nice, but perhaps a lighter
pudding for tonight?   Baked custard?   Or some fruit?
ETHEL: Very good, ma'am.†
ISOBEL: Ethel, I've been putting it off but there's
something you ought to know and you will need to think
about.

Ethel waits.

ISOBEL: Lady Grantham, the Dowager, that is, has been
concerned that your history here has left you lonely.
ETHEL: She's kind to concern herself.
ISOBEL: It's not just that.   She believes that you've
made this house a local topic of unwelcome conversation.
ETHEL: Ah.
ISOBEL: So she's placed an advertisement for you and
she's got some replies.
ETHEL: She did this without telling me?
ISOBEL: She did it without telling *me*.

She brings out a packet of envelopes and gives them over.

ISOBEL (CONT'D):   The point is, you would go to your new
position with references from me and from Mrs Hughes, and
you would not have to refer to your earlier life.   In
effect, you'd be washed clean.

....

* Mrs Hughes defines herself as a reasonably just person because she is not
tremendously on anyone's side, and even Thomas is capable of seeing that. I
felt that he had to have someone in the authority structure whom he could
talk to, and it seemed to me that Mrs Hughes was the one he would think
most likely to give him a reasonably sympathetic hearing.

† I was sorry this went because I always like to remind people that these
characters are working in service. This is a workplace drama. Here we have
Ethel doing her work. We know she's been a tart, but here she's working as a
cook and producing menus like any cook.

ETHEL: So are you sacking me?

ISOBEL: Not at all. But I'm now persuaded that the decision to stay or go must be yours and not mine.

22 INT. MARY'S BEDROOM. DOWNTON. EVE.

Edith enters. Mary is getting ready in front of her mirror.

EDITH: Yes?

MARY: Is the new maid working out?

EDITH: No, not really. I don't think she'll stay. I miss Anna… What do you call her now she's your maid?

MARY: Anna, I'm afraid. I can't very well call her Bates.

EDITH: No. What's this about?

MARY: Well… You know Matthew wants to come with you to London…

EDITH: Why shouldn't he?

MARY: I just need to check which train you're planning to come back on.

EDITH: The three o'clock on Thursday. Why?

MARY: Can you promise not to let him catch an earlier one?

EDITH: Of course not. What reason would I give?

MARY: You can think of something. Please.

EDITH: Oh, all right. But why is everything always so complicated?*

23 INT. HALL. DOWNTON. NIGHT.

This is only the core family, without Violet, Isobel or Rose. They've had dinner, and are disposed about the room.

MATTHEW: When are we leaving tomorrow?

EDITH: Eleven. We'll lunch on the train.

MATTHEW: Goodnight. I'll see you upstairs.

He touches Mary's cheek and slips out. Edith looks at Mary.

....

* Here we have one of our invisible characters, Edith's new maid who isn't working out. And we plant more drama. Matthew wants to go to London, so Mary needs to check what train Edith is planning to come back on. 'Can you promise not to let him catch an earlier one?' Knowing Mary's feelings about Edith, to ask a favour must be a clear indication that she is fairly desperate.

EDITH: What do you think Rose is up to? Planning her so-called surprise?

MARY: I'm not sure. I'm beginning to suspect Lady Rose MacClare may prove to be rather a handful.

EDITH: And she's *my* handful, worse luck.

Robert is with Branson.

BRANSON: We'll talk about it when Matthew gets back from London.

ROBERT: Can't I even have a clue?

BRANSON: He should tell you. It's his idea.

ROBERT: God. It sounds ominous.

CORA: What does?

She has joined them.

ROBERT: Matthew has some ghastly scheme for the estate and Tom's too frightened to say what it is. I need a drink.

He goes off to fetch one.

CORA: Is this the big plan?

BRANSON: Yes. And it's going to come off.

CORA: Well done. You must be pleased.

BRANSON: I am pleased, but I worry that Lord Grantham will be angry we've taken it so far without involving him.

CORA: You have to see his point… Have you started planning the move?

BRANSON: Not really. Not yet.

CORA: I do wish you weren't going. Are you sure it's what you want? The two of you alone in an empty house?

BRANSON: I think it's for the best.*

....

* Should Branson and Sybbie move out to the agent's house? As I've said before, I've always had a problem with those American series where everyone lives in one house, even though they've got seventeen billion. Nevertheless, dramatically, you don't want them to keep moving into different houses. So we've stopped Matthew and Mary moving away from *Downton*. Now I've got to stop Branson and Sybbie going into a different house and find a reason to do so. And it seemed to me the only emotional excuse I could find was if he were convinced it would be good for the child to stay.

**24 INT. MRS HUGHES'S SITTING ROOM. DOWNTON.
NIGHT.**

*Mrs Hughes is with Carson. The door is shut. He pours them
a sherry.*

MRS HUGHES: You cannot allow him to blackmail you like
this. And before you ask, Thomas has told me the whole
story.
CARSON: I'm only sorry you had to listen to such
horrors.
MRS HUGHES: Why? Do you think Thomas is the first man
of… that sort, that I've ever come across?
CARSON: I would hope so.
MRS HUGHES: Well, he isn't. And I'll tell you something
else. I think James may have led him on —
CARSON: What! Oh, I cannot listen to such… allegations —
MRS HUGHES: Oh, calm down. I don't mean deliberately.
But he's a vain and silly flirt. He may have given
Thomas the wrong impression without meaning to.
CARSON: I can hardly believe we're having this
conversation.
MRS HUGHES: Maybe not, but I won't sit by and let that
young whippersnapper ruin a man for the rest of his life.
Not a man who was wounded in the service of King and
Country.
CARSON: We may have no choice. These practices, with
which you are apparently so familiar, are against the
law.
MRS HUGHES: I know that!
CARSON: Very well, then. If we stand up to James and he
goes to the police, it will only put Thomas in prison,
which he will not thank you for.*

....

* What I am sure was true at that time was that people were protected by
their own prejudice. Because everyone knew they'd disapprove frightfully,
they weren't told. Carson in a long life of service has lived and worked
alongside several homosexual men, but none has given himself away to him.
Whereas Mrs Hughes, as an essentially sympathetic person, has not been so
protected. She is aware that she has come across several other people who are
the same. That's what we explore here. Carson is uncomfortable with being
blackmailed, there's no question about that, but he doesn't see how they can
let James go to the police, given that his motivation is at all costs to keep the

25   EXT.   THE BATESES' COTTAGE.   DOWNTON.   NIGHT.

Bates comes out of the cottage, holding a candle in a funnel.
Bates stops and finds Thomas, smoking in the shadows.

THOMAS: Inspecting the love nest?
BATES: Just fetching some coal.
THOMAS: I envy you.
BATES: Whatever you say.
THOMAS: No. I mean it. The happy couple and everyone
so pleased for you. Can't imagine what that's like.
BATES: Perhaps you should try being nicer.
THOMAS: It's being nice that got me into trouble.
BATES: What do you mean?
THOMAS: Never mind. I'll be gone soon and out of your
hair. You'll be glad of that.
BATES: Yes, I will be.

Thomas stubs his cigarette out and walks away. But Bates is
troubled by this exchange.

END OF ACT TWO

ACT THREE

26   INT.   SERVANTS' HALL.   DOWNTON.   DAY.

Carson is addressing them all.

CARSON: I assume I can count on you, Mr Molesley?
MOLESLEY: Oh, I'll say. There's not much I don't know
about cricket.
CARSON: You make me quite nervous. So, with you, me,
James, Alfred, both you hall boys, that makes six from
down here. What about Mr Stark?

....

Continued from page 428:

family out of the papers. That's the nightmare. And in fact it would become
more of a nightmare the more intrusive the press became as the century wore
on.

MRS HUGHES: He'll play. He's always kicking a ball around by the garages.

CARSON: It's not quite the same thing.

MRS HUGHES: It is to me.*

BATES: I can't play, Mr Carson. But I can keep score.

CARSON: Good. Very good. So, with his lordship, Mr Crawley and 'Mr' Branson, we're already ten.

IVY: What about you, Mr Barrow?

There is a slight silence at the table.

THOMAS: I think I'll be gone by then.

JIMMY: Yes. You will.

O'Brien smiles at this, which Bates sees.

27 INT. LIBRARY/HALL. DOWNTON. DAY.

Robert is with Cora.

ROBERT: Where's Mary? I was looking for her, but Anna said she'd gone out.

CORA: She's away for the night. She'll be back tomorrow.

ROBERT: Oh?

But Cora does not provide any more information than this.

ROBERT (CONT'D): Cora, is everything… as it should be between them?

CORA: Between Mary and Matthew? Oh, yes, I think so. Why do you ask?

ROBERT: I find I'm rather impatient to get the succession settled.

CORA: Robert, it's still early days.

The door opens and Carson appears.

CARSON: Luncheon is served, m'lady.

ROBERT: Is it just us?

....

* As we have said, chauffeurs lived outside the house and brought the car to the front when it was required. Of course, in real life the staff would have known Mr Stark well, but we'd taken one chauffeur (Branson) into the house and we didn't really want to replace him as a character. So we now make references to Mr Stark and every now and then we see Mr Stark, but we never get to know him.

CORA: Yes. Tom's on the other side of the estate, so he said he'd eat in a pub.

They get up and head out.

ROBERT: He's hiding from me until Matthew's told me the worst.
CORA: Probably.
CARSON: May I take the opportunity to bring your lordship up to date with the team?
ROBERT: Are we in good shape?
CARSON: I reckon that with three family players and seven from downstairs, we're only one short.
ROBERT: Two short. Branson won't play.
CORA: Mr Branson is busy at the moment.
CARSON: Is he, m'lady? Might I point out that we're all busy, but we still find time to support the honour of the house.
ROBERT: Yes. But that is not the right road to travel, Carson, if we want to remain in her ladyship's good graces.*

....

* This is all part of Branson's struggle for personal definition. It's always a choice when you go into a different environment. I was talking to an actress recently who had been a deb when I was a debs' delight and we had both gone on the stage later on. She'd reinvented herself and, without ever lying, suggested that she came from quite a different background to fit in more. She adopted the politics and the mores of show business as it was in the early Seventies. I made the opposite choice; I didn't do any of that. Looking back, she felt her decision had been right professionally but more complicated privately, whereas mine, not to present a different picture of who I was, had taken me towards a good marriage and the rest of it, but erected a lot of hurdles in my work. People have to deal with this. You must work out who you want to be; how much do you want to fit in and how much do you want to change? Actually, in retrospect, I think I was rather inflexible. My difficulty was that I simply didn't believe in the popular politics in showbiz at that time. I didn't see how you could support a party that couldn't manage the economy. I failed to realise it was all about club membership and I was refusing to be a member. I suppose it would have helped if I hadn't been very political, but I was, and it was a problem I had to overcome. That is what Branson is going through. How far does he have to go in order for everyone to be comfortable, and how uncomfortable will he make himself in the process?

28 INT. HALL. ROSAMUND'S HOUSE. LONDON. DAY.

Rosamund is greeting them all as they arrive.

ROSAMUND: Now, I know you're here because you all have
lots of things to do, so just run about and do them.
EDITH: I'll go up and change.
ROSAMUND: But I did think we'd have dinner together.
And then we can have a proper catch-up.
MATTHEW: If that's what you'd like, but please don't let
me be a nuisance.
ROSE: We could always just —
ROSAMUND: I insist. A good family gossip will be my
payment in kind.
EDITH: Then of course we'd be delighted.
ROSAMUND: Good. We dine at half past eight.

*As they all head upstairs, Rose sneaks off into another room
and picks up the telephone.*

ROSE: Hello, operator? Knightsbridge 4056…

29 INT. DRAWING ROOM. CRAWLEY HOUSE. DAY.

*Isobel walks in the door with a basket of flowers, and Ethel
is waiting for her.*

ETHEL: I've been through those replies to her ladyship's
advertisement. And I don't think there's one where I
should be happier than here.

....

* Samantha Bond (Rosamund) is a very busy actress, so we always have to
check whether or not she's up for an episode or two. On the whole, if you see
her at all she's got something real to do in that episode. She's never an also-
ran. Her role in the family essentially means they don't have to open
Grantham House every time they go to London. She's got a house that is
easily big enough to accommodate them. She also has money, and to host
them in the capital is a way of staying at the centre of the group. In my own
life I had a grandmother with a flat in Queen's Gate, and since it was very
central we would leave things there and sleep the night there and meet each
other there, and I would drop something off and my mother could pick it up
in the afternoon, and so on. So she became a kind of 'Forsyte Change' for us,
and that's really what Rosamund is based on. She's a convenience in a way,
but I don't think she minds. I believe she is fully aware of the role she plays.

ISOBEL: That's very flattering.

ETHEL: You don't mind if I stay, then?

ISOBEL: Quite the reverse. I'm delighted.

ETHEL: There was a nice letter from a Mrs Watson. But it was near Cheadle.

Isobel realises some response is expected, but what?

ETHEL (CONT'D): Cheadle's very close to where Mr and Mrs Bryant live.

ISOBEL: Oh, I see. And you feel that would defeat the purpose, if the goal is to leave your past behind you?

ETHEL: Don't you, Ma'am?

ISOBEL: Yes, I'm afraid I do. It's a pity if it was the only one that was appealing.

Ethel covers her face with her hands and starts to weep.

ETHEL: I'll never see Charlie again. I know I won't. I know it.

ISOBEL: No, you don't. And in the meantime, you have made a great sacrifice for his happiness. No mother could do more than that.

Ethel nods. She has pulled herself together.

ETHEL: So it looks as if I'll be staying on. I'm sorry if it makes trouble between you and the Dowager.

ISOBEL: Oh, don't worry about that. If you'd gone, she'd have found some other bone for us to fight over.

30 INT. GREGSON'S OFFICE. LONDON. DAY.

Gregson and Edith are standing over some pages. Edith is looking especially nice with her hair freshly done.

GREGSON: You look very pretty today. I'm not sure how, er, professional it is of me to point that out.

EDITH: Well, it's jolly nice of you.

GREGSON: So, er, business. Now, I've read your piece. Of course the plight of ex-soldiers — it's not an obvious topic for a woman's column.

EDITH: I knew you were going to say that. I know it isn't very feminine, but I felt so strongly about it I thought it was worth a try.

GREGSON: No, no. You misunderstand me. I like the idea of a woman taking a position on a 'man's' subject. And I was going to say: 'Don't be afraid of being serious when it feels right.'
EDITH: Really?
GREGSON: Really. You know, I think we're onto something new here. *The mature female voice in debate.*
EDITH: I don't like the sound of 'mature'.
GREGSON: No. Er… 'Balanced'?
EDITH: Yes. Let's go with 'balanced'.

They laugh. They are very well suited.

GREGSON: Are you in town tonight and by any chance looking for something to do?
EDITH: I am, but sadly I'm spoken for. I'm staying with my aunt and I'm chaperoning a cousin's daughter, so it's complicated.
GREGSON: That's a pity… But you will let me know when you're up in London again?*

31   INT. THE BATESES' COTTAGE. DOWNTON. DAY.

Bates and Anna, in overalls, have covered the furniture with sheets, and they are distempering the room.

ANNA: But why are you bothering with Thomas? He's going. Good riddance.
BATES: I don't know. Something he said. And I feel funny taking his job.
ANNA: You haven't taken his job. He filled in for you, while you were away, that's all.
BATES: Hmm. I might ask Mrs Hughes. She usually knows what's going on.

He splashes his face with distemper.

ANNA: Which is more than you do.

....

* Gregson gives Edith permission to be herself, which is what makes her fall in love with him. That seems to me to be realistic. We have only ever seen Edith being essentially thwarted or ignored, and the mere fact that he is interested in her opinions is probably the most seductive thing about him.

32 EXT. ROSAMUND'S HOUSE. EVE.

Rose emerges. She looks like a different person, in a snappy coat and a bright silk scarf. She runs down the street, hailing a taxicab.

    ROSE: Taxi!

The taxi pulls up, horn beeping.

    ROSE: Warwick Square, please.*

Rose climbs in and the car drives away.

33 EXT. WARWICK SQUARE. LONDON. EVE.

The taxi driver waits patiently. Rose appears, with a sleek lounge lizard of a man, Terence Margadale. She leans in.

    ROSE: I'm afraid I've been hours. You're an angel to wait.
    TAXI DRIVER: I've not been paid, Miss.
    ROSE: No. Well, could you take us to the Blue Dragon? It's in Greek Street.

34 INT. MRS HUGHES'S SITTING ROOM. DOWNTON. NIGHT.

Mrs Hughes is with Bates.

    BATES: Now I understand it.
    MRS HUGHES: You're not too shocked, then?
    BATES: No, but why is Mr Carson? It's not as if none of us knew.

....

* Rose is revealing the real Rose now and her true reason for coming to London. We present how wild she is in a slightly veiled way; whether she sleeps with this man or not we never really know. Maybe she does, maybe she doesn't. She certainly flirts like billy-o and her mother sent her to Yorkshire to get rid of him, so they have all fallen for her tricks.

Originally, Rose gave a particular number in Warwick Square to the taxi driver, but the production team got worried that the number exists and someone who lives there might take offence, which I thought was unnecessary, like a directive from Health and Safety. But I lost, so I had to take the number out and leave her simply saying, 'Warwick Square, please.' But actually you often don't say a number until you get there, so I didn't mind much.

MRS HUGHES: I think the point is we didn't know *officially*. That's what Mr Carson finds hard. He can't avoid the subject any longer, because it's lying there on the mat.*

BATES: And he can't stand up to Jimmy?

MRS HUGHES: He says he's powerless. And it's true we won't help Thomas by putting him in prison.

BATES: I wouldn't wish that on any man. Hah. Imagine me feeling sorry for Thomas.

MRS HUGHES: Life is full of surprises.

35   INT. DINING ROOM. ROSAMUND'S HOUSE. LONDON. NIGHT.

Rosamund, Matthew and Edith are dining at a table laid for four in this grand apartment. A butler waits on them.

ROSAMUND: You don't think we should have waited?

MATTHEW: No. Why should your delicious dinner be spoiled just because Rose has forgotten the time? How long was she here when she came back?

ROSAMUND: I was out, but my maid said she just ran in and out to change her frock and make a telephone call. She swore she'd be back by eight. But it's past ten now.

EDITH: It's my fault. I shouldn't have let her out of my sight.

MATTHEW: Nonsense. You had stuff to see to. That's why we're in London at all.

ROSAMUND: Talking of which, how did you get on today? With your editor?

EDITH: Oh. Quite well, I think. How about you, Matthew?

MATTHEW: Oh, I was only running errands. My main thing is tomorrow.

....

* Mrs Hughes makes the distinction about not knowing officially, which I believe is key. My parents were always very keen on this. When we were older and we used to bring girlfriends down to the country, we were never given the same bedroom. Ever. I once asked my mother about it. My brother Rory had arrived with a girl and I said, 'Why don't you put them in the same room? You know they are going to sleep together.' She said, 'I may know it, but I don't know it officially.' And that was that.

He is distracted as the butler has been called in a whisper
to the door. Rosamund raises her voice.

    ROSAMUND: Mead? What is it?

The man turns back. He is a little flustered. A rather
rough-looking man hovers behind him, clutching his cap.

    MEAD: Come on. This is the driver who took up Lady Rose
    from outside the house, m'lady.
    TAXI DRIVER: I came back because she left a scarf in the
    back of my cab.
    MATTHEW: How very good of you.
    MEAD: Well, go on. Tell them why they sent you up to
    the dining room.
    TAXI DRIVER: I know where she is, m'am. Your maid
    downstairs said you might like to hear.
    ROSAMUND: And she was right. Where did she go?
    TAXI DRIVER: First to Warwick Square. To pick up a…
    friend.
    EDITH: And then you took her on somewhere?
    TAXI DRIVER: Eventually. I was sat outside for the best
    part of two hours.
    ROSAMUND: How very expensive.
    TAXI DRIVER: When they came out, they said they wanted
    to go to a club. The Blue Dragon, on Greek Street.
    ROSAMUND: And what sort of club is that?
    TAXI DRIVER: Well… you know.
    ROSAMUND: That's the point. I don't.

    36   INT. THE BLUE DRAGON. SOHO. NIGHT.

A band of black musicians plays jazz in the crowded, smoky
basement. The clientele is mostly, but not entirely, young,
with vividly made-up women and sleek, lounge-lizard men.
Rose is on the floor with an older man. They're dancing the
faster, jazzier version of the foxtrot that was popular in
the 1920s. Matthew, Rosamund and Edith enter.*

....

* The Blue Dragon is the first of the new clubs that *Downton* characters visit,
but they were being opened all over London by people like the famous Mrs
Meyrick, who managed to marry all her daughters into the peerage, despite
spending quite a lot of time in jug as an illegal seller of drink and God knows
what else besides. These clubs were a new kind of night life. There had been

MATTHEW: This is like the outer circle from Dante's
Inferno.
ROSAMUND: The *outer* circle?
EDITH: There she is.
ROSAMUND: Heavens. What a transformation.

Some 'bright young things' push past Rosamund.

ROSAMUND (CONT'D): And that, presumably, is the 'friend'
she spent two hours with in Warwick Square.
MATTHEW: Let's not start down that track.

*As they watch she kisses her partner passionately. Rose and
the man then make their way to a table, where…*

ROSE: Oh, my G— How on earth did you find me?

The dancing partner has stood. Rosamund addresses him firmly.

ROSAMUND: How do you do. I am a cousin of Rose's
mother.
MATTHEW: Lady Rosamund Painswick…
ROSE: Terence Margadale.
MARGADALE: Well, how do you do. Please sit down.

They do. He speaks to a passing waiter.

MARGADALE (CONT'D): Can you bring some more glasses?
ROSAMUND: Tell me, where is Mrs Margadale?
MARGADALE: She's in the country at the —

He and Rose realise he has been tricked. There is a silence.

....

Continued from page 437:

bars before the war, and places you would take your girlfriend, with a private
dining room and a couch behind the curtain. But now respectable women
were allowed in, they could go dancing without a chaperone, so the clubs
were part of that general loosening of the stays. Most of their time was spent
dancing in hotels: Claridge's, the Ritz and the rest all had top dance bands,
and you went to one of them perhaps two or three times a week. But at times
that was not enough and you wanted something more cutting edge. That's
where the clubs came in. The most famous was probably the Embassy,
because it was the one that the Prince of Wales enjoyed.

ROSE: Er… Terence used to work for Daddy so he's more
of a family friend, really.
EDITH: Oh, so Cousin Shrimpie'll be pleased to hear
about him, won't he?
ROSE: No, please —
MATTHEW: Why don't we dance?

*To the bewilderment of the others, he takes Rose's arm and
leads her onto the floor. He talks as they dance.**

MATTHEW (CONT'D): Now, look. I think I can just about
get Rosamund and Edith to keep their mouths shut, if you
come back with us now and have nothing more to do with
this man, at least not until you are out of our charge.
ROSE: But you know, he's — he's — he's terribly unhappy
and it's not his fault at all. His wife is absolutely
horrid —
MATTHEW: Married men who wish to seduce young women
always have horrid wives. I suggest you meet Mrs
Margadale before you come to any final conclusions.
ROSE: You're wrong. He's in love with me. He wants to
marry me just as soon as he can get a divorce.
MATTHEW: And when will that be?
ROSE: Well, you see, it's terribly difficult.†
MATTHEW: Yes, I thought it might be. Now are you going
to accept my conditions, or do I throw you to Lady
Rosamund?

....

* We wanted to feature some black musicians here, because the 1920s was the
moment when black musicians and singers really became fashionable and
popular. It seemed a nice visual statement that the world is becoming more
recognisably modern. Later, in Season Four, we would develop this theme
into a major storyline.

† It always fascinates me the number of sentient adults, men and women,
who will tell you how incredibly unhappy the person they have just run off
with was in their marriage. You always want to say, 'But if they were so
incredibly unhappy, why were they still together?' I asked someone the other
day if her lover was living with his wife when their affair started. She said,
'Oh yes, but it was completely finished.' When the truth is that if he was still
living with her, then it wasn't finished. It is the one rather objectionable fact
that they never want to address.

ROSE: Why are you helping me?
MATTHEW: I'm on the side of the downtrodden.*

He leads her from the dance floor.

MATTHEW: Excuse me.

Back at the table, the women are struggling.

EDITH: I rather like Warwick Square. Sort of Belgravia
without the bustle.
MARGADALE: Oh, we haven't been there very long.

They look up. Matthew and Rose are approaching.

MATTHEW: Rose is feeling rather tired, so we're leaving.
MARGADALE: But won't you at least stay for a —

But they have gone, leaving him to his bottle of champagne.

37   INT. DRAWING ROOM. DOWNTON. DAY.

Cora, Violet and Isobel are together, without servants.

VIOLET: Well, no. No, I'm glad she's staying, but one
forgets about parenthood. The on-and-on'ness of it.
ISOBEL: Were you a very involved mother with Robert and
Rosamund?
VIOLET: Does it surprise you?
ISOBEL: A bit. I'd imagined them surrounded by nannies
and governesses, being starched and ironed to spend an
hour with you after tea.
VIOLET: Yes, but it was an hour *every day*.
ISOBEL: I see. Yes. How tiring.†
CORA: Rose seems a nice young woman.
VIOLET: Nice, I give you, and placid, but…

....

* For Matthew, of course, this place is hell; for Rosamund, it's double hell; but it's a pretty truthful version of what was going on then. Matthew and Rose forge a sort of alliance here that will pay off in the Special.

† I was always rather fascinated by that sort of upbringing. When I was young, a few of my contemporaries were still living something similar. For most people – most British people, anyway – it really has gone now, but in the 1950s and 1960s there were still children in England being taken down to the drawing room for an hour after tea. I can't pretend they have grown up any more messed up than the rest of us.

CORA: But what?

VIOLET: I'm not sure. A sense that we're only being shown half the picture. I wish I could talk to Susan.

ISOBEL: If you do speak to Lady Flintshire, you must be careful not to mention the trip to London.

CORA: We did all promise not to tell.

VIOLET: Not me. I never did any such thing.

38 INT. CARSON'S PANTRY. DOWNTON. DAY.

Carson is with Bates.

CARSON: After the money turned up from Mr Swire, things went back to normal.

Jimmy knocks. They look up.

JIMMY: Mr Carson, may I have a word?

BATES: I'll leave you.

JIMMY: You can stay. I'm not bothered.

There is an insolence in his manner which infuriates Carson. Carson motions for Bates to stay.

CARSON: Well?

JIMMY: When's Mr Barrow leaving?

CARSON: I'm not sure.

JIMMY: He's lost his job. Why can't he just go? I find it very awkward.

CARSON: I am sorry to hear that.

JIMMY: If you think I'll change my mind about the reference, I won't.

BATES: Are you always so unpleasant?

JIMMY: I'm not unpleasant, but you don't know what he did.

BATES: He made a mistake. You're still in one piece. Why do you have to be such a big girl's blouse about it?*

JIMMY: I'm sorry, Mr Carson, but I won't change my mind.

Jimmy looks at Bates furiously and leaves.

....

* A Yorkshire phrase that I've always rather liked. I am assuming it was already going in the 1920s, but I haven't got proof of that. As nobody has been in touch to complain, I think I'm in the clear.

BATES: I suppose you know who's put him up to this, Mr
Carson?

39 INT. SERVANTS' HALL. DOWNTON. DAY.

Jimmy has come in to find Alfred and some of the others.
Molesley is practising with his bat. O'Brien is sewing.

JIMMY: That Mr Bates is gobby, isn't he?*
IVY: Why do you say that?
JIMMY: Well, everyone used to talk about him as if he
could walk on water, but he's got a mouth on him.
ALFRED: What did he say?
JIMMY: He was sticking up for Mr Barrow.
IVY: Is this because of Mr Carson not giving him a
reference? I don't think it's right, do you?
JIMMY: Yes, I bloody well do think it's right! You know
nothing about it!

He storms out. Ivy is bewildered.

IVY: What's happened? What did I say?
O'BRIEN: I shouldn't get involved, dear. If you'll take
my advice, I should stay out of it.†

40 INT. MOTOR CAR. DAY.

Violet and Isobel are being driven home.

VIOLET: Stark, I wonder if we could have the window up.
It's a bit draughty.

The chauffeur nods and the dividing window is raised.

....

* 'Gobby' is a Yorkshire term for someone who speaks his mind noisily and
continually. I used to hear quite a lot of these northern phrases during my
school years at Ampleforth, and my grandmother's family is based in North
Yorkshire, which used to be called the North Riding. I am often asked why
we set *Downton* in that part of Yorkshire, and various houses there have
claimed to be the inspiration for it, but the truth is, ITV wanted it set in the
North and the North Riding was the one part of the North I knew well.

† They are all disturbed by the fact that Thomas is not to have a reference.
As working servants that would be more or less the worst thing anyone could
do to you, so it is a very, very serious business. Jimmy, of course, does not
want to be chivvied over it because he is responsible for the trouble.

VIOLET: Tell me, has there been any progress with Ethel?

ISOBEL: No. I'm sorry to disappoint you but she doesn't want to go.

VIOLET: Not one of them was right?

ISOBEL: One. A Mrs Watson. But the house was near where the Bryants live and, to be honest, I suspect that was the reason. A chance to see little Charlie from time to time.

VIOLET: Well, I can't blame her for that.

ISOBEL: Of course not. But the Bryants would be bound to find out, which would only lead to more heartbreak.

41   INT.   DOCTOR RYDER'S CONSULTING ROOMS.   LONDON. DAY.

Matthew is with the doctor.

RYDER: I'll write to you as soon as I hear, but it's extremely unlikely there is anything wrong at all. This may prove an expensive journey for you.*

MATTHEW: May I ask you a question, Doctor Ryder? Has my wife been to see you?

RYDER: I'm not aware of treating a Mrs Crawley, but even if I had I could not possibly comment on it.

MATTHEW: I only want to know if she was here for the same purpose as me.

RYDER: I don't mean to be rude but, just supposing she has been one of my patients, surely if she wanted you to know, she'd have told you.

MATTHEW: Of course. It's only… I can't bear to think of her being worried, when I know very well that if anyone's to blame, it's me.

RYDER: I'm not sure 'blame' is a very useful concept in this area.

He stands to indicate that the interview is over.

....

* We are not specific about what Matthew is being tested for, as it wouldn't be very *Downton* to go into detail. He wants to know why Mary isn't getting pregnant and so he has had some tests run. That is quite enough for us to be going on with.

RYDER (CONT'D): Please believe me that probability and logic indicate a Crawley baby yowling in its crib before too long.
MATTHEW: Thank you. Goodbye.
RYDER: Goodbye. I'll show you out.

Matthew leaves and walks down the stairs, where he is shocked to see Mary standing in front of the receptionist.

MARY: Mrs Levinson for Doctor Ryder.

Mary turns and finds Matthew standing there.

END OF ACT THREE

ACT FOUR

42   INT.   CAFE.   LONDON.   DAY.

A waitress carries a pot of tea to Matthew and Mary's table.

MATTHEW: This should buck you up.
MARY: Buck me up or kill me. It looks like treacle.

He sits. They are not angry, but it is a strange moment.

MATTHEW: Why did you go without saying? When I knew all along it was me.
MARY: You know nothing of the sort… In fact, it was *me*.
MATTHEW: What do you mean?
MARY: There *was* something wrong. With… Actually, I can't talk about this sort of thing. Even to you.*
MATTHEW: You sound like Robert.

....

* There is a modern idea that if you are in love with someone you want to tell them everything, but I don't believe that. I always remember the story of a husband whose wife had died and they were going through her things and they found this box, and the son said, 'Oh, it's her false teeth.' And the father said, 'Don't show me. I never knew in life; it would be disloyal to know in death.' I thought that was rather good. In fact, if Matthew hadn't found her at Doctor Ryder's, I doubt she would have told him anything at all.

MARY: Well, I am his daughter. The fact is, it meant a small operation —

MATTHEW: What!

MARY: It's all right. It was weeks ago. That's why I've been keeping you at arm's length.

MATTHEW: What a relief. I thought you'd gone off me.

MARY: Anyway, today was just to see if all is well and he says it is. He says I'm to get in touch with him in six months' time, but that I'll be pregnant before then.

MATTHEW: So, now we can start making babies.

They smile warmly at one another. He takes her hand and kisses it.

MATTHEW (CONT'D): What do you think we'd have done if there had been a problem?

MARY: God knows. Track down the next heir after you and adopt him.

She starts to laugh and, after a moment, so does he.

MATTHEW: We'd be okay. That's the main thing.

MARY: Yes. I think it is.

MATTHEW: How did you explain your absence?

MARY: Mama knows. She'll cover for me.

MATTHEW: You told your mother but you wouldn't tell me?

MARY: Any woman would understand.

MATTHEW: Now you can join our merry band for the ride home. I have much to tell of young Lady Rose, who proved quite as troublesome as you suspected.

MARY: What about Edith and her editor?

MATTHEW: I think she's rather taken with him. She had her hair done.

MARY: Oh, dear. He'll obviously turn out to be wildly unsuitable. Either that, or a complete rotter.

MATTHEW: You're very harsh.

MARY: No, I'm not. We all conform to a pattern, and that's hers.

43 INT. HALL. LADY ROSAMUND'S HOUSE. LONDON. DAY.

They are in the hall. Mary is with them.

ROSAMUND: Right. Have you got everything?

MARY: You're so sweet to put them all up.

ROSAMUND: Not a bit. I only wish you'd been here with us.
MARY: I know. It was silly of me.

Rosamund turns to Rose.

ROSAMUND: I feel very guilty not telling Susan about last night.
ROSE: Mummy wouldn't understand.
ROSAMUND: Nor do I. What were you thinking? A respectable, well-born young woman going out with a *married man*?*

The camera finds Edith's face. But Matthew continues to talk.

MATTHEW: Rose knows that it all depends on her behaviour for the rest of her stay. One false step and I shall personally telephone Lady Flintshire.
ROSAMUND: Very well. But I don't approve. Now hurry or you'll miss your train. I'll see you at the cricket match.

Rose sighs and walks off.

MATTHEW: Edith, you're in a daze. What is it?
EDITH: Oh, just something we were talking about last night. Aunt Rosamund reminded me of it. That's all.

44 EXT/INT. THE DOWER HOUSE. HALL. EVE.

The car has arrived at the Dower House. All four get out.

MATTHEW: We thought we'd walk from here.

They set off, leaving the other two.

ROSE: I don't need to be escorted inside. What are you afraid of? That I'll make a run for it?

* I have already talked about this loosening up for unmarried women. And because they were suddenly without chaperones for so much of the time and allowed to go out with young men for the evening, in the end exactly what all those Victorian chaperones were afraid of did start to happen – not as it would later, once the pill had essentially liberated women sexually in the 1960s, but love affairs for the unmarried and posh were no longer totally unknown, as they had been in the previous century. Of course, it was still a big thing, because it was a very, very bad move to get pregnant, so that did keep them in check, but it was beginning to kick off.

EDITH: Rose, you've obviously read too many novels about young women admired for their feistiness.

As they talk, they open the door and go into the hall.

ROSE: Do you think they will keep quiet?
EDITH: I expect so. As long as you stick to your side of the bargain.
ROSE: Even Cousin Rosamund? She didn't like being made to keep the secret.
EDITH: Probably because she knows that Granny would be furious.

The camera travels on, to find Violet on the stairs. Hearing this, Violet turns and climbs the staircase out of sight.

45   INT.   KITCHENS.   DOWNTON.   NIGHT.

Daisy and Ivy are working as Molesley is demonstrating moves with a cricket bat for Jimmy and Mrs Patmore.

MOLESLEY: It's all in the wrist. Don't tighten your grip until you're ready to take the stroke. Just keep it light. You see? How I turn it, first this way and now that.
JIMMY: Why not just whack it for six?
MOLESLEY: It's not the battle of the Titans, Jimmy. A little grace, please, a little art. Cricket is a spectator sport, so let's give the spectators something worth looking at.

He demonstrates some noble footwork.

MRS PATMORE: By heaven, Mr Molesley. You should be on the stage.*

Alfred walks in.   He seems downcast.

MRS PATMORE: Alfred? What's the matter?
ALFRED: Nothing. I'm not easy about this business with Mr Barrow.

....

* There is something in Kevin Doyle (Molesley), a kind of pathos, a dignified sorrow, that I now write for and he mines. It is interesting to see as, before *Downton*, he usually played serial killers, so we have released the lovable, sensitive side of him.

MRS PATMORE: Well, why not take a turn with Mr
Molesley's bat? That'll put a smile on your face.
DAISY: Is Mr Carson really not giving Mr Barrow a
reference? That's what I heard.
IVY: Why ever not?
MRS PATMORE: It's complicated, Ivy. And very difficult
for Mr Carson.
IVY: What will he do? If he hasn't got a reference?
MRS PATMORE: Well, he could always go abroad. He might
do well in America, Mr Barrow.
DAISY: Seems a bit drastic. Why should he go abroad?
JIMMY: Keep your nose out of it.
IVY: Why won't someone tell us what's going on?
MRS PATMORE: Because you wouldn't understand it. I very
much hope.

46 EXT. DRIVE. DOWNTON. EVE.

Mary and Matthew are walking along, hand in hand. The car
overtakes them and stops. Edith looks out of the window.

EDITH: Sure you don't want a lift?
MARY: Quite sure.

The car moves off.

MATTHEW: The big meeting with Robert is in the morning
and I need you there. He trusts you more than me.
MARY: Papa trusts you.
MATTHEW: But he thinks I don't understand the
responsibilities of this way of life. He thinks I'm a
bean-counter.
MARY: Well, you are in a way.
MATTHEW: Darling, it's the bean-counters who'll survive
and, anyway, I'm a bean-counter with a heart.

This makes her smile. She kisses his hand.

MARY: I'll be there. But Mama ought to join us, to be
on his side.
MATTHEW: I agree. Now hurry up.
MARY: Why?
MATTHEW: Because there isn't long before dinner. We've
got work to do.
MARY: You should have thought of that before you sent
the car away.

47   INT.   ROBERT'S DRESSING ROOM.   DOWNTON.   DAY.

Bates is dressing Robert for a new day.

ROBERT: It's not very fragrant, is it?

BATES: No, m'lord.

ROBERT: Why didn't Carson tell me? He's the one who's being undermined.

BATES: It's a very difficult subject for him to discuss.

ROBERT: I can imagine. But it's not as if we didn't all know. About Barrow.*

BATES: That's what I said to Mrs Hughes.

ROBERT: I mean, if I'd shouted blue murder every time someone tried to kiss me at Eton, I'd have gone hoarse in a month. What a tiresome fellow.†

BATES: It's not the boy's fault. He's been whipped up, told that if he doesn't see it through, we'd all suspect him of batting for the same team.

ROBERT: Crikey. But who'd do that? Who's got it in for Barrow?

BATES: Miss O'Brien.

ROBERT: O'Brien? I thought they were as thick as thieves.

BATES: Not now, m'lord.

ROBERT: Well, if that's true, it seems like a good place to start.

48   INT.   DRAWING ROOM.   DOWER HOUSE.   DAY.

Violet and Rose are alone.

VIOLET: I've spoken to your mother. She has a new plan for when you leave here.

ROSE: Aren't I going back to London?

VIOLET: Oh, no, no. It's so horrid and dusty…

....

* Robert's attitude to all this is very like my father's (he can often be glimpsed in Robert's opinions). There was a good quote from an MP not long ago when the tabloids, in their charity and mercy, decided to reveal that his brother was gay. The journalists asked the MP whether he objected, to which he replied: 'Why should I object? It's like objecting to rain.' I think my father felt that; it was like objecting to rain. And that's the attitude that I've given Robert.

† This line brought me a lot of letters, I can tell you.

ROSE: What is Mummy's plan?

VIOLET: They're opening Duneagle early; you're to go there.

ROSE: On my own?

VIOLET: No. Your Aunt Agatha will keep you company.

ROSE: *Alone in Scotland with Aunt Agatha!* She can't be serious!

VIOLET: I know, I know. Lady Agatha isn't much of a party person, I admit —

ROSE: A *party person?* It's like being guarded by Quasimodo and the Witch of Endor rolled into one! This is all because I went up to London to see Terence, isn't it? How did she find out? Who gave me away?

VIOLET: I don't know who 'Terence' is —

ROSE: Of course, it's not your fault, Aunt Violet. But they promised!

VIOLET: Don't shoot the messenger, my dear. I'm only relaying your mother's orders. You're to stay for the cricket match and head north the next day.

ROSE: Perhaps I'll run away.

VIOLET: Not this time. My maid will travel with you. So you have someone to talk to on the journey.

ROSE: I won't be held a prisoner forever.

VIOLET: No. One day you'll be older and out of our power. But not yet.

*They lock eyes. But Rose knows her mother, through Violet, has won.**

49 INT. THOMAS'S BEDROOM. ATTICS. DOWNTON. DAY.

Thomas is sitting on the bed, while Bates stands there.

THOMAS: Prison's changed you. There was a time when nothing was too bad for me, as far as you were concerned.

BATES: Prison has changed me.

....

* At one point I thought I was going to do something with Aunt Agatha, but then I came to the conclusion that a battle-axe might trample on Maggie Smith's feet. She'd have to be comedic, and once she was a comedic old battle-axe then isn't what Maggie's doing much better than that? So I never went forward with it. But anyway, she is a background character here. Violet is pretending she found out legitimately.

Thomas sinks back on his pillow.

> THOMAS: The hell with it. I'm finished and there's nothing to be done for me.
>
> BATES: You do know Miss O'Brien is behind it?
>
> THOMAS: I knew someone was. Jimmy'd never think of it for himself.
>
> BATES: Doesn't it bother you that she'll get away with it?
>
> THOMAS: Not really. To tell you the truth, I'm tired. Tired of fighting my corner, tired of being disliked. Wouldn't it be better if I just go?
>
> BATES: Without a reference after ten years here, you'll never work again.
>
> THOMAS: Not in England, but elsewhere maybe, yeah. I've a cousin in Bombay. I might go there. I like the sun.
>
> BATES: But you must fight fire with fire, Mr Barrow. There must be something you know about Miss O'Brien you could use against her.
>
> THOMAS: You've heard of the phrase 'To know when you're beaten'? Well, I'm beaten, Mr Bates. I am well and truly beaten.
>
> BATES: Then give me the weapon and I'll do the work. What can I say that would make her change her mind?

Thomas looks at him. He almost speaks… and then:

> THOMAS: I couldn't. She made me promise on everything I hold sacred.
>
> BATES: I'm glad to hear there are things you hold sacred, Mr Barrow.

But he waits…*

....

* I always think it is interesting emotionally to make a character in a drama sympathise with another character whom they don't like, if they've been betrayed or wrongfully accused. Just as in life, you may not like someone, but that doesn't alter the fact that in certain instances you're on their side. Besides which, when they're very young most people feel they have to dislike anyone who dislikes them, but as you get older you don't necessarily dislike people who dislike you, and that is really what we are exploring here. Of course, Bates is right in thinking that Thomas will know something about O'Brien that can be used against her.

50 INT. LIBRARY. DOWNTON. DAY.

Robert is with Branson, Cora, Matthew and Mary.

ROBERT: It is not how we do things! Many of the
farmers' families have been at Downton for as long as we
have!

BRANSON: But we need to see more profits from the farms —

ROBERT: Here we go! Profit! Profit! Profit!

MATTHEW: Profit is also called income. We cannot go
forward with no income.*

ROBERT: But why not tackle it gradually? Perhaps buy
some time by investing your capital. I hear of schemes
every day that'll double whatever's put into them or
treble it or more.

MATTHEW: Many schemes offer high rewards; very few
deliver them.

ROBERT: There's a chap in America — what's his name?
Charles Ponzi — who offers a huge return after ninety
days. Now, Harry Stoke has gone in with a bundle —†

MATTHEW: Then Harry Stoke, whoever he is, is a fool!

ROBERT: But if I could find out about —

MATTHEW: Robert, the last time you took an interest in
investments you ruined the family!

He has shouted. This silences Robert, and enrages Cora.

CORA: Now, look here! Robert's been the captain of this
ship long enough to be entitled to some respect!

MARY: He didn't mean to be disrespectful.

ROBERT: Well, he does a marvellous impression of it!

....

* Robert is making the mistake a lot of the intelligentsia of our own day make regularly, which is to assume anything that is run commercially and makes a profit has no merit. A film that is popular must be a bad film, because a good film would not have a large audience. A popular book is a trashy book, because a good book would not be easily accessible, and so on. This prejudice has really dominated our artistic life to quite a degree for a long time. For me, it is the position that has held the film industry back in this country, and as a result it is not level pegging with the national film industries of many other lands.

† Charles Ponzi was a real fellow who became briefly rich before heading for a lengthy term in gaol. His name would enter the language meaning false pyramid selling. He was in action at this time.

BRANSON: We are giving the farmers a choice. That's
all. If they want to sell, the larger units will let us
meet the challenges of the modern world.
MARY: We need to build something that will last, Papa.
Not stand by and watch it crumble into dust.
ROBERT: What about the tenants? What about the men and
women, who put their trust in us? Is this fair to them?
I don't believe so.
CORA: But isn't the most important thing, for them or
us, to maintain Downton as a source of employment?
ROBERT: So you're against me, too.
CORA: It seems to me your plan adds up to carrying on as
if nothing's changed, to spend Matthew's money keeping up
the illusion. Then when we've fallen into a bottomless
pit of debt, we'll sell up and go.

They are all silent at this assessment. Cora nods.

CORA (CONT'D): But I don't think the tenants will thank
us for that, nor the farm workers, nor the servants, nor
the village, nor the county. So, yes, I believe Matthew
is right.
ROBERT: I see. You seem to be agreed that there's no
place for me in all this. So obviously it's time for me
to take a back seat.

*He is very, very hurt and he walks out, leaving them to it.**

51   INT.   HALL.   DOWNTON.   DAY.

*As Robert strides across the hall, behind him, in the outer
hall, Edith is on the telephone. Someone has answered.*

....

* This is a good *Downton* argument, because we agree with and like Robert's
concern for the tenants and the estate, which someone like him would feel.
We are on his side. On the other hand, as Cora says, they have to maintain
the estate as a source of employment and income, which can only happen if it
is run efficiently. So in a sense they are both in strong positions, but they are
pulling in opposite directions. Here, Cora does come down on the other
side, and Robert is wounded, but in his wounding he's convinced.
Sometimes in an argument you go on after you know you've lost, because
actually you have been convinced, even though you don't want to admit it
quite yet.

EDITH: Hello? Is that the *Daily Telegraph* Information Desk? I want to find out about a London editor... Michael Gregson... Of *The Sketch*... Just some general stuff, his education, what he's done since then, and a little about his... private life.*

52 EXT. BACK DOOR. DOWNTON. DAY.

O'Brien comes out of the door and sets off.

53 EXT. THE BATESES' COTTAGE. DOWNTON. DAY.

O'Brien arrives at the Bates cottage.

54 INT. THE BATESES' COTTAGE. DOWNTON. DAY.

The little room is painted. Anna is up a ladder pinning a frilly pelmet to a board. Bates stands by the fireplace.

ANNA: But why here? I don't like the idea of her being our first visitor.
BATES: I want to be away from the others.
ANNA: I don't know why you're doing this. You don't even like Thomas.
BATES: Because I know what it is to feel powerless. To see your life slide away and there's nothing you can do to stop it.
ANNA: Quite the orator. Have you thought about standing for Parliament?

There is a knock at the door. It is O'Brien. She looks round.

O'BRIEN: Oh, yes. Very nice. It'll be even better with a bit of money spent on it.
ANNA: Can I get you some tea?
O'BRIEN: If I'm staying long enough. I don't know what it is Mr Bates wants to see me about.
BATES: You'll have time for tea.

....

* In the days before the internet the *Telegraph*'s Information Desk was a first port of call when you wanted to know something. *The Sketch* was a weekly glossy illustrated magazine. The nearest equivalent today is *Hello!*, but it had other articles besides the celebrity gossip, although there was quite a lot of that.

55   INT. DRAWING ROOM. CRAWLEY HOUSE. DAY.

Ethel is collecting a tray of tea things.

ETHEL: Will that be all, ma'am?
ISOBEL: There is one thing. There was a letter
delivered by hand this afternoon. It's from the Dowager.
ETHEL: Oh, yes?
ISOBEL: She wants us to call on her in the morning.
ETHEL: I don't understand.
ISOBEL: Nor I. She wants us both to go to the Dower
House at eleven.
ETHEL: But why would she want me?
ISOBEL: No doubt we'll find out in the morning.

56   INT. THE BATESES' COTTAGE. DOWNTON. DAY.

Bates and O'Brien are together, watched by Anna.

O'BRIEN: Well, I am surprised to find that you're a fan
of Mr Oscar Wilde.
BATES: You've known about Mr Barrow all along, so what's
changed now?
O'BRIEN: Perhaps I've come to my senses.
ANNA: You mean you've found a way to be even nastier
than usual.
O'BRIEN: Oh. Get back in the knife box, Miss Sharp.
BATES: I want you to persuade Jimmy to let Mr Barrow have
a reference, so when he leaves here he can start again.
O'BRIEN: Why would Jimmy listen to me?

Bates just looks at her.

O'BRIEN (CONT'D): I won't do it.
BATES: I think you will. And to persuade you, I'm going
to whisper three words into your ear.
O'BRIEN: It won't make any difference.

*But when Bates walks round the table and whispers something,
the blood drains from her face.* She stands.*

....

*'... the blood drains from her face'. When you write that kind of direction it
is always a little unfair on the actor. I remember a wonderful stage direction,
although I've forgotten the play, where the text describes the character as
entering from stage left and 'in his eyes is written the fall of Rome'. Can you
imagine the feelings of the poor actor at the read-through?

O'BRIEN (CONT'D): I'm going.

BATES: Sort it out by this evening.

O'BRIEN: Or?

BATES: Or you'll find your secret is no longer safe with me.

57 INT. SERVANTS' HALL. DOWNTON. NIGHT.

O'Brien is with Jimmy.

O'BRIEN: I'm just saying I think you've made your point. To let it go now would be the gentlemanly thing to do.

JIMMY: You said if I let it go they'd think I was up to the same thing. That I wasn't a proper man.

O'BRIEN: If you'd done nothing, yes, but this way you'll come across as merciful and not vindictive, do you see?

JIMMY: I never wanted to push it this far.

O'BRIEN: Then you'll be glad to stop it.

JIMMY: You're sure I won't be made to look a fool?

O'BRIEN: Far from it. I think they'll hold you higher in their estimation.

CARSON: Ah, James? Upstairs, please.

JIMMY: May I have a word with you, please, Mr Carson, before we go up?

58 INT. DINING ROOM. DOWNTON. NIGHT.

The family is at dinner. The atmosphere is strained.

CORA: But why London? You've only just got back.

EDITH: Something's come up.

MARY: What?

MATTHEW: She doesn't have to justify herself whenever she leaves the house.

EDITH: Thank you, Matthew, but I don't mind. I've had some bad news, that's all. I need to go up to London to sort it out.

MARY: What sort of bad news?

MATTHEW: Never mind. It's not our business. How's the cricket team coming along?

ROBERT: We're still two short.

MARY: I wrote to Evelyn Napier, but he can't get away on that Saturday.

MATTHEW: Why him?

MARY: Evelyn's a whizz at cricket. He's on some team or other.*

MATTHEW: What about the chaps at the office?

ROBERT: But it should be men who are connected to Downton in some way. Napier would be all right, as he used to stay here, but recruiting in the office seems a bit desperate.

MATTHEW: And you're still determined not to play?

BRANSON: It's not that I won't play. I can't play. I don't know how.

CORA: Stop twisting his arm… Any news on the move, Tom? We're going to miss you both so much.

EDITH: You told Matthew not to twist his arm, now you're doing exactly the same thing.

CORA: I just think children are happier in families. I'm sorry, but I do.

59 INT. ROBERT'S DRESSING ROOM. DOWNTON. NIGHT.

Bates is getting Robert changed for bed.

ROBERT: Well, I'm glad that's settled, but I suppose Barrow will have to go?

BATES: M'lord?

ROBERT: He's so good at cricket. I know we were soundly beaten last year, but he did get most of our runs.

BATES: I thought we just wanted him to have a reference, so he could find work when he leaves.†

ROBERT: I know, but, now that I think about it, Carson ought to insist that he stays on. He needs to re-establish his authority over James.

BATES: Couldn't Mr Barrow just stay till after the match, m'lord? And then go?

ROBERT: That seems rather unkind. Wouldn't we be using him?

....

* This was cut and it doesn't matter much, but I like to mention characters whom we have met earlier in the series, but who have not been in it for a while. In some shows, no vanished character is ever mentioned who is not immediately coming back.

† Bates has made his own life much more complicated by winning a reprieve for Thomas. He didn't think it through. Which of us will think ill of him for that, when we've all done something similar at one time or another?

BATES: But what would he stay as?

ROBERT: You're a clever fellow. You'll think of something. Just tell him it's conditional on his playing.

BATES: He might not want to stay, m'lord. After the unpleasantness.

ROBERT: I think he will. Then he won't have to leave with a nasty taste in his mouth. But don't forget the cricket.

BATES: I won't, m'lord.

60 INT. SERVANTS' HALL. DOWNTON. NIGHT.

Molesley is demonstrating how to bowl the ball.

MOLESLEY: You see how my grip is firm but tender. Cherish the ball, don't crush it.

JIMMY: Do you know how to bowl a googly?

MOLESLEY: Can I bowl a googly? I should say so, although I prefer to call it a Bosie, after Bernard Bosanquet who first invented it. I saw him play once at Lord's. I've tried to model my style on his.

MRS PATMORE: Have you, now? How proud he'd be.*

Jimmy is distracted by Alfred beckoning him. He leaves Molesley instructing the hall boys and goes over to him.

ALFRED: Is it true you've given in? And let Mr Barrow get away with it?

JIMMY: It was dragging on and on. At least this way we'll be rid of him.

ALFRED: I heard his lordship wants him to stay for the cricket match.

JIMMY: And even if he does, it won't be for much longer. Then he'll get his reference and go. Good riddance.

....

* B. T. Bosanquet (1877–1936) was an Old Etonian who played cricket for Middlesex and England. His 'Bosie' is a legbreak ball delivered out of the back of the hand that becomes an offbreak, not that I know what the phrase means. I wonder if the name was a kind of in-joke. Oscar Wilde's tragedy was still quite recent and he had been brought down by his love for Lord Alfred Douglas, otherwise known as Bosie.

Even so, Alfred seems really troubled by this.*

61 INT. DINING ROOM. DOWNTON. DAY.

Robert, Matthew and Branson are at breakfast.

ROBERT: Where's Lady Edith, Carson?

CARSON: She went to the station first thing, m'lord.

MATTHEW: Her mystery mission... I'm going over to Windmill Farm, to see what we can do with the outbuildings. Would you like to come with me?

ROBERT: I'm sure you can manage on your own.

Matthew does not prolong the awkward moment. He leaves.

ROBERT (CONT'D): Aren't you going?

BRANSON: I'll meet him there later... He's putting a good face on it, but you know he wants you with him on this. More than anything.

ROBERT: I should not serve him well. I don't have the instincts for what he wants to do.

BRANSON: You mean you're not a tradesman.

ROBERT: Your word, not mine.

BRANSON: Shall I tell how I look at it? Every man or woman who marries into this house, every child born into it, has to put their gifts at the family's disposal. I'm a hard worker, and I've some knowledge of the land. Matthew knows the law and the nature of business.

ROBERT: Which I do not.

BRANSON: You understand the responsibilities we owe to the people round here, those who work for the estate and those that don't. It seems to me if we could manage to pool all of that, if we each do what we can do, then Downton has a real chance.

Robert is both surprised and rather moved by this outburst.

ROBERT: You're very eloquent.

BRANSON: I'm not usually.

Branson looks down, a little embarrassed.

....

* Every now and then you want to give a few false resolutions to stories, to stop the audience feeling too comfortable. They thought that storyline was done and dusted but... it's not.

ROBERT: You're a good spokesman for Matthew's vision.
Better than he has been, lately.
BRANSON: So you'll give us your backing?
ROBERT: I'll think about it. On one condition.

Branson waits to hear.

ROBERT (CONT'D): You play cricket for the house. You
said it yourself: we all have to do what we can do.

Branson knows when he is beaten.

BRANSON: For God's sake. If it means that much to you.

*Robert has his team.**

62 EXT. DOWER HOUSE. DOWNTON. DAY.

Isobel and Ethel approach the front door.

63 INT. DRAWING ROOM. DOWER HOUSE. DAY.

They are shown in, to find Violet… and Mrs Bryant.

ETHEL: Oh.
MRS BRYANT: You didn't expect to find me here.
ISOBEL: No.
VIOLET: I thought the only person who could tell us with
any accuracy the Bryants' response to Ethel's working
nearby were the Bryants themselves.
MRS BRYANT: Lady Grantham wrote to me, explaining your
wish.
ETHEL: Well, it was only that Mrs Watson had answered
the advertisement…
MRS BRYANT: I know the circumstances. Just as I know
that you would like to see how Charlie's getting on.
ISOBEL: But surely Mr Bryant —
MRS BRYANT: Mr Bryant will know nothing about it. As it
happens, I've been uncomfortable about keeping a mother
from her son. And although I would not want to confuse
him, until he's much older, if then —

....

* This analysis by Branson that they all have to get behind the wheel and try
to make it turn is meant to show how there is a place for Robert in this new
Downton, which we will go on with.

ETHEL: We wouldn't have to confuse him. I've already worked it out. I'm his old nanny who was employed by you when he was first born.

ISOBEL: But what about when he talks about you to Mr Bryant?

MRS BRYANT: You will please leave Mr Bryant to me. Now, Ethel, you must write to Mrs Watson today and get it settled.

ETHEL: And I'll be able to see Charlie.

ISOBEL: It won't be easy.

ETHEL: It'll be easier than not seeing him. Very much easier.*

64 INT. MRS HUGHES'S SITTING ROOM. DOWNTON. DAY.

Mrs Hughes, Carson, Bates and Anna are all in there.

MRS HUGHES: His lordship is quite correct. You must re-establish your authority.

CARSON: That's all very well. But there's still nothing to stop James going to the police.

....

* In films, people aren't often allowed to live a compromise; they normally have to have a total resolution. In reality, on the other hand, a false position is often the best option available. Almost all of us are living in a false position to some degree, and so it seems to me quite realistic to give Ethel a compromised conclusion. She will keep an eye on her son and he will probably never know she is his mother until the end, if then. Certainly not until he's a grown man. This is not too bad for him and a definite improvement for her.

I was sad to lose Amy Nuttall. Her performance was extremely strong and hers was a very moving story, to me anyway. But sometimes with a character you feel you have accomplished their journey; you've got there. It is very difficult to explain, and not everyone agrees. On a show like *Coronation Street*, one producer will see tremendous potential in certain characters, and then the next producer will come along a year or two later and feel differently. Suddenly an actor who thought they would be running the Rovers Return for the rest of time is out on their ear. But worse than going is staying with nothing to do, and we all agreed we had reached Ethel's conclusion. Amy is an extremely talented actress. We loved having her and I wish her more than well.

BATES: He won't do that now. Miss O'Brien won't let him.
MRS HUGHES: I wish I knew why she keeps changing direction.
ANNA: I agree. It's funny, isn't it?

She stares at Bates but he says nothing.

CARSON: And if Mr Barrow is to stay on... what would he be? My valet?
MRS HUGHES: You can make him under butler. Then your dinners will be grand enough for Chu Chin Chow, and he can apply to be a butler when he does leave.*
BATES: But that would make him my superior.
CARSON: Oh, I don't know. Under butler, head valet. There's not much in it.
MRS HUGHES: The question remains. How do we convince James?
CARSON: Well, it's his lordship who wants Mr Barrow to stay on, so I think his lordship can bring it about.

65 EXT. CRICKET GROUND. DOWNTON ESTATE. DAY.

Branson, padded up, and Matthew are practising in the nets. Matthew is bowling. Branson misses.

BRANSON: Is this worth it? I've no time to learn anything. Shouldn't I just trust to beginner's luck?
MATTHEW: Certainly not. I want you to profit from my skills in gratitude for bringing Robert round.
BRANSON: Not completely. Not yet.

Matthew bowls again. Branson misses.

MATTHEW: Elbow up.
BRANSON: You won't make a gentleman of me, you know. You can teach me to fish, to ride and to shoot, but I'll still be an Irish Mick in my heart.

....

* The musical *Chu Chin Chou* (by Oscar Asche, with music by Frederic Norton) opened in London in 1916 and ran for five years, then considered a triumph. I was in one of its very rare revivals when I was in Rep in Northampton in 1973. I know it well, because I was made understudy to the juvenile lead. I was so terrified I might have to go on that if he developed the mildest sniffle I would run to the chemist and spend half my weekly salary on cold remedies for him.

MATTHEW: So I should hope. There. See? You're getting the hang of it.*

It is true. Branson has hit the ball hard.

66 INT. GREGSON'S OFFICE. LONDON. DAY.

Gregson is surprised to find Edith standing before him.

EDITH: I'm sorry if this is inconvenient.
GREGSON: It's unexpected, not inconvenient.

She sits, gathering her nerve.

EDITH: I suppose I'd better just say it.
GREGSON: Please do.
EDITH: I had the impression on my last visit that you were flirting… giving signs that you found me attractive. If I'm wrong, then I apologise —
GREGSON: You're not wrong.

This makes things both better and worse.

EDITH: But, since then I have discovered you are in fact married.

This elicits a long pause. Then he nods.

GREGSON: Yes.
EDITH: I'm afraid I find the idea of a married man flirting with me wholly repugnant, so you'll see I must hand in my resignation at once. I've enjoyed the work and thank you for the opportunity. But now we must part.

She stands, keen to get out before she loses it. He stands.

GREGSON: No. It's true, I am married, but I hope you'll allow me to explain.

....

* What we've really done with Matthew is to make him the happiest married man alive, we've made him the one person that Branson loves, the one person that Edith loves and the man who saved Downton. All of this has been done within three episodes because we know we've got to knock him on the head at the end of the series. So we are trying to make it as sad when he goes as we possibly can, and also to put them all into dramatic relationships that will give them something to play after he's dead. It's all quite deliberate, building him up and up until the end of the Special… And then he gets it in the neck.

EDITH: Explain what? I am familiar with the institution of marriage.

GREGSON: Yes. But not with this one. My wife is in an asylum. And she has been for some years. It's an odd business. Lizzie was a wonderful person and I loved her very much. It took me a long time to accept that the woman I knew was gone and wouldn't be coming back.

EDITH: Then why haven't you got a divorce?

GREGSON: I can't. Under our present legal system a lunatic is not deemed responsible; she's neither the guilty nor the innocent party.

He is sad rather than bitter.

EDITH: So it means that…

Edith sits again. This revelation has changed everything.

GREGSON: It means that I'm tied for the rest of my life to a mad woman who doesn't even know me.

EDITH: I see.

GREGSON: Do you? Because if you do, I hope you'll consider staying on. I can't begin to tell you how much it cheers me to read your column and to meet when we do. I hope very much you'll consider staying on.*

....

* I've long been interested in this question. There was a so-called screwball comedy (what does that mean?) made at the end of the 1930s, starring Claudette Colbert, Don Ameche, John Barrymore and Mary Astor, titled *Midnight*. I remember watching it with my parents when I was a boy. There was lots of mistaken identity and wackiness, but at the end Don Ameche pretended to be mad to prevent his wife from divorcing him, because you couldn't divorce a mad person. This seemed so odd to me, but it was true, as my mother explained, and the law wasn't changed for some years after the film was made.

In fact, later on, I had a relation of my own with a wife who went mad. He did eventually divorce her, but it was incredibly difficult, because there are all these safeguards for the welfare of the mad party who is unable to look after him- or herself. By comparison, a normal divorce between two adults is a walkover. Culturally, we have grown up on mad wives you can't get rid of. That's why Rochester could not divorce Mrs Rochester and had to hide her in the attic, which I think is lost on most young readers today. A Victorian reading *Jane Eyre* would not have needed an explanation. Anyway, Gregson is a 1920s Mr Rochester.

66A EXT. VILLAGE AND CICKET PITCH. DOWNTON
ESTATE. DAY.

The cricketers march through the village and onto the field of play.

67 EXT. CRICKET PITCH. DOWNTON ESTATE. DAY.

Robert tosses the coin, while Clarkson makes the call.

CLARKSON: Heads.
ROBERT: Ah. Well, there we are.

The House Team is batting and Bates keeps score. Jimmy and Matthew stride out to the crease. All the male servants are in whites. Violet and Isobel are among the spectators. Old Mr Molesley is the umpire, in a white coat. We join them at the moment that Matthew hits the ball for four. Bates hangs the score.

VIOLET: I'm glad everything's settled with Ethel. But I trust you can find another cook without too much difficulty.
ISOBEL: Preferably one with a blameless record so my house ceases to be a topic of gossip, which is really what this is all about.
VIOLET: If Ethel wants to be part of her son's life, even a little part, who are we to stand in her way?
ISOBEL: Of course, if you'd had to sell Charlie to the butcher to be chopped up as stew to achieve the same ends, you would have done so.
VIOLET: Happily, it was not needed.

But she does not deny it. Back to the cricket, and Matthew is out, Carson comes out to bat, and finally it is Robert and Thomas at the crease. Thomas's skill lives up to its billing as a series of elegant strokes sees him make a century.

ROBERT: Oh, shot, sir.

Everyone rises to their feet to applaud. A beaming Robert shakes his hand.

ROBERT: Well played, Barrow.
THOMAS: Thank you.
ROBERT: Excellent innings.

Bates is with Anna.

ANNA: I knew you'd regret it. He'll be up to his old
tricks before too long.
BATES: I thought I was helping him get out of our lives
for good. And now he ranks higher than I do. I've been
a damn fool.
ANNA: I've no sympathy.

But she is as amused as cross.

ANNA (CONT'D): By the way, what was that phrase he gave
you to say to Miss O'Brien? You can tell me now, surely?
BATES: If you keep it under your hat. It was: 'Her
ladyship's soap.'
ANNA: What?
BATES: I can't make any sense of it, either, but that's
what he said. 'Her ladyship's soap.' And it worked.*

*Robert and Thomas are running, but the ball has been returned
fast and it is smashed against the wicket just before Robert
reaches the crease. Robert is out and walks from the crease.
On his way to the marquee he greets Molesley.*

ROBERT: It's down to you, Molesley. Last man in. We're
in good shape thanks to Barrow, but we could do with a
bonus.
MOLESLEY: Don't you worry about me, m'lord. I'll show
them a thing or two.
ROBERT: That's the spirit.

He joins Mary at the edge of the field.

MARY: Well done, Papa.
ROBERT: Well, I did my best. We'll just have to hope
it's enough.
MARY: Anna says we are to expect great things of
Molesley.

*Molesley takes his place. The bowler bowls. Molesley draws
himself up, muttering fiercely under his breath.*

....

* I knew we had to tell the audience what Bates had said, what the three
words were, and I needed to rely on the viewers' memory, because otherwise
'Her ladyship's soap' doesn't make any sense, as it doesn't to either Anna or
Bates. But we know it is the bar of soap that O'Brien placed for Cora to slip
on, causing the miscarriage, which O'Brien so bitterly regretted. I didn't
have any complaints actually, so I think most people did piece it together.

MOLESLEY: This time. Oh, Lord, I beg you. Make it happen for me *this time!*

The ball arrives and he steps forward to play it as it whacks into the wicket and sends the bails flying.

CLARKSON: 'Owzat!
MOLESLEY: Well bowled.

Mr Molesley holds up his hand to mark his son out.

ROBERT: As usual, our expectations are disappointed. Let's have some tea.

As his team walks off the pitch, he leads the way back to the tent where tea is being dispensed by Mrs Hughes, Mrs Patmore, Ivy and Daisy. Rose walks up to Edith and Rosamund.

ROSE: Who gave me away? Was it you?
EDITH: Certainly not.
ROSE: Because, in case you don't know, I'm being sent north tomorrow, with a monster for a gaoler!

Rosamund is rather uncomfortable as Rose stalks off. Violet approaches.

VIOLET: Well, what did she expect? Carrying on with a married man, as if her home were in a tree.
EDITH: Granny? Who told you?

Violet is silent, but she glances at Rosamund.

EDITH (CONT'D): How could you have done that? After you promised?
ROSAMUND: But Mama said *you* told her! I just filled in the details.
EDITH: I never said a word.
ROSAMUND: Have you tricked me, Mama?
VIOLET: Tricked? I am not a conjuror. I only did what was necessary to preserve the honour of the family.
ROSAMUND: In other words, you tricked me.

Robert approaches Jimmy. Carson is nearby.

ROBERT: James, you put up a very good show out there. Well done.

Jimmy stands, unused to the pseudo informality.

JIMMY: Thank you, m'lord.

ROBERT: As a matter of fact, I wanted to thank *you* for your generosity with Barrow. Letting him stay on shows a real largeness of spirit.

JIMMY: Stay on? Mr Barrow's staying on?

ROBERT: As under butler. I was given the impression you'd allowed it.

JIMMY: I allowed him to have a decent reference, for when he left.

ROBERT: But you won't mind too much, will you? Oh, and by the way, congratulations on your appointment as first footman.

CARSON: What?

JIMMY: Thank you, m'lord. Very much.

Two men in dark clothing get out of a car and walk across the pitch. Alfred looks very nervous. Branson catches sight of them first but he is looking around.

BRANSON: Have you seen Sybbie?

MRS HUGHES: Lady Mary had her the last time I saw them.

He nods and goes off in search as Thomas arrives. They are watching Robert calming Carson down.

THOMAS: How do you think it's going?

MRS HUGHES: I'm sure it'll go well for you. You're like a cat with your nine lives, Mr Barrow. But if you've scraped by this time, watch your back in future.

THOMAS: You know me, Mrs Hughes. Always try to stay light on my feet.

MRS HUGHES: Too light, if you ask me.

Carson and Robert are now alone. The two men are nearer.

CARSON: I'm not comfortable, m'lord. Promoting that young jackanapes over Alfred.

ROBERT: It needn't be for ever. And James won't do anything to rock the boat now. Isn't that the main thing?

CARSON: If you say so, m'lord. But I'm not comfortable.

The men have reached them. Robert raises an enquiring brow.

FIRST OFFICER: Lord Grantham, I believe?

ROBERT: The same.

FIRST OFFICER: We're looking for a Mr Alfred Nugent, m'lord.

ROBERT: And you are?

FIRST OFFICER: Inspector Stanford and Sergeant Brand, York Police.

ROBERT: Alfred can't have got into trouble with the police. That's not possible.

FIRST OFFICER: He's made a complaint concerning a Mr Thomas Barrow making an assault of a criminal nature on another of your employees.

Robert and Carson exchange a glance.

ROBERT: That is a very serious allegation.

FIRST OFFICER: It is, m'lord. Serious enough to bring us here to interrupt your cricket match. If you'd like to point out the young gentleman?

CARSON: He's over —

ROBERT: I'll fetch him.

Before the Inspector can argue with this, Robert walks off with a firm, admonitory look at Carson.

FIRST OFFICER: Well, we'll go with —

CARSON: I think it's better if you leave it to his lordship. I'm sure he can get to the bottom of it.

FIRST OFFICER: I'm *not* sure we want him to.

Robert is with Alfred.

ALFRED: But I know what I saw, m'lord, and it weren't right.

ROBERT: I'm not asking you to abandon your beliefs, Alfred. Just to introduce a little kindness into the equation.

ALFRED: Am I not to stand up against evil?

ROBERT: Evil? Thomas does not choose to be the way he is, and what harm was done, really, that his life should be destroyed for it?

ALFRED: Well…

ROBERT: Let he who is without sin cast the first stone. Are you without sin, Alfred? For I am certainly *not*.*

....

* Robert strong-arming Alfred is, I think, realistic. The police must often find it difficult when they are dealing with authority figures who essentially expect to live by their own laws. I am sure they come up against it all the time when they interview a big employer, the head of a corporation, a major

Old Bill Molesley is taking a cup of tea from Mrs Patmore.
Doctor Clarkson is there.

CLARKSON: Sorry about your son, Mr Molesley.
BILL MOLESLEY: Don't be.
MRS PATMORE: But he talked such a lovely game.
BILL MOLESLEY: He could always talk a good game of
cricket. He just couldn't play it.

Robert is approaching the policemen with Alfred.

ROBERT: Just as I thought. There's been a mix-up.
Alfred here witnessed some rough-housing between two of
the staff and misinterpreted it. Isn't that the case,
Alfred?
ALFRED: If you say so, m'lord.
FIRST OFFICER: With all due respect, we're not
interested in his lordship's version of events. We want
yours.
ALFRED: It's like he says. They were fighting and
joking and I got the wrong end of the stick.
FIRST OFFICER: But why did you make the telephone call
without checking your facts?

....

Continued from page 469:

landowner… The downside of this is the story of Cyril Smith, the Liberal MP, where clearly, not once but time and again, some bigwig stepped in to shelter him. That was peculiarly offensive because it involved not just children, but children with no defenders, in homes where they were kept for others' pleasure, like the Emperor Tiberius's minnows. It is very horrible to think how many men went along with it – men who were not evil so much as weak, too weak to make trouble. And actually, although I am not a big fan of the cases where something dubious happened in 1961, there are crimes that seem to scream across that divide, and the Cyril Smith case, like Jimmy Savile's, is one of them. There's nothing we can do to him now, but his victims deserve some acknowledgement.

Here, there's nothing the police can do, and on the whole I hope we are on Robert's side. We don't want to see Thomas dragged off. Nevertheless, it must sometimes be difficult when the police feel they're being blocked and their only option is just to wait until the next time. In this instance, they are of course also dealing with an aristocrat. They know Robert would telephone the Chief Constable: 'Bobby, my dear chap, do you know what's going on…?'

ROBERT: I'm very much afraid to say he was a bit squiffy, weren't you, Alfred?

ALFRED: If that's how we're telling it. I made the call before I knew what I were doing. I'd been at the cider.

CARSON: You *what?*

ROBERT: Oh, I think we can overlook it this once, don't you, Carson?

His look tells Carson to shut up, which he does.

ROBERT (CONT'D): So, you see, I'm afraid there's really nothing to investigate. I'm terribly sorry to have wasted your time. Would you care to have some tea?

The policemen know they are on a hiding to nothing.

FIRST OFFICER: No, thank you, Lord Grantham. I think we've got the measure of it. Good luck with your match.

They walk away, muttering and shaking their heads.
Robert puts his hand on Alfred's shoulder.

ROBERT: You did the right thing, Alfred. Judge not, lest ye be judged. Don't you agree, Carson?

CARSON: Do I have any choice, m'lord?

Branson walks round the corner of the tent and there is a family group. Mary, on a low deck chair, arranges a daisy chain around the neck of Sybbie who sits on her lap, while Matthew looks on. Rosamund and Edith are chatting, but we cannot hear what they say, while Isobel sits with Violet. All Branson can see is his baby at the centre of this large, social family. Cora watches from a seat nearby. She is drinking tea. *

....

* Originally, I intended a bit more of a tableau than I got here. I don't think I explained it clearly enough. I wanted Branson to see Sybbie as a member of the family, not just as his daughter – an image of how all these people were related to her and she was part of something. A sort of 'Holy Family' icon. There was a nice shot of Mary and Matthew with the child, but the rest were quite spaced out. Anyway, it worked. His daughter is shown as safe in her group of protectors, none of whom will harm her, and that's the security of leaving her there. So he decides to stay, at least until she's older. This is what Cora wants and what she believes Sybil would have wanted. I'm not so sure, but I'm glad they're all happy.

BRANSON: Where's Nanny?

MARY: Gone to get some baby paraphernalia. Shall I tell her you're looking for her?

BRANSON: No, no. I'll be here anyway.

He walks over and sits next to Cora.

CORA: You're very good to play.

BRANSON: I don't know why I made such a fuss about it. Can I ask you something?

CORA: Of course.

BRANSON: If I were to say I'd live with you while Sybbie's little, and that we wouldn't move out until she's older, would you mind?

CORA: I should be delighted. And I know it's what Sybil would want.

BRANSON: I think you're right. And that's why I'm suggesting it.

Matthew is with Mary, drinking tea.

MATTHEW: Tom says Robert's ready to get behind the plan.

MARY: I'm glad. So we'll be building a new kingdom, while we make our little prince.

MATTHEW: I'm looking forward to both enormously.

He kisses her hand with a chuckle as he looks round.

ROBERT: Right, gentlemen. Time's up to resume play.

MATTHEW: We're about to start again. I hope I can count on you not to laugh when I drop the ball.

MARY: You can always count on me.

MATTHEW: I know that.

ROBERT: Gentlemen! Time's up!

He and the others are all walking back out onto the pitch.

MATTHEW: I didn't know it was possible to love as much as I love you.

ROBERT: Matthew! Hurry up! You're keeping everyone waiting!

MATTHEW: I've got to go.

MARY: Of course you have.

MATTHEW: Though I'd rather stay here for the rest of my life, holding your hand.

MARY: Go.

He kisses her. Matthew runs onto the pitch. He stops when he reaches Robert. He has something he wants to say.

MATTHEW: Tom seems to think you might be coming round.
ROBERT: Well, he's brought me round more like. But, yes. All right. Let's give it a go, and see what the future brings.
MATTHEW: Thank you.

Robert takes up his place as wicket-keeper and Matthew drops into his place as, at a sign from the umpire, Carson bowls. Clarkson hits the ball high.

MOLESLEY: Catch it!

And Branson catches it. The crowd and players applaud, and Matthew, Branson and Robert run together, shake hands and embrace. *

END OF EPISODE EIGHT

....

* I rather disagreed with the slow-motion shot here as it seemed sentimental and not quite right for the style of *Downton*, but I was overruled and now I'm not sure I was correct. This is, after all, Matthew's last happy ending, and perhaps it was good to celebrate it in a kind of self-consciously perfect way.

CHRISTMAS SPECIAL

ACT ONE*

1 EXT. DOWNTON. DAY.

A cart is being loaded with luggage, including fishing rods, hat boxes, the lot. A caption reads: One Year Later.

2 INT. PASSAGE. DOWNTON. DAY.

Anna is carrying a suitcase. O'Brien, who is carrying cases of her own, approaches.

  O'BRIEN: Anna. What have you got for hair in the evening?
  ANNA: Er… Diamond stars and one tiara. We may not use it, but I'd rather be safe than sorry.

A new, pretty maid, Edna, walks down the passage, passing Branson, and giving him a good looking over.

3 INT. KITCHENS. DOWNTON. DAY.

Daisy and Mrs Patmore make sandwiches and peel boiled eggs.

  MRS PATMORE: Wrap it all in brown paper so they won't have a basket to worry about at the other end.

....

*This Special is one of our excursion episodes, and this year we decided to make it about stalking. I am an unashamed supporter of the country way of life, and stalking particularly is easy to defend because it is essential for the health of the herds. Without stalking it would be necessary for the people in charge of the deer to undertake ever more culling. I like to shake the rather simplistic opinions that you come up against, and we thought Scotland would be a nice change of scenery. We looked at various houses and, prompted by our indefatigable advisor, Alastair Bruce, who is a friend of the family, we thought the most appropriate was Inverarary, the seat of the Dukes of Argyll. As always, it is necessary for us to take houses where the family is still there, because we cannot create convincing interiors otherwise, and happily the Argylls seemed pleased to welcome us, being hospitable and nice throughout the filming. It is a very beautiful place.

4 INT. KITCHEN PASSAGE. DOWNTON. DAY.

Bates comes in to find Jimmy.

BATES: The suitcases are finished.

JIMMY: Okay. I'll go up and get them now.*

He starts up the stairs. Ivy has overheard this.

IVY: It's quite a palaver, isn't it? Do they go to Duneagle every year?

BATES: Not last year after Lady Sybil died, and not during the war. But otherwise, it's the high spot of his lordship's calendar.

5 INT/EXT. ENTRANCE. DOWNTON. DAY.

Cases are being packed. Thomas oversees the equipment being carried outside.

THOMAS: Come on, quickly, quickly. Straight onto the wagonette.

Alfred's loading cases. Molesley, in a panic, is with Carson.

MOLESLEY: Why aren't we taking the guns?

CARSON: Because you're going stalking, Mr Molesley. And stalking does not involve shotguns.

MOLESLEY: Well, maybe we should take them, just to be sure.

CARSON: I am already sure.†

Branson looks on, with his baby in his arms. Alfred, Jimmy and Thomas struggle to get a particularly heavy case onto the cart. Thomas and Jimmy walk back into the house awkwardly, and in silence. Jimmy walks away.

....

* We always like to remind the audience of the mechanics of how these houses worked, that the valets and the ladies' maids tell the footmen that the cases are ready to go down and so on. And the maids swap information as to what they will need for the stay.

† Here we make a distinction for the audience: stalking does not involve shotguns.

6 INT. MARY'S BEDROOM. DOWNTON. DAY.

Anna is dressing a pregnant Mary, under Matthew's gaze.

MARY: We can't possibly chuck now. We couldn't be so
rude.
MATTHEW: Why don't I go on my own?
MARY: Darling, this isn't 1850. No one expects me to
hide indoors until the baby's born.
MATTHEW: Of course not… Well, all right. If you're
certain. But if you change your mind at any point and
want to come home, just tell me.

He leaves. Anna looks at Mary.

ANNA: I hope you know what you're doing.
MARY: *Et tu, Brute?**

7 INT. SERVANTS' HALL. DOWNTON. DAY.

*Thomas reads a newspaper. Bates, Molesley and O'Brien are in
overcoats as Ivy comes in with a large parcel. Anna follows.*

IVY: There you are. That's your lunch for the train.
ANNA: I've four evening dresses for ten nights. Do you
think it's enough?
O'BRIEN: I've put in five.
IVY: It all seems very formal. I thought they were
going stalking.
O'BRIEN: How do you think they eat their dinner?
Wrapped in a towel?
THOMAS: I envy you, Mr Bates. I'd love to go stalking
at Duneagle. But then I suppose you won't be out on the
hill much. Not with your leg.

Mrs Hughes arrives. She addresses the new maid.

MRS HUGHES: Edna, they're almost out of the dining room.
EDNA: I thought I was doing the bedrooms.
MRS HUGHES: We clear the dining room first and clean the
bedrooms when they're out of them. Like any other house.

....

* We start to touch, very lightly I hope, on the wisdom of Mary's making this
journey when she is extremely pregnant. Everyone is going to think it a
mistake by the time we're finished.

EDNA: Not any house in 1921.*

MRS HUGHES: I can't help that. We still do things properly at Downton Abbey.

8 INT. OUTER HALL. DOWNTON. DAY.

Edith is on the telephone. She is smiling, despite herself.

EDITH: Well, no, we'd be thrilled to see you… It just seems an awfully long way to come for a walk…

9 INT. DINING ROOM. DOWNTON. DAY.

Carson and Thomas attend the whole family at breakfast, including all the women, as Edith walks back in and sits down.

CORA: Who was it?

EDITH: My editor, Michael Gregson… He's realised he's going to be in Scotland at the same time as us.

MARY: Don't tell me he'll be near Duneagle?

EDITH: Apparently.

MARY: What a coincidence.

Mary and Matthew share a look.

EDITH: Yes, isn't it?

CORA: Maybe we can ask him over. We want to meet him, don't we, Robert?†

MATTHEW: Why are the Flintshires based in Scotland when the title's Welsh?

ROBERT: Oh, Shrimpie's grandmother was Countess of Newtonmore in her own right; it's now their courtesy title. She was chiefly heiress of that strand of the MacClares and they took her name. Shrimpie's the chief now.‡

....

* The breaking up of the old rules is one of the main themes of the show.

† Gregson has invited himself up to Scotland because he wants to know them all. It is quite deliberate. So I think their suspicions that he's done it to get in with them are true, but not quite in the way Mary believes.

‡ That the Countess of Newtonmore was 'chiefly heiress' was a phrase I rather liked, which I got from our historical advisor, Alastair Bruce. Peerages that may pass through women are much more common in Scotland than in

MATTHEW: Dare one ask why he's called Shrimpie?
ROBERT: It was a nursery game. Louisa was a lobster,
Agatha was a shark, which is easy to believe, and I
suppose Shrimpie was a shrimp.
BRANSON: Is he very small?
MARY: No, but he was the youngest.*
CORA: I'm sorry you won't be with us.
BRANSON: Why should they ask me? I don't know them at
all.†
MATTHEW: Nor do I, really.
ROBERT: Are you sure you should be going?
MARY: Don't be a spoilsport. I still have a month.

She notices that Carson is watching her intently.

MARY (CONT'D): You don't want me to go, either.
CARSON: I think you should take good care of yourself,
m'lady. That's all.
ROBERT: I agree. Right. Let's get started. I told
Mama we'd be on the platform at quarter to, and we're
late.

....

Continued from page 479:

England. Scottish titles created before the Act of Union can be inherited by women in default of a male heir, which for me is an argument for extending the custom to England. As for the title itself, Newtonmore was one of the towns I knew well when I was making *Monarch of the Glen*. It is a lovely part of Inverness-shire and it was a privilege to be working there.

* Nicknames should make things easier and more informal, but instead they often make them stickier. They are a defensive mechanism of the upper classes. You soon reach a point where you could call someone like Lord Flintshire by his Christian name, but you really cannot bring yourself to call him Shrimpie. Maybe these days this is less true because we are so much more relaxed, but in those days, whatever such people may pretend, it was a way of keeping outsiders out.

† Branson has been left out partly for plot reasons, but partly because I want to remind the audience that his has not been an easy journey. The family may have now got to the point of accepting him, but once he leaves the sheltering umbrella of Downton he is back up against the values of the English upper class.

10 EXT. RAILWAY STATION. DOWNTON VILLAGE. DAY.

Bates, Molesley, O'Brien and Anna are walking by the luggage van.

ANNA: It feels like a holiday, doesn't it?

O'BRIEN: Oh, don't worry. It won't feel like a holiday once we get there.

MOLESLEY: Oh! Let me just retrieve the briefcase. He might need it for the journey.

He darts back into the van as O'Brien walks off down the platform, leaving Anna and Bates alone.

BATES: I ought to check their dining-car seats for luncheon.

ANNA: Do you like Scotland?

BATES: Have you really never been?

ANNA: They didn't go last year, and you know I wasn't a proper lady's maid before that.

BATES: No, I meant as a child, or when you were growing up… My mother's mother was Scottish. She was a Keith. Did I tell you that?*

Further down, Robert is talking to Branson, while Isis sniffs around.

ROBERT: Now, you won't forget to take her for some decent walks? She can be lazy.

BRANSON: Don't worry. She'll be fine.†

Violet has met the others. Isobel is there.

ISOBEL: Have you got everything?

VIOLET: Well, if I haven't it's too late now. Do you think it's wise? To leave him here unsupervised?

She is looking at Branson, who is chatting to Robert.

CORA: What do you mean?

....

* Bates has Scottish blood, just to give him a bit of back story.

† Robert has always been more worried about his dog than he is about his house or estate or son-in-law or anything else. I think that's fairly truthful. Certainly it would be in my family.

VIOLET: Well, I know he's housebroken, more or less, but I don't want freedom to go to his head.*
ISOBEL: I'll keep an eye on him. He can come to dinner tonight.
VIOLET: Oh, well. That's one day taken care of. Only nine to go.

They climb in. The whistle blows. Isobel waves them off, Matthew blows his mother a kiss and Branson stands with Isis.

11   INT.   SERVANTS' HALL.   DOWNTON.   DAY.

The servants are eating lunch.

ALFRED: So, will we have a bit of a break while they're away, Mr Carson?
CARSON: What?
JIMMY: He meant can we expect some time off? For an outing or something.
CARSON: I don't understand. Has someone forgotten to pay your wages?
JIMMY: No.
CARSON: Exactly. Now, we will start with the ceremonial ware. And when that's done, I want all the silver brought down for cleaning, one room at a time.

The three maids at the table snigger.

MRS HUGHES: And don't you maids think you're out of it. We'll give every room a thorough cleaning while they're away…

She lowers her voice as she whispers to Carson.

MRS HUGHES (CONT'D): But you can let them have a bit of free time, can't you?
CARSON: If they get the extra work done, then I'll think about it.†

....

* Violet is much more aware of Branson's vulnerability than the others are.

† In the nineteenth century when the family was away the servants would usually go on what were called board wages, where they would get extra money but the daily food supply would stop. They wouldn't be catered for because, with the family absent, the kitchens were not operating at full tilt. That is one of the reasons for the huge number of pubs in London's

12   INT.   BRANSON'S BEDROOM.   DOWNTON.   DAY.

Edna picks up a picture of Sybil as Mrs Hughes comes in.

MRS HUGHES: Edna?

Edna puts down the picture and starts on the bed.

EDNA: Why hasn't Mr Branson been asked to go with the others?
MRS HUGHES: I'm sure I don't know.
EDNA: I wonder what Lady Flintshire made of her cousin's daughter eloping with a chauffeur.
MRS HUGHES: It's not your place to wonder.

Mrs Hughes adjusts the picture.

EDNA: What was she like?
MRS HUGHES: She was a sweet, kind person, and a real beauty, inside and out.
EDNA: You'd think she could have done better.
MRS HUGHES: But *she* didn't think she could do better, and that's what matters.
EDNA: He's nice looking. I'll give him that.
MRS HUGHES: I don't think you're required to give him anything.*

....

Continued from page 482:

Belgravia, because many houses in the area would be on board wages for chunks of the year while the families were at their country estates or travelling. Those servants who remained in London would get extra money to feed themselves, so pubs serving food were quite an important part of the local economy. As for how much of a rest they had, these breaks from the family were generally seen as an opportunity to clean things that don't normally get cleaned and to go through the rooms really thoroughly. So the work continued.

* Edna, for my money, has what they call 'sussed' the situation. She's an ambitious girl who wants to get on. I don't blame her for that. And she sees that her best bet is Branson, because he comes from her own people. She is right that he is a legitimate target for a girl like her, especially as he is considered by the others to be a bridge between upstairs and down.

13 INT. DRAWING ROOM. CRAWLEY HOUSE. DAY.

Isobel is having tea with Doctor Clarkson.

CLARKSON: She'll be a long way off.
ISOBEL: But not in the middle of nowhere. There are hospitals in Inverness.
CLARKSON: You mean I'm being an old woman.
ISOBEL: Well… After Sybil, who could blame you?
CLARKSON: It'll be very quiet for you, with them all gone.
ISOBEL: It will. Why not come to supper tomorrow? I daren't call it dinner as I don't know what we can conjure up. But do come.
CLARKSON: I don't want to be a nuisance.
ISOBEL: You won't be. Tom Branson's here this evening, so I shall be back in training.
CLARKSON: Thank you. I'd be delighted.

14 INT. DINING ROOM. DOWNTON. DAY.

Branson sits at the table, when Edna comes in with a tray.

EDNA: Oh. Mr Carson sent me up to clear. He thought you'd be out of here.
BRANSON: I should be.
EDNA: It seems sad for you to be left behind, all on your own.
BRANSON: I'm used to it.
EDITH: Yes. Yes, of course, you would be… It must be very hard.

She has spoken with feeling, and he's slightly taken aback. He gets up.

BRANSON: Don't worry about me. I've got plenty to do… You're the new maid, aren't you? What's your name?
EDNA: Edna. Edna Braithwaite.

15 EXT/INT. DUNEAGLE CASTLE/HALL. DAY.

This is a fairytale castle, with turrets and battlements and secret windows. The family party climbs out of two cars as Shrimpie, his wife, Susan, and Rose greet them.*

> ROBERT: Shrimpie. This is so nice of you.
> SHRIMPIE: Nonsense. I can't tell you how glad we are. Cora. Edith.

He kisses the two women (on one cheek only).†

> ROSE: Daddy, this is Matthew. Defender of the downtrodden. Including me.
> MATTHEW: I don't know why I've earned that.
> SHRIMPIE: We met at your wedding. Mary.

He kisses Mary as Susan kisses Violet.

> SUSAN: Aunt Violet. We feel so privileged to have lured you this far north.

....

* Inverarary looks like Sleeping Beauty's castle, but the entrance has a cumbersome covered glass porch that was put up for Queen Victoria. Her daughter, Princess Louise, married the then Marquis of Lorne – later Duke of Argyll – which was quite contentious at the time, being the first marriage between royalty and a commoner for centuries. The union was not in fact all that happy and they had no children, but anyway, Victoria used to visit. For our purposes the decision was made that, because the entrance was slightly ugly, we would use one of the other entrances round the side. I can't say it's a decision I completely agree with, because all the vehicles are crowded onto what were essentially garden paths, as opposed to a big forecourt like at Highclere. Left to me, I would have gone with the covered glass porch, but we seem to have got away with it. In the story, this is our first example of a house running on empty, of which in 1921 there were many. For those families, the money was gone but everything would continue as normal for a period before it all caved in. In this very year the agricultural subsidies would be ended by the Government and people would sink further into debt, without knowing what was going to happen next.

† They kiss on one cheek only. I had a bit of trouble on *Gosford Park* when once or twice the actresses would kiss on two cheeks, forgetting that the custom only came here in the 1970s from the continent. Personally, I prefer the one-cheek kiss because I feel you get it over without banging noses and general awkwardness, but that isn't how it's done these days. It is a bit of a giveaway in period drama when you see the double kiss.

VIOLET: Oh, my dear. You flatter me, which is just as it should be.

Rose, Mary and Edith lead the way into a splendid hall.

ROSE: We've got lots of things planned — oh, and there's the Ghillies' Ball, which Mary's always the star of —*
SUSAN: Rose, don't wear them out.†

But she catches herself and turns, smiling, to Cora.

SUSAN (CONT'D): We remembered how you liked our mountain loch; we've arranged for luncheon to be taken up there one day.
SHRIMPIE: That was my idea.

Clearly, Susan is infuriated by this, which Cora sees.

CORA: Well, whoever's idea it was, it's a lovely one.
SUSAN: Tea is in the library when you're ready to come down.

They all continue their conversations as they file into the grand hallway.

....

* The Ghillies' Ball is one of those moments where, like a Servants' Ball, you can, quite genuinely, mix the two elements in the house: the family and the staff. It was on the whole a wilder affair than the English Servants' Ball, where the family left comparatively early in the evening. Not so those at the Ghillies' Ball. It was run on whisky and half of them would be as drunk as lords. Queen Victoria in particular enjoyed these gatherings very much, because she didn't often get to witness people just having a good time in an abandoned way. Of course, like so many of those Scottish traditions that underpinned her love affair with the Highlands, the Ghillies' Ball really began in the 1840s. Here, I knew we would get some mileage out of it, because it certainly wouldn't be just another Servants' Ball.

† The character of Rose MacClare is now going to come into the series proper, and this episode will deliver the reason why she moves to Downton for Season Four. Of course, in a way, she replaced Sybil as the young woman in the family mix, but Lily James, who plays her, has her own very distinctive style (by now spotted by Walt Disney to star in their new version of *Cinderella*), and we felt she would be a very rewarding inclusion in her own right, which she has proved.

16   INT.   CORRIDOR.   DUNEAGLE CASTLE.   DAY.

Molesley wanders down the passage, looking slightly haunted.
A voice makes him jump.   It is the butler, Mr McCree.*

> MCCREE: What's the matter, Mr Crawley?   Looking for the
> servants' hall?
> MOLESLEY: I feel like Ariadne.   Only I've lost me
> thread.
> MCCREE: Duneagle's quite a maze.   They do say, on dark
> nights, you can hear the ghost of a young girl who never
> found her way back to her room.
> MOLESLEY: Really?   They say that, do they?

The thought has not calmed him down.

17   INT.   SERVANTS' HALL/KITCHEN.   DOWNTON.   EVE.

Some of the servants, including Thomas, are reading and
sewing when a robust man in his sixties appears in the
doorway.

> TUFTON: I'm looking for a Mrs Patmore.
> THOMAS: Why's that, then?
> TUFTON: I've got some deliveries for her.
> THOMAS: Really?   Where from?
> TUFTON: You're not very curious, are you?
> THOMAS: And you're not one of our regulars.
> TUFTON: Well, if you must know, I've taken over from Mr
> Cox in Thirsk.   Mrs Patmore sent an order in to him.
> MRS PATMORE: What's this?   Do I hear my name taken in
> vain?

She, Daisy and Ivy have arrived, carrying the tea things.

....

* This scene was cut, which was rather a shame because it was shot very well
as a spooky, haunted, Dracula's castle moment with a nice colour to it. But
you always know scenes that add atmosphere but not much else will normally
go in the edit. The mention of Ariadne shows that Molesley is quite well
read and later, in the fifth series, he will lend Daisy a book on the reign of
Queen Anne. For me, Molesley is someone who, with a different education
and a different class system operating, could have gone far. He's a clever
man, but the system has defeated him.

TUFTON: I was just explaining. You sent an order in to
Mr Cox. Well, I've bought the shop and all the stock so
I thought I'd take the liberty of filling it out.
THOMAS: It *was* a liberty. How do you know she wants to
do business with you?
MRS PATMORE: All right, Mr Barrow. I can fight my own
battles, thank you. So, where is this order, then?

He walks into the passage and picks up a large box.

MRS PATMORE (CONT'D): Bring it to the kitchen. And
what's your name, since you know mine?
TUFTON: It's Tufton. Jos Tufton.

They walk off. In the servants' hall, Alfred speaks.

ALFRED: What was Mr Cox's shop?
THOMAS: A grocer's, but finer than Bakewell's in the
village. Spices and foreign oils and special cheese and
such.
ALFRED: I'd like to see that.

In the kitchen, Mrs Patmore is unpacking the wares.

TUFTON: What's this?
MRS PATMORE: Some Vichyssoise. Left over from last
night.

*He does not wait for permission, sticking his fingers in and
tasting it.*

TUFTON: Oh, that's heaven. Have you any more leftovers
going begging?
MRS PATMORE: Have a bit of the tart if you like.

He helps himself.

TUFTON: Don't mind if I do.

It is a great success.

TUFTON: I've not had food that good since the last time
I were in London.
MRS PATMORE: Oh, I'm not just a pretty face.
TUFTON: This family's fallen on its feet and no mistake.
I wouldn't mind eating food like that every day.
MRS PATMORE: Enough of the flannel; I'll keep the order.
But if there's owt amiss, you'll be hearing from me.

TUFTON: Let's just hope that there's something not quite up to scratch.

MRS PATMORE: Why do you say that?

TUFTON: Because I'd like to hear from you again, Mrs Patmore. I would.

MRS PATMORE: Be off with you, you cheeky devil. Go on.

He snatches another sliver of the tart as he goes. Ivy and Daisy giggle as they look on.*

END OF ACT ONE

ACT TWO

18 INT. SERVANTS' HALL. DUNEAGLE CASTLE. EVE.

The servants, visitors and employees are eating supper. The butler, Mr McCree, is next to Anna.

MCCREE: Are you not hungry?

ANNA: It's a bit early for us. We eat our dinner after the family's.

WILKINS: Oh, I agree with you, Miss Crawley. In London we eat last thing when all the work is done, and I prefer it.

MCCREE: How about you, Miss Grantham?

O'BRIEN: Me? Oh, I do what I'm told.

ANNA: It makes me laugh when I hear Miss O'Brien and Mr Bates called Mr and Miss Grantham.

BATES: Mrs Bates and I don't often work in the same house party.

MCCREE: Of course, you two are married, Miss Crawley. How do you manage at home, being called Bates and Bates?

ANNA: We're not. They still call me Anna, like when I was a housemaid.

....

* Lesley Nicol wanted a little love interest after three years of chastity and decorum, and Mr Tufton arrives with that in mind, and we were very lucky that the marvellous John Henshaw agreed to play him. Of course, Mrs Patmore is aware that she's being chatted up, but she doesn't mind a bit.

O'BRIEN: Which isn't right. I do so hate to see a
lady's maid downgraded.
WILKINS: Oh, I so agree, Miss Grantham, but then we
would think alike, wouldn't we? It's a treat to have a
kindred spirit come to stay. It really is.
MCCREE: Tell Mrs Crane I've gone up. I'll announce
dinner in ten minutes.*

19 INT. DINING ROOM. DUNEAGLE CASTLE. NIGHT.

*The men are in white tie, the married women with diamonds in
their hair. It is a real pre-war image. A piper circles the
table, then he finishes and leaves. Robert is thrilled.*

ROBERT: How marvellous.
SUSAN: I should remind you that he'll be back to pipe us
awake at eight o'clock.
ROSE: And he keeps it up through breakfast.†
SHRIMPIE: So the chances of getting back to sleep again
are nil.

....

* There's a point I wanted to make here. You often hear people talking about these houses, and this life, as if everything was done in the same way everywhere. They would always gather in the library before dinner and in the drawing room afterwards. It was always the second footman who wound the clock… Except that there was no 'always'. Every household was different and had its different customs. Here we have the servants eating an early supper before the family dinner, which is how I managed it in *Gosford Park*. That was done in some houses, but in others they had a late supper at about half past ten when the work for the day was done for most of them. This is what we do at Downton. Arthur Inch, my advisor on *Gosford*, had experienced both. He said he miles preferred eating late, because then the feed was a jolly one where everyone, apart from the valets and maids, had finished their work. So they could finally relax.

By calling O'Brien Miss Grantham I went on with the tradition of the visiting maids and valets taking the names from their employers. You have to remember it just made things much less complicated for the staff of the house they were staying in.

† Like Robert, I enjoy pipers circling the table, which still goes on in some houses, although interestingly Scotland is now much more left-wing than England, with a war on the landed classes being waged by the Scottish Parliament. But at the time, before and after the First World War, they changed more slowly from the old ways, because it was a very rooted way of

SUSAN: All right, Shrimpie. The point has been made.*

Her annoyance has been noticed. Robert salvages the moment.

ROBERT: You've no need to apologise. I'm glad to see
the old ways being maintained.
SHRIMPIE: Tomorrow we'll kit you out with some rifles
for some practice.
VIOLET: And what is planned for the women?
ROSE: Well, there's a picnic by the loch the day after
tomorrow, and the Ghillies' Ball on Friday is always good
fun.
SUSAN: As long as it's not too *much* fun.

Rose rolls her eyes and giggles, which irritates Susan.

EDITH: As a matter of fact, a friend of mine is staying
quite nearby. I thought I might telephone him.

....

Continued from page 490:

life. It may be that the clan system affected the relationship between the
classes, which was rather different from that in England. Serving the chief of
your own clan is more dignified and less uncomfortable than just being a gun
for hire to be taken on as a footman. All of which gave a slightly different
taste to it, which Queen Victoria, for one, enjoyed very much. She liked the
greater ease with the tenants and the farming people. With John Brown
she'd visit the crofters' houses for cups of tea, which she really wouldn't have
done much of at Windsor.

* Now we start to set up an unhappy upper-class marriage between Susan and
Shrimpie. When we talk about how that generation had so much less divorce
and so much more discipline – all of which is true – we can forget that the
price of it was people having to live for many, many years with partners they
couldn't bear. It was a price that, increasingly during the Twenties, they were
unwilling to pay. And as houses got smaller and couples lived in greater
intimacy, it became even harder for them to stick it out. I think one of the
toughest things for young couples now is that they usually have to live in such
constricted surroundings. I always say to my nieces or their contemporaries
that they should try to find one little area – even if it's a bit of the kitchen –
which is their own, a private space, where they can do what they want. Both
halves of a couple should have the same. Otherwise you're always being
jostled and cramped. Admittedly, Susan and Shrimpie are not very cramped
at Inverarary, but they are isolated, which is another thing. We begin to
understand that, by this point, she can't even be polite to him.

ROSE: Oh, but you must ask him here.

ROBERT: She doesn't have to.

CORA: Oh, please do. I'd like to meet him.

SHRIMPIE: Right, that's settled then. Invite him to dinner tomorrow night. Unless, of course, Susan objects.

SUSAN: Of course I don't object. Why on earth would I object?

We can see that Shrimpie tries to wrong-foot her, too.

20   INT.   HALL/SERVANTS' HALL.   DOWNTON.   NIGHT.

Ivy is carrying a tray of late-night tea things when she passes Edna standing in the staircase hall, pulling the petals off a flower, muttering under her breath.

IVY: Well, does he love you? Or not?

EDNA: I think I could make him, whatever the flowers says, and I mean to try.*

They are overtaken by Mrs Patmore who enters the servants' hall, talking. Ivy and Edna follow her in.

MRS PATMORE: I thought it was too good to be true. He's sent dried ginger instead of fresh. Oh, it's my fault. I just put 'ginger' because Mr Cox knew what I liked.

THOMAS: I might go into Thirsk tomorrow. I can take it back for you if you want.

MRS PATMORE: Would you? You should go with him, Alfred. You'd like that shop.

CARSON: Who's doing what tomorrow?

MRS PATMORE: Mr Barrow's going into Thirsk. I said Alfred should go with him.

CARSON: Who says I can spare them? What about Mr Branson's luncheon?

THOMAS: I doubt he needs an under butler, Mr Carson, or two footmen.

MRS HUGHES: He told me he'd get lunch at the Grantham Arms. So, can they go?

CARSON: I suppose so. But there's a lot to be done, and don't forget it.

....

* 'He loves me, he loves me not.' But it was cut.

*He shakes out his newspaper. Edna is thinking.**

21 INT. DRAWING ROOM. CRAWLEY HOUSE. NIGHT.

Isobel is drinking coffee with Branson.

> ISOBEL: I hope you'll come here whenever you like. It
> must be odd, being alone in that great house.
> BRANSON: Well, I'm *not* alone. There's people I know
> well, except they're all downstairs and I'm up.
> ISOBEL: Why not take the opportunity to spend some time
> with them?
> BRANSON: I don't think old Lady Grantham would approve
> of that.
> ISOBEL: No, but I doubt she approves of the working
> class learning to read... Tom, can I take this chance to
> say you've managed a very delicate transition superbly?
> BRANSON: Thank you.
> ISOBEL: But don't be too eager to please. You have a
> new identity and I don't mean because you're not a
> chauffeur any more. You are the agent of this estate,
> and as the agent you have a perfect right to talk to
> anyone who works under you. Anyone you choose.
> BRANSON: That's quite a speech.
> ISOBEL: I mean it. You have a position now and you're
> entitled to use it.†

....

* Here, Carson is demonstrating not double values but that his disapproval of
Branson does not undermine the fact that Branson is the son-in-law of the
house and must be accorded the treatment the son-in-law of the house is
entitled to. But it's all obviated by the fact that he's going out to the pub.

† Isobel supports Branson's change in his social position. But because she
supports it and she is essentially a liberal, it doesn't mean she's not aware of
the journey that he's had to make. I felt this was important, because there are
moments when there's a danger that Isobel can appear so modern that she is
not aware of the society in which she is living. Here, she clearly understands
the problems that he faces. She congratulates him on managing the
transition and, in doing so, defines herself as his ally.

22 INT. KITCHEN PASSAGE. DOWNTON. NIGHT.

Branson closes the back door behind him and walks down the kitchen passage. He seems rather wrapped up in himself. Then Mrs Hughes appears behind him.

> MRS HUGHES: Mr Branson.
> BRANSON: I didn't want to drag one of you upstairs to open the door.
> MRS HUGHES: That was kind. Oh, I wonder if you would allow the maids to clean during the day, while the family is in Scotland?
> BRANSON: You don't need my permission.
> MRS HUGHES: But I do. And if you want to use a particular room, then please let me know, and we'll vacate it at once.

He looks at her. He understands she is telling him his role.

> BRANSON: Thank you, Mrs Hughes. Goodnight.
> MRS HUGHES: Goodnight, Mr Branson.

He climbs the stairs as Carson comes into the passage.

> CARSON: What was he doing down here?
> MRS HUGHES: Showing a bit of consideration.
> CARSON: But he's still not at ease, is he?
> MRS HUGHES: I expect he's lonely. Rattling about in this great barn.
> CARSON: Then he should ask a friend in for a drink, and not come snuffling round the servants' quarters.
> MRS HUGHES: We don't all have your standards, Mr Carson, as you never tire of pointing out.*

23 INT. MARY'S BEDROOM. DUNEAGLE CASTLE. NIGHT.

Anna is brushing Mary's hair. Mary seems uncomfortable.

....

* I was sorry this went because I think it was quite complicated. By coming in downstairs Branson is breaking the rules, which Mrs Hughes does not agree with. But her motives aren't unkind, which is not quite true of Carson. So when Carson attacks Branson her instinct is to defend him, but we know she thinks Carson is right and Branson should stick to the rules of the game.

MARY: I was a bit shaken up on the train, but please
don't say anything. I don't want to worry Mr Crawley.
ANNA: You don't want to give him the satisfaction, you
mean.
MARY: I can't spoil his last treat before fatherhood
claims him.
ANNA: Not that he'll change his ways much, if he's like
most men.

Mary laughs at Anna through the glass.

MARY: Are they looking after you?
ANNA: Oh, yes. But I'm a bit nervous about this
Ghillies' Ball.
MARY: Why?
ANNA: I suppose I just feel so *English*. I don't want to
look a fool.
MARY: I love reeling.* If I weren't pregnant, I'd dance
until dawn.
ANNA: But you *are* pregnant, m'lady.

24 EXT. DUNEAGLE CASTLE. DAY.

A piper walks along the terrace, playing his pipes.

25 INT. CORA'S BEDROOM. DUNEAGLE CASTLE. DAY.

*The caterwauling continues. Robert, in bed with Cora,
groans.*

ROBERT: Bloody hell.

He turns over. Cora laughs.

CORA: Welcome to the Highlands.

He pulls a pillow over his head.†

....

* That is a reference to my wife Emma, who is passionate on this subject, and
the phrase 'Scottish country dancing' makes her see red. The correct term is
'reeling' and that's all there is to it.

† It's the disadvantage of pipers that they go round the house at seven in the
morning.

26 INT. KITCHENS. DOWNTON. DAY.

Jimmy is watching Daisy and Ivy work to get breakfast ready.

IVY: Are you going into Thirsk? With Mr Barrow and
Alfred? Because if you are, you might get me some
ribbon.

JIMMY: Me? Larking about with Mr Barrow?

MRS PATMORE: Careful. You know Mr Carson won't put up
with any bad feeling.

JIMMY: I can work with him. He's the under butler here
and I don't argue with it, but he's not my choice of
playmate and that's flat.

DAISY: Oh, go. What harm can it do?

JIMMY: If I do go I'm not speaking to him.

MRS PATMORE: Then take a pad and pencil.

27 EXT. PARK. DUNEAGLE CASTLE. DAY.

*One flat cast-iron stag is set about 100 yards from a raised
and mown shooting point. A shot rings out and the head
ghillie, Nield, who is tight in beside Matthew, is leaning
back on something with his telescope trained on the target.
Robert is standing beside them, watching the fall of shot.*

NIELD: Take your time. You're not chasing a pheasant.
Be calm and confident.*

MATTHEW: I thought I was.

NIELD: These are noble beasts. We must take them out
for the good of the herd, but they've earned our respect
and they deserve a clean death.

ROBERT: Fine words.†

....

* Nield is a name taken from a friend of mine from my time in Kingussie
(filming *Monarch of the Glen*). Shirley Nield and her husband have remained
pals since that time. Emma collects different versions of the famous 'Your
Country Needs You' poster featuring her great-uncle, Lord Kitchener. And
whenever they see one used in the Scottish press or a magazine or even
locally, they always send it down to her. In short, they are very nice people
and so I use their surname here.

† This is the difference between stalking and shooting. You are performing a
service, which you're not really doing when you shoot a game bird. If you hit
a pheasant and it comes down, then hopefully someone will eat it, but that's
it. With a stag, you are preserving the health of the herd and so the kill is

Shrimpie and Rose arrive.

SHRIMPIE: How are you getting on?

NIELD: Not too bad, your lordship.

ROSE: That's high praise from Nield.

MATTHEW: He's being kind... I don't suppose your father needs much practice.

NIELD: His lordship was born with a rod in one hand and a gun in the other.

SHRIMPIE: That sounds rather uncomfortable.

But Nield turns his attention to Matthew.

ROBERT: I love to hear your ghillie speak. It's like a voice from a bygone age... Where's Susan?

ROSE: Aunt Violet wanted to see the gardens. So I left them to it.

She wanders off. Shrimpie glances at Robert.

SHRIMPIE: Rose is not anxious for her mother's company.

ROBERT: How's it going with you?

SHRIMPIE: I'm in for an adventure. I'm to don a ceremonial uniform and hold mighty sway on some distant shore.

ROBERT: You won't mind a foreign posting?

SHRIMPIE: Why not? They say a change of sink is as good as a rest...

28 EXT. GARDENS. DUNEAGLE CASTLE. DAY.

Susan Flintshire is walking with Violet.

VIOLET: Do you know where it will be?

....

Continued from page 496:

important, and a clean kill is the best, all of which Robert endorses. I like that sense of consideration for the game. If you shoot in France, for instance, the birds are all laid out in geometric patterns at the end of the day in front of the house, so the guns can pay their respects to them. It's like an instant memorial and there is something appealing about giving the birds their due. So I hope this scene is full of respect for the deer. That is what was intended.

SUSAN: No, but it'll be filthy and dirty and the food
will be awful and there'll be no one to talk to for a
hundred square miles.*
VIOLET: That sounds like a week with my mother-in-law.
Will Rose go, too?
SUSAN: Why? What's she been saying?
VIOLET: My dear, no one can accuse me of being modern,
but even I can see it's no crime to be young.
SUSAN: I know that, Aunt Violet. But you don't see how
they gang up on me.
VIOLET: Then I shall strive to keep the peace.
SUSAN: That's all very well, but you are my mother's
sister, and you can jolly well be on my side.

29 INT. SERVANTS' HALL. DUNEAGLE CASTLE. DAY.

*The bell rings. O'Brien is talking to Wilkins, Lady
Flintshire's maid.*

O'BRIEN: I'd like to travel more. We see a bit of
London in the Season, but otherwise, it's Yorkshire.†
WILKINS: What about the House of Lords?
O'BRIEN: When his lordship goes up, he just takes Mr Bates
with him and stays in his club, which is no use to me.
WILKINS: We're headed for an outpost of Empire. Her
ladyship's dreading it and so am I.
O'BRIEN: Oh, I don't know. Something different. I
could quite fancy that.
WILKINS: Oh. Not me. All sweat and gippy tummy. Oh,
no.‡

....

* Phoebe Nicholls, who plays Susan Flintshire, didn't like saying that line.
She thought it rather insulting, but I felt her character would not feel much
respect for foreign climes or customs, certainly not the kind of respect that
Phoebe feels today.

† The news had just been broken to me that, to my great sorrow, Siobhan
Finneran was leaving us. She was already one of the leads on *Benidorm*, and
what with children and various other matters, she felt she couldn't keep doing
both series. I was very, very sorry, as I thought her creation of O'Brien was
one of the best things in our show.

‡ I mentioned earlier the famous letter written by Lady Curzon from India
saying how hard it was to fasten buttons because her fingers were slippery

29A INT. SERVANTS' HALL. DOWNTON. DAY.

Jimmy and Alfred sit in front of a table full of silver and give one another an unhappy look. Carson appears at the doorway and dramatically clears his throat, at which the two footmen frantically begin cleaning the silver.

30 INT. DRAWING ROOM. DUNEAGLE CASTLE. DAY.

Mary and Cora are reading as Edith comes in.

CORA: Did you get him?

EDITH: I did. He said he'd love to come.

MARY: I'm sure he would.

EDITH: What do you mean by that?

MARY: Well, I can't imagine Mr Gregson finds himself at Duneagle Castle very often. Or anywhere like it.

CORA: Mary, that sounds very snobbish.

MARY: Well, what's he doing up here?

EDITH: He's on a sketching holiday. He's sketching and fishing.

MARY: Fishing? Oh, well. That's something, I suppose.

MATTHEW: What do you suppose?

He has just come in.

EDITH: For some reason, Mary has decided to be nasty about Michael Gregson.

MARY: I was simply questioning his motives for being in the Highlands.

EDITH: He's brought his pencils and his rods. What's wrong with that?

MATTHEW: Nothing at all. So there.

This last is to Mary, but he strokes her shoulder and cheek. *

....

Continued from page 498:

with sweat. How did they manage it? Getting into those corsets, interlined and padded, the men in stiffened uniform, the women laced into whale bone and four or five layers, all under the boiling Indian sun – I think it was an extraordinary discipline and I doubt we could do it today.

* Mary is a snob, which is why her journey towards Branson is interesting; she is, though, able to see beyond her own snobbery, all of which was quite deliberate. Of course she's not interested in Gregson's sketching, only in his

31   EXT.   GRANTHAM ARMS.   DOWNTON VILLAGE.   DAY.

Branson is walking towards the pub.   Isis is with him.

32   INT.   BAR.   GRANTHAM ARMS.   DOWNTON VILLAGE.
                 DAY.

Branson walks into the bar.

BRANSON: Afternoon, George. The usual and a sandwich,
please.

*He catches sight of Edna, smiles and strolls over to join
her.*

BRANSON: This is very daring. Sitting in a pub on your
own? Won't the village cut you dead forever?
EDNA: I knew you were coming in. And I don't care about
all that stuff.
BRANSON: Do you have the day off?
EDNA: I'll fudge it but not really. We've extra
cleaning to do while the family's away… Of course,
you're family.
BRANSON: Well, I am and I'm not, as I'm sure you know.
EDNA: Anna said when you first came back as Lady Sybil's
husband you refused to dress the part, but you do now.
BRANSON: I was tired of talking about my clothes every
time I came downstairs, but I'm still the same man
inside.
EDNA: Then why not join us for dinner one night, instead
of eating alone?*

....

Continued from page 499:

fishing, which gives him a better claim to be a member of their tribe. Mary
reminds me of Cynthia French-McGrath in M. J. Farrell's novel *The Rising
Tide*, when she asks if anyone has seen her son. 'He's in the orchard, reading,'
says one of the guests. 'Oh dear,' sighs Cynthia. 'I do hope he's not going to
be clever.' That self-conscious and rather smug philistinism was absolutely
typical of the upper class at that time.

* For Branson, the neutral setting of the pub for a talk with Edna feels more
natural than it would have done on a staircase at Downton. He is seduced
into intimacy by the situation, as she knew he would be.

33 EXT. TUFTON'S SHOP. THIRSK. DAY.

Thomas, Jimmy and Alfred are leaving Tufton's shop. Thomas carries a brown paper bag. Tufton has followed them out.

TUFTON: I'll tell her, and I'll not forget again.

ALFRED: By 'eck, it were worth the visit, Mr Tufton. What a range. I've never heard of some of those spices.

TUFTON: I tell you what: we've a fair here, starting Friday. I run a stall and so do some of the suppliers. Why not come?

THOMAS: What sort of fair?

TUFTON: Well, the usual sort of fair. Food, games, Morris dancers and a brass band. But they do it well.

ALFRED: Could we get the time off?

THOMAS: I don't see why not. Jimmy?

JIMMY: I might come if there's a crowd of us, but not otherwise.

TUFTON: Have you got a minute? I'll just put a note in that bag for Mrs Patmore.

THOMAS: Go on, then.

Tufton hurries back inside his shop.

34 INT. SERVANTS' HALL. DUNEAGLE CASTLE. DAY.

The dinner is being cleared away.

ANNA: I don't think I'd realised we'd all be expected at the Ghillies' Ball.*

BATES: Why wouldn't we be? It's only a Scottish Servants' Ball.

ANNA: It's my own fault. I just wish I'd done more to prepare. Especially now I know my husband's Scottish.

BATES: Not very.

WILKINS: I dare say it'll be a bit wilder than any Servants' Ball at Downton.

....

* Anna is nervous of the Ghillies' Ball for a simple reason, as we later learn. She doesn't know how to dance any of the reels, because she's never travelled. We make the point that a lady's maid who was only a housemaid often didn't travel, and real ladies' maids would often double up to look after a mother and her daughters if it was for a few days somewhere, rather than bringing too cumbersome a party.

MOLESLEY: Not too wild, I hope.

BATES: Come on, Mr Molesley. We're hoping to see you let your hair down. What there is of it.

35 INT. CORA'S BEDROOM. DUNEAGLE CASTLE. DAY.

Cora is with O'Brien and Robert. She looks splendid in a grand evening dress and a tiara. O'Brien is just leaving.

CORA: Judging by my last experience of a Ghillies' Ball, I'm terrified, but I dare say we'll get through it.

ROBERT: You'll enjoy it. I know I will.

CORA: Of course, you're in your element, given that life at Duneagle is just as it was in the 1850s.

ROBERT: It may be nostalgia, but can't you indulge me?

CORA: I wish you could see that what Tom and Matthew and even Mary are doing at home is so much more interesting than anything happening here.

ROBERT: I'm not fighting the changes.

CORA: No. But you're sad. Sad that the estate isn't run as it used to be. When I think it's so much better.

ROBERT: I'm afraid we must agree to differ.

CORA: Yes, but we don't *agree* to differ, do we? We just differ.

36 INT. MRS HUGHES'S SITTING ROOM. DOWNTON.
DAY.

Carson is with Mrs Hughes.

CARSON: I can't let them go gallivanting off to every fair at the drop of a hat. I mean, what are we paying them for?

MRS HUGHES: But they've been working very hard. Don't they deserve a treat?

Mrs Patmore arrives.

MRS PATMORE: Excuse me! On Friday, can I take the afternoon off? I'll make the servants' dinner and Ivy and Daisy can serve it.

MRS HUGHES: Mrs Patmore doesn't often take the time she's allowed.

CARSON: What about Mr Branson?

MRS HUGHES: I'll see to Mr Branson. Where are you going? Or shouldn't we ask?

MRS PATMORE: There's a fair in Thirsk. A friend of mine
has asked me to meet him there.
CARSON: I don't believe it! Must I be undermined at
every turn?

He storms out. Mrs Patmore is amazed.

MRS PATMORE: What's got into him?
MRS HUGHES: Mr Barrow and the boys have asked to go to
the same fair and he was trying to find a way to say no.
MRS PATMORE: Why don't we all go? I'll make Mr Branson
a tray and he can keep charge of the house. He won't
mind. Come on. It'll be fun.

37 INT. DRAWING ROOM. DUNEAGLE CASTLE. NIGHT.

*They stand about, with no drinks. The butler announces Mr
Gregson. He comes in. Gregson is also in white tie.**
Gregson is greeting his hostess.

GREGSON: This is very kind of you, Lady Flintshire.
SUSAN: Not a bit. It's a pleasure to welcome a friend
of dear Edith's.

Across the room, Mary is with Matthew.

MATTHEW: What a disappointment. He looks perfectly
normal.
MARY: Since he came here with the express purpose of
dining at Duneagle, he obviously bought a set of tails.
EDITH: Come and meet my parents. Mama, Granny, Papa,
this is Mr Gregson.
GREGSON: Lady Grantham.

....

* No drinks. Essentially Robert is enjoying being transported back to 1880
for a blessed few days, and at Duneagle they do observe the customs of fifty
years earlier. Here, Gregson comes in looking normal and being normal.
One of the things that interests me is when posh people pretend they find the
upper middle classes very different from themselves when, in most cases,
they're not different at all. It's an invented difference, but they want to
preserve it in their mind. You see less of it now, but thirty years ago there was
still a lot of pretence that when a nice banker and his wife came in for a drink
from the village they were almost talking a different language, which of
course they weren't.

CORA: You know, I started to read your magazine because of Edith's column, but now I wouldn't miss it. We read it from cover to cover, don't we?
ROBERT: It puzzles me why you choose to employ amateurs like my daughter.
MARY: I agree.
GREGSON: Well, is the distinction very meaningful? Surely the most important thing is whether or not people have something to say.
EDITH: Come and meet my sister, Mary.

Across the room, Susan is with Rose.

SUSAN: Do stand up. You're slouching like a field hand.
ROSE: Might I just have five minutes without being criticised?

Violet and Cora have observed this. Violet speaks softly.

VIOLET: We knew things were awkward between them, but now that I'm here I don't think Susan handles it very well.
CORA: But it's so complicated with a young daughter who's full of new ideas. She thinks you're fighting her, when all the time you're just frightened and — I'm sorry.

She breaks off, as her eyes fill with tears.

VIOLET: We all miss her. Every single day.
SUSAN: We're going in, everyone.

Cora is taken in by Shrimpie as Mary draws alongside Violet.

MARY: Granny? You look very *sérieuse*, this evening.
VIOLET: I've been thinking. And you know what an effort that can be.*

....

* It's important in a show like this to keep these prickly relationships, like Violet and Cora, from going past the point of no return, because then they're much less useful dramatically. However much they may fall out, you must never let the fall-out be to a degree where they cannot mend their fences for the purposes of another story.

38 INT. DINING ROOM. DOWNTON. NIGHT.

Branson is sitting with Sybbie on his lap. There is a knock at the door.

BRANSON: Come in.

Edna arrives.

EDNA: Would you like me to take Miss Sybbie up to the nursery?
BRANSON: Thank you. Go with Edna, darling. Oh, go on…
EDNA: Come here.

Edna takes the child, rocks her gently and walks towards the door, then stops.

EDNA: Can I ask you something?
BRANSON: Be my guest. Please.
EDNA: Are you ashamed of who you are? Or of who you were? Is that why you won't eat your dinner with us?
BRANSON: No. It is not.
EDNA: Well, I'd better be going.

She leaves with Sybbie as Alfred comes in. Branson whispers.

BRANSON: It is *not*.

END OF ACT TWO

ACT THREE

39 EXT. DUNEAGLE CASTLE. DAY/NIGHT.

Anna and Bates are together in the evening light.

ANNA: It never really gets dark here, does it?
BATES: Not like further south, no.*
ANNA: I never asked you what your room's like. Is it nice?

....

* This is true. The summer nights aren't ever really dark in the Highlands. It never goes much further than a sort of dusk.

He reaches up and strokes her cheek.

    BATES: It's fine, but it feels funny being on my own
    again… Let's take a picnic out tomorrow. Just the two
    of us. They'll be gone for the day. What do you say?
    ANNA: I'd love it.

But they see a lone figure. It is Rose, smoking and crying.

    BATES: Is everything all right, m'lady?
    ROSE: It will be, if you don't tell my mother you saw me
    smoking.
    ANNA: Don't worry. You're safe with us.
    BATES: Would you like a peppermint?*

He has taken out a paper bag. Rose smiles and takes one.

    ROSE: I better had. Thank you. Oh, sorry. It's just
    my mother has been unusually impossible this evening.
    BATES: My whole childhood would seem impossible to you,
    m'lady. But I survived; so will you.

There is a movement at the front door.

    SUSAN: Rose? Who are you talking to? Come inside at
    once! Everyone's in the drawing room!
    ROSE: Yes, Mummy.

She starts towards the entrance, but looks round as she goes.

    ROSE (CONT'D): Thanks for the mint.

40   INT. DRAWING ROOM. CRAWLEY HOUSE. NIGHT.

Clarkson and Isobel are in the drawing room.

    CLARKSON: I should be away.
    ISOBEL: Oh, don't go just yet.
    CLARKSON: Heaven knows, I've no desire to. It makes a
    welcome change from reading a medical journal and going
    to bed with a glass of whisky.
    ISOBEL: Goodness. I wondered what you were going to say
    for a moment.

Which makes them both laugh.

....

* By giving Rose a peppermint they are setting up a later alliance.

CLARKSON: I sometimes forget, when we meet in the splendour of the Abbey, that you were a doctor's wife. That you know what my life consists of in a way that no one else does. At any rate, not round here.

ISOBEL: I know. It's a relief, sometimes, to be able to talk without having to explain one's self, isn't it?

CLARKSON: A relief and a privilege. I hope we can do it again, soon.*

41 INT. DRAWING ROOM. DUNEAGLE CASTLE. NIGHT.

The company is in there, after dinner. Edith is with Gregson.

GREGSON: Matthew's asked me to go out stalking with him tomorrow, so I thought I would.

EDITH: Michael, can I ask you why you're here? Tell me the truth. Please.

She is in earnest, almost severe. He decides to be honest.

GREGSON: I want to get to know your family.

EDITH: What do you hope to achieve?

GREGSON: I thought if they knew me — if they came to like me — I'd — they might find it easier to be on my side.

EDITH: It won't change the basic facts, though, will it?

GREGSON: Edith. My basic fact is that I'm in love with you. You know that already.

EDITH: Do I? Yes, I suppose I do.

....

* Clarkson is starting to dream that he might have another life with Isobel, who is, after all, a doctor's widow. She, I think, is in one of the most delicate positions of any of the characters, because the family have made her feel part of them and she is now quite relaxed in their midst and will say what she likes. But at the same time the life she has actually led is much closer to Clarkson's, and although her husband and father were rather grand doctors, nevertheless they spent their time healing and dealing with patients. Like Clarkson. So she can talk to him without having to explain, because he understands the things she's saying. From which you may infer we're getting set to put her in a predicament. All the way through a show, you're trying to put the characters into predicaments that need to be resolved.

GREGSON: I want you in my life and I want to be in yours.

EDITH: That's all very well, but —

GREGSON: Somehow, I've got to work out how to make it possible.

EDITH: When will you tell them the truth?

GREGSON: Not yet. I want them to let me in first. Then we can all deal with it together. Later. When they know me.

She says nothing and he is not encouraged by her expression.

GREGSON (CONT'D): You don't think it's a good plan.

EDITH: I just can't see a happy ending.*

VIOLET: Edith, dear, stop fascinating that young man and come and make a four at Bridge.

42 INT. MARY'S BEDROOM. DUNEAGLE CASTLE. NIGHT.

Matthew is looking out of the window as Mary gets into bed.

MATTHEW: I wonder what the weather will be like tomorrow.

MARY: You know the golden rule in England or Scotland. Dress for rain.† Are you looking forward to it?

MATTHEW: Yes. Though I hope my chap's less frightening than the head ghillie.

MARY: Just tell him you're a novice and all will be well. Papa says you must never pretend with these people. They're always better at it than you'll ever be.

Matthew leaves the window and climbs into bed.

MATTHEW: I've asked Gregson to come. I won't see you all day so he'll be company.

MARY: He was right to invest in those tails, wasn't he? You know Susan's invited him to the Ghillies' Ball? He probably had reeling classes before he left London.

....

* Edith is very torn. In some ways she is pleased and in other ways she just doesn't quite know what can come of it.

† That was my grandmother.

MATTHEW: Don't dislike him before you know him. That's the hallmark of our parents' generation, and I forbid it. Just be as nice as you are.*
MARY: You think me nice, but nobody else does. What makes you so sure I am?
MATTHEW: Because I've seen you naked and held you in my arms, and I know the real you.

He strokes her pregnant belly.

MARY: Goodness, what a testimonial.

They kiss.

43 INT. SERVANTS' PASSAGE/CARSON'S PANTRY. DOWNTON. NIGHT.

Mrs Hughes is with Carson.

MRS HUGHES: Oh, go on. You were young once.
CARSON: I'm young now. Well, I'm not old.
MRS HUGHES: All the more reason to say yes. Oh, you'll enjoy yourself.
CARSON: No, I won't be coming.

He shuts the door to his pantry.

CARSON (CONT'D): If I came, *they* wouldn't have fun. They'd spend the day looking over their shoulder.
MRS HUGHES: Well, I'm going. Whether I spoil their fun or not.
CARSON: That's different. They respect you, of course. But I am their leader.
MRS HUGHES: Well, that's put me in my place.
CARSON: Don't envy me, Mrs Hughes. You know what they say. Uneasy lies the head that wears the crown.†

....

* Mary is slightly mocking him, because in a sense he is going along with Gregson's plan. 'Don't dislike him before you know him': that assumption of dislike because this person is not their type is something I used to come up against. Not from my mother, who was fairly wild, but my father would just assume that so-and-so was not his sort of person and that was that. The trouble was, sometimes they *were* his type of person if he would only open his eyes. He had to be led to it gently.

† The awareness that your presence makes people slightly uncomfortable can be rather sobering.

44 EXT. DUNEAGLE CASTLE. DAY.

Two traps are waiting for the men, all in tweeds.*
Susan is there. She has not yet changed. Nield is talking to Shrimpie.

NIELD: The wind is north-west and getting stronger. We should get started.

Robert is with Matthew, Gregson and Shrimpie.

GREGSON: Well, good hunting, everyone.
ROBERT: Oh, Shrimpie's not stalking. He's coming with me.
NIELD: Mr Crawley? Mr Gregson?

Matthew and Gregson climb into a trap with their beat's stalker and they head off. Shrimpie's with Susan.

SHRIMPIE: Is your picnic under control?
SUSAN: Of course.
ROBERT: I'm worried about Mary, bumping through the glen.
SUSAN: She doesn't have to come.
ROBERT: No, I know, but she will, I'm afraid.

Nield has the reins of the trap in his hands and is waiting to head off to the other beat. Shrimpie is aware of Nield's eyes upon him.

SHRIMPIE: We'd best get going, otherwise we're in for some stick.

45 INT. KITCHENS. DOWNTON. DAY.

Mrs Patmore, Daisy and Ivy work. Alfred, Jimmy and Thomas watch.

....

* If you weren't in a pelting hurry, and particularly for riding over an estate, using traps continued well into the motor age. My great-great-aunt, Lady Sydenham, whom I've talked about before, had a Daimler for long journeys and for going up and down to London, but a trap to meet the train in Lamberhurst and to drive her into the town for shopping or to a neighbour's for lunch. She thought she saw more of the countryside and benefited from the air. In a way it was quite modern – petrol saving was part of it – but also the pace of life suited horse-drawn travel. For Aunt Phyllis, her guests were met off the train by a trap until her death in 1952.

DAISY: I'm not sure I'm going to go tomorrow. It's such a waste of money.

MRS PATMORE: Oh, come on. You've enough for a few rides and a beef sandwich, I suppose?

THOMAS: I can buy you all a bottle of pop, if you like.

MRS PATMORE: What an offer. Let's take him up on it before he's time to think again.

JIMMY: Thank you, Mr Barrow, but I can buy my own pop.

DAISY: Don't pretend you've money to burn.

JIMMY: I can always get money.

The others just roll their eyes as Mrs Hughes comes in.

MRS HUGHES: The store cupboard's open if you need anything.

MRS PATMORE: No, but I do have something to ask you. Now, where did I put that box?

IVY: This one?

She gives the box to Mrs Patmore, who leaves with Mrs Hughes.

IVY (CONT'D): Did you see the lid? Mrs Curley's dress shop in Ripon. She's got a fancy man. I'm telling you.

ALFRED: *Mrs Patmore?*

DAISY: Why not? She's a woman, isn't she?

THOMAS: Only technically.

46   INT.   MARY'S BEDROOM.   DUNEAGLE CASTLE.   DAY.

Anna is putting some clothes away when Rose comes in.

ROSE: Oh. I was looking for Lady Mary. To tell her we're going.

ANNA: She's already gone down, m'lady.

ROSE: You were kind to cheer me up yesterday. I did feel terribly blue.

ANNA: That's all right.

ROSE: You must let me know if I can return the favour.

ANNA: As a matter of fact, there *is* something you could help me with…*

....

*These slight friendships are really part of the fabric of the show.

47 EXT. ON THE HILL. DAY.

A proud stag lifts his head and sniffs the air. On the hill above, Nield has set the rifle in place and gently indicates with his finger for Robert to crawl forward and take up the weapon. Robert moves forward, carefully keeping his head down, and Shrimpie follows.

    ROBERT: Shall I take it from here?

But the chance is gone.

    NIELD: We can bring you to a better place. We don't rush things at Duneagle.
    SHRIMPIE: Well, that's true, God knows.

48 INT. MRS HUGHES'S SITTING ROOM. DOWNTON. DAY.

Mrs Hughes is watching as Mrs Patmore holds up a pink shirt.

    MRS PATMORE: You don't think it's too girlish?
    MRS HUGHES: And what's the matter with being girlish once in a while? Heaven knows, we don't have much opportunity.
    MRS PATMORE: I'd wear a coat over it, you know, so it wouldn't jump out at you.
    MRS HUGHES: I hope he's worth it.

Mrs Patmore takes a letter from her apron pocket.

    MRS PATMORE: Read that.
    MRS HUGHES: 'I hope you will allow me the honour of squiring you through the day.'
    MRS PATMORE: No man's wanted to squire me since the Golden Jubilee. Even then he expected me to buy the drinks.
    MRS HUGHES: Suppose he wants something more?
    MRS PATMORE: I *beg* your pardon!
    MRS HUGHES: There is only one reason why a man his age courts a respectable woman. He finds himself in need of a wife.

This does make Mrs Patmore pause.

49 EXT. CASTLE BRIDGE. DAY.

Bates and Anna are unpacking a modest picnic.

BATES: Is there anything to drink?

ANNA: There certainly is.

She takes out a bottle and two glasses, and starts to pour.

BATES: Beer? That's very racy of you.

ANNA: I am racy.

BATES: What shall we drink to?

ANNA: The future and your Scottish blood.

She almost giggles. He looks at her.

BATES: What are you up to?

ANNA: Nothing.

He takes the picnic basket and holds it out of her reach.

BATES: What are you up to?

ANNA: Nothing!

*She laughs, he hands the basket back and they kiss.**

50 INT. SERVANTS' HALL. DUNEAGLE CASTLE. DAY.

Some of the staff are here, eating their lunch.

WILKINS: We should all have taken a picnic out, on a day like this.

O'BRIEN: It's a lot of bother, though, isn't it? I'd rather just have a walk.

MCCREE: Have you asked Miss Grantham yet?

O'BRIEN: Asked me what?

MCCREE: Go on.

WILKINS: There's really no need.

O'BRIEN: What is it you want to ask?

MCCREE: Her ladyship — our ladyship, that is — was very taken with Lady Grantham's hair last night. She asked if you'd show Miss Wilkins how to do it.

WILKINS: I know how to do it. I just didn't know she liked that style. I'd have thought it was too old-fashioned.

....

* If you have lovers in a show, every now and then you want to show them enjoying a romantic moment. Which was the purpose of this scene.

O'BRIEN: *Old-fashioned?*

WILKINS: Well, shall we say 'traditional'?

O'BRIEN: You'd better not say old-fashioned.*

MOLESLEY: It's rather flattering to think we're causing a stir with our up-to-the-minute ways. If you need any tips from me, you have only to ask.

MCCREE: We won't want anything from you, Mr Molesley. Mr Bolt can manage very well without any help from you.

51 EXT. ON THE HILL. DAY.

A pony, laden with a stag, leads the way. Nield carries the rifle. Some way behind, Robert is following with Shrimpie.†

SHRIMPIE: Well, you managed that very well. When the time comes for me to go, I'll ask them to send for you.

Once again, there is a bitter undertone. Robert looks at him.

ROBERT: Is everything all right, Shrimpie? Ah, of course, impertinent to ask.

SHRIMPIE: No, it's not all right. But what's the point in talking about it when there's nothing to be done?

Shrimpie has stopped and hands Robert his hipflask.

ROBERT: I'm not so sure these days. The Marlboroughs have got a divorce, and you still see them around.‡

....

* I was sorry this had to go because the visit gave us a chance to explore this sort of petty rivalry, which, I am sure, was very much part of that way of life, and very undermining when it happened.

† I was pleased we were allowed the pony laden with the stag, which might have been a victim of television's sometimes rather prim and townie attitudes. The truth is, when you are stalking you are taking out stags and they have to be brought down from the hill. That's why ponies go up there with you. To show all of that but not the stag coming down would have been false and overprotective. I don't think we had any backlash at all, actually, but that was the reason for doing it visually and truthfully.

‡ There were many unhappy marriages that stuck it out during the late-Victorian and Edwardian eras, but, as I have said, after the war a lot of them began to come unstuck because society was loosening up. It was the Jazz Age, wild and free, and the whole business of living with someone you

SHRIMPIE: But Sunny Marlborough has no official post. He hasn't been in office since the end of the war.

ROBERT: While you must have Susan next to you under the tropical sun?

SHRIMPIE: She'll do it well. She's born to grace a ballroom and she could teach diplomacy to experts.

ROBERT: But?

SHRIMPIE: We don't like each other.

He has said enough. He walks on briskly.

52   INT.   SERVANTS' HALL.   DOWNTON.   DAY.

Several servants are in here. Mrs Hughes is pinning pieces of a tissue pattern over some cloth, ready to be cut out.

DAISY: Is it for the outing tomorrow?

MRS HUGHES: I'm not that quick with a needle.

But the room has fallen silent. Branson has entered.

MRS HUGHES (CONT'D): How can I help, Mr Branson?

The others stand but Edna does not, which Mrs Hughes sees.

BRANSON: I was thinking... It's just...

MRS HUGHES: Yes?

BRANSON: I thought I'd come down for supper tonight. Catch up with your news.

This is a surprise to all of them.

MRS HUGHES: If you'd like to, of course you'd be very welcome. We don't eat late while the family's away so dinner will be at about eight o'clock.

BRANSON: I'll see you then.

He smiles a little nervously and goes. Mrs Hughes looks at Edna.

....

Continued from page 514:

Continued from page 514:

detested for the look of the thing was increasingly seen as ridiculous. But one of the absolute milestones in this development was the 1921 divorce of the Duke and Duchess of Marlborough, as we discuss in several episodes. It really changed things, paving the way for many others; from then on divorce among the upper classes became more and more common.

DAISY: Well.

THOMAS: Fains I tell Mr Carson.

ALFRED: You're looking very pleased with yourself, Edna.

But Edna just smiles.

53 EXT. A LOCH IN THE GLEN. DAY.

Two traps stand by and another two ponies wait, with huge baskets on either side, while footmen in their livery are setting up a picnic under a pavilion.

Robert, Shrimpie and Nield walk down the hill towards a simple shelter with a table at its centre, laid with a cloth and all the glass and china necessary. It seems very out of place.*

Susan, Violet, Cora, Mary, Edith and Rose are there.

EDITH: How tiny the glens make one feel.

VIOLET: That is the thing about nature. There's so much of it.

CORA: Must be lovely to be queen of such a kingdom.

SUSAN: You're right. We're very lucky in this.

She looks up. Shrimpie and Robert are walking towards them.

SUSAN (CONT'D): Goodness. We weren't expecting male company for our feasting.

SHRIMPIE: I'm sorry to disappoint you.

This is unfair to Susan, who had only spoken the truth.

EDITH: How did you get on?

SHRIMPIE: Very well. Not too long a trail and death by a single shot at the end of it. Nield is cock-a-hoop.

MARY: Well done, Papa. Your reward will be to join the ladies' lunch.

....

* This was a lovely scene, the simple picnic. I've talked before of my experience as a boy when I thought I was going on a picnic in a T-shirt and jeans and we ended up in a Gothic pavilion on the edge of a canal, waited on by servants. We are making a similar joke here. They talk about the Duneagle picnic, which turns out to be a stately and formal affair. They had a certain amount of trouble with midges – midges being the bane of the glens – but we managed to lose them in the edit.

ROBERT: An added bonus. I hope it's venison [pronounced venson].*
ROSE: Quite right. We ought to eat what we kill.
SUSAN: Rose, stop talking nonsense and tell McCree to lay two more places.

END OF ACT THREE

ACT FOUR

54 EXT. THE GLEN. EVE.

Matthew and Gregson walk together at dusk. Two ponies are behind them, with two ghillies, but no dead stag. Gregson carries his sketching block and a shoulder bag.

MATTHEW: Ten hours crawling through heather and nothing to show for it. Perhaps it's a parable of life.
GREGSON: It reminds me of the trenches, rather. Hours of inching through mud with no discernible purpose.
MATTHEW: Why don't you come fly fishing tomorrow? We might see a bit more activity. You could bring your evening clothes and change at Duneagle.
GREGSON: It's rather an imposition.
MATTHEW: But that's what you're here for, isn't it? To get to know us all… Besides, you didn't bring your tails all the way to Scotland to dine in a country pub.
GREGSON: No. I suppose not.

55 INT. BEDROOM PASSAGE. DUNEAGLE CASTLE. NIGHT.

O'Brien comes out of a door. Wilkins is waiting.

WILKINS: Have you got a minute? Because if you haven't, it's perfectly fine.

....

* I made a point of dropping the 'i' of venison, because 'venson' is the pronunciation I grew up with. If you spell it correctly, you always risk the wrong sound.

```
O'BRIEN:  A minute for what?
WILKINS:  Her ladyship would like a word.
O'BRIEN:  Why?  What does she want with me?
WILKINS:  Well, what do you think?  She wants to make a
fuss, like she always does.
```

All this is whispered. She reaches a door and opens it.

56   INT. SUSAN'S BEDROOM. DUNEAGLE. NIGHT.

Susan is sitting before her glass. She greets O'Brien.

```
SUSAN:  This is so kind of you…
O'BRIEN:  O'Brien, m'lady.
SUSAN:  O'Brien.  It's just that Wilkins here isn't quite
able to understand what I'm getting at when I'm
describing the shape of Lady Grantham's hair.
WILKINS:  I understand, m'lady, it's just —
SUSAN:  Could you help her?  You'll know exactly what I
mean.
O'BRIEN:  Er, well…  It's a question of body, m'lady.
You need more volume to begin, before you sculpt it, so
to speak.
SUSAN:  I knew you'd have the answer.
O'BRIEN:  If I could…*
SUSAN:  Oh, please, please, please.  Wilkins, pay close
attention to what she's doing.
WILKINS:  Yes, your ladyship.
```

But she looks daggers at the visiting maid.

57   INT. DRAWING ROOM. DUNEAGLE CASTLE. NIGHT.

*It is before dinner. Everyone is there around the fire.
Shrimpie is with Robert and Violet.*

```
ROBERT:  Bombay?  That sounds rather modest for a
marquess.†
```

....

* We continue to lay the circumstances of O'Brien's subsequent departure, revealed the following year, which is the purpose of this plot.

† I chose Bombay because my own great-great-uncle, Sir George Sydenham Clarke, later Lord Sydenham, was made Governor of Bombay and he was there to welcome the King and Queen for the great Delhi Durbar of 1911, the only time that an Emperor and Empress of India visited the country. It

VIOLET: Well, no. Not if it's a step towards the Viceroy's crown.

SHRIMPIE: I don't know about that. All I do know is that it's going to be very hot.

VIOLET: And all the costumes of imperial rule are always so peculiarly unsuited to the climate. Will you take Rose?

SHRIMPIE: I don't think we should but... Susan won't discuss it.

VIOLET: Unless you want her married to a third-rate colonial official with no money and bad teeth, Susan had better think again.

Mary, Edith and Matthew are together.

MATTHEW: Just as he stood, a gust of wind comes into the corrie from behind us. A hind got our scent and they were away.*

MARY: Really, darling, it's boring enough to hear about when you succeed.

EDITH: What did you think of Michael?

MATTHEW: Well, he seems like a nice chap. We're going fishing tomorrow.

EDITH: He's had such a lot to put up with.

MARY: Oh, God, not one of your hard-luck cases, is he?

EDITH: Why must you sound so heartless?

Rose is sitting with Cora.

ROSE: Actually, I think India would be fascinating, but I know that Mummy and I will drive each other mad.

Behind them, Susan has heard this. She continues to listen.

....

Continued from page 518:

was such a high point in Uncle George's career that he had ambitions of the Vice-Regal Crown, which did not come to pass. Let us hope he was satisfied with his peerage and his subsequent life at Lamberhurst Priory in Kent. Anyway, that's why I decided to send Shrimpie to Bombay and, in his case, as a much grander chap than Uncle George, it probably would have been seen as a test run for the Vice-Regalty. But they will mess everything up by getting divorced.

* All this came from our historical advisor Alastair Bruce, who is a very keen stalker. I wrote outline dialogue and he just filled it in.

CORA: You mustn't be too hard on your mother. You know it's natural for her to be concerned.
ROSE: Concerned? Is that what she is?
CORA: I'm sure she loves you very much.
SUSAN: What's this?

She has made her presence known.

CORA: Rose was just saying how nice your hair looks tonight.
MCCREE: Dinner is served, your ladyship.

58   INT.   CARSON'S PANTRY.   DOWNTON.   NIGHT.

Mrs Hughes is faced by an irate Carson.

CARSON: *He's what?*
MRS HUGHES: It's only meant to be friendly.

There is a knock at the door.

BRANSON: Good evening, Mr Carson. I don't expect you to approve.

He is standing in the passage. Carson does not answer, so Mrs Hughes speaks up.

MRS HUGHES: As long as you don't tell tales upstairs.
BRANSON: That goes for me, too.
MRS HUGHES: Good. Well, now, come along in.*

Branson starts down the passage, but Mrs Hughes turns back to Carson.

MRS HUGHES (CONT'D): I hope you won't show an example of rudeness to the younger staff.

Carson's face is a picture of resignation as he follows.

59   INT.   HALLWAY.   CRAWLEY HOUSE.   NIGHT.

Isobel is with Doctor Clarkson.

CLARKSON: I was hoping to catch you.
ISOBEL: What about a glass of something?

....

* As I've repeatedly said, servants always knew more about the family than the other way round, because they were often privy to private conversations, whereas the family never overheard their servants talking informally.

CLARKSON: No, I won't stay, but I've had an idea. I saw Mrs Hughes in the village today and she told me the servants have got up a party for the Thirsk fair. And, erm, I was wondering if you'd like to go.

ISOBEL: What? With the servants?

CLARKSON: No, of course not, but I could drive us over for an hour or two… I'm told they do it well.

ISOBEL: Why not? It might be fun.

CLARKSON: Good. I'll come for you at five.*

60 INT. SERVANTS' HALL. DOWNTON. NIGHT.

Branson is in their midst as they eat. The girls are talking about what they will wear to the fair.

BRANSON: I'll keep an eye on the place.

EDNA: Oh, don't say you're not coming! I thought you could drive us in the wagonette.

MRS HUGHES: There is no need for impertinence, Edna, thank you.

BRANSON: You're all right. I'm happy to drive them. But who'll stay here?

CARSON: I will.

ALFRED: You don't want to come to the fair?

CARSON: I would sooner chew broken glass.

But his look at Mrs Hughes reminds us of the real reason.

61 INT. MARY'S BEDROOM. DUNEAGLE CASTLE. NIGHT.

Anna is with Mary, who is dressed for bed.

ANNA: It was lovely, m'lady. But what about you? Did you enjoy your day?

MARY: I was stupid to go to the picnic. We were shaken about in that trap like dice in a cup.

ANNA: Stay in bed for the morning and take it easy at the ball.

MARY: Are you looking forward to it?

ANNA: I am rather. I've been planning a bit of a surprise for Mr Bates.

....

* Clarkson's come with his invitation to the fair, so the audience is gradually being told that this is going to be the big finish for the characters who stayed at Downton, while the Ghillies' Ball will be the Duneagle big finish.

MARY: Why? What sort of surprise?

ANNA: No. It's a surprise for you, too. Don't forget what I said.

MARY: I won't.

Matthew enters in his dressing gown as Anna leaves.

MATTHEW: What was that?

MARY: Just that I've promised to rest tomorrow, which is annoying because I'd rather come out with you and interrogate Mr Gregson. Is he going to propose?

MATTHEW: I think so. But he's quite opaque.

MARY: A man of mystery? Edith could use some of that.

MATTHEW: You are horrid when you want to be.

MARY: I know. But you love me, don't you?

MATTHEW: Madly.

He is in bed by now, and he pulls her into his arms and kisses her, before turning to his book.

62 INT. BALLROOM. DUNEAGLE CASTLE. DAY.*

Rose is with Anna. They are reeling, with Rose humming.

ANNA: So. Let me do it. One last time.

ROSE: You've got it now.

ANNA: The man on my left first.

She demonstrates the move.

ROSE: And then the man on your right… And then round in a figure of eight.

Rose's clapping and singing becomes louder and more frantic before the two fall about laughing.

63 INT. DRAWING ROOM/HALL. DOWNTON. DAY.

Alfred is with Jimmy, collecting the silver.

ALFRED: You take it easy with Mr Barrow today. I don't mean crawl all over him, but don't spoil things.

....

* Some of the Duneagle interior scenes – and this is one of them – were shot at Wrotham Park, where we filmed *Gosford Park* in 2001. This was to avoid needless expense on overnights up North. It's a lovely house, actually.

JIMMY: You're a fine one to talk. Who rang the police
in the first place? Oh, sod this. I'm bushed.

He puts the silver on a tray and sits down in a chair,
putting his feet up on a stool.

ALFRED: Suppose someone comes in?
JIMMY: They'll find a man sitting in an armchair.
They'll survive it.

Alfred gets his nerve up and sits, but more stiffly.

ALFRED: The funny thing with Mr Barrow is he won't hear
a bad word about you.
JIMMY: Why? What have I done?
ALFRED: I only meant he won't let anyone speak against
you.
MRS HUGHES: What on earth is going on here?*

Alfred jumps to his feet. Jimmy gets up more slowly.

ALFRED: We were just —
MRS HUGHES: You were just taking advantage of the cat's
absence. We'll see what Mr Carson has to say.
BRANSON: Mrs Hughes?
MRS HUGHES: Mr Branson.

He is there. She walks with him out into the hall. Some
maids, including Edna, are cleaning in different parts of the
room.

BRANSON: What time are we leaving?
MRS HUGHES: About half past four, but Mr Stark can
easily drive us.
BRANSON: Because I'm so high and mighty?

....

* To Mrs Hughes, servants sitting down in a drawing room is an intolerable
breach of discipline. In fact, servants never sat in any room used by the
family or in the family's presence right through my growing-up years. You
could go and see an old cook in her cottage and you would both be sitting
down, but in the big house no servant ever sat. Queen Victoria took it
further – her Prime Ministers didn't sit (something we got wrong in the film
Young Victoria when Sir Robert Peel sat down while talking to the Queen) –
but Edward VII changed the rules and he allowed some people to be seated.
Even so, for a servant to sit in front of you was considered calculated
impertinence.

MRS HUGHES: You're part of the family now. There's nothing false in that.

BRANSON: I know.

MRS HUGHES: I hope you do. Because if someone is trying to make you feel awkward, they're in the wrong, not you.

BRANSON: I'll be there at half past four.

He goes. Mrs Hughes glances at Edna, who is smiling.

END OF ACT FOUR

ACT FIVE

64 EXT. THIRSK FAIR. DAY.

There are stalls and a merry-go-round and a brass band. Mrs Patmore is with Mrs Hughes.

MRS PATMORE: I said I'd meet him at his stall.

MRS HUGHES: What's that?

She points at a package Mrs Patmore is carrying.

MRS PATMORE: Oh. He asked me to bring sandwiches.

ALFRED: Oh, can I come? I want to find out where the best food stalls are.

MRS HUGHES: Why don't we all go?

They have stopped by a poster for a tug-of-war contest. The slogan is 'Beat the Champions! Cash Prizes to Win!'

JIMMY: Here's something for us. Alfred? Mr Branson? Let's give it a go.

BRANSON: I don't mind.

ALFRED: Well…

MRS HUGHES: Go on. I'll find out where your spice stall is.

ALFRED: What about you?

He has addressed this to Thomas, but Jimmy sniggers.

JIMMY: Isn't it a bit rough for Mr Barrow?

THOMAS: Oh, I think I could manage.

The men start to walk off, as Edna spots her moment.

EDNA: I'll come cheer you on, if that's all right.

She puts her arm through Branson's. Daisy watches them go.

DAISY: Wait till Mrs Hughes sees that.
IVY: Come on. I don't care about any tug-of-war. Let's
go find some games.
DAISY: You do know they're all fixed?
IVY: I don't think they are.
DAISY: They must have seen you coming.

65 EXT. TUFTON'S STALL. THIRSK. DAY.

*Jos Tufton is delighted to welcome his visitors. He has
equipped them with a glass of punch.*

TUFTON: Come on, ladies. Drink up, drink up. We can go
and join in the fun then…
MRS PATMORE: Well, what about your stall?
TUFTON: Don't worry about that. Lucy can look after the
stall, can't you, Lucy?

*Tufton walks behind Lucy, an attractive young woman, who
flinches and squeals as he walks by. Mrs Hughes is not
impressed.*

TUFTON (CONT'D): I hope you don't mind my saying so, Mrs
Patmore, but in that blouse you look as though you've
stepped off the pages of *Vogue*.
MRS PATMORE: I don't mind. I don't believe you, but I
don't mind your saying it at all. Eh, Mrs Hughes?
MRS HUGHES: You're generous with compliments.
TUFTON: I love to be in love, Mrs Hughes. I'll not deny
it. Any time, any place. I love to be in love.
MRS PATMORE: Get away with you, you daft beggar!
MRS HUGHES: I must go and find Alfred and tell him where
to look for the spice stall. If you don't mind my
leaving you?
MRS PATMORE: No, I don't mind that, either.

66 EXT. THIRSK FAIR. DAY.

The tug-of-war is under way. A team of thugs is about to pull against the Downton team. A self-appointed judge is in charge.

JUDGE: Any side bets? Before we begin?

FIRST MAN: Who'd bet on them?

Jimmy speaks up.

JIMMY: What odds would you give us?

JUDGE: Ten to one.

JIMMY: Right. A quid on the Downton team.

This is greeted by a laugh. He produces a one-pound note and hands it over.

JUDGE: Any more?

ALFRED: That's enough money down the drain.

JUDGE: Ready?

JIMMY: One moment.

He hails Tufton and Mrs Patmore who have just arrived.

JIMMY (CONT'D): Mr Tufton! You'll join our team, won't you? As a Downton supplier?

TUFTON: If you want us, lad, aye.

He hands his jacket to Mrs Patmore. The other team are irritated by his arrival. Alfred whispers to Jimmy.

ALFRED: Had you already seen him when you made the bet?

JIMMY: What do you think?

Tufton also hands his hat to Mrs Patmore.

TUFTON: If you'd be so kind.

Then he jogs down the line of the Downton team.

TUFTON: Tufton's at your service.

He approaches a couple of young ladies in the crowd.

TUFTON: Good afternoon, ladies. They needed a bit of muscle so they sent for Tufton.

The ladies are quite amused as he flexes his bicep.

TUFTON: Go on, feel that muscle.

They oblige, still giggling.

LADIES: Very strong!
TUFTON: That's my name, Jos Tufton. You see that stall over there with the spices on?
LADIES: Oh, yeah.

Mrs Hughes watches this scene with some interest.

TUFTON: That's me. If you want a bit of spice in your life, send for Tufton.
ALFRED (V.O.): Mr Tufton, come on!
TUFTON: I'm coming.
JUDGE: Gentlemen, take the strain…

The Downton team, with Tufton at the rear, still chuntering away, get ready.

JUDGE (CONT'D): Pull!

67 EXT. GARRON RIVER. DAY.

Matthew and Gregson are fishing. But they have been distracted by their conversation.*

GREGSON: Of course it's a lot to ask, but what else can I do? I'm prevented from divorcing a woman who doesn't even know who I am. Does the law expect me to have no life at all, until I die? Would Lord Grantham?
MATTHEW: I'm sure my father-in-law would be the first to understand that you have to make some sort of life for yourself, beyond the pale. I do.
GREGSON: Well, then.
MATTHEW: You can't expect him to want you to involve his own daughter! Not when all you have to offer is a job as your mistress.
GREGSON: No. I love her. I'm offering my love.

....

* Charles Edwards, who plays Gregson, knew exactly what he was up to and did a perfect cast, whereas Dan Stevens had to learn how to do it from Alastair Bruce, so we had to rifle through the shots in the edit to find a moment where they both looked as if they had got it right.

MATTHEW: You've been misled by our surroundings. We're not in a novel by Walter Scott.*

68 EXT. THIRSK FAIR. DAY.

Mrs Hughes has reached the tug-of-war. As she arrives, something catches her eye in the crowd. Her attention is drawn back to Mrs Patmore, who calls encouragement, wildly.

MRS HUGHES: Mrs Patmore —

MRS PATMORE: Don't tell me to calm down.

MRS HUGHES: Should I not?

MRS PATMORE: No. Because I can't remember having a better time than this!

Each team is straining and the crowd is shouting encouragement. The judge is in the ear of the leader of the opposing team.

JUDGE: Pull it. Pull the rope!

But with a shout the other team falls. The judge raises his hand.

JUDGE: I declare the Downton team the winner! Have a drink, lads!

A tray of beer is brought forward as the judge pulls out a wad of notes and gives them to Jimmy. The judge and the other team do not look amused.

BRANSON: Well done, Jimmy.

He shakes his hand.

JIMMY: Thank you, Mr Branson.

....

* This and Scene 69 are useful scenes for Matthew. We think of him as a nice and progressive young man, but the danger is that we might forget he takes his duties as Edith's brother-in-law seriously. The fact is, he can't stand by and let Edith enter an illicit relationship, however much he likes the man. This is the kind of responsibility that, in those days, your role in a family placed on you. We've rather abandoned that now and a young man today who was married to one sister might not feel morally responsible for another, but that wasn't true then. Particularly in a family where there is no brother. Rather like Mrs Hughes, however much he is a modern man, Matthew is only modern in that context. He is still a child of his own time, as we all are.

69 EXT. GARRON RIVER. DAY.

Matthew is amazed by what he has been listening to.

GREGSON: So the laws of Society should be preserved, no matter what? Edith gave me the impression you were a freer soul than that.

MATTHEW: I find that hard to believe. I agree, your position is tragic, and I'm very sorry. But you can't imagine I would let Edith slide into a life of scandal without lifting a finger to stop her.

GREGSON: Will you tell Lord Grantham?

MATTHEW: I'm not going to tell anyone. But you must see it's quite hopeless.

GREGSON: Are you saying I should leave now? And not stay for the ball?

MATTHEW: No. Use it to say a proper goodbye. You owe her that.

GREGSON: It's odd the way we're punished for things, when we're not to blame.

MATTHEW: But we also get rewards we don't deserve. It's called luck. And I'm afraid you've had rotten luck.

GREGSON: More than you, I suspect.

MATTHEW: Perhaps, touch wood, but you never know what's coming.

70 EXT. THIRSK FAIR. DAY.

Mrs Patmore is on the swings with Tufton. Branson and Edna ride the merry-go-round as Mrs Hughes looks on. Jimmy is throwing his money around at the bar, while Ivy and Daisy are walking through the stalls.

DAISY: Look at all these people wasting their hard-earned cash.

IVY: But what's it for, if it's not to have a bit of fun?

They've stopped by a stall proclaiming 'Win a Golden Sovereign!' Squares of wood hold prizes and at the top is a sovereign on its own base. A man carries the wooden rings.

IVY (CONT'D): How much is it?

STALL KEEPER: Hook yourselves a fortune, ladies. Thruppence for three.

DAISY: Thruppence? Never in this world!

STALL KEEPER: Look at the prizes, eh? Not fairground rubbish here, you know. When did you last see a gold sovereign?
DAISY: When did you last win one?
JIMMY: What's the matter?

He has turned up by their side.

IVY: I want a go but Daisy thinks it's too expensive.
JIMMY: Ah, have it on me.

He pulls out the wad of his winnings, takes a sixpence and hands it over.

JIMMY (CONT'D): One go for each of them.
DAISY: Are you drunk?*
JIMMY: 'Ah, thank you, Jimmy. How kind of you.'
IVY: It is kind. Thanks very much.
DAISY: Don't flash your money about.
JIMMY: It's my money, won fair and square. I'll do what I want with it.
STALL KEEPER: Remember, the ring must go over the base and lie flat.

Jimmy goes, colliding with someone as he walks away.

STALL KEEPER: Now you.

Ivy has failed and so Daisy starts to throw.

DAISY: I don't believe it!

She has won the sovereign.

DAISY (CONT'D): I've never won nothing before!
STALL KEEPER: Don't let it make a gambler of you.

She takes her prize eagerly.

IVY: See. I told you they were honest.

....

* If you live where drink is limited, there is always a great temptation when you go into a free bar at a wedding or a party to overindulge, because normally you have neither the money nor the opportunity to drink too much. It's why I have to say I'm a believer in keeping drink in the house, because if it's always there and it's always available, no one needs to feel they have to get six glasses down their neck as soon as they have the chance. But there are others who would no doubt disagree.

They move off. The keeper's mood darkens for his assistant.

STALL KEEPER: Didn't I say to make the blocks too wide
for the bally rings!

Mrs Hughes and Alfred are at the food stall.

ALFRED: Thanks for not telling Mr Carson about us
sitting down in the drawing room. We'd not be here now.
MRS HUGHES: Don't let me catch you again. Oh, there's
Mrs Crawley with Doctor Clarkson.

Sure enough, Clarkson and Isobel are there.

ALFRED: This is where I belong. I know it.
MRS HUGHES: What? At a fairground stall?
ALFRED: No. Working with food. Cooking. Preparing.
It's what I love.
MRS HUGHES: Don't sound so tragic. Your time at Downton
won't be wasted. You know how a great house runs now.
That'll come in handy.

*Just then she is distracted by Tufton flirting with another
woman. She looks worried.*

ALFRED: What's the matter? What have you found now?
MRS HUGHES: Nothing. Mr Tufton.
ALFRED: What about him?

But she doesn't answer. Isobel is chatting to Clarkson.

ISOBEL: Well, that was great fun, with the music and
everything. I'm glad we came.
CLARKSON: I'm *very* glad you came.
ISOBEL: Shall we sit down for a bit?
CLARKSON: Let me fetch you a drink… I've got something
I want to ask you. Punch?
ISOBEL: That would be lovely.

Jos Tufton is bringing a glass of wine to Mrs Patmore.

TUFTON: You wouldn't miss service.
MRS PATMORE: I've not been unhappy, you know. I can't
pretend I have.
TUFTON: But taking orders from a husband, it's got to be
better than taking them from some jumped-up lord or lady.
MRS PATMORE: Hmm. It's still orders, isn't it? Wait a
minute. Is that you, James?

Jimmy does not hear her. He is really drunk as he walks by, picking up another tankard of beer. Tufton is tucking into the sandwiches.

> TUFTON: Did you make this pâté as well?
> MRS PATMORE: All with my own fair hand.
> TUFTON: Well, fair hand or red flipper, you're the cook for me.

Jimmy walks down an alley under a bridge. An opposing team member steps out.

> FIRST MAN: Where d'you think you're going, m'laddo?
> JIMMY: Get out of my way!

But the man does not move. Instead he pushes Jimmy back. Another man appears.

> FIRST MAN: Take him!

The second man seizes Jimmy.

> THOMAS: Let him go!

He also appears to have come from nowhere. He stands there.

> FIRST MAN: And who's going to make me?
> THOMAS: I am.

Catching them out, he launches a punch not at the first, but at the second tough who holds Jimmy. Taken by surprise, he releases Jimmy. Thomas shouts as the first man grabs him.

> THOMAS (CONT'D): I mean it, Jimmy! Run! Run!*

Jimmy does run, leaving Thomas to his fate. The first man holds his arms, and the second lays in with a vengeance. Back by the wine stall, Clarkson drains a glass for courage, and then takes two more to where Isobel is sitting.

> CLARKSON: There.
> ISOBEL: Thank you.
> CLARKSON: I'm so sorry. The queue was a mile long.

....

* This is one of those moments when Thomas is allowed to redeem himself. He is taller and older than Jimmy and he has no other motive than to protect the younger man. I hope that is clear. There is nothing in it for him. And the audience should be able to deduce that he is genuinely fond of Jimmy, who runs off – hopefully feeling rather guilty.

ISOBEL: What was it you wanted to ask me?

CLARKSON: Ah. Well, I'm not sure I have the right…

ISOBEL: If you'd like me to come back to the hospital, I was thinking —

CLARKSON: No, it's not the hospital… I'd be interested to know if you've ever thought of marrying again?

Suddenly everything is clear.

ISOBEL: Are you thinking of getting married, Doctor Clarkson? Because if you are, you're a better man than I am, Gunga Din.

CLARKSON: Why?

ISOBEL: Well, with good friends like you, I enjoy my life as it is and I wouldn't want to risk things by changing it.*

Before Clarkson can reply, Jimmy, who has barged through the crowd, runs up.

JIMMY: Doctor! Doctor! You've got to come now!

His tone brings Isobel and Clarkson sharply to their feet.

CLARKSON: What is it?

JIMMY: It's Thomas, please!

71 INT. BEDROOM LANDING. DUNEAGLE CASTLE. EVE.

Rose is arguing with her mother.

SUSAN: Rose, you are not wearing that dress and that is final. You are not a street girl from a slum.

Shrimpie, in Highland dress, arrives with Violet.

ROSE: Oh, Daddy, please stick up for me!

SUSAN: She looks like a slut.

VIOLET: Heavens. That's not a word you often hear among the heather.

....

* Isobel understands that once Clarkson has proposed and she has turned him down, their relationship will be altered. So she is determined to stop it ever getting to that if she can. Something I've observed in life, with admiration, is when women – or even men these days – turn off a potentially embarrassing situation before it can develop into one, and that is what she is doing here. She is saying no, but it is well wrapped up.

ROSE: But Princess Mary has one just like it! It's the fashion now!

SUSAN: Then it is a mad fashion. Aunt Violet, tell her.

VIOLET: Oh, my dear, in my time I wore the crinoline, the bustle and the leg-of-mutton sleeve. I'm not in a strong position to criticise.*

SHRIMPIE: Rose, take Aunt Violet through to the ballroom. Now.

VIOLET: Do you know, Rose, dear, the first Ghillies' Ball I ever attended was at Balmoral… in 1860. Yes, I'd not long been married, and I confess I was a little alarmed because all the men were as tight as ticks, but the amusing thing was that the Queen resolutely refused to notice…†

During this speech Rose has walked off down the passage with Violet, leaving Shrimpie and Susan alone.

SUSAN: Don't blame me if she is the object of ridicule.

SHRIMPIE: I won't. Whatever else I might blame you for.

SUSAN: You are a fool to indulge her. Have you never stopped —

SHRIMPIE: No, you stop! Stop making everyone so unhappy all the bloody time!

Her eyes look beyond him. Now Robert stands there, in tails.

ROBERT: I'm just on my way down. Forgive me. I think I know where I'm going.

SHRIMPIE: I'll come with you.

....

* Rose is in fact wearing a dress very like one that was worn by the Princess Royal, as King George V's daughter Princess Mary later became. She was photographed in it. Violet's line, 'I wore the crinoline, the bustle and the leg-of-mutton sleeve. I am not in a strong position to criticise,' is a reminder that a woman then in her late seventies had been through a series of vastly different fashions, because of the changing role of women. By 1921 modern women would have found the crinoline totally impractical. And this change has happened within Violet's lifetime.

† Violet would have been seventy-nine in 1921. She was born in 1842, married at eighteen, and that year, 1860, she went to her first Ghillies' Ball at Balmoral. It is true that the Queen never objected to the ghillies getting drunk, even though it used to drive the courtiers mad.

The two men walk away, leaving Susan alone.

72 EXT. THIRSK FAIR. EVE.

Thomas has been badly beaten. He is a mess, with his face bruised and bleeding. Branson, Edna, Mrs Hughes, Jimmy and Alfred hover as Clarkson and Isobel tend to him.

> MRS HUGHES: Thank God I saw you, Doctor.
> ISOBEL: Is there any chance of apprehending these men?
> ALFRED: Not really.
> MRS HUGHES: But why did you get into a fight? It's not like you.

Thomas glances at Jimmy but says nothing.

> BRANSON: What have they taken?
> THOMAS: Every penny I had, but it weren't much.
> MRS HUGHES: Is there anything broken?
> CLARKSON: I don't think so.
> JIMMY: So he'll be all right?
> ISOBEL: We ought to get him home.
> BRANSON: I'll fetch the wagonette. Can you make it back to the road?
> ALFRED: I'll help him.

Clarkson and Alfred lift Thomas to his feet. He is in severe pain.

> ALFRED (CONT'D): Lean on me.

Watched by a troubled Jimmy, the group staggers off.*

73 INT. BEDROOM PASSAGE/SYBBIE'S NURSERY. DOWNTON. DAY.

Carson is walking along when he hears the sound of crying. He pushes the door open and goes in. The child is weeping.

> CARSON: Hello? What's the matter with you, eh? Where's your nanny?

The child continues to cry and he lifts her out of the crib.

....

* Jimmy is troubled by the fact that he is in debt to someone whom he felt happier disliking, which I believe is truthful.

CARSON (CONT'D): Let's have a little chat about it.

And he rocks her gently in his arms.

74 INT. BALLROOM. DUNEAGLE CASTLE. NIGHT.

A band plays and the reeling has begun. The party is lively but not out of control. Anna is with Bates, Mary and Matthew.

MARY: Oh, we must all join in.
BATES: Not me, m'lady. And I have a cast-iron alibi.
MATTHEW: I can manage an eightsome and the Dashing White Sergeant but that's about it.
MARY: Well, I'm very good. Hamilton House is my favourite but I know most of them. Our dancing master was a Scot for this very reason.*
MATTHEW: But you won't be doing any tonight.
MARY: Spoilsport.
ANNA: I think Mr Crawley's right, m'lady.
MATTHEW: Will you be staying out of it?
ANNA: We'll have to see.

Molesley is putting on quite a show. O'Brien approaches Susan and Wilkins.

SUSAN: O'Brien. Wilkins has been trying her best to imitate you. What do you think?
O'BRIEN: It looks very nice, your ladyship.
SUSAN: Yes, well, it's not right yet, but we're trying our best. Aren't we, Wilkins?

She drifts away, leaving Wilkins almost too angry to speak.

O'BRIEN: I might go find a drink.
WILKINS: I'll fetch you one.
O'BRIEN: There's no need. I'll go.
WILKINS: No. I insist. You're the guest.

....

* Matthew and Mary here are based on me and Emma. Actually, Emma used to go off to a house nearby in Hampshire, where she grew up, and they would have reeling parties that included Alastair Bruce. She took it very seriously and went up for the Skye balls for years. All of which I am afraid I have taken from her. But marriage is compromise, isn't it?

She moves off towards a drinks table where the punch is being ladled out.

Violet and Rose are with Cora as Rose takes a passing glass, having just finished her previous one.

CORA: You must be careful. Matthew says it's rather strong.

ROSE: I should jolly well hope so.

She gulps it down. Cora looks at Violet.

VIOLET: Rose's evening had a bumpy start. I'm afraid Susan isn't herself.

ROSE: But she's absolutely herself. That's the problem.

She walks off. Violet looks after her.

VIOLET: Poor souls. It's bad enough parenting a child when you like each other.

Wilkins is at the drinks table. She takes a glass as she turns to Nield.

WILKINS: Can I trouble you for a drop of whisky, Mr Nield?

NIELD: Certainly, Miss Wilkins, but I'm surprised if it's for you.

WILKINS: Oh, no. For a guest from the South.

He gives her a bottle and turns away to talk to someone. Wilkins takes it and pours about four inches into the glass.

75 INT. LIBRARY. DOWNTON. NIGHT.

Mrs Hughes stops. Someone is singing 'Rock-a-Bye Baby'. She pushes a half-open door and goes in. Carson is rocking the baby in his arms. Mrs Hughes watches him for a few moments. Then he turns.

CARSON: Ah, you're back, then.

MRS HUGHES: We are, and we've a few stories to tell. But you've spent your day more productively, I see. Where's Nanny?

CARSON: I'm not sure. She must have had some washing to do or something. But she'll find us in a moment.

He stares down at the now placid child in his arms.

CARSON (CONT'D): I was thinking about Lady Sybil, when she was this age.

MRS HUGHES: All we can do for her now is to cherish her bairn, and it's lovely to watch you doing just that.

CARSON: Well, there's no need to get sentimental, Mrs Hughes. Right, let's get this one back to bed. Come on, shall we go look for Nanny?*

76   INT.   BALLROOM.   DUNEAGLE CASTLE.   NIGHT.

Robert has joined Cora and his mother.

CORA: Where have you been?

ROBERT: Trying to calm Shrimpie. You missed some fun and games earlier.

CORA: So I gather.

ROBERT: How is Rose?

VIOLET: In need of rescue.

She looks at Cora, but the latter shakes her head.

CORA: No. I know what you're thinking, but I won't do that to Susan.†

She moves away.

ROBERT: What was she talking about?

VIOLET: Never mind. Now, where is Shrimpie?

ROBERT: Hiding and licking his wounds. I'll go in search of him in a bit, poor fellow, if he hasn't come back.

Across the room, Wilkins arrives with the drink.

O'BRIEN: That's very kind. Thank you.

Wilkins leaves as O'Brien takes one sip, wrinkles her nose and puts the glass down. Molesley has joined her.

....

* Carson allows himself to demonstrate a softness of heart with the child that I think is quite useful to us. We indulge in a little bit of nostalgia, as we know we're boiling up to the end of the show for the year.

† I was sad to lose this as I wanted to make it clear that Cora is reluctant to take Rose without Susan's cooperation, which would put her on the moral high ground. But I suppose we know she's going to do it.

MOLESLEY: Don't you want it?

O'BRIEN: No. I wouldn't drink that if I were you, Mr —

But Molesley has finished it off in one draught.

MOLESLEY: Oh, that slipped down a treat. Think I'll get another one.

O'BRIEN: Each to his own.

77   INT.   BILLIARDS ROOM.   DUNEAGLE CASTLE.   NIGHT.

Robert is with Shrimpie by the billiards table.

ROBERT: Shrimpie, I think you've got to come and show your face —

Shrimpie is standing by the window with a gun in his hand.

ROBERT (CONT'D): For Christ's sake, *don't!*

Shrimpie is puzzled until he notices the gun in his own hand.

SHRIMPIE: My dear fellow, it's not what you think. There's a fox who's been giving us some trouble. But I don't think he's coming tonight.

He places the gun on the desk, shaking his head.

SHRIMPIE (CONT'D): And don't worry. I'd never do that to the children. I'm far too much of a coward.

ROBERT: You make me feel as if I've been blind. Was it always as bad?

SHRIMPIE: Not at the beginning. We weren't madly in love, but there was a job to be done and we both believed in it. Then the children came along, and for years we hardly had time to think.

ROBERT: What went wrong?

SHRIMPIE: First James left and then Annabel got married, and we started to learn just how little we had in common.

ROBERT: Why is Susan so hard on Rose?

SHRIMPIE: Who knows? Perhaps Rose reminds her of me. As I used to be. Me, when I had something to live for.

ROBERT: Oh, you have a great deal to live for. Duneagle. I can't remember being as envious as I have been these past few days.

SHRIMPIE: Don't be. It'll all have to go.

ROBERT: What?

SHRIMPIE: It's my own fault. If I'd had any gumption and modernised as you did… But I sat on my hands as the money drained away. Now it's all gone.

ROBERT: What will you do?

SHRIMPIE: Go to India first and then London. Oh, it'll be all right. What, with the club and the Lords, Susan and I needn't see too much of each other.

ROBERT: Shrimpie, my dear chap, I'm so sorry.

SHRIMPIE: Question is: Rose. What are we going to do about Rose?

Shrimpie rolls the ball he has been holding down the table.*

END OF ACT FIVE

ACT SIX

78 INT. BALLROOM. DUNEAGLE CASTLE. NIGHT.

The band strikes up. Rose runs over to Anna and Bates.

ROSE: Anna! Come on. This is it.

BATES: This is what?

ROSE: You'll see!

She pulls Anna to the circle of dancers. They start.

MARY: Look at Anna! She never said she could reel. Bates? Did you know?

BATES: No, m'lady. I never knew.

MARY: But isn't she marvellous?

....

* I have a good deal of sympathy for Shrimpie in this scene, because he represents many people in the 1920s who suddenly, one dark day, realised the game was up. They had received one too many bank statements written, as they used to be so charmingly, in red ink and they had to wake up to the fact that their way of life could not go on indefinitely. This is when the great sales and demolitions got under way. And, whatever one feels about the rights and wrongs of the system, it must have been very sad for them to watch it crumble away on every side when it was all they'd ever known.

It's true. Anna is whirling round with the best of them.
Bates looks at her, as she laughs and skips through the
figures of the reel. He smiles.

BATES: Yes. She is marvellous.

79 INT. MRS HUGHES'S SITTING ROOM. DOWNTON. NIGHT.

Mrs Hughes is reading when Mrs Patmore arrives, carrying a
tea tray with cups for two.

MRS HUGHES: Oh, Mrs Patmore, how kind of you.
MRS PATMORE: I want a word, so I thought we could have some tea while I get it.

She shuts the door and pours out two cups, and she gives one
to Mrs Hughes while she talks.

MRS PATMORE (CONT'D): You were right. He says he loves me and he can't live without me.
MRS HUGHES: Oh, dear.
MRS PATMORE: What do you mean, 'Oh, dear'? It's a long time since anyone wanted to share my seat on the bus, never mind my heart and home.
MRS HUGHES: I don't know how to say it.
MRS PATMORE: Find a way.

They sit down.

MRS HUGHES: Well, I first noticed it when I was standing at the stall. He was flirting with that young assistant and stroking her… well… bottom.
MRS PATMORE: What?
MRS HUGHES: It's true. Then I saw him making eyes at some other women when he was pulling in the tug-of-war.
MRS PATMORE: While I was cheering him?
MRS HUGHES: And later, when I was with Alfred, I saw Mr Tufton in the crowd, and he seemed to be chewing the mouth off some poor woman…
MRS PATMORE: Where was I all this time?
MRS HUGHES: I don't know. Dreaming of a better life… Oh, Mrs Patmore, I am sorry. I don't know if he wanted to eat a few dinners before he told you the truth, or if he planned to marry you and chain you to the stove…

MRS PATMORE: Either way, it was the cooking he was after. And not me.

MRS HUGHES: I feel terrible. I should've pulled you away then and there, but you were having such a good time.

She covers her face with her hands and sits, silent.

MRS HUGHES (CONT'D): Is there anything I can do?

Mrs Patmore shakes her head and we hear, 'No.' Then she removes her hands. She is grinning from ear to ear.

MRS PATMORE: Because I've never felt more relieved in all my life!

MRS HUGHES: What?

MRS PATMORE: The more he said about how he liked his beef roasted and his eggs fried and his pancakes flipped, the more I wondered how to get away.

MRS HUGHES: And what if he comes back?

MRS PATMORE: He'll get a thick ear and no mistake. But how could he do such a thing, Mrs Hughes? How could he lead a poor woman on like that?

MRS HUGHES: You heard him, Mrs Patmore. Any time, any place. He loves to be in love.

And the two of them burst into peals of laughter.*

80 INT. BALLROOM. DUNEAGLE CASTLE. NIGHT.

Robert is with Violet.

ROBERT: We ought to get it settled.

VIOLET: We'll talk to her tomorrow.

ROBERT: The thing is, I believe it would do her good. To have someone like Rose to look after.

Violet regards this dear simpleton of a son.

VIOLET: Now, why didn't I think of that?

Edith is with Gregson.

EDITH: And that was really his reaction? How disappointing.

....

* I like to emphasise the friendship between Mrs Patmore and Mrs Hughes. I'm sure those workplace alliances got you through this life.

GREGSON: I wasn't going to tell you until I was leaving.
EDITH: Why not?
GREGSON: Because I wanted us to have a last evening together.
EDITH: This is not our last evening.
GREGSON: Isn't it?
EDITH: It's odd. If you'd asked before tonight how I felt about you, I'm not sure what I would have answered, but now I'm absolutely sure. And this is not our last evening.*

The couples form an eightsome and she leads Gregson onto the floor. As the dance starts, Mary is with Matthew. The ballroom is filled with a blood-curdling cry.

MARY: What in God's name —?

At the centre of a circle, Molesley has gone mad. He dances like a dervish, arms stretched above him, screaming and yelling, terrifying the maid opposite him. He swings her round like a cape. O'Brien is standing with Wilkins.

O'BRIEN: Are you proud of your handiwork? Seeing as he's taken my punishment.
WILKINS: I don't know what you mean.
O'BRIEN: Never mind, Miss Wilkins. It might do him good to let it all go for once. And I'm grateful. I am.
WILKINS: What for?
O'BRIEN: Because I need never be held back by any sense of loyalty to you.†

She walks off to speak to Susan Flintshire as Wilkins wonders if she's been smart. Violet and Robert are watching Molesley.

ROBERT: They do say there's a wild man inside all of us.
VIOLET: If only he would *stay* inside.

....

* This is one of our first indications that the war really has changed Edith, that she will no longer necessarily do what she is told. This is her crunch time. In simple terms, she is not prepared to give him up.

† This means that O'Brien will now happily pinch Wilkins's job when it comes to it.

81   INT.   BRANSON'S BEDROOM.   DOWNTON.   NIGHT.

Branson is bare-chested, in pyjama trousers, when the door opens.   It is Edna.

BRANSON: What in the —?

EDNA: I thought you'd like to know Mr Barrow is feeling much better.

BRANSON: Thank you, but you should go now.

EDNA: I just wanted to tell you what a lovely day I've had. Really lovely. Shall we meet for lunch tomorrow? In the Grantham Arms?

Taking him unawares, she quickly kisses his mouth and hurries out.   And now he sees what he has done.

82   INT.   BALLROOM.   DUNEAGLE CASTLE.   NIGHT.

Mary is finishing Hamilton House.   She rubs her tummy, looking concerned, and returns to sit with Matthew.

MARY: I don't think I should have done that, but I couldn't resist.

MATTHEW: Which is just what I was afraid of —

MARY: Calm down. Everything's fine, but I wonder: would you mind terribly if I went home tomorrow?

MATTHEW: Of course not. I'll tell Shrimpie tonight that we're leaving and —

MARY: No, not you. You must stay here.

MATTHEW: What do you mean? I don't want to let you out of my sight.

MARY: But if you come, Mama and Papa will think they have to leave, and the party will break up.

MATTHEW: So what? I'm coming with you.

MARY: But it's very unfair on Susan and Shrimpie when I'm perfectly all right. It's only a couple more days. Let me go, and I'll see you when I see you. Please.*

She glances across the room to where Molesley has passed out.

....

* The British upper classes on the whole – and of course it's a generalisation – like to minimise what's wrong with them physically, whereas there are other nationalities and other social groups who like to maximise it. Here, Mary deliberately trivialises her anxiety and she is mistaken to do so.

MARY (CONT'D): Besides, Molesley may need a little time before he's fit to travel.

83 INT. HALL. DUNEAGLE CASTLE. NIGHT.

Bates and Anna emerge from the ballroom.

ANNA: Let's get away before we have to carry him upstairs.

She is laughing, as Bates looks at her in wonder.

ANNA (CONT'D): Why are you being funny? You're not angry with me, are you?
BATES: Angry? Good God, no.
ANNA: I hope I haven't upset you, Mr MacBates. I thought the sight of me reeling would make you smile.
BATES: It does make me smile, but it also fills me with wonder.
ANNA: How so?
BATES: That an old peg-leg like me should find himself married to a creature made of quicksilver and light.

Anna is very moved by this. Rose comes down the stairs.

ROSE: Isn't she terrific, Bates? She said you'd never believe she could do it.
BATES: She was wrong, m'lady.

Anna looks up at him, a little concerned.

BATES (CONT'D): There's nothing I don't believe she could do. Nothing at all.
ROSE: Good. I shall have pleasure telling Mummy I've done something right.

She goes into the ballroom.

ANNA: Oh, that reminds me. Lady Mary wants to leave in the morning, so I may not see you for a day or two.
BATES: Do you think I could sneak into the maids' quarters tonight?
ANNA: I'm afraid not. But you know what my mother says?
BATES: No. What does your mother say?
ANNA: That it's always nice to leave something for another time.*

*That was a phrase of Nanny's.

She takes his face in her hands and kisses him. Behind them, the door opens and a wretched, green Molesley appears.

ANNA (CONT'D): Are you all right, Mr Molesley?
MOLESLEY: 'All right' is not the first phrase that springs to mind.

He staggers upstairs, leaving the other two laughing.

84 INT. SERVANTS' HALL. DOWNTON. DAY.

Mrs Hughes is with Edna and some others when Carson looks in.

CARSON: That was Mr Bates on the telephone. Lady Mary and Anna are coming back today. They're already on the train so we need to be prepared.
MRS HUGHES: Well, we'd better look sharp. Edna, air the room and make up the bed, while I go and talk to Mrs Patmore.
EDNA: Must I?

This brings them up short, both Mrs Hughes and Carson.

CARSON: Why? Do you have you other plans, Edna?
EDNA: I said I'd meet Tom Branson for lunch in the village.
CARSON: Did you, indeed? 'Tom' Branson?*

But Mrs Hughes ushers Carson to the passage outside.

MRS HUGHES: Before you start, it may not be his fault.
CARSON: Whether it's his fault or not, she has to go.
MRS HUGHES: Oh, yes. Of course she has to go. Will you tell him or will I?
CARSON: You'd better do it. I'd only be rude, which wouldn't help anyone.

85 INT. CORA'S BEDROOM. DUNEAGLE CASTLE. DAY.

Cora sits in bed with a breakfast tray. There is a knock and Susan comes in. She is dressed.

....

* Edna is beginning to overplay her hand. Carson knows that she will have to be sacked, because it's all got out of control. This aspect of her character is based on a maid of my mother's before the war. She was called Esther. One evening she made it clear that she thought she was now indispensable to the family and so she didn't have to do what she was asked any more, unless she chose to. She left the following day.

SUSAN: You've heard about Mary?

CORA: I have. Her maid left a message with O'Brien. I hope you don't think her rude. I know you haven't always approved of Mary.

SUSAN: She's having a baby. We all need a little leeway when it comes to our babies. And as for the other business, I'm not as harsh as I was. Rose is proving quite an education.

CORA: I can imagine.

SUSAN: Annabel was so straightforward. But I find myself worrying about Rose before I open my eyes for the morning. Do you think I'm being stupid?

CORA: Not at all. I understand better than anyone else here could.

Cora is becoming aware that Susan has come to say something.

SUSAN: Shrimpie wants her to live at Downton while we're in India.

CORA: I've told Robert I would never agree to that against your wishes.

SUSAN: I know. Thank you. It's not often that I get support in this house.

She smiles wearily.

SUSAN (CONT'D): But I wonder now if he isn't right and that we need a rest from one another. Apart from anything else, I can't bring her out from Bombay. But would you be prepared for all that?

CORA: If you want me to be. And only if you want it. But what about you and Shrimpie?

SUSAN: Oh, we'll soldier on. Our sort never accept defeat… Even if I wish we could.

She walks to the door. Then she pauses.

SUSAN (CONT'D): Will you speak well of me to her? Not every day, but sometimes?

CORA: Of course I will. I promise.*

....

* Susan is a sort of villain in the story, because we must have some villains and it's good to have an upstairs villain instead of only Thomas downstairs. But I put in this scene so we would understand that there is another side to her story, that it isn't all her fault.

86 INT. LIBRARY. DOWNTON. DAY.

Branson is with Mrs Hughes.

BRANSON: So I've spoiled things for her?

MRS HUGHES: I'm afraid the work would no longer satisfy her. I've seen it before. She'd unsettle the other maids.

BRANSON: I didn't encourage her, you know.

MRS HUGHES: Maybe. But if I may say it, you didn't discourage her, either.

BRANSON: Can I ask one thing? That you give her a decent reference. Please.

MRS HUGHES: I will. Though I don't think she's cut out to be a housemaid… Would you allow me to speak as I would have in the old days?

BRANSON: Go on, then.

MRS HUGHES: You let Edna make you ashamed of your new life, but you've done well and Lady Sybil would be so proud.

At this, Branson's eyes fill with tears. He shakes his head.

BRANSON: I can't bear to be without her.

MRS HUGHES: You must bear it. And one day I hope — and so would she — you'll find someone to bear it with you. But until then, be your own master and call your own tune.*

87 INT. GRANTHAM ARMS. DOWNTON VILLAGE. DAY.

Edna sits alone, attracting puzzled glances.

88 EXT. RAILWAY STATION. DOWNTON VILLAGE. DAY.

Mary is helped onto the platform by a guard. Anna and the chauffeur are supervising the removal of the luggage. Mary approaches.

ANNA: M'lady? Is something the matter?

....

* Branson acknowledges here that he's made a mess of things by abandoning the rules, and he immediately makes another mistake by asking Mrs Hughes to falsify the reference and make it a glowing one. This will, we already know, come back to bite him in the bottom. I suppose I was saying that it is necessary to be tough in this life, which seems a bit harsh.

MARY: I don't want to alarm anyone, but would you leave the cases here for now and take me straight to the hospital?
CHAUFFEUR: M'lady.
ANNA: What?
MARY: Let Mrs Crawley know and get a message to Mr Crawley straight away.

Mary and Anna exchange a look. They know what's happening.

89 EXT. THE GLEN. DAY.

Matthew is lying, with Nield nearby, preparing to shoot a stag. A man rides up behind them. He shouts and a stag panics at the noise and runs.

HORSEMAN: Mr Crawley! Mr Crawley!
NIELD: What in God's name —?

The man gets off his horse and rushes towards them.

90 INT. SERVANTS' HALL/KITCHEN PASSAGE. DOWNTON. NIGHT.

Carson is in a frenzy. Mrs Hughes and the others are there.

CARSON: Right. All change. The whole family is coming back tomorrow. And we must be ready to receive them.
DAISY: Is it because Lady Mary's in the hospital?
CARSON: It is.
DAISY: Does that mean she's in danger?
CARSON: No! It doesn't mean any such thing!

He storms out. Mrs Hughes takes over.

MRS HUGHES: Lady Mary will be perfectly fine, but we have to make allowances.

She walks out into the passage. Edna is there with her case.

MRS HUGHES (CONT'D): Now, do you have everything?
EDNA: But what have I done wrong? I'm as good as Mr Branson and there was nothing improper, nothing at all.
MRS HUGHES: I'm sure. But there are rules to this way of life, Edna. And if you're not prepared to live by them, then it's not the right life for you.

Edna picks up her bags and leaves.

91 INT. CORA'S BEDROOM. DUNEAGLE CASTLE. DAY.

Cora and O'Brien are packing.

O'BRIEN: I'll leave this case open to finish off tomorrow, and I'll tell them to come for the others now.

As she goes out, she passes Robert.

ROBERT: It's organised. We've got tickets for the first train in the morning. There isn't one before then.
CORA: I just wish I was there with her.

He watches her for a moment.

ROBERT: Shrimpie's so happy you've taken pity on Rose. Thank you.
CORA: It was different when Susan asked me. But Rose won't replace Sybil.
ROBERT: Of course not. No one will.
CORA: Because that's what your mother believes.

By way of answer, he takes her hand and kisses it.

ROBERT: I can't wait to get home.
CORA: Aren't you enjoying your Victorian idyll any longer?
ROBERT: I'm glad I was jealous of Shrimpie. It's made me realise what a fool I've been. Downton will survive because of Matthew's vision.
CORA: I'm so pleased to hear you say it.
ROBERT: You always knew how lucky we are in Matthew, and now I give thanks for him. As I give thanks for my home and my family, and most of all I give thanks for my wife.

He takes her into his arms and kisses her.

92 EXT. DUNEAGLE CASTLE. DAY.

A new day. Violet, Robert, Edith, Rose and Matthew are joined by Bates, O'Brien and Molesley, with luggage stowed into cars and onto the wagonette. Shrimpie, Susan and Cora stand by.

SHRIMPIE: Send us the news as soon as you know it. And thank you for taking in Rose.
SUSAN: We'll make firm plans as soon as we know when we're leaving.

CORA: I'm glad to have her now I know it's what you both want.

Cora walks towards the car, but Shrimpie follows her.

SHRIMPIE: What *I* want is for her to know that family can be a loving thing.
CORA: We'll do our best.
SHRIMPIE: Love is like riding or speaking French. If you don't learn it young, it's hard to get the trick of it later.
CORA: Well said, Shrimpie. And good luck.

She smiles and joins Robert and Violet by a waiting car.

VIOLET: You've taken such a weight off their minds, my dear.
CORA: But you're wrong, Mama. She won't help me get over Sybil. For the simple reason I don't want her to.

She climbs into the car. Violet turns to Robert.

VIOLET: Why does Cora always think I have an ulterior motive?
ROBERT: Because she knows you.

Edith is with Matthew.

EDITH: What did you tell Mary about Michael Gregson?
MATTHEW: Nothing. But I hope he made it clear what has to happen.
EDITH: Oh, yes. We both know what happens next.

They climb in, too. Rose runs up to Robert.

ROSE: I'll see you at Downton very soon. And thank you both so much.
ROBERT: We look forward to it. Are we all ready, Bates?
BATES: We are, m'lord.

As the servants climb aboard the wagonette, Susan catches O'Brien's eye and nods. O'Brien nods back. The procession of vehicles heads off.*

....

* This is where we indicated, economically and visually and without dialogue, that O'Brien and Susan had reached an understanding. I thought the actresses did it rather well.

93 INT. SERVANTS' PASSAGE. DOWNTON. DAY.

Carson is there. Anna is with him, in her coat.

ANNA: Mr Carson? I'm going down to the hospital. I
think I have what she needs.
CARSON: If there's anything else, anything at all, just
telephone.
ANNA: According to the doctor, there's nothing to worry
about.
CARSON: Well, of course I worry. After Lady Sybil how
could I not worry? Now, should I meet the others off the
train?
ANNA: Get Mr Matthew's car taken to the station and have
the others brought here. Mr Matthew can drive himself to
the hospital and come back with the news when he's
ready.*
CARSON: Yes. Good, good. Very good. And Anna, thank
you.

He is so grateful that someone is thinking straight.

94 INT. DOWNTON HOSPITAL/HOSPITAL PASSAGE. DAY.

*Mary sits up on her bed, looking troubled. A nurse pats her
back and leaves. Clarkson and Isobel are in the passage.*

CLARKSON: Would you help to prepare, while I make sure
everything's ready?

Isobel moves towards the door.

CLARKSON (CONT'D): Erm… You saved me from making a fool
of myself at the fair. I'm afraid I'd had too much to
drink.
ISOBEL: I don't know what you mean.
CLARKSON: Well, I think you do. And thank you.

Isobel smiles and goes in to find Mary in bed.

MARY: I wish Matthew were here. It's funny. I feel as
if I'm only half myself without him.

....

* Anna, most unfortunately, decides to say, 'Get Mr Matthew's car taken to
the station and have the others brought here. Mr Matthew can drive himself
to the hospital and come back with the news when he is ready.' So here the
death sentence has been passed on Matthew.

ISOBEL: He'll be on the train by now. And you won't want him in the room till it's all over. You can trust me.
MARY: It's so strange. I must have known something, or why did I sense that I had to get home?

Mary has another spasm.

MARY: Oh!

Isobel strokes her hand.

ISOBEL: It won't be long now.
MARY: We must ring Carson. He'll be in such a state.
ISOBEL: I will.
MARY: I shouldn't have gone up North. All that bumping around in those carts. How could I be so stupid?
ISOBEL: My dear, the baby will be perfectly well. Slightly early, but not very. We'll have to take a little extra care, that's all.

There is a knock. She looks up to see Clarkson in the doorway. He nods.

95   INT. THOMAS'S ROOM. DOWNTON. DAY.

Thomas, black and blue, is in bed. Jimmy knocks and enters. For a moment they stare at each other.

THOMAS: What are you doing up here?
JIMMY: I just wanted to make sure there wasn't too much harm done.
THOMAS: Well, there was enough harm done.

He laughs rather painfully, and winces.

JIMMY: You were brave, Mr Barrow. Very brave. I feel badly. I… I shouldn't have run off.
THOMAS: No, you should have. Otherwise, what was I bloody doing it for?
JIMMY: Were you following me?
THOMAS: I like to keep an eye out… I could see you'd had a bit to drink and so… Yes, yes, I did follow you.
JIMMY: Why?
THOMAS: You know why.

Now they have come to the nub of it. Jimmy pulls up a chair.

JIMMY: I can never give you what you want.

THOMAS: I understand that. I do. And I don't ask for it. But I'd like it if we could be friends.

This is both a surprise and a relief to Jimmy.

JIMMY: Right you are, Mr Barrow. If that's all, I think I could manage that.

THOMAS: Thank you, Jimmy. Thank you. Now make yourself useful…

Thomas hands him the paper to read to him, and they chat warmly. *

95A INT. HALL. DOWNTON. DAY.

Carson is on the telephone.

CARSON: Thank you. Thank you very much. Thank you very much indeed.

He hangs up and looks overwhelmed.

96 INT. MRS HUGHES'S SITTING ROOM. DOWNTON. DAY.

Mrs Hughes is with Mrs Patmore when Carson looks in.

CARSON: That was Mrs Crawley. It's over. Lady Mary's very tired but she's come through it. They both have.

MRS PATMORE: Thank the Lord.

MRS HUGHES: And what about the baby?

CARSON: What about it?

MRS HUGHES: What sex is it?

CARSON: I never thought to ask.

He ducks away and hurries off.

MRS PATMORE: Men.

....

* This resolution – that Jimmy and Thomas are going to be friends – has been set up to be mined in the next series. They will be in cahoots more or less from now on.

97 INT. DOWNTON HOSPITAL. DAY.

Mary holds the baby.

MATTHEW: Can this hot and dusty traveller come in?

Anna leaves as Matthew sits on the bed.

MARY: Say hello to your son and heir.

He takes the baby.

MATTHEW: Hello, my dearest little chap… I wonder if he has any idea how much joy he brings with him?

He takes his wife gently by the shoulders.

MATTHEW (CONT'D): My darling, how are you? Really?
MARY: Tired. And pretty relieved. But just think. We've done our duty. Downton is safe. Papa must be dancing a jig.
MATTHEW: *I'm* dancing a jig. I feel like I've swallowed a box of fireworks.

She strokes his hair, as he looks at her in wonder.

MATTHEW (CONT'D): You are going to be such a wonderful mother.
MARY: How do you know?
MATTHEW: Because… Because you're such a wonderful woman.
MARY: I hope I'm allowed to be *your* Mary Crawley for all eternity, and not Edith's version, or anyone else's for that matter.
MATTHEW: You'll be my Mary, always, because mine is the true Mary. Do you ever wonder how happy you've made me?
MARY: You sound rather foreign. Shouldn't you be saying things like, 'You'll be up and about in no time'?
MATTHEW: I'll do all that tomorrow, but right now I want to tell you that I fall more in love with you every day that passes.
MARY: I'll remind you of that next time I scratch the car.
MATTHEW: Do. I give you full permission.
MARY: Where are the others?
MATTHEW: Back at the house, panting to see you — to see you both — but I've sent Mother to keep them at bay. I wanted the chance to be alone with my family.

MARY: You'd better go and tell them I'm still alive.
But first, I think I've earned a decent kiss.
MATTHEW: You certainly, certainly have.

*They kiss.**

98   INT.   DRAWING ROOM.   DOWNTON.   DAY.

*Edith is with Branson. They are chatting. Branson has
Sybbie in his arms.*

EDITH: First Sybbie, now her little cousin. It's rather
wonderful the ways that families just keep unrolling.
BRANSON: But did you have a good time?
EDITH: I did. Very good, in a way. How about you?
BRANSON: I've been on a bit of a learning curve, as it
happens.
EDITH: Me, too. And it isn't over yet.†

....

* The demonstration of Matthew's and Mary's happiness was the scene I wanted to end the episode with. And so I spoke to Dan Stevens. He had been very definite about leaving the show, as we know, but I asked him if he would reconsider, let this episode end happily before coming back in Season Four to be killed, or die in some way, right at the start. He thought about it, but finally he just felt he couldn't. I was very sorry, but I also sympathised with what he was trying to do, and so I had quite mixed feelings. Anyway, I knew I had to kill him by the end. Then I woke up one morning and I realised that his decision meant we could have a six-month gap between his death and resuming the story the following year. We wouldn't need to have funerals or memorials and Mary reeling at the onset of her grief. We could pick it up again when Mary was beginning to come out of it, which actually had far more dramatic potential than her just sobbing. And so although I was very, very sorry to spoil a lot of Christmas evenings, nevertheless it allowed us a far more interesting role for Mary, both to act and to watch, in Season Four.

† 'Learning curve' was one of the phrases that the press pounced on, saying it came from the 1960s. In fact, one journalist wrote a half-page article on how ridiculous it was that I had used it. The truth is, 'learning curve' was coined in 1879 and originally used as a scientific term. But by twenty years later it had entered popular slang. Its meaning was the same – accelerated learning – but used to describe social situations, 'that was a learning curve', in an unscientific way. I pointed this out to the journalist, who acknowledged that he'd been wrong, but he never wrote a retraction. I thought that was rather disappointing. Not surprising, given what they're like, but disappointing.

Isobel is talking to Robert.

ISOBEL: These things are always rather nerve-racking.
But all's well that ends well, and it won't be long
before you'll be able to say hello to your very own
grandson.
ROBERT: My grandson? Oh, my dear, how sweet and
miraculous that sounds!
CORA: *Our* grandson. And, yes, it does sound miraculous.

99 EXT. COUNTRY ROAD. DAY.

Matthew, as happy as a man can be, drives along at a lick.

100 INT. DRAWING ROOM. DOWNTON. DAY.

ROBERT: Life is strange, isn't it?
VIOLET: In so many different ways.
ROBERT: No, I mean, I think of all the uncertainty
between Matthew and Mary, or when the money was lost, and
everything was so dark.

100A EXT. COUNTRY ROAD. DAY

Matthew continues driving at speed.

ROBERT (CONT'D: V.O.): Yet now, here we are, with two
healthy heirs…

*Matthew hums a tune as he drives over the hill and taps his
hands on his steering wheel in time, looking to the heavens.
A huge lorry, also travelling at speed, is coming the other
way.**

ROBERT (CONT'D: V.O.): … an estate in good order, and I
wonder what I've done to deserve it.

The lorry seems to fill the road ahead.

....

* Matthew hums a tune as he drives over the hill… That is the moment when
we tell the audience what's about to happen. The moment following is put in
to make it quite clear to the audience that darling Matthew has had it.
Before the truck has appeared, though, they already know it's all over.

100B   INT.   DRAWING ROOM.   DOWNTON.   DAY.

VIOLET: I agree.   But then we don't always get our just
deserts.

101   EXT.   A COUNTRY LANE.   DAY.

*Skid marks on the road lead to a row of broken sycamores and
the overturned wreck of the roadster.   The driver, badly
shaken, gets out of the cab and runs towards the crashed car.
He stops at the sight of Matthew lying, broken and bleeding,
under the vehicle.   He is quite, quite dead.* *

102   INT.   DOWNTON HOSPITAL.   DAY.

*Mary sits, in a pretty bed jacket, holding the baby, flowers
beside her.   Anna finishes tidying the sheet.*

ANNA: You look lovely, m'lady.   Motherhood on a
monument.
MARY: You'd better go down.   They'll be here in a
minute.   And tell Mr Matthew he must wait his turn…

102A   EXT.   COUNTRY ROAD.   DAY

Matthew lies dead, with blood trickling down his cheek.

MARY (CONT'D: V.O.):   He's seen the baby and they
haven't.

102B   INT.   DOWNTON HOSPITAL.   DAY.

*Anna has left.   How charming Mary looks with the child.   And
how happy.* †

THE END

....

* It was very sad for me, too – the man what done it. This nice, handsome
young man that we'd all grown so fond of was dead. We loved Matthew and
we loved his journey. And Dan Stevens, of course, was terrific throughout.

† And now, for a moment of maximum and pure sorrow, we mount this
iconic tableau of mother and child. Mary has become the Madonna.

CAST LIST

Charlie Anson	Larry Grey
Edward Baker-Duly	Terence Margadale
Robert Bathurst	Sir Anthony Strallan
Neil Bell	Durrant
Samantha Bond	Lady Rosamund Painswick
Hugh Bonneville	Robert, Earl of Grantham
Jessica Brown Findlay	Lady Sybil Crawley
Kenneth Bryans	Nield
Myanna Buring	Edna
Laura Carmichael	Lady Edith Crawley
Jim Carter	Mr Carson
Michael Cochrane	Reverend Mr Travis
Ruairi Conaghan	Kieran Branson
Paul Copley	Mr Mason
Jonathan Coy	George Murray
Brendan Coyle	Mr Bates
Sarah Crowden	Lady Manville
Michael Culkin	Archbishop of York
Michelle Dockery	Lady Mary Crawley
Ron Donachie	McCree
Kevin Doyle	Mr Molesley
Charles Edwards	Michael Gregson
Peter Egan	Marquess of Flintshire
Siobhan Finneran	Miss O'Brien
Joanne Froggatt	Anna Bates
Jason Furnival	Craig
Bernard Gallagher	Bill Molesley
Terence Harvey	Jarvis
Karl Haynes	Dent
Shaun Hennessy	Judge
John Henshaw	Jos Tufton

Claire Higgins	Mrs Bartlett
Lily James	Lady Rose MacClare
Rob James-Collier	Thomas Barrow
Edmund Kente	Mead
Simone Lahbib	Wilkins
Allen Leech	Tom Branson
Phyllis Logan	Mrs Hughes
Christine Lohr	Mrs Bird
Jordan Long	Taxi driver
Christine Mackie	Mrs Bryant
Shirley MacLaine	Martha Levinson
Elizabeth McGovern	Cora, Countess of Grantham
Kevin R. McNally	Mr Bryant
Sophie McShera	Daisy Mason
Matt Milne	Alfred Nugent
Phoebe Nicholls	Marchioness of Flintshire
Lesley Nicol	Mrs Patmore
Amy Nuttall	Ethel Parks
Mark Penfold	Mr Charkham
Tim Pigott-Smith	Sir Philip Tapsell
Douglas Reith	Lord Merton
David Robb	Doctor Clarkson
Lucille Sharp	Reed
Ged Simmons	Turner
Maggie Smith	Violet, Dowager Countess of Grantham
Ed Speleers	Jimmy Kent
Dan Stevens	Matthew Crawley
Richard Teverson	Doctor Ryder
Cara Theobold	Ivy Stuart
William Travis	Stall keeper
Tony Turner	Inspector Stanford
John Voce	Photographer
Stuart Ward	First man
Penelope Wilton	Isobel Crawley

PRODUCTION CREDITS

Writer & Creator	Julian Fellowes
Executive Producers	Gareth Neame
	Julian Fellowes
Co-Executive Producer	Nigel Marchant
Series Producer	Liz Trubridge
Director (Episodes 1 & 2)	Brian Percival
Director (Episodes 3, 4 & Christmas Special)	Andy Goddard
Director (Episodes 5 & 6)	Jeremy Webb
Director (Episodes 7 & 8)	David Evans
Production Designer	Donal Woods
Director of Photography	Nigel Willoughby
Editors	John Wilson A.C.E.
	Al Morrow
Assembly/Assistant Editor	Dan Crinnion
Costume Designer	Caroline McCall
Costume Supervisor	Dulcie Scott
Assistant to Costume Designer	Poli Kyriacou
Wardrobe Master	Jason Gill
Principal Costume Standby	Emma Bevan Hyde
Costume Trainee	Jessica Phillips
Make-up & Hair Designer	Magi Vaughan
Make-up & Hair Supervisor	Vanya Pell
Hair Dresser	Julio Cesar Parodi
Make-up & Hair Artist	Sue Newbould
Make-up & Hair Trainee	Doone Forsyth
Casting Director	Jill Trevellick C.D.G.
Casting Associate	Robert Morris
Music	John Lunn
First Assistant Directors	Chris Croucher
	Cordelia Hardy

Second Assistant Director	Danielle Bennett
Third Assistant Director	Eddie Williams
Script Supervisors	Sam Donovan
	Sarah Garner
	Vicki Howe
Location Manager	Mark 'Sparky' Ellis
Assistant Location Manager	John Prendergast
Unit Manager	Holly Baird
Head of Security	Christian De Vos
Security	Andy Davies
Line Producer	Charles Hubbard
Production Accountant	Denis Wray
First Assistant Accountant	Matthew Lawson
Assistant Accountant	Ellie Downham
Production Coordinator	Jonathan Houston
Assistant Production	
Coordinator	Oliver Cockerham
Camera Operators/Steadicam	Andy Speller
	Jonathan Beacham
Focus Pullers	George Grieve
	Milos Moore
Clapper Loaders	Joanne Smith
	Alba Moran Ruiz
Grips	Simon Fogg
	Peter Olney
Gaffer	Phil Brookes
Best Boy	David Staton
Supervising Art Director	Charmian Adams
Art Director	Mark Kebby
Buyer	Sue Morrison
Set Decorator	Gina Cromwell
Standby Art Director	Laura Conway-Gordon
Assistant Art Director	Chantelle Valentine
Art Department Assistant	Steven Granger
Graphic Artist	Aoife McKim
Prop Master	Charlie Johnson
Dressing Props	Don Santos
Standby Props	Damian Butlin
	Mark Quigley
Storeman	Tom Pleydell Pearce
Special Effects	Mark Holt Special Effects
Digital Imaging Technician	Villing Chong
Historical Advisor	Alastair Bruce

Medical Advisors	John Powell
	Dr Alasdair Emslie
Health & Safety Advisor	Dave Sutcliffe
Script Editor	Claire Daxter
Production Executive	Kimberley Hikaka
Business Affairs	David O'Donoghue
	Aliboo Bradbury
Picture Post Producer	Portia Napier
Unit Publicity	Milk Publicity
Post-production Supervisor	Jessica Rundle
Post-production Script Services	Ilana Epstein
Sound Maintenance Engineer	Martin Ireland
Sound Assistant	Jackson Milliken
Colourist	Aidan Farrell
Online Editor	Clyde Kellet
Sound Mixers	Chris Ashworth
	Brian Milliken
Re-recording Mixer	Nigel Heath
Assistant Re-recording Mixer	Alex Fielding
Sound FX Editors	Adam Armitage
	Darren Banks
Dialogue Editors	Alex Sawyer
	Tom Williams
Titles	Huge Design
Visual Effects	The Senate Visual Effects

ACKNOWLEDGEMENTS

Once again, I must voice my undying gratitude to Gareth Neame and Liz Trubridge, as it is we three who are at the heart of the show, and it would be quite impossible for these scripts to have come together in the way they have without their help. As always, Dr Alasdair Emslie has supplied us with ailments, most particularly with the plot of Sybil's demise, where his mastery of the details of eclampsia was invaluable. I have had advice on estate management from Conroy Harrowby and others, while Alastair Bruce, whose names recurs often in this text, is a mainstay of every part of the production. But of course I rely most on my son, Peregrine, for his well-considered criticism, and on my wife, Emma. She sees the pages first and stamps her mark on them before they get any further. Thank you all.

Immerse yourself in the world of
DOWNTON ABBEY

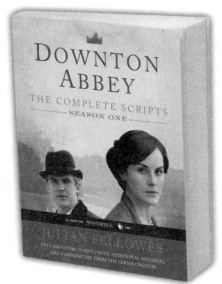

THE COMPLETE SCRIPTS
SEASON ONE

THE COMPLETE SCRIPTS
SEASON TWO

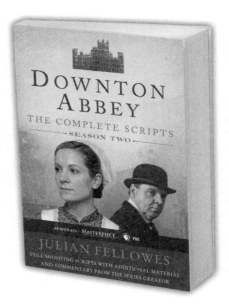

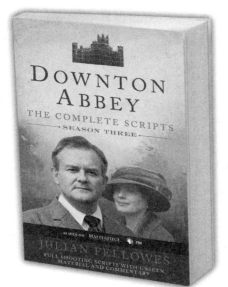

THE COMPLETE SCRIPTS
SEASON THREE

Created by Oscar-winning writer Julian Fellowes, *Downton Abbey* has delighted viewers with stellar performances, ravishing sets and costumes, and above all, a gripping plot.

Each handsome volume includes the full shooting scripts as well as introductions, additional material and commentary from Julian Fellowes, and eight pages of full-color behind-the-scenes photos!

Available in Paperback and eBook wherever books are sold.